THE COLLECTED STORIES OF
GREG BEAR

Tor Books by Greg Bear

THE COLLECTED STORIES OF GREG BEAR

GREG BEAR

A Tom Doherty Associates Book
New York

To Astrid, Alexandra, and Erik
With all my love

and

To my editors, who gave me courage

THE COLLECTED STORIES OF GREG BEAR

Copyright © 2002 by Greg Bear

Edited by Beth Meacham

An Orb Book
Published by Tom Doherty Associates, LLC
175 Fifth Avenue
New York, NY 10010

www.tor.com

Library of Congress Cataloging-in-Publication Data

Bear, Greg, 1951–
      [Short stories. Selections]
      The collected stories of Greg Bear / Greg Bear.
            p. cm.
      "A Tom Doherty Associates book."
      ISBN 0-765-30160-1 (hc)
      ISBN 0-765-30161-X (pbk)
      1. Science fiction, American. I. Title.

   PS3552.E157 A6 2002
   813'.54—dc21   2002020466

First Tor Edition: September 2002
First Orb Edition: March 2003

Printed in the United States of America

0 9 8 7 6 5 4 3 2 1

Copyright Acknowledgments

Contents

Introduction: The Blank Space

Being a writer is a peculiar life. Like an actor, a good writer has days when he doesn't know who he is. He becomes a book or a story, and his surroundings seem like a dream. Some writers (I name no names) become so engrossed in this other world that they are insufferable to those around them.

When a writer is with book, he is filled with different people and voices. When the book is good, the voices haunt his waking moments and clog his dreams. Near the end of a long and involved novel, I have stopped dreaming entirely.

A short story is not so filling, but it is equally demanding; it can drain all emotion and energy for a week or a month or longer, as I birth a small, intense universe.

Some writers can't wait to go back to the computer or the typewriter and rejoin this stream of characters and fictitious life. Often, however, we feel as if the unreal world vampirizes the real, and we are reluctant to submit. But the most painful time of all is when we need to see the other, unreal world as clearly as the real, and it *does not come*. It will not be summoned. A deadline looms, a story must be written; the subterranean talents can't work fast enough. The cart gallops on without the horse, and stories come crashing down, perhaps because they have been tinkered up from emotions that are false, characters that are unformed, plots that seemed grand at first, but ultimately turned out to be puerile and forced.

Remember that, the next time you think about being a writer. We spend days and weeks alone, and as someone (a French writer) once said, to be alone is to be in bad company. I don't find the company so bad, but I miss not being able to see my family. I miss not being able to see my family when they are all around me. The subterranean forces are at work building things, covering so many acres of my mental real estate that the iceberg tip of me becomes a little artificial and frail. I joke and the jokes are fragile; the world I am spinning, underground, is frightening because it is not clear. It is not finished.

I look around, frantic at the thought that this time, the story will be a fraud, I will be found out, my career—my income—the support of my family will collapse. Readers will finally catch on to my weakness. Everything I have done will be clearly perceived as a lineup of shams, pretensions, monstrosities . . .

Whoops! In comes a bad review for a recent novel, or the news that a competitor's novel (or worse, a good friend's novel) has climbed high on the bestseller lists . . . I wallow in the depths of creative despair . . .

And then, suddenly, at ten or eleven o'clock at night, I see a clear path. I see a way to bring the characters and situations into stark relief. I know the emotions will be true and compelling, the scene or chapter *will* work—at least for me—and for that evening, all is resolved, and I am happy.

Then comes the morning. I must write the scene that was so clear the night before. I stare at the blank space that must be filled. I back off, confused. There are problems I had not considered. There are logistical frames and setups to be resolved. I prowl around my office, tinker with other things, watch the news, scowl at the inanities and brilliancies of popular culture on TV. I do not know what oppresses me more: the clumsiness or the talent. The vicious idiocy of the world weighs on me. I become angry at politics, disgruntled at the way Americans refuse to understand how powerful and rich they really are. I see frightened, uninformed Americans worried about losing the things they never really needed and insist on distorting their lives to have. I build to a quiet rage. I am disappointed in all of them, because I have not done my work for the day.

I take a bath. Lying back in the tub, I nap silently; the water cools and is still. My knees shift from side to side. If the phone does not ring, I come back after half an hour, blink, wonder if there is anything ready to emerge, anything solved, a few pages to put down in the blankness.

I wash and dry my hair, it is afternoon, I wander into the office and sit in the chair. Anybody home, down there? I begin to write. Something has been resolved. Maybe only a few pages emerge. Maybe there is much dialog, a scene with clear emotions and follow-through, and seven or eight pages roll out. Maybe only three or four. Or two. Or none. But often, there is enough. The story or the novel grows. It is assembled like a clay sculpture, pasted together one small piece at a time. The sculpture has a rough shape that begins to please.

I go back to my family, driving carefully across the freeway, for I am a little stunned. Something has been drained out of me. I have written, but again I am not sure . . . Was it good? Will it read well the next day?

I have lived this way, crossing my daily tightrope, since the age of eight years. I have never had a choice. I think I was born a storyteller.

Storytellers grow, and their stories change. Sometimes they improve, sometimes they don't. But what may improve the least is the short story, and what may improve the most is the novel. For the short story works best with the emotions and fears and joys of the young. The novel is wiser and longer and slower, and it often improves as the writer ages. It is filled with longer and more difficult emotions, more convoluted and lovely and mellow.

The short story is bright and quick and sharp, like a song. To have written any successful short stories, any at all, is something of a miracle. To try to write a short story later in life is to reclaim a difficult thing: youth. Sometimes I manage. There is a joy in the accomplishment, but my real joy remains the novel. I can't easily condense my emotions and train my wandering thoughts. The short story remains difficult. Maybe I was always a little old, or at least unwilling to give in entirely to my youth.

All my life I have tried to explain the difference between writing imaginative literature—science fiction and fantasy—and writing contemporary fiction. My explanations usually fail. There is no real difference; there is only class distinction, distortions caused by historical trauma and literary snobbery (science fiction is the literature of "tradesmen," not "gentlemen").

All literature is fantasy. We do not understand who we are and perhaps never shall; we do not understand the world we live in, and perhaps never will. We make up the so-called real world as we grow and learn to see, but as we mature, we are horrified to realize that this world, so beautiful and necessary, will turn on us, that it will kill us and those we love. So perhaps this is the difference. The real world will kill us. But the unreal world kills us by its absence. We need vacations from death and certainty, from hard facts and distorted lives. Fantasy is part of our inner survival, our inner growth; it feeds the need to believe there is something more, strange and wonderful and affirming. We need to go where these strange things grow wild and free.

We also need to model and prepare for the future. This is how living things differ from the dead; we model the future. We anticipate. Science fiction is a living, Promethean thing. By describing the possible that does not yet exist, we help avoid it—or create it.

The best science fiction explores the truly blank pages, those on which no one has *ever* written. Filling those blank pages is one of the great joys in my life—next to raising my kids, the most delightful and demanding job I'll ever do.

The writers I read as a boy helped give birth to the future I live in today. I can only hope I'll have a fraction of their influence.

This book is for friends, family, readers, all who put up with me, and for storytellers in general. Thanks.

Soon, Now

Introduction to "Blood Music"

"Blood Music" was the big one—the idea that crept up on me, staggered me, and eventually helped shape my career.

There's a joke that when you join the Science Fiction Writers of America, you get a little envelope in the mail, and in that envelope there is a slip of paper on which is scrawled the idea that will haunt you for the rest of your days. For Frank Herbert, it was "Dune, desert planet." For Isaac Asimov, it might have been, "Robots work by the rules."

For me, it was "intelligent cells."

As it turns out, the read-write DNA of "Blood Music" is a natural reality, and this was known to a fair number of biologists even in 1982, when the idea for the story first occurred to me. HIV and other retroviruses, which incorporate their genome into host DNA, were just on the horizon of the lay public, however, and the Central Dogma of molecular biology—that DNA is transcribed to RNA, and RNA is translated into proteins, and that the reverse never happens; that DNA is a fixed template and can only be altered by "mistakes," random mutations—still ruled.

"Blood Music" has been described as a parable about AIDS. I don't think that's the case, really; we shouldn't throw all biological transformations into one pot. The point about this story, and many of my subsequent forays into genetics and evolution, is that what at first seems an unmitigated horror is in fact much more, if we could only take off the blinders of our mortal individuality.

I submitted this story to a number of high-paying magazines, including *Playboy* and *Omni*, and they rejected it with either no comment or wry grimaces. *Analog* was more receptive, but editor Stanley Schmidt wanted to know if the idea of a smart cell was even possible. I looked up the number of nucleotide base pairs in the human genome, about three billion, loosely compared that to the number of nerve cells in the human brain—trillions—and decided it was possible. What are factors of a thousand or ten thousand among friends?

Stan published the story. It went on to win a Hugo and a Nebula, my first prizes in the field.

As I wrote the novel version (published in 1985), I scrawled myself a note asking "what do cold viruses do for us?" In other words, why do we allow them to give us the sniffles, or worse? Some ten years later, while researching my novel *Darwin's Radio*, I asked that question again, and concocted a subplot in which a scientist discovers the remains of ancient retroviruses in the human genome. Not long after, I learned about HERV—Human Endogenous Retroviruses. They're real, many of them are primordial—tens of millions of years or older—

and they could play a major role in human birth, autoimmune diseases, cancer, and even in evolution.

So much for trying to write science fiction.

Cells are self-making and self-regulating in ways we never imagined only a few decades ago. In other words, our cells are intelligent, in their way, and sometimes even break loose from their slavery and assert their individuality.

We call such things tumors.

I wonder—do tumor cells read the genetic equivalent of Ayn Rand?

Blood Music
Analog, Stanley Schmidt, 1983

There is a principle in nature I don't think anyone has pointed out before. Each hour, a myriad of trillions of little live things—bacteria, microbes, "animalcules"—are born and die, not counting for much except in the bulk of their existence and the accumulation of their tiny effects. They do not perceive deeply. They do not suffer much. A hundred billion, dying, would not begin to have the same importance as a single human death.

Within the ranks of magnitude of all creatures, small as microbes or great as humans, there is an equality of "elan," just as the branches of a tall tree, gathered together, equal the bulk of the limbs below, and all the limbs equal the bulk of the trunk.

That, at least, is the principle. I believe Vergil Ulam was the first to violate it.

It had been two years since I'd last seen Vergil. My memory of him hardly matched the tan, smiling, well-dressed gentleman standing before me. We had made a lunch appointment over the phone the day before, and now faced each other in the wide double doors of the employees' cafeteria at the Mount Freedom Medical Center.

"Vergil?" I asked. "My God, Vergil!"

"Good to see you, Edward." He shook my hand firmly. He had lost ten or twelve kilos and what remained seemed tighter, better proportioned. At university, Vergil had been the pudgy, shock-haired, snaggle-toothed whiz kid who hot-wired doorknobs, gave us punch that turned our piss blue, and never got a date except with Eileen Termagent, who shared many of his physical characteristics.

"You look fantastic," I said. "Spend a summer in Cabo San Lucas?"

We stood in line at the counter and chose our food. "The tan," he said, picking out a carton of chocolate milk, "is from spending three months under a sunlamp. My teeth were straightened just after I last saw you. I'll explain the rest, but we need a place to talk in private."

I steered him to the smoker's corner, where three diehard puffers were scattered among six tables.

"Listen, I mean it," I said as we unloaded our trays. "You've changed. You're looking good."

"I've changed more than you know." His tone was motion-picture ominous, and he delivered the line with a theatrical lift of his brows. "How's Gail?"

Gail was doing well, I told him, teaching nursery school. We'd married the year before. His gaze shifted down to his food—pineapple slice and cottage cheese, piece of banana cream pie—and he said, his voice almost cracking, "Notice something else?"

I squinted in concentration. "Uh."

"Look closer."

"I'm not sure. Well, yes, you're not wearing glasses. Contacts?"

"No. I don't need them anymore."

"And you're a snappy dresser. Who's dressing you now? I hope she's as sexy as she is tasteful."

"Candice isn't—wasn't responsible for the improvement in my clothes," he said. "I just got a better job, more money to throw around. My taste in clothes is better than my taste in food, as it happens." He grinned the old Vergil self-deprecating grin, but ended it with a peculiar leer. "At any rate, she's left me, I've been fired from my job, I'm living on savings."

"Hold it," I said. "That's a bit crowded. Why not do a linear break-down? You got a job. Where?"

"Genetron Corp.," he said. "Sixteen months ago."

"I haven't heard of them."

"You will. They're putting out common stock in the next month. It'll shoot off the board. They've broken through with MABs. Medical—"

"I know what MABs are," I interrupted. "At least in theory. Medically Applicable Biochips."

"They have some that work."

"What?" It was my turn to lift my brows.

"Microscopic logic circuits. You inject them into the human body, they set up shop where they're told and troubleshoot. With Dr. Michael Bernard's approval."

That was quite impressive. Bernard's reputation was spotless. Not only was he associated with the genetic engineering biggies, but he had made news at least once a year in his practice as a neurosurgeon before retiring. Covers on *Time, Mega, Rolling Stone*.

"That's supposed to be secret—stock, breakthrough, Bernard, every-thing." He looked around and lowered his voice. "But you do whatever the hell you want. I'm through with the bastards."

I whistled. "Make me rich, huh?"

"If that's what you want. Or you can spend some time with me before rushing off to your broker."

"Of course." He hadn't touched the cottage cheese or pie. He had, however, eaten the pineapple slice and drunk the chocolate milk. "So tell me more."

"Well, in med school I was training for lab work. Biochemical re-search. I've always had a bent for computers, too. So I put myself through my last two years—"

"By selling software packages to Westinghouse," I said.

"It's good my friends remember. That's how I got involved with Ge-netron, just when they were starting out. They had big money backers, all the lab facilities I thought anyone would ever need. They hired me, and I advanced rapidly.

"Four months and I was doing my own work. I made some break-throughs—" he tossed his hand nonchalantly—"then I went off on tan-gents they thought were premature. I persisted and they took away my lab, handed it over to a certifiable flatworm. I managed to save part of the experiment before they fired me. But I haven't exactly been cautious . . . or judicious. So now it's going on outside the lab."

I'd always regarded Vergil as ambitious, a trifle cracked, and not ter-ribly sensitive. His relations with authority figures had never been smooth. Science, for him, was like the woman you couldn't possibly have, who suddenly opens her arms to you, long before you're ready for mature love—leaving you afraid you'll forever blow the chance, lose the prize. Apparently, he did. "Outside the lab? I don't get you."

"Edward, I want you to examine me. Give me a thorough physical. Maybe a cancer diagnostic. Then I'll explain more."

"You want a five-thousand-dollar exam?"

"Whatever you can do. Ultrasound, NMR, thermogram, everything."

"I don't know if I can get access to all that equipment. NMR full-scan has only been here a month or two. Hell, you couldn't pick a more expensive way—"

"Then ultrasound. That's all you'll need."

"Vergil, I'm an obstetrician, not a glamour-boy lab-tech. OB-GYN, butt of all jokes. If you're turning into a woman, maybe I can help you."

He leaned forward, almost putting his elbow into the pie, but swing-ing wide at the last instant by scant millimeters. The old Vergil would have hit it square. "Examine me closely and you'll . . ." He narrowed his eyes. "Just examine me."

"So I make an appointment for ultrasound. Who's going to pay?"

"I'm on Blue Shield." He smiled and held up a medical credit card. "I messed with the personnel files at Genetron. Anything up to a hundred thousand dollars medical, they'll never check, never suspect."

He wanted secrecy, so I made arrangements. I filled out his forms myself. As long as everything was billed properly, most of the examination could take place without official notice. I didn't charge for my services. After all, Vergil had turned my piss blue. We were friends.

He came in late at night. I wasn't normally on duty then, but I stayed late, waiting for him on the third floor of what the nurses called the Frankenstein wing. I sat on an orange plastic chair. He arrived, looking olive-colored under the fluorescent lights.

He stripped, and I arranged him on the table. I noticed, first off, that his ankles looked swollen. But they weren't puffy. I felt them several times. They seemed healthy but looked odd. "Hm," I said.

I ran the paddles over him, picking up areas difficult for the big unit to hit, and programmed the data into the imaging system. Then I swung the table around and inserted it into the enameled orifice of the ultrasound diagnostic unit, the *humhole,* so-called by the nurses.

I integrated the data from the humhole with that from the paddle sweeps and rolled Vergil out, then set up a video frame. The image took a second to integrate, then flowed into a pattern showing Vergil's skeleton. My jaw fell.

Three seconds of that and it switched to his thoracic organs, then his musculature, and, finally, vascular system and skin.

"How long since the accident?" I asked, trying to take the quiver out of my voice.

"I haven't been in an accident," he said. "It was deliberate."

"Jesus, they beat you to keep secrets?"

"You don't understand me, Edward. Look at the images again. I'm not damaged."

"Look, there's thickening here"—I indicated the ankles—"and your ribs—that crazy zigzag pattern of interlocks. Broken sometime, obviously. And—"

"Look at my spine," he said. I rotated the image in the video frame.

Buckminster Fuller, I thought. It was fantastic. A cage of triangular projections, all interlocking in ways I couldn't begin to follow, much less understand. I reached around and tried to feel his spine with my fingers. He lifted his arms and looked off at the ceiling.

"I can't find it," I said. "It's all smooth back there." I let go of him and looked at his chest, then prodded his ribs. They were sheathed in something tough and flexible. The harder I pressed, the tougher it became. Then I noticed another change.

"Hey," I said. "You don't have any nipples." There were tiny pigment patches, but no nipple formations at all.

"See?" Vergil asked, shrugging on the white robe, "I'm being rebuilt from the inside out."

In my reconstruction of those hours, I fancy myself saying, "So tell me about it." Perhaps mercifully, I don't remember what I actually said.

He explained with his characteristic circumlocutions. Listening was like trying to get to the meat of a newspaper article through a forest of sidebars and graphic embellishments.

I simplify and condense.

Genetron had assigned him to manufacturing prototype biochips, tiny circuits made out of protein molecules. Some were hooked up to silicon chips little more than a micrometer in size, then sent through rat arteries to chemically keyed locations, to make connections with the rat tissue and attempt to monitor and even control lab-induced pathologies.

"That was something," he said.

"We recovered the most complex microchip by sacrificing the rat, then debriefed it—hooked the silicon portion up to an imaging system. The computer gave us bar graphs, then a diagram of the chemical char-acteristics of about eleven centimeters of blood vessel . . . then put it all together to make a picture. We zoomed down eleven centimeters of rat artery. You never saw so many scientists jumping up and down, hugging each other, drinking buckets of bug juice." Bug juice was lab ethanol mixed with Dr Pepper.

Eventually, the silicon elements were eliminated completely in favor of nucleoproteins. He seemed reluctant to explain in detail, but I gath-ered they found ways to make huge molecules—as large as DNA, and even more complex—into electrochemical computers, using ribosome-like structures as "encoders" and "readers" and RNA as "tape." Vergil was able to mimic reproductive separation and reassembly in his nucle-oproteins, incorporating program changes at key points by switching nucleotide pairs. "Genetron wanted me to switch over to supergene en-gineering, since that was the coming thing everywhere else. Make all kinds of critters, some out of our imagination. But I had different ideas." He twiddled his finger around his ear and made theremin sounds. "Mad scientist time, right?" He laughed, then sobered. "I injected my best nucleoproteins into bacteria to make duplication and compounding eas-ier. Then I started to leave them inside, so the circuits could interact with the cells. They were heuristically programmed; they taught them-selves. The cells fed chemically coded information to the computers, the computers processed it and made decisions, the cells became smart. I mean, smart as planaria, for starters. Imagine an *E. coli* as smart as a planarian worm!"

I nodded. "I'm imagining."

"Then I really went off on my own. We had the equipment, the techniques; and I knew the molecular language. I could make really dense, really complicated biochips by compounding the nucleoproteins, making them into little brains. I did some research into how far I could go, theoretically. Sticking with bacteria, I could make a biochip with the computing capacity of a sparrow's brain. Imagine how jazzed I was! Then I saw a way to increase the complexity a thousandfold, by using something we regarded as a nuisance—quantum chit-chat between the fixed elements of the circuits. Down that small, even the slightest change could bomb a biochip. But I developed a program that actually predicted and took advantage of electron tunneling. Emphasized the heuristic aspects of the computer, used the chit-chat as a method of increasing complexity."

"You're losing me," I said.

"I took advantage of randomness. The circuits could repair themselves, compare memories, and correct faulty elements. I gave them basic instructions: Go forth and multiply. Improve. By God, you should have seen some of the cultures a week later! It was amazing. They were evolving all on their own, like little cities. I destroyed them all. I think one of the petri dishes would have grown legs and walked out of the incubator if I'd kept feeding it."

"You're kidding." I looked at him. "You're not kidding."

"Man, they knew what it was like to improve! They knew where they had to go, but they were just so limited, being in bacteria bodies, with so few resources."

"How smart were they?"

"I couldn't be sure. They were associating in clusters of a hundred to two hundred cells, each cluster behaving like an autonomous unit. Each cluster might have been as smart as a rhesus monkey. They exchanged information through their pili, passed on bits of memory, and compared notes. Their organization was obviously different from a group of monkeys. Their world was so much simpler, for one thing. With their abilities, they were masters of the petri dishes. I put phages in with them; the phages didn't have a chance. They used every option available to change and grow."

"How is that possible?"

"What?" He seemed surprised I wasn't accepting everything at face value. "Cramming so much into so little. A rhesus monkey is not your simple little calculator, Vergil."

"I haven't made myself clear," he said, obviously irritated. "I was using nucleoprotein computers. They're like DNA, but all the information can interact. Do you know how many nucleotide pairs there are in the DNA of a single bacteria?"

It had been a long time since my last biochemistry lesson. I shook my head.

"About two million. Add in the modified ribosome structures—fifteen thousand of them, each with a molecular weight of about three million—and consider the combinations and permutations. The RNA is arranged like a continuous loop paper tape, surrounded by ribosomes ticking off instructions and manufacturing protein chains . . ." His eyes were bright and slightly moist. "Besides, I'm not saying every cell was a distinct entity. They cooperated."

"How many bacteria were in the dishes you destroyed?"

"Billions. I don't know." He smirked. "You got it, Edward. Whole planetsful of *E. coli.*"

"But Genetron didn't fire you then?"

"No. They didn't know what was going on, for one thing. I kept compounding the molecules, increasing their size and complexity. When bacteria were too limited, I took blood from myself, separated out white cells, and injected them with the new biochips. I watched them, put them through mazes and little chemical problems. They were whizzes. Time is a lot faster at that level—so little distance for the messages to cross, and the environment is much simpler. Then I forgot to store a file under my secret code in the lab computers. Some managers found it and guessed what I was up to. Everybody panicked. They thought we'd have every social watchdog in the country on our backs because of what I'd done. They started to destroy my work and wipe my programs. Ordered me to sterilize my white cells. Christ." He pulled the white robe off and started to get dressed. "I only had a day or two. I separated out the most complex cells—"

"How complex?"

"They were clustering in hundred-cell groups, like the bacteria. Each group as smart as a four-year-old kid, maybe." He studied my face for a moment. "Still doubting? Want me to run through how many nucleotides there are in the human genome? I tailored my computers to take advantage of the white cells' capacity. Tens of thousands of genes. Three billion nucleotides, Edward. And they don't have a huge body to worry about, taking up most of their thinking time."

"Okay," I said. "I'm convinced. What did you do?"

"I mixed the cells back into a cylinder of whole blood and injected myself with it." He buttoned the top of his shirt and smiled thinly at me. "I'd programmed them with every drive I could, talked as high a level as I could using just enzymes and such. After that, they were on their own."

"You programmed them to go forth and multiply, improve?" I repeated.

"I think they developed some characteristics picked up by the biochips in their *E. coli* phases. The white cells could talk to each other with extruded memories. They found ways to ingest other types of cells and alter them without killing them."

"You're crazy."

"You can see the screen! Edward, I haven't been sick since. I used to get colds all the time. I've never felt better."

"They're inside you, finding things, changing them."

"And by now, each cluster is as smart as you or I."

"You're absolutely nuts."

He shrugged. "Genetron fired me. They thought I was going to take revenge for what they did to my work. They ordered me out of the labs, and I haven't had a real chance to see what's been going on inside me until now. Three months."

"So . . ." My mind was racing. "You lost weight because they improved your fat metabolism. Your bones are stronger, your spine has been completely rebuilt—"

"No more backaches even if I sleep on my old mattress."

"Your heart looks different."

"I didn't know about the heart," he said, examining the frame image more closely. "As for the fat—I was thinking about that. They could increase my brown cells, fix up the metabolism. I haven't been as hungry lately. I haven't changed my eating habits that much—I still want the same old junk—but somehow I get around to eating only what I need. I don't think they know what my brain is yet. Sure, they've got all the glandular stuff—but they don't have the big picture, if you see what I mean. They don't know I'm in here. But boy, they sure did figure out what my reproductive organs are."

I glanced at the image and shifted my eyes away.

"Oh, they look pretty normal," he said, hefting his scrotum obscenely. He snickered. "But how else do you think I'd land a real looker like Candice? She was just after a one-night stand with a techie. I looked okay then, no tan but trim, with good clothes. She'd never screwed a techie before. Joke time, right? But my little geniuses kept us up half the night. I think they made improvements each time. I felt like I had a goddamned fever."

His smile vanished. "But then one night my skin started to crawl. It really scared me. I thought things were getting out of hand. I wondered what they'd do when they crossed the blood-brain barrier and found out about me—about the brain's real function. So I began a campaign to keep them under control. I figured, the reason they wanted to get into the skin was the simplicity of running circuits across a surface. Much easier than trying to maintain chains of communication in and around muscles, organs, vessels. The skin was much more direct. So I bought a quartz lamp." He caught my puzzled expression. "In the lab, we'd break down the protein in biochip cells by exposing them to ultraviolet light. I alternated sunlamp with quartz treatments. Keeps them out of my skin and gives me a nice tan."

"Give you skin cancer, too," I commented.

"They'll probably take care of that. Like police."

"Okay. I've examined you, you've told me a story I still find hard to believe . . . what do you want me to do?"

"I'm not as nonchalant as I act, Edward. I'm worried. I'd like to learn how to control them before they find out about my brain. I mean, think of it, they're in the trillions by now, each one smart. They're cooperating to some extent. I'm probably the smartest thing on the planet, and they haven't even begun to get their act together. I don't really want them to take over." He laughed unpleasantly. "Steal my soul, you know? So think of some treatment to block them. Maybe we can starve the little buggers. Just think on it." He buttoned his shirt. "Give me a call." He handed me a slip of paper with his address and phone number. Then he went to the keyboard and erased the image on the frame, dumping the memory of the examination. "Just you," he said. "Nobody else for now. And please . . . hurry."

It was three o'clock in the morning when Vergil walked out of the examination room. He'd allowed me to take blood samples, then shaken my hand—his palm was damp, nervous—and cautioned me against ingesting anything from the specimens.

Before I went home, I put the blood through a series of tests. The results were ready the next day.

I picked them up during my lunch break in the afternoon, then destroyed all of the samples. I did it like a robot. It took me five days and nearly sleepless nights to accept what I'd seen. His blood was normal enough, though the machines diagnosed the patient as having an infection. High levels of leukocytes—white blood cells—and histamines. On the fifth day, I believed.

Gail came home before I did, but it was my turn to fix dinner. She slipped one of the school's disks into the home system and showed me video art her nursery kids had been creating. I watched quietly, ate with her in silence.

I had two dreams, part of my final acceptance. In the first, that evening, I witnessed the destruction of the planet Krypton, Superman's home world. Billions of superhuman geniuses went screaming off in walls of fire. I related the destruction to my sterilizing the samples of Vergil's blood.

The second dream was worse. I dreamed that New York City was raping a woman. By the end of the dream, she gave birth to little embryo cities, all wrapped up in translucent sacs, soaked with blood from the difficult labor.

I called him on the morning of the sixth day. He answered on the fourth ring. "I have some results," I said. "Nothing conclusive. But I want to talk with you. In person."

"Sure," he said. "I'm staying inside for the time being." His voice was strained; he sounded tired.

Vergil's apartment was in a fancy high-rise near the lake shore. I took the elevator up, listening to little advertising jingles and watching dancing holograms display products, empty apartments for rent, the building's hostess discussing social activities for the week.

Vergil opened the door and motioned me in. He wore a checked robe with long sleeves and carpet slippers. He clutched an unlit pipe in one hand, his fingers twisting it back and forth as he walked away from me and sat down, saying nothing.

"You have an infection," I said.

"Oh?"

"That's all the blood analyses tell me. I don't have access to the electron microscopes."

"I don't think it's really an infection," he said. "After all, they're my own cells. Probably something else . . . some sign of their presence, of the change. We can't expect to understand everything that's happening."

I removed my coat. "Listen," I said, "you really have me worried now." The expression on his face stopped me: a kind of frantic beatitude. He squinted at the ceiling and pursed his lips.

"Are you stoned?" I asked.

He shook his head, then nodded once, very slowly. "Listening," he said.

"To what?"

"I don't know. Not sounds . . . exactly. Like music. The heart, all the blood vessels, friction of blood along the arteries, veins. Activity. Music in the blood." He looked at me plaintively. "Why aren't you at work?"

"My day off. Gail's working."

"Can you stay?"

I shrugged. "I suppose." I sounded suspicious. I glanced around the apartment, looking for ashtrays, packs of papers.

"I'm not stoned, Edward," he said. "I may be wrong, but I think something big is happening. I think they're finding out who I am."

I sat down across from Vergil, staring at him intently. He didn't seem to notice. Some inner process involved him. When I asked for a cup of coffee, he motioned to the kitchen. I boiled a pot of water and took a jar of instant from the cabinet. With cup in hand, I returned to my seat. He twisted his head back and forth, eyes open. "You always knew what you wanted to be, didn't you?" he asked.

"More or less."

"A gynecologist. Smart moves. Never false moves. I was different. I had goals, but no direction. Like a map without roads, just places to be. I didn't give a shit for anything, anyone but myself. Even science. Just a means. I'm surprised I got so far. I even hated my folks."

He gripped his chair arms.

"Something wrong?" I asked.

"They're talking to me," he said. He shut his eyes.

For an hour he seemed to be asleep. I checked his pulse, which was strong and steady, felt his forehead—slightly cool—and made myself more coffee. I was looking through a magazine, at a loss what to do, when he opened his eyes again. "Hard to figure exactly what time is like for them," he said. "It's taken them maybe three, four days to figure out language, key human concepts. Now they're on to it. On to me. Right now."

"How's that?"

He claimed there were thousands of researchers hooked up to his neurons. He couldn't give details. "They're damned efficient, you know," he said. "They haven't screwed me up yet."

"We should get you into the hospital now."

"What in hell could other doctors do? Did you figure out any way to control them? I mean, they're my own cells."

"I've been thinking. We could starve them. Find out what metabolic differences—"

"I'm not sure I want to be rid of them," Vergil said. "They're not doing any harm."

"How do you know?"

He shook his head and held up one finger. "Wait. They're trying to figure out what space is. That's tough for them: They break distances down into concentrations of chemicals. For them, space is like intensity of taste."

"Vergil—"

"Listen! Think, Edward!" His tone was excited but even. "Something big is happening inside me. They talk to each other across the fluid, through membranes. They tailor something—viruses?—to carry data stored in nucleic acid chains. I think they're saying 'RNA.' That makes sense. That's one way I programmed them. But plasmidlike structures, too. Maybe that's what your machines think is a sign of infection—all their chattering in my blood, packets of data. Tastes of other individuals. Peers. Superiors. Subordinates."

"Vergil, I still think you should be in a hospital."

"This is my show, Edward," he said. "I'm their universe. They're amazed by the new scale." He was quiet again for a time. I squatted by his chair and pulled up the sleeve to his robe. His arm was crisscrossed with white lines. I was about to go to the phone when he stood and stretched. "Do you realize," he said, "how many body cells we kill each time we move?"

"I'm going to call for an ambulance," I said.

"No, you aren't." His tone stopped me. "I told you, I'm not sick, this is my show. Do you know what they'd do to me in a hospital? They'd be like cavemen trying to fix a computer. It would be a farce."

"Then what the hell am I doing here?" I asked, getting angry. "I can't do anything. I'm one of those cavemen."

"You're a friend," Vergil said, fixing his eyes on me. I had the impression I was being watched by more than just Vergil. "I want you here to keep me company." He laughed. "But I'm not exactly alone."

He walked around the apartment for two hours, fingering things, looking out windows, slowly and methodically fixing himself lunch. "You know, they can actually feel their own thoughts," he said about noon. "I mean, the cytoplasm seems to have a will of its own, a kind of subconscious life counter to the rationality they've only recently acquired. They hear the chemical 'noise' of the molecules fitting and unfitting inside."

At two o'clock, I called Gail to tell her I would be late. I was almost sick with tension, but I tried to keep my voice level. "Remember Vergil Ulam? I'm talking with him right now."

"Everything okay?" she asked.

Was it? Decidedly not. "Fine," I said.

"Culture!" Vergil said, peering around the kitchen wall at me. I said good-bye and hung up the phone. "They're always swimming in that bath of information. Contributing to it. It's a kind of gestalt thing. The hierarchy is absolute. They send tailored phages after cells that don't interact properly. Viruses specified to individuals or groups. No escape. A rogue cell gets pierced by the virus, the cell blebs outward, it explodes and dissolves. But it's not just a dictatorship. I think they effectively have more freedom than in a democracy. I mean, they vary so differently from individual to individual. Does that make sense? They vary in different ways than we do."

"Hold it," I said, gripping his shoulders. "Vergil, you're pushing me to

the edge. I can't take this much longer. I don't understand, I'm not sure
I believe—"

"Not even now?"

"Okay, let's say you're giving me the right interpretation. Giving it to
me straight. Have you bothered to figure out the consequences yet?
What all this means, where it might lead?"

He walked into the kitchen and drew a glass of water from the tap
then returned and stood next to me. His expression had changed from
childish absorption to sober concern. "I've never been very good at
that."

"Are you afraid?"

"I was. Now, I'm not sure." He fingered the tie of his robe. "Look, I
don't want you to think I went around you, over your head or something. But I met with Michael Bernard yesterday. He put me through
his private clinic, took specimens. Told me to quit the lamp treatments.
He called this morning, just before you did. He says it all checks out.
And he asked me not to tell anybody." He paused and his expression
became dreamy again. "Cities of cells," he continued. "Edward, they
push tubes through the tissues, spread information—"

"Stop it!" I shouted. "Checks out? What checks out?"

"As Bernard puts it, I have 'severely enlarged macrophages' throughout my system. And he concurs on the anatomical changes."

"What does he plan to do?"

"I don't know. I think he'll probably convince Genetron to reopen
the lab."

"Is that what you want?"

"It's not just having the lab again. I want to show you. Since I stopped
the lamp treatments, I'm still changing." He undid his robe and let it
slide to the floor. All over his body, his skin was crisscrossed with white
lines. Along his back, the lines were starting to form ridges.

"My God," I said.

"I'm not going to be much good anywhere else but the lab soon. I
won't be able to go out in public. Hospitals wouldn't know what to do,
as I said."

"You're . . . you can talk to them, tell them to slow down," I said,
aware how ridiculous that sounded.

"Yes, indeed I can, but they don't necessarily listen."

"I thought you were their god or something."

"The ones hooked up to my neurons aren't the big wheels. They're
researchers, or at least serve the same function. They know I'm here,
what I am, but that doesn't mean they've convinced the upper levels of
the hierarchy."

"They're disputing?"

"Something like that. It's not all that bad, anyway. If the lab is re-opened, I have a home, a place to work." He glanced out the window, as if looking for someone. "I don't have anything left but them. They aren't afraid, Edward. I've never felt so close to anything before." The beatific smile again. "I'm responsible for them. Mother to them all."

"You have no way of knowing what they're going to do."

He shook his head.

"No, I mean it. You say they're like a civilization—"

"Like a thousand civilizations."

"Yes, and civilizations have been known to screw up. Warfare, the environment—"

I was grasping at straws, trying to restrain a growing panic. I wasn't competent to handle the enormity of what was happening. Neither was Vergil. He was the last person I would have called insightful and wise about large issues.

"But I'm the only one at risk."

"You don't know that. Jesus, Vergil, look what they're doing to you!"

"To me, all to me!" he said. "Nobody else."

I shook my head and held up my hands in a gesture of defeat. "Okay, so Bernard gets them to reopen the lab, you move in, become a guinea pig. What then?"

"They treat me right. I'm more than just good old Vergil Ulam now. I'm a goddamned galaxy, a super-mother."

"Super-host, you mean." He conceded the point with a shrug.

I couldn't take any more. I made my exit with a few flimsy excuses, then sat in the lobby of the apartment building, trying to calm down. Somebody had to talk some sense into him. Who would he listen to? He had gone to Bernard . . .

And it sounded as if Bernard was not only convinced, but very interested. People of Bernard's stature didn't coax the Vergil Ulams of the world along unless they felt it was to their advantage.

I had a hunch, and I decided to play it. I went to a pay phone, slipped in my credit card, and called Genetron.

"I'd like you to page Dr. Michael Bernard," I told the receptionist.

"Who's calling, please?"

"This is his answering service. We have an emergency call and his beeper doesn't seem to be working."

A few anxious minutes later, Bernard came on the line. "Who the hell is this?" he asked. "I don't have an answering service."

"My name is Edward Milligan. I'm a friend of Vergil Ulam's. I think we have some problems to discuss."

We made an appointment to talk the next morning.

I went home and tried to think of excuses to keep me off the next day's hospital shift. I couldn't concentrate on medicine, couldn't give my patients anywhere near the attention they deserved.

Guilty, angry, afraid.

That was how Gail found me. I slipped on a mask of calm and we fixed dinner together. After eating, holding onto each other, we watched the city lights come on in late twilight through the bayside window. Winter starlings pecked at the yellow lawn in the last few minutes of light, then flew away with a rising wind which made the windows rattle.

"Something's wrong," Gail said softly. "Are you going to tell me, or just act like everything's normal?"

"It's just me," I said. "Nervous. Work at the hospital."

"Oh, lord," she said, sitting up. "You're going to divorce me for that Baker woman." Mrs. Baker weighed three hundred and sixty pounds and hadn't known she was pregnant until her fifth month.

"No," I said, listless.

"Rapturous relief," Gail said, touching my forehead lightly. "You know this kind of introspection drives me crazy."

"Well, it's nothing I can talk about yet, so . . ." I patted her hand.

"That's disgustingly patronizing," she said, getting up. "I'm going to make some tea. Want some?" Now she was miffed, and I was tense with not telling.

Why not just reveal all? I asked myself. An old friend was turning himself into a galaxy.

I cleared away the table instead. That night, unable to sleep, I looked down on Gail in bed from my sitting position, pillow against the wall, and tried to determine what I knew was real, and what wasn't.

I'm a doctor, I told myself. A technical, scientific professional. I'm supposed to be immune to things like future shock.

Vergil Ulam was turning into a galaxy.

How would it feel to be topped off with a trillion intelligences speaking a language more mysterious than Chinese? I grinned in the dark and almost cried at the same time. What Vergil had inside him was unimaginably stranger. Stranger than anything I—or Vergil—could easily understand. Perhaps ever understand.

But I knew what was real. The bedroom, the city lights faint through gauze curtains. Gail sleeping. Very important. Gail in bed, sleeping.

The dream returned. This time the city came in through the window and attacked Gail. It was a great, spiky lit-up prowler, and it growled in a language I couldn't understand, made up of auto horns, crowd noises, construction bedlam. I tried to fight it off, but it got to her—and turned into a drift of stars, sprinkling all over the bed, all over everything. I jerked awake and stayed up until dawn, dressed with Gail, kissed her, savored the reality of her human, unviolated lips.

I went to meet with Bernard. He had been loaned a suite in a big downtown hospital; I rode the elevator to the sixth floor, and saw what fame and fortune could mean.

The suite was tastefully furnished, fine serigraphs on wood-paneled walls, chrome and glass furniture, cream-colored carpet, Chinese brass, and wormwood-grain cabinets and tables.

He offered me a cup of coffee, and I accepted. He took a seat in the breakfast nook, and I sat across from him, cradling my cup in moist palms. He wore a dapper gray suit and had graying hair and a sharp profile. He was in his mid sixties and he looked quite a bit like Leonard Bernstein.

"About our mutual acquaintance," he said. "Mr. Ulam. Brilliant. And, I won't hesitate to say, courageous."

"He's my friend. I'm worried about him."

Bernard held up one finger. "Courageous—and a bloody damned fool. What's happening to him should never have been allowed. He may have done it under duress, but that's no excuse. Still, what's done is done. He's talked to you, I take it."

I nodded. "He wants to return to Genetron."

"Of course. That's where all his equipment is. Where his home probably will be while we sort this out."

"Sort it out—how? Why?" I wasn't thinking too clearly. I had a slight headache.

"I can think of a large number of uses for small, superdense computer elements with a biological base. Can't you? Genetron has already made breakthroughs, but this is something else again."

"What do you envision?"

Bernard smiled. "I'm not really at liberty to say. It'll be revolutionary. We'll have to get him in lab conditions. Animal experiments have to be conducted. We'll start from scratch, of course. Vergil's . . . um . . . colonies can't be transferred. They're based on his own white blood cells. So we have to develop colonies that won't trigger immune reactions in other animals."

"Like an infection?" I asked.

"I suppose there are comparisons. But Vergil is not infected."

"My tests indicate he is."

"That's probably the bits of data floating around in his blood, don't you think?"

"I don't know."

"Listen, I'd like you to come down to the lab after Vergil is settled in. Your expertise might be useful to us."

Us. He was working with Genetron hand in glove. Could he be objective? "How will you benefit from all this?"

"Edward, I have always been at the forefront of my profession. I see no reason why I shouldn't be helping here. With my knowledge of brain and nerve functions, and the research I've been conducting in neurophysiology—"

"You could help Genetron hold off an investigation by the government," I said.

"That's being very blunt. Too blunt, and unfair."

"Perhaps. Anyway, yes: I'd like to visit the lab when Vergil's settled in. If I'm still welcome, bluntness and all." He looked at me sharply. I wouldn't be playing on his team; for a moment, his thoughts were almost nakedly apparent.

"Of course," Bernard said, rising with me. He reached out to shake my hand. His palm was damp. He was as nervous as I was, even if he didn't look it.

I returned to my apartment and stayed there until noon, reading, trying to sort things out. Reach a decision. What was real, what I needed to protect.

There is only so much change anyone can stand: innovation, yes, but slow application. Don't force. Everyone has the right to stay the same until they decide otherwise.

The greatest thing in science since . . .

And Bernard would force it. Genetron would force it. I couldn't handle the thought. "Neo-Luddite," I said to myself. A filthy accusation.

When I pressed Vergil's number on the building security panel, Vergil answered almost immediately. "Yeah," he said. He sounded exhilarated. "Come on up. I'll be in the bathroom. Door's unlocked."

I entered his apartment and walked through the hallway to the bathroom. Vergil lay in the tub, up to his neck in pinkish water. He smiled vaguely and splashed his hands. "Looks like I slit my wrists, doesn't it?" he said softly. "Don't worry. Everything's fine now. Genetron's going to take me back. Bernard just called." He pointed to the bathroom phone and intercom.

I sat on the toilet and noticed the sunlamp fixture standing unplugged next to the linen cabinets. The bulbs sat in a row on the edge of the sink counter. "You're sure that's what you want," I said, my shoulders slumping.

"Yeah, I think so," he said. "They can take better care of me. I'm getting cleaned up, going over there this evening. Bernard's picking me up in his limo. Style. From here on in, everything's style."

The pinkish color in the water didn't look like soap. "Is that bubble bath?" I asked. Some of it came to me in a rush then and I felt a little weaker; what had occurred to me was just one more obvious and necessary insanity.

"No," Vergil said. I knew that already.

"No," he repeated, "it's coming from my skin. They're not telling me everything, but I think they're sending out scouts. Astronauts." He looked at me with an expression that didn't quite equal concern; more like curiosity as to how I'd take it.

The confirmation made my stomach muscles tighten as if waiting for a punch. I had never even considered the possibility until now, perhaps because I had been concentrating on other aspects. "Is this the first time?" I asked.

"Yeah," he said. He laughed. "I've half a mind to let the little buggers down the drain. Let them find out what the world's really about."

"They'd go everywhere," I said.

"Sure enough."

"How . . . how are you feeling?"

"I'm feeling pretty good now. Must be billions of them." More splashing with his hands. "What do you think? Should I let the buggers out?"

Quickly, hardly thinking, I knelt down beside the tub. My fingers went for the cord on the sunlamp and I plugged it in. He had hot-wired doorknobs, turned my piss blue, played a thousand dumb practical jokes and never grown up, never grown mature enough to understand that he was sufficiently brilliant to transform the world; he would never learn caution.

He reached for the drain knob. "You know, Edward, I—"

He never finished. I picked up the fixture and dropped it into the tub, jumping back at the flash of steam and sparks. Vergil screamed and thrashed and jerked and then everything was still, except for the low, steady sizzle and the smoke wafting from his hair.

I lifted the toilet lid and vomited. Then I clenched my nose and went into the living room. My legs went out from under me and I sat abruptly on the couch.

After an hour, I searched through Vergil's kitchen and found bleach, ammonia, and a bottle of Jack Daniel's. I returned to the bathroom, keeping the center of my gaze away from Vergil. I poured first the booze, then the bleach, then the ammonia into the water. Chlorine started bubbling up and I left, closing the door behind me.

The phone was ringing when I got home. I didn't answer. It could have been the hospital. It could have been Bernard. Or the police. I could envision having to explain everything to the police. Genetron would stonewall; Bernard would be unavailable.

I was exhausted, all my muscles knotted with tension and whatever name one can give to the feelings one has after—

Committing genocide?

That certainly didn't seem real. I could not believe I had just murdered a hundred trillion intelligent beings. Snuffed a galaxy. It was laughable. But I didn't laugh.

It was easy to believe that I had just killed one human being, a friend. The smoke, the melted lamp rods, the drooping electrical outlet and smoking cord.

Vergil.

I had dunked the lamp into the tub with Vergil.

I felt sick. Dreams, cities raping Gail. (And what about his girlfriend, Candice?) Draining the water filled with them. Galaxies sprinkling over us all. What horror. Then again, what potential beauty—a new kind of life, symbiosis and transformation.

Had I been thorough enough to kill them all? I had a moment of panic. Tomorrow, I thought, I will sterilize his apartment. Somehow, I didn't even think of Bernard.

When Gail came in the door, I was asleep on the couch. I came to, groggy, and she looked down at me.

"You feeling okay?" she asked, perching on the edge of the couch. I nodded.

"What are you planning for dinner?" My mouth didn't work properly. The words were mushy. She felt my forehead.

"Edward, you have a fever," she said. "A very high fever.'

I stumbled into the bathroom and looked in the mirror. Gail was close behind me. "What is it?" she asked.

There were lines under my collar, around my neck. White lines, like freeways. They had already been in me a long time, days.

"Damp palms," I said. So obvious.

I think we nearly died. I struggled at first, but in minutes I was too weak to move. Gail was just as sick within an hour.

I lay on the carpet in the living room, drenched in sweat. Gail lay on the couch, her face the color of talcum, eyes closed, like a corpse in an embalming parlor. For a time I thought she was dead. Sick as I was, I raged—hated, felt tremendous guilt at my weakness, my slowness to understand all the possibilities. Then I no longer cared. I was too weak to blink, so I closed my eyes and waited.

There was a rhythm in my arms, my legs. With each pulse of blood, a kind of sound welled up within me, like an orchestra thousands strong, but not playing in unison; playing whole seasons of symphonies at once. Music in the blood. The sound became harsher, but more co-ordinated, wave-trains finally canceling into silence, then separating into harmonic beats.

The beats seemed to melt into me, into the sound of my own heart.

First, they subdued our immune responses. The war—and it was a war, on a scale never before known on Earth, with trillions of combatants—lasted perhaps two days.

By the time I regained enough strength to get to the kitchen faucet, I could feel them working on my brain, trying to crack the code and find the god within the protoplasm. I drank until I was sick, then drank more moderately and took a glass to Gail. She sipped at it. Her lips were cracked, her eyes bloodshot and ringed with yellowish crumbs. There was some color in her skin. Minutes later, we were eating feebly in the kitchen.

"What in hell is happening?" was the first thing she asked. I didn't have the strength to explain. I peeled an orange and shared it with her. "We should call a doctor," she said. But I knew we wouldn't. I was already receiving messages; it was becoming apparent that any sensation of freedom we experienced was illusory.

The messages were simple at first. Memories of commands, rather than the commands themselves, manifested themselves in my thoughts. We were not to leave the apartment—a concept which seemed quite abstract to those in control, even if undesirable—and we were not to have contact with others. We would be allowed to eat certain foods and drink tap water for the time being.

With the subsidence of the fevers, the transformations were quick and drastic. Almost simultaneously, Gail and I were immobilized. She was sitting at the table, I was kneeling on the floor. I was able barely to see her in the corner of my eye.

Her arm developed pronounced ridges.

They had learned inside Vergil; their tactics within the two of us were very different. I itched all over for about two hours—two hours in hell—before they made the breakthrough and found me. The effort of ages on their timescale paid off and they communicated smoothly and directly with this great, clumsy intelligence who had once controlled their universe.

They were not cruel. When the concept of discomfort and its undesirability was made clear, they worked to alleviate it. They worked too effectively. For another hour, I was in a sea of bliss, out of all contact with them.

With dawn the next day, they gave us freedom to move again; specifically, to go to the bathroom. There were certain waste products they could not deal with. I voided those—my urine was purple—and Gail followed suit. We looked at each other vacantly in the bathroom. Then she managed a slight smile. "Are they talking to you?" she asked.

I nodded.

"Then I'm not crazy."

For the next twelve hours, control seemed to loosen on some levels. I suspect there was another kind of war going on in me. Gail was capable of limited motion, but no more.

When full control resumed, we were instructed to hold each other. We did not hesitate.

"Eddie . . ." she whispered. My name was the last sound I ever heard from outside.

Standing, we grew together. In hours, our legs expanded and spread out. Then extensions grew to the windows to take in sunlight, and to the kitchen to take water from the sink. Filaments soon reached to all corners of the room, stripping paint and plaster from the walls, fabric and stuffing from the furniture.

By the next dawn, the transformation was complete.

I no longer have any clear view of what we look like. I suspect we resemble cells—large, flat, and filamented cells, draped purposefully across most of the apartment. The great shall mimic the small.

Our intelligence fluctuates daily as we are absorbed into the minds within. Each day, our individuality declines. We are, indeed, great clumsy dinosaurs. Our memories have been taken over by billions of them, and our personalities have been spread through the transformed blood.

Soon there will be no need for centralization.

Already the plumbing has been invaded. People throughout the building are undergoing transformation.

Within the old time frame of weeks, we will reach the lakes, rivers, and seas in force.

I can barely begin to guess the results. Every square inch of the planet will teem with thought. Years from now, perhaps much sooner, they will subdue their own individuality—what there is of it.

New creatures will come, then. The immensity of their capacity for thought will be inconceivable.

All my hatred and fear is gone now.

I leave them—us—with only one question.

How many times has this happened, elsewhere? Travelers never came through space to visit the Earth. They had no need.

They had found universes in grains of sand.

Afterword

In the early eighties, a brilliant visionary named K. Eric Drexler proposed that very tiny machines could change the nature of the human race. Physicist Richard Feynman (of course) had come up with the idea first, imagining a series of "assemblers" that could make smaller versions of themselves, capable of making smaller versions still, down to the molecular scale. Drexler refined these ideas and called his new field of endeavor "nanotechnology." His first book on the subject, *Engines of Creation*, appeared from Doubleday in 1985.

To many, "Blood Music" and the novel of the same name suggested the first appearance of nanotechnology in science fiction, which is perhaps true. But Drexler's vision, while it encompasses biology, relies to this day on the replacement of biology with something more certain, "harder" as it were and less "squishy," less subject to the vagaries of death and decay.

I tend to believe that since protein molecules already perform many of the tasks of Drexler's nanomachines, biology will rule—for the time being. But Eric and his colleagues could ultimately be correct. They've certainly caught the attention of industry and the government. And they regard a story like "Blood Music" as not so much inspirational as a warning: Avoid processes that can turn the world into "gray goo."

But the novel version of *Blood Music* ends on a very upbeat note. Very few people die, and we're all biologically uploaded into a new kind of heaven, where we can do almost anything we want, even live forever.

What's so bad about that?

I like squishy. Always have. I still think squishy will win.

Introduction to "Sisters"

Brian Thomsen was my editor at Warner Books during the late 1980s and early 1990s. To help promote my second collection of short stories, *Tangents,* Brian suggested I write an original story. I had been thinking for some time about the day-to-day effects of the genetic revolution—as opposed to the more spectacular possibilities described in *Blood Music* and *Eon*—and also, what sort of tribal distinctions might arise between those who have been genetically enhanced and those who have not. The beginning of our acute awareness of tribes is often in high school.

"Sisters" was the result.

Fortunately, this story preceded the excellent film *Gattaca,* which I highly recommend. It's one of the best science fiction films of the last decade.

Sisters
Tangents (author collection), Brian Thomsen, 1989

B ut you're the only one, Letitia." Reena Cathcart lay a light, slender hand on her shoulder with a look of utmost sincerity. "You know none of the others can. I mean . . ." She stopped, the slightest hint of awareness of her *faux pas* dawning. "You're simply the only one who can play the old—the older—woman."

Letitia Blakely looked down at the hall floor, eyes and face hot, then circled her gaze up to the ceiling, trying to keep the fresh tears from spilling over. Reena tossed her long black hair, perfect hazel eyes imploring. A few stragglers sauntered down the clean and carpeted hall of the new school wing to their classes. "We're late for first period," Letitia said. "Why the old woman? Why didn't you come to me when there was some other part to play?"

Reena was too smart not to know what she was doing. Smart, but not terribly sensitive. "You're the type."

"You mean frowsy?"

Reena didn't react. She was intent on a yes answer, the perfect solution to her problems.

"Or just dumpy?"

"You shouldn't be ashamed of how you look."

"I look frowsy and *dumpy!* I'm perfect for the old woman in your lysing play, and you're the only one with the guts to ask me."

"We'd like to give you a chance. You're such a loner, and we want you to feel like you're part—"

"Bullmusk!" The moisture spilled over and Reena backed away. "Leave me alone. Just leave me alone."

"No need to swear." Petulant, offended.

Letitia raised her hand as if to strike. Reena swung her hair again defiantly and turned to walk away. Letitia leaned against the tile wall and wiped her eyes, trying to avoid damage to her carefully applied makeup. The damage was already done, however. She could feel the tear-tracks of her mother's mascara and the smudged eyeshadow. With a sigh, she walked off to the bathroom, not caring how late she was. She wanted to go home.

Coming into class fifteen minutes after the bell, Letitia was surprised to find the students in self-ordered discussion, with no sign of Mr. Brant. Several of Reena's drama group gave her frosty looks as she took her seat.

"TB," Edna Corman said beneath her breath from across the aisle.

"RC you," Letitia replied, head cocked to one side and tone matching Edna's precisely. She poked John Lockwood in the shoulder. Lockwood didn't much care for socializing; he seldom noticed the exchanges going on around him. "Where's Mr. Brant?"

"Georgia Fischer blitzed and he took her to the counselors. He told us to plug in and pursue."

"Oh." Georgia Fischer had transferred two months ago from a super-whiz class in Oakland. She was brighter than most but she blitzed about once every two weeks. "I may be fat and ugly," Letitia said for Lockwood's ears only. "But I never blitz."

"Nor I," Lockwood said. He was PPC, like Georgia, but not a super-whiz. Letitia liked him, but not enough to feel threatened by him. "Better pursue."

Letitia leaned back in her seat and closed her eyes to concentrate. Her mod activated and projections danced in front of her, then steadied. She had been cramming patient psych for a week and was approaching threshold. The little Computer Graphics nursie in whites and pillcap began discussing insanouts of terminal patient care, which all seemed very TB to Letitia; who died of disease now, anyway? She made her decision and cut to the same CG nursie discussing the shock of RoR— replacement or recovery. What she really wanted to study was colony medicine, but how could she ever make it Out There?

Some PPCs had been designed by their parents to qualify physically and mentally for space careers. Some had been equipped with bichemistries, one of which became active in Earth's gravity, the other in space. How could an NG compete with that?

Of the seven hundred adolescents in her high school training programs, Letitia Blakely was one of ten NGs—possessors of natural, unaltered genomes. Everyone else was the proud bearer of juggled genes, PPCs or Pre-Planned Children, all lovely and stable with just the proper amount of adipose tissue and just the proper infusion of parental characteristics and chosen features to be beautiful and different; tall, healthy, hair manageable, skin unblemished, well-adjusted (except for the occasional blitzer) with warm and sunny personalities. The old derogatory slang for PPCs was RC—Recombined.

Letitia, slightly overweight, skin pasty, hair frizzy, bulbous-nosed and weak-chinned, one breast larger than the other and already showing a droop pronounced enough to grip a stylus—with painful menstrual periods and an absolute indisposition to athletics—was the Sport. That's what they were called. NG Sports. TBs—Throwbacks. Neanderthals.

All the beautiful PPCs risked a great deal if they showed animosity toward the NGs. Her parents had the right to sue the system if she was harassed to the detriment of her schooling. This wasn't a private school where all parents paid astronomical tuitions; this was an old-fashioned public school, with public school programs and regulations. Teachers tended to nuke out on raggers. And, she admitted to herself with a painful loop of recrimination, she wasn't making it any easier for them.

Sure, she could join in, play the old woman—how much realism she would contribute to their little drama, with her genuine TB phys! She could be jolly and self-deprecating like Helen Roberti, who wasn't all that bad-looking anyway—she could pass if she straightened her hair. Or she could be quiet and camouflaged like Bernie Thibhault.

The CG nursie exited from RoR care. Letitia had hardly absorbed a thing. Realtime mod education was a bore, but she hadn't yet qualified for experience training. She had only one course of career study now—no alternates—and two aesthetic programs, individual orchestra on Friday afternoon and LitVid publishing on alternating weekends.

For pre-med, she was a washout, but she wouldn't admit it. She was NG. Her brain took longer to mature; it wasn't as finely wired.

She thought she was incredibly slow. She doubted whether she would ever be successful as a doctor; she was squeamish, and nobody, not even her fellow NGs, would want to be treated by a doctor who grew pale at the sight of blood.

Letitia silently told nursie to start over again, and nursie obliged.

Reena Cathcart, meanwhile, had dropped into her mod with a vengeance. Her blissed expression told it all. The realtime ed slid into her so smooth, so quick, it was pure joy.

No zits on her brain.

Mr. Brant returned ten minutes later with a pale and bleary-eyed Georgia Fischer. She sat two seats behind Letitia and over one aisle. She plugged in her mod dutifully and Brant went to his console to bring up the multimedia and coordinate the whole class. Edna Corman whispered something to her.

"Not a bad blitz, all in all," Georgia commented softly.

"How are you doing, Letitia?" the autocounselor asked. The CG face projected in front of her with some slight wirehash, which Letitia paid no attention to. CG ACs were the jams and she didn't appreciate them even in pristine perfection.

"Poorly," she said.

"Really? Care to elaborate?"

"I want to talk to Dr. Rutger."

"Don't trust your friendly AC?"

"I'd like some clear space. I want to talk to Dr. Rutger."

"Dr. Rutger is busy, dear. Unlike your friendly AC, humans can only be in one place at a time. I'd like to help if I may."

"Then I want program sixteen."

"Done, Letitia." The projection wavered and the face changed to a real-person simulation of Marian Tempesino, the only CG AC Letitia felt comfortable with.

Tempesino had no wirehash, which indicated she was a seldom-used program, and that was just fine with Letitia. "Sixteen here. Letitia? You're looking cut. More adjustment jams?"

"I wanted to talk with Dr. Rutger but he's busy. So I'll talk to you. And I want it on my record. I want out of school. I want my parents to pull me and put me in a special NG school."

Tempesino's face didn't wear any particular expression, which was one of the reasons Letitia liked Program 16 AC. "Why?"

"Because I'm a freak. My parents made me a freak and I'd like to know why I shouldn't be with all the other freaks."

"You're a natural, not a freak."

"To look like any of the others even to look like Reena Cathcart—I'd have to spend the rest of my life in bioplasty. I can't take it anymore. They asked me to play an old lady in one of their dramas. The only part I'm fit for. An old lady."

"They tried to include you in."

"That hurt!" Letitia said, tears in her eyes.

Tempesino's image wavered a bit as the emotion registered and a higher authority AC kicked in behind 16.

"I just want out. I want to be alone."

"Where would you like to go, Letitia?"

Letitia thought about it for a moment. "I'd like to go back to when being ugly was normal."

"Fine, then. Let's simulate. Sixty years should do it. Ready?"

She nodded and wiped away more mascara with the back of her hand.

"Then let's go."

It was like a dream, somewhat fuzzier than plugging in a mod. CG images compiled from thousands of miles of old films and tapes and descriptive records made her feel as if she were flying back in time, back to a place she would have loved to call home. Faces came to her—faces with ugly variations, growing old prematurely, wearing glasses, even beautiful faces which could have passed today—and the faces pulled away to become attached to bodies. Bodies out of shape, in good condition, overweight, sick and healthy, red-faced with high blood pressure: the whole variable and disaster-prone population of humanity, sixty years past. This was where Letitia felt she belonged.

"They're beautiful," she said.

"They didn't think so. They jumped at the chance to be sure their children were beautiful, smart, and healthy. It was a time of transition, Letitia. Just like now."

"Everybody looks alike now."

"I don't think that's fair," the AC said. "There's a considerable variety in the way people look today."

"Not my age."

"Especially your age. Look." The AC showed her dozens of faces. Few looked alike, but were handsome or lovely. Some made Letitia ache; faces she could never be friends with, never love, because there was always someone more beautiful and desirable than an NG.

"My parents should have lived back then. Why did they make me a freak?"

"You're developmentally normal. You're not a freak."

"Sure. I'm a DNG. Dingy. That's what they call me."

"Don't you invite the abuse sometimes?"

"No!" This was getting her nowhere.

"Letitia, we all have to adjust. Not even today's world is fair. Are you sure you're doing all you can to adjust?"

Letitia squirmed in her seat and said she wanted to leave. "Just a moment," the AC said. "We're not done yet." She knew that tone of voice. The ACs were allowed to get a little rough at times. They could make unruly students do grounds duty or detain them after hours to work on assignments usually given to computers. Letitia sighed and settled back. She hated being lectured.

"Young woman, you're carrying a giant chip on your shoulder."

"That's all the more computing capacity for me."

"Quiet and listen. We're all allowed to criticize policy, whoever makes it. Dignity of office and respect for superiors has not survived very well into Century Twenty-one. People have to earn respect. That goes for students, too. The average student here has four major talents, each of them fitting into a public planning policy which guarantees them a job incorporating two or more of those talents. They aren't forced to accept the jobs, and if their will falters, they may not keep those jobs. But the public has tried to guarantee every one of us a quality employment opportunity. That goes for you, as well. You're DNG, but you also show as much intelligence and at least as many developable talents as the PPCs. You are young, and your maturation schedule is a natural one—but you are not inferior or impaired, Letitia. That's more than can be said for the offspring of some parents even more resistive than your own. You at least were given prenatal care and nutrition adjustment, and your parents let the biotechs correct your allergies."

"So?"

"So for you, it's all a matter of will. If your will falters, you won't be given any more consideration than a PPC. You'll have to choose secondary or tertiary employment, or even . . ." The AC paused. "Public support. Do you want that?"

"My grades are up. I'm doing fine."

"You are choosing career training not matching your developable talents."

"I like medicine."

"You're squeamish."

Letitia shrugged.

"And you're hard to get along with."

"Just tell them to lay off. I'll be civil . . . but I don't want them treating me like a freak. Edna Corman called me . . ." She paused. That could get Edna Corman into a lot of trouble. Among the students, TB was a casual epithet; to school authorities, applied to an NG, it might be grounds for a blot on Corman's record. "Nothing. Not important."

The AC switched to lower authority and Tempesino's face took a different counseling track. "Fine. Adjustment on both sides is necessary. Thank you for coming in, Letitia."

"Yeah. I still want to talk with Rutger."

"Request has been noted. Please return to your class in progress."

"PAY ATTENTION TO YOUR BROTHER WHEN HE'S TALKING," JANE SAID. ROALD was making a nuisance of himself by chattering about the preflight training he was getting in primary. Letitia made a polite comment or two, then lapsed back into contemplation of the food before her. She didn't eat. Jane regarded her from the corner of her eye and passed a bowl of sugared berries. "What's eating you?"

"I'm doing the eating," Letitia said archly.

"Ha," Roald said. "Full load from this angle." He grinned at her, his two front teeth missing. He looked hideous, she thought. Any other family would have given him temporaries; not hers.

"A little more respect from both of you," said Donald. Her father took the bowl from Roald and scooped a modest portion into his cup, then set it beside Letitia. "Big fifteen and big eight." That was his homily; behave big whether eight or fifteen.

"Autocounselor today?" Jane asked. She knew Letitia much too well.

"AC," Letitia affirmed.

"Did you go in?"

"Yes."

"And?"

"I'm not tuned."

"Which means?" Donald ask.

"It means she hisses and crackles," Roald said, mouth full of berries, juice dripping down his chin. He cupped his hand underneath and sucked it up noisily. Jane reached out and finished the job with a napkin. "She complains," Roald finished.

"About what?"

Letitia shook her head and didn't answer.

The dessert was almost finished when Letitia slapped both palms on the table. "Why did you do it?"

"Why did we do what?" her father asked, startled.

"Why are Roald and I normal? Why didn't you design us?"

Jane and Donald glanced at each other quickly and turned to Letitia. Roald regarded her with wide eyes, a bit shocked himself.

"Surely you know why by now," Jane said, looking down at the table, either nonplussed or getting angry. Now that she had laid out her course, Letitia couldn't help but forge ahead.

"I don't. Not really. It's not because you're religious."

"Something like that," Donald said.

"No," Jane said, shaking her head firmly.

"Then why?"

"Your mother and I—"

"I am *not* just their mother," Jane said.

"Jane and I believe there is a certain plan in nature, a plan we shouldn't interfere with. If we had gone along with most of the others and tried to have PPCs—participated in the boy-girl lotteries and signed up for the prebirth opportunity counseling—why, we would have been interfering."

"Did you go to a hospital when we were born?"

"Yes," Jane said, still avoiding their faces.

"That's not natural," Letitia said. "Why not let nature decide whether we'd be born alive?"

"We have never claimed to be consistent," Donald said.

"Donald," Jane said ominously.

"There are limits," Donald expanded, smiling placation. "We believe those limits begin when people try to interfere with the sex cells. You've had all that in school. You know about the protests when the first PPCs were born. Your grandmother was one of the protesters. Your mother and I are both NGs; of course, our generation has a much higher percentage of NGs."

"Now we're freaks," Letitia said.

"If by that you mean there aren't many teenage NGs, I suppose that's right," Donald said, touching his wife's arm. "But it could also mean you're special. Chosen."

"No," Letitia said. "Not chosen. You played dice with both of us. We could have been DDs. Duds. Not just dingies, but retards or spazzes."

An uncomfortable quiet settled over the table. "Not likely," Donald said, his voice barely above a whisper. "Your mother and I both have good genotypes. Your grandmother insisted your mother marry a good genotype. There are no developmentally disabled people in our families."

Letitia had been hemmed in. There was no way she could see out of it, so she pushed back her chair and excused herself from the table.

As she made her way up to her room, she heard arguing below. Roald raced up the stairs behind her and gave her a dirty look. "Why'd you have to bring all that up?" he asked. "It's bad enough at school, we don't have to have it here."

She thought about the history the AC had shown her. Back then, a family with their income wouldn't have been able to live in a four-bedroom house. Back then, there had been half as many people in the United States and Canada as there were now. There had been more unemployment, much more economic uncertainty, and far fewer automated jobs. The percentage of people doing physical labor for a living—simple construction, crop maintenance and harvesting, digging ditches and hard work like that—had been ten times greater then than it was now. Most of the people doing such labor today belonged to religious sects or one of the Wendell Barry farming communes.

Back then, Roald and Letitia would have been considered gifted children with a bright future.

She thought about the pictures and the feeling of the past, and wondered if Reena hadn't been right.

She would be a perfect old woman.

Her mother came into her room while Letitia was putting up her hair. She stood in the door frame. It was obvious she had been crying. Letitia watched her reflection in the mirror of her grandmother's dressing table, willed to her four years before. "Yes?" she asked softly, ageless bobby pins in her mouth.

"It was more my idea than your father's," Jane said, stepping closer, hands folded before her. "I mean, I am your mother. We've never really talked about this."

"No," Letitia said.

"So why now?"

"Maybe I'm growing up."

"Yes." Jane looked at the soft and flickering pictures hung on the walls, pastel scenes of improbable forests. "When I was pregnant with you, I was very afraid. I worried we'd made the wrong decision, going against what everybody else seemed to think and what everybody was advising or being advised. But I carried you and felt you move . . . and I knew you were ours, and ours alone, and that we were responsible for you body and soul. I was your mother, not the doctors."

Letitia looked up with mixed anger and frustration . . . and love.

"And now I see you. I think back to what I might have felt, if I were your age again, in your position. I might be mad, too. Roald hasn't had time to feel different yet; he's too young. I just came up here to tell you; I know that what I did was right, not for us, not for them"—she indicated the broad world beyond the walls of the house—"but right for you. It will work out. It really will." She put her hands on Letitia's shoulders. "They aren't having an easy time either. You know that." She stopped for a moment, then from behind her back revealed a book with a soft brown cover. "I brought this to show you again. You remember Great-Grandma? Her grandmother came all the way from Ireland, along with her grandpa." Jane gave her the album. Reluctantly, Letitia opened it up. There were real photographs inside, on paper, ancient black and white and faded color. Her great-grandmother did not much resemble Grandmother, who had been big-boned, heavy-set. Great-grandmother looked as if she had been skinny all her life. "You keep this," Jane said. "Think about it for a while."

The morning came with planned rain. Letitia took the half-empty metro to school, looking at the terraced and gardened and occasionally neglected landscape of the extended suburbs through raindrop-smeared glass. She came onto the school grounds and went to one of the older buildings in the school, where there was a little-used old-fashioned lavatory. This sometimes served as her sanctuary. She stood in a white stall and breathed deeply for a few minutes, then went to a sink and washed her hands as if conducting some ritual. Slowly, reluctantly, she looked at herself in the cracked mirror. A janitorial worker went about its duties, leaving behind the fresh, steamy smell of clean fixtures.

The early part of the day was a numb time. Letitia began to fear her own distance from feeling, from the people around her. She might at any minute step into the old lavatory and simply fade from the present, find herself sixty years back . . .

And what would she really think of that?

In her third period class she received a note requesting that she appear in Rutger's counseling office as soon as was convenient. That was shorthand for immediately; she gathered up her mods and caught Reena's unreadable glance as she walked past.

Rutger was a handsome man of forty-three (the years were registered on his desk life-clock, an affectation of some of the older PPCs) with a broad smile and a garish taste in clothes. He was head of the counseling department and generally well-liked in the school. He shook her hand as she entered the counseling office and offered her a chair. "Now. You wanted to talk to me?"

"I guess," Letitia said.

"Problems?" His voice was a pleasant baritone; he was probably a fairly good singer. That had been a popular trait in the early days of PPCs.

"The ACs say it's my attitude."

"And what about it?"

"I . . . am ugly. I am the ugliest girl . . . the only girl in this school who is ugly."

Rutger nodded. "I don't think you're ugly, but which is worse, being unique or being ugly?" Letitia lifted the corner of one lip in snide acknowledgment of the funny.

"Everybody's unique now," she said.

"That's what we teach. Do you believe it?"

"No," she said. "Everybody's the same. I'm . . ." She shook her head. She resented Rutger prying up the pavement over her emotions. "I'm TB. I wouldn't mind being a PPC, but I'm not."

"I think it's a minor problem," Rutger said quickly. He hadn't even sat down; obviously he was not going to give her much time.

"It doesn't feel minor," she said, anger poking through the cracks he had made.

"Oh, no. Being young often means that minor problems feel major. You feel envy and don't like yourself, at least not the way you look. Well, looks can be helped by diet, or at the very least by time. If I'm any judge, you'll look fine when you're older. And I am something of a judge. As for the way the others feel about you . . . I was a freak once."

Letitia looked up at him.

"Certainly. Bona fide. Much more of a freak than you. There are ten NGs like yourself in this school now. When I was your age, I was the only PPC in my school. There was still suspicion and even riots. Some PPCs were killed in one school when parents stormed the grounds."

Letitia stared.

"The other kids hated me. I wasn't bad-looking, but they knew. They had parents who told them PPCs were Frankenstein monsters. Do you remember the Rifkin Society? They're still around, but they're extreme fringies now. Just as well. They thought I'd been grown in a test tube somewhere and hatched out of an incubator. You've never experienced real hatred, I suspect. I did."

"You were nice-looking," Letitia said. "You knew somebody would like you eventually, maybe even love you. But what about me? Because of what I am, the way I look, who will ever want me? And will a PPC ever want to be with a Dingy?"

She knew these were hard questions and Rutger made no pretense of answering them. "Say it all works out for the worst," he said. "You end up a spinster and no one ever loves you. You spend the rest of your days alone. Is that what you're worried about?"

Her eyes widened. She had never quite thought those things through. Now she really hurt.

"Everybody out there is choosing beauty for their kids. They're choosing slender, athletic bodies and fine minds. You have a fine mind, but you don't have an athletic body. Or so you seem to be convinced; I have no record of you ever trying out for athletics. So when you're out in the adult world, sure, you'll look different. But why can't that be an advantage? You may be surprised how hard we PPCs try to be different. And how hard it is, since tastes vary so little in our parents. You have that built in."

Letitia listened, but the layers of paving were closing again. "Icing on the cake," she said.

Rutger regarded her with his shrewd blue eyes and shrugged. "Come back in a month and talk to me," he said. "Until then, I think auto-counselors will do fine."

Little was said at dinner and less after. She went upstairs and to bed at an early hour, feeling logy and hoping for escape.

Her father did his usual bedcheck an hour after she had put on her pajamas and lain down. "Rolled tight?" he asked.

"Mmph," she replied.

"Sleep tighter," he said. Rituals and formulas. Her life had been shaped by parents who were comfortable with nightly rituals and formulas.

Almost immediately after sleep, or so it seemed, she came abruptly awake. She sat up in bed and realized where she was, and who, and began to cry. She had had the strangest and most beautiful dream, the finest ever without a dream mod. She could not remember details now, try as she might, but waking was almost more than she could bear.

In the first period class, Georgia Fischer blitzed yet again and had to go to the infirmary. Letitia watched the others and saw a stony general cover-up of feelings. Edna Corman excused herself in second period and came back with red puffy eyes and pink cheeks. The tension built through the rest of the day until she wondered how anyone could concentrate. She did her own studying without any conviction; she was still wrapped in the dream, trying to decide what it meant.

In eighth period, she once again sat behind John Lockwood. It was as if she had completed a cycle beginning in the morning and ending with her last class. She looked at her watch anxiously. Once again, they had Mr. Brant supervising. He seemed distracted, as if he, too, had had a dream, and it hadn't been as pleasant as hers.

Brant had them cut mods mid-period and begin a discussion on what had been learned. These were the so-called integrative moments when the media learning was fixed by social interaction; Letitia found these periods a trial at the best of times. The others discussed their economics, Reena Cathcart as usual standing out in a class full of dominant personalities.

John Lockwood listened intently, a small smile on his face as he presented a profile to Letitia. He seemed about to turn around and talk to her. She placed her hand on the corner of her console and lifted her finger to attract his attention.

He glanced at her hand, turned away, and with a shudder looked at it again, staring this time, eyes widening. His mouth began to work as if her hand was the most horrible thing he had ever seen. His chin quivered, then his shoulder, and before Letitia could react he stood up and moaned. His legs went liquid beneath him and he fell to the console, arms hanging, then slid to the floor. On the floor, John Lockwood— who had never done such a thing in his life—twisted and groaned and shivered, locked in a violent blitz.

Brant pressed the class emergency button and came around his desk. Before he could reach Lockwood, the boy became still, eyes open, one hand letting go its tight grip on the leg of his seat. Letitia could not move, watching his empty eyes; he appeared so horribly *limp*.

Brant grabbed the boy by the shoulders, swearing steadily, and dragged him outside the classroom. Letitia followed them into the hall, wanting to help. Edna Corman and Reena Cathcart stood beside her, faces blank. Other students followed, staying well away from Brant and the boy.

Brant lowered John Lockwood to the concrete and began pounding his chest and administering mouth-to-mouth. He pulled a syringe from his coat pocket and uncapped it, shooting its full contents into the boy's skin just below the sternum. Letitia focused on the syringe, startled. Right in his pocket; not in the first aid kit.

The full class stood in the hallway, silent, in shock. The medical arrived, Rutger following; it scooped John Lockwood onto its gurney and swung around, lights flashing. "Have you administered KVN?" the robot asked Brant.

"Yes. Five cc's. Direct to heart."

Room after room came out to watch, all the PPCs fixing their eyes on the burdened medical as it rolled down the hall. Edna Corman cried. Reena glanced at Letitia and turned away as if ashamed.

"That's five," Rutger said, voice tired beyond grimness. Brant looked at him, then at the class, and told them they were dismissed. Letitia hung back. Brant screwed up his face in grief and anger. "Go! Get out of here!"

She ran. The last thing she heard Rutger say was, "More this week than last."

Letitia sat in the empty white lavatory, wiping her eyes, ashamed at her sniveling. She wanted to react like a grown-up—she saw herself being calm, cool, offering help to whoever might have needed it in the classroom—but the tears and the shaking would not stop.

Mr. Brant had seemed angry, as if the entire classroom were at fault. Not only was Mr. Brant adult, he was PPC.

So did she expect adults, especially adult PPCs, to behave better?

Wasn't that what it was all about?

She stared at herself in the cracked mirror. "I should go home, or go to the library and study," she said. Dignity and decorum. Two girls walked into the lavatory, and her private moment passed.

Letitia did not go to the library. Instead, she went to the old concrete and steel auditorium, entering through the open stage entrance, standing in darkness in the wings. Three female students sat in the front row, below the stage level and about ten meters away from Letitia. She recognized Reena but not the other two; they did not share classes with her.

"Did you know him?"

"No, not very well," Reena said. "He was in my class."

"No ducks!" the third snorted.

"Trish, keep it *interior*, please. Reena's had it rough."

"He hadn't blitzed. He wasn't a superwhiz. Nobody expected it."

"When was his incept?"

"I don't know," Reena said. "We're all about the same age, within a couple of months. We're all the same model year, same supplements, if it's something in the genotype, in the supplements . . ."

"I heard somebody say there had been five so far. I haven't heard anything," the third said.

"I haven't either," said the second.

"Not in our school," Reena said. "Except for the superwhizzes. And none of them have died before now."

Letitia stepped back in the darkness, hand on mouth. Had Lockwood actually died?

She thought for a mad moment of stepping out of the wings, going into the seats and telling the three she was sorry. The impulse faded fast. That would have been intruding.

They weren't any older than she was, and they didn't sound much more mature. They sounded scared.

In the morning, at the station room for pre-med secondary, Brant told them that John Lockwood had died the day before. "He had a heart attack," Brant said. Letitia intuited that was not the complete truth. A short eulogy was read, and special hours for psych counseling were arranged for those students who felt they might need it.

The word "blitzing" was not mentioned by Brant, nor by any of the PPCs throughout that day. Letitia tried to research the subject but found precious few materials in the libraries accessed by her mod. She presumed she didn't know where to look; it was hard to believe that *nobody* knew what was happening.

The dream came again, even stronger, the next night, and Letitia awoke out of it cold and shivering with excitement. She saw herself standing before a crowd, no single face visible, for she was in light and they were in darkness. She had felt, in the dream, an almost unbearable happiness, grief mixed with joy, unlike anything she had ever experienced before. She *loved* and did not know what she loved—not the crowd, precisely, not a man, not a family member, not even herself.

She sat up in her bed, hugging her knees, wondering if anybody else was awake. It seemed possible she had never been awake until now; every nerve was alive. Quietly, not wanting anybody else to intrude on this moment, she slipped out of bed and walked down the hall to her mother's sewing room. There, in a full-length cheval mirror, she looked at herself as if with new eyes.

"Who are you?" she whispered. She lifted her cotton nightshirt and stared at her legs. Short calves, lumpy knees, thighs not bad—not fat, at any rate. Her arms were softlooking, not muscular, but not particu-

larly plump, a rosy vanilla color with strawberry blotches on her elbows
where she leaned on them while reading in bed. She had Irish ancestors
on her mother's side; that showed in her skin color, recessed cheekbones, broad face. On her father's side, Mexican and German; not much
evidence in her of the Mexican. Her brother looked more swarthy.
"We're mongrels," she said. "I look like a mongrel compared to PPC
purebreds." But PPCs were not purebred; they were *designed*.

She lifted her nightshirt higher still, pulling it over her head finally
and standing naked. Shivering from the cold and from the memory of
her dream, she forced herself to focus on all of her characteristics.
Whenever she had seen herself naked in mirrors before, she had blurred
her eyes at one feature, looked away from another, special-effecting her
body into a more acceptable fantasy. Now she was in a mood to know
herself for what she was.

Broad hips, strong abdomen—plump, but strong. From her pre-med,
she knew that meant she would probably have little trouble bearing
children. "Brood mare," she said, but there was no critical sharpness in
the words. To have children, she would have to attract men, and right
now there seemed little chance of that. She did not have the "Attraction
Peaks" so often discussed on the TV, or seen faddishly headlined on the
LitVid mods; the culturally prescribed geometric curves allocated to so
few naturally, and now available to so many by design. *Does Your Child
Have the Best Design for Success?*

Such a shocking triviality. She felt a righteous anger grow—another
emotion she was not familiar with—and sucked it back into the excitement, not wanting to lose her mood. "I might never look at myself like
this again," she whispered.

Her breasts were moderate in size, the left larger than the right and
more drooping. She could indeed hold a stylus under her left breast,
something a PPC female would not have to worry about for decades, if
ever. Rib cage not really distinct; muscles not distinct; rounded, soft,
gentle-looking, face curious, friendly, wide-eyed, skin blemished but not
so badly it wouldn't recover on its own; feet long and toenails thick,
heavily cuticled. She had never suffered from ingrown toenails.

Her family line showed little evidence of tendency to cancer—cor-
rectible now, but still distressing—or heart disease or any of the other
diseases of melting pot cultures, of mobile populations and changing
habits. She saw a strong body in the mirror, one that would serve her
well.

And she also saw that with a little makeup, she could easily play an
older woman. Some shadow under the eyes, lines to highlight what
would in thirty or forty years be jowls, laugh lines . . .

But she did not look old *now*.

Letitia walked back to her room, treading carefully on the carpet. In the room, she asked the lights to turn on, lay down on the bed, pulled the photo album Jane had given her from the top of her nightstand and gingerly turned the delicate black paper pages. She stared at her great-grandmother's face, and then at the picture of her grandmother as a little girl.

INDIVIDUAL ORCHESTRA WAS TAUGHT BY THREE INSTRUCTORS IN ONE OF THE older drama classrooms behind the auditorium. It was a popular aesthetic; the school's music boxes were better than most home units, and the instructors were very popular. All were PPCs.

After a half-hour of group, each student could retire to box keyboard, order up spheres of countersound to avoid cacophony, and practice.

Today, she practiced for less than half an hour. Then, tongue between her lips, she stared into empty space over the keyboard. "Countersound off, please," she ordered, and stood up from the black bench. Mr. Teague, the senior instructor, asked if she were done for the day.

"I have to run an errand," she said.

"Practice your polyrhythms," he advised.

She left the classroom and walked around to the auditorium's stage entrance. She knew Reena's drama group would be meeting there.

The auditorium was dark, the stage lighted by a few catwalk spots. The drama group sat in a circle of chairs in one illuminated corner of the stage, reading lines aloud from old paper scripts. Hands folded, she walked toward the group. Rick Fayette, a quiet senior with short black hair, spotted her first but said nothing, glancing at Reena. Reena stopped reading her lines, turned, and stared at Letitia. Edna Corman saw her last and shook her head, as if this were the last straw.

"Hello," Letitia said.

"What are you doing here?" There was more wonder than disdain in Reena's voice.

"I thought you might still . . ." She shook her head. "Probably not. But I thought you might still be able to use me."

"*Really,*" Edna Corman said.

Reena put her script down and stood. "Why'd you change your mind?"

"I thought I wouldn't mind being an old lady," Reena said. "It's just not that big a deal. I brought a picture of my great-grandmother." She took a plastic wallet from her pocket and opened it to a copy she had made from the photo in the album. "You could make me up like this. Like my great-grandmother."

Reena took the wallet. "You look like her," she said.

"Yeah. Kind of."

"Look at this," Reena said, holding the picture out to the others. They gathered around and passed the wallet from hand to hand, staring in wonder. Even Edna Corman glanced at it briefly. "She actually *looks* like her great-grandmother."

Rick Fayette whistled with wonder. "You," he said, "will make a really great old lady."

Rutger called her into his office abruptly a week later. She sat quietly before his desk. "You've joined the drama class after all," he said. She nodded.

"Any reason?"

There was no simple way to express it. "Because of what you told me," she said.

"No friction?"

"It's going okay."

"Very good. They gave you another role to play?"

"No. I'm the old lady. They'll use makeup on me."

"You don't object to that?"

"I don't think so."

Rutger seemed to want to find something wrong, but he couldn't. With a faintly suspicious smile, he thanked her for her time. "Come back and see me whenever you want," he said. "Tell me how it goes."

The group met each Friday, an hour later than her individual orchestra. Letitia made arrangements for home keyboard hookup and practice. After a reading and a half hour of questions, she obtained the permission of the drama group adviser, a spinsterish non-PPC seldom seen in the hallways, Miss Darcy. Miss Darcy seemed old-fashioned and addressed all of her students as either "Mister" or "Miss," but she knew drama and stagecraft. She was the oldest of the six NG teachers in the school.

Reena stayed with Letitia during the audition and made a strong case for her late admittance, saying that the casting of Rick Fayette as an older woman was not going well. Fayette was equally eager to be rid of the part; he had another nonconflicting role, and the thought of playing two characters in this production worried him.

Fayette confessed his appreciation at their second Friday meeting. He introduced her to an elfishly handsome, large-eyed, slender group member, Frank Leroux. Leroux was much too shy to go on stage, Fayette said, but he would be doing their makeup. "He's pretty amazing."

Letitia stood nervously while Leroux examined her. "You've really got a *face*," he said softly. "May I touch you, to see where your contours are?"

Letitia giggled and abruptly sobered, embarrassed. "Okay," she said. "You're going to draw lines and make shadows?"

"Much more than that," Leroux said.

"He'll take a video of your face in motion," Fayette said. "Then he'll digitize it and sculpt a laserfoam mold—much better than sitting for a life mask. He made a life mask of *me* last year to turn me into the Hunchback of Notre Dame. No fun at all."

"This way is much better," Leroux said, touching her skin delicately, poking under her cheeks and chin, pulling back her hair to feel her temples. "I can make two or three sculptures showing what your face and neck are like when they're in different positions. Then I can adjust the appliance molds for flex and give."

"When he's done with you, you won't know yourself," Fayette said.

"Reena says you have a picture of your great-grandmother. May I see it?" Leroux asked. She gave him the wallet and he looked at the picture with squint-eyed intensity. "What a wonderful face," he said. "I never met my great-grandmother. My own grandmother looks about as old as my mother. They might be sisters."

"When he's done with you," Fayette said, his enthusiasm becoming a bit tiresome, "you and your *great-grandmother* will look like sisters!"

When she went home that evening, taking a late pay metro from the school, she wondered just exactly what she was doing. Throughout her high school years, she had cut herself off from most of her fellow students; the closest she came to friendship had been occasional banter while sitting at the mods with John Lockwood, waiting for instructors to arrive. Now she actually liked Fayette, and strange Leroux, whose hands were thin and pale and strong and slightly cold. Leroux was a PPC, but obviously his parents had different tastes; was he a superwhiz? Nobody had said so; perhaps it was a matter of honor among PPCs that they pretended not to care about their classifications.

Reena was friendly and supportive, but still distant.

As Letitia walked up the stairs, across the porch into the door of their home, setting her keyboard down by the closet, she saw the edge of a news broadcast in the living room. Nobody was watching; she surmised everybody was in the kitchen.

From this angle, the announcer appeared translucent and blue, ghostly. As Letitia walked around to the premium angle, the announcer solidified, a virtual goddess of Asian-negroid features with high cheekbones, straight golden hair and copper-bronze skin. Letitia didn't care what she looked like; what she was saying had attracted her attention.

"—revelations made today that as many as one-fourth of all PPCs inceived between sixteen and seventeen years ago may be possessors of a defective chromosome sequence known as T56-WA 5659. Originally part of an intelligence enhancement macrobox used in ramping creativity and mathematical ability, T56-WA 5659 was refined and made a standard option in virtually all pre-planned children. The effects of this defective sequence are not yet known, but at least twenty children in our city have already died. They all suffered from initial symptoms similar to grand mal epilepsy. Nationwide casualties are as yet unknown. The Rifkin Society is charging government regulatory agencies with a wholesale coverup.

"The Parental Pre-Natal Design Administration has advised parents of PPC children with this incept to immediately contact your medicals and design specialists for advice and treatment. Younger children may be eligible to receive wholebody retroviral therapy. For more detailed information, please refer to our LitVid online at this moment, and call—"

Letitia turned and saw her mother watching with a kind of grim satisfaction. When she noticed her daughter's shocked expression, she suddenly appeared sad. "How unfortunate," she said. "I wonder how far it will go."

Letitia did not eat much dinner. Nor did she sleep more than a couple of hours that night. The weekend seemed to stretch on forever.

LEROUX COMPARED THE LASERFOAM SCULPTURES TO HER FACE, TURNING HER chin this way and that with gentle hands before the green room mirror. As Leroux worked to test the various molds on Letitia, humming softly to himself, the rest of the drama group rehearsed a scene that did not require her presence. When they were done, Reena walked into the green room and stood behind them, watching. Letitia smiled stiffly through the hastily applied sheets and mounds of skinlike plastic.

"You're going to look great," Reena said.

"I'm going to look *old*," Letitia said, trying for a joke.

"I hope you aren't worried about that," Reena said. "Nobody cares, really. They all like you. Even Edna."

"I'm not worried," Letitia said.

Leroux pulled off the pieces and laid them carefully in a box. "Just about got it," he said. "I'm getting so good I could even make *Reena* look old if she'd let me."

Letitia considered for a moment. The implication, rather than the meaning, was embarrassingly obvious. Reena blushed and stared angrily at Leroux. Leroux caught her stare, looked between them, and said, "Well, I could." Reena could not argue without sinking them all deeper. Letitia blinked, then decided to let them off this particular hook. "She wouldn't look like a grandmother, though. I'll be a much better old lady."

"Of course," Leroux said, picking up his box and the sculptures. He walked to the door, a mad headsman. "Like your great-grandmother."

For a long silent moment, Reena and Letitia faced each other alone in the green room. The old incandescent makeup lights glared around the cracked mirror, casting a pearly glow on the white walls behind them. "You're a good actress," Reena said. "It really doesn't matter what you look like."

"Thank you."

"Sometimes I wished I looked like somebody in my family," Reena said.

Without thinking, Letitia said, "But you're beautiful." And she meant it. Reena *was* beautiful; with her Levantine darkness and long black hair, small sharp chin, large hazel-colored almond eyes and thin, ever-so-slightly bowed nose, she was simply lovely, with the kind of face and bearing and intelligence that two or three generations before would have moved her into entertainment, or pushed her into the social circles of the rich and famous. Behind the physical beauty was a sparkle of reserved wit, and something gentle. PPCs were healthier, felt better, and their minds, on the average, were more subtle, more balanced. Letitia did not feel inferior, however; not this time.

Something magic touched them. The previous awkwardness, and her deft destruction of that awkwardness, had moved them into a period of charmed conversation. Neither could offend the other; without words, that was a given.

"My parents are beautiful, too. I'm second generation," Reena said.

"Why would you want to look any different?"

"I don't, I suppose. I'm happy with the way I look. But I don't look much like my mother or my father. Oh, color, hair, eyes, that sort of thing . . . Still, my mother wasn't happy with her own face. She didn't get along well with my grandmother . . . She blamed her for not match-ing her face with her personality." Reena smiled. "It's all rather silly."

"Some people are never happy," Letitia observed.

Reena stepped forward and leaned over slightly to face Letitia's mirror image. "How do you feel, looking like your grandmother?"

Letitia bit her lip. "Until you asked me to join, I don't think I ever knew." She told about her mother giving her the album, and looking at herself in the mirror—though she did not describe being naked—and comparing herself with the old pictures.

"I think that's called an epiphany," Reena said. "It must have been nice. I'm glad I asked you, then, even if I was stupid."

"Were you . . ." Letitia paused. The period of charm was fading, re-grettably; she did not know whether this question would be taken as she meant it. "Did you ask me to give me a chance to stop being so silly and stand-offish?"

"No," Reena said steadily. "I asked you because we needed an old lady."

Looking at each other, they laughed suddenly, and the charmed moment was gone, replaced by something steadier and longer-lasting: friendship. Letitia took Reena's hand and pressed it. "Thank you," she said.

"You're welcome." Then, with hardly a pause, Reena said, "At least you don't have to worry."

Letitia stared up at her, mouth open, eyes searching.

"Got to go home now," Reena said. She squeezed Letitia's shoulder with more than gentle strength, revealing a physical anger or jealousy that ran counter to all they had said and done thus far. She turned and walked through the green-room door, leaving Letitia alone to pick off a few scraps of latex and adhesive.

The disaster grew. Letitia listened to the news in her room late that night, whispers in her ear, projected ghosts of newscasters and doctors and scientists dancing before her eyes, telling her things she did not really understand, could only feel.

A monster walked through her generation, but it would not touch her.

Going to school on Monday, she saw students clustered in hallways before the bell, somber, talking in low voices, glancing at her as she passed. In her second period class, she learned from overheard conversation that Leroux had died during the weekend. "He was superwhiz," a tall, athletic girl told her neighbor. "They don't die, usually, they just blitz. But he died."

Letitia retreated to the old lavatory at the beginning of lunch break, found it empty, but did not stare into the mirror. She knew what she looked like and accepted it.

What she found difficult to accept was a new feeling inside her. The young Letitia was gone. She could not live on a battlefield and remain a child. She thought about slender, elfin Leroux, carrying her heads under his arms, touching her face with gentle, professional admiration. Strong, cool fingers. Her eyes filled but the tears would not fall, and she went to lunch empty, fearful, confused.

She did not apply for counseling, however. This was something she had to face on her own.

Nothing much happened the next few days. The rehearsals went smoothly in the evenings as the date of the play approached. She learned her lines easily enough. Her role had a sadness that matched her mood. On Wednesday evening, after rehearsal, she joined Reena and Fayette at a supermarket sandwich stand near the school. Letitia did not tell her parents she would be late; she felt the need to not be responsible to anybody but her immediate peers. Jane would be upset, she knew, but not for long; this was a *necessity*.

Neither Reena nor Fayette mentioned the troubles directly. They were fairylike in their gaiety. They kidded Letitia about having to do without makeup now, and it seemed funny, despite their hidden grief. They ate sandwiches and drank fruit sodas and talked about what they would be when they grew up.

"Things didn't used to be so easy," Fayette said. "Kids didn't have so many options. Schools weren't very efficient at training for the real world; they were academic."

"Learning was slower," Letitia said.

"So were the kids," Reena said, tossing off an irresponsible grin.

"I resent that," Letitia said. Then, together, they all said, *"I don't deny it, I just resent it!"* Their laughter caught the attention of an older couple sitting in a corner. Even if the man and woman were not angry, Letitia wanted them to be, and she bowed her head down, giggling into her straw, snucking bubbles up her nose and choking. Reena made a disapproving face and Fayette covered his mouth, snorting with laughter.

"You could paste rubber all over your face," Fayette suggested.

"I'd look like Frankenstein's monster, not an old woman," Letitia said.

"So what's the difference?" Reena said.

"Really, you guys," Letitia said. "You're acting your age."

"Don't have to act," Fayette said. "Just *be.*"

"I wish we could act our age," Reena said.

Not once did they mention Leroux, but it was as if he sat beside them the whole time, sharing their levity.

It was the closest thing to a wake they could have.

"HAVE YOU GONE TO SEE YOUR DESIGNER, YOUR MEDICAL?" LETITIA ASKED Reena behind the stage curtains. The lights were off. Student stagehands moved muslin walls on dollies. Fresh paint smells filled the air.

"No," Reena said. "I'm not worried. I have a different incept."

"Really?"

She nodded. "It's okay. If there was any problem, I wouldn't be here. Don't worry." And nothing more was said.

The night of dress rehearsal came. Letitia put on her own makeup, drawing pencil lines and applying color and shadow; she had practiced and found herself reasonably adept at aging. With her great-grandmother's photograph before her, she mimicked the jowls she would have in her later years, drew laugh lines around her lips, and completed the effect with a smelly old gray wig dug out of a prop box.

The actors gathered for a prerehearsal inspection by Miss Darcy. They seemed quite adult now, dressed in their period costumes, tall and handsome. Letitia didn't mind standing out. Being an old woman gave her special status.

"This time, just relax, do it smooth," said Miss Darcy. "Everybody expects you to flub your lines, so you'll probably do them all perfectly.

We'll have an audience, but they're here to forgive our mistakes, not laugh at them. This one," Miss Darcy said, pausing, "is for Mr. Leroux."

They all nodded solemnly.

"Tomorrow, when we put on the first show, that's going to be for you."

They took their places in the wings. Letitia stood behind Reena, who would be first on stage. Reena shot her a quick smile, nervous.

"How's your stomach?" she whispered.

"Where's the bag?" Letitia asked, pretending to gag herself with a finger.

"TB," Reena accused lightly

"RC," Letitia replied. They shook hands firmly.

The curtain went up. The auditorium was half-filled with parents and friends and relatives. Letitia's parents were out there. The darkness beyond the stagelights seemed so profound it should have been filled with stars and nebulae. Would her small voice reach that far?

The recorded music before the first act came to its quiet end. Reena made a move to go on stage, then stopped. Letitia nudged her. "Come on."

Reena pivoted to look at her, face cocked to one side, and Letitia saw a large tear dripping from her left eye. Fascinated, she watched the tear fall in slow motion down her cheek and spot the satin of her gown.

"I'm sorry," Reena whispered, lips twitching. "I can't do it now. Tell. Tell."

Horrified, Letitia reached out, tried to stop her from falling, to lift her, paste and push her back into place, but Reena was too heavy and she could not stop her descent, only slow it. Reena's feet kicked out like a horse's, bruising Letitia's legs, all in apparent silence, and her eyes were bright and empty and wet, fluttering, showing the whites.

Letitia bent over her, hands raised, afraid to touch her, afraid not to, unaware she was shrieking.

Fayette and Edna Corman stood behind her, equally helpless.

Reena lay still like a twisted doll, face upturned, eyes moving slowly to Letitia, vibrating, becoming still.

"Not you!" Letitia screamed, and barely heard the commotion in the audience. "Please, God, let it be me, not her!"

Fayette backed away and Miss Darcy came into the light, grabbing Letitia's shoulders. She shook free.

"Not her," Letitia sobbed. The medicals arrived and surrounded Reena, blocking her from the eyes of all around. Miss Darcy firmly, almost brutally, pushed her students from the stage and herded them into the green room. Her face was stiff as a mask, eyes stark in the paleness.

"We have to *do* something!" Letitia said, holding up her hands, be-seeching.

"Get control of yourself," Miss Darcy said sharply. "Everything's being done that can be done."

Fayette said, "What about the play?"

Everyone stared at him.

"Sorry," he said, lip quivering. "I'm an idiot."

Jane, Donald, and Roald came to the green room and Letitia hugged her mother fiercely, eyes shut tight, burying her face in Jane's shoulder. They escorted her outside, where a few students and parents still milled about in the early evening. "We should go home," Jane said.

"We have to stay here and find out if she's all right." Letitia pushed away from Jane's arms and looked at the people. "They're so frightened. I know they are. She's frightened, too. I saw her. She told me—" Her voice hitched. "She told me—"

"We'll stay for a little while," her father said. He walked off to talk to another man. They conversed for a while, the man shook his head, they parted. Roald stood away from them, hands stuffed into his pockets, dismayed, young, uncomfortable.

"All right," Donald said a few minutes later. "We're not going to find out anything tonight. Let's go home."

This time, she did not protest. Home, she locked herself in her bedroom. She did not need to know. She had seen it happen; anything else was self-delusion.

Her father came to the door an hour later, rapped gently. Letitia came up from a troubled doze and got off the bed to let him in.

"We're very sorry," he said.

"Thanks," she murmured, returning to the bed. He sat beside her. She might have been eight or nine again; she looked around the room, at toys and books, knickknacks.

"Your teacher, Miss Darcy, called. She said to tell you, Reena Cathcart died. She was dead by the time they got her to the hospital. Your mother and I have been watching the vids. A lot of children are very sick now. A lot have died." He touched her head, patted the crown gently. "I think you know now why we wanted a natural child. There were risks."

"That's not fair," she said. "You didn't have us . . ." She hiccupped. "The way you did, because you thought there would be risks. You talk as if there's something wrong with these . . . people."

"Isn't there?" Donald asked, eyes suddenly flinty. "They're defective."

"They're my friends!" Letitia shouted.

"Please," Donald said, flinching.

She got to her knees on the bed, tears coming again. "There's nothing wrong with them! They're people! They're just sick, that's all."

"You're not making sense," Donald said.

"I talked to her," Letitia said. "She must have known. You can't just say there's something wrong with them. That isn't enough."

"Their parents should have known," Donald pursued, voice rising. "Letitia . . ."

"Leave me alone," she demanded. He stood up hastily, confused, and walked out, closing the door behind him. She lay back on the bed, wondering what Reena had wanted her to say, and to whom.

"I'll do it," she whispered.

In the morning, breakfast was silent. Roald ate his cereal with caution, glancing at the others with wide, concerned eyes. Letitia ate little, pushed away from the table, said, "I'm going to her funeral."

"We don't know—" Jane said.

"I'm going."

LETITIA WENT TO ONLY ONE FUNERAL: REENA'S. WITH A PUZZLED EXPRESSION, she watched Reena's parents from across the grave, wondering about them, comparing them to Jane and Donald. She did not cry. She came home and wrote down the things she had thought.

That school year was the worst. One hundred and twelve students from the school died. Another two hundred became very ill.

John Fayette died.

The drama class continued, but no plays were presented. The school was quiet. Many students had been withdrawn from classes; Letitia watched the hysteria mount, listened to rumors that it was a plague, not a PPC error.

It was not a plague.

Across the nation, two million children became ill. One million died.

Letitia read, without really absorbing the truth all at once, that it was the worst disaster in the history of the United States. Riots destroyed PPC centers. Women carrying PPC babies demanded abortions. The Rifkin Society became a political force of considerable influence.

Each day, after school, listening to the news, everything about her existence seemed trivial. Their family was healthy. They were growing up normally.

Edna Corman approached her in school at the end of one day, two weeks before graduation. "Can we talk?" she asked. "Someplace quiet."

"Sure," Letitia said. They had not become close friends, but she found Edna Corman tolerable. Letitia took her into the old bathroom and they stood surrounded by the echoing white tiles.

"You know, everybody, I mean the older people, they stare at me, at us," Edna said. "Like we're going to fall over any minute. It's really bad. I don't think I'm going to get sick, but . . . It's like people are afraid to touch me."

"I know," Letitia said.

"Why is that?" Edna said, voice trembling.

"I don't know," Letitia said. Edna just stood before her, hands limp.

"Was it our fault?" she asked.

"No. You know that."

"Please tell me."

"Tell you what?"

"What we can do to make it right."

Letitia looked at her for a moment, and then extended her arms, took her by the shoulders, drew her closer, and hugged her. "Remember," she said.

Five days before graduation, Letitia asked Rutger if she could give a speech at the ceremonies. Rutger sat behind his desk, folded his hands, and said, "Why?"

"Because there are some things nobody's saying," Letitia told him. "And they should be said. If nobody else will say them, then . . ." She swallowed hard. "Maybe I can."

He regarded her dubiously for a moment. "You really think there's something important that you can say?"

She faced him down. Nodded.

"Write the speech," he said. "Show it to me."

She pulled a piece of paper out of her pocket. He read it carefully, shook his head—she thought at first in denial—and then handed it back to her.

Waiting in the wings to go on stage, Letitia Blakely listened to the low murmur of the young crowd in the auditorium. She avoided the spot near the curtain.

Rutger acted as master of ceremonies. The proceedings were somber, low-energy. She began to feel as if she were making a terrible mistake. She was too young to say these things; it would sound horribly awkward, even childish.

Rutger made his opening remarks, then introduced her and motioned for her to come on stage. Letitia deliberately walked through the spot near the curtain, paused briefly, closed her eyes and took a deep breath, as if to infuse herself with whatever remained there of Reena. She walked past Miss Darcy, who seemed to glare at her.

Her throat seized. She rubbed her neck quickly, blinked at the bright lights on the catwalk overhead, tried to see the faces beyond the lights. They were just smudges in great darkness. She glanced out of the corner of her eye and saw Miss Darcy nodding, *Go ahead.*

"This has been a bad time for all of us," she began, voice high and scratchy. She cleared her throat. "I've lost a lot a friends, and so have you. Maybe you've lost sons and daughters. I think, even from there, looking at me, you can tell I'm not . . . designed. I'm natural. I don't have to wonder whether I'll get sick and die. But I . . ." She cleared her throat again. It wasn't getting easier. "I thought someone like me could tell you something important.

"People have made mistakes, bad mistakes. But you are not the mistakes. I mean . . . they weren't mistaken to make you. I can only dream about doing some of the things you'll do. Some of you are made to live in space for a long time, and I can't do that. Some of you will think things I can't, and go places I won't . . . travel to see the stars. We're different in a lot of ways, but I just thought it was important to tell you . . ." She wasn't following the prepared speech. She couldn't. "I love you. I don't care what the others say. We love you. You are very important. Please don't forget that."

The silence was complete. She felt like slinking away. Instead, she straightened, thanked them, hearing not a word, not a restless whisper, then bowed her head from the catwalk glare and the interstellar darkness beyond.

Miss Darcy, stiff and formal, reached her arm out as Letitia passed by. They shook hands firmly, and Letitia saw, for the first time, that Miss Darcy looked upon her as an equal.

Letitia stood backstage while the ceremonies continued, examining the old wood floor, the curtains, counterweights, and flies, the catwalk.

It seemed very long ago, she had dreamed what she felt now, this unspecified love, not for family, not for herself. Love for something she could not have known back then; love for children not her own, yet hers none the less. Brothers.

Sisters.

Family.

Introduction to "A Martian Ricorso"

In 1976, the *Viking* lander settled down on Mars, scooped up a shovel full of soil, and tested it. The results were negative ... or inconclusive. But for a brief moment, following a radio announcement that organic chemistry had been revealed in the samples, I was positive life had been discovered on another planet. The feeling was unforgettable.

"A Martian Ricorso" scored my first magazine cover, a beautiful piece by Rick Sternbach on the February 1976 issue of *Analog*. I carried a copy of the magazine around for days, then wrote a letter to Rick. We became friends. The original cover art graces our house.

Today, there are still headlines about water being discovered on Mars. A cyclical Mars, as proposed in this story, seems less likely now, but current discoveries do not rule it out—and may actually lend it some support. Mars is probably more like I described it in *Moving Mars* (1993), with a rich, wet past eventually giving way to steady aridity and cold. But this was my first bold attempt to stick a scientific hypothesis into a story of hard science fiction, and who knows?

I might still win the lottery.

A Martian Ricorso
Analog, Ben Bova, 1976

Martian night. The cold and the dark and the stars are so intense they make music, like the tinkle of ice xylophones. Maybe it's my air tank hose scraping; maybe it's my imagination. Maybe it's real.

Standing on the edge of Swift Plateau, I'm afraid to move or breathe deeply, as I whisper into the helmet recorder, lest I disturb something holy: God's sharp scrutiny of Edom Crater. I've gone outside, away from the lander and my crewmates, to order my thoughts about what has happened.

The Martians came just twelve hours ago, like a tide of five-foot-high laboratory rats running and leaping on their hind legs. To us, it seemed as if they were storming the lander, intent on knocking it over. But it seems now we were merely in their way.

We didn't just sit here and let them swamp us. We didn't hurt or kill any of them—Cobb beat at them with a roll of foil and I used the parasol of the damaged directenna to shoo them off. First contact, and we must have looked like clowns in an old silent comedy. The glider wings came perilously close to being severely damaged. We foiled and doped what few tears had been made before nightfall. They should suffice, if the polymer sylar adhesive is as good as advertised.

But our luck this expedition held true to form. The stretching frame's pliers broke during the repairs. We can't afford another swarm, even if they're just curious.

Cobb and Link have had bitter arguments about self-defense. I've managed to stay out of them so far, but my sympathies at the moment lie with Cobb. Still, my instinctual desire to stay alive won't stop me from feeling horribly guilty if we *do* have to kill a few Martians.

We've had quite a series of revelations the last few days. Schiaparelli was right. And Percival Lowell, the eccentric genius of my own home state. He was not as errant an observer as we've all thought this past century.

I have an hour before I have to return to the lander and join my mates in sleep. I can last here in the cold that long. Loneliness may weigh on me sooner, however. I don't know why I came out here; perhaps just to clear my head, we've all been in such a constrained, tightly controlled, oh-so-disguised panic. I need to know what I think of the whole situation, without benefit of comrades.

The plateau wall and the floor of Edom are so barren. With the exception, all around me, of the prints of thousands of feet. . . . Empty and lifeless.

Tomorrow morning we'll brace the crumpled starboard sled pads and rig an emergency automatic release for the RATO units on the glider. Her wings are already partially spread for a fabric inspection—accomplished just before the Winter Troops attacked—and we've finished transferring fuel from the lander to the orbit booster. When the glider gets us up above the third jet stream, by careful tacking we hope to be in just the right position to launch our little capsule up and out. A few minutes' burn and we can dock with the orbiter if Willy is willing to pick us up.

If we don't make it, these records will be all there is to explain, on some future date, why we never made it back. I'll feed the helmet memory into the lander telterm, stacked with flight telemetry and other data in computer-annotated garble, and instruct the computer to store it all on hard-copy glass disks.

The dust storm that sand-scrubbed our directenna and forced me to this expedient subsided two days ago. We have not reported our most recent discovery to mission control; we are still organizing our thoughts. After all, it's a momentous occasion. We don't want to make any slips and upset the folks back on Earth.

Here's the situation. We can no longer communicate directly with Earth. We are left with the capsule radio, which Willy can pick up and boost for re-broadcast whenever the conditions are good enough. At the moment, conditions are terrible. The solar storm that dogged our Icarus heels on the way out, forcing us deep inside Willy's capacious hull, is still active. The effect on the Martian atmosphere has been most surprising.

There's a communicator on the glider body as well, but that's strictly short-range and good for little more than telemetry. So we have very garbled transmissions going out, reasonably clear coming back, and about twenty minutes of complete blackout when Willy is out of line of sight, behind or below Mars.

We may be able to hit Willy with the surveyor's laser, adapted for signal transmission. For the moment we're going to save that for the truly important communications, like time of launch and approximate altitude, calculated from the fuel we have left after the transfer piping exploded. . . . was it three days ago? When the night got colder than the engineers thought possible and exceeded the specs on the insulation.

I'm going back in now. It's too much out here. Too dark. No moons visible.

Now at the telterm keyboard. Down to meaningful monologue.

Mission Commander Linker, First Pilot Cobb, and myself, Mission Specialist Mercer, have finished ninety percent of the local survey work and compared it with Willy's detailed mapping. What we've found is fascinating.

At one time there were lines on Mars, stripes like canals. Until a century ago, any good telescope on Earth, on a good night, could have revealed them for a sharp-eyed observer. As the decades went by, it was not the increased skill of astronomers and the quality of instruments that erased these lines, but the end of the final century of the *Anno Fecundis.* Is my Latin proper? I have no dictionary to consult.

With the end of the Fertile Year, a thousand centuries long, came the first bleak sandy winds and the lowering of the Martian jet streams. They picked up sand and scoured.

The structures must have been like fairy palaces before they were swept down. I once saw a marketplace full of empty vinegar jugs in the Philippines, made from melted Coca-Cola bottles. They used glass so thin you could break them with a thumbnail tap in the right place—but they easily held twenty or thirty gallons of liquid. These colonies must have looked like grape-clusters of thousands of thin glass vinegar bottles, dark as emeralds, mounted on spider-web stilts and fed with water pumped through veins as big as Roman aqueducts. We surveyed one field and found the fragments buried in red sand across a strip thirty miles wide. From a mile or so up, the edge of the structure can still be seen, if you know where to look.

Neither of the two previous expeditions found them.

They're *ours*.

Linker believes these ribbons once stretched clear around the planet. Before the sand storm, Willy's infrared mapping proved him correct. We could trace belts of ruins in almost all the places Lowell had mapped— even the civic centers some of his followers said he saw. Aqueducts laced the planet like the ribs on a basketball, meeting at ocean-sized black pools covered with glassy membranes. The pools were filled by a thin purple liquid, a kind of resin, warming in the sun, undergoing photosynthesis. The resin was pumped at high pressure through tissue and glass tubes, nourishing the plantlike colonies inhabiting the bottles. They probably lacked any sort of intelligence. But their architectural feats put ours to shame, nonetheless.

Sandstorms and the rapidly drying weather of the last century are still bringing down the delicate structures. Ninety-five percent or more have fallen already, and the rest are too rickety to safely investigate. They are still magnificent. Standing on the edge of a plain of broken bottles and shattered pylons stretching to the horizon, we can't help but feel very young and very small.

A week ago, we discovered they've left spores buried deep in the red-orange sand, tougher than coconuts and about the size of medicine balls.

Six days ago, we learned that Mars provides children for all his seasons. Digging for ice lenses that Willy had located, we came across a cache of leathery eggshells in a cavern shored up with a translucent organic cement. We didn't have time to investigate thoroughly. We managed to take a few samples of the cement—scrupulously avoiding disturbing the eggs—and vacated before our tanks ran out. While cutting out the samples, we noticed that the walls had been patterned with hexagonal carvings, whether as a structural aid or decoration we couldn't tell.

Yesterday, that is, about twenty-six hours ago, we saw what we believe must be the hatchlings: the Winter Troops, five or six of them, walking along the edge of the plateau, not much more than white specks from where we sat in the lander.

We took the sand sled five kilometers from the landing to investigate the cache again, and to see what Willy's mapping revealed as the last standing fragments of an aqueduct bridge in our vicinity. We didn't locate our original cache. Collapsed caverns filled with leathery egg skins pocked the landscape. More than sandstorms had been at the ruins. The bridges rested on the seeds of their own destruction—packs of kangaroo-rat Winter Troops crawled over the structure like ants on a carcass, breaking off bits, eating or just cavorting like sand fleas.

Linker named them. He snapped pictures enthusiastically. As a trained exobiologist, he was in a heat of excitement and speculation. His current theory is that the Winter Troops are on a binge of destruction, programmed into their genes and irrevocable. We retreated on the sled, unsure whether we might be swamped as well.

Linker babbled—pardon me, expounded—all the way back to the lander. "It's like Giambattista Vico resurrected from the historian's bone-yard!" We barely listened; Linker was way over our heads. "Out with the old, in with the new! Vico's historical *ricorso* exemplified."

Cobb and I were much less enthusiastic. "Indiscriminate buggers," he grumbled. "How long before they find us?"

I had no immediate reaction. As in every situation in my life, I decided to sit on my emotions and wait things out.

Cobb was prescient. Unluckily for us, our lander and glider rise above the ground like a stray shard of an aqueduct-bridge. At that stage of their young lives, the Winter Troops couldn't help but swarm over everything. An hour ago, I braved the hash and our own confusion and sent out descriptions of our find. So far, we've received no reply to our requests for First Contact instructions. The likelihood was so small nobody planned for it. The message was probably garbled.

But enough pessimism. Where does this leave us, so far, in our speculations?

Gentlemen, we sit on the cusp between cycles. We witness the end of the green and russet Mars of Earth's youth, ribbed with fairy bridges and restrained seas, and come upon a grimmer, more practical world, buttoning down for the long winter.

We haven't studied the white Martians in any detail, so there's no way of knowing whether or not they're intelligent. They may be the new masters of Mars. How do we meet them—passively, as Linker seems to think we should, or as Cobb believes: defending ourselves against creatures who may or may not belong to our fraternal order of Thinkers?

What can we expect if we *don't* defend ourselves?

Let your theologians and exobiologists speculate on *that*. Are we to be the first to commit the sin of an interplanetary Cain? Or are the Martians?

It will take us nine or ten hours tomorrow to brace the lander pads. Our glider sits with sylar wings half-flexed, crinkling and snapping in the rising wind, silver against the low sienna hills of the Swift Plateau.

Sunlight strikes the top of the plateau. Pink sky to the East; fairy bridges, fairy landscape! Pink and dreamlike. Ice-crystal clouds obscure a faded curtain of aurora. The sky overhead is black as obsidian. Between the pink sunrise and the obsidian is a band of hematite, a dark rainbow like carnival glass, possibly caused by crystalline powder from the aqueduct bridges elevated into the jetstreams. From our vantage on the plateau, we can see dust devils crossing Edom's eastern rim and the tortured mounds and chasms of the Moab-Marduk range, rising like the pillars of some ancient temple. Boaz and Jachin, perhaps.

Since writing the above, I've napped for an hour or so. Willy relayed a new chart. He's found construction near the western rim of Edom Crater—recent construction, not there a few days ago when the area was last surveyed. Hexagonal formations—walls and what could be roads. From his altitude, they must rival the Great Wall of China. How could such monumental works be erected in just days? Were they missed on the previous passes? Not likely.

So there we have it. The colonies that erected the aqueduct-bridges were not the only architects on Mars. The Winter Troops are demonstrating their skills. But are they intelligent, or just following some instinctual imperative? Or *both?*

Both men are sleeping again now. They've been working hard, as have I, and their sleep is sound. The telterm clicking doesn't wake them. I can't sleep much—no more than an hour at a stretch before I awake in a sweat. My body is running on supercharge and I'm not ready to resort to tranquilizers. So here I sit, endlessly observing. Linker is the largest of us. Though I worked with him for three years before this mission, and we have spent over eight months in close quarters, I hardly know the man. He's not a quiet man, and he's always willing to express his opinions, but he still surprises me. He has a way of raising his eyebrows when he listens, opening his dark eyes wide and wrinkling his forehead, that reminds me of a dog cocking its ears. But it would have to be a devilishly bright dog. Perhaps I haven't plumbed Linker's depths because I'd go in over my head if I tried. He's certainly more dedicated than either Cobb or I. He's been in the USN for twenty-one years, fifteen of them in space, specializing in planetary geology and half a dozen other disciplines.

Cobb, on the other hand, can be read like a book. He tends toward bulk, more in appearance than mass; he weighs only a little more than I do. He's shorter and works with a frown; it seems to take twice his normal concentration to finish some tasks. I do him no injustice by saying that; he gets the work done, and well, but it costs him more than it would Linker. The extra effort sometimes takes the edge off his nonessential reasoning. He's not light on his mental feet, particularly in a situation like this. Doggedness and quick reflexes brought him to his prominence in the Mars lander program; I respect him nonetheless for that, but. . . . He tends to the technical, loving machines more than men, I've often thought, and from my more liberal arts background, I've resented that.

Linker and I once had him close to tears on the outward voyage. We conversed on five or six subjects at once, switching topics every three or four minutes. It was a cruel game and neither of us are proud of it, but I for one can peg part of the blame on the mission designers. Three is too small a community for a three-year mission in space. Hell. Space has been billed as making children out of us all, eh? A two-edged sword.

I have (as certain passages above might indicate) been thinking about the Bible lately. My old childhood background has been stimulated by the danger and moral dilemmas—hair of the dog that bit me. The maps of Mars, with their Biblical names, have contributed to my thoughts. We're not far from Eden as gliders go. We sit in fabled Moab, above the Moab-Marduk range, Marduk being one of the chief "baals" in the Old Testament. Edom Crater—Edom means red, an appropriate name for a Martian crater. I have red hair. Call me Esau!

Mesogaea—Middle Earth. Other hair, other dogs.

BACK ON THE RECORDER AGAIN. TIME WEIGHS HEAVILY ON ME. I'VE RE-treated to the equipment bay to weather a bit of grumpiness between Linker and Cobb. Actually, it was an out-and-out argument. Linker, still the pacifist, expressed his horror of committing murder against another species. His scruples are oddly selective—he fought in Eritrea in the nineties. Neither has been restrained by rank; this could lead to really ugly confrontations, unless danger straightens us all out and makes brothers of us.

Three comrades, good and true, tolerant of different opinions.

Oh, God, here they come again! I'm looking out the equipment bay port, looking East. They must number five or six thousand, lining a distant hill like Indians. That many attacking. . . . Cobb can have his way, and it won't matter, we'll still have had the course. If they rip a section of wing sylar larger than we can stretch by hand, we're stuck.

THAT WAS CLOSE. COBB FIRED BURSTS OF THE SURVEYOR'S LASER OVER THEIR heads. Enough dust had been raised by their movement and by the wind to make a fine display. They moved back slowly and then vanished behind the hill. The laser is powerful enough to burn them should the necessity arise.

Linker has as much as said he'd rather die than extend the sin of Cain. I'm less worried about that sin than I am about lifting off. We have yet to brace the sled pad. Linker's out below the starboard hatch now, rigging the sling that will keep one section of the glider body level when the RATOs fire.

More dust to the East now. Night is coming slowly. After the sun sets, it'll be too cold to work outside for long. If the Winter Troops are water-based, how do they survive the night? Antifreeze in their blood, like Arctic fish? Can they keep up their activity in temperatures between fifty and one hundred below? Or will we be out of danger until sunrise, with the Martians warm in their blankets, and we in our trundle-bed, nightmaring?

I'VE HELPED LINKER RIG THE SLING. WE'VE ALL WORKED ON THE SLED PAD. Cobb has mounted the laser on a television tripod—clever warrior. Linker advised him to beware of the fraying power cable. Cobb looked at him with a sad sort of resentment and went about his work. Other than the few bickerings and personality games of the trip out, we managed to keep respect for one another until the last few days. Now we're slipping. At one time, I had the fantasy we'd all finish the mission life-time friends, visiting each other years after, comparing pictures of our grandchildren and complaining about the quality of young officers after our retirement. What a dream.

Steam rises from the hoarfrost accumulated during the night. It vanishes like a tramp after dinner.

Should we wish to send a message to Willy now, we shall have to unship the laser and remount it. The hash has increased and Willy says his pickup is deteriorating.

More ice falls during the night. Linker kept track of them. My insomnia has communicated itself to him—ideal for standing long watches. Ice falls are more frequent here than on Earth—the leavings of comets and the asteroids come through this thin atmosphere more easily. A small chunk came to within a sixty meters of our site, leaving an impressive crater.

ANOTHER BREAK. WILLY HAS RELAYED A MESSAGE FROM CONTROL. THEY managed to pick up and reconstruct our request for instructions on first contact. They must have thought we were joking. Here's part of the transmission:

We think you're not content with finding giant vegetables on Mars. Dr. Wender advised on Martians . . . (hash) . . . some clear indications of their ability to fire large cylindrical bodies into space. Beware tripod machines. Second opinion from Frank: Not all green

Martians are Tharks. He wants sample from Dejah Thoris—can you arrange for egg?

I put on a pressure suit and went for a walk after the disappointment of the transmission. Linker suited up after me and followed for a while. I armed myself with a piece of aluminum from the salvaged pad. He carried nothing.

Swift Plateau is about four hundred kilometers across. At its northern perimeter, an aqueduct had once hoisted itself a kilometer or so and vaulted across the flats, covering fifteen kilometers of upland before dropping over the south rim into the Moab-Marduk Range. Our landing site is a kilometer from the closest stretch of fragments. Linker followed me to the edge of the field of green and blue grass, keeping quiet, looking behind apprehensively as if he expected something to pop up between us and the lander.

I had a notebook in my satchel and paused to sketch some of the piers the Winter Troops hadn't yet brought down. None of them were over four meters tall.

"I'm afraid of them," Linker said over the suit radio. I stopped my sketching to look at him.

"So?" I inquired with a touch of irritation. "We're all afraid of them."

"I'm not afraid because they'll hurt me. It's because of what they might bring out in me, if I give them half a chance. I don't want to hate them."

"Not even Cobb *hates* them," I said.

"Oh, yes he does," Linker said, nodding his head within the bulky helmet. "But he's afraid for his life. I fear for my self-respect."

I shook my helmet to show I didn't understand.

"Because I can't understand them. They're irrational. They don't seem to *see* us. They run around us, fulfilling some mission . . . they don't care whether we live or die. Yet I have to respect them—they're *alien*. The first intelligent creatures we've ever met."

"If they're intelligent," I reminded him.

"Come on, Mercer, they must be. They build."

"So did these," I said, waving a gloved hand at the field of shattered green bottles."

"I'm trying to make myself clear," he said, exasperated. "When I was in Eritrea, I didn't understand the nationalists. Or the communists. Both sides were willing to kill their own people or allow them to starve if it won some small objective. It was sick. I even hated the ones we were supporting."

"The Martians aren't Africans," I said. "We can't expect to understand their motives."

"Comes back double, then, don't you see? I want to understand, to know why—" He suddenly switched his radio off, raised his hands in frustration and turned to walk back to the lander.

Our automatic interrupts clicked on and Cobb spoke to us. "That's it, friends. We're blanketed by hash. I can't get through to Willy. We'll have to punch through with the laser."

"I'm on my way back," Linker said. "I'll help you set it up."

In a few minutes, I was alone on the field of ruins. I sat on a weather-pocked boulder and took out my sketchbook again. I mapped the directions from which we had been approached and attacked and compared them with the site of the eggs we had found. What I was looking for, with such ridiculously slim evidence, was a clear pattern of migration—say, from the hatcheries in a line with the sunrise. Nothing came of it.

Disgusted at my desperation, I was lost in a fog of something approaching misery when I glanced up. . . . And jumped to my feet so fast I leaped a good three feet into the air, twisting my ankle as I came down. Two white Martians stared at me with their wide, blank gray eyes, eyelashes as long and expressive as a camel's. The fingers on their hands—each had three arms, but only two legs—shivered like mouse-whiskers, not nervous but seeking information. We had been too involved fending them off before to take note of their features. Now, at a loss what to do, I had all the time in the world.

Three long webbed toes, leathery and dead-looking like sticks, met at an odd two-jointed ankle, which even now I can't reproduce on paper. Their thighs were knotted with muscles and covered with red and white stippled fur. They could hop or run like frightened deer—that much I knew from experience. Their hips were thickly furred. They defied my few semesters of training in biology by having trilateral symmetry between hips and neck, and bilateral below the hips. Three arms met at ingenious triangular shoulders, rising to short necks and mouselike faces. Their ears were mounted atop their heads and could fan out like unfolded directennas, or hide away if rough activity threatened them.

The Martians were fast when they wanted to be, and I had no idea what else they could eat besides the ruins, so I made no false moves.

One whickered like a horse, its voice reedy and distant in the thin atmosphere. The noise must have been impressively loud to reach my small, helmeted ears. It looked behind itself, twisting its head one-eighty to look as its behind-arm scratched a tuft of hair on its right shoulder. The back fur rippled appreciatively. Parrot-like, the head returned to calmly stare at me.

After half an hour, I sat down again on the boulder. I could still see the lander and the linear glint of the glider wings, but there was no sign of Cobb or Linker. Nobody was searching for me.

My suit was getting cold. Slowly, I checked my battery pack gauge and saw it was showing a low charge. Cautiously, in distinct stages, I stood and brushed my pressure suit. The Martian to my right jerked, fingers trembling, and I held my pose, apprehensive. With a swift motion, it pulled a green, fibrous piece of aqueduct-bridge girder from its stiff rump fur with its behind-arm and held it out to me. The piece was about thirty centimeters long, chewed all around. I straightened, extended one hand and accepted the gift.

Without further ado, the Martians twisted around and leaped across the plateau, running and leaping simultaneously.

Clutching my gift, I returned to the lander. My feet and fingers were numb when I arrived.

The tripod lay on the ground, legs spraddled. The laser was nowhere to be seen. I had a moment's panic, thinking the lander had been attacked—but since I had kept it in sight, that didn't seem likely. I climbed into the lander's primary lock.

Inside, Linker clutched the laser in both hands, one finger resting lightly, nervously, on the unsheathed and delicate scandium-garnet rod. Cobb sat on the opposite side of the cabin, barely two meters from Linker, fuming.

"What in hell is going on?" I asked, puffing on my fingers and stamping my feet.

"Listen, Thoreau," Cobb said bitterly, "while you were out communing with nature, Mr. Gandhi here decided to make sure we can't harm any of the sweet little creatures."

I turned to Linker, focusing on his uncertain finger and the garnet. "What are you doing?"

"I'm not sure, Dan," he answered calmly, face blank. "I have a firm conviction, that's all I know. I have to be firm. Otherwise I'll be just like you and Cobb."

"I have a conviction, too," Cobb said. "I'm convinced you're nuts."

"You're seriously thinking about breaking that garnet?" I asked.

"Damned serious."

"We can fight them off with other things if we have to," I reasoned. "The assay charges, the core sample gun—"

"Don't give Cobb any more ideas," Linker said.

"But we can't talk to Willy if you break that garnet."

"Cobb saw two of the Winter Troops. He was going to take a pot-shot at them with this." Linker lifted the laser, face still blank.

I blinked for a few seconds, feeling myself flush with anger. "Jesus. Cobb, is that true?"

"I was sighting on them, in case there were more—"

"Were you going to shoot?"

"It was convenient. They might have been a vanguard."

"That's not very rational," I observed.

"I'm not sure I'm being rational, either," Linker said, fully aware how fragmented we were now, the sadness we all felt coming to the surface. His eyes were doglike, searching my face for understanding, or at least a way to understand himself.

"I'll do anything necessary to make sure we all survive," Cobb said. "If that means killing a few Martians, then I'll do it. If it means over-ruling the mission commander, then I'll do that, too."

"He refused to put the laser down, even when I gave him a direct order. That's mutiny."

"This isn't getting us anywhere," Cobb said.

"I won't vouch for your sanity," I said to Linker. "Not if you break that garnet. And I won't vouch for Cobb's, either. Taking pot-shots at possibly intelligent aliens." I remembered the stick. Damn it, they *were* intelligent! They had to be, advancing on a stranger and giving him a gift. . . . "I don't know what sort of speculative first-contact training we should have had, but in spirit if not in letter, Linker has to be closer to the ideal than you."

"We should be testing the brace on the pad and leveling the field in front of the glider. When we get out of here, we can argue philosophy all the way home. And to get home, we *need the laser.*"

Linker nodded. "We'll just agree not to use it for anything but com-munication."

I looked at Cobb, finally making my decision, and wondering whether I was crazy, too. "I think Linker's right."

"Okay," Cobb said softly. "But there's going to be a hell of a row after we debrief."

"That's an understatement," I said.

This record, even if it survives, will probably be kept in the admin-istration files for fifty or sixty years—or longer—to "protect the feelings of the families." But who can gainsay the judgment of the folks who put us here? Not I, humble Thoreau on Mars, as Cobb described me.

I did not reveal the gift to my crewmates until the laser had been remounted in the lander. I simply lay it on the table, wrapped in an airtight transparent sylar specimen bag, while we rested and sipped hot chocolate. Linker was the first to pick it up, glancing at me, puzzled.

"We have enough of these, don't we?" he asked.

"It's been chewed on," I pointed out, reaching to run my finger along the stick's surface. I told them about the two Martians. Cobb looked decidedly uncomfortable.

"Did they chew on it in your presence?" Linker asked.

"No."

"Maybe they were offering food," Cobb said. "A peace offering?" His expression was sad, as if all the energy and anger had been drained and nothing much was left but regret.

"It's more than food," Linker said. "It's like stick-writing. . . . Ogham. The Irish and Britons used something similar centuries ago. Notches on the side of a stone or stick—a kind of alphabet. But this is much more complex. Here—there's an oval—"

"Unless it's a tooth-mark," I said.

"Whether it's a tooth-mark or not, it isn't random. There are five long marks beside it, and one mark about half the length of the others. That's about equal to one Deimotic month—five and a half days." My respect for Linker increased. He raised his eyebrows, looking for confirmation, and started to hand the stick to me, then stopped and swung it around to Cobb. Mission commander, reintegrating a disgruntled crewmember. A mist of tears came to my eyes.

"I don't think they've reached a high level of technology yet," Linker said.

Cobb looked up from the gift and grinned. "Technology?"

"They built the walls and structures Willy saw. I don't think any of us can argue that they're not intent on changing their environment. Unless we make asses out of ourselves and say their work is no more significant than a beaver dam, it's obvious they're advancing rapidly. They might use notched sticks for relaying information."

"So what's this?" I asked, pointing to the gift.

"Maybe it's a subpoena," Linker said.

While I've been recording the above, Cobb has gone outside to see how long it will take to clear the glider path. The field was chosen to be free of boulders—but anything bigger than a fist could skew us around dangerously. The sleds have been deployed. I've finished tamping the braces on the pad.

The glider and capsule check out. In an hour we'll lase a message to Willy and give our estimate on launch and rendezvous.

Willy tells us that most of Mesogaea and Memnonia are covered with walls. Meridiani Sinus, according to his telescope observations, has been crisscrossed with roads or trails. The white Martians are using the sand-filled black old resin reservoirs for some purpose unknown.

Edom Crater is as densely packed as a city. All this in less than two days. There must be millions of hatchlings at work.

I'll break again and supervise the glider powerup.

———

LINKER AND COBB ARE DEAD.

Jesus, that hurts to write.

We had just tested the RATO automatic timers when a horde of Winter Troops marched across the plateau, about ninety deep and a good four kilometers abreast. I'm certain they weren't out to get us. It was one of those migrational sweeps, a screwball mass survey of geography, and incidentally a leveling of all the aqueduct-bridges from the last cycle.

They gave us our chance. We didn't reply.

Linker had finished clearing the path. They caught him a half-kilometer from the lander. I think they just trampled him to death. They were moving much faster than a man can run. I imagine his face, eyebrows rising in query, maybe he even tried to smile or greet them, lifting a hand. . . .

I can't get that out of my head. I have to concentrate.

Cobb knew exactly what to do. I think he didn't mount the laser solidly, leaving a few brackets loose enough so he could unship it and bring it down, ready for hand use at a minute's notice. He took it outside the ship with just helmet and oxygen on—it's about five or six degrees outside, daylight—and fired on the Winter Troops just before they reached the glider. There are dead and dying or blinded Martians all along the edge of the path.

They paid their casualties no heed. They did not bother with us, just pushed around and through, touching nothing, staying away from the area he was sweeping—the edge of the path.

They can climb like monkeys. They dropped over the rim of the plateau.

They didn't touch Cobb. The frayed cord on the laser killed him when he stepped on it coming back in.

Where was I? Inside the glider, monitoring the powerup. I couldn't hear a thing. It was all over by the time I got outside.

The laser is gone, but we've already sent our data to Willy. I have the return message. That's all I need for the moment. The glider and capsule are powered and ready.

I'll launch it by myself. I can do that.

When Willy's position is right. The timer is going. Everything will be automatic.

I'll make it to orbit.

Two hours. Less. I can't bring them in. I could, but what use? There are no facilities for dead astronauts aboard the orbiter. What hurts is I'll have a better margin with them gone, more fuel. I did not want it that way, I never thought of that, I swear to God.

The glider wings are crackling in the wind. The wind is coming at a perfect angle, thin but fast, about two hundred kilometers an hour. Enough to feel if I were outside.

I trust in an awful lot now that Linker and Cobb are gone. Maybe it'll be over soon and I can stop this writing and stop feeling this pain.

Waiting. Just the right instant for launch. Timers, everything on auto. I sit helpless and wait. My last instructions: three buttons and an instruction to the remotes to expand the wings to take-off width and increase tension. Like a square-rigger. They check okay, flat now, waiting for the best gust and RATO fire. Then they'll drop into the proper configuration, dragonfly wings, for high atmosphere.

I spent some time learning Martian anatomy as I cleared the path of the few Cobb had let through. There are still a couple out there. I don't think I'll hit them.

I killed one. I hit it over the head with a rock pick. Pain/Cain. It was in the Martian equivalent of pain. It died just like we do.

Linker died innocent.

I think I'm going to be sick.

Here it comes. RATOs on.

I'm in the first jet-stream. Second wing mode—fore and aft foils have been jettisoned. I'm riding directly into the black wind. I can see stars, can see Mars red and brown and gray below.

Third wing mode. All wings jettisoned. Falling, my stomach says. Main engines on capsule are firing and I'm through the glider framework. I can see the glare and feel the punch and the wings are far down to port, twirling like a child's toy.

In low, uncertain orbit.

Willy's coming.

Last orbit before going home. Willy looked awfully good. I climbed inside of him through the transfer tunnel and requested a long drink of miserable orbiter water. "Hey, Willy Ley," I said, "you're the most beautiful thing I've ever seen." Of course, all he did was take care of me. No accusations.

He's the only friend I have now.

I spoke to mission control. That was not easy. An hour ago. I'm sitting by the telescope, having pushed Willy's sensors out of the way, doing my own surveying and surmising.

So far, the Winter Troops—I *assume* they're responsible—have zoned and partially built up Mare Tyrennhum, Hesperia, and Mare Cimmerium. They've done something I can't decipher or really describe in Aethiopis. By now I'm sure they've got to the old expedition landers in

Syrtis Major and Minor. I don't know what they'll do with them. Maybe add them to the road-building material.

Maybe *understand* them.

I have no idea what they're like, no idea at all. I can't. We can't. They move too fast, grow along instinctive lines, perhaps. Instinct for culture and technology. They may not be intelligent in the way we define intelligence, not as individuals, anyway. But they do *move*.

Perhaps they're just resurrecting what their ancestors left them fifty, a hundred thousand years ago, before the long, warm, wet Spring of Mars drove them underground and brought up the sprouts of aqueduct-bridges.

At any rate, I've been in orbit for a week and a half. They've gone from cradle to sky in that time.

I've seen their balloons.

And I've seen the distant fires of their rockets, icy blue and sharp like hydroxy torches. They seem to be testing. In a few days, they'll have it.

Beware, Control. These brave lads will go far.

Introduction to "Schrödinger's Plague"

I rarely get ideas that can be expressed in 2,500 words or less. Short fiction is difficult at best, but short short fiction is damned near impossible for me. I've only managed the trick a couple of times. This one is the best of my efforts. It's also my only epistolary story—a tale told through letters.

One of my fondest memories is of handing this story to Poul Anderson, my father-in-law, when Astrid and I were in Orinda for a family visit. Poul took the issue of *Analog* into his back office to read the story. A few minutes later, I heard a loud guffaw. Perfect!

I think I know the point in the story where Poul laughed.

According to some physicists (Gregory Benford and John Cramer) the physics behind this story is bogus. Your assignment for the week is to find out why. Your only clue: John Bell.

Schrödinger's Plague
Analog, Stanley Schmidt, 1982

Interdepartmental Memo—Werner Dietrich to Carl Kranz

Carl:

I'm not sure what we should do about the Lambert journal. We know so little about the whole affair—but there's no doubt in my mind we should hand it over to the police. Incredible as the entries are, they directly relate to the murders and suicides, and they even touch on the destruction of the lab. Just reading them in your office isn't enough: I'll need copies of the journal. And how long did it circulate in the system before you noticed it?

Kranz to Dietrich

Werner:

It must have been in the system since just before the events, so a month at least. Copies enclosed of the appropriate entries. The rest, I think, is irrelevant and private. I'd like to return the journal to Richard's estate. The police would probably hold it. And—well, I have other reasons for wanting to keep it to ourselves. For the moment, anyway. Examine the papers carefully. As a physicist, tell me if there's anything in them you find completely unbelievable. If not, more thought should be applied to the whole problem.

P.S. I'm verifying the loss from Bernard's lab now. Lots of hush-hush over there. It's definite Bernard was working on a government CBW contract, apparently in defiance of the university's guidelines. ?—How did Goa get access to the materials? Tight security over there.

Enc.: five pages.

The Journal
April 15, 1981

Today has been a puzzler. Marty convened an informal meeting of the Hydroxyl Radicals for lunch—on him. In attendance, the physics contingent: Martin Goa himself, Frederik Newman, and the new member, Kaye (pr: *Kie*) Parkes; the biologists, Oscar Bernard and yours truly; and the sociologist, Thomas Fauch. We met outside the lounge, and Marty took us to the auxiliary physics building to give us a brief tour of an experiment. Nothing spectacular. Then back to the lounge for lunch. Why he should waste our time thus is beyond me. Call it intuition, but something is up. Bernard is a bit upset for reason or reasons unknown.

May 14, 1981

Radicals convened again today, at lunch. Some of the most absurd shit I've ever heard in my life. Marty at it again. The detail is important here.

"Gentlemen," Marty said in the private lounge, after we had eaten. "I have just destroyed an important experiment. And I have just resigned my position with the university. I'm to have all my papers and materials off campus by this date next month."

Pole-axed silence.

"I have my reasons. I'm going to establish something once and for all."

"What's that, Marty?" Frederik asked, looking irritated. None of us approve of theatrics.

"I'm putting mankind's money where our mouth is. Our veritable collective scientific mouth. Frederik, you can help me explain. You are all aware how good a physicist Frederik is. Better at grants, better at subtleties. Much better than I am. Frederik, what is the most generally accepted theory in physics today?"

"Special relativity," Frederik said without hesitating.

"And the next?"

"Quantum electrodynamics."

"Would you explain Schrödinger's cat to us?"

Frederik looked around the table, obviously a bit put-upon, then shrugged his shoulders. "The final state of a quantum event—an event on a microcosmic scale—appears to be defined by the making of an observation. That is, the event is indeterminate until it is measured. Then it assumes one of a variety of possible states. Schrödinger proposed linking quantum events to macrocosmic events. He suggested putting a cat in an enclosed box, and also a device which would detect the decay of a single radioactive nucleus. Let's say the nucleus has a fifty-fifty chance of decaying in an arbitrary length of time. If it does decay, it triggers the device, which drops a hammer on a vial of cyanide, releasing the gas into the box and killing the cat. The scientist conducting this experiment has no way of knowing whether the nucleus decayed or not without opening the box. Since the final state of the nucleus is not determined without first making a measurement, and the measurement in this case is the opening of the box to discover whether the cat is dead, Schrödinger suggested that the cat would find itself in an undetermined state, neither alive nor dead, but somewhere in between. Its fate is uncertain until a qualified observer opens the box."

"And could you explain some of the implications of this thought experiment?" Marty looked a bit like a cat himself—one who has swallowed a canary.

"Well," Frederik continued, "if we dismiss the cat as a qualified observer, there doesn't seem to be any way around the conclusion that the cat is neither alive nor dead until the box is opened."

"Why not?" Fauch, the sociologist, asked. "I mean, it seems obvious that only one state is possible."

"Ah," Frederik said, warming to the subject, "but we have linked a quantum event to the macrocosm, and quantum events are tricky. We have amassed a great deal of experimental evidence to show that quantum states are not definite until they are observed, that in fact they fluctuate, interact, as if two or more universes each containing a potential outcome—are meshed together, until the physicist causes the collapse into the final state by observing. Measuring."

"Doesn't that give consciousness a godlike importance?" Fauch asked.

"It does indeed," said Frederik. "Modern physics is on a heavy power trip."

"It's all just theoretical, isn't it?" I asked, slightly bored.

"Not at all," Frederik said. "Established experimentally."

"Wouldn't a machine—or a cat—serve just as well to make the measurement?" Oscar, my fellow biologist, asked.

"That depends on how conscious you regard a cat as being. A machine—no, because its state would not be certain until the physicist looked over the record it had made."

"Commonly," said Parkes, his youthful interest piqued, "we substitute

Wigner's friend for the cat. Wigner was a physicist who suggested putting a man in the box. Wigner's friend would presumably be conscious enough to know whether he was alive or dead, and to properly interpret the fall of the hammer and the breaking of the vial to indicate that the nucleus has, in fact, decayed."

"Wonderful," Goa said. "And this neat little fable reflects the attitudes of those who work with one of the most accepted theories in modern science."

"Well, there are elaborations," Frederik said.

"Indeed, and I'm about to add another. What I'm about to say will probably be interpreted as a joke. It isn't. I'm not joking. I've been working with quantum mechanics for twenty years now, and I've always been uncertain—pardon the pun—whether I could accept the foundations of the very discipline which provided my livelihood. The dilemma has bothered me deeply. It's more than bothered me—it's caused sleepless nights, nervous distress, made me go to a psychiatrist. None of what Frederik calls 'elaborations' have provided any relief. So I've used my influence—and my contacts—to somewhat crooked advantage. I've begun an experiment. Not being happy with just a cat, or with Wigner's friend, I've involved all of you in the experiment, and myself, as well. Ultimately, many more people—conscious observers—will be involved."

Oscar smiled, trying to keep from laughing. "I do believe you've gone mad, Martin."

"Have I? Have I indeed, my *dear* Oscar? While I have been driven to distraction by intellectual considerations, why haven't you been driven to distraction by ethical ones?"

"What?" Oscar asked, frowning.

"You are, I believe, trying to locate a vial labeled DERVM-74."

"How did you—"

"Because I stole the vial while looking over your lab. And I cribbed a few of your notes. Now. You're among friends, Oscar. Tell us about DERVM—74. Tell them, or I will."

Oscar looked like a carp out of water for a few seconds. "That's classified," he said. "I refuse."

"DERVM-74," Marty said, "stands for Dangerous Experimental RhinoVirus, Mutation 74. Oscar does some moonlighting on contract for the government. This is one of his toys. Tell us about its nature, Oscar."

"You have the vial?"

"Not anymore," Marty said.

"You idiot! That virus is deadly. I was about to destroy it when the culture disappeared. It's of no use to anybody!"

"How does it work, Oscar?"

"It has a very long gestation period—about 330 days. Much too long for military uses. After that time, death is certain in ninety-eight percent of those who have contracted it. It can be spread by simple contact, by breathing the air around a contaminated subject." Oscar stood. "I must report this, Martin."

"Sit down." Marty pulled a broken glass tube out of his pocket, with a singed label still wrapped around it. He handed it to Oscar, who paled. "Here's my proof. You're much too late to stop the experiment."

"Is this all true?" Parkes asked.

"That's the vial," Oscar said.

"What in *hell* have you done?" I asked, loudly.

The other Radicals were as still as cold agar.

"I made a device which measures a quantum event, in this case the decay of a particle of radioactive Americium. Over a small period of time, I exposed an instrument much like a Geiger counter to the possible effects of this decay. In that time, there was exactly a fifty-fifty chance that a nucleus in the particle would decay, triggering the Geiger counter. If the Geiger counter was triggered, it released the virus contained in this vial into a tightly sealed area. Immediately afterward, I entered the area, and an hour later, I gave all five of you a tour through the same area. The device was then destroyed, and everything in the chamber sterilized, including the vial. If the virus was not released, it was destroyed along with the experimental equipment. If it was released, then we have all been exposed."

"Was it released?" Fauch asked.

"I don't know. It's impossible to tell—yet."

"Oscar," I said, "it's been a month since Marty did all this. We're all influential people—giving talks, attending meetings, we all travel a fair amount. How many people have been exposed—potentially?"

"It's very contagious," Oscar said. "Simple contact guarantees passage from one vector . . . to another."

Fauch took out his calculator. "If we exposed five people each day, and they went on to expose five more . . . Jesus Christ. By now, everyone on Earth could have it."

"Why did you do this, Marty?" Frederik asked.

"Because if the best mankind can do is come up with an infuriating theory like this to explain the universe, then we should be willing to live or die by our belief in the theory."

"I don't get you," Frederik said.

"You know as well as I. Oscar, is there any way to detect contamination by the virus?"

"None. Marty, that virus was a mistake—useless to everybody. Even my notes were going to be destroyed."

"Not useless to me. That's unimportant now, anyway. Frederik, what

I'm saying is, according to theory, nothing has been determined yet. The nucleus may or may not have decayed, but that hasn't been decided. We may have better than a fifty-fifty chance—if we truly believe in the theory."

Parkes stood up and looked out the window. "You should have been more thorough, Marty. You should have researched this thing more completely."

"Why?"

"Because I'm a hypochondriac, you bastard. I have a very difficult time telling whether I'm sick or not."

"What does that have to do with anything?" Oscar asked.

Frederik leaned forward. "What Marty is implying is, since the quantum event hasn't been determined yet, the measurement that will flip it into one state or another is our sickness, or health, about three hundred days from now."

I picked up on the chain of reasoning. "And since Parkes is a hypochondriac, if he believes he's ill, that will flip the event into certainty. It will determine the decay, after the fact—" My head began to ache. "Even after the particle has been destroyed, and all other records?"

"If he truly believes he's ill," Marty said. "Or if any of us truly believes. Or if we actually become ill. I'm not sure there's any real difference, in this case."

"So you're going to jeopardize the entire world—" Fauch began, then he started to laugh. "This is a diabolical joke, Martin. You can stop it right here."

"He's not joking," Oscar said, holding up the vial. "That's my handwriting on the label."

"Isn't it a beautiful experiment?" Marty asked, grinning. "It determines so many things. It tells us whether our theory of quantum events is correct, it tells us the role of consciousness in determining the universe, and, in Parkes's case, it—"

"Stop it!" Oscar shouted. At that point, we had to restrain the biologist from attacking Marty, who danced away, laughing.

May 17, 1981

Today all of us—except Marty—convened. Frederik and Parkes presented documentary evidence to support the validity of quantum theory, and, perversely enough, the validity of Marty's experiment. The evidence was impressive, but I'm not convinced. Still, it was a marathon session, and we now know more than we ever cared to know about the strange world of quantum physics.

The physicists—and Fauch, and Oscar, who is very quiet nowadays—are completely convinced that Marty's nucleus is—or was—in an undetermined state, and that all the causal chains leading to the potential release of the rhinovirus mutation are also in a state of flux. Whether the human race will live or die has not been decided yet.

And Parkes is equally convinced that, as soon as the gestation period passes, he will begin having symptoms, and he will feel—however irrationally—that he has contracted the disease. We cannot convince him otherwise.

In one way, we were very stupid. We had Oscar describe the symptoms—the early signs—of the disease to us. If we had thought things out more carefully, we would have withheld the information, at least from Parkes. But since Oscar knows, if he became convinced he had the disease, that would be enough to flip the state, Frederik believes. Or would it? We don't know yet how many of us will need to be convinced. Would Marty alone suffice? Is a consensus necessary? A two-thirds majority?

It all seemed—seems—totally preposterous to me. I've always been suspicious of physicists, and now I know why.

Then Frederik made a horrible proposal.

May 23, 1981

Frederik made the proposal again at today's meeting.

The others considered the proposal seriously. Seeing how serious they were, I tried to make objections but got nowhere. I am completely convinced that there is nothing we can do, that if the nucleus decayed, then we are doomed. In three hundred days, the first signs will appear—backache, headache, sweaty palms, piercing pains behind the eyes. If they don't, we won't. Even Frederik saw the ridiculous nature of his proposal, but he added, "The symptoms aren't that much different from flu, you know. And if just one of us becomes convinced . . ."

Indicating that the flipping of the state, because of human frailty, was almost certainly going to result in release of the virus. Had resulted.

His proposal—I write it down with great difficulty—is that we should all commit suicide, all six of us. Since we are the only ones who know about the experiment, we are the only ones, he feels, who can flip the state, make things certain. Parkes, he says, is particularly dangerous, but we are all potential hypochondriacs. With the strain of almost ten months waiting between now and the potential appearance of symptoms, we may all be near the breaking point.

May 30, 1981

I have refused to go along with them. Everyone has been extremely quiet, stayed away from each other. But I suspect Parkes and Frederik are doing something. Oscar is morose—he seems suicidal anyway, but is too much of a coward to go it alone. Fauch . . . I can't reach him.

—Ah, Christ. Frederik called. He said I can't hold out. They've killed Marty and destroyed the lab building to wipe out all traces of the experiment, so that no one will know it ever took place. The group is coming over to my apartment now. I just have time to put this in the university pick-up box. What can I do, run?

They're too close.

———

Dietrich to Kranz

Carl:
I've read the journal, although I'm not sure I've assimilated it. What have you found out about Bernard?

Kranz to Dietrich

Werner:
Oscar Bernard was indeed working on a rhinovirus mutation around the time of the incident. I haven't been able to find out much—lots of people in gray suits wandering through the corridors over there. But the rumor is that all his notes on certain projects are missing.

Do you believe it? I mean—do you believe the theory enough to agree with me, that word about the journal should end here? I feel both scared and silly.

Dietrich to Kranz

Carl:
We have to find out the complete list of symptoms—besides headache, sweaty palms, backache, pains behind the eyes.

Yes. I'm a firm believer in the theory. And if Goa did what the journal says . . . you and I can flip the state.

Anyone who reads this can flip the state.

What in God's name are we going to do?

THE MIDDLE DISTANCE

INTRODUCTION TO *HEADS*

In 1989, Deborah Beale at Random Century/Legend, my United Kingdom publisher, commissioned a novella for a series of short illustrated science fiction books. I had to pull together a plot and propose it to Deborah, and then write it, all within a few months. The novella turned out longer than I had expected, and has been in print in England, the United States, and various other countries ever since.

My good friend Gregory Benford had described to me the operations of Alcor, a foundation set up to harvest the bodies of recently deceased members and slip them, very carefully, into liquid nitrogen bottles for preservation, hopeful of resurrection and repair at a later date, in a more medically advanced society. A cheaper option is to simply have your head frozen.

Other friends and acquaintances became involved, or joined the society. I never did. Timothy Leary apparently showed interest, but when time came to make a final decision, Leary decided on cremation, instead.

Benford, writing as Sterling Blake, wrote an excellent novel based on Alcor's legal and scientific experiences: *Chiller*. For a more sanguine take on the process, though not without some grim prognostications, I highly recommend this book. There are, of course, quite a few speculative nonfiction discussions of cryopreservation, and there is Alcor on the Web, as well.

At the time, I wasn't convinced it was feasible for humans, and I still have severe doubts, and not just about the technology. These doubts are expressed in *Heads*.

A later and much more paranoid critique of the quest for biological immortality can be found in my novel *Vitals,* published in 2002.

HEADS IS DISTINGUISHED BY A LINKED PAIR OF TECHNOLOGICAL FORECASTS. QUANTUM LOGIC computers (thinkers, actually) appear here for the first time in science fiction. The phrase "quantum logic" with reference to computation may also be my invention: any challengers?

Quantum computing is now standard fare in research, industry, and science magazines, and will probably, when made completely practical, transform the computer industry. Searching on the Web for quantum logic computers produces too many hits to track!

I did not invent the idea, however; that credit goes to Paul Benioff and Richard Feynman, and to David Deutsch.

"Its from Bits" is a phrase coined by J. A. Wheeler to broadly describe information-based theories of physics. It's that approach to physics (inspired in my case by reading Frederick Kantor's *Information Mechanics* in the early seventies) that led me to describe what happens at or near absolute zero in *Heads*. This presaged to some extent the results of physics experiments that proved the reality of a Bose-Einstein condensate, a new state of matter in which supercooled atoms joining together in a single quantum state.

"Its from Bits" was later used in my novels *Anvil of Stars* and *Moving Mars*. I'm not done with this approach, and am still working over the possibility of deriving various forces, particularly gravitation, from the data refresh rate of interacting masses.

Heads begins with that most subtle and difficult branch of the physical sciences, thermodynamics . . .

HEADS

1990, Deborah Beale, Random Century UK, Greg Bear

O rder and cold, heat and politics. The imposition of wrong order: anger, death, suicide, and destruction. I lost loved ones, lost my illusions and went through mental and physical hell, but what still haunts my dreams, thirty years after, are the great silvery refrigerators four stories tall hanging motionless in the dark void of the Ice Pit; the force disorder pumps with their constant sucking soundlessness; the dissolving ghost of my sister, Rho; and William Pierce's expression when he faced his lifetime goal, in the Quiet . . .

I believe that Rho and William are dead, but I will never be sure. I am even less sure about the four hundred and ten heads.

FIFTY METERS BENEATH THE CINEREOUS REGOLITH OF OCEAN PROCELLARUM, in the geographic center of the extensive and largely empty Sandoval territories, the Ice Pit was a volcanic burp in the Moon's ancient past, a natural bubble almost ninety meters wide that had once been filled with the aqueous seep of a nearby ice fall.

The Ice Pit had been a lucrative water mine, one of the biggest pure water deposits on the Moon, but it had long since tapped out.

Loathe to put family members out of work, my family, the binding multiple of Sandoval, had kept it as a money-losing farm station. It supported three dozen occupants in a space that had once housed three hundred. It was sorely neglected, poorly managed, and worst of all for a lunar establishment, its alleys and warrens were *dirty*. The void itself was empty and unused, its water-conserving atmosphere of nitrogen long since leaked away and its bottom littered with rubble from quakes.

In this unlikely place, my brother-in-law William Pierce had proposed seeking absolute zero, the universal ultimate in order, peace, and quiet. In asking for the use of the Ice Pit, William had claimed, he would be turning a sow's ear into a scientific silk purse. In return, Sandoval BM would boast a major scientific project, elevating its status within the Triple, and therefore its financial standing. The Ice Pit Station would have a real purpose beyond providing living space for several dozen idled ice miners masquerading as farmers. And William would have something uniquely his own, something truly challenging.

Rho, my sister, supported her husband by using all her considerable energy and charm—and her standing with my grandfather, in whose eyes she could do no wrong.

Despite grandfather's approval, the idea was subjected to rigorous examination by the Sandoval syndics—the financiers and entrepreneurs, as well as the scientists and engineers, many of whom had worked with William and knew his extraordinary gifts. Rho skillfully navigated his proposal through the maze of scrutiny and criticism.

By a five to four decision of the syndics, with much protest from the financiers and grudging acceptance from the scientists, William's project was approved.

Thomas Sandoval-Rice, the BM's director and chief syndic, gave his own approval reluctantly, but give it he did. He must have seen some use for a high-risk, high-profile research project; times were hard, and prestige could be crucial even for a top-five family.

Thomas decided to use the project as a training ground for promising young family members. Rho spoke up on my behalf, without my knowledge, and I found myself assigned to a position far above what my age and experience deserved: the new station's chief financial manager and requisitions officer.

I was compelled by family loyalties—and the pleas of my sister—to cut loose from formal schooling at the Tranquil and move to the Ice Pit Station. At first I was less than enthusiastic. I felt my calling to be liberal arts rather than finance and management; I had, in family eyes, frittered away my education studying history, philosophy, and the Terrestrial classics. But I had a fair aptitude for the technical sciences—less aptitude for the theoretical—and had taken a minor in family finances. I felt I could handle the task, if only to show my elders what a liberal mentality could accomplish.

Ostensibly I was in charge of William and his project, answerable to the syndics and financial directors alone; but of course, William quickly established his own pecking order. I was twenty years old at the time; William, thirty-two.

Inside the void, foamed rock was sprayed to insulate and seal in a breathable atmosphere. I oversaw the general cleanup, refitting of already-existing warrens and alleys, and investment in a relatively spartan laboratory.

Large refrigerators stored at the station since the end of ice mining had been moved into the void, providing far more cooling capacity than William actually needed for his work.

Vibration is heat. The generators that powered the Ice Pit laboratory lay on the surface, their noise and reverberation isolated from the refrigerators and William's equipment and laboratory. What vibration remained was damped by suspension in an intricate network of steel springs and field levitation absorbers.

The Ice Pit's heat radiators also lay near the surface, sunk six meters deep in the shadow of open trenches, never seeing the sun, faces turned toward the all-absorbing blackness of space.

Three years had passed since the conversion. Again and again, William had failed to meet his goal. His demands for equipment had become more extravagant, more expensive, and more often than not, rejected. He had become reclusive, subject to even wider mood swings.

I met William at the beginning of the alley that led to the Ice Pit, in the main lift hollow. We usually saw each other only in passing as he whistled through the cold rock alleys between home and the laboratory. He carried a box of thinker files and two coils of copper tubing and looked comparatively happy.

William was a swarthy stick of a man, two meters tall, black eyes deep-set, long narrow chin, lips thin, brows and hair dark as space, with a deep shadow on his jaw. He was seldom calm or quiet, except when working; he could be rude and abrasive. Set loose in a meeting, or conversing on the lunar com net, he sometimes seemed contentious to the point of self-destruction, yet still the people closest to him loved and respected him. Some of the Sandoval engineers considered William a genius with tools and machines, and on those rare occasions when I was privileged to see his musician's hands prodding and persuading, seducing all instrumentality, designing as if by willing consensus of all the material parts, I could only agree; but I loved him much less than I respected him.

In her own idiosyncratic way, Rho was crazy about him; but then, she was just as driven as William. It was a miracle their vectors added.

We matched step. "Rho's back from Earth. She's flying in from Port Yin," I said.

"Got her message," William said, bouncing to touch the rock roof three meters overhead. His glove brought down a few lazy drifts of foamed rock. "Got to get the arbeiters to spray that." He used a distracted tone that betrayed no real intent to follow through. "I've finally straightened out the QL, Micko. The interpreter's making sense. My problems are solved."

"You always say that before some new effect cuts you down." We had come to the large, circular, white ceramic door that marked the entrance to the Ice Pit and stopped at the white line that William had crudely painted there, three years ago. The line could be crossed only on his invitation.

The hatch opened. Warm air poured into the corridor; the Ice Pit was always warmer than ambient, being filled with so much equipment. Still, the warm air *smelled* cold; a contradiction I had never been able to resolve.

"I've licked the final source of external radiation," William said. "Some terrestrial metal doped with Twentieth Century fallout." He zipped his hand away. "Replaced it with lunar steel. And the QL is really tied in. I'm getting straight answers out of it—as straight as quantum logic can give. Leave me my illusions."

"Sorry," I said. He shrugged magnanimously. "I'd like to see it in action."

He stopped, screwed up his face in irritation, then slumped a bit. "I'm sorry, Mickey. I've been a real wart. You fought for it, you got it for me, you deserve to see it. Come on."

I followed William over the line and across the forty-meter-long, two-meter-wide wire and girder bridge into the Ice Pit.

William walked ahead of me, between the force disorder pumps. I stopped to look at the ovoid bronze toruses mounted on each side of the bridge. They reminded me of abstract sculptures, and they were among the most sensitive and difficult of William's tools, always active, even when not connected to William's samples.

Passing between the pumps, I felt a twitch in my interior, as if my body were a large ear listening to something it could barely discern: an elusive sucking silence. William looked back at me and grinned sympathetically. "Spooky feeling, hm?"

"I hate it," I said.

"So do I, but it's sweet music, Micko. Sweet music indeed."

Beyond the pumps and connected to the bridge by a short, narrow walkway, hung the Cavity, enclosed in a steel Faraday cage. Here, within a meter-wide sphere of perfect orbit-fused quartz, the quartz covered with a mirror coating of niobium, were eight thumb-sized ceramic cells, each containing approximately a thousand atoms of copper. Each cell was surrounded by its own superconducting electromagnet. These were the mesoscopic samples, large enough to experience the macroscopic qualities of temperature, small enough to lie within the microscopic realm of quantum forces. They were never allowed to reach a temperature greater than one millionth Kelvin.

The laboratory lay at the end of the bridge, a hundred square meters of enclosed work space made of thin shaped steel framing covered by black plastic wall. Suspended by vibration-damping cords and springs and field levitation from the high dome of the Ice Pit, three of the four cylindrical refrigerators surrounded the laboratory like the pillars of a tropical temple, overgrown by a jungle of pipes and cables. Waste heat was conveyed through the rubble net at the top of the void and through the foamed rock roof beyond by flexible tubes; the buried radiators on the surface then shed that heat into space.

The fourth and final and largest refrigerator lay directly above the Cavity, sealed to the upper surface of the quartz sphere. From a distance the refrigerator and the Cavity might have resembled a squat, old-fashioned mercury thermometer, with the Cavity serving as bulb.

The T-shaped laboratory had four rooms, two in the neck of the T, one extending on each side to make the wings. William led me through the laboratory door—actually a flexible curtain—into the first room, which was filled with a small metal table and chair, a disassembled nano-works arbeiter, and cabinets of cubes and disks. In the second room, the QL thinker occupied a central platform about half a meter on a side. On the wall to the left of the table were a manual control board—seldom used now—and two windows overlooking the Cavity. The second room was quiet, cool, a bit like a cloister cell.

Almost from the beginning of the project, William had maintained to the syndics—through Rho and myself; we never let him appear in person—that his equipment could not be perfectly tuned by even the most skilled human operators, or by the most complicated of computer controllers. All of his failures, he said in his blackest moods, were due to this problem: the failure of macroscopic controllers to be in sync with the quantum qualities of the samples.

What he—what the *project*—needed was a Quantum Logic thinker. Yet these were being manufactured only on Earth, and they were not being exported. Because so few were manufactured, the black market of the Triple had none to offer, and the costs of purchasing, avoiding Earth authorities, and shipping to the Moon were vast. Rho and I could not convince the syndics to make such a purchase. William had seemed to blame me personally.

Our break came with news of an older-model QL thinker being offered for sale by an Asian industrial consortium. William had determined that this so-called obsolete thinker would suit our needs—it was suspiciously cheap, however, and almost certainly out of date. That didn't bother William.

The syndics had approved this request, to everybody's surprise, I think. It might have been Thomas's final gift and test for William—any more expensive requisitions without at least the prospect of a success and the Ice Pit would be closed.

Rho had gone to Earth to strike a deal with the Asian consortium. The thinker had been packaged, shipped, and had arrived six weeks before. I had not heard from her between the time of the purchase and her message from Port Yin that she had returned to the Moon. She had spent four weeks extra on Earth, and I was more than a little curious to find out what she had been doing there.

William leaned over the platform and patted the QL proudly. "It's running almost everything now," he said. "If we succeed, the QL will take a large share of the credit."

The QL itself covered perhaps a third of the platform's surface. Beneath the platform lay the QL's separate power supplies; by Triple common law, all thinkers were equipped with supplies capable of lasting a full year without outside replenishment.

"Who'll get the Nobel, you or the QL?" I asked. I bent to the QL's level to peer at its white cylindrical container. William shook his head.

"Nobody off Earth has ever gotten a Nobel, anyway," he said. "Surely I get some credit for *telling* the QL about the problem." I felt the most affection for my brother-in-law when he reacted positively to my acidulous humor.

"What about this?" I asked, touching the interpreter lightly with a finger. Connected to the QL by fist-thick optical cables, covering another half of the platform, the interpreter was a thinker in itself. It addressed the QL's abstruse contemplations and rendered them, as closely as possible, in language humans could understand.

"A marvel all by itself."

"Tell me about it," I said.

"You didn't study the files," William chided.

"I was too busy fighting with the syndics to *study*," I said. "Besides, you know theory's never been my greatest strength."

William knelt behind the opposite side of the table, his expression contemplative, reverent. "Did you read about Huang-Yi Hsu?"

"Tell me," I said patiently.

He sighed. "You paid for it out of ignorance, Mickey. I could have misled you grievously."

"I trust you, William."

He accepted that with generous dubiety. "Huang-Yi Hsu invented post-Boolean three-state logic before 2010. Nobody paid much attention to it until 2030. He was dead by then; had committed suicide rather than submit to Beijing's Rule of Seven. Brilliant man, but I think a true anomaly in human thought. Then a few physicists in the University of Washington's Cramer Lab Group discovered they could put Hsu's work to use solving problems in quantum logic. Post-Boolean and quantum logic were made for each other. By 2060, the first QL thinker had been built, but nobody thought it was successful.

"Fortunately, it was against the law by then to turn off activated thinkers without a court order, but nobody could talk to it. Its grasp of human languages was inadequate; it couldn't follow their logic. It was a mind in limbo, Mickey; brilliant but totally alien. So it sat in a room at Stanford University's Thinker Development Center for five years before Roger Atkins—you know about Roger Atkins?"

"William," I warned.

"Before Atkins found the common ground for any functional real logic, the Holy Grail of language and thought . . . His CAL interpreter. Comprehensible All Logics. Which lets us talk to the QL. He died a year later." William sighed. "Swan song. So this," he patted the interpreter, a flat gray box about fifteen centimeters square and nine high, "let's us talk to *this*." He patted the QL.

"Why hasn't anybody used a QL as a controller before?" I asked.

"Because even with the interpreter, the QL—*this* QL at any rate—is a monster to work with," he said. He tapped the display button and a prismatic series of bars and interlacing graphs appeared over the thinker. "That's why it was so cheap. It has no priorities, no real sense of needs or goals. It thinks, but it may not *solve*. Quantum logic can outline the center of a problem before it understands the principles and questions, and then, from our point of view, everything ends in confusion. More often that not, it comes up with a solution to a problem not yet stated. It does virtually everything but linear, time's arrow ratiocination. Half of its efforts are meaningless to goal-oriented beings like ourselves, but I can't prune those efforts, because somewhere in them lies the solution to my problems, even if I haven't stated the problem or aren't aware that I have a problem. A post-Boolean intelligence. It functions in time and space, yet ignores their restrictions. It's completely in tune with the logic of the Planck-Wheeler continuum, and that's where the solution to my problem lies."

"So when's your test?"

"Three weeks. Or sooner, if there aren't any more *interruptions*."

"Am I invited?"

"All doubters, front-row seats," he said. "Call me when Rho gets in. Tell her I've got it."

MY OFFICE LAY ALONG A NORTH WARREN, IN AN INSULATED CYLINDRICAL chamber that had once been a liquid water tank. It was much larger than I needed, cavernous in fact, and my bed, desk, slate files, and other furnishings occupied one small section of about five meters square near the door. I entered, set myself down in a wide air-cushion seat, called up the Triple Exchange—monetary rates within the Greater Planets economic Sphere of Earth, Moon, and Mars—and began my daily check on the Sandoval Trust. I could usually gauge the Ice Pit's annual operating expenses by such augurs.

Rho's shuttle landed at Pad Four an hour later. I was engrossed in trust investment performances; she buzzed my line second. William was not answering his.

"Micko, congratulate me! I've got something wonderful," she said.

"A new terrestrial virus we can't set for," I said.

"Mickey. This is serious."

"William says to tell you he's very very close."

"All right. That's good. Now listen."

"Where are you?"

"In the personnel lift. *Listen*."

"Yes."

"How much extra cooling capacity does William have?"

"You don't know?"

"*Mickey . . .*"

"About eight billion calories. Cold is no problem here. You know that."

"I have a load of twenty cubic meters coming in. Average density like fatty water, I assume. What would that be, point nine? It's packed in liquid nitrogen at sixty K. Keeping it colder would be much better, especially if we decide on long-term storage . . ."

"What is it? Smuggled nano prochines to liberate lunar industry?"

"You wish. Nothing quite so dangerous. Forty stainless steel Dewar containers, quite old, vacuum insulated."

"Anything William would be interested in?"

"I doubt it. Can he spare the extra capacity now?"

"He's never used it before, even when he was close, very close. But he's in no mood for—"

"Meet me at home, then we'll go to the Ice Pit and tell him."

"You mean ask."

"I mean *tell*," Rho said.

The Pierce/Sandoval home was two alleys south of my office, not far from the farms, off a nice double-width heated mining bore with smooth white walls of foamed rock. I palmed their home doorplate a half hour later, allowing her time to freshen from the Copernicus trip, never a luxury run.

Rho came out of the bathnook in lunar cotton terry and turban, zaftig by lunar standards, shook out her long red hair, and waved a brochure at me as I entered.

"Have you ever heard of the StarTime Preservation Society?" she asked, handing me the ancient glossy folio.

"Paper," I said, hefting the folio carefully. "Heavy paper."

"They had boxes full of these on Earth," she said. "Stacked up in a dusty office corner. Leftovers from their platinum time. Have you heard of it?"

"No," I said, looking through the brochure. Men and women in cold suits; glass tanks filled with mysterious mist; bare rooms blue with cold. A painting of the future as seen from the early twenty-first century; the moon oddly enough, glass domes and open-air architecture. *"Resurrection in a time of accomplishment, human maturity and wonder . . ."*

"Corpsicles," Rho explained when I cast her a blank look.

"Oh," I said.

"Society capacity of three hundred and seventy; they took in fifty extra before close of term in 2064."

"Four hundred and twenty bodies?" I asked.

"Heads only. Voluntarily harvested individuals. Each paid half a million terrestrial U.S. dollars. Four hundred and ten survivals, well within the guarantees."

"You mean, they were *revived*?"

"No," she said disdainfully. "Nobody's ever brought back a corpsicle. You know that. Four hundred and ten theoretically revivable. We can't bring them back, but Cailetet BM has complete facilities for brain scan and storage . . ."

"So I've heard—for live individuals."

She waved that off. "And doesn't Onnes BM have new solvers for the groups of human mental languages? You study their requests from the central banks, their portfolios. Don't they?"

"I've heard something to that effect."

"If they do, and if we can work a deal between the three BMs, just give me a couple of weeks, and I can read those heads. I can tell you what their memories are, what they were thinking. Without hurting a single frozen neuron. We can do it before anyone on Earth—or anywhere else."

I looked at her with less than brotherly respect. "Dust," I said.

"Flip your own dust, James. I'm serious. The heads are coming. I've signed Sandoval to store them."

"You signed a BM contract?"

"I'm allowed."

"Who says? Christ, Rho, you haven't talked with anybody—"

"It will be the biggest anthropological coup in lunar history. Four hundred and ten terrestrial heads . . ."

"Dead meat!" I said.

"Expertly stored in deep cold. Minor decay at most."

"Nobody wants corpsicles, Rho—"

"I had to bid against four other anthropologists, three from Mars and one from the minor planets."

"Bid?"

"I won," she said.

"You don't have *that* authority," I said.

"Yes I do. Under family preservation charter. Look it up. 'All family members and legal heirs and etc., etc. free hand to make reasonable expenditures to preserve Sandoval records and heritage; to preserve the reputations and fortunes of all established heirs.' "

She had lost me. "What?"

Her look of triumph was carnivorous.

"Robert and Emilia Sandoval," she said. "They died on Earth. Remember? They were members of StarTime."

My jaw dropped. Robert and Emilia Sandoval, our great grandparents, the first man and woman to make love on the moon; nine months later, they became the first parents on the moon, giving birth to our grandmother, Deirdre. In their late middle age, they had returned to Earth, to Oregon in the old United States, leaving their child on the Moon.

"They joined the StarTime Preservation Society. Lots of famous people did," she said.

"So . . . ?" I asked, waiting for my astonishment to peak.

"They're in this batch. Guaranteed by the society."

"Oh, *Rhosalind*," I said, as if she had just told me someone had died. I felt an incredulous hollow sense of doom. "They're coming back?"

"Don't worry," she said. "Nobody knows but the society trustees and me, and now you."

"Great-Grandpa and Grandma," I said.

Rho smiled the kind of smile that had always made me want to hit her. "Isn't it wonderful?"

WILLIAM CAME FROM AN UNBOUND LUNAR FAMILY, THE PIERCES OF COPERnicus Research Center Three. A lunar family—then as even more so now—was not just those born of a single mother and father, but tight associations of sponsored settlers, working their way across the lunar surface in newly-dug warrens, adding children and living space as they burrowed. Individuals usually kept their own surnames, or added surnames, but claimed allegiance to the central family, even when all the members of the central family had died, as sometimes happened.

As with our own family, the Sandovals, the Pierces were among the original fifteen families established on the moon in 2019. The Pierces were an odd lot, unofficial histories tell us—aloof and unwilling to pull together with the newer settlers. The original families—called primes—spread out across the Moon, forming and breaking alliances, eventually coming together—under pressure from Earth—into the financial associations later called binding multiples. The Pierces did not bind with any of the nascent multiples, though they formed loose alliances with other families.

The unbound families did not flourish. The Pierces lost influence, despite being primes. Their final disgrace was cooperation with terrestrial governments during the Split, when Earth severed ties with the Moon to punish us for our presumptuous independence. Thereafter, for decades, the Pierces and their kind were social outcasts.

By contrast, the allied superfamilies handily survived the crisis.

The Pierces, and most unbound families like them, driven by destitution and resentment, contracted their services in 2094 to the Franco-Polish technological station at Copernicus. They became part of the Copernicus binding multiple of nine families and finally joined the mainstream economy of the post–Split Moon.

Still, the Pierces' descendants faced real prejudice in lunar society. They became known as a wild, churlish lot, and kept to themselves in and around the Copernicus station.

These difficulties had obviously affected William as a child, and made him something of an enigma.

When my sister met William at a Copernicus mixer barn dance, courted him (he was too shy and vulnerable to court her in turn) and finally asked him to join the Sandoval BM as her husband, he had to face the close scrutiny of dozens of dubious family members. William lacked the almost instinctive urge to unity of a BM-bred child; in an age of rugged individuals tightly fitted into even more rugged and demanding multiples, he was a loner, quick-tempered yet prone to sentimentality, loyal yet critical, brilliant but prone to choosing tasks so difficult he seemed doomed to always fail.

Yet in those tense months, with Rho's constant coaching, he put on a brilliant performance, adopting a humble and pleasant attitude. He was accepted into the Sandoval Binding Multiple.

Rho was something of a lunar princess. Biologically of the Sandoval line, great-grandchild of Robert and Emilia Sandoval, her future was the concern of far too many, and she developed a closeted attitude of defiance. That she should reach out for the hand of a Pierce was both expected, considering her character and upbringing, and shocking.

But old prejudices had softened considerably. Despite the doubts of Rho's very protective "aunts" and "uncles," and the strains of initiation and marriage, and despite his occasional reversion to prickly form, William was quickly recognized as a valuable adjunct to our family. He was a brilliant designer and theoretician. For four years he contributed substantially to many of our scientific endeavors, yet adjunct he was, playing a subservient role that must have deeply galled him.

I was fifteen when Rho and William married, and nineteen when he finally broke through this more or less obsequious mask to ask for the Ice Pit. I had never quite understood their attraction for each other; lunar princess drawn to son of outcast family. But one thing was certain: whatever William did to strain Rho's affections, she could return with interest.

I walked to the Ice Pit with Rho after an hour of helping her prepare her case.

She was absolutely correct; as Sandovals, we had a duty to preserve the reputation and heirs of the Sandoval BM, and even by an advocate's logic that would include the founders of our core family.

That we were also taking in four hundred and eight outsiders was quite another matter . . . But as Rho pointed out, the Society could hardly sell individuals. Surely nobody would think it a *bad* idea, bringing such a wealth of potential information to the Moon. Tired old Earth didn't want it; just more corpsicles on a world plagued by them. Anonymous heads, harvested in the mid-twenty-first century, declared dead, stateless, very nearly outside the law, without rights except under the protection of their money and their declining foundation.

The StarTime Preservation Society was actually not *selling* anything or anyone. They were transferring members, chattels and responsibilities to Sandoval BM pending dissolution of the original Society; in short, they were finally, after one hundred and ten years, going cold blue belly up. Bankruptcy was the old term; pernicious exhaustion of means and resources was the new. Well and good; they had guaranteed to their charter members only sixty-one years (inclusive) of tender loving care. After that, they might just as well be out in the warm.

"The societies set up in 2020 and 2030 are declaring exhaustion at the rate of two and three a year now," Rhosalind said. "Only one has actually buried dead meat. Most have been bought out by information entrepreneurs and universities."

"Somebody hopes to make a profit?" I asked.

"Don't be noisy, James," she said, by which she meant incapable of converting information to useful knowledge. "These aren't just dead people; they're huge libraries. Their memories are theoretically intact; at least as intact as death and disease allow them to be. There's maybe a five percent degradation; we can use natural language algorithms to check and reduce that to maybe three percent."

"Very noisy," I said.

"Nonsense. That's usable recall. Your memories of your seventh birthday have degraded by fifty percent."

I tried to remember my seventh birthday; nothing came to mind. "Why? What happened on my seventh birthday?

"Not important, Mickey" Rho said.

"So who wants that sort of information? It's out of date, it's noisy, it's going to be hard to prove provenance . . . Much less check it out for accuracy."

She stopped, brow cloudy, clearly upset. "You're resisting me on this, aren't you?"

"Rho, I'm in charge of project finances. I *have* to ask dumb questions. What value are these heads to us, even if we can extract information? And—" I held up my hand, about to make a major point, "What if extraction of information is intrusive? We can't dissect these heads— you've assumed the contracts."

"I called Cailetet from Tampa, Florida, last week. They say the chance of recovery of neural patterns and states from frozen heads is about eighty percent, using nonintrusive methods. No nano injections. Lamb shift tweaking. They can pinpoint every molecule in every head from *outside* the containers."

However outlandish Rho's schemes, she always did a certain amount of planning ahead. I leaned my head to one side and lifted my hands, giving up. "All right," I said. "It's fascinating. The possibilities are—"

"Luminous," Rho finished for me.

"But who will buy historical information?"

"These are some of the finest minds of the twentieth century," Rho said. "We could sell shares in future accomplishments."

"*If* they're revivable." We were coming up to the white line and the big porcelain hatch to the Ice Pit. "They're currently not very active and not very creative," I commented.

"Do you doubt we'll be able to revive them someday? Maybe in ten or twenty years?"

I shook my head dubiously. "They talked revival a century ago. High-quality surgical nano wasn't enough to do the trick. You can make a complex machine shine like a gem, fix it up so that everything fits, but if you don't know where to kick it . . . Long time passing, no eyelids cracking to light of a new day."

Rho palmed the hatch guard. William took his own sweet time answering. "I'm an optimist," she said. "I always have been."

"Rho, you've come when I'm busy," William said over the com.

"Oh, for Christ's sake, William. I'm your wife and I've been gone for three months." She wasn't irritated; her tone was playfully piqued. The hatch opened, and again I caught the smell of cold in the outrush of warm.

"The heads are ancient," I said, stepping over the threshold behind her. "They'll need retraining, re-everything. They're probably elderly, inflexible . . . But those are hardly major handicaps when you consider that right now, they're *dead*."

She shrugged this off and walked briskly across the steel bridge. She'd once told me that William, in his more tense and frustrated moments, enjoyed making love on the bridge. I wondered about harmonics. "Where's the staff?" she asked.

"William told me to let them go. He said we didn't need them with the QL in control." We had been working for the past three years with a team of young technicians chosen from several other families around Procellarum. William had informed me two days after the QL's installation that these ten colleagues were no longer needed. He was coldly blunt about it, and he made no dust about the fact that I was the one who would have to arrange for their severance.

His logic was strong; the QL would not need additional human support, and we could use the BM exchange for other purchases. Despite my instincts that this was bad manners between families, I could not stand alone against William; I had served the notices and tried to take or divert the brunt of the anger.

Rho cringed as she sidled between the double tori of the disorder pumps, whether in reaction to her husband's blunt efficiency or the pumps' effect on her body. She glanced over her shoulder sympathetically. "Poor Micko."

William opened the door, threw out his arms in a peremptory fashion, and enfolded Rho.

I love my sister. I do not know whether it was some perverse jealousy or a sincere desire for her well-being that motivated my feeling of unease whenever I saw William embrace her.

"I've got something for us," Rho said, looking up at him with high-energy, complete-equality adoration.

"Oh," William said, eyes already wary. "What?"

I LAY IN BED, UNABLE TO GET THE NOISELESS SUCK OF THE PUMPS OUT OF MY thoughts, purged from my body. After a restless time I began to slide into my usual lunar doze, made a half-awake comparison between seeing William embrace Rho and feeling the pumps embrace me; thought of William's reaction to Rho's news; smiled a little; slept.

William had not been pleased. An unnecessary intrusion; yes there was excess cooling capacity; yes his arbeiters had the time to construct a secure facility for the heads in the Ice Pit; but he did not need the extra stress now nor any distractions because he was *this close* to his goal.

Rho had worked on him with that mix of guileless persuasion and unwavering determination that characterized my sister. I have always equated Rho with the nature-force shakers of history; folks who in their irrational stubbornness shift the course of human rivers, whether for good or ill perhaps not even future generations could decide.

William had given in, of course. It was after all a small distraction, so he finally admitted; the raw materials would come out of the Sandoval BM contingency fund; he might even be able to squeeze in some mutually advantageous equipment denied him for purely fiscal reasons. "I'll do it mostly for the sake of your honored ancestors, of course," William had said.

The heads came by shuttle from Port Yin five days later. Rho and I supervised the deposit at Pad Four, closest to the Ice Pit lift entrance. Packed in cubic steel boxes with their own refrigerators, the heads were slightly bulkier than Rho had estimated. Six cartloads and seven hours after landing, we had them in the equipment lift.

"I've had Nernst BM design an enclosure for William's arbeiters to build," Rho said. "These'll keep for another week as is." She patted the closest box, peering through her helmet with a wide grin.

"You could have chosen someone cheaper," I groused. Nernst had gained unwarranted status in the past few years; I would have chosen the more reasonable, equally capable Twinning BM.

"Nothing but the best for our progenitors," Rho said. "Christ, Mickey. Think about it." She turned to the boxes, mounted in a ring of two crowded stacks in the round lift, small refrigerators sticking from the inward-pointing sides of the boxes. We descended in the shaft. I could not see her face, but I heard the emotion in her voice. "Think of what it would mean to access them . . ."

I walked around and between the boxes. High quality, old fashioned bright steel, beautifully shaped and welded. "A lot of garrulous old-timers," I said.

"Mickey." Her chide was mild. She knew I was thinking.

"Are they labelled?" I asked.

"That's one problem," Rho said. "We have a list of names, and all the containers are numbered; but StarTime says it can't guarantee a one-to-one match. Records were apparently jumbled after the closing date."

"How could that happen?" I was shocked by the lack of professionalism more than by the obvious ramifications.

"I don't know."

"What if StarTime goofed in other ways, and they really *are* just cold meat?" I asked.

Rho shrugged with a casualness that made me cringe, as if, after all her efforts and the expenditure of hard-earned Sandoval capital, such a thing might not be disastrous. "Then we're out of some money," she said. "But I don't think they made that big a goof."

We slowly pressurized at the bottom of the shaft, Rho watching the containers for any sign of buckling. There was none; they had been expertly packed. "Nernst BM says it will take two days for William's machines to make this enclosure. Can you supervise? William refuses . . ."

I pulled off my helmet, kicked some surface dust from my boots against a vacuum nozzle, and grinned miserably. "Sure. I have nothing better to do."

Rho put her gloved hands on my shoulders. "Mickey. Brother."

I looked at the boxes, intrigue growing alarmingly. What if they were alive inside there, and could—in their own deceased way—tell us of their lives? That would be extraordinary; historic. Sandoval BM could gain an enormous amount of publicity, and that would reflect on our net worth in the Triple. "I'll supervise," I said. "But you get Nernst BM to send a human over here and not just an engineering arbeiter. It should be in their design contract; I want someone to personally inspect upon completion."

"No fear," Rho said. Gloves removed but skinsuit still on, she gave me a quick hug. "Let's roll!" She guided the first cartload of stacked boxes through the gate into the Ice Pit storage warren, where they'd be kept for the time being.

THE FIRST SIGN OF TROUBLE CAME QUICKLY. JANIS GRANGER, ASSISTANT TO Fiona Task-Felder, visited barely six hours after the unloading of the heads.

I had neglected to inform Rho about what had happened in lunar politics since her departure to Earth: Fiona Task-Felder's election to president of the Multiple Council, something I would have said was impossible only a year before.

Janis Granger made a meeting request through the Sandoval BM secretary in Port Yin. I okayed the request, though I didn't have the slightest idea what she wanted to talk about. I could hardly refuse to speak with a representative of the council president.

Her private bus landed at Pad Three six hours after I gave permission.

I received her in my spare but spacious formal office in the farm management warrens.

Granger was twenty-seven, black-haired with Eurasian features and Amerindian skin—all tailored. She wore trim flag-blue denims and a white ruffled-neck blouse, the ruffles projecting a changing pattern of delicate white-on-white geometrics. Janis, like her boss and "sister" Fiona, was a member of Task-Felder BM.

Task-Felder had been founded on Earth as a lunar BM, an unorthodox procedure that had raised eyebrows fifty years before. Membership was allegedly limited to Logologists—nobody knew of any exceptions, at any rate—which made it the only lunar BM founded on religious principles. For these reasons, Task-Felder BM had been outside the loop and comparatively powerless in lunar politics, if such could be called politics: a weave of mutual advantage, politeness, small-community cooperation in the face of clear financial pressures.

The Task-Felder Logologists tended their businesses carefully, played their parts with scrupulous attention to detail and quality, and had carefully distributed favors and loans to other BMs and the council, working their way with incredible speed up the ladder of lunar acceptance, all at the same time they believed six impossible things before breakfast.

"I have the BM Project Status report from the council," Janis Granger said, seating herself gracefully in a chair across from mine. I did not sit behind a desk; that was reserved for contract talks or financial dealings. "I wanted to discuss it with you, since you manage the major scientific project undertaken by Sandoval BM at this time."

I had heard something about this council report; in its early drafts, it had seemed innocuous, another BM mutual-activity consent agreement.

"We've gotten a consensus of the founding BMs to agree to consult with each other on projects which may affect lunar standing in the Triple," Granger said.

Why hadn't she gone to the family syndics in Port Yin? Why come all this way to talk with me? "All right," I said. "I assume Sandoval's representative has looked over the agreement."

"She has. She told me there might be a conflict with a current project, not your primary project. She advised me to send a representative of the president to talk with you; I decided this was important enough I would come myself."

Granger had an intensity that reminded me of Rho. She did not take her eyes off mine. She did not smile. She leaned forward, elbows still on the chair rests, and said, "Rhosalind Sandoval has signed a contract to receive terrestrial corpsicles."

"She has. She's my direct sister, by the way."

Granger blinked. With any family-oriented BM member, such a comment would have elicited a polite "Oh, and how is your branch?" She neglected the pleasantry.

"Are you planning resuscitation?" she finally asked.

"No," I said. *Not as yet.* "We're speculating on future value."

"If they're not resuscitated, they have no future value."

I disagreed with a mild shake of my head. "That's our worry, nobody else's."

"The Council has expressed concern that your precedent could lead to a flood of corpsicle dumping. The Moon can't possibly receive a hundred thousand dead. It would be a major financial drain."

"I don't see how a precedent is established," I said, wondering where she was going to take this.

"Sandoval BM is a major family group. You influence new and offshoot families. We've already had word that two other families are considering similar deals, in case you're on to something. And all of them have contacted Cailetet BM. I believe Rhosalind Sandoval-Pierce has tried to get a formal exclusion contract with Cailetet. Have you approved all this?"

I hadn't; Rho hadn't told me she'd be moving so quickly, but it didn't surprise me. It was a logical step in her scheme. "I haven't discussed it with her. She has Sandoval priority approval on this project."

This seemed to take Granger by surprise. "BM charter priority?"

"Yes."

"Why?"

I saw no reason to divulge family secrets. If she didn't already know, my instincts told me, she didn't need to know. "Business privilege, ma'am."

Granger looked to one side and thought this over for an uncomfortably long time, then returned her eyes to me. "Cailetet is asking Council advice. I've issued a chair statement of disapproval. We think it might adversely effect our currency ratings in the Triple. There are strong moral and religious feelings on Earth now about corpsicles; revival has been outlawed in seven nations. We feel you've been taken advantage of."

"We don't think so," I said.

"Nevertheless, the Council is considering issuing a restraining order against any storage or use of the corpsicles."

"Excuse me," I said. I reached across to the desk and brought out my manager's slate. "Auto counselor, please," I requested aloud. I keyed in instructions I didn't want Granger to hear, asking for a legal opinion on this possibility. The auto counselor quickly reported: "Not legal at this time" and gave citations.

"You can't restrain an autonomous chartered BM," I said. I read out the citations, "Mutual benefit agreement 35 stroke 2111, reference to charter family agreements, 2102."

"If sufficient BMs can be convinced of the unwisdom of your actions, and if the financial result could be ruinous to any original charter BM, our council thinker has issued an opinion that you can be restrained."

It was my turn to pause and think things over.

"Then it seems we might be heading for council debate," I said.

"I'd regret causing so much fuss," Granger said. "Perhaps we can reach an agreement outside of council."

"Our syndics can discuss it," I allowed. My backbone was becoming stubbornly stiff. "But I think it should be openly debated in Council."

She smiled. If, as was alleged by the Logologists, their philosophy removed all human limitations, judging by Janis Granger, I opposed such benefits. There was a control about her that suggested she had nothing to control, neither stray whim nor dangerous passion; automatonous. She chilled me.

"As you wish," she said. "This is really not a large matter, It's not worth a lot of trouble."

Then why bother? "I agree," I said. "I believe the BMs can resolve it among themselves."

"The council represents the BMs," Granger said.

I nodded polite agreement. I wanted nothing more than to have her out of my office, out of the Ice Pit Station.

"Thank you for your time," she said, rising. I escorted her to the lift. She did not say good-bye; merely smiled her unrevealing mannequin smile.

Back in my office, I put through a request for an appointment with Thomas Sandoval-Rice at Port Yin. Then I called Rho and William and Rho answered. "Mickey! Cailetet has just accepted our contract."

That took me back for a second. "I'm sorry," I said, confused. "What?"

"What are you sorry about? It's good news. They think they can manage it. They say it's a challenge. They're willing to sign an exclusive."

"I just had a conversation with Janis Granger."

"Who's she?"

"Task-Felder. Aide to the president of the council," I said. "I think they're going to try to shut us down."

"Shut down Sandoval BM?" Rho laughed. She thought I was joking.

"No. Shut down your heads project."

"They can't do that," she said, still amused.

"Probably not. At any rate, I have a call in to the director." I was thinking over what Rho had told me. If Cailetet had accepted our contract, then they were either not worried about the council debate, or . . .

Granger had lied to me.

"Mickey, what's this all about?"

"I don't know," I said. "I'll field it. The new Council president is a Task-Felder. You should keep up on these things, Rho."

"Who gives a rille? We haven't had any complaints from other BMs. We keep to our boundaries. Task-Felder. Dust them, they're not even a lunar-chartered BM Aren't they Logologists?"

"They have the talk seat in Council," I said.

"Oh, for the love of," Rho said. "They're crazier than mud. When did they get the seat?"

"Two months ago."

"How did they get it?"

"Careful attention to the social niceties," I said, tapping my palm with a finger.

Rho considered. "Did you record your meeting?"

"Of course." I filed an automatic BM-priority request for Rho and transferred the record to her slate address.

"I'll get back to you, Mickey. Or better yet, come on down to the Ice Pit. William needs someone besides me to talk to, I think. He's having trouble with the QL again, and he's still a little irritated about our heads."

MY BROTHER-IN-LAW WAS IN A CONTEMPLATIVE MOOD. "ON EARTH," HE said, "In India and Egypt, centuries before they had refrigerators, they had ice, cold drinks. Air-conditioning. All because they had dry air and clear night skies."

I sat across the metal table from him in the laboratory's first room. Outside, William's arbeiters were busily, noisily constructing an enclosure for Rho's heads, using the Nernst BM design. William sat in a tattered metal sling chair, leaving me the guest's cushioned armchair.

"You mean, they used storage batteries or solar power or something," I said, biting on his nascent anecdote.

He smiled pleasantly, relaxing into the story. "Nothing so obvious," he said. "Pharaoh's servants could have used flat, broad, porous earthenware trays. Filled them with a few centimeters of water, hoping for a particularly dry evening with clear air."

"Cold air?" I suggested.

"Not particularly important. Egypt was seldom cold. Just dry air and a clear night. Voila. Ice."

I looked incredulous.

"No kidding," he said, leaning forward. "Evaporation and radiation into empty space. Black sky at night, continuous evaporation cooling the tray and the liquid, temperature of the liquid drops, and given almost no humidity, the tray freezes solid. Harvest the ice in the morning, fill the tray again for the next night. Air conditioning, if you had enough surface area, enough trays, and some caves to store the ice."

"It would have worked?"

"Hell, Micko, it *did* work. Before there was electricity, that's how they made ice. Anyplace dry, with clear night skies . . ."

"Lose a lot of water through evaporation, wouldn't you?"

William shook his head. "You haven't a gram of romance in you, Micko. Not at all tempted by the thought of a frosty mug of beer for the Pharaoh."

"Beer," I said. "Think of all the beer you could store in Rho's annex." Beer was a precious commodity in a small lunar station.

He made a face. "I saw the record of that Granger woman. Is she going to give Rho trouble?"

I shook my head.

"Serves Rho right," William said. "Sometimes . . ." He stood and wiped his face with his hands, then squeezed thumb and pointing finger together, squinting at them. "You were right. A new problem, Micko, a new *effect*. The QL says the disorder pumps have to be tuned again. It'll take a week. Then we'll hit the zeroth state of matter. Nothing like it since before we were all a twinkle in God's eye."

We had been through this before. My teasing seemed a necessary anodyne to him when he was bumping against another delay. "Violation of third law," I said casually.

He waved that away. "William, you're an infidel. The Third Law's a mere bagatelle, like the sound barrier—"

"What if it's more like the speed of light?"

William shut one eye half-way and regarded me balefully. "You've laid out the money this far. If I'm a fool, you're a worse fool."

"From your point of view, I wouldn't find that reassuring," I said, smiling. "But what do I know. I'm a dry accountant. Set me out under a clear terrestrial night sky and my brain would freeze."

William laughed. "You're smarter than you need to be," he said. "Violating the third law of thermodynamics—no grief there. It's a sitting duck, Micko. Waiting to be shot."

"It's been sitting for a long time. Lots of hunters have missed. *You've* missed for three years now."

"We didn't have quantum logic thinkers and disorder pumps," William said, staring out into the darkness beyond the small window, face lit orange by flashes of light from the arbeiters at work in the pit below.

"The pumps make me twitch," I confessed, not for the first time.

William ignored that and turned to me, suddenly solemn. "If the council tries to stop Rho, you'd better fight them with all you've got.

I'm not a Sandoval by birth, Mickey, but by God, this BM better stand by her."

"It won't get that far, William," I said. "It's all dust. A burble of politics."

"Tell them to cut the damned politics," William said softly. The rallying cry of all the Moon's families, all our tightly-bound, yet ruggedly individual citizens; how often had I heard that phrase? "This is Rho's project. If I—if *we* let her have the Ice Pit for her heads, nobody should interfere. Damn it, that's what the Moon is all about. Do you believe all you hear about the Logologists?"

"I don't know," I said. "They certainly don't think like you and I."

I joined William at the window. "Thank you," I said.

"For what?"

"For letting Rho do what she wants."

"She's crazier than I am," William said with a sigh. "She says you weren't too pleased at first, either."

"It's pretty gruesome," I admitted.

"But you're getting interested?"

"I suppose."

"The Task-Felder woman made you even more interested."

I nodded.

William tapped the window's thick glass idly. "Mickey, Rho has always been protected by Sandoval, by living here on the Moon. The Moon has always encouraged her; free spirit, small population, place for young minds to shine. She's a little naive."

"We're no different," I said.

"Perhaps you aren't, but I've seen the rough."

I leaned my head to one side, giving him that much. "If by *naive*, you mean she doesn't know what it's like to be in a scrap, you're wrong."

"She knows intellectually," William said. "And she's sharp enough that may be all she needs. But she doesn't know what a dirty fight really is."

"You think this is going to get dirty?"

"It doesn't make sense," William said. "Four hundred heads is gruesome, but it isn't dangerous, and it's been tolerated on Earth for a century . . ."

"Because nothing ever came of it," I said. "And apparently the toleration is wearing thin."

William rubbed thumb and forefinger along his cheeks, narrowing his already narrow mouth. "Why would anyone object?"

"For philosophical reasons, maybe," I said.

William nodded. "Or religious reasons. Have you read Logologist literature?"

I admitted that I hadn't.

"Neither have I, and I'm sure Rho hasn't. Time we did some research, don't you think?"

I shrugged dubiously, then shivered. "I don't think I'm going to like what I find."

William clucked. "Prejudice, Micko. Pure prejudice. Remember *my* origins. Maybe the Task-Felders aren't all that forbidding."

Being accused of prejudgment irritated me. I decided to change the subject and scratch an itch of curiosity. He had shown the QL to me earlier, but had seemed to deliberately avoid demonstrating the thinker. "Can I talk to it?"

"What?" William asked, then, following my eyes, looked behind him at the table. "Why not. It's listening to us now. QL, I'd like to introduce my friend and colleague, Mickey Sandoval."

"Pleased to meet you," the QL said, its gender neutral, as most thinker voices were. I raised an eyebrow at William. Normal enough, house-trained, almost domestic. He understood my expression of mild disappointment.

"Can you describe Mickey to me?" he asked, challenged now.

"In shape and form it is not unlike yourself," the thinker said.

"What about his extensions?"

"They differ from yours. Its state is free and dynamic. Its link with you is not primary. Does he want controlling?"

William smiled triumphantly. "No, QL, he is not an instrumentality. He is like myself."

"You are instrumentality."

"True, but for convenience's sake only," William said.

"It thinks you're part of the lab?" I asked.

"Much easier to work with it that way," William assured me.

"May I ask another question?"

"Be my guest," William said.

"QL, who's the boss here?"

"If by boss you mean a node of leadership, there is no leader here. The leader will arise at some later date, when the instrumentalities are integrated."

"When we succeed," William explained, "then there will be a boss, a node of leadership; and that will be the successful result itself."

"You mean, QL thinks that if you achieve absolute zero, that will be the boss?"

William smiled. "Something like that. Thank you, QL."

"You're welcome," the QL replied.

"Not so fast," I said. "I have another question."

William extended his hand, be my quest.

"What do you think will happen if the cells in the Cavity reach absolute zero?"

The interpreter was silent for a moment, and then spoke in a subtly different voice. "This interpreter is experiencing difficulties translating the QL thinker's response," it said. "Do you wish a statement in post-Boolean mathematical symbols by way of direct retinal projection, or the same transferred to a slate address, or an English interpretation?"

"I've already asked this question, of course," William told me. "I have the mathematics already, several different versions, several different possibilities."

"I'd like an English interpretation," I said.

"Then please be warned that response changes from hour to hour in significant ways," the interpreter said. "This might indicate a chaotic wave-mode fluctuation of theory within the QL. In other words, it has not yet formulated an adequate prediction, and cannot. This thinker will present several English language responses, but warns that they are inadequate for full understanding, which may not be possible for organic human minds at any rate. Do you wish possibly misleading answers?"

"Give us a try," I said, feeling a sting of resentment. William sat at the manual control console, willing to let this be my own contest.

"QL postulates that achievement of absolute zero within a significant sample of matter will result in a new state of matter. Since there is a coupling between motion of matter in spacetime and other forces within matter, particularly within atomic nuclei—the principle upon which the force disorder pumps operate—then this new state of matter may be stable, and may require substantial energy input to return to a thermodynamic state. There is a small possibility that this new state may be communicable by quantum forces, and may induce a similar state in closely associated atoms."

I glanced at William. "A very small possibility," William said. "And I've protected against it. The copper atoms are isolated in a Penning trap and can't come in contact with anything else."

"Please go on," I told the interpreter.

"Another possibility involves a hitherto undiscovered coupling between states of spacetime itself and thermodynamic motion of matter. If thermodynamism ceases within a sample, the nature of spacetime around the sample may change. Quantum ground states may be affected. Restraints on probabilities of atomic positions may induce an alignment of virtual particle activities, with amplification of other quantum effects, including remote release of quantum information normally communicated between particles and inaccessible to noncommunicants."

"All right," I said, defeated. "William, I need an interpreter for your interpreter."

"What the math says," William said, eyes shining with what must have been joy or pride—it could not have been sadness—"is that a kind of crystallization of spacetime will occur."

"So?"

"Spacetime is naturally amorphous, if we can poetically use terms reserved for matter. Crystallized space would have some interesting properties. Information of quantum states and positions normally communicated only between particles—through the so-called exclusive channels—could be leaked. There could even be propagation of quantum information backwards in time."

"That doesn't sound good," I said.

"It would be purely local," William said. "Fascinating to study. You could think of it as making space a superconductor of information, rather than the highly limited medium it is now."

"But is it likely?"

"No," William said. "From what I can understand, no QL prediction is likely or unlikely at this point."

THE ICE PIT FARMS AND SUPPORT WARRENS OCCUPIED SOME THIRTY-FIVE HECtares and employed ninety family members. That was moderately large for an isolated research facility, but old habits die hard—on the Moon, each station large and small is designed to be autonomous, in case of emergency, natural or political. Stations are more often than not spread so far apart that the habit makes hard sense. Besides, each station must act as an independent social unit, like a village on Earth. The closest major station to us, Port Yin, was six hours away by shuttle.

I had been assigned twelve possible in-family girlfriends at the age of thirteen. Two resided at the Ice Pit. I had met one only casually, but the other, Lucinda Bergman-Sandoval, had been a love friend since we were sixteen. Lucinda worked on the farm that grew the station's food. We saw each other perhaps once a month now, my focus having shifted to extra-family women, as was expected when one approached marriage age. Still, those visits were good times, and we had scheduled a chat dinner date at the farm cafe this evening.

I've never cared much what women looked like. I mean, extraordinary beauty has never impressed me, perhaps because I'm no platinum sheen myself. The Sandoval family had long since accepted pre- and post-birth transforms as a norm, as had most lunar families, and so no son or daughter of Sandoval BM was actively unpleasant to look at. Lucinda's family had given her normal birth, and she had chosen a light transform at age seventeen: she was black-haired, coffee-skinned, purple-eyed, slender and tall, with a long neck, and pleasant, wide face. Like most lunar kids, she was bichemical—she could go to Earth or other higher gravity environments and adjust quickly.

We met in the cafe, which overlooked the six hectare farm spread on the surface. Thick field-reinforced windows separated our table from high vacuum; a brass bar circled the enclosure to reassure our instincts that we would not fall off to the regolith or the clear polystone dome below.

Lucinda was a quiet girl, quick and sympathetic. We talked relationships for a while—she was considering an extra-family marriage proposal from a Nernst engineer named Hakim. I had some prospects but was still barn dancing a lot.

"Hakim's willing to be name-second," she said. "He's very generous."

"Wants kids?"

"Of course. He told me they could be ex-utero if I was squeamish." Lucinda smiled.

"Sounds rad," I said.

"Oh, he's not. Just . . . generous. I think he's really sweet on me."

"Advantages?"

She smirked lightly. "Lots of advantages. His branch controls Nernst Triple Contracts."

"Nernst's done some work for us," I said.

"Tell," she instructed me softly.

"I probably shouldn't. I haven't even thought it through . . ."

"Sounds serious."

"It could be, I suppose. The council president may try to stop something my blood-sister is doing."

Lucinda raised her wide, thin eyebrows. "Really? On what grounds?"

"I'm not sure. The president is Task-Felder . . ."

"So?"

"She's a Logologist."

"Mm-hmm. So? They have to play by the rules, too."

"Of course. I'm not making any accusations. . . . But what do you know about Logologists?"

Lucinda thought for a moment. "They're tough on contracts. Daood—that's Hakim's brother—he administered a design contract to the Independence Station near Fra Mauro. That's a Task-Felder station."

"I know. I was invited to a barn dance there last month."

"Did you go?"

I shook my head. "Too much work."

"Daood says they rode the Nernst designers for eight weeks, jumped them between three different specs. Seemed to be a management lag—Task-Felder niggles from the top down. No independent thinking from on-site managers. Daood was not impressed."

I smiled. "We've upset some Nernst people ourselves. Last year, on the refrigerator repairs and radiator upgrades."

"Hakim mentioned that. . . . Daood said we were saints compared to Task-Felder."

"Good to know we're appreciated by our brother BMs."

She mused for a moment. Our food came on an arbeiter delivery cart. "I've heard about Io, of course. That was hard to believe. Have you read any of Thierry's works?" Lucinda asked. "They were popular when we were kids."

"I managed to avoid them," I said. K. D. Thierry, an Earth-born movie producer who called himself a philosopher and acted like a dictatorial guru, had founded Chronopsychology in the late twentieth century, and then had spun it off into Logology.

"He must have written about three hundred books and LitVids. I read two—*Planetary Spirit* and *Whither Mind?* They were pretty strange. He tried to lay down rules for everything from what to dream to toilet training."

I laughed. "Why did you read them?"

Lucinda shrugged. "I used to scan a lot of LitVids. They were in the library—I called them up, paid the fee—about half what most LitVids cost. Lots of pretty video stuff. Sparkling lakes and rivers on Earth . . . pictures of Thierry riding his solar-powered yacht around the world. That sort of thing. All very attractive to a Moon girl."

"Did you read anything that explained what happened on Io?"

"I remember something about Thierry being told by an angel that humans were the spawn of warring gods, superbeings. They lived before the birth of our Sun. He said that deep within us were pieces of the personalities of some of these gods."

"I'll buy that," I said.

"The rest of the god's minds had been imprisoned, buried by their enemies under sulfur on the 'Hellmoon.' They were waiting for us to liberate them and join with them again. Something like that." She shook her head.

I knew the rest of the story; it was in files on recent history I had studied in secondary. In 2090, Logologists on Mars had taken out a thousand-year development lease on Io from the Triple; violent useless Io, visited only twice in history by human explorers. The new lease-holders set up a human-occupied station on Io in 2100. The station was lost with all occupants during the formation of a new Pelean-class sulfur lake. Seventy-five loyal Logologists died and were never recovered; they are still there, entombed in black sulfur.

The Logologists had never admitted to looking for lost gods.

I shuddered. "I didn't know what they were after. That's interesting."

"It's spooky," Lucinda said. "I stopped reading him when I realized he thought he was writing history. These folks think he's practically a god himself."

"They do?"

"You're dealing with them, and you don't know what they think?"

"My shortcomings are legendary," I said, raising my hands. "What kind of god?"

"They say he didn't die, that he was in perfect health. He just left his body behind like a husk. Now he's supposed to advise the Logologists through spiritual messages to his chosen disciples, each generation. He anoints them with blue cold, they say. Whatever that is. So what does Rho want to do that they don't like?"

"My lips are sealed. Rho gives the press conferences around here."

"But the president knows."

"I presume she must."

"Thanks for trusting me, Micko." She gave me a narrow grin to let me know she was teasing. Still, I felt uncomfortable.

"I can say I don't like any of it," I confessed. "It makes things a lot more complicated."

"Better get on your homework, then," she advised.

THE DEEPER I DUG INTO LOGOLOGY, THE MORE FASCINATED I BECAME. AND repelled—though fascination won out in the end. Here was a creed without a coherent philosophy—a system without a sensible metaphysic. Here was puerile hypothesis and even outright fantasy masquerading as revealed truth. And it was all based on a single supposed insight into the human mind, something so audacious—and so patently ridiculous—that it was fascinating.

K. D. Thierry had exploited everybody's deeply held wish to participate in the unfolding of a Big Event. In this he was little different from other prophets and messiahs; the real differences lay in how much we knew about Thierry, and how ridiculous it seemed that such a man could be vouchsafed any great truth.

Thierry had been an actor in his youth. He had played small roles in bad chemstock films, one or two tiny appearances in good ones. He was known to film buffs but not to many others. In time he found his real strength lay in putting together deals, and so he began to produce and even direct films not so much bad as lusterless, soon forgotten.

By the late 1980s he had made a reputation as the director of a series of bizarre mystery films in which a peculiar flavor, half lunacy, half ironic humor, attracted a faithful following. He began to lecture at colleges and universities. He allegedly once told a screenwriter in New York that "Movies are a weak shadow. Religion is where we ought to go."

And so he went. Not an uneducated man, he joined the chorus of psychologists then intent on knocking the last crumbling chunks of Freudian doctrine from its pedestal. He tried to add all the rest of psychology to the scraps; his first wife had been a psychotherapist, and the parting had been memorably cruel to both.

Then, when he was forty-three years old, came a night of revelation. Sitting on a beach near the California city of Newport, he was confronted—so he claimed—by a massive figure, tall as a skyscraper, who gave him a piece of rock crystal the size of his fist. The figure was female in shape, but masculine in strength, and it said to him, "I don't have much time. I've been dead too long to stay here and talk to you in person. This crystal tells the entire story."

Thierry surmised that the huge figure was a *hologram*—which seemed to me to be primitive technology for a god to use when manifesting herself, but then, Thierry's imagination was limited by his times, and to reach his presumed audience of scientific naives, he used the jargon and concepts of the 1990s.

He stared into the crystal, wrote down what he saw in a series of secret books not published in his lifetime, and then produced an epitome for public consumption. That epitome was called *The Old and the New Human Race*, and in it he revealed the cosmic science of Chromopsychology.

The enormous hologram had been the last of the True Humans, and the crystal she had given him had helped him unlock the power of his mind.

He published and promoted the book personally. It sold ten thousand copies the first year, and five hundred thousand copies the next. Later editions revised the name and some of the doctrines of the cosmic science: it became Logology, his final break with even the name *psychology*.

The Old and the New Human Race was soon available not just in paper, but in cube text, LitVid, Vid, and five interactive media.

Through a series of seminars, he converted a few disciples at first, then multitudes, to the belief that humanity had once been godlike in its powers, and was now shackled by ancient chains which made us small, dependent on our bodies, and stupid. Thierry said that all humans were capable of transforming themselves into free-roving, very powerful spirits. The crystal told him how to break these chains through a series of mental exercises, and how to realize that humanity's ancient enemies—all but one, whom he called Shaytana—were dead, powerless to stop our self-liberation. All one's personal liberation required was concentration, education, and discipline—and a lifetime membership in the Church of Logology.

Shaytana was Loki and a watered-down Satan combined, too weak to destroy us or even stop strong individuals from breaking free of the chains, wily enough and persistent enough to convince the great majority of humans that death was our destiny and weakness our lot. Those who opposed Thierry were dupes of Shaytana, or willing cohorts (as Freud, Jung, Adler, and all other psychiatrists and psychologists had been). There were many dupes of Shaytana, including presidents, priests, and fellow prophets.

In 1997, Thierry tried to purchase a small South Pacific island to create a community of Unchained. He was rebuffed by the island's inhabitants and forced to move his seedling colony to Idaho, where he started his own small town, Ouranos, named after the progenitor of human consciousness. Ouranos became a major political center in Idaho; Thierry was in part responsible for the separation of the state into two sections in 2012, the northern calling itself Green Idaho.

He wrote massively, still made movies occasionally. His later books covered all aspects of a Logologist's life, from prenatal care to funeral rites and design of grave site. He packaged LitVid on such topics as world economics and politics. Slowly, he became a recluse; by 2031, two years before his death, he saw no one but his mistress and three personal secretaries.

Thierry claimed that a time of crisis would come after his own "liberation," and that within a century he would return, "freed of the chains of flesh," to put the Church of Logology into a position of "temporal power over the nations of the Earth." "Our enemies will be cinderized," he promised, "and the faithful will see an eon of spiritual ecstasy."

At his death, he weighed one hundred and seventy-five kilograms and had to move with the aid of a massive armature part wheelchair, part robot. Press releases, and reports to his hundreds of thousands of disciples in Ouranos and around the world, described his death as voluntary release. He was accompanying the spirit who had first appeared to him on the beach in California on a tour of the galaxy.

His personal physician—a devoted disciple—claimed that despite his bulk, he was in perfect health, and that his body had changed its internal constitution in such a way as to build up massive amounts of energy necessary to power him in the first few years of his spiritual voyage.

Thierry himself they called the Ascended Master. Allegedly he had made weekly reports to his mistress on his adventures. She lived to a ripe old age, eschewed rejuvenation legal or otherwise, grew massive in bulk and so the story went, joined her former lover on his pilgrimage.

A year after his death, one of his secretaries was arrested in Green Idaho on charges of child pornography. There was no evidence that Thierry had ever participated in such activities; but the ensuing scandal nearly wrecked the Church of Logology.

The Church recovered with remarkable speed when it sponsored a program of supporting young LitVid artists. Using the program as a steppingstone to acceptance among politicians and the general public, Logology's past was soon forgotten, and its current directors—anonymous, efficient, and relatively colorless—finished the job that Thierry had begun. They made Logology a legitimate alternative religion, for those who continued to seek such solace.

The church prospered and made its beginning moves on Puerto Rico. Logologists established a free hospital and "psychiatric" training center on the island in 2046, four years before Puerto Rico became the fifty-first state. The island was soon controlled by a solid 60 percent majority population of Logologists, the greatest concentration of the religion on Earth. Every Puerto Rican representative in the United States Congress since statehood had been a Logologist.

The rest was more or less familiar, including an in-depth history of the Io purchase and expedition.

When I finished poring over the massive amounts of material, I was drained and incredulous. I felt that I understood human nature from a somewhat superior perspective—as someone who was not a Logologist, who had not been taken in by Thierry's falsehoods and fantasies.

I DREAMED THAT NIGHT OF WALKING ALONG AN IRRIGATION CANAL IN EGYPT. Dawn came intensely blue in the east, stars still out overhead. The canal had frozen during the night, which pleased me; it lay in jumbled cubes of ice, clear as glass, and the cubes were rearranging themselves like living things into perfect flat sheets. *Order*, I thought. *The Pharaoh will be pleased.* But as I looked into the depths of the canal, I saw fish pinned in by the layers of cubes, unable to move, gills flexing frantically, and I realized that I had sinned. I looked up to the stars, blaming them, but they refused to accept responsibility; then I looked to the sides of the canal, among the reeds, and saw copper double tori on each side, sucking soundlessly. All my dream-muscles twitched and I came awake.

It was eight hundred hours and my personal line was blinking politely. I answered; there were two messages, one from Rho, left three hours earlier, and one from Thomas Sandoval-Rice, an hour after hers.

Rho's message was voice only, and brief. "Mickey, the director wants to meet with both of us today in Port Yin. He's sending an executive shuttle for us at ten hundred."

The director's message was extensive text and a vocal from his secretary. "Mickey, Thomas Sandoval-Rice would like you to meet with him in Port Yin as soon as possible. We'd like Rhosalind to be there as well." Accompanying the message was text and LitVid on Logology, much of the same material I'd already studied.

I arranged my affairs for the day and canceled a meeting with family engineers on generator maintenance.

RHO WAS UNCHARACTERISTICALLY SOMBER AS WE WAITED IN THE PAD FOUR lounge. Outside, it was lunar night, the brilliant glow of field lights blanking out the stars. Earth was at full above us, a thumbnail-sized spot of bluish light through the overhead ports. All we could see through the lounge windows was a few hectares of ashen churned lunar soil, a pile of rubble dug out from the Ice Pit warrens decades before, the featureless gray concrete of the field itself.

"I feel like they're pushing my nose in the dust," Rho said. The lights of the executive bus became visible above the horizon. "This is pretty fancy treatment. The director has never paid us so much attention before."

I tried to reassure her. "You've never reeled in great-grandma and grandpa before," I said.

She shook her head. "That isn't it. He sent a stack of research on Logologists."

I nodded. "Me, too. You've read it?"

"Of course."

"What did you think?"

"They're odd people, but I can't find anything that would make them object to this project. They say death isn't liberation unless you're enlightened—so frozen heads could just be more potential converts . . ."

"Maybe Thomas knows something more," I said.

The bus landed, sleek and bright red, an expensive full-pressure, full-cabin late model Lunar Rover. I had never ridden on the Sandoval limo before. The interior was very impressive; automatic adjustment seats, restaurant unit—I regretted I'd already eaten breakfast, but nibbled on Rho's eggs and mock ham—and complete communications center. We could have called Earth or Mars or any of the asteroids using Lunar Cooperative or even the Triple satellites if we'd wished.

"Makes you realize how far out of the Sandoval mainstream we are at the Ice Pit," I said as Rho slipped her plate into the return.

"I haven't missed it," she said. "We get what we need."

"William might not agree."

Rho smiled. "It's not luxury he's after."

Port Yin was Procellarum's main interplanetary commerce field and largest city, hub for all the stations in the ocean. Procellarum was the main territory of Sandoval BM, though we had some twenty stations and two smaller ports in the Earthside highlands. Besides being a transportation hub, Port Yin was surrounded by farms; it fed much of the Earthside Moon south and west of the ocean. For lunar citizens, a farm station of sufficient size also acts as a resort—a chance to admire forests and fields.

We passed over the now-opaqued rows of farm domes, thousands of hectares spaced along the southeast edge of the port, and came in at the private Sandoval field half an hour before our appointment. That gave us little time to cross by rail and walkway through Yin City's crowds to Center Port.

The director's secretary led us down the short hall to his small personal office, centrally located among the Sandoval syndic warrens. Thomas Sandoval-Rice was trim, resolutely gray-haired, with a thin nose and ample lips, a middling seventy-five years old, and he wore a formal black suit with red sash and mooncalf slippers. He stood to greet us. There was barely room for three chairs and a desk; this was his inner sanctum, not the show office for Sandoval clients or other BM reps. Rho looked at me forlornly as we entered; this did indeed seem like the occasion for a dressing-down.

"I'm pleased to see both of you again," Thomas said as he offered us chairs. "You're looking well. Mickey, it's been three years, hasn't it, since we approved your position at the Ice Pit?"

"Yes, sir," I said.

Thomas looked at Rho's wary face and smiled reassurance. "This is not a visit to a dental mechanic," he said. "Rho, I smell a storm coming, and I'd like to have you tell me what kind of storm it might be, and why we're sailing into it."

"I don't know, sir," Rho said steadily.

"Mickey?"

"I've read your text, sir. I'm puzzled, as well."

"The Task-Felder BM is behind all this, everybody's assured me of that. I have friends in the United States of the Western Hemisphere Senate. Friends who are in touch with California Logology, the parent church, as it were. Task-Felder BM is less independent than they want to appear; if California Logology nods its hoary head, Task-Felder jumps. Now, you know that no lunar BM is supposed to operate as either a terrestrial representative or to promote purely religious principles. . . . That's in the Lunar Binding Multiples Agreements. The Constitution of the Moon."

"Yes, sir," I said.

"But Task-Felder BM has managed to avoid or ignore a great many of those provisions, and nobody's called them on it, because no BM likes the image of making a council challenge of another fully chartered BM, even one with terrestrial connections. Bad for business, in brief. We all like to think of ourselves as rugged individualists, family first, Moon second, Triple third . . . and to hell with the Triple if push comes to shove. Understood?"

"Yes, sir," I said.

"I've served as chief syndic and director of Sandoval BM for twenty-nine years, and in that time, I've seen Task-Felder grow powerful *despite* the distaste of the older, family-based binding multiples. They're sharp, they're quick learners, they have impressive financial backing, and they have a sincerity and a drive that can be disconcerting."

"I've noticed that, sir," I said.

Thomas pursed his lips. "Your conversation with Janis Granger was not pleasant?"

"No, sir."

"We've done something to offend them, and my sources on Earth tell me they're willing to take off their gloves, get down in the dust and spit up a volcano if they have to. Mud, mud, mud, crazier than."

"I don't understand why, sir," Rho said.

"I was hoping one or both of you could enlighten me. You've gone through the brief on their history and beliefs. You don't find anything suggestive?"

"I certainly don't," Rho said.

"Our frozen great-grandma and great-grandpa never did anything to upset them?"

"Not that we know of."

"Rho, we've got some two-facing from our fellow family BMs, haven't we? Nernst and Cailetet are willing to design something for us and take our cash, but they may not stand up for us in the Council." He rubbed his chin for a moment with his finger, making a wry face. "Is there anybody else interesting in the list of heads, besides great-grandma and great-grandpa?"

"I've brought along my files, including the list of individuals preserved by StarTime. There's a lacuna I was not aware of, sir—three viable individuals—and I've asked StarTime's advocate in New York for an accounting, but I haven't gotten an answer yet."

"You've correlated the list?"

"Pardon?" Rho asked.

"You've run crosschecks between Logology connections and the list? In history?"

"No."

"Mickey?"

"No, sir."

Thomas glanced at me reproachfully. "Let me do it now, then," he said. He took Rho's slate and plugged it into his desktop thinker. With a start, I realized this small green cube was Ellen C, *the* Sandoval thinker, adviser to all the syndics. Ellen C was one of the oldest thinkers on the Moon, somewhat obsolete now, but definitely part of the family. "Ellen, what do we have here?"

"No interesting strikes or correlations in the first or second degree," the thinker reported. "Completed."

Thomas raised his eyebrows. "Perhaps a dead end."

"I'll look into the unnamed three," Rho said.

"Do that. Now, I'd like to rehearse a few things with you folks. Do you know our weaknesses—your own weaknesses? And the weaknesses of the lunar BM system?"

I could not, in my naivete, come up with any immediate comments to this question. Rho was equally blank.

"Allow an older fool to lecture you a bit, then. Grandpa Ian Reiker-Sandoval favored Rho, doted on her. Gave her anything she wanted. So Rho has the man she wanted, someone from outside who doesn't meet the usual Sandoval criteria for eligible matches. Still, William has done his work admirably, and we all look forward to a breakthrough. However—"

"I'm spoiled," Rho anticipated him.

"Let's say . . . that you've had a rich girl's leeway, without the corruption of free access to fabulous wealth," Thomas said. "Nevertheless, you have substantial BM resources at your disposal, and you have a way of getting us into trouble without really seeing it coming."

"I'm not sure that's fair," I said.

"As judgments go, it's extremely fair," Thomas said, staring at me sharply. "This is not the first time . . . or are memories short in the younger Sandovals?"

Rho looked up at the ceiling, then at me, then at Thomas. "The tulips," she said.

"Sandoval BM lost half a million Triple dollars. Fortunately, we were able to convert the farms to tailored pharmaceuticals. But that was before your marriage to William, and it was minor. . . . Although typical of your early adventures. You've matured considerably since then, as I'm sure you'll both agree. Still, Rho has never been caught up in a freefall scuffle. She has always had Sandoval BM firmly behind her. To her credit, she's never brought in the kind of trouble that could reflect badly on the BM. Until now, and I can't pin the blame on her for this, except to say she's not terribly prescient."

"You blame her for *any* aspect of this?" I asked, still defensive before Thomas's relaxed gaze.

"No," Thomas said after a pregnant pause. "I blame you. You, my dear lad, are a focused dilettante, very good in your area, which is the Ice Pit, but not widely experienced. You don't have Rho's ambition, and you haven't shown many signs of her innovative spark. . . . You've never even taken advantage of your Earth sabbatical. Micko, if I may be familiar, you've done the job of managing the Ice Pit well enough, certainly nothing for us to complain about, but you've had very little experience in the bigger arena of the Triple, and you've grown a little soft sitting out there. You didn't check out Rho's scheme."

I straightened in my chair. "It had BM charter—"

"You should *still* have checked it out. You should have smelled something coming. There may be no such thing as prescience, but honed instincts are crucial in our game, Micko.

"You've cultivated fine literature—terrestrial literature—fine music, and a little history in the copious time you've had between your bursts of economic activity. You've become something of a lady's man in the barn dances. Fine; you're of an age where such things are natural. But now it's time that you put on some muscle. I'd like you to handle this matter as my accessory. You'll go to the council meetings—one is scheduled in a couple of days—and you'll study up on the chinks in our system's armor."

I settled back, suddenly more than just uneasy, and not about my impending debut in larger BM politics. "You think we're approaching a singularity?"

Thomas nodded. "Whatever your failings, Micko, you are sharp. That's exactly right. A time when all the rules could fail, and all our past oversights come back to haunt us. It's a good possibility. Care to lecture me for a minute?"

I shrugged. "Sir, I—"

"Stretch your wings, lad. You're not ignorant, else you wouldn't have made that last remark. What singularity faces the BMs now?"

"I can't really say, sir. I don't know which weakness you're referring to, specifically, but—"

"Go on." Thomas smiled like a genial tiger.

"We've outgrown the lunar constitution. Two million people in fifty-four BMs, that's ten times as many as lived on the Moon when the constitution was written. And actually, it was never written by an individual. It was cobbled together by a committee intent on not stretching or voiding individual BM charters. I think that *you* think Task-Felder isn't above forcing a constitutional crisis."

"Yes?"

"If they are planning something like that, now's the time to do it. I've been studying the Triple's performance for the past few years. Lunar BMs have gotten increasingly conservative, sir. Compared with Mars, we've been . . ." I was on a nervous high; I waved my hands, and smiled placatingly, hoping not to overwhelm or offend.

"Yes?"

"Well, a little like you accuse me of being, sir. Self-contented, taking advantage of the lull. But the Triple is going through a major shakeup now, Earth's economy is suffering its expected forty-year cyclic decline, and the lunar BMs are vulnerable. If we stop cooperating, the Moon could be put into a financial crisis worse than the Split. So everybody's being very cautious, very . . . conservative. The old rough-and-tumble has given way to don't-prick-the-seal."

"Good," Thomas said.

"I haven't been a worm, sir," I said with a pained expression.

"Glad to hear it. And if Task-Felder convinces a significant number of BMs that we're rocking the boat in a way that could lower the lunar rating in the Triple?"

"It could be bad. But why would they do that?" I asked, still puzzled.

Rho picked up my question. "Tom, how could a few hundred heads bring this on? What's Task-Felder got against us?"

"Nothing at all, dear daughter," Thomas said. BM elders often referred to family youngsters as if they were their own children. "That's what worries me most of all."

RHO RETURNED TO THE ICE PIT TO SUPERVISE COMPLETION OF THE CHAMBER for the heads; I stayed behind to prepare for the council meeting. Thomas put me up in Sandoval guest quarters reserved for family, spare but comfortable. I felt depressed, angry with myself for being so vulnerable.

I *hated* disappointing Thomas Sandoval-Rice.

And I took no satisfaction in the thought that perhaps he had stung me to get my blood moving, to spur me to action.

I wanted to avoid any circumstance where he would need to sting me again.

THOMAS WOKE ME UP FROM AN ERRATIC SLEEP OF ONE HOUR, POST TWELVE hours of study. My head felt like a dented air can. "Tune to general net lunar news," he said. "Scroll back the past five minutes."

I did as he told me and watched the LitVid image.

News of the quarter-hour. Synopsis: Earth questions jurisdiction of Moon in Sandoval BM buy-out of StarTime Preservation Society Contract and transfer of corpsicles.

Expansion 1: The United States Congressional Office of Triple Relations has issued an advisory alliance alert to the Lunar Council of Binding Multiples that Sandoval BM purchase of preservation contracts of four hundred and ten frozen heads of deceased twenty-first-century individuals may be invalid, under a late twentieth-century law regarding retention of archaeological artifacts within cultural and national boundaries. StarTime Preservation Society, a deceased-estate financed partnership group now dissolved on Earth, has already transferred "members, chattels, and responsibilities" to Sandoval BM. Sandoval Chief Syndic Thomas Sandoval-Rice states that the heads are legally under control of his binding multiple, subject to . . .

The report continued in that vein for eight thousand words of text and four minutes of recorded interviews. It concluded with a kicker, an interview with Puerto Rican Senator Pauline Grandville: *"If the Moon can simply ignore the feelings and desires of its terrestrial forebears, then that could call into question the entire matrix of Earth-Moon relations."*

I transferred to Thomas's line. "It's amazing," I said.

"Not at all," Thomas said. "I've run a search of the Earth-Moon LitVids and terrestrial press. It's in your hopper now."

"I've been reading all night, sir—"

Thomas glared at me. "I wouldn't have expected any less. We don't have much time."

"Sir, I'd be able to pinpoint my research if you'd let me know your strategy, your plan of battle."

"I don't have one yet, Micko. And neither should you. These are just the opening rounds. Never fire your guns before you've chosen a target."

"Did you know about this earlier? That California would tell Puerto Rico to do something like this?"

"I had a hint, nothing more. But my sources are quiet now. No more tattling from Earth, I'm afraid. We're on our own."

I wanted to ask him why the sources were quiet, but I sensed I'd used up my ration of questions.

NEVER IN MY LIFE HAD I FACED A PROBLEM WITH INTERPLANETARY IMPLICATIONS. I finished a full eighteen hours of research, hardly more enlightened than when I had started, though I was full of facts: facts about Task-Felder, facts about the council president and her aide, yet more facts about Logology.

I was depressed and angry. I sat head in hands for fully an hour, wondering why the world was picking on me. At least I had a partial answer to Thomas's criticisms—short of actual precognition, I didn't think anybody could have intuited such an outcome to Rho's venture.

I lifted my head to answer a private line call, routed to the guest quarters.

"I have a live call direct from Port Yin for Mister Mickey Sandoval."

"That's me," I said.

The secretary connected and the face of Fiona Task-Felder, president of the council, clicked into vid. "Mr. Sandoval, may I speak to you for a few minutes?"

I was stunned. "I'm sorry, I wasn't expecting . . . a call. Not here."

"I like to work direct, especially when my underlings screw up, as I trust Janis did."

"Uh . . ."

"Do you have a few minutes?"

"Please, Madame President . . . I'd much rather hold this conversation with our chief syndic tied in . . ."

"I'd rather not, Mr. Sandoval. Just a few questions, and maybe we can patch all this up."

Fiona Task-Felder could hardly have looked more different from her aide. She was gray-haired, in her late sixties, with a muscular build that showed hours of careful exercise. She wore stretch casuals beneath her short council collar and seal. She looked vigorous and friendly and motherly, and was a handsome woman, but in a natural way, quite the reverse of Granger's studied, artificial hardness.

I should have known better, but I said, "All right. I'll try to answer as best I can . . ."

"Why does your sister want these heads?" the president asked.

"We've already explained that."

"Not to anybody's satisfaction but your own, perhaps. I've learned that your grandparents—pardon me, your great-grandparents—are among them. Is that your sole reason?"

"I don't think now's the time to discuss this, not without my sister being available, and certainly not without our director."

"I'm trying hard to understand, Mr. Sandoval. I think we should meet casually, without any interference from aides and syndics, and straighten this out quickly, before somebody else screws it up out of all proportion. Is that possible?"

"I think Rho could explain—"

"Fine, then, bring her."

"I'm sorry, but—"

She gave me a motherly expression of irritation, as if with a wayward son—or irritating lover. "I'm giving you a rare opportunity. In the old lunar spirit of one-on-one, and cut the politics. I think we can work it out. If we work fast."

I felt way out of my depth. I was being asked to step outside of formal procedures. . . . To make a decision immediately.

I knew the only way to play *that* game was to ignore her unexpressed rules.

"All right," I said.

"I have an appointment available on the third at ten hundred. Is that acceptable?"

That was three days away. I calculated quickly; I'd be back in the Ice Pit station by then, and that meant I'd have to hire a special shuttle flight. "I'll be there," I said.

"I'm looking forward to it," Task-Felder said, and left me alone in the guest room to think out my options.

I DID NOT BREAK THE UNEXPRESSED RULES OF HER GAME. I DID NOT TALK TO Thomas Sandoval-Rice. Nor did I tell Rho what I was doing. Before leaving Port Yin for a return trip to the Ice Pit, I secretly I booked an unscheduled round-trip shuttle, spending a great deal of Sandoval money on one passenger; thankfully, because of my position at the station, I did not have to give details.

I doubted that Thomas or Rho would look for me during the time I was gone; six hours going, a few hours there, and six back. I could leave custom messages for whoever might call, including Rho or Thomas or—much less likely—William.

To this day I experience a sick twist in my stomach when I ask myself why I did not follow through with my original thought, and tell Thomas about the president's call. I think perhaps it was youthful ego, wounded by Thomas's dressing-down; ego plus a strange gratification that the council *president* was going to see me personally, to put aside a block of her time to speak to someone not even an assistant syndic. Me. To speak to *me*.

I knew I was not doing what I should be doing, but like a mouse entranced by a snake, I ignored them all—a tendency of behavior I have since learned I was not unique in possessing. A tendency common in some lunar citizens.

We habitually cry out, "Cut the politics." But the challenge and intrigue of politics seduces us every time.

I honestly thought I could beat out Fiona Task-Felder.

AS OUR ARBEITERS EXECUTED THE NERNST DESIGN, THE REPOSITORY FOR THE heads resembled a flattened doughnut lying on its side, a wide circular passageway with heads stored in seven tiers of cubicles around the outer perimeter. It would lie neatly in the bottom cup of the void, seven meters below the laboratory, out of range of whatever peculiar fluctuations might occur in the force disorder pumps during William's tests, and easily connected to the refrigerators. Lunar rock would insulate the outer torus; pipes and other fittings could be neatly dropped from the refrigerators above. A small elevator from the side of the bridge opposite the Cavity would give access.

It was a neat design, as we expected from Nernst BM. Our arbeiters performed flawlessly, although they were ten years out of date.

Not once did anyone mention problems with the Council. I started to feel cocky; the plans I'd had of talking to Thomas about the visit with the president faded in and out with my mood. I could handle her; the threat was minimal. If I was sufficiently cagey, I could drop right in, leap right out, no harm although perhaps no benefits, either.

The day after I finished oversight and inspection on the chamber, and received a Nernst designer's inspection report, and after the last of Rho's heads had been installed in their cubicles, I stamped my approval for final payment to Nernst, called in the Cailetet consultants to look over the facilities, packed my travel bag, and was off.

THERE IS A GRAY SAMENESS TO A LUNAR OCEAN'S SURFACE THAT INDUCES A state of hypnosis, a mix of fascination at the lifeless expanse, never quite encompassed by memory, and incredible boredom. Parts of the moon are beautiful in a rugged way, even to a citizen. Crater walls, rilled terrain, even the painted flats of ancient vents.

Life on the Moon is a process of turning inward, toward interior living spaces, toward an interior you. Lunar citizens are exceptional at introspection and decoration and indoor arts and crafts. Some of the finest craftsmen and artists in the solar system reside on the Moon; their work commands high prices throughout the Triple.

Two hours into the journey, I fell asleep and dreamed of Egypt again, endless dry deserts beyond the thin greenbelts of the Nile, deserts populated by mummies leading camels. Camels carrying trays of ice, making sounds like force disorder pumps . . .

I awoke quickly and cursed William for that story, for its peculiar fascination. What was so strange about space sucking heat from trays of water? That was the principle behind our own heat exchangers on the surface above the Ice Pit. Still, I could not conceive of a sky on Earth as black as the Moon's, as all forgiving, all absorbing.

The shuttle made a smooth landing minutes later at Port Yin, and I disembarked, part of me still believing I would go to Thomas's office first, an hour before my appointment.

I did not. I spent that hour shopping for a birthday present for a girl in Copernicus Station. A girl I was not particularly courting at the time; something to pass an hour. My mind was blank.

The offices of the council president were located in the council annex to Port Yin's western domicile district; in the suburbs, as it were, and away from the center of BM activity, as befitted a political institution. The offices were numerous but not sumptuous; the syndics of many small BMs could have displayed more opulence.

I walked and took the skids, using the time to prepare myself. I was not stupid enough to believe there was no danger; I even felt with one part of my mind that what I was doing was more likely to turn out badly than otherwise. But I skidded along toward the council president's offices regardless, and in my defense I must say that my self-assurance still overcame my doubts. On the average, I felt more confident than ill-at-ease.

It was politics. My entire upbringing had ingrained in me the essential triviality of lunar politics. Council officers were merely secretaries to a bunch of congenial family businesses, dotting the i's and crossing the t's of rules of cooperation that probably would have been followed anyway, out of simple courtesy and for the sake of mutual benefit.

Most of our ancestors had been engineers and miners exported from the Earth; conservative and independent, suspicious of any authority, strongly convinced that large groups of people could live in comparative peace and prosperity without layers of government and bureaucracy.

My ancestors worked to squash the natural growth of such layers: "Cut the politics" was their constant cry, followed by shaking heads and raised eyes. Political organization was evil, representative government an imposition. Why have a representative when you could interact personally? Keep it small, direct, and uncomplicated, they believed, and freedom would necessarily follow. They couldn't keep it small. The moon had already grown to such a point that layers of government and representation were necessary. But as with sexual attitudes in some Earth cultures, necessity was no guarantee of responsibility and planning.

From the beginning, our prime families and founders—including, I must say, Emilia and Robert—had screwed up the lunar constitution, if the patched-up collations of hearsay and station charters could even be called such.

When complex organization did come, it was haphazard, unenthusiastically organic, undisciplined. When the Split broke our economic supply lines with Earth, and when the first binding multiples came, the Moon was a reservoir of naively amenable suckers, but blessedly lucky—at first. The binding multiples weren't political organizations—

they were business families, extensions of individuals, the Lunars said. Lunar citizens saw nothing wrong with family structures or even syndicates; they saw nothing wrong with the complex structures of the binding multiples, because somehow they did not qualify as government.

When the binding multiples had to set up offices to work with each other, and share legal codes written and unwritten to prevent friction, that was not government; it was pragmatism. And when the binding multiples formed a council, why, that was nothing more sinister than business folks getting together to talk and achieve individual consensus. (That oxymoron—individual consensus—was actually common then.) The Council of Binding Multiples was nothing more than a committee organized to reduce frictions between the business syndicates—at first. It was decorative and weak.

We were still innocent and did not know that the price of freedom—of individuality—is attention to politics, careful planning, careful organization; philosophy is no more a barrier against political disaster than it is against plague.

Think me naive; I was. We all were.

I ENTERED THE RECEPTION AREA, A CUBICLE BARELY FOUR METERS SQUARE, with a man behind a desk to supplement an automated appointments system.

"Good day," the man said. He was perhaps fifty, gray-haired, blunt-nosed, with a pleasant but discriminating expression.

"Mickey Sandoval," I said. "I have an invitation from the president."

"Indeed you do, Mr. Sandoval. You're about three minutes early, but I believe the president is free now." The automated appointments clerk produced a screenful of information. "Yes, Mr. Sandoval. Please go in." He gestured toward a double door on his left, which opened to a long hallway. "At the end. Ignore the mess, please; the administration is still moving in."

Boxes of information cubes and other files lined the hallway in neat stacks. Several young women in Port Yin drabs—a style I did not find attractive—were moving files into an office along the hallway by electric cart. They smiled at me as I passed. I returned their smiles.

I was full of confidence, walking into the attractive, the seductive and yet trivial inner sanctum. These were all doubtless Logologists. The council presidents could choose all staff members from their own BM if they so desired. Binding multiples worked together; there would never be any accusations of nepotism or favoritism in a political climate where such was the expected, the norm.

Fiona Task-Felder's office was at the end of the hall. Wide lunar oak doors opened automatically as I approached, and the president herself stepped forward to shake my hand.

"Thanks for shuttling in," she said. "Mr. Sandoval—"

"Mickey, please," I said.

"Fiona to you, as well. We're just getting settled here. Come sit; let's talk and see if some sort of accommodation can be reached between the council and Sandoval."

Subtly, she had just informed me that Sandoval was on the outs, that we somehow stood apart from our fellow BM's. I did not bristle at the suggestion. I noted it, but assumed it was unintentional. Lunar politics was almost unfailingly polite, and this seemed too abrupt.

"Fruit juice? That's all we're serving here," Fiona said with a smile. She was even more fit-looking in person, solid and square-shouldered, hair strong and stiff and cut short, eyes clear blue and surrounded by fine wrinkles, what my mother had once called "time's dividends." I took a glass of apple juice and sat at one end of the broad curved desk, where two screens and two keyboards waited.

"I understand the installation is already made, and that Cailetet is beginning its work now," the president said.

I nodded.

"How far along?" she asked.

"Not very," I said.

"Have you revived any heads?"

That set me aback; she knew as well as I, she *had* to know, that it was not our plan to revive any heads, that nobody had the means to do so. "Of course not," I said.

"If you had, you'd have violated council wishes," she said.

From the very beginning, she had me off balance. I tried to recover. "We've broken no rules."

"Council has been informed by a number of BM's syndics that they're concerned about your activities."

"You mean, they think we might try to bring more corpsicles up from Earth."

"Yes," she said, nodding once, firmly. "That will not be allowed if I have anything to do with it. Now, please explain what you plan to do with these heads."

I was aghast. "Excuse me? That's—"

"It's not confidential at all, Mickey. You've agreed to come here to speak with me. A great many BMs are awaiting my report on what you say."

"That isn't what I understood, Fiona." I tried to keep my voice calm. "I'm not here testifying under oath, and I don't have to reveal family business plans to any council member, even the president." I settled more firmly into my seat, trying to exude the confidence I had already scattered to the winds.

Her face hardened. "It would be simple courtesy to your fellow BMs to explain what you intend to do, Mickey."

I hoped to give her a tidbit sufficient to put her off. "The heads are being preserved in the Ice Pit, in the void where my brother does his work."

"You're brother in-law, you mean."

"Yes. He's family now. We dispense with such modifiers." *When talking with outsiders*, I might have added.

She smiled, but her expression was still hard. "William Pierce. He's doing BM funded research on extremely low temperatures in copper, no?"

I nodded.

"Has he been successful?"

"Not yet," I said.

"It's simple coincidence that his facilities are capable of preserving the heads."

"I suppose so, yes. My sister probably would not have brought them to the Moon otherwise, however. I think of it more as opportunity than coincidence."

Fiona instructed the screens to bring up displays of lunar binding multiples who were pushing for an investigation of the Sandoval corpsicle imports. They were platinum names indeed: the top four BM's, except for Sandoval, and fifteen others, spaced around the Moon, including Nernst and Cailetet. "Incidentally," she said, "You know about the furor on Earth."

"I've heard," I said.

"Did you know there's a ruckus starting on Mars now?"

I did not.

"They want Earth's dead kept on Earth," the president said. "They think it's bad precedent to export corpsicles and make the outer planets responsible for the inner's problems. They think the Moon must be siding with Earth in some fashion to get rid of this problem."

"It's not a problem," I said, exasperated. "Nobody on Earth has made a fuss about this in decades."

"So what's causing the fuss now?" she asked.

I tried to think my way through to a civil answer. "We think Task-Felder is behind it," I said.

"You accuse me of carrying my BM's interests into the council with me, despite my oath of office?"

"I'm not accusing anybody of anything," I said. "We have evidence that the representative, the . . . the . . . United States national assembly representative from Puerto Rico—"

"Congressional representative," she corrected.

"Yes . . . You know about that?"

"He's a Logologist. So is most of Puerto Rico. Are you accusing members of my religion of instigating this?"

She spoke with such complete shock and indignation that I thought for a moment, could we be wrong? Were our facts misleading, poorly analyzed? Then I remembered Janis Granger and her tactics in our first interview. Fiona Task-Felder was no more gentle, no more polite. I was here at her invitation to be raked over the coals.

"Excuse me, Madame President," I said. "I'd like for you to get to your point."

"The point is, Mickey, that you've agreed by coming here to testify before the full council and explain your actions, your intentions, everything about this mess, at the next meeting, which will be in three days."

I smiled and shook my head, then brought up my slate. "Auto counselor," I said.

Her smile grew harder her blue eyes more intense.

"Is this some new law you've cooked up for the occasion?" I asked, trying for a tough and sophisticated manner.

"Not at all," she said with an air of closing claws on the kill. "You may think what you wish about Task-Felder BM, or about Logologists— about my people—but we do not play outside the rules. Ask your auto counselor about courtesy briefings and formal council meetings. This is a courtesy briefing, Mickey, and I've logged it as such."

My auto counselor found the relevant council rules on courtesy briefings, and the particular rule passed thirty years before, by the council, that mandated the council's right to hear just what the president heard, as testimony, under oath. A strange and parochial law, so seldom invoked that I had never heard of it. Until now.

"I'm ending this discussion," I said, standing.

"Tell Thomas Sandoval-Rice that you and he should be at the next full council meeting. Under council agreements, you don't have any choice, Mickey."

She did not smile. I left the office, walked quickly down the hall, avoided looking at anyone, especially the young women still moving files.

"SHE'S SNARED HER RABBIT," THOMAS SAID AS HE POURED ME A BEER.

He had been unusually quiet all evening, since I had announced myself at his door and made my anguished confession of gross ineptitude.

Far worse than being blasted by his rage was facing his quiet disappoint-ment. "Don't blame yourself entirely, Micko." He seemed somehow de-flated, withdrawn, like an aquarium anemone touched by an uncaring finger. "I should have guessed they'd try something like this."

"I feel like an idiot."

"That's the third time you've said that in the past ten minutes," Tho-mas said. "You have been an idiot, of course, but don't let that get you down."

I shook my head; I was already down about as far as it was possible to fall.

Thomas lifted his beer, inspected the large bubbles, and said, "If we don't testify, we're in much worse trouble. It will look as if we're ig-noring the wishes of our fellow BMs, as if we've gone renegade. If we do testify, we'll have been maneuvered into breaking the BM's sacred right to keep business and research matters private . . . and that will make us look like weaklings and fools. No doubt about it, she's pushed us into a deep rille, Mickey. If you had refused to go in, and had claimed family privilege, she'd have tried something else . . ."

"At least now we can be sure what we're in store for. Isolation, re-crimination, probable withdrawal of contracts, maybe even boycott of services. That's never happened before, Micko. We're going to make history this week, no doubt about it."

"Is there anything I can do?"

Thomas finished his glass and wiped his lips. "Another?" he asked, gesturing at the keg. I shook my head. "No. Me neither. We need clear heads, Micko, and we need a full family meeting. We're going to have to build internal solidarity here; this has gone way beyond what the director and all the syndics can handle by themselves."

I flew back from Port Yin, head cloudy with anguish. It seemed some-how I had been responsible for all of this. Thomas did not say as much, not this time; but he had hinted it before. I halfway hoped the shuttle would smear itself across the regolith; that the pilot would survive and I would not. Then, anguish began to be replaced by a grim and deter-mined anger. I had been twisted around by experts; used by those who had no qualms about use and abuse. I had seen the enemy and under-estimated the strength of their resolve, whatever their motivations, whatever their goals. These people were not following the lunar way; they were playing us all, all of the BMs, me, Rho, the Triple, the Western Hemispheric United States, the corpsicles, like fish on a line, single-mindedly dedicated to one end.

The heads were just an excuse. They had no real importance; that much was obvious.

This was a power play. The Logologists were intent on dominating the Moon, perhaps the Earth. I hated them for their ambition, their evil presumption, for the way they had lowered me in the eyes of Thomas.

Having erred on the side of underestimation, I was now swinging in the opposite direction, equally in error; but I would not realize that for a few more days yet.

I came home, and knew for the first time how much the station meant to me.

I met a Cailetet man in the alley leading to the Ice Pit. "You're Mickey, right?" he asked casually. He held a small silver case in front of him dangling from one hand. He seemed happy. I looked at him as if he might utter words of absolute betrayal.

"We've just investigated one of your heads," he said, only slightly put off by my expression. "You've been shuttling, eh?"

I nodded. "How's Rho?" I asked, somewhat irrelevantly; I hadn't spoken to anybody since my arrival.

"She's ecstatic, I think. We've done our work well."

"You're sticking with us?" I asked suspiciously.

"Beg your pardon?"

"You haven't been recalled by your family syndics?"

"No," he said, drawling the word dubiously. "Not that I've heard."

The families were being incredibly two-faced. "Just curious," I said. "What's it going to cost us?"

"In the long term? That's *right*," he said, as if the reason for my surliness had finally been solved. "You're financial manager for the Ice Pit. I'm sorry; I'm a bit slow. Believe me, we're interested in this as a research project. If we perfect our techniques here, we can market the medical applications all over the Triple and beyond. We're charging you expenses and nothing else, Mickey. This is platinum opportunity."

"Does it work?" I asked, still sullen.

He thumped the case. "Data right here. We're checking it with history on Earth. I'd say it works, yes. Talking with the dead—I don't think anybody's done that before!"

"Who was it?" I asked.

"One of the three unknowns. Rho decided we'd work with them first, to help solve the mystery. Please go right in, Mickey. Nernst has designed a very nice facility. Ask questions, see what they're doing. They're working on unknown number two right now."

"Thanks," I said, wondering what distortion of protocol could lead this man to invite me into my own BM's facility. "I'm glad it's working."

"All right," the man said, with a short intake of breath. "Must be off. Check this individual out, correlate . . . on our own nickel, Mickey. Good to have met you."

I stopped at the white line and queried. "Goddamn it, yes!" William's voice roared from the speaker. "It's open. Just cross the goddamn line and stop bothering me."

"It's me, Mickey," I said.

"Well then come on in and join the party! Everybody else is here."

William had locked himself in the laboratory. Three Onnes and Cailetet techs were on the bridge standing well away from the force disorder pumps, chatting and eating lunch. I passed them by with casual nods.

William sounded in no mood for visitors—this time of day was usually his phase of most intense activity. I swung onto the lift and descended to Rho's facility, twenty feet below the laboratory. The Ice Pit echoed with voices from above and below; the sounds seemed to come from all directions as I descended in the open lift, first to the right, then the left, canceled, returned, grew soft, then immediate. Rho came through the hatch at the top of the chamber and rushed forward excitedly. "William's pissed, but we're leaving him alone, mostly, so it will pass." She fairly brewed over with enthusiasm. *"Oh, Mickey!"* She threw her arms around me.

"Yes?"

"Did you hear upstairs? We tuned in to a head! It works! Come on in. We're working on the second head now."

"An unknown," I said with polite interest, her enthusiasm not infecting me. (How much could I blame *her* for these problems?)

"Yes. Another unknown. I still can't get a response from the StarTime trustees. Do you think they've lost all their backup records? That would be something, wouldn't it?" She ushered me down the hatch into the chamber. Within the chamber, all was quiet but for a faint song of electronics and the low hiss of refrigerants.

I recognized Armand Cailetet-Davis, the balding, slight-figured powerhouse of Cailetet research. Beside him stood Irma Stolbart of Onnes, a reputed lunar-born superwhiz whom I had heard of but never met: thirty or thirty-five, tall and thin with reddish brown hair and chocolate skin. They stood beside a tripod-mounted piece of equipment, three horizontal cylinders strapped together, pointed at the face of one of the forty stainless steel boxes mounted in the racks.

Rho introduced me to Cailetet-Davis and Stolbart. I felt a little thrill of something—a realization of what was actually going on here, penetrating my dark mood.

"We're selecting one of the seventy-three known natural mind languages," Armand explained, pointing at a thinker prism in Irma Stolbart's hands. She smiled, quick glance at me, at Armand, distracted, then continued to work on her thinker, which was about a tenth the size of

William's QL, easily portable. "We'll test some uploaded data for patterns—"

"Patterns from the head," I said, stating the obvious.

"Yes. A masculine individual, age sixty-five at death, apparently in good condition considering the medical standards of the time. Very little deterioration."

"Have you looked inside?" I asked.

Rho lifted her brows. "Brother, nobody looks inside. Not by actually opening the box. We don't care what they *look* like." She laughed nervously. "It's not the head, it's what's locked up in the brain."

A soul, still? Now I was shivering from fatigue, as well as something like superstitious awe. "Sorry," I said to nobody in particular. They ignored me, concentrating on their work.

"We find northern Europeans tend to cluster in these three program areas," Stolbart explained. She showed me a slate screen on which a diagram had been sketched. The diagram showed twelve different rectangles, each labeled with a cultural-ethnic group. Her finger underlined three boxes: *Finn/ Scand/ Teut/.* "Mind memory storage languages are among the genetic traits most rigidly adhered to. We think they change very little across thousands of years. That makes sense, considering the necessity of immediate infant adaptation to its milieu."

"Indeed," Rho said, smiling at me, squeezing my arm again gently. "So he's of northern European stock?"

"He's definitely not Levantine, African, or Asian," Irma Stolbart said. I watched her curiously, focusing on her face, lean and intent, with lovely, skeptical brown eyes.

"Have you spoken with your syndics?" I asked out of the blue, startling even myself.

Armand had clearly earned his position in Cailetet through quick thinking and adaptability. With no hesitation whatsoever, he said, "We work here until somebody tells us to leave. Nobody has yet. Maybe you administrators can work it all out in the council."

You administrators. That put us in our place. Paper pushers, bureaucrats, politicians. Cut the politics. We were the ones who stood in the way of the scientist's goal of unrestrained research and intellection.

"I see a fourteen Penrose cipher trace algorithm in the cerebral cortex," Irma said. "Definitely Northern European."

Rho looked troubled, examined my face for signs. With a tug of my ear and a gesture up into the air I indicated that we should talk. She drew me aside. "Are you tired?" she asked.

"Dead on my feet," I said. "I'm an idiot, Rho, and maybe I've augered this whole thing right into a rille."

"I have faith in the family. We'll make it. I have faith in you, Micko," she said, grasping my arm. I felt vaguely sick, seeing her expression of support, her trust. "I'd like you to stay and watch . . . this is really something . . . if you're up to it?"

"Wouldn't miss it," I said.

"It's almost religious, isn't it?" she whispered in my ear.

"All right," Armand said. "We have the locale. Let's take a picture, upload into the translator, and see if we can draw a name from the file."

Armand adjusted the position on the triple cylinders and tuned his slate to their output, getting a picture of a vague gray mass suspended by a thin sling in a sharp black square—the head resting in its cubicle and cradle within the larger box. "We're centered," he said. "Irma, if you could . . ."

"Field guide on," she said, flipping a switch on a tiny disk taped to the box.

"Recording," Armand said nonchalantly. There was no noise, no visible or audible sign that anything was happening. Squares appeared on Armand's slate in the upper right hand portion of the mass. I was able to make out that the head had slumped to one side, whether facing us or not, I could not tell. I kept staring at the image, the squares flashing one by one in sequence around the cranium, and I realized with a gruesome tingle that the head was misshapen, that during its decades in storage it had deformed in the presence of Earth gravity, nestling deeper into its sling like a frozen melon.

"Got it," Armand said. "One more—the third unknown—and we'll call it a session."

For Rho's sake, I stayed to watch the third head be scanned and its neural states and patterns recorded. I kissed Rho's cheek, congratulated her, and took the lift to the bridge. Again, the voices flowed around me, soft technical chatter from the chamber below, the technicians on the bridge above.

I went to my water tank room and collapsed.

Strangely enough, I slept well.

RHO CAME INTO MY ROOM AND WOKE ME UP AT TWELVE HUNDRED, EIGHT hours after I'd dropped onto my bed. Obviously, she had not slept at all; her hair was matted with finger-tugs and rearrangement, her face shiny with long hours.

"We got a name on the number one unknown," she said. "It's a female, not a male, we think. But we haven't done chromosome check through their sensors. Irma located a few minutes of pre-death short-term memory and translated it into sound. We heard . . ." She suddenly wrinkled her face, as if about to cry, and then lifted her head and laughed. "Micko, we *heard* a voice, it must have been a doctor, a voice speaking out loud, 'Inchmore, can you hear me? Evelyn? We need your permission . . .' "

I sat up on the bed and rubbed my eyes. "That's . . ." I couldn't find a good word.

"Yeah, amen," Rho said, sitting on the edge of the bed. "Evelyn Inchmore. I've sent a query to StarTime's trustees on Earth. Evelyn Inchmore, Evelyn Inchmore . . ." She spoke the name out loud several more times, her voice dropping in exhaustion and wonder. "Do you know what this means, Micko?"

"Congratulations," I said.

"It's the first time anybody has ever communicated with a corpsicle," Rho said distantly.

"She hasn't answered back," I said. "You've just accessed her memories." I shrugged my shoulders. "She's still dead."

"Yeah," Rho said. " '*Just* accessed her memories.' Wait a minute." She looked up at me, startled by some inner realization. "Maybe it's a male after all. We thought the name was female. . . . But didn't Evelyn used to be a male's name? Wasn't there a male author centuries ago named Evelyn?"

"Evelyn Waugh," I said.

"We could have it all wrong again," she said, too tired to build up much concern. "I hope we can straighten it out before this goes to the press."

My level of alertness went up several notches. "Have you told Thomas what's happened?"

"Not yet," she said.

"Rho, if word gets out that we've already accessed the heads. . . . But who's going to stop Cailetet or Onnes from trumpeting this?"

"You think it would cause problems?" Rho asked.

I felt vaguely proud that finally I was starting to anticipate trouble, as Thomas would want me to. "It would probably cook off the bomb," I said.

"All right, then. I don't want to cause more trouble than is absolutely necessary." She looked at me with loving sympathy. "You've been in a rough, Micko."

"You heard what happened in Port Yin?"

"Thomas talked to me while you were shuttling home." She pushed out her lips dubiously and shook her head. "Fapping pol. Someone should impeach her and take away the Task-Felder charter."

"I appreciate the sentiments, but neither is likely. Could you keep this quiet for a few more days?"

"I'll do my damnedest," Rho said. "Cailetet and Onnes are under contract. We control the release of the results, even if they get full scientific credit. I'll tell them we want to confirm with the Earth trustees, back up our findings, analyze the third unknown head . . . Work on a few known heads and see if the process is reliable."

"What about Great-grandmother and Great-grandfather?" I asked.

Rho's smile was conspiratorial. "We'll save them until later," she said.

"We don't want to experiment on family, right?"

She nodded. "When we're sure the whole thing works, we'll do something with Robert and Emilia. As for me, Micko, in a few minutes I'm going to get some induced sleep. Right after I lay down some rules to the Cailetet and Onnes folks. Now. William wants to talk with you."

"About the interruptions?"

"I don't think so. He says work is going well."

She hugged me tightly and then stood. "To sleep," she said. "No dreams, I think . . ."

"No ancient voices," I said.

"Right."

WILLIAM SEEMED TIRED BUT AT PEACE, PLEASED WITH HIMSELF. HE SAT IN the laboratory control center, patting the QL thinker as if it were an old friend.

"It did me proud, Micko," he said. "It's tuned everything to a fare-thee-well. It keeps the universe's quantum bugs from nibbling at my settings, controls the rebuilt disorder pumps, anticipates virtual fluctuations and corrects for them. I'm all set now; all I have to do is bring the pumps to full capacity."

I tried to show enthusiasm, but couldn't. I felt sick at heart. The disaster in Port Yin, the upcoming council meeting, Rho's success with the first few heads . . .

With a little time to think about what had happened, I realized now that it all felt *bad*. Thomas was scrambling furiously to convince the council to reverse its action. And here I was, cut out of the drift of things, watching William gloat about an upcoming moment of triumph. William caught my mood and reached out to tap my hand.

"Hey," he said. "You're young. Fapping up is part of the game."

I screwed my face up at first in anger, then in simple grief, and turned away, tears running down my cheeks. To have William name the card so openly—*fapping up*—was not what I needed right now. It was neither circumspect nor sensitive. "Thank you so very much," I said.

William kept tapping my hand until I jerked it away. "I'm sorry, Micko," he said, his tone unchanged—telling it like is. "I've never been afraid to admit when I've made a mistake. It nearly drives me nuts sometimes, making mistakes, I keep telling myself I should be perfect, but that isn't what we're here for. Perfection isn't an option for us; perfection is death, Micko. We're here to learn and change and that means making mistakes."

"Thanks for the lecture," I said, glancing at him resentfully.

"I'm twelve years older than you are. I've made maybe twelve times more major mistakes. What can I tell you? That it gets any easier to fap up? Well, yes, it gets easier and easier with more and more responsibilities—but hell, Micko, it doesn't feel any better."

"I can't just think of it as a mistake," I said softly. "I was betrayed. The president was dishonest and underhanded."

William leaned back in his chair and shook his head, incredulous. "Hay-soos, Micko. Who expects anything different? That's what politics is all about—coercion and lies."

Suddenly my anger reached white heat. "Goddamn it, *no*, that isn't what politics is all about, William, and people thinking that it is has gotten us into this mess!"

"I don't understand."

"Politics is management and guidance and feedback, William. We seem to have forgotten *that* on the Moon. Politics is the art of managing large groups of people in good times and bad. When the people know what they want and when they don't know what they want. 'Cut the politics . . .' Hay-soos yourself, William!" I waved my arm out and shook my fist in the air. "You can't get rid of politics, any more than you can . . ." I struggled to find a metaphor. "Any more than you can cut out *manners* and *talking* and all the other ways we interact."

"Thanks for the lecture, Micko," William said, not unpleasantly.

I dropped my fist on the table.

"What you're saying is, the whole Moon is screwing this up," William said. "I agree. And the Task-Felder BM is leading us all into temptation. But my point is, I'm never going to be a politician or an administrator. Present company excepted, I hate the breed, Micko. They're put on this Moon to stand in my way. This council stuff only reinforces my prejudices. So what can you do about it?" He looked at me with frank inquiry.

"I can wise up," I said. "I can be a better . . . administrator, politician."

William smiled ironically. "More devious? Play their own game?"

I shook my head. Deviousness and playing the Task-Felder game were not what I meant. I was thinking of some more idealistic superiority, playing within the ethical boundaries as well as the law.

William continued. "We can plan ahead for the worse yet to come. They might cut off our resources, beyond just stopping other BMs from helping us. We can survive an interdict for some time, maybe even forge a separate business alliance within the Triple."

"That would be . . . very dangerous," I said.

"If we're forced into it, what can we do? We have business interests all over the Triple. We have to survive."

The QL toned softly on the platform. "Temperature stability has been broken," it said.

William jerked up in his chair. "Report," he said.

"Unknown effect has caused temperature to rotate in unknown phase. The cells have no known temperature at this time."

"What's that mean?" I asked.

William grabbed his thinker remote and pushed through the curtain to the bridge. He walked out to the Cavity and I followed, glad to have an interruption. The Cailetet and Onnes techs had retired to get some rest; the Ice Pit was quiet.

"What's wrong?" I asked.

"I don't know," William said in a low voice, concentrating on the Cavity's status display. "There are drains on four of the eight cells. The QL refuses to interpret temperature readings. QL, please explain."

The remote said, "Phase rotation in lambda. Fluctuation between banks of four cells."

"Shit," William said. "Now the other four cells are absorbing, and the first four are stable. QL, do you have any idea what's happening here?" He looked up at me with a worried expression.

"Second bank is now in down cycle of rotation. Up cycle in three seconds."

"It's reversed," William said after the short interval had passed. "Back and forth. QL, what's causing a power drain?"

"Temperature maintenance," the QL said.

"Explain, please," William pursued with waning patience.

"Energy is being accepted by the phase down cells in an attempt to maintain temperature."

"Not by the refrigerators or the pumps?"

"It is necessary to put energy directly into the cells in the form of microwave radiation to try to maintain temperature."

"I don't understand, QL."

"I apologize," the QL said. "The cells accept radiation to remain stable, but they have no temperature this thinker can interpret."

"We have to *raise* the temperature?" William guessed, face slack with incredulity.

"Phase down reversal," the QL said.

"QL, the temperatures have jumped to *below* absolute zero?"

"That is an interpretation, although not a very good one."

William swore and stood back from the Cavity.

The QL reported, "All eight cells have stabilized in lambda phase down. Fluctuation has stopped."

William went pale. "Micko, tell me I'm not dreaming."

"I don't know what the hell you're doing," I said, starting to become frightened.

"The cells are draining microwave energy and maintaining a stable temperature. Christ, they must be accessing new spin dimensions, radiating into a direction outside status geometry . . . does that mean they're operating in negative time? Micko, if any of Rho's outsiders have messed with the lab, or if their goddamn equipment is causing this . . ." He balled his fists up and shook them at the darkness above. "God help them! I was this close, Micko . . . All I had to do was connect the pumps, align the cells, turn the magnetic fields off . . . I was going to do that tomorrow."

"I don't think anybody's messed with your equipment," I told him, trying to calm him. "These are pros, William, and besides, Rho would kill them . . ."

William lowered his head and swung it back and forth helplessly. "Micko, something has to be wrong. Negative temperature is meaningless."

"It didn't *say* temperatures were negative," I reminded him.

"This thinker does not interpret the data," the QL chimed in.

"That's because you're a coward," William accused it.

"This thinker does not relay false interpretation," it responded.

Suddenly, William laughed, a rocking angry laugh that seemed to hurt. He opened his eyes wide and patted the QL remote with gritted-teeth paternalism. "Micko, as God is my witness, nothing on this Moon is ever easy, no?"

"Maybe you've got something even more important than absolute zero," I suggested. "A new state of matter."

The idea sobered him. "That . . ." He ran his hand through his hair, making it even more unruly. "A big idea, that."

"Need help?" I asked.

"I need time to think," he said softly. "Thanks, Micko. I need time without interruptions . . . a few hours at least."

"I can't guarantee anything," I said.

He squinted at me. "I'll let you know if I've discovered something big, okay? Now get out of here." He pushed me gently along the bridge.

THE COUNCIL ROOM WAS CIRCULAR, PANELED WITH LUNAR FARM OAK, CENtrally lighted, with a big antique display screen at one end, lovingly preserved from the year of the Council's creation. Politicians like to keep an eye on each other; no corners, no chairs facing away from the center.

I shuffled in behind Thomas and two freelance advocates from Port Yin, hired by Thomas to offer him extrafamilial advice. Within the Triple it has often been said that lunar advocates are the very worst money can rent; there is some truth to that, but Thomas still felt the need of an objective and critical point of view.

The room was mostly empty. Three representatives had already taken their seats—interestingly enough, they were from Cailetet, Onnes, and Nernst BMs. Other representatives talked in the hall outside the room. The president and her staff would not enter until just before the meeting began.

The council thinker, a large, antique terrestrial model encased in gray ceramic, rested below the president's dais at the north end of the room. Thomas nudged me as we sat, pointed at the thinker, and said, "Don't underestimate an old machine. That son of a glitch has more experience in this room than anybody. But it's the president's tool, not ours; it will not contradict the president, and it will not speak out against her."

We sat quietly while the room slowly filled. At the appointed time of commencement, Fiona Task-Felder entered through a door behind the president's dais, Janis Granger and three council advocates in train.

I knew many of the BM representatives. I had spoken to ten or fifteen of them over the years while doing research for my minor; others I knew by sight from lunar news reports and council broadcasts. They were honorable women and men all; I thought we might not do so badly here after all.

Thomas's expression revealed a less favorable opinion.

The Ice Pit controversy was not first on the council agenda. There were matters of who would get contracts to parent lucrative volatiles supply deliveries from the Outer; who had rights in a BM border dispute to sell aluminum and tungsten mining claims to Richter BM, the huge and generally silent tri-family merger that had taken over most lunar mining operations. These problems were discussed by the representatives in a way that struck me as exemplary. Resolutions were reached, contracts vetted and cleared, shares assigned. The president remained silent most of the time. When she did speak, her words were well-chosen and to the point. She impressed me.

Thomas seemed to sink into his chair, chin in hand, gray hair in disarray. He glanced at me once, gave me something like a leer, and retreated into glum contemplation.

Our two outside advocates sat plumbline in their chairs, hardly blinking.

Janis Granger read out the next item on the agenda: "Inter-family disputes regarding purchase by Sandoval BM of human remains from terrestrial preservation societies."

Societies. That was a subtlety that could speak volumes of misinterpretation. Thomas closed his eyes, opened them again after a long moment.

"The representative from Gorrie BM would like to address this issue," the president said. "Chair allots five minutes to Achmed Bani Sadr of Gorrie BM."

Thomas straightened, leaned forward. Bani Sadr stood with slate held at waist-level for prompting.

"The syndics of Gorrie BM have expressed some concern over the strain on Triple relations this purchase might provoke. As the major transportation utility between Earth and Moon, and on many translunar links, our business would be very adversely affected by any shift in terrestrial attitudes . . ."

And so it began. Even I in my naivete could see that this had been brilliantly orchestrated. One by one, politely, the BMs stood in council and voiced their collective concern. Earth had rattled its pocketbooks at us; Mars had chided us for rocking the Triple boat in a time of economic instability. The United States of the Western Hemisphere had voted to restrict lunar trade if this matter was not resolved to its satisfaction.

Thomas's expression was intense, sorrowful but alert. He had not been inactive. Cailetet had expressed an interest in pursuing potentially very lucrative, even revolutionary, research on the deceased; Onnes BM testified that there was no conceivable way these heads could be resurrected and made active members of society within the next twenty years; the technology simply did not yet exist, despite decades of promising research.

Surprisingly, the representative from Gorrie BM reversed himself and expressed an interest in the medical aspects of this research; he asked how long such work might take to mature, in a business sense, but the president—not unreasonably—ruled that this was beyond the scope of the present discussion.

The representative from Richter BM expressed sympathy for Sandoval's attempts to open a new field of lunar business, but said that disturbances in lunar raw materials supply lines to Earth could be disastrous in the short term. "If Earth boycotts lunar minerals, the Outer can supply them almost immediately, and we lose one third of our gross lunar export business."

Thomas requested time to speak in reply. The president granted him ten minutes to state Sandoval's case.

He conferred briefly with the advocates. They nodded agreement to several whispered comments, and he stood, slate at waist-level, the formal posture in this room, to begin his reply.

"Madame President, honored Representatives, I'll be brief, and I'll be blunt. I am ashamed of these proceedings, and I am ashamed that this council has been so blind as to make them necessary. I have never, in my thirty-nine years of service to the Sandoval BM, and in my seventy-five years of lunar citizenship, felt the anguish I feel now, knowing what is about to happen. Knowing what is about to be done to lunar ideals in the name of expediency.

"Sandoval BM has made an entirely reasonable business transaction with a fully authorized terrestrial legal entity. For reasons none of us can fathom, Task-Felder BM, and Madame President, have raised a flare of protest and carefully planned and executed a series of maneuvers to force an autonomous lunar family to divest itself of legally acquired resources. To my knowledge, this has never before been attempted in the history of the Moon."

"You speak of actions not yet taken, perhaps not even contemplated," the president said.

Thomas looked around the room and smiled. "Madame President, I address those who have already received their instructions."

"Are you accusing the president of participating in this so-called conspiracy?" Fiona Task-Felder continued.

Calls of, "Let him speak," "Let him have his say." She nodded and motioned for Thomas to resume.

"I have not much more to say, but to recount a tale of masterful politics, conducted by an extra-lunar organization across the Solar System, in support of a policy that has nothing to do with lunar well-being or business. Even my assistant, Mickey Sandoval, has been trapped into giving testimony on private family affairs, through a ruse involving an old council law not invoked since its creation. My fellow citizens, he will testify under protest if this council so wishes—but think of the precedent! Think of the power you give to this council, and to those who have the skills to manipulate it—skills which we have not ourselves acquired, and are not likely to acquire, because such activity goes against our basic nature. We are naive weaklings in such a fight, and because of our weakness, our lack of foresight and planning, we will give in, and my family's activities will be interfered with, perhaps even forbidden—all because a religious organization, based on our home planet, does not wish us to do things we have every legal right to do. I voice my protest now, that it may be put in the record before the council votes. Our shame will be complete by day's end, Madame President, and I will not wish to show my face here thereafter."

The president's face was cold and pale. "Do you accuse me, or my chartered BM, of being controlled by extra-lunar interests?"

Thomas, who had sat quickly after his short talk, stood again, looked around the council, and nodded curtly. "I do."

"It is not traditional to libel one's fellow BMs in this council," the president said.

Thomas did not answer.

"I believe I must reply to the charge of manipulation. At my invitation, Mickey Sandoval came to Port Yin to render voluntary testimony to the president. Under old council rules, designed to prevent the president from keeping information that rightfully should be given to the council, the president has the duty to request testimony be given to the council as a whole. If that is manipulation, then I am guilty."

Our first extra-familial advocate stood up beside Thomas. "Madame President, a tape of Mickey Sandoval's visit to your office is sufficient to fulfill the requirements of that rule."

"Not according to the council thinker's interpretation," the president said. "Please render your judgment."

The thinker spoke. "The spirit of the rule is to encourage more open testimony to the council than to the president in private meetings. A voluntary report to the president implies willingness to testify in full to the council. Such testimony must always be voluntary, and not under threat of subpoena." Its deep, resonating voice left the council room in silence.

"So much for our auto counselors," the first advocate muttered to Thomas. Again he addressed the council. "Mickey Sandoval's testimony was solicited under guise of casual conversation. He was not aware he would later be forced to divulge family business matters to the entire council."

"The president's conversations on council matters can hardly be called casual. I am not concerned with your assistant's lack of education," the president said. "This council deserves to hear Sandoval BM's plans for these deceased individuals."

"In God's name, why?" Thomas stood, jaw thrust out. "Who asks these questions? Why is private Sandoval business of concern to anybody but us?"

The president did not react as strongly to this outburst as I expected. I cringed, but Fiona Task-Felder said, "The freedom of any family to swing its fist ends at our nose. How the inquiry has arisen is irrelevant; what *is* relevant is the damage that might occur to lunar interests. Is that enough, Mr. Sandoval-Rice?"

Thomas sat down without answering. I looked at him curiously; how much of this was show, how much loss of control? Seeing his expression, I realized that show and inner turmoil were one. Only then did I understand, gut-level, that he knew things I did not know, and that our situation was truly desperate. Thomas was a consummate and seasoned professional syndic, a true lunar citizen in the old sense of concerned and responsible free spirit, quickly losing all of his few illusions as to power and government and lunar politics.

I turned my gaze to the president's dais, to Fiona Task-Felder, feeling for the first time a flash of real hatred. I date my present self to that moment; it was as if I had been reborn, more cynical, more calculating, sharper, no longer young. My hands trembled. I made them still, wiped their dampness on my pants, swiftly calculated what I might give in testimony and what I might withhold.

The representative from Richter BM stood and was recognized by Janis Granger. "Madame President, I move that we have Mr. Mickey Sandoval stand forward and testify, as required by the rules, but that Mr. Sandoval's testimony be restricted to those areas that will not reveal information that could adversely affect future profit potential for his family. That is, should this council vote to allow the project to continue."

Thomas's expression brightened the merest of a mere. I hoped for the president to falter, to acknowledge this limitation to her success, but she hardly blinked an eye before saying, "Is there a second?"

Cailetet and Nernst reps seconded in unison. A quick vote was taken and the decision was unanimous; even the Task-Felder rep joined the flow.

This was the first block in the path of the juggernaut. It was a small block; it was quickly crushed; but it provided us with an immense amount of needed relief.

I testified, following an outline quickly prepared by Thomas and vetted by the advocates; the council listened attentively. I did not discuss our success in deciphering some of the mental contents of one of the dead.

The Task-Felder rep stood at the end of my testimony and urged the council to vote now on whether our project would continue. The motion was seconded. Thomas did not object or ask for delay.

Cailetet, Nernst, and Onnes voted for the project to continue.

The remaining fifty-one reps voted for the project to be shut down.

History was made, political paradigms shifted, all according to the rules.

After adjournment, Thomas and I went out to a Port Yin pub and sat over two schooners of fresh ale, saying very little for the first five minutes.

"Not so bad," Thomas commented after draining the last of his glass. "We didn't go down in glorious flames. Bless massive old Richter; draw and quarter us, but leave us our dignity before we're spiked."

"I don't want to tell Rho," I said.

"She already knows, Mickey. My office has called the Ice Pit. She wants to talk with you, but I don't want you to talk to anyone until we chat a while. All right?"

I nodded.

"Do I detect a change in your attitudes?" Thomas asked gently.

I smiled. "Yes. And in yours?"

"I'm not as good a syndic as you might believe, Micko." He waved off my weak objection. "Save it for your memoirs. I couldn't stop this. But I can delay the results. The council is going to have to design a plan for us, some way to end the project with minimal loss of resources. That will take a few weeks, and I don't think Task-Felder—Fiona or her BM—can speed things up. I'll make sure they don't if I have to resort to assassination."

He didn't smile. In my present frame of mind, I didn't care whether he was serious or not.

"You know, Micko, I've always had my doubts about this project. I think the reasons we lost in the council are less political and more psychological, perhaps even mystical. Deep down, I think they believe— and maybe even I believe—we're interfering where we shouldn't. If Rho succeeds, it's going to change a lot of things. We're a peculiar kind of conservative lot here on the Moon, spiritually, however much we keep our religious observances to ourselves."

"She has," I said.

"She has what?"

"Succeeded. They have, actually."

"Yes?"

"They've accessed a head. They're working on a second head now. We know their names. We—"

My face contorted and I shivered, cursed, half-stood. Something walked over my future grave; I almost literally saw a ghost sitting beside us at the table, the image of an immensely fat Pharaoh covered with ice, watching us all balefully. Thomas reached out to take hold of my arm and I sat. The ghost was gone.

"Don't lose it now, Mickey," Thomas said. Other customers stared at us. "What's wrong?"

"Christ, I don't know. Thomas, I've got to go back. To the Ice Pit. Something just occurred to me, something really bad."

"Can you tell me?"

"Hell, no," I said, shaking my head. "It's too stupid and wild. But I have to go back." I stood. "Please forgive me. It's a hunch, a ridiculous hunch."

"You're forgiven," Thomas said and credited the tab to his personal account.

I CAUGHT THE REGULAR ICE PIT SHUTTLE; LUCK AND THE TIMETABLE WERE ON my side. I was in a fever of inspired unease. I could not shake my theory. My head spun with disbelief; this could not be, yet it all fit together so smoothly, yet again the chances were more than astronomical; and I realized if I were wrong, and I had to be, no doubt about it, I wouldn't be worthy of my position in the Sandoval BM. I would have to resign. If I played such wild hunches, if I could become so obsessed by them, I was a useless crank.

We flew over the external generation plant, a bright red building against pale gray dust and rock. The shuttle banked over the Ice Pit radiators, hunkering in their shadowy trenches, glowing dull red-orange as they broadcast heat into the darkness of space.

We landed and I disembarked, small case in hand. I was eight hours past reasonable sleep time but did not stop to stimulate or simulate. I barely took time to drop my case off in my water tank.

I rang up Rho, waking her.

"Have they pulled their equipment yet?" I asked.

"Who?" she responded sleepily. "Stolbart and Cailetet-Davis? No. They're waiting to get orders from their BMs. Thomas said you'd fill me in on some things—he was going to talk with you."

"Yes, well there are delays, and I have to do some research. Have you accessed the third head yet?"

"We've downloaded some patterns, but they're not translated. This mess has kind of put a crimp in our enthusiasm, Micko."

"I understand. Rho, get them to translate what you have."

"You sound a bit crazed, brother. Don't take this personally. This is my screw-up, not yours. Tulips, remember?"

"Just get those patterns translated. Please. Humor me."

I leaned back in my chair, stunned by all that was happening, assessing my position, our position, if my hunch was correct.

Then I began yet more research. There was no way around it—what I needed to know would very likely be found only on Earth, and it would cost me dearly.

I would charge it to my personal account.

I CROSSED THE WHITE LINE SIX HOURS LATER. I STILL HADN'T SLEPT. My world of warrens and alleys and water tanks and volcanic bubbles and bridges and force disorder pumps was taking on a quality of bitter dream; I do not know why I felt William was the still point in the center of my life, but he was, and I needed above all else to find out how his project was proceeding. There seemed something almost holy and pure in his quest, above human quibbling; I sensed I could take comfort in his presence, in his words.

But William himself was not comfortable. He looked a wreck. He, too, had not slept. I entered the laboratory, ignoring the soft voices from the chamber below, and found him standing by the QL thinker, eyes closed, lips moving as if in prayer. He opened his eyes and faced me with a jerk of his shoulders and head. "Christ," he said softly. "Are they done down there?"

I shook my head. "I'm afraid I've set them on to something new."

"I heard you've been checkmated," he said.

I shrugged. "And you?"

"My opponent is far more subtle than any human conspiracy," he said. "I've gone so far as to be able to switch between plus and minus." He chuckled. "I can access this new state at will, but there's real resistance to reaching the no man's land between. I have the QL cogitating now. It's been working five hours on the problem."

"What's the problem?" I asked.

"Micko, I haven't even engaged the force disorder pumps to achieve this new state. No magnetic field cut-off, no special efforts—just a sudden jerk-down to this negative state, absorbing energy to maintain an undefined temperature."

"But why?"

"The best the QL can come up with is we're approaching some key event that sends signals back in time, affecting our experiment now."

"So neither of you know what's actually happened?"

He shook his head. "It's not only undefined, it's incomprehensible. Even the QL is befuddled by it and can't give me straight answers."

I sat on the edge of the QL's platform and caressed the machine with an open palm as if in sympathy. "Everything's screwed, top to bottom," I said. "The center cannot hold."

"Ah, Micko—there's the question. What is the center? What is this event we're approaching that can reach subtle fingers back and befuddle us now?"

I smiled. "We're a real pair of loons," I said.

"Speak for yourself," William said defensively, prickly. "I'll solve this dustover, by God, Micko." He pointed down. "Solve your little problem, and I'll solve mine."

As if on cue, Rho stood on the open laboratory door, face ashen. "Mickey," she said. "How did you know?"

The shock of confirmation—and confirmation was not in doubt— made me tremble. I glanced at William. "A little ghost told me. A fat nightmare on ice."

"We don't have too much translated," she said. "But we know his name."

"What are you talking about?" William asked.

"Our third unknown," I explained. "We have three unknown heads below, three among four hundred and ten. Alleged bad record keeping."

"Do you know something, Mickey?" Rho asked.

"There were four Logologists employed by StarTime Preservation between 2079 and 2094," I said. "Two worked in records, two were in administration. None were ever given access to the heads themselves; they were kept in cold vaults in Denver."

"You think they screwed up the records?"

"It was the most they could manage."

"It's so *cynical*," Rho said. "I can't believe such a thing. It would be like our . . . trying to kill Robert and Emilia. It's sickening."

William uttered a wordless curse of frustration. "Dammit, Rho, what are you talking about?"

"We know why we're having such problems with Task-Felder. I've hit the jackpot, William. I've brought a real wolf into our fold. I apologize."

"What wolf?"

"K. D. Thierry," I said, the breath going out of me. I didn't know whether I might laugh or cry.

"You've got *him* down there?" William asked.

Rho and I hugged each other and laughed, near hysteria. "Kimon David Thierry," Rho said when we had recovered. She wiped her eyes. "Mickey, you're brilliant. But it still doesn't make sense. Why are they so afraid of him?"

I spread my arms. I couldn't come up with an immediate answer.

"The Logologist himself?" William still couldn't grasp the whole of the truth.

Rho sat and put her legs up on the QL stand. She leaned her head back. "William, could you get my neck, please? I'm going to twist my head off with a muscle cramp if someone doesn't massage me soon."

William stood behind her and rubbed her neck.

"What are we going to do, Micko?" Rho asked.

"They're afraid of him because they think we can access secrets, truths," I said, finally articulating what I had known for hours. "We can look into his memories, his private thoughts. They suppose if we go far enough, we can access what he was thinking when he wrote their great books, when he organized their faith . . ."

"They know he was a fraud," Rho said. "They're doing all this because they know they're living a lie. I can't believe how cynical that is."

"They're managers," I said. "They're politicians, shepherds of their flock."

" 'Cut the politics,' " William said. "Rho, you've stirred a snake pit."

"Ice Pit. Frozen snakes. Heaven save us," she said, and I think she meant it as a genuine request.

" 'A prophet is not without honor, save in his own country.' Matthew." William seemed to surprise himself with his own erudition. "Do you think Fiona Task-Felder wants Thierry disposed of?"

"She may not even know," I said. "She's been given orders from Earth. All the puppets are dancing because somebody high in the Church of Logology knew all along where Thierry was, knew that he had had himself frozen by StarTime upon his death. . . . That his cremation was a hoax, not to mention his joining the Ascended Masters as a galaxy-roaming spirit."

"Then why didn't they outbid me on Earth?" Rho asked. "Why didn't the Logologists buy StarTime decades ago and bury dead meat?"

"You can't buy what somebody refuses to sell." I took out my slate and scrolled through a list of names and biographies, from public records and old Triple Financial Disclosure files. Any individual or group on Earth who had invested in Triple enterprises in the late twenty-first and early twenty-second centuries had had to file extensive disclosures with suspicious and reluctant terrestrial authorities. Those had been the bad old days of embargoes and the Split.

StarTime Preservation Society had maintained a wide folio of investments, including investments in the Triple. "Here's my prime suspect," I said. "His name was Frederick Jones. He was director of StarTime from 2097 until his death four years ago. He was a lapsed Logologist. In fact, he had sued the church for thirty million dollars in 2090. He lost. Did StarTime select its bidders?"

"They could have," Rho said.

"Jones probably knew that K. D. Thierry was a member of StarTime. He might not have known *where* he was, since he seemed at no particular pains to straighten out the records after the Logologist employees scrambled them. Think of what qualms Jones must have had, protecting the man he most hated from his own church . . .

"To fulfill the contracts with Thierry, Jones's successors locked the church out of the bidding, allowing only legitimate concerns. Jones had fought them off for decades. I'd say that eventually the church just gave up. There didn't seem to be any scientific breakthroughs on the horizon. The heads were just frozen meat. No foreseeable threat. New church directors came into power. Memories lapsed. Then they discovered what had happened. It's all supposition, but it makes sense."

"Pandora came along," Rho said. "Pandora of the tulips. What are we going to do, Mickey?"

"Obviously, we're legally required to defend the interests of these corpsicles—but I'm not sure under what law. Earth law and Triple Law don't exactly mesh, let alone Earth law and lunar law."

"What about Robert and Emilia?" Rho asked. "If we're forced to divest, what happens to *them*?"

The QL Thinker interrupted us with a gentle chiming. "William, a comprehensible stability has returned. All cells are stable at one to the minus twentieth Kelvin. No energy input is required to maintain stability."

William stopped his massage. "Don't think me unconcerned," he said, "but this means I can get back to work."

"I haven't even kept track of what you're doing," Rho told him sorrowfully.

"No fear," he said, bending over to kiss her on the forehead. I had never seen William more gentle, more sympathetic with Rho, and I was touched. "So long as I'm left alone *most* of the time, I'll get my own work done. Save Robert and Emilia. This family is important to me, too."

I told Thomas about our discovery ten minutes later. He hardly reacted at all—the family meeting was to be that evening, his job was in the balance, and he was thinking.

"The family syndics voted full confidence," Thomas told me over the phone early in the morning. "They've left this matter entirely in my hands." He had left his vid off. I interpreted this to mean that he looked too tired, too defeated to be seen by an underling; his voice confirmed my suspicion. "I wish to hell they'd kicked me out and taken over, Mickey, but they've got their own work to do at a higher level."

"That means they have confidence in you," I said.

"No," he said slowly. "Not at all, Mickey. Think. What does it *really* mean?"

I considered for a moment. "They think Sandoval BM, under your direction, can't do much more damage than we've already done, and the other family syndics will work behind the scenes with the BMs and the council to patch things up."

"Give Mickey long enough, and he gets the answer," Thomas said.

"But that doesn't make sense, not entirely," I said, my voice rising at this sting. "Why not tell us to just butt out?"

Thomas suddenly switched on his vid. He looked ten years older and exhausted, but his eyes were twin points of fever brightness. "I didn't tell them about Thierry, Mickey. We're going to try one more thing. You think the president doesn't know why she's been ordered to shut down our project. Well, why don't we tell her? Better yet, Mickey, why don't you play the cocky little bastard and tell her yourself?"

If he had been in the room with me, I might have reached out and hit him. "You're the bastard," I said. "You're a goddamned sanctimonious and cruel old bastard."

"That's what I want, Mickey: conviction," he said. "I'm putting a lot of faith in you. I think this will shock the lunar Logologists into a useful confusion. The leaders of the Church are counting on our not knowing; if we don't know, Fiona and the lunar branch won't know. Let's upset the balance of ignorance."

I was still angry enough to keep my finger on the cutoff. But his words and his plan started to become clear to me. "You want me to play the upstart again," I said.

"You got it, Mickey. Angry. Insulted. I've just fired you. Tell Fiona Task-Felder that we know we have Thierry, and that we're going to debrief his head unless they back off."

"Thomas, that's . . . a little scary."

"I think it will knock Fiona into a stupor and give us some much-needed time. You know what the next step is, Mickey?"

"We announce it to the solar system."

Thomas laughed out loud. "Damn you to hell, my boy, you're getting the hang of it now. We could set the Logologists back fifty years. 'Church seeks to destroy remains of prophet and founder.' " His hands ascribed lit headlines. "I think Sandoval's directors are correct to leave this to us, don't you?"

I felt like a rat in a hole. "If you say so, Thomas."

"We have our orders. Sic her, Mickey."

I waited thirty hours, just to give myself time to think, to feel my way through to some independence from Thomas. I was not at all sure he hadn't broken under this strain. The thought of calling the president, after my last defeat at her hands, was nauseating. I thought of all the poor idiots throughout human history who had been caught in political traps, logistical traps, traps of any kind; all rats in a common hole.

I felt myself growing older. I didn't see it as an improvement.

And who was behind it all? Whom could I blame?

Ultimately, one man who had started a strangely secular church, attracting people good and bad, faithful and cynical, starting an organization too large and too well-financed and organized to simply fade: promulgating a series of lies become sacred truths. How often had that happened in human history, and how many had suffered and died?

I had dipped into records of past prophets during my Earth research. Zarathustra. Jesus. Mohammed. Shabbetai Tzevi, the seventeenth cen-

.urkish Jew who had claimed to be Messiah, and who in the end
. apostatized and become a Moslem. Al Mahdi, who had defeated
.ıe British at Khartoum. Joseph Smith, who had read the Word of God
from golden tablets with special glasses, and Brigham Young. Dozens of
nineteenth- and twentieth-century founders of radical branches of
Christianity and Islam. The nameless, faceless prophet of the Binary
Millennium. And all the little ones since, the pretenders whose religions
had eventually foundered, the charlatans of small talent, of skewed messages too foul even for human mass consumption. To which rank did
Thierry belong?

I swung back from this dark vision, asking myself how much such
humans had contributed to human philosophy and order, to civilization.
Judaism, Christianity, and Islam had ordered and divided the Western
world. I myself admired Jesus.

But what I had learned about Thierry made it impossible for me to
give him top rank. He had been petty, a philanderer, a malicious prosecutor of those who had fallen from his grace. He had written ridiculous
laws to govern the lives of his followers. He had been cruel and intem-
perate. Eventually, instead of going on a galactic cruise and joining the
Ascended Masters, as he had claimed he would do upon "discorpora-
tion," Thierry had been frozen by StarTime Preservation. He had donated his head to the ages, in the hopes of a purely secular immortality.

I visited the Ice Pit and rode the elevator to the chamber. Stolbart
and Cailetet-Davis had been recalled, finally, but they had left their
equipment in place, since the recall was tentative, pending final decision
for disposition of the project.

Rho had been instructed in some of the fundamentals of the instruments. She could play back the recordings already made, and with some
effort make crude translations of other patterns.

We sat in the near-silence, squatting on the steel decking. Rho cursed
and fumbled her way through the equipment settings.

"I'm going to have to interpret some of this," Rho said. "The translations aren't perfect."

We listened to Kimon Thierry's last few minutes of conscious memory. There were, as yet, no visual translations. The sound that came
from the equipment was distorted, human voices barely recognizable.

"*Mr. Thierry, a* . . . (crackling whicker) *longtime friend of Mrs. Win-
ston* . . ."

"We think he's talking on the phone," Rho explained.

"*Yes, I know her. What's she want?*"

That was Thierry himself, speaking aloud, heard from within his own
head: voice deeper and more resonant.

"She's asked about the (something) *logos point meeting in January. Is there going to be an XYZ mind discourse?*"

"*I don't see why not. Who is she? Not another bitch from the Staten Island instrumentality, is she?*"

"*No, sir. She's a platinum contributor. She brought her five children to the Taos Campus Logos in September . . .*"

"Just day-to-day business," Rho suggested. She rested her chin in her hands, squatting lotus on the floor, elbows on knees, as I remembered her sitting when she was a young girl. She looked at me with a be-patient expression; more coming.

"*Tell her the mind discourse takes a lot of my mental energy. If I'm going to hold an XYZ, we'll need ten new contributors, each at the platinum level. Takes a lot of energy to contact the lost gods.*"

Even through his own filter, Thierry sounded more than just physically tired; he sounded like a man trapped in boredom, mouthing the words with no hope for relief.

"*Can you guarantee contact with them?*"

"*What in hell kind of question is that?*"

"*Sir, I mean, do you have the wherewithal? Your health hasn't been that good recently. The last logos point . . .*"

"*Tell Mrs. Whats-her-name I'll have her swimming in Delta Wisdom, I'll have the gods evacuate her mental sinuses back to her conception. Tell her whatever she needs to be convinced to work for us. We need ten new platinums. What the hell else have you got?*"

"*I'm sorry to upset you, Mr. Thierry, but I'd like this to go well—*"

"*I appreciate your concern, but I know what my strength is now. I rest . . . on my own theos charge. What else? Ahhh . . .*"

"*Sir?*" (Distorted.)

A long groan, followed by sharp clatters, other voices in his immediate vicinity, one female voice coming to the fore, "*Kimon, Kimon, what's wrong?*"

No answer from Thierry, just another groan; something like plumbing rattling, fireworks exploding in a muffled room. The same female voice barely audible over Thierry's final memories of a drastically failing body: "*Kimon, what is this—*"

And Thierry's final words, issued in a whispered moan, "*Get Peter.*"

The translation ended and Rho shut off the tape.

We stared at each other without speaking for a moment. "I can see . . . why some people think this is wrong," I said quietly. "I can see maybe why the Logologists on Earth wouldn't want this."

"It's a real intrusion, not like just opening a diary," Rho admitted.

"We should seal them off until they can be resurrected," I said. Rho looked away, at the neat tiers of steel boxes stretching around the curve of the chamber, at the Cailetet and Onnes equipment stacked beside us.

"We have to have courage," she said. "And if we're allowed to continue, we have to work out our own ethics. We're the first to do this. It isn't wrong, I think, but it *is* dangerous."

"Rho, I'm exhausted by this whole thing. We could call Task-Felder and offer to give them Thierry. Let them have what they want."

"What do you think they'd do?" Rho asked.

I bit my lower lip and shrugged. "They'd send him back to Earth, probably. Let the directors decide whether he should be . . ."

"Released," Rho suggested. "To join the Ascended Masters."

"He doesn't have any descendants, any family I could discover . . . Just the Logologists."

"And they don't want him," Rho said.

"They don't want anybody else to have him," I said.

She unwound from her lotus and got to her knees, turning off the power on the translator. "Do you agree with Thomas's plan?"

I didn't move or speak for a moment, not wanting to commit myself. "We need the time."

"Mickey, Sandoval has signed for the whole lot, a binding agreement. We have to protect them, keep them, all of them . . . and if there's a way to revive them, we have to do that, too."

"All right," I said. "I don't think I was being serious, anyway."

"I wish Robert and Emilia had chosen another preservation society," she said. "Hell, I wish I'd never heard about StarTime."

"Amen," I said.

I HATE DUPLICITY. THOMAS'S PLAN WAS THE BEST; AT LEAST I COULD THINK of no better. We were being forced to the wall, and desperate measures were necessary, but I didn't like what I was about to do: to play the clumsy innocent with Fiona Task-Felder. To smell like meat before the wolf.

Again, I took the shuttle to Port Yin. I did not visit Thomas's offices, however; we had planned things in advance by phone two hours before I left, with contingencies, prevarications, fallbacks.

The first part of the plan was for me to arrive at the office of the president unannounced, defeated and out of a job, straying from the established course of the elders in my family. I mussed my hair, put on a strained look, and entered the president's reception area, asking in a halting voice for an audience with Fiona Task-Felder.

The receptionist knew who I was and asked me to take a seat. He did not appear to speak with Fiona or to type anything; I assume she was simply notified there was someone interesting out front and that I was being scanned by hidden camera. I acted my part with some flair, appearing ill-at-ease.

The receptionist turned to me after a moment and said, "The president will have time to meet with you later this afternoon. Could you be back here by fifteen?"

I said that I could. I lost three hours and returned. This round of the dance was going well; the preliminary steps, the shufflings and determinations of who would lead, who would follow.

I walked the long corridor to the president's inner sanctum. The young women were still shifting files. The replay was hauntingly exact. They smiled at me. I half-heartedly returned their smiles.

The door to the president's office opened, and there sat the fit, blue-eyed Madame President behind her desk, hands folded, prepared to accept surrender and nothing else.

"Please sit," she said. "What can I do for you, Mr. Sandoval?"

"I'm taking a big risk," I said. "You must know that I've been reassigned. . . . Fired. But I feel there's still some room for negotiation . . ."

"Negotiation between who?"

"Myself . . . and you," I said.

"Who are you representing, Mr. Sandoval? Whom do you think I represent? The council, or my binding multiple?"

I smiled weakly. "That doesn't matter to me, now."

"It matters to me. If you wish to speak to the president of the council, I'm all ears. If you wish to speak to the Task-Felder BM—"

"I want to talk to you. I need to tell you something . . ."

She lifted her eyes to the ceiling. "You've screwed up before, Mr. Sandoval. Apparently it's cost you dearly. Family BMs are dens of nepotism and incompetents. Do you have your syndics' authorization?"

"No, I don't."

"It does neither of us any good for you to be here, then."

"You used me before . . ." I began. Real anger and nervousness added a conviction to my act I could not have faked. "I'm trying to redeem myself before our syndics, our director, and to give you a chance, some information you might want to know . . ."

She looked me over shrewdly, not unkindly, wolf surveying a highly suspect meal. "Would you be willing to testify before the council? Tell them whatever you're about to tell me?"

Thomas was right.

"I'd prefer not to . . ."

"I will not listen to you unless you are willing to testify, in open session."

"Please."

"That's my requirement, Mickey. It would be best if you consulted with your syndics before you went any further." She stood to dismiss me.

"All right," I said. "I'll let you judge whether you want me to testify."

"I'll record this as a voluntary meeting, just like the last time you were here."

"Fine," I said, caving in disconsolately.

"I'm listening."

"We've started accessing the patterns, the memories inside the heads," I said.

She seemed to swallow something bitter. "I hope all of you know what you're doing," she said slowly.

"We've discovered something startling, something we didn't expect at all . . ."

"Go on," she said.

I told her about StarTime's apparent bookkeeping errors, I told her about learning the names of the first two unknowns from short-term memory and other areas in the dead but intact brains.

She showed a glimmer of half-fascinated, half disgusted interest.

"Only a couple of days ago, we learned who the third unknown was." I swallowed. Drew back before leaping into the abyss. "He's Kimon Thierry. K. D. Thierry. He joined StarTime."

Fiona Task-Felder rocked back and forth slowly in her chair. "You're lying," she said softly. "That is the foulest, most ridiculous story I've. . . . It's more than I imagined you were capable of, Mr. Sandoval. I am . . ." She shook her head, genuinely furious, and stood up at her desk. "Get out of here."

I laid a slate on her desk. "I d-don't think you should d-dismiss me," I said, shaking, stuttering, teeth knocking together. My own contradic-tory emotions again supported my play-acting. "I've put together a lot of evidence, and I have recordings of Mr. Thierry's . . . last moments."

She stared at me, at the slate. She sat again but still said nothing.

"I can show you the evidence very quickly," I said, and I laid out my trail of evidence. The employment of the Logologists, Frederick Jones's suit against the church, the three unknown members of the group of dead transported from Earth, our triumph in playing back and translat-ing the last memories of each. I thought there might be facts and re-membrances clicking, meshing, in her head, but her face betrayed nothing but cold, tightly controlled rage.

"I see nothing conclusive here, Mr. Sandoval," she said when I had finished.

I played her a tape made by Thierry when he'd been alive, in his later years. Than I played the record of his last moments, not just the short-term memories of sounds, but the visual memories, which Rho had clumsily processed and translated at Thomas's request. Faces, oddly inhuman at first, and then fitting a pattern, being recognized; the memories not buffered by the personal mind's own interpreters, raw and immediate and therefore surprisingly crude. The office where he died, his bulky hands on the table, the twitching and shifting of his eyes from point to point in the room, difficult to follow. The fading. The end of the record.

The president looked down at the slate, eyebrows raised, hands tightly clenched on the desktop.

I leaned forward to retrieve the slate. She grabbed it herself, held it shakily in both hands, and suddenly threw it across the office. It banged against a foamed rock wall and caromed to the metabolic carpet.

"It's not a hoax," I said. "We were shocked, as well."

"Get out," she said. "Get the hell out, now."

I turned to leave, but before I could reach the door, she began to cry. Her shoulders slumped and she buried her face in her hands. I moved toward her to do something, to say I was sorry again, but she screamed at me to leave, and I did.

"HOW DID SHE REACT?" THOMAS ASKED. I SAT IN HIS PRIVATE QUARTERS, MY mind a million miles away, contemplating sins I had never imagined I would feel guilty for. He handed me a glass of terrestrial madeira and I swallowed it neat, then looked over the cube files on his living room wall.

"She didn't believe me," I said.

"Then?"

"I convinced her. I played the tape."

Thomas filled my glass again.

"And?"

I still would not face him.

"Well?"

"She cried," I said. "She began to cry."

Thomas smiled. "Good. Then?"

I gave him a look of puzzlement and disapproval. "She wasn't faking it, Thomas. She was devastated."

"Right. What did she do next?"

"She ordered me out of her office."

"No setup for a later meeting?"

I shook my head.

"Sounds like you really knocked a hole in her armor, Mickey."

"I must have," I said solemnly.

"Good," Thomas said. "I think we've got our extra time. Go home now, Mickey, and get some rest. You've redeemed yourself a hundred times over."

"I feel like a shit, Thomas."

"You're an honorable shit, doing only when others do unto you," Thomas said. He offered his hand to me but I did not accept it. "This is for your *family*," he reminded me, eyes flinty.

I could not forget the tears coming, the fierce, shattering anger, the dismay and betrayal.

"Thank you again, Micko," Thomas said.

"Call me Mickey, please," I said as I left.

ALIENATION WITHOUT MUST BE ACCOMPANIED BY ALIENATION WITHIN; THAT is the law for every social level, even individuals. To harm one's fellows, even one's enemies, harms you, takes away some essential element from your self respect and self image. This must be the way it is when fighting a full-fledged war, I told myself, only worse. Gradually, by killing your enemies, you kill your old self. If there is room for a new self, for an extraordinary redevelopment then you grow and become more mature though sadder. If there is no room, you die inside or go crazy.

Alone in my dry warm water-tank, creature comforts aplenty and mind in a state of complete misery, I played my own Shakespearean scene of endless unvoiced soliloquy. I held a party of all my selves and we gathered to argue and fight.

I felt badly for my anger toward Thomas. Still, the anger was inevitable; he had turned me into a weapon and I had been effective and that hurt. I learned the hard way that Fiona Task-Felder was not a heartless monster; she was a human, playing her cards as she thought they must be played, not for reasons of self-aggrandizement, but following orders.

What effect would our news have on her superiors, the directors of the political and secular arms of the Logologist Church?

If Thomas actually leaked the news to the public of the Triple, what would the effect be on millions of faithful Logologists?

Logology was a personal madness expanded by chance and the laws of society into an institution, self-perpetuating, even growing with time. We could eventually tap the experiences, the memories, of the man at the fount of the madness. We could in time disillusion the members, perhaps even destroy the Church.

None of this gave me the least satisfaction.

I longed for the innocence I had known but not been aware of, three months past.

Ten hours after returning from Port Yin, I left my water tank to cross the white line.

We had bought our extra time, and here it was; the Task-Felder arm of Logology was quiet. On the Triple nets, there was nary a murmur from the Earthside forces.

William was jubilant. "You just missed Rho," he told me as I entered the laboratory. "She'll be back in an hour, though. I have it now, Micko. Tomorrow I'll do the trial run. Everything's stable—"

"Did you find out what caused your last problem?"

William pursed his lips as if I'd mentioned something dirty. "No," he said. "I'd just as soon forget it. I can't reproduce the effect now, and the QL is no help."

"Beware those ghosts," I said mordantly. "They come back."

"You're both so cheerful," he said. "You'd think we were all waiting doomsday. What did Thomas have you do, assassinate somebody?"

"No," I said. "Not literally."

"Well, try to cheer up a little—I'd like to have both of you help me tomorrow."

"Doing what?" I asked.

"I'll need more than one pair of hands, and I'll also need official witnesses. The record-keepers aren't emotionally satisfying; real human testimony can shake loose more grant money, I suspect, especially if you and Rho are giving the testimony to possible financiers."

We'll be too controversial to squeeze dust from any financiers, I thought. "Are we going to market absolute zero?"

"We'll market something new and rare. Never in the history of the universe—until tomorrow—has matter been cooled and tricked to reach a temperature of zero Kelvin. It will make the nets all over the Triple, Mickey. It might even take some of the heat off Sandoval BM, if I may pun. But you know that; why are you being *so* pessimistic?"

"My apologies, William."

"Judging from your face, you'd think we've already lost," he said.

"No. We may have won," I said.

"Then cheer up a little, if only to give me some breathing room in all this gloom."

He returned to work; I walked out on the bridge and deliberately stood between the force disorder pumps to punish my body with their fingernail-on-slate sensation of deep displacement.

RHO AND I JOINED WILLIAM IN THE ICE PIT LABORATORY AT EIGHT HUNDRED. He assigned Rho to monitoring the pumps, which he ramped to full activity. I sat watch on the refrigerators. There didn't seem to be any real practical need for either Rho or I to be there. It soon became obvious we had been invited more to provide company than to help or witness.

William was outwardly calm, inwardly very nervous, which he betrayed by occasional short bursts of mild pique, quickly apologized for and retracted. I didn't mind facing pique; somehow it made me feel better, took my mind off events happening outside the Ice Pit.

We were a strange crew; Rho even more subdued than William, unaffected by the grating of the disorder pumps; I getting progressively drunker and drunker with an uncalled-for sense of separation and relief from our troubles; William making a circuit of all the equipment, ending at the highly polished Cavity containing the cells, mounted on levitation absorbers just beyond the left branch of the bridge.

Far above us, barely visible in the spilled light from the laboratory and the bridge, hung the dark gray vault of the volcanic void, obscured by a debris net.

At nine hundred, William's calm cracked wide open when the QL announced another reverse in the lambda phase, and conditions within the cells that it could not interpret. "Are they the same conditions as last time?" William asked, fingers of both hands drumming the top surface of the QL.

"The readings and energy requirements are the same," the QL said. Rho pointed out that the force disorder pumps were showing chaotic fluctuations in their "draw" from the cells. "Has that happened before?"

"I've never had the pumps ramped so high before. No, it hasn't happened," William explained. "QL, what would happen to our cells if we just turned off the stabilizing energy?"

"I cannot guess," the QL replied. It flatly refused to answer any similar questions, which irritated William.

"You said something earlier about this possibly reflecting future events in the cells," I reminded him. "What did you mean by that?"

"I couldn't think of any other explanation," William said. "I still can't. QL won't confirm or deny the possibility."

"Yes, but what did you *mean*? How could that happen?"

"If we achieved some hitherto unstudied state in the cells, there might be a chronological backwash, something reflected in the past, our now."

"Sounds pretty speculative to me," Rho commented.

"It's more than speculative, it's desperate rille dust," William said. "Without it, however, I'm completely lost."

"Have you correlated times between the changes?" Rho asked.

"Yes," William said, sighing impatiently.

"Okay. Then try changing your scheduled time for achieving zero."

William looked across the lab at his wife, both eyebrows raised, mouth open, giving his long face a simian appearance. "What?"

"Re-set your machines. Make the zero-moment earlier or later. And don't change it back again."

William produced his most sardonic, pitying smile. "Rho, my sweet, you're crazier than I am."

"Try it," she said.

He swore but did as she suggested, setting his equipment for five minutes later.

The lambda phase reversal ended. Five minutes later, it began again.

"Christ," he whispered. "I don't dare touch it now."

"Better not," Rho said, smiling. "What about the previous incident?"

"It was continuous, no lapses," he said.

"There. You're going to succeed, and this is a prior result, if such a thing is possible in quantum logic."

"QL?" William queried the thinker.

"Time reverse circumstances are only possible if no message is communicated," it said. "You are claiming to receive confirmation of experimental success."

"But success at what?" William said. "The message is completely ambiguous. . . . We don't know what our experiment will do to cause this condition in the past."

"I'm dizzy, having to think with those damned pumps going," I said.

"Wait'll they're completely tuned to the cells," William warned, enjoying my discomfort. His grin bared all his teeth. He made final preparations, calling out numbers and settings to us, all superfluously. We echoed just to keep his morale up. From here on, the experiment was automatic, controlled by the QL.

"I think the reversal will end in a few minutes," William said, standing beside the polished Cavity. "Call it a quantum hunch."

A few minutes later, the QL reported yet again the end of reversal. William nodded with mystified satisfaction. "We're not scientists, Micko," he said cheerily. "We're magicians. God help us all."

The clocks silently counted their numbers. William walked down the bridge and made a final adjustment in the right hand pump with a small hex wrench. "Cross your fingers," he said.

"Is this it?" Rho asked.

"In twenty seconds I'll tune the pumps to the cells, then turn off the magnetic fields . . ."

"Good luck," Rho said. He turned away from her, turned back and extended his arms, folding her into them, hugging her tightly. His face shined with enthusiasm; he seemed gleeful, childlike.

I clenched my teeth when he tuned the pumps. The sensation was trebled; my long bones seemed to become flutes piping a shrill unmelodic quantum tune. Rho closed her eyes and groaned. "That's atrocious," she said. "Makes me want to crap my pants."

"It's sweet music," William said, shaking his head as if to rid himself of a fly. "Here goes." He beat the seconds with his upheld finger. "Field . . . off." A tiny green light flashed in the air over the main lab console, the QL's signal.

"Unknown phase reversal. Lambda reversal," the QL announced.

"Goddamn it all to hell!" William shrieked, stamping his foot.

Simultaneously with his shout, there came the sound of four additional footstamps above the cavern overhead, precisely as if gigantic upstairs neighbors had jumped on a resonant floor. William held his left foot in the air, astonished by what seemed to be echoes of his anger. His expression had cycled beyond frustration, into something like expectant glee: *Yes by God, what next?*

Rho's personal slate called for her attention in a thin voice. My own slate chimed; William was not wearing his.

"There is an emergency situation," our slates announced simultaneously. "Emergency power reserves are in effect." The lights dimmed and alarms went off throughout the lab. "There have been explosions in the generators supplying power to this station."

Rho looked at me with eyes wide, lips drawn into a line.

The mechanical slate voices announced calmly, in unison, "There has been apparent damage to components above the Ice Pit void, including heat radiators." This information came from auto sentries around the station. Every slate in the station—and emergency speaker systems throughout the warrens and alleys—would be repeating the same information.

A human voice interrupted them, someone I did not recognize, perhaps the station watch attendant. Somebody was always assigned to observe the sentries, a human behind the machines. "William, are you all right? Anybody else in there with you?"

"Mickey and I are in here with William. We're fine," Rhosalind said.

"A shuttle has dropped bombs into the trenches. They've taken out your radiators, William, and all of our generators are damaged. Your pit is drawing a lot more power than normal—I was worried perhaps—"

"It shouldn't be," William said.

"William says it shouldn't be drawing more power," Rho informed the anonymous watch attendant.

"But it is," William continued, turning to look at his instruments.

"Phase down lambda reversal in all cells," the QL announced.

"—you folks might be injured," the voice concluded, overlapping.

"We're fine," I said.

"You'd better get out of there. No way of knowing how much damage the void has sustained, whether—"

"Let's go," I said, looking up.

Chunks of rock and dust drifted into the overhead net, making it belly in and out like the upside-down bell of a jellyfish..

"Lambda reversal ending in all cells," the QL said.

"Wait—" William said.

I stood on the bridge between the Cavity and the disorder pumps. The refrigerators hung motionless in their intricate suspensions. Rho stood in the door to the lab. William stood beside the Cavity.

"Zero attained," the QL announced.

Rho glanced at me, and I started to say something, but my throat caught. The lights dimmed all around.

Distantly, our two slates said, *Time to evacuate . . .*

I turned to leave, stepping between the pumps, and that saved my life . . . or at any rate made it possible for me to be here, now, in my present condition.

The pump jackets fluoresced green and vanished, revealing spaghetti traceries of wire and cable and egg-shaped parcels. My eyes hurt with the green glare, which seemed to echo in glutinous waves from the walls of the void. I considered the possibility that something had fallen and hit me on the head, making me see things, but I felt no pain, only a sense of being stretched. I could not see Rho or William, as I was now facing down the bridge toward the entrance to the Ice Pit. I could not hear them, either. When I tried to swivel around again, parts of my being seemed to separate and rejoin. Instinctively, I stopped moving, waiting for everything to come together again.

It was all I could do to concentrate on one of my hands grasping the bridge railing. The hand shed dark ribbons which curled toward the deck of the bridge. I blinked and felt my eyelids separate and rejoin with each rise and fall. Fear deeper than thought forced me to stop all motion until only my blood and the beat of my heart threatened to sunder me from the inside.

Finally I could stand it no more. I slowly turned in the deepening quiet, hearing only the slide of my shoes on the bridge and the serpent's hiss of my body separating and rejoining as I rotated.

Please do not take my testimony from this point on as having any kind of objective truth. Whatever happened, it affected my senses, if not my mind, in such a way that all objectivity fled.

The Cavity sphere had cracked like an egg. I saw Rho standing between the Cavity and the laboratory, perfectly still, facing slightly to my left as if caught in mid-turn, and she did not look entirely real. The light that reflected from her was not familiar, not completely useful to my eyes, whether because the light had changed or my eyes had changed, I do not know. In addition there came from her—radiated is not the right word, it is deceptive, but perhaps there is no better—a kind of communication of her presence that I had never experienced before, a shedding of skins that *lessened* her as I watched. I think perhaps it was the information that comprised her body, leaching away through a new kind of space that had never existed before: space made crystalline, a superconductor of information. With the shedding of this essence Rho became less substantial, less real. She was dissolving like a piece of sugar in warm water.

I tried to call out her name, but could make no sound. I might have been caught in a vicious gelatin, one that stung me whenever I tried to move. But I could not see myself dissolving, as I saw Rho. I seemed immune at least to that danger.

William stood behind her, becoming more clear as Rho dissipated. He was farther from the Cavity; the effect, whatever it might be, had not worked quite as strongly on him. But he too began to shed this essence, the hidden music that communicates each particle's place and quantum state to other particles, that holds us in one shape and one condition from this moment to the next. I think he was trying to move, to get back inside the laboratory, but he succeeded only in evaporating this essence more rapidly, and he stopped himself, tried instead to reach out for Rho, his face utterly intent, like a child facing down a tiger.

His hand passed through her.

I saw something else flee from my sister at that moment. I apologize in advance for describing this; I do not wish to spread any more or less hope, to offer encouragement to mystical interpretations of our existence, for as I said, what I saw might be a function of hallucination, not objective reality.

But I saw two, then three, versions of my sister standing on the bridge, the third like a cloud maintaining its rough shape, and this cloud-shape managed to move toward me, and touch me with an outstretched limb.

Are you all right, Micko? I heard in my head if not in my ears. *Don't move. Please don't move. You seem to be . . .*

Suddenly I saw myself from her perspective, her experience leaching from her, passing into me, like a taste of her dissipating self in the superconducting medium.

The cloud passed through me, carried by some unknown momentum of propagation through the bridge rail and out over the void where it fell like rain. Was I to fade as well? The other images of Rho and William had become mere blurs against the laboratory which was itself blurring, casting away fluid tendrils.

Oddly, the Cavity containing the copper samples—I assumed they were the cause of this, their new condition, announced by the QL, *zero Kelvin*—seemed more solid and stable than anything else, despite the fine cracks across its surface.

Because of my position between the disorder pumps—and I repeat, this is only my speculation—I seemed to have suffered as much dissolution as I was due, whereas everything else became even less real, less material.

The bridge slumped, stretching beneath my weight as if I stood on a sheet of rubber. I performed some gymnastic and caught the rails with both hands. I could not stop the plunge downward, however. I was dropping toward the lower structure built to hold the heads. I tried to climb but could not gain purchase with my feet.

My descent continued until the bridge and my legs actually passed through the ceiling of the lower chamber. A sharp pain shoved like a spear through both limbs, gouging through my bones into my hips. Looking up for some new handhold, some way of stalling my fall, I saw the laboratory rotating loosely at the center of the void, shedding vapors. Rho and William I could not see at all.

A sensation of deep cold surrounded me, then faded. The refrigerators fell silently all around me, passing through the chamber and casting up slow ripples of some cold blue liquid that had filled the bottom of the pit. The liquid washed over me.

I describe the rest knowing perfectly well it cannot be anything more than delirium.

How is it that instinct can be aware of dangers from a situation no human being could ever have faced before? I felt a terrified loathing of that wash of unknown liquid, abhorrence so strong I crushed the bridge railing between my hands like thin aluminum. Yet I knew that it was not liquified gas from the refrigerators; *I was not afraid of being frozen.*

My feet pulled up from the mire and I hooked one onto a stanchion, lifting myself perhaps a meter higher. Still, I was not out of that turbulent pool, and it seeped into me.

I began to fill with sensations, remembrances not my own.

Memories from the dead.

From the heads, four hundred and ten of them, leaking their patterns and memories across a transformed and crystalline spacetime, the information slumping into a thick lake not of matter, not of anything anyone had ever experienced before, like an essence or a cold brew.

I carry some of these memories with me still. In most cases I do not know who or what they might come from, but I see things, hear voices, remember scenes on Earth that I could not possibly know. I have never sought verification, for the same reasons I have never told this story until now—because if I am a chalice of such memories, they have changed *me*, replacing some parts of my own memories shed in the first few instants of the Quiet, and I do not wish that confirmed.

There is one memory in particular, the most disturbing I think, that I must record, even though it is not verifiable. It must have come from Kimon Thierry himself. It has a particular flavor that matches the translated voices and visual memories I played for Fiona Task-Felder. I believe that in this terrible pond, the last thoughts of his dying moment permeated me. I loathe this memory: I loathe *him*.

To suspect, even deeply believe, in the duplicity and the malice and the greed—in the evil—of others is one thing. To know it for a fact is something no human being should ever have to face.

Kimon Thierry's last thoughts were not of the glorious journey awaiting him, the translation to a higher being. He was terrified of retribution. In his last moment before oblivion, he knew he had constructed a lie, knew that he had convinced hundreds of thousands of others of this lie, had limited their individual growth and freedom, and he feared going to the hell he had been taught about in Sunday school . . .

He feared another level of lie, created by past liars to punish their enemies and justify their own petty existences.

The memory ends abruptly with, I suppose, his death, the end of all recorded memories, all physical transformations. Of that I am left with no impressions whatsoever.

I rose above this hideous pool by climbing up the stanchions, finding the bars stronger the farther from the Cavity they had initially been, stronger but losing their strength and shape rapidly. I scrambled like an insect, mindless with terror, and somehow I climbed the twenty yards to the lip of the doorway in complete silence.

Perhaps three minutes had elapsed since the bombing, if time had any function in the Ice Pit void.

A group of rescuers found me crawling over William's white line. When they tried to go through the door and rescue the others, I told them not to, and because of my condition, they did not need much persuasion.

I had lost the first half centimeter of skin around my body from the neck down, and all my hair, precisely as if I had been sprayed with supercold gas.

FOR TWO MONTHS I LAY IN DREAMLESS SUSPENDED SLEEP IN THE YIN CITY Hospital, wrapped in healing liquid, skin-cells and muscle cells and bone cells migrating under the guidance of surgical nano machines, knitting my surface. I came awake at the end of this time, and fancied myself—with not a hint of fear, as if I had lost all my emotions—still in the Ice Pit, floating in the pool, spreading through the spherical void like water through an eager sponge, dissolving slowly and peacefully in the Quiet.

Thomas came to my room when I had a firmer grasp of who I was and where. He sat by my cradle and smiled like a dead man, eyes glassy, skin pale.

"I didn't do so well, Mickey," he told me.

"We didn't do so well," I said in a hoarse whisper, the strongest I could manage. My body felt surrounded by ice cubes. The black ceiling above me seemed to suck all my substance up and out, into space.

"You were the only one who escaped," Thomas said. "William and Rho didn't make it."

I had guessed that much. Still, the confirmation hurt.

Thomas looked down at the cradle and ran his gnarled, pale hand along the suspension frame. "You're going to recover completely, Mickey. You'll do better than I. I've resigned as director."

His eyes met mine and his mouth betrayed the presence of an ironic smile, fleeting, small, self-critical. "The art of politics is the art of avoiding disasters, of managing difficult situations for the benefit of all, even for your enemies, whether they know what's good for them or not. Isn't it, Mickey?"

"Yes," I croaked.

"What I had you do . . ."

"I did it," I said.

He acknowledged that much, gave me the gift of that much complicity but no more. "The word has spread, Mickey. We really hurt them, worse than they know. They hurt themselves."

"Who dropped the bombs?"

He shook his head. "It doesn't matter. No evidence, no arrests, no convictions."

"Didn't somebody see?"

"The first bomb took out the closest surface sentries. Nobody saw. We think it was a low-level shuttle. By the time we were able to get a search team off, it must have been hundreds of klicks away."

"No arrests . . . what about the president? Who's going to make her pay?"

"We don't know she ordered it, Mickey. Besides, you and I, we really zapped her. She's no longer president."

"She resigned?"

Thomas shook his head. "Fiona walked out of an airlock four days after the bombing. She didn't wear a suit." He rubbed the back of one hand with the fingers of his other hand. "I think I can take the blame for that."

"Not just you," I said.

"All right," he said, and that was all. He left me to my thoughts, and again and again, I told myself:

William and Rho did not escape.

Only I remember the pool.

Whether they are dead, or simply dissolved in the Ice Pit, floating in that incomprehensible pond or echoing in the space above, I do not know. I do not know whether the heads are somehow less dead than before.

THERE IS THE PROBLEM OF ACCOUNTABILITY.

In time, I was interrogated to the limits of my endurance, and still there were no prosecutions. The obvious suspicions—that the bombers had acted on orders from Earth, if not from Fiona Task-Felder herself— were never formalized as charges. The binding multiples wished to return to normal, to forget this hideous anomaly.

But Thomas was right. The story made its rounds, and it became legend: of Thierry's having himself harvested and frozen, an obvious apostasy from the faith he had established, and the violent reluctance of his followers to have him return in any form.

In the decades since, that has hurt the faith he founded in ways that even a court case and conviction could not have. The truth is less vigorous a prosecutor than legend. Neither masterful politics nor any number of great lies can stand against legend.

Task-Felder ceased being a Logologist multiple twenty years ago. The majority of members voted to open it to new settlers, of whatever beliefs; their connections with Earth were broken.

I have healed, grown older, worked to set lunar politics aright, married and contributed my own children to the Sandoval family. I suppose I have done my duty to family and Moon, and have nothing to be ashamed of. I have watched lunar politics and the lunar constitution change and reach a form we can live with, ideal for no one, acceptable to most, strong in times of crisis.

Yet until this record I have never told everything I knew or experienced in that awful time.

Perhaps my time in the Quiet was an internal lie, my own fantasy of justification, my own kind of revenge dreamed in a moment of pain and danger.

I still miss Rho and William. Writing this, I miss them so deeply I put my slate aside and come back to it only after a time of grieving all over. The sorrow never dies; it is merely pearled by time.

No one has ever duplicated William's achievement, leading me to believe that had it not been for the bombs, perhaps he would have failed, as well. Some concatenation of his brilliance, the guidance of the perverse QL and an unexpected failure of equipment, a serendipity that has not been repeated, led to his success, if it can be called such.

On occasion I return to the blocked-off entrance of the Ice Pit. Before I began writing, I went there, passing the stationed sentries, the single human guard—a young girl, born after the events I describe. As director of Sandoval BM, participant in the mystery, I am allowed this freedom.

The area beyond the white line is littered with the deranged and abandoned equipment of dozens of fruitless investigations. I have gone there to pray, to indulge in my own apostasy against rationalism, to hope that my words can reach into the transformed matter and information beyond.

Trying to reconcile my own feeling that I sinned against Fiona Task-Felder, as Thierry had sinned against so many . . . I cannot make it sensible.

No one will understand, not even myself, but when I die, I want to be placed in the Ice Pit with my sister and William. God forgive me, even with Thierry, Robert and Emilia, and the rest of the heads . . .

In the Quiet.

Afterword

Writing *Heads*

One of the strengths of nineteenth- and twentieth-century lit has been the emphasis on the little guy, the underdog. Dickens, Joyce, Faulkner, Steinbeck, James Jones, Vonnegut, Pynchon, King, William Gibson—all focus their attentions and sympathies on characters at the bottom of political and economic (or metaphysical) forces. The problems of leaders, politicians, robber barons—people wielding real power—are not dealt with nearly as often, perhaps because writers naturally feel themselves to be "put upon," at the receiving end of the forces of history and nature. Some—Vidal and Drury come to mind—have written about the corridors of power. In science fiction, however, the literature of masters and power-wielders is even sparser. Popular fiction almost demands an underdog as a main character.

Never willing to give in to the obvious, or to popular wisdom—and following the lead of Poul Anderson and Shakespeare, among others—I often choose people in positions of responsibility and power as sympathetic central characters in my works. They're human, too, and their internal conflicts are just as complex. Leadership is a dirty job, but some-body has to do it—even though he or she may, with the best of inten-tions, leave crushed bodies and broken souls strewn across the landscape.

In *Heads*, the opening sentences define the conflict and theme: "Order and cold, heat and politics. The imposition of wrong order: anger, death, suicide, and destruction." Politics is a kind of ordering, with the laws of human behavior and interaction giving shape to the social body much as chemical bonds, hormones, and enzymes give shape to the individual. Wrong order—the rule of the incompetent or the corrupt—is a constant danger, akin to cancer or disease. But unlike the individual body, society is made what it is by decisions both instinctive and conscious. Will and resolve and training are important aspects; the people in power must be vigilant, educated, and resourceful. The people who are governed must also be informed and responsible, especially in a democracy. The failure to take these responsibilities seriously—or to denigrate all political ac-tivities—or to advocate change at any cost—can lead to calamity.

Mickey Sandoval, the narrator of *Heads*, is a leader-in-training. His instincts are good; he passionately believes that politics is a necessity, when his lunar society—made up of rugged individualists, descendants of settlers and miners—tends to discredit all politics. Such disdain is a reflection of opinions generally held in the United States, where a sub-stantial portion of the population never votes, and believes in letting somebody else take the blame for everything.

But what immediately brought these facts home to me—and probably led to this story being written—was seven years of service to the Science Fiction Writers of America. I served on the grievance committee, edited a publication, acted as vice-president, and finally as president; and there are few individualists more rugged and contentious, or more suspicious of politics and politicians, than writers.

The level of political naivete in the SFWA—my own as well as oth-ers'—was astonishing. Constantly heartrending were the letters which arrived from member writers, claiming, in paraphrase, "I can't serve as an officer, or in any other capacity, because I am unqualified by reason of my philosophical opposition to governments and politics—but here's what I think *you* should do . . ." When important votes came up (or, at least, votes which *I* thought were important), much less than half of the active membership voted.

Tossed through the muse's meat-grinder, the emotions and frustra-tions aroused by this service emerged as *Heads*.

The other aspects of "Heads"—the echoing themes of science, nature, and human nature so important in science fiction—came from reading science magazines. An article on the search for absolute zero in *The*

Sciences—unfortunately, the issue is not immediately at hand, nor the author's name—kicked off idea and plot. Reading the entry for *Principles of Thermodynamics* in the *Encyclopedia Britannica* (1986) provided the wonderfully evocative picture of ancient Egypt and ice trays. Ice, freezing, the ideas of order and disorder, information and nonsense . . . *What if?*

I've also expelled a hairball associated with young religious groups, one of which—undecided as to whether it is a science or a religion—has tried to have an impact on science fiction, in the name of its founder. This group represents just the sort of "wrong order" which must *not* gain power. Complacency and over-tolerant pluralism—which not just tolerates, but tacitly condones—could lead to political disaster. We've seen it happen before, and the beginnings are often deceptively benign.

As Deep Throat is alleged to have said, *Follow the money . . .*

None of this was on my mind when Deborah Beale of Legend proposed I should write a novella for their line. But what irks me for a long enough time will inevitably emerge.

Often, the origins seem remote from the final product, as wine is remote from microbes and grape juice. Less remote, I think, in *Heads*.

Simply put twelve hundred science fiction and fantasy writers on the Moon, expand them two or three thousandfold, and stir . . .

Introduction to "The Wind from a Burning Woman"

This story is the first in my longest and most successful sequence of stories and novels—the Thistledown series. The asteroid starships described here will later form the setting for *Eon, Eternity*, and portions of *Legacy*, as well as the novella "The Way of All Ghosts."

"Wind" was written in Long Beach and first published in *Analog* by Ben Bova, who gave it a fine cover and interior illustrations by Mike Hinge. It would become the title story for my first collection from Arkham House, and thereby hangs another tale.

Jim Turner, at that time the editor of Arkham House, the most venerable small press publisher in SF and fantasy, was one of the most important people in my career. In 1980, he wrote a letter asking if I had a short story collection in the works. Jim had this silly notion that he wanted to publish SF writers, and not just modern horror. (Some horror writers regarded this as a betrayal of Arkham House's roots as the publisher of H. P. Lovecraft, Robert E. Howard, and Clark Ashton Smith. But in fact August Derleth, cofounder of the small press, had published science fiction long before—notably, A. E. Van Vogt's *Slan*.)

I was not just an avid fan of Lovecraft et al., I was a collector of Arkham House books, and I was thrilled when Jim approached me about a collection of short fiction—thrilled and amazed, as I was still pretty much an unknown. We assembled a tentative collection, but he wanted to top it off with something phenomenal—a story better than anything I had ever done before. I obliged with "Hardfought," which left him nonplussed for a couple of months—until he decided it met his requirements. The collection was finally published in 1983, and sold out its first printing faster than any previous book in Arkham House's history.

The irony of course was that Jim had approached a virtual unknown rather than the obvious up-and-comers and the established giants of the field. A then-famous agent asked him, pointblank, "Why Greg Bear? Who's he? Why not so-and-so or so-and-so?"

Jim just grinned—and passed the comment on to me, just to keep me in my place.

He continued to do that, surprising people and grinning at their reactions, publishing collections from promising new sf writers as well as neglected established writers, along with the core program at Arkham House of keeping Lovecraft and Clark Ashton Smith in print.

Jim was a visionary in a very restricted pond, and what he did must have rankled many, but he was right. He pulled Arkham House up in the seventies and eighties from a publisher of old classics and collectibles to one of the major forces in small-press publishing, doing, in his own way, just what Derleth had done in the thirties and forties.

I HAD READ A POEM BY MICHAEL BISHOP THAT CONTAINS THE LINE, "THE WIND FROM A burning woman is always a Chinook." I knew instantly I had the title for the following story, so I asked permission from Michael to use part of the line, which he very kindly gave me. Later, in his scrupulous attention to details and permissions, Jim Turner wrote to Michael. They struck up a friendship, and Jim bought two collections and a novel from Michael.

Jim Turner was a remarkable man, a conscientious editor, a fine raconteur, prickly and contentious on the surface and loving underneath. I will miss him.

THE WIND FROM A BURNING WOMAN
Analog, Ben Bova, 1978

Five years later the glass bubbles were intact, the wires and pipes were taut, and the city—strung across Psyche's surface like a dewy spider's web wrapped around a thrown rock—was still breathtaking. It was also empty. Hexamon investigators had swept out the final dried husks and bones. The asteroid was clean again. The plague was over.

Giani Turco turned her eyes away from the port and looked at the displays. Satisfied by the approach, she ordered a meal and put her work schedule through the processor for tightening and trimming. She had six tanks of air, enough to last her three days. There was no time to spare. The robot guards in orbit around Psyche hadn't been operating for at least a year and wouldn't offer any resistance, but four small pursuit bugs had been planted in the bubbles. They turned themselves off whenever possible, but her presence would activate them. Time spent in avoiding and finally destroying them: one hour forty minutes, the processor said. The final schedule was projected in front of her by a pen hooked around her ear. She happened to be staring at Psyche when the readout began; the effect—red numerals and letters over gray rock and black space—was pleasingly graphic, like a film in training.

Turco had dropped out of training six weeks early. She had no need for a final certificate, approval from the Hexamon, or any other nicety. Her craft was stolen from Earth orbit, her papers and cards forged, and her intentions entirely opposed to those of the sixteen corporeal desks. On Earth, some hours hence, she would be hated and reviled.

The impulse to sneer was strong—pure theatrics, since she was alone—but she didn't allow it to break her concentration. (Worse than sheep, the cowardly citizens who tacitly supported the forces that had driven her father to suicide and murdered her grandfather; the seekers-after-security who lived by technology but believed in the just influences: Star, Logos, Fate, and Pneuma . . .)

To calm her nerves, she sang a short song while she selected her landing site.

The ship, a small orbital tug, touched the asteroid like a mote settling on a boulder and made itself fast. She stuck her arms and legs into the suit receptacles, and the limb covers automatically hooked themselves to the thorax. The cabin was too cramped to get into a suit any other way. She reached up and brought down the helmet, pushed until all the semifluid seals seized and beeped, and began the evacuation of the cabin's atmosphere. Then the cabin parted down the middle, and she floated slowly, fell more slowly still, to Psyche's surface.

She turned once to watch the cabin clamp together and to see if the propulsion rods behind the tanks had been damaged by the unusually long journey. They'd held up well.

She took hold of a guidewire after a flight of twenty or twenty-five meters and pulled for the nearest glass bubble. Five years before, the milky spheres had been filled with the families of workers setting the charges that would form Psyche's seven internal chambers. Holes had been bored from the Vlasseg and Janacki poles, on the narrow ends of the huge rock, through the center. After the formation of the chambers, materials necessary for atmosphere would have been pumped into Psyche through the bore holes while motors increased her natural spin to create artificial gravity inside.

In twenty years, Psyche's seven chambers would have been green and beautiful, filled with hope—and passengers. But now the control bubble hatches had been sealed by the last of the investigators. Since Psyche was not easily accessible, even in its lunar orbit, the seals hadn't been applied carefully. Nevertheless it took her an hour to break in. The glass ball towered above her, a hundred feet in diameter, translucent walls mottled by the shadows of rooms and equipment. Psyche rotated once every three hours, and light from the sun was beginning to flush the top of the bubbles in the local cluster. Moonlight illuminated the shadows. She pushed the rubbery cement seals away, watching them float lazily to the pocked ground. Then she examined the airlock to see if it was still functioning. She wanted to keep the atmosphere inside the bubble, to check it for psychotropic chemicals; she would not leave her suit at any rate.

The locked door opened with a few jerks and closed behind her. She brushed crystals of frost off her faceplate and the inner lock door's port. Then she pushed the button for the inner door, but nothing happened. The external doors were on a different power supply, which was no longer functioning—or, she hoped, had only been turned off.

From her backpack she removed a half-meter pry bar. The break in took another fifteen minutes. She was now five minutes ahead of schedule.

ACROSS THE VALLEY, THE FUSION POWER PLANTS THAT SUPPLIED POWER TO the Geshel populations of Tijuana and Chula Vista sat like squat mountains of concrete. By Naderite law, all nuclear facilities were enclosed by multiple domes and pyramids, whether they posed any danger or not. The symbolism was two-fold—it showed the distaste of the ruling Naderites for energy sources that were not nature-kinetic, and it carried on the separation of Naderites-Geshels. Farmer Kollert, adviser to the North American Hexamon and ecumentalist to the California corporeal desk, watched the sun set behind the false peak and wondered vaguely if there was any symbolism in the act. Was not fusion the source of power for the sun? He smiled. Such things seldom occurred to him; perhaps it would amuse a Geshel technician.

His team of five Geshel scientists would tour the plants two days from now and make their report to him. He would then pass on *his* report to the desk, acting as interface for the invariably clumsy, elitist language the Geshel scientists used. In this way, through the medium of advisers across the globe, the Naderites oversaw the production of Geshel power. By their grants and control of capital, his people had once plucked the world from technological overkill, and the battle was ongoing still—a war against some of mankind's darker tendencies.

He finished his evening juice and took a package of writing utensils from the drawer in the veranda desk. The reports from last month's energy consumption balancing needed to be edited and revised, based on new estimates—and he enjoyed doing the work himself rather than giving it to the library computer persona. It relaxed him to do things by hand. He wrote on a positive feedback slate, his scrawly letters adjusting automatically into script, with his tongue between his lips and a pleased frown creasing his brow.

"Excuse me, Farmer." His ur-wife, Gestina, stood by the French doors leading to the veranda. She was as slender as when he had married her, despite fifteen years and two children.

"Yes, cara, what is it?" He withdrew his tongue and told the slate to store what he'd written.

"Josef Krupkin."

Kollert stood up quickly, knocking the metal chair over. He hurried past his wife into the dining room, dropped his bulk into a chair, and drew up the crystalline cube on the alabaster tabletop. The cube adjusted its picture to meet the angle of his eyes and Krupkin appeared.

"Josef! This is unexpected."

"Very," Krupkin said. He was a small man with narrow eyes and curly black hair. Compared to Kollert's bulk, he was dapper—but thirty years behind a desk had given him the usual physique of a Hexamon backroomer. "Have you ever heard of Giani Turco?"

Kollert thought for a moment. "No, I haven't. Wait—Turco. Related to Kimon Turco?"

"Daughter. California should keep better track of its radical Geshels, shouldn't it?"

"Kimon Turco lived on the Moon."

"His daughter lived in your district."

"Yes, fine. What about her?" Kollert was beginning to be perturbed. Krupkin enjoyed roundabouts even in important situations and to call him at this address, at such a time, something important had happened.

"She's calling for you. She'll only talk to you, none of the rest. She won't even accept President Praetori."

"Yes. Who is she? What has she done?"

"She's managed to start up Psyche. There was enough reaction mass left in the Beckmann motors to alter it into an Earth-intersect orbit." The left side of the cube was flashing bright red, indicating the call was being scrambled.

Kollert sat very still for a few seconds. There was no need acting incredulous. Krupkin was in no position to joke. But the enormity of what he said—and the impulse to disbelieve, despite the bearer of the news—froze Kollert for an unusually long time. He ran his hand through lank blond hair.

"Kollert," Krupkin said. "You look like you've been—"

"Is she telling the truth?"

Krupkin shook his head. "No, Kollert, you don't understand. She hasn't claimed these accomplishments. She hasn't said anything about them yet. She just wants to speak to you. But our tracking stations say there's no doubt. I've spoken with the officer who commanded the last inspection. He says there was enough mass left in the Beckmann drive positioning motors to push—"

"This is incredible! No precautions were taken? The mass wasn't drained, or something?"

"I'm no Geshel, Farmer. My technicians tell me the mass was left on Psyche because it would have cost several hundred million—"

"That's behind us now. Let the journalists worry about that, if they ever hear of it." He looked up and saw Gestina still standing near the French doors. He held up his hand to tell her to stay where she was. She was going to have to keep to the house, incommunicado, for as long as it took to straighten this out.

"You're coming?"

"Which center?"

"Does it matter? She's not being discreet. Her message is hitting an entire hemisphere, and there are hundreds of listening stations to pick it up. Several aren't under our control. Once anyone pinpoints the source, the story is going to be clear. For your convenience, go to Baja Station. Mexico is signatory to all the necessary pacts."

"I'm leaving now," Kollert said. Krupkin nodded, and the cube went blank.

"What was he talking about?" Gestina asked. "What's *Psyche?*"

"A chunk of rock, dear," he said. Her talents lay in other directions—she wasn't stupid. Even for a Naderite, however, she was unknowledgeable about things beyond the Earth.

He started to plan the rules for her movements, then thought better of it and said nothing. If Krupkin was correct—and he would be—there was no need. The political considerations, if everything turned out right, would be enormous. He could run as Governor of the Desk, even President of the Hexamon . . .

And if everything didn't turn out right, it wouldn't matter where anybody was.

TURCO SAT IN THE MIDDLE OF HER GRANDFATHER'S CONTROL CENTER and cried. She was tired and sick at heart. Things were moving rapidly now, and she wondered just how sane she was. In a few hours she would be the worst menace the Earth had ever known, and for what cause? Truth, justice? They had murdered her grandfather, discredited her father and driven him to suicide—but all seven billion of them, Geshels and Naderites alike?

She didn't know whether she was bluffing or not. Psyche's fall was still controllable, and she was bargaining it would never hit the Earth. Even if she lost and everything was hopeless, she might divert it, causing a few tidal disruptions, minor earthquakes perhaps, but still passing over four thousand kilometers from the Earth's surface. There was enough reaction mass in the positioning motors to allow a broad margin of safety.

Resting lightly on the table in front of her was a chart that showed the basic plan of the asteroid. The positioning motors surrounded a crater at one end of the egg-shaped chunk of nickel-iron and rock. Catapults loaded with huge barrels of reaction mass had just a few hours earlier launched a salvo to rendezvous above the crater's center. Beckmann drive beams had then surrounded the mass with a halo of energy, releasing its atoms from the bonds of nature's weak force. The blast had bounced off the crater floor, directed by the geometric patterns of heat-resistant slag. At the opposite end, a smaller guidance engine was in position, but it was no longer functional and didn't figure in her plans. The two tunnels that reached from the poles to the center of Psyche opened into seven blast chambers, each containing a fusion charge. She hadn't checked to see if the charges were still armed. There were so many things to do.

She sat with her head bowed, still suited up. Though the bubbles contained enough atmosphere to support her, she had no intention of unsuiting. In one gloved hand she clutched a small ampule with a nozzle for attachment to air and water systems piping. The Hexamon Nexus's trumped-up excuse of madness caused by near-weightless conditions was now a shattered, horrible lie. Turco didn't know why, but the Psyche project had been deliberately sabotaged, and the psychotropic drugs still lingered.

Her grandfather hadn't gone mad contemplating the stars. The asteroid crew hadn't mutinied out of misguided Geshel zeal and space sickness.

Her anger rose again, and the tears stopped. "You deserve whoever governs you," she said quietly. "Everyone is responsible for the actions of their leaders."

The computer display cross-haired the point of impact. It was ironic—the buildings of the Hexamon Nexus were only sixty kilometers from the zero point. She had no control over such niceties, but nature and fate seemed to be as angry as she was.

"MOVING AN ASTEROID IS LIKE CARVING A DIAMOND," THE GESHEL ADVISER said. Kollert nodded his head, not very interested. "The charges for initial orbit change—moving it out of the asteroid belt—have to be placed very carefully or the mass will break up and be useless. When the asteroid is close enough to the Earth-Moon system to meet the major crew vessels, the work has only begun. Positioning motors have to be built—"

"Madness," Kollert's secretary said, not pausing from his monitoring of communications between associate committees.

"And charge tunnels drilled. All of this was completed on the asteroid ten years ago."

"Are the charges still in place?" Kollert asked.

"So far as I know," the Geshel said.

"Can they be set off now?"

"I don't know. Whoever oversaw dismantling should have disarmed to protect his crew—but then, the reaction mass should have been jettisoned, too. So who can say? The report hasn't cleared top secrecy yet."

And not likely to, either, Kollert thought. "If they haven't been disarmed, can they be set off now? What would happen if they were?"

"Each charge has a complex communications system. They were designed to be set off by coded signals and could probably be set off now, yes, if we had the codes. Of course, those are top secret, too."

"What would happen?" Kollert was becoming impatient with the Geshel.

"I don't think the charges were ever given a final adjustment. It all depends on how well the initial alignment was performed. If they're out of true, or the final geological studies weren't taken into account, they could blow Psyche to pieces. If they are true, they'll do what they were intended to do—form chambers inside the rock. Each chamber would be about fifteen kilometers long, ten kilometers in diameter—"

"If the asteroid were blown apart, how would that affect our situation?"

"Instead of having one mass hit, we'd have a cloud, with debris twenty to thirty kilometers across and smaller."

"Would that be any better?" Kollert asked.

"Sir?"

"Would it be better to be hit by such a cloud than one chunk?"

"I don't think so. The difference is pretty moot—either way, the surface of the Earth would be radically altered, and few life forms would survive."

Kollert turned to his secretary. "Tell them to put a transmission through to Giani Turco."

The communications were arranged. In the meantime Kollert tried to make some sense out of the Geshel adviser's figures. He was very good at mathematics, but in the past sixty years many physics and chemistry symbols had diverged from those used in biology and psychology. To Kollert, the Geshel mathematics was irritatingly dense and obtuse.

He put the paper aside when Turco appeared on the cube in front of him. A few background beeps and noise were eliminated, and her image cleared. "Ser Turco," he said.

"Ser Farmer Kollert," she replied several seconds later. A beep signaled the end of one side's transmission. She sounded tired.

"You're doing a very foolish thing."

"I have a list of demands," she said.

Kollert laughed. "You sound like the Good Man himself, Ser Turco. The tactic of direct confrontation. Well, it didn't work all the time, even for him."

"I want the public—Geshels and Naderites both—to know why the Psyche project was sabotaged."

"It was not sabotaged," Kollert said calmly. "It was unfortunate proof that humans cannot live in conditions so far removed from the Earth."

"Ask those on the Moon!" Turco said bitterly.

"The Moon has a much stronger gravitational pull than Psyche. But

I'm not briefed to discuss all the reasons why the Psyche project failed."

"I have found psychotropic drugs—traces of drugs and containers in the air and water the crew breathed and drank. That's why I'm maintaining my suit integrity."

"No such traces were found by our investigating teams. But, Ser Turco, neither of us is here to discuss something long past. Speak your demands—your price—and we'll begin negotiations." Kollert knew he was walking a loose rope. Several Hexamon terrorist team officers were listening to everything he said, waiting to splice in a timely splash of static. Conversely, there was no way to stop Turco's words from reaching open stations on the Earth. He was sweating heavily under his arms. Stations on the Moon—the bastards there would probably be sympathetic to her—could pick up his messages and relay them back to the Earth. A drop of perspiration trickled from armpit to sleeve, and he shivered involuntarily.

"That's my only demand," Turco said. "No money, not even amnesty. I want nothing for myself. I simply want the people to know the truth."

"Ser Turco, you have an ideal platform to tell them all you want them to hear."

"The Hexamons control most major reception centers. Everything else—except for a few ham and radio-astronomy amateurs—is cabled and controlled. To reach the most people, the Hexamon Nexus will have to reveal its part in the matter."

Before speaking to her again, Kollert asked if there was any way she could be fooled into believing her requests were being carried out. The answer was ambiguous—a few hundred people were thinking it over.

"I've conferred with my staff, Ser Turco, and I can assure you, so far as the most privy of us can tell, nothing so villainous was ever done to the Psyche project." At a later time, his script suggested, he might indicate that some tests had been overlooked, and that a junior officer had suggested lunar sabotage on Psyche. That might shift the heat. But for the moment, any admission that drugs existed in the asteroid's human environments could backfire.

"I'm not arguing," she said. "There's no question that the Hexamon Nexus had somebody sabotage Psyche."

Kollert held his tongue between his lips and punched key words into his script processor. The desired statements formed over Turco's image. He looked at the camera earnestly. "If we had done anything so heinous, surely we would have protected ourselves against an eventuality like this—drained the reaction mass in the positioning motors—" One of the terrorist team officers was waving at him frantically and scowling. The screen's words showed red where they were being covered by static. There was to be no mention of how Turco had gained control of Psyche.

The issue was too sensitive, and blame hadn't been placed yet. Besides, there was still the option of informing the public that Turco had never gained control of Psyche at all. If everything worked out, the issue would have been solved without costly admissions.

"Excuse me," Turco said a few seconds later. The time lag between communications was wearing on her nerves, if Kollert was any judge. "Something was lost there."

"Ser Turco, your grandfather's death on Psyche was accidental, and your actions now are ridiculous. Destroying the Hexamon Nexus"— much better than saying *Earth*—"won't mean a thing." He leaned back in the seat, chewing on the edge of his index finger. The gesture had been approved an hour before the talks began, but it was nearly genuine. His usual elegance of speech seemed to be wearing thin in this encounter. He'd already made several embarrassing misjudgments.

"I'm not doing this for logical reasons," Turco finally said. "I'm doing it out of hatred for you and all the people who support you. What happened on Psyche was purely evil—useless, motivated by the worst intentions, resulting in the death of a beautiful dream, not to mention people I loved. No talk can change my mind about those things."

"Then why talk to me at all? I'm hardly the highest official in the Nexus."

"No, but you're in an ideal position to know who the higher officials involved were. You're a respected politician. And I suspect you had a great deal to do with suggesting the plot. I just want the truth. I'm tired. I'm going to rest for a few hours now."

"Wait a moment," Kollert said sharply. "We haven't discussed the most important things yet."

"I'm signing off. Until later."

The team leader made a cutting motion across his throat that almost made Kollert choke. The young bastard's indiscreet symbol was positively obscene in the current situation. Kollert shook his head and held his fingertips to his temples. "We didn't even have time to begin," he said.

The team leader stood and stretched his arms.

"You're doing quite well so far, Ser Kollert," he said. "It's best to ease into these things."

"I'm Adviser Kollert to you, and I don't see how we have much time to take it easy."

"Yes, sir. Sorry."

SHE NEEDED THE REST, BUT THERE WAS FAR TOO MUCH TO DO. SHE PUSHED off from the seat and floated gently for a few moments before drifting down. The relaxation of weightlessness would have been welcome, and

Psyche's pull was very weak, but just enough to remind her there was no time for rest.

One of the things she had hoped she could do—checking the charges deep inside the asteroid to see if they were armed—was impossible. The main computer and the systems board indicated the transport system through the bore holes was no longer operative. It would take her days to crawl or float the distance down the shafts, and she wasn't about to take the small tug through a tunnel barely fifty meters wide. She wasn't that well-trained a pilot.

So she had a weak spot. The bombs couldn't be disarmed from where she was. They could be set off by a ship positioned along the axis of the tunnels, but so far none had shown up. That would take another twelve hours or so, and by then time would be running out. She hoped that all negotiations would be completed.

The woman desperately wanted out of the suit. The catheters and cups were itching fiercely; she felt like a ball of tacky glue wrapped in wool. Her eyes were stinging from strain and sweat buildup on the lids. If she had a moment of irritation when something crucial was happening, she could be in trouble. One way or another, she had to clean up a bit—and there was no way to do that unless she risked exposure to the residue of drugs. She stood unsteadily for several minutes, vacillating, and finally groaned, slapping her thigh with a gloved palm. "I'm *tired*," she said. "Not thinking straight."

She looked at the computer. There was a solution, but she couldn't see it clearly. "Come on, girl. So simple. But what?"

The drug would probably have a limited life, in case the Nexus wanted to do something with Psyche later. But how limited? Ten years? She chuckled grimly. She had the ampule and its cryptic chemical label. Would a Physician's Desk Reference be programmed into the computers?

She hooked herself into the console again. "PDR," she said. The screen was blank for a few seconds. Then it said, "Ready."

"Iropentaphonate," she said. "Two-seven diboltene."

The screen printed out the relevant data. She searched through the technical maze for a full minute before finding what she wanted. "Effective shelf life, four months two days from date of manufacture."

She tested the air again—it was stale but breathable—and unhooked her helmet. It was worth any risk. A bare knuckle against her eye felt so good.

The small lounge in the Baja Station was well-furnished and comfortable, but suited more for Geshels than Naderites—bright rather than natural colors, abstract paintings of a mechanistic tendency, modernist furniture. To Kollert it was faintly oppressive. The man sitting across from him had been silent for the past five minutes, reading through a sheaf of papers.

"Who authorized this?" the man asked.

"Hexamon Nexus, Mr. President."

"But who proposed it?"

Kollert hesitated. "The advisory committee."

"Who proposed it to the committee?"

"I did."

"Under what authority?"

"It was strictly legal," Kollert said defensively. "Such activities have been covered under the emergency code, classified section fourteen."

The president nodded. "She came to the right man when she asked for you, then. I wonder where she got her information. None of this can be broadcast—why was it done?"

"There were a number of reasons, among them financial—"

"The project was mostly financed by lunar agencies. Earth had perhaps a five percent share, so no controlling interest—and there was no connection with radical Geshel groups, therefore no need to invoke section fourteen on revolutionary deterrence. I read the codes, too, Farmer."

"Yes, sir."

"What were you afraid of? Some irrational desire to pin the butterflies down? Jesus God, Farmer, the Naderite beliefs don't allow anything like this. But you and your committee took it upon yourselves to covertly destroy the biggest project in the history of mankind. You think this follows in the tracks of the Good Man?"

"You're aware of lunar plans to build particle guidance guns. They're canceled now because Psyche is dead. They were to be used to push asteroids like Psyche into deep space, so advanced Beckmann drives could be used."

"I'm not technically minded, Farmer."

"Nor am I. But such particle guns could have been used as weapons—considering lunar sympathies, probably would have been used. They could cook whole cities on Earth. The development of potential weapons *is* a matter of concern for Naderites, sir. And there are many studies showing that human behavior changes in space. It becomes less Earth-centered, less communal. Man can't live in space and remain human. We were trying to preserve humanity's right to a secure future. Even now the Moon is a potent political force, and war has been suggested by our strategists . . . it's a dire possibility. All this because of the separation of a group of humans from the parent body, from wise government and safe creed."

The president shook his head and looked away. "I am ashamed such a thing could happen in my government Very well, Kollert, this remains your ball game until she asks to speak to someone else. But my advisers are going to go over everything you say. I doubt you'll have the chance to botch anything. We're already acting with the Moon to stop this before it gets any worse. And you can thank God—for your life, not your career, which is already dead—that our Geshels have come up with a way out."

Kollert was outwardly submissive, but inside he was fuming. Not even the President of the Hexamon had the right to treat him like a child or, worse, a criminal. He was an independent adviser, of a separate desk, elected by Naderites of high standing. The ecumentalist creed was apparently much tighter than the president's. "I acted in the best interests of my constituency," he said.

"You no longer have a constituency, you no longer have a career. Nor do any of the people who planned this operation with you, or those who carried it out. Up and down the line. A purge."

Turco woke up before the blinking light and moved her lips in a silent curse. How long had she been asleep? She panicked briefly—a dozen hours would be crucial—but then saw the digital clock. Two hours. The light was demanding her attention to an incoming radio signal.

There was no video image. Kollert's voice returned, less certain, almost cowed. "I'm here," she said, switching off her camera as well. The delay was a fraction shorter than when they'd first started talking.

"Have you made any decisions?" Kollert asked.

"I should be asking that question. My course is fixed. When are you and your people going to admit to sabotage?"

"We'd—I'd almost be willing to admit, just to—" He stopped. She was about to speak when he continued. "We could do that, you know. Broadcast a worldwide admission of guilt. A cheap price to pay for saving all life on Earth. Do you really understand what you're up to? What satisfaction, what revenge, could you possibly get out of this? My God, Turco, you—" There was a burst of static. It sounded suspiciously like the burst she had heard some time ago.

"You're editing him," she said. Her voice was level and calm. "I don't want anyone editing anything between us, whoever you are. Is that understood? One more burst of static like that, and I'll . . ." She had already threatened the ultimate. "I'll be less tractable. Remember—I'm already a fanatic. Want me to be a hardened fanatic? Repeat what you were saying, Ser Kollert."

The digital readout indicated one-way delay time of 1.496 seconds. She would soon be closer to the Earth than the Moon was.

"I was saying," Kollert repeated, something like triumph in his tone, "that you are a very young woman, with very young ideas—like a child leveling a loaded pistol at her parents. You may not be a fanatic. But you aren't seeing things clearly. We have no evidence here on Earth that you've found anything, and we won't have evidence—nothing will be solved—if the asteroid collides with us. That's obvious. But if it veers aside, goes into an Earth orbit perhaps, then an—"

"That's not one of my options," Turco said.

"—investigating team could reexamine the crew quarters," Kollert continued, not to be interrupted for a few seconds, "do a more detailed search. Your charges could be verified."

"I can't go into Earth orbit without turning around, and this is a one-way rock, remember that. My only other option is to swing around the Earth, be deflected a couple of degrees, and go into a solar orbit. By the time any investigating team reached me, I'd be on the other side of the sun, and dead. I'm the daughter of a Geshel, Ser Kollert—don't forget that. I have a good technical education, and my training under Hexamon auspices makes me a competent pilot and spacefarer. Too bad there's so little long-range work for my type, just Earth-Moon runs. But don't try to fool me or kid me. I'm far more expert than you are. Though I'm sure you have Geshel people on your staff." She paused. "Geshels! I can't call you traitors—you in the background—because you might be thinking I'm crazy, out to destroy all of you. But do you understand what these men have done to our hopes and dreams? I've never seen a finished asteroid starship, of course—Psyche was to have been the first. But I've seen good simulations. It would have been like seven Shangri-las inside, hollowed out of solid rock and metal, seven valleys separated by walls four kilometers high, each self-contained, connected with the others by tube trains. The valley floors reach up to the sky, like magic, everything wonderfully topsy-turvy. And quiet—so much insulation none of the engine sounds reach inside." She was crying again.

"Psyche would consume herself on the way to the stars. By the time she arrived, there'd be little left besides a cylinder thirty kilometers wide, and two hundred ninety long. Like the core of an apple, and the passengers would be luxurious worms—star travelers. Now ask why, why did these men sabotage such a marvelous thing? Because they are blind unto pure evil—blind, ugly-minded, weak men who hate big ideas . . ." She paused. "I don't know what you think of all this, but remember, they took something away from you. I know. I've seen the evidence here. Sabotage and murder." She pressed the button and waited wearily for a reply.

"Ser Turco," Kollert said, "you have ten hours to make an effective course correction. We estimate you have enough reaction mass left to extend your orbit and miss the Earth by about four thousand kilometers. There is nothing we can do here but try to convince you—"

She stopped listening, trying to figure out what was happening behind the scenes. Earth wouldn't take such a threat without exploring a large number of alternatives. Kollert's voice droned on as she tried to think of the most likely action, and the most effective.

She picked up her helmet and placed a short message, paying no attention to the transmission from Earth. "I'm going outside for a few minutes."

THE ACCELERATION HAD BEEN STEADY FOR TWO HOURS, BUT NOW THE weightlessness was just as oppressive. The large cargo handler was fully loaded with extra fuel and a bulk William Porter was reluctant to think about. With the ship turned around for course correction, he could see the Moon glowing with Earthshine, and a bright crescent so thin it was almost a hair.

He had about half an hour to relax before the real work began, and he was using it to read an excerpt from a novel by Anthony Burgess. He'd been a heavy reader all his memorable life, and now he allowed himself a possible last taste of pleasure.

Like most inhabitants of the Moon, Porter was a Geshel, with a physicist father and a geneticist mother. He'd chosen a career as a pilot rather than a researcher out of romantic predilections established long before he was ten years old. There was something immediately effective and satisfying about piloting, and he'd turned out to be well suited to the work. He'd never expected to take on a mission like this. But then, he'd never paid much attention to politics, either. Even if he had, the disputes between Geshels and Naderites would have been hard to spot—they'd been settled, most experts believed, fifty years before, with the Naderites emerging as a ruling class. Outside of grumbling at restrictions, few Geshels complained. Responsibility had been lifted from their shoulders. Most of the population of both Earth and Moon was now involved in technical and scientific work, yet the mistakes they made would be blamed on Naderite policies—and the disasters would likewise be absorbed by the leadership. It wasn't a hard situation to get used to.

William Porter wasn't so sure, now, that it was the ideal. He had two options to save Earth, and one of them meant he would die.

He'd listened to the Psyche-Earth transmissions during acceleration, trying to make sense out of Turco's position, to form an opinion of her character and sanity, but he was more confused than ever. If she was right—and not a raving lunatic, which didn't seem to fit the facts—then the Hexamon Nexus had a lot of explaining to do and probably wouldn't do it under the gun. The size of Turco's gun was far too imposing to be rational—the destruction of the human race, the wiping of a planet's surface.

He played back the computer diagram of what would happen if Psyche hit the Earth. At the angle it would strike, it would speed the rotation of the Earth's crust and mantle by an appreciable fraction. The asteroid would cut a gouge from Maine to England, several thousand kilometers long and at least a hundred kilometers deep. The impact would vault hundreds of millions of tons of surface material into space, and that would partially counteract the speedup of rotation. The effect would be a monumental jerk, with the energy finally being released as heat. The continents would fracture in several directions, forming new faults, even new plate orientations, which would generate earthquakes on a scale never before seen. The impact basin would be a hell of molten crust and mantle, with water on the perimeter bursting violently into steam, altering weather patterns around the world. It would take decades to cool and achieve some sort of stability.

Turco may not have been raving, but she was coldly suggesting a cataclysm to swat what amounted to a historical fly. That made her a lunatic in anyone's book, Geshel or Naderite. And his life was well worth the effort to thwart her.

That didn't stop him from being angry, though.

KOLLERT IMPATIENTLY LET THE PHYSICIAN CHECK HIM OVER AND ADMINISTER a few injections. He talked to his wife briefly, which left him more nervous than before, then listened to the team leader's theories on how Turco's behavior would change in the next few hours. He nodded at only one statement: "She's going to see she'll be dead, too, and that's a major shock for even the most die-hard terrorist."

Then Turco was back on the air, and he was on stage again.

"I've seen your ship," she said. "I went outside and looked around in the direction where I thought it would be. There it was—treachery all around. Goddamned hypocrites! Talk friendly to the little girl, but shiv her in the back! Public face cool, private face snarl! Well, just remember, before he can kill me, I can destroy all controls to the positioning engines. It would take a week to rewire them. You don't have the time!" The beep followed.

"Giani, we have only one option left, and that's to do as you say. We'll admit we played a part in the sabotage of Psyche. It's confession under pressure, but we'll do it." Kollert pressed his button and waited, holding his full chin with one hand.

"No way it's so simple, Kollert. No public admission and then public denial after the danger is over—you'd all come across as heroes. No.

There has to be some record-keeping, payrolls if nothing else. I want full disclosure of all records, and I want them transmitted around the world—facsimile, authenticated. I want uninvolved government officials to see them and sign that they've seen them. And I want the actual documents put on display where anyone can look at them—memos, plans, letters, whatever. All of it that's still available."

"That would take weeks," Kollert said, "if they existed."

"Not in this age of electronic wizardry. I want you to take a lie detector test, authenticated by half a dozen experts with their careers on the line—and while you're at it, have the other officials take tests, too."

"That's not only impractical, it won't hold up in a court of law."

"I'm not interested in formal courts. I'm not a vengeful person, no matter what I may seem now. I just want the truth. And if I still see that goddamn ship up there in an hour, I'm going to stop negotiations right now and blow myself to pieces."

Kollert looked at the team leader, but the man's face was blank.

"LET ME TALK TO HER, THEN," PORTER SUGGESTED. "DIRECT PERSON-TO-person. Let me explain the plans. She really can't change them any, can she? She has no way of making them worse. If she fires her engines or does any positive action, she simply stops the threat. So I'm the one who holds the key to the situation."

"We're not sure that's advisable, Bill," Lunar Guidance said.

"I can transmit to her without permission, you know," he said testily.

"Against direct orders, that's not like you."

"Like me, hell," he said, chuckling. "Listen, just get me permission. Nobody else seems to be doing anything effective." There was a few minutes' silence, then Lunar Guidance returned.

"Okay, Bill. You have permission. But be very careful what you say. Terrorist team officers on Earth think she's close to the pit."

With that obstacle cleared away, he wondered how wise the idea was in the first place. Still, they were both Geshels—they had something in common compared to the elite Naderites running things on Earth.

Far away, Earth concurred and transmissions were cleared. They couldn't censor his direct signal, so Baja Station was unwillingly cut from the circuit.

"Who's talking to me now?" Turco asked when the link was made.

"This is Lieutenant William Porter, from the Moon. I'm a pilot—not a defense pilot usually, either. I understand you've had pilot's training."

"Just enough to get by." The lag was less than a hundredth of a second, not noticeable.

"You know I'm up here to stop you, one way or another. I've got two options. The one I think more highly of is to get in line-of-sight of your bore holes and relay the proper coded signals to the charges in your interior."

"Killing me won't do you any good."

"That's not the plan. The fore end of your rock is bored with a smaller hole by thirty meters. It'll release the blast wastes more slowly than the aft end. The total explosive force should give the rock enough added velocity to get it clear of the Earth by at least sixty kilometers. The damage would be negligible. Spectacular view from Greenland, too, I understand. But if we've miscalculated, or if one or more charges doesn't go, then I'll have to impact with your aft crater and release the charge in my cargo hold. I'm one floating megaboom now, enough to boost the rock up and out by a few additional kilometers. But that means I'll be dead, and not enough left of me to memorialize or pin a medal on. Not too good, hm?"

"None of my sweat."

"No, I suppose not. But listen, sister—"

"No sister to a lackey."

Porter started to snap a retort, but stopped himself. "Listen, they tell me to be soft on you, but I'm under pressure, too, so please reciprocate. I don't see the sense in all of it. If you get your way, you've set back your cause by God knows how many decades—because once you're out of range and blown your trump, they'll deny it all, say it was manufactured evidence and testimony under pressure—all that sort of thing. And if they decide to hard-line it, force me to do my dirty work, or God forbid let you do yours—we've lost our homeworld. You've lost Psyche, which can still be salvaged and finished. Everything will be lost, just because a few men may or may not have done a very wicked thing. Come on, honey. That isn't the Geshel creed, and you know it."

"What is our creed? To let men rule our lives who aren't competent to read a thermometer? Under the Naderites, most of the leaders on Earth haven't got the technical expertise to . . . to . . . I don't know what. To tie their goddamn shoes! They're blind, dedicated to some half-wit belief that progress is the most dangerous thing conceived by man. But they can't live without technology so we provide it for them. And when they won't touch our filthy nuclear energy, we get stuck with it—because otherwise we all have to go back four hundred years, and sacrifice half the population. Is that good planning, sound policy? And if they do what I say, Psyche won't be damaged. All they'll have to do is fetch it back from orbit around the sun."

"I'm not going to argue on their behalf, sister. I'm a Geshel, too, and a Moonman besides. I never have paid attention to Earth politics because it never made much sense to me. But now I'm talking to you one-to-one, and you're telling me that avenging someone's irrational system is worth wiping away a planet?"

"I'm willing to take that risk."

"I don't think you are. I hope you aren't. I hope it's all bluff, and I won't have to smear myself against your backside."

"I hope you won't, either. I hope they've got enough sense down there to do what I want."

"I don't think they have, sister. I don't put much faith in them, myself. They probably don't even know what would happen if you hit the Earth with your rock. Think about that. You're talking about scientific innocents—flat-Earthers almost, naive. Words fail me. But think on it. They may not even know what's going on."

"They know. And remind them that if they set off the charges, it'll probably break up Psyche and give them a thousand rocks to contend with instead of one. That plan may backfire on them."

"What if they—we—don't have any choice?"

"I don't give a damn what choice you have," Turco said. "I'm not talking for a while. I've got more work to do."

Porter listened to the final click with a sinking feeling. She was a tough one. How would he outwit her? He smiled grimly at his chutzpah for even thinking he could. She'd committed herself all the way—and now, perhaps, she was feeling the power of her position. One lonely woman, holding the key to a world's existence. He wondered how it felt.

Then he shivered, and the sweat in his suit felt very, very cold. If he would have a grave for someone to walk over . . .

FOR THE FIRST TIME, SHE REALIZED THEY WOULDN'T ACCEDE TO HER DEMANDS. They were more traitorous than even she could have imagined. Or— the thought was too horrible to accept—she'd misinterpreted the evidence, and they weren't at fault. Perhaps a madman in the Psyche crew had sought revenge and caused the whole mess. But that didn't fit the facts. It would have taken at least a dozen people to set all the psychotropic vials and release them at once—a concerted preplanned effort. She shook her head. Besides, she had the confidential reports a friend had accidentally plugged into while troubleshooting a Hexamon computer plex. There was no doubt about who was responsible, just uncertainty about the exact procedure. Her evidence for Farmer Kollert's guilt was circumstantial but not baseless.

She sealed her suit and helmet and went outside the bubble again, just to watch the stars for a few minutes. The lead—gray rock under her feet was pitted by eons of micrometeoroids. Rills several kilometers across attested to the rolling impacts of other asteroids, any one of which would have caused a major disaster on Earth. Earth had been hit before, not often by pieces as big as Psyche, but several times at least, and had survived. Earth would survive Psyche's impact, and life would start anew. Those plants and animals—even humans that survived would eventually build back to the present level, and perhaps it would be a better world, more daunted by the power of past evil. She might be a force for positive regeneration.

The string of bubbles across Psyche's surface was serenely lovely in the starlight. The illumination brightened slowly as Earth rose above the Vlasseg pole, larger now than the Moon. She had a few more hours to make the optimum correction. Just above the Earth was a tiny moving point of light—Porter in his cargo vessel. He was lining up with the smaller bore hole to send signals, if he had to.

Again she wanted to cry. She felt like a little child, full of hatred and frustration, but caught now in something so immense and inexorable that all passion was dwarfed. She couldn't believe she was the controlling factor, that she held so much power. Surely something was behind her, some impersonal, objective force. Alone she was nothing, and her crime would be unbelievable—just as Porter had said. But with a cosmic justification, the agreeing nod of some vast all-seeing God, she was just a tool, bereft of responsibility.

She grasped the guide wires strung between the bubbles and pulled herself back to the airlock hatch. With one gloved hand she pressed the button. Under her palm she felt the metal vibrate for a second, then stop. The hatch was still closed. She pressed again and nothing happened.

PORTER LISTENED CAREFULLY FOR A FULL MINUTE, TRYING TO PICK UP THE weak signal. It had cut off abruptly a few minutes before, during his final lineup with the bore hole through the Vlasseg pole. He called his director and asked if any signals had been received from Turco. Since he was out of line-of-sight now, the Moon had to act as a relay.

"Nothing," Lunar Guidance said. "She's been silent for an hour."

"That's not right. We've only got an hour and a half left. She should be playing the situation for all it's worth. Listen, LG, I received a weak signal from Psyche several minutes ago. It could have been a freak, but I don't think so. I'm going to move back to where I picked it up."

"Negative, Porter. You'll need all your reaction mass in case Plan A doesn't go off properly."

"I've got plenty to spare, LG. I have a bad feeling about this. Something's gone wrong on Psyche." It was clear to him the instant he said it. "Jesus Christ, LG, the signal must have come from Turco's area on

Psyche! I lost it just when I passed out of line-of-sight from her bubble."

Lunar Guidance was silent for a long moment. "Okay, Porter, we've got clearance for you to regain that signal."

"Thank you, LG." He pushed the ship out of its rough alignment and coasted slowly away from Psyche until he could see the equatorial ring of domes and bubbles. Abruptly his receiver again picked up the weak signal. He locked his tracking antenna to it, boosted it, and cut in the communications processor to interpolate through the hash.

"This is Turco. William Porter, listen to me! This is Turco. I'm locked out. Something has malfunctioned in the control bubble. I'm locked out . . ."

"I'm getting you, Turco," he said. "Look at my spot above the Vlasseg pole. I'm in line-of-sight again." If her suit was a standard model, her transmissions would strengthen in the direction she was facing.

"God bless you, Porter. I see you. Everything's gone wrong down here. I can't get back in."

"Try again, Turco. Do you have any tools with you?"

"That's what started all this, breaking in with a chisel and a pry bar. It must have weakened something, and now the whole mechanism is frozen. No, I left the bar inside. No tools. Jesus, this is awful."

"Calm down. Keep trying to get in. I'm relaying your signal to Lunar Guidance and Earth." That settled it. There was no time to waste now. If she didn't turn on the positioning motors soon, any miss would be too close for comfort. He had to set off the internal charges within an hour and a half for the best effect.

"She's outside?" Lunar Guidance asked when the transmissions were relayed. "Can't get back in?"

"That's it," Porter said.

"That cocks it, Porter. Ignore her and get back into position. Don't bother lining up with the Vlasseg pole, however. Circle around to the Janacki pole bore hole and line up for code broadcast there. You'll have a better chance of getting the code through, and you can prepare for any further action."

"I'll be cooked, LG."

"Negative—you're to relay code from an additional thousand kilometers and boost yourself out of the path just before detonation. That will occur—let's see—about four point three seconds after the charges receive the code. Program your computer for sequencing; you'll be too busy."

"I'm moving, LG." He returned to Turco's wavelength. "It's out of your hands now," he said. "We're blowing the charges. They may not be enough, so I'm preparing to detonate myself against the Janacki pole crater. Congratulations, Turco."

"I still can't get back in, Porter."

"I said, congratulations. You've killed both of us and ruined Psyche for any future projects. You know that she'll go to pieces when she drops below Roche's limit? Even if she misses, she'll be too close to survive. You know, they might have gotten it all straightened out in a few administrations. Politicos die, or get booted out of office—even Naderites. I say you've cocked it good. Be happy, Turco." He flipped the switch viciously and concentrated on his approach program display.

FARMER KOLLERT WAS SLUMPED IN HIS CHAIR, EYES CLOSED BUT STILL AWAKE, half-listening to the murmurs in the control room. Someone tapped him on the shoulder, and he jerked up in his seat.

"I had to be with you, Farmer." Gestina stood over him, a nervous smile making her dimples obvious. "They brought me here to be with you."

"Why?" he asked.

Her voice shook. "Because our house was destroyed. I got out just in time. What's happening, Farmer? Why do they want to kill me? What did I do?"

The team officer standing beside her held out a piece of paper, and Kollert took it. Violence had broken out in half a dozen Hexamon centers, and numerous officials had had to be evacuated. Geshels weren't the only ones involved—Naderites of all classes seemed to share indignation and rage at what was happening. The outbreaks weren't organized—and that was even more disturbing. Wherever transmissions had reached the unofficial grapevines, people were reacting.

Gestina's large eyes regarded him without comprehension, much less sympathy. "I had to be with you, Farmer," she repeated. "They wouldn't let me stay."

"Quiet, please," another officer said. "More transmissions coming in."

"Yes," Kollert said softly. "Quiet. That's what we wanted. Quiet and peace and sanity. Safety for our children to come."

"I think something big is happening," Gestina said. "What is it?"

PORTER CHECKED THE ALIGNMENT AGAIN, PUT UP HIS VISUAL SHIELDS, AND instructed the processor to broadcast the coded signal. With no distinguishable pause, the ship's engines started to move him out of the path of the particle blast.

Meanwhile Giani Turco worked at the hatch with a bit of metal bracing she had broken off her suitpack. The sharp edge just barely fit into the crevice, and by gouging and prying she had managed to force the door up half a centimeter. The evacuation mechanism hadn't been activated, so frosted air hissed from the crack, making the work doubly difficult. The Moon was rising above the Janacki pole.

Deep below her, seven prebalanced but unchecked charges, mounted on massive fittings in their chambers, began to whir. Four processors checked the timings, concurred, and released safety shields.

Six of the charges went off at once. The seventh was late by ten thousandths of a second, its blast muted as the casing melted prematurely. The particle shock waves streamed out through the bore holes, now pressure release valves, and formed a long neck and tail of flame and ionized particles that grew steadily for a thousand kilometers, then faded. The tail from the Vlasseg pole was thinner and shorter, but no less spectacular. The asteroid shuddered, vibrations rising from deep inside to pull the ground away from Turco's boots, then swing it back to kick her away from the bubble and hatch. She floated in space, disoriented, ripped free of the guidewires, her back to the asteroid, faceplate aimed at peaceful stars, turning slowly as she reached the top of her arc.

Her leisurely descent gave her plenty of time to see the secondary plume of purple and white and red forming around the Janacki pole. The stars were blanked out by its brilliance. She closed her eyes. When she opened them again, she was nearer the ground, and her faceplate had polarized against the sudden brightness. She saw the bubble still intact, and the hatch wide open now. It had been jarred free. Everything was vibrating . . . and with shock she realized the asteroid was slowly moving out from beneath her. Her fall became a drawn-out curve, taking her away from the bubble toward a ridge of lead-gray rock, without guidewires, where she would bounce and continue on unchecked. To her left, one dome ruptured and sent a feathery wipe of debris into space. Pieces of rock and dust floated past her, shaken from Psyche's weak surface grip. Then her hand was only a few meters from a guidewire torn free and swinging outward. It came closer like a dancing snake, hesitated, rippled again, and came within reach. She grabbed it and pulled herself down.

"Porter, this is Lunar Guidance. Earth says the charges weren't enough. Something went wrong."

"She held together, LG," Porter said in disbelief. "She didn't break up. I've got a fireworks show like you've never seen before."

"Porter, listen. She isn't moving fast enough. She'll still impact."

"I heard you, LG," Porter shouted. "I heard! Leave me alone to get things done." Nothing more was said between them.

TURCO REACHED THE HATCH AND CRAWLED INTO THE AIRLOCK, EXHAUSTED. She closed the outer door and waited for equalization before opening the inner. Her helmet was off and floating behind as she walked and bounced and guided herself into the control room. If the motors were still functional, she'd fire them. She had no second thoughts now. Something had gone wrong, and the situation was completely different.

In the middle of the kilometers-wide crater at the Janacki pole, the bore hole was still spewing debris and ionized particles. But around the perimeter, other forces were at work. Canisters of reaction mass were flying to a point three kilometers above the crater floor. The Beckmann drive engines rotated on their mountings, aiming their nodes at the canister's rendezvous point.

Porter's ship was following the tail of debris down to the crater floor. He could make out geometric patterns of insulating material. His computers told him something was approaching a few hundred meters below. There wasn't time for any second guessing. He primed his main cargo and sat back in the seat, lips moving, not in prayer, but repeating some stray, elegant line from the Burgess novel, a final piece of pleasure.

One of the canisters struck the side of the cargo ship just as the blast began. A brilliant flare spread out above the crater, merging with and twisting the tail of the internal charges. Four canisters were knocked from their course and sent plummeting into space. The remaining six met at the assigned point and were hit by beams from the Beckmann drive nodes. Their matter was stripped down to pure energy.

All of this, in its lopsided, incomplete way, bounced against the crater floor and drove the asteroid slightly faster.

When the shaking subsided, Turco let go of a grip bar and asked the computers questions. No answers came back. Everything except minimum life support was out of commission. She thought briefly of returning to her tug, if it was still in position, but there was nowhere to go. So she walked and crawled and floated to a broad view window in the bubble's dining room. Earth was rising over the Vlasseg pole again, filling half her view, knots of storm and streaks of brown continent twisting slowly before her. She wondered if it had been enough—it hadn't felt right. There was no way of knowing for sure, but the Earth looked much too close.

"IT'S TOO CLOSE TO JUDGE," THE PRESIDENT SAID, DELIBERATELY STANDING with his back to Kollert. "She'll pass over Greenland, maybe just hit the upper atmosphere."

The terrorist team officers were packing their valises and talking to each other in subdued whispers. Three of the president's security men looked at the screen with dazed expressions. The screen was blank except for a display of seconds until accession of picture. Gestina was asleep in the chair next to Kollert, her face peaceful, hands wrapped together in her lap.

"We'll have relay pictures from Iceland in a few minutes," the president said. "Should be quite a sight." Kollert frowned. The man was almost cocky, knowing he would come through it untouched. Even with survival uncertain, his government would be preparing explanations. Kollert could predict the story: a band of lunar terrorists, loosely tied with Giani Turco's father and his rabid spacefarers, was responsible for the whole thing. It would mean a few months of ill-feeling on the Moon, but at least the Nexus would have found its scapegoats.

A communicator beeped in the room, and Kollert looked around for its source. One of the security men reached into a pocket and pulled out a small earplug, which he inserted. He listened for a few seconds, frowned, then nodded. The other two gathered close, and they whispered.

Then, quietly, they left the room. The president didn't notice they were gone, but to Kollert their absence spoke volumes.

Six Nexus police entered a minute later. One stood by Kollert's chair, not looking at him. Four waited by the door. Another approached the president and tapped him on the shoulder. The president turned.

"Sir, fourteen desks have requested your impeachment. We're instructed to put you under custody, for your own safety."

Kollert started to rise, but the officer beside him put a hand on his shoulder.

"May we stay to watch?" the president asked. No one objected.

Before the screen was switched on, Kollert asked, "Is anyone going to get Turco, if it misses?"

The terrorist team leader shrugged when no one else answered. "She may not even be alive."

Then, like a crowd of children looking at a horror movie, the men and women in the communications center grouped around the large screen and watched the dark shadow of Psyche blocking out stars.

FROM THE BUBBLE WINDOW, TURCO SAW THE SUDDEN AURORAE, THE SPRAY of ionized gases from the Earth's atmosphere, the awesomely rapid passage of the ocean below, and the blur of white as Greenland flashed past. The structure rocked and jerked as the Earth exerted enormous tidal strains on Psyche.

Sitting in the plastic chair, numb, tightly gripping the arms, Giani looked up—down—at the bright stars, feeling Psyche die beneath her.

Inside, the still-molten hollows formed by the charges began to collapse. Cracks shot outward to the surface, where they became gaping chasms. Sparks and rays of smoke jumped from the chasms. In minutes the passage was over. Looking closely, she saw roiling storms forming over Earth's seas and the spreading shock wave of the asteroid's sudden atmospheric compression. Big winds were blowing, but they'd survive.

It shouldn't have gone this far. They should have listened reasonably, admitted their guilt—

Absolved, girl, she wanted her father to say. She felt him very near. *You've destroyed everything we worked for—a fine architect of Pyrrhic victories.* And now he was at a great distance, receding.

The room was cold, and her skin tingled.

One huge chunk rose to block out the sun. The cabin screamed, and the bubble was filled with sudden flakes of air.

Afterword

Researching this story in 1977 led me back to a science article by J. E. Enever, "Giant Meteor Impact," published in *Analog* in March 1966. J. E. Enever—no biography or credentials are given in the magazine, and he published, as far as I can discover, only a couple of items later—started something really big with this piece. To my knowledge, nobody before the mysterious Mr. Enever had ever written realistically about the effects of a large rocky mass striking the Earth. It's hard to imagine now, but in those years, Catastrophism—the belief that the Earth had ever been subjected to short, sharp shocks—was not in favor in mainstream geology. Most geologists were only beginning to seriously consider the theory of continental drift, espoused by Alfred L. Wegener. It's possible Enever could not have published this article in any respectable science journal.

That left John W. Campbell, Jr., and *Analog.*

Within a few years, Walter Alvarez would begin thinking about giant asteroids and dinosaur extinction . . .

In his 1972 novel, *Rendezvous with Rama,* Arthur C. Clarke (now Sir Arthur) would propose Spaceguard, a security system designed to watch for meteorites and asteroids that could collide with Earth.

Jerry Pournelle and Larry Niven would write the bestselling *Lucifer's Hammer* . . .

Gregory Benford and William Rotsler would write *Shiva Descending.*

Scientists would begin looking for the Big Ones, the impact craters that would provide the evidence for Alvarez's hypothesis. They would find several such craters, and the public imagination would be altered forever. We would watch a calved comet fall into Jupiter's atmosphere, and imagine our own possible fate.

We would feel very mortal.

Decades later, *Deep Impact* and *Armageddon* would compete for big bucks in the movie marketplace. Nearly every documentary on dino-saurs would show them peering up, squinty-eyed, at that bright light descending from the sky . . .

Today, Spaceguard exists, in a rudimentary form. It has been orga-nized by J. R. Tate in the United Kingdom, where it is struggling to procure funding to *keep watching the skies.*

All, possibly, because of J. E. Enever.

Introduction to "The Venging"

I wrote "The Venging" in 1973, while I was working at the Reuben H. Fleet Space Theater in San Diego, California. With this story, I created my first major female character, Anna Sigrid Nestor, and the first episode in a future history that would come to include two novels—*Beyond Heaven's River* and *Strength of Stones*—and two short stories, the second being "Perihesperon."

In the late 1960s and early '70s, black holes—collapsed stars so dense that their gravitational field traps all light—were hot. Literally. (Well, warmer than the background of deep space, at any rate—but very popular, no doubt about that.) Stephen Hawking had just shown how black holes could radiate heat from their event horizons. The truly hip debated whether or not black holes had "hair," whether there could be naked singularities—black holes without event horizons—and other weighty matters. Kip Thorne was speculating on time travel and wormholes, and lots of us were writing stories about this fascinating topic in physics.

I bought and read a copy of the monumental textbook *Gravitation* by Thorne, Misner, and Wheeler, and managed to understand about a third of it. I read all the popular articles and books I could find on the subject. Somehow I absorbed much of the theory and proceeded to both paint portraits of black holes and write about them.

Here's a black hole story such as Jean Paul Sartre might have written, with no exit. I fancy there's also a touch of Jack Vance. The language is enthusiastically and unabashedly science fictional, and I was quite proud of it at the time.

And wrapped around it all is the tale of my first brush with Jim Baen, *Galaxy* Magazine, published hard science fiction, my opinions about living forever, and the Walt Disney Studios.

First, the story, and then the aftermath.

The Venging
Galaxy, James Baen, 1975

W*altz the night away, woman,* Kamon thought, exuding a base undersmell of fury. *Your husband will be dead soon, and all your property scattered like seeds to hungry birds.* He coiled near the parapet, watching the dancers below execute their moves to strains of Ravel's *La Valse.* He focused on one dancer in particular, dressed in a simple, sheer blue gown, brown hair cut close to her head, thin arms graceful, delicate face lost in the ecstasy of the waltz: Lady Edith Fairchild.

Three small moons hung above the etched glass lamps surrounding the dance floor, one at the horizon above labyrinths of hedgerows, another to the west topping the Centrum Minara, and a third at zenith, the largest. The moonlight gleamed from the polished dance floor, shaded by swirling gowns and white breeches.

"Enjoying the view, I hope," an old woman said. She had moved up behind him quietly. Kamon swiveled his head and regarded her through multifaceted eyes, then turned back to look down from the parapet. The old woman wore a plain black robe, revealing by dress if not manner that she was an Abstainer. He recognized her, but he did not wish to release his fury yet.

"It is a bit limited," he said, his words clipped by a nonhuman vocal apparatus.

"You can see the entire floor from here," the woman said. Despite the ominous black in his skin, she would not leave him be.

"The *subject* is limited," he clarified. "Their pleasures are mindless, don't you think?"

"When I was young I enjoyed such pleasures, and I wasn't mindless. Foolish, to be sure; very foolish."

"I find it difficult to believe Anna Sigrid Nestor was ever foolish."

"Kamon, you're getting old, too. You must be twice as old as I am. You know how foolish the young are. No awareness of death."

"I have been aware of death since I was a few brief days old, Baroness. Do you forget that my kind have no juvenates?" He turned one jewellike green eye on her but kept the other on the dance floor.

"You'll probably still outlive me." Nestor stepped up to the parapet and put her hands on the railing. "Keeping an eye on Edith Fairchild, or just dreaming of assassinations and seizures?"

"Your exalted status gives you no right to show me human sarcasm," Kamon said. "You are not so strong you can feel secure against my kind."

Nestor's face tightened, wrinkles deepening. "You're a *wretch*, Kamon." She turned to stare into his leathery face, dominated by the triangular mouth that articulated so many languages, human and otherwise, so well. Teeth like a lamprey, mind to match: vicious by design.

I am not a bigot, but dear God, I despise his class of Aighors, Anna thought. "Our pact compels my silence, but I weary of the support of your kind," she said. "I'm here to rescind our agreement."

"That will be of advantage no one," Kamon said, skin turning a dismal shade of gray-brown.

She took some satisfaction from his discomfiture. "Be quiet until I've finished. I'm disgusted that I've let self-interest blind me to your plans for so long. Disjohn Fairchild is my friend. He is a good man, perhaps a better human than I. I have a duty to such a man, Kamon. Among all of us, his kind is rare. You and I are proof of that."

Kamon bowed elegantly, long upraised torso supple as a snake. "I will convey your message to the Administers. I am sure they will wish to alter the performance of the next auspices, knowing you are no longer a partner."

Administers performed auspices—rituals of forward-seeing and propitiation—for dozens of species associated with the mercantile consolidations. Like the Romans of ancient Earth, they sought signs in the deeply imbedded patterns of nature. But none were as fanatically devoted to the practice as the Aighor members of Hafkan Bestmerit.

Anna abhorred judging other species by human standards. If the Aighors wished to sacrifice the most perfect of their young and seek signs in their bowels, so be it. Human considerations meant nothing to them. But she had once attended a ceremony, and the memory still sickened her.

"Hear me," she said, drawing herself up. She was pitifully small compared to the Aighor. "I deny the support of Hafkan Bestmerit, and rescind the oath of noninterference. I will do everything I can to prevent your kind from stripping Fairchild of his life and holdings. I will defend him with all my power. That's no small force, Kamon."

"The Baroness is influential," the Aighor acknowledged, resorting to third person now that the honorable relationship had been formally ended. He bowed and swung the anterior half of his body into a coil. "But she is not omnipotent. Her weapons are registered. She must answer to the Combine, as all of us do. This makes an interesting challenge."

Anna fumed at the reminder. "Hafkan Bestmerit wishes to establish stronger ties with United Stars, my allies. Strike against me, and you offend them. You're perched on the horizon of a very dark singularity, Kamon. Beware falling in."

She walked off, leaving the Aighor to resume his scrutiny of the dance as it came to a close. His three lips pressed tight over forty-eight needle-sharp teeth, an expression of thoughtful concern.

AFTER THE FINAL DANCE, LADY FAIRCHILD MADE HER WAY THROUGH THE throngs with a nod here and a word there, smiling to all, face flushed, deporting herself as if in a Jane Austen novel or a scene from Imperial Russia. As soon as she was off the dance floor, however, her demeanor changed. She looked around like a bird, head moving nervously jerk, jerk, jerk. Her hands trembled. Tiny rivulets glistened on her neck and cheek as she entered the gilded elevator. Her shoulders slumped.

In the upper reaches of the hotel, she climbed a flight of stairs edged with malachite, and at the top, found the door to the Fairchild suite and spoke her name. The door opened.

Inside, she reached to pull up the hem of her gown and sat on the padded bar ringing the sleep field as she undid her shoes. One finger prodded the sleep field button. The bed hummed and she fell back, hair fanning.

Disjohn Fairchild stood over her, his entrance quieter than the sleep field. "What's wrong?" he asked.

"I saw the Aighor," she answered. "He watched me from the balcony above the dance floor." Her voice quavered with anger. "They could at least have the decency to hide themselves while they scheme!"

"They're too honest and above-board for that," Disjohn said, sitting beside her. He frowned at the ceramic wall mural, then at his shelves of old books—all as familiar as his own hands. He had no official connections with the Centrum, but his value to them was such that he had used this suite and his billet on the Centrum world for twenty years. It was more than home; it was the repository for his life's work. *Christ,* he thought. *It's my world and all I am, and it can't save me.*

But what was there to be afraid of in the short term? The Aighors would not do anything drastic now. They would wait for weeks, months, even years, for a time when he was offworld and away from all his protections. Likely enough they would strike when he went to Shireport to deliver his personal lectures.

They would declare a cultural insult, announce the terms of the vendetta, commandeer his ship if they could, and do away with him cleanly—in deep space. There wasn't a thing Dallat or United Stars could do about that. Complex diplomacy was involved, and Fairchild was not so important that his friends and allies would risk the anger of the Centrum to defend him.

Of course, if he could reach Shireport safely, there were Crocerians who might consent to go with him—paid, say, in data trade preferences for two years. The Aighors wouldn't touch his ship from Shireport to Ansinger with the Crocerians aboard.

When he delivered his lectures at Shireport, he would apply for United Stars zone protection to Ansinger. Ansinger was the largest USC stellar province, ten systems. He could transfer his funds and data banks—those parts he could mobilize and take with him—convert his lands and holdings to transferrable commodities, perhaps yet more data, and establish himself on a terraformed world in undeveloped Ansinger. Buy a continent on Kresham Elak. Set up a school for diplomats' off-spring. "Get the hell *away*!" he shouted.

Edith flinched.

He apologized and stroked her short, silky hair. "Thinking about alternatives." But going to Ansinger meant the loss of most of what he had accomplished here, the subtle nets of interpersonal relations; he would not be able to return to the Centrum world, ever. His wife's life would change, as well.

"Why are they so vindictive?" Edith asked. "You did such a simple thing, so . . . *innocuous.* You meant no harm or insult. Why go after you, anyway? Why not just ask you to remove the station?"

He shook his head. "Not so simple from their point of view." That had to be their reason; that he had pioneered and promoted the construction of the Precipice Five station. He could think of no other.

The station studied black hole emissions from the Pafloshwa Rift. The Aighors called such emissions *thrina*, and had constructed extensive religious rituals around them. In some way the station had violated taboo—who could know what human words applied, if any?—and the Aighors held Disjohn Fairchild accountable.

"They can't destroy the station," he said. "It's under United Stars jurisdiction now, thanks to Anna Nestor. If they attack USC personnel, the Centrum has to intervene. That would result in severe restrictions. But I'm under Dallat protection, and Dallat hasn't yet signed a full agreement with the Centrum. . . . Still a renegade consolidation. Until an agreement is signed, the Aighors can resort to prehuman law and call a cultural vendetta."

With their early half-understanding of human tongues, the Aighors had called it a "venging."

"Their laws are so damned complicated," Edith said, staring at the night-sky ceiling.

"Not really, once you've been around them for a while."

"You almost make it sound just."

"Their laws kept interspecies conflict to a minimum for a thousand years before we came," Disjohn said quietly. "Roger Bacon was messing around with crude lenses when the original pacts were established."

Edith stood up from the sleepfield and unhitched her gown in the back, letting the folds pile themselves automatically into a tight, square pile. At fifty she wasn't doing at all badly, he thought, and without yet relying on juvenates.

As if she were reading his mind in part, she said, "They don't have any way of staying young."

"So?"

"They don't have any way to prevent death. Maybe that's why they cling to old religions and rituals. It means personal survival after death, or whatever their equivalent is."

"You mean, what I've done blocks their chances of immortality?"

"They bury their dead in black holes, don't they?"

"Yes, but before they die. Pilgrim ships of old and sick."

"Maybe studying the thing takes it out of religion and puts it into science. Science still says nobody survives after death. Maybe the intellect can't accept what the subconscious—"

"That's archaic," he said. "And they aren't human, besides. Their psychology is nothing like ours."

Edith shrugged and lay back on the bed. He crawled in beside her and the lights automatically went out.

What if his actions *had* condemned the Aighors to eternal darkness? He shuddered and closed his eyes tight, trying not to think, above all, not to empathize with his enemies.

KAMON LOOKED ACROSS THE MESSAGE SPHERES ON THE FLOOR BEFORE HIM and crossed his eyes in irritation. This gave him a double view of the opposite sides of the octagonal room—*gepter* knives hung ceremonially on one wall, over the receiver-altar which periodically reproduced the radio noise of the Thrina as sound; wooden tub next to another wall, filled with mineral water smelling of sulfur and iodine salts.

He picked up a sphere and put it in the depression in his tape-pad, then instructed the little machine to record all the successive layers of information and display them linearly. The method tasted too much of human thought patterns for his liking, but it had been adopted by Hafkan Bestmerit as a common method of using interculture information.

It was disgusting that a single cultural method should control information techniques stretching halfway across the galaxy.

But such was the dominance pattern of the young humans.

The pad's read-out began immediately. The first message was from the council at Frain, the Aighor birth-world. The council had examined the theological and ethical problem of Fairchild and his sacrilege, and supported the judgment of the district priests.

Fairchild's alien origins and upbringing did not exempt him from the Venging.

He had condemned millions of Aighors to oblivion after death. He had profaned the major region of Thrina pilgrimage by treating it as an area for rational investigation, and not of deep reverence.

The death-ships could no longer drop the assembled dying pilgrims below the event horizons of their chosen black holes. They would no longer experience the redemption of Zero, or bathe themselves in the source of the Thrina song.

Kamon seethed. He was one of those potential pilgrims.

He had wanted so much to live forever.

"FAIRCHILD HAS BITTEN OFF MORE THAN HE CAN CHEW, BUT I SEE NO WAY USC can interfere. We're conducting high-level talks with Hafkan Best-merit, very delicate. If I were to start an incident I would forego my employment quick as that."

Kiril Kondrashef snapped his fingers in demonstration and stared at Anna Sigrid-Nestor with large, woeful eyes. His jowly face gleamed pale in the white light of his reading bureau.

"So I can expect no support from USC?" Anna said, anger coloring her cheeks.

"At the moment, no."

"Then what do you suggest?"

"Fairchild could make his way to some immunity zone like Ansinger. He can seek USC support, but only by renouncing his associations with Dallat. As I understand it, that would mean giving up most of his wealth."

"What can I do to help him now?"

"Give him the advice I've given you. But keep your nose out of it. Stay clear unless you want USC to renounce its connections with you."

"Kiril, I've known you for over a century now. We're about as friendly as two old wolves can be. You bailed me out of my doldrums after the death of my first husband. More even, we're both Abstainers. For us, immortality is no desirable thing. Yet now you tell me you won't do anything to help a man who has done more good for colonists and the consolidations than anyone, Dallat associations or no. You're being incredibly two-faced, I think."

Kiril chuckled ruefully. "I don't like your tactics much and I never have. You tend to stamp when you should tread softly. A good many fragile and important deals hang on this matter. Do you have any idea— you must have, you're no idiot—how difficult it is for species to coexist when all they have in common is the fact that they're alive? Whole civilizations walking on tiptoes through trip-wires, all the time. Anna, you could start a collapse you can hardly imagine."

She sat in front of his desk, hands gripping the edge as if to push it aside. Her forearms were rigid but her facial expression hadn't changed from the mild, grandmotherly smile she'd put on when she came in.

"Besides," he continued in an undertone, "your weapons are registered whenever fired, in defense or otherwise, and the situation is recorded in stasis memory. You can't get around that. We'll have you on the carpet if you do anything that can't be strictly considered defensive."

"I've never been able to figure out a bureaucrat," Anna said. She sighed and picked up her silk duffel bag to leave. "I've never used my weapons. Ever."

"Garden tools, once," Kiril reminded her.

She stared at him, shocked that he would mention that.

"I'm frightened, Anna," he said. "Very frightened. The fates of individuals mean nothing in this kind of dispute."

SHE TOOK A TRANSIT TUBE BENEATH THE MODULAR CITY AS ANY PEDESTRIAN might have, nothing more than an old woman. In her bag she carried several pictures of young men, one of whom attracted her very much. She glanced at them several times as she rode, trying to lose herself in reverie and allow her limbic mind to feel its way through to an action. Gut-level thought had carried her through crises before.

She picked out one photograph and tapped it against her cheek as she left the tube at an underground terminal. She walked below the Myriadne starport, largest on Tau Ceti II. Shuttles landed and departed dozens by the hour overhead, bronze and silver smooth bullets homing for their mother ships.

One such bullet, small and utilitarian, waited for her. She rode a wheeled maneuvering tug out to it. In ten minutes it was off-planet.

Disjohn Fairchild was an intelligent man. He would already be implementing some of the suggestions Kiril had made. They were the only outs he had for the moment, with or without her help. She calmly analyzed her own reaction to the suggestions, watching sun, planets and stars form a glittering bow around her ship. Then she smiled grimly and went to sleep as the stars winked out.

When she came awake three hours later, dark still surrounded her. It grew muddied and started to take on form. There was a queasy moment, a tiny shiver, and the outer universe returned. Occasional wisps of color appeared and vanished streamer-like along the forty-five-degree rotated starbow.

She began to wonder what Kamon had meant by the reminder that his kind had no juvenates. She went to the ship's library to do research. On her way, she lifted the photograph to a ship's eye and told it, "Hire him."

They would pick him up at Shireport.

EDITH GREW TIRED OF THE VIEWSCREEN'S TRANSLATION OF WHAT WAS HAPpening outside the ship. She frowned and closed her eyes, trying to wipe her mind clear for a moment. The books in front of her ghosted and darkened, and she swam in a small red sea of interior designs.

After a moment, she no longer thought in words, and pictures came to her clearly.

Three large, very fast starships all moved across hyperspatial geodesics toward a common goal. They left tracks—she could see them in an allegorical fashion—in amorphous higher geometries. They were aware of each other's presence and direction.

Edith wondered what Anna Sigrid-Nestor's purpose was, beyond friendship. They'd communicated briefly a few hours before, and Disjohn had told her to leave well enough alone. But Edith was sure she wouldn't.

One ship carried a being not classifiable in terms of terrestrial biology, having aspects of many phyla. Kamon was called "he" by default—a cultural tendency to view the convex sexual form as male. But Kamon was neither male nor female in the reproductive process of his kind. He gestated young. His children, by human standards, were not his children.

His neurological makeup differed radically from a human's. The arrangement of his nervous system was central, not dorsal. He had three brains spaced around his esophagus.

One of his brains was an evolutionary vestige, in charge of autonomic and emotive functions. Very powerful in influence despite its size, it connected with the two other portions by fibers substantially larger than any human nervous connection—networks of medullae, each marvelously complex.

He could contemplate at least four different things at once while involved in a routine action. While driven by what humans might consider a mania, the Aighor could think as rationally as any calm human. He was a dangerous enemy, highly motivated. In this match, Kamon had the upper hand. He would know everything they had planned—with benefit of manic certainty and calm intellection—and he'd act without hesitation.

But Kamon was not supernatural. They could elude him. They could survive him.

Perhaps Sigrid-Nestor could help by distracting him. There was at least hope, and perhaps even a good chance. So why did she feel so dark inside, and cold?

She closed her books, stood up slowly from the table, and went to join her husband on the bridge.

"A ship riding protogeometry has three options in case of attack," Graetikin, the captain, was telling Disjohn as she entered. Graetikin nodded at her and continued. "It can drop into half-phase, that is, fluctuate between two geometries . . ." His finger lightly sketched an equation on the tapas pad. "Or drop into status geometry, our normal continuum. Or it can dispatch part of its mass and create pseudo-ships like squid's ink. This happens to some extent during any transfer of geometries, to satisfy the Dirac corollaries, but the mass loss is extremely low, on the order of fifty or sixty trillion atomic units, randomly scattered."

"What about protection from shields?"

"Shields only operate in status geometry. They're electromagnetic and that implies charge-holes in hyperspatial manifolds."

"It would have been easier if we'd had a few Crocerians," Fairchild said wistfully. When the ship had put in at Shireport, all the Crocerians he'd asked had politely refused, not wishing to gamble, or, if gambling, betting on the Aighors. The Crocerians were a pragmatic species.

"I'd never fight Aighors if I could avoid it," Graetikin said. "I would avoid it by not having them challenge me."

"We're forced to take that risk."

"It's up to you. Once committed to a protogeometry vector we can't back down."

"How far ahead of us is he?"

"About four light-hours, following a parallel course."

"How much of a jump can we get if we take one of these protogeometries?"

"He'll learn about our jump about a tenth of a second status time after we make it. That gives us a good hour or two at the other end of the pierce."

"They might take that as an affront," Disjohn said, looking at Edith.

"Why, for God's sake?" Graetikin said. "We'd have to jump into some manifold or another anyway."

"Protogeometry jumps are a waste of energy, unless one wants to gain a certain advantage." Fairchild pushed away from the anchored chair and drifted across the cabin. "Cat and mouse. If I give any clue that I think they're after me, they'll interpret it as a cultural insult. Kamon won't miss a trick."

Graetikin shrugged. While talking about things that could mean life or death, he had doodled an equation among the others on the tapas. He had been working on this problem in his head for months, unaware he was so close to a solution. His eyes widened. He had just described what the Thrina were in terms of deep proto-geometries.

He quickly branched off with another equation, and saw that in any geometry outside of status—any universe beyond their continuum—the Thrina would be ubiquitous.

That, he idly thought, did qualify them for godhood somewhat.

He would transmit the equations and solutions to Precipice 5 when he had a chance, and see what they made of it. But for the moment, it wasn't relevant. He folded the tapas and put it into his shirt pocket.

"We're four light-days out from Shireport, and sixty parsecs from the Ansinger systems. We made it to Shireport without harassment, and that makes me suspicious. So far we've only been tailed." Graetikin turned to look at Fairchild floating on his back in mid-air. "They're usually more punctual."

THE AIGHOR CAPTAIN LAY AGAINST THE WALL WITH HIS THROAT AND THREE brains smashed flat. He managed a final gasp of query before Kamon pressed the slammer button again and laid his head out. The thorax and tail twitched and the arms writhed slowly, then all motion stopped. Kamon's mate-of-ship huddled against the back of the cabin and croaked tightly, regularly, her face black as blood with fear. Kamon put the slammer down and sent his message to the Council at Frain.

"The diplomatic team has caused damage to the Venging," he said. The hazy, distorted image of the Auspiseer chided him for his vehemence.

"They have called the meeting at Precipice 5 partly for your advantage," the Auspiseer said. "The human Fairchild's ship has been notified en route to Ansinger, and he cannot refuse."

"But I have already had several chances to attack—"

"The captain's reluctance to destroy the Fairchild ship was part of his training. You should have been more gentle with him."

"He is of the governing breed. They've become almost human in the past centuries."

"The Council allowed the meeting at Precipice 5 to be called for a number of reasons. For one, it eases our relations with the humans temporarily. And for another, it puts you in a better position should the discussions be unsuccessful.

"The Council cannot discount your premature release of Captain Liiank, without benefit of pilgrimage. You will execute yourself upon completion of your mission."

"The release of Fairchild will sanctify the Rift Thrina, and I will take my end there."

"Wise and good."

"But I have lost the Fairchild ship now because of the Captain's reluctance. It will take time to recapture the advantage."

"What else has offended besides Fairchild?"

"His station."

"Kamon, you are officially declared rogue. We are not answerable for your actions. We will broadcast suitable warnings to that effect."

"That is how I've planned, Auspiseer." He ended the communication and turned to speak to his mate. She had regained her composure and was adjusting her belts of prefertilized egg capsules. "We will gestate no more young," he said.

So far, three things have gone wrong with the predictions," the Heuritex said. "I've calculated based on all known constants and variables, all options open, but the trend is against the predicted results. I must remind you that there are large areas of the problem of which I am totally ignorant, making the model inadequate."

"In short, you're useless," Anna told the machine.

"That is as it may be."

"I should replace you with my gigolo."

"He's a handsome bastard, I'll say that for him."

"What if we assume that Kamon is going to behave erratically, say, deranged by being denied an afterlife?"

"We have more options."

"Then that's our operating hypothesis. No, wait. Use this—Kamon will behave *as if* he is deranged, by human standards. I never underestimate opponents."

"Do you wish that to be an hypothesis, or an assumption? There is a difference, you know."

"Whichever way it works. You know what you're doing better than I do, dearie."

"Incorporated. The resulting future-model, still highly inadequate, indicates that the meeting at Precipice 5—course corrected for that destination, by the by—will not take place. The station will be destroyed. Kamon will probably be the destroyer, and the Aighors will claim Kamon has gone rogue to deny responsibility."

She paced in front of the panel, then asked for gravitation to be shut off, and floated at ease. "Warn Precipice 5 to be on full alert when Disjohn arrives."

"Done."

"And contact USC, division of Martial Aids, at Shireport. Tell them there is going to be a confrontation in the Pafloshwa Rift, coordinates unknown."

"Such an action will mark you as a rogue agent as well," the machine said, a speculative tone in its voice.

"Whatever for?"

"It indicates a willingness to engage in battle, since you are heading toward the Rift of your own free will."

"Not exactly my free will. USC doesn't know I'm aboard this vessel, so they'll assume—will have to assume, and believe me are smart enough to assume—that whoever advises the Captain is not playing with a full deck of cards."

"I advise the Captain."

"I will have you overhauled when we get back to Ansinger."

"That will be a good time to install the new Parakem function modules. Where are you, since you're not here?"

"On Tau Ceti II. I made an appointment with Jessamyn Negras for a business talk, and she hates me enough to keep me waiting for at least a month. She will refuse to believe anyone would miss out on the blessed chance to talk to her. And appropriately deluded recorders are going at all times in my apartments. I'm there, that's certain."

"I see," said the Heuritex.

KAMON REGRETTED KILLING THE CAPTAIN BEFORE LEARNING ALL THERE WAS to know about ship operation. The Aighors who crewed the vessel were all competent in their special tasks, and the computers were helpful, but an overall cohesiveness was, if not lacking, at least shaky. Kamon absorbed the captain's library rapidly.

He was gratified to know an Aighor pilgrimage fleet was forming on the borders of the Rift. His kind cheered him on, and the government—diplomats and rulers alike—had not yet sent a ship to stop him. It would be useless if they did.

Coldly, precisely, he figured where difficulties would arise. First would be the protection of Precipice 5—negligible defenses, all things considered. Second would be the presence of Anna Sigrid-Nestor, whom of all the humans he had met he most admired. Third—the final battleground would not be Precipice 5. He would have to chase Fairchild across the Rift.

The station would be destroyed before the human ships arrived.

FAIRCHILD'S SHIP SAW THE DEAD RUIN, ISSUED A DISTRESS SIGNAL ON THE station's behalf, and headed at full power for deep space. It was away from the major gravitational effects of the small system in hours and shamelessly relied on protogeometry jumps to take it deep into the Rift. It shut down all activities not connected with life-support, went into half-phase, and laid ghost images of itself across a wide range of continua.

Graetikin silently cursed the Dallat conventions which made all private ships carry nothing more offensive than meteoroid deflection shields. He had spent his first thirty years in space as an apprentice commander in the Centrum Astry, helping to command ships armed to the teeth with all conceivable weapons, from rocket projectiles to stasis-shielded neutronium blocks which, when warped into the center of another vessel, quickly gravitated everything into super-dense spheres.

Now he was facing a violent confrontation with nothing more offensive than flare rockets and half-phase warps.

It was like the final charge of an old lion against warriors wielding assegais. Fairchild's motives and the Aighor's motives didn't concern him. Both in their own ways were altruistic and noble, concerned with good tasks. But he was concerned with surviving to captain another ship, or at least continue captaining this one.

He didn't mind Fairchild's employ. The man was reasonably sharp and knew how to provide for the upkeep of his own ships. If he had the tact of a young bull in dealing with alien cultures, that was usually not Graetikin's concern.

Between and around these thoughts, he reworked his equations describing the Thrina. There was a cool, young hypothesis on the horizons of his mind, and it tantalized him. In reworking the expressions on his notepad, he found four connections with Parakem functions which he hadn't noticed earlier. These implied that the Thrina, though ineffectual in a cause-effect relation in most geometries, had interesting properties in coincidence-controlled geometries. They could influence certain aspects of status geometry, where cause-effect and synchronicity operated in struggling balance. And that implied . . .

He raised his eyebrows.

"THERE IS A GOOD POSSIBILITY WE CAN CONTACT FAIRCHILD IF HE CHOOSES to coast free within the next thirty-five hours," the Heuritex said.

Anna grumbled out of a light doze. "What was that?"

"We can join forces with him at points I have calculated along geodesics meeting in higher geometries."

"Translate for us mortals, please." She straightened in her command chair and rubbed her face with her hands.

"I think we can join with Fairchild's ship before Kamon reaches it. Here is our condition: fifth standard day of flight; all three ships are deep into the Rift. Fairchild is inert, following a least-energy geodesic in half-phase. Kamon is matching the most likely direction of that geodesic, though I'm certain he has no clear picture of the ship's present position along such a path. We follow Kamon closely. And we are constantly correcting our charts with observations of the Rift pulsars and singularities."

"Yes, but what's this about joining Fairchild?"

"His vessel alone is not sufficient to propel itself away from Kamon. He has little or no chance of escape in the long run. But with our two ships linked, we can create a broader affect-beam in protogeometry—"

"You can arrange this in more than just theory?"

"I think so, madame. I can contact Disjohn Fairchild's ship in a code only it can understand, and arrange for the rendezvous without the Aighor knowing."

"You're a maker of wonders, and you draw my curiosity like a magnet . . . into areas I'm sure will baffle me. I'll think on it," she said.

Why hesitate? she asked herself. Because now, faced with the possibility of doing what she had started out to do—save Disjohn Fairchild at any cost—a miserable, cold sensibility started to creep in. She needed to think about it, long and hard. There were too many considerations to weigh for a hasty decision.

She made her way to the ship's observation chamber. Far out on the needlelike boom which extended from the crew ball, an isolated multisense chamber seemed to hang in dark space. But its walls were transparent only by illusion. Millions of luminous cells provided adjustable images of anything within range of the ship's sensors, down to the finest detail a human eye could perceive. Images could be magnified, starbows undistorted into normal starfields for quick reference, or high-frequency energy shifted into visual regions. If need demanded, such subtle effects as light distortion in higher geometries could be brought within human interpretation. The sphere could also synthesize programmed journeys and sound effects, or any combination of fictions and synaesthesias.

Anna requested a tour of the nearby singularities. "Will there be a specific sequence, madame?" the media computer asked.

"Only an introductory tour. Explain what I'm seeing."

The visual journey started.

"Some singularities are made obvious by surrounding nebulae," the voice-over began. "These are veils of supernova dust and gas that have been expanding for hundreds of millions of years." Fading in, wisps like mare's-tail clouds in a sunset, backed by velvet space. Hidden within, a tiny spinning and glowing cloud, a pinprick, not worth noticing . . . geometric jaws gaping wide, tides deadly as any ravening star furnace.

"Others are companions to dim red stars, and thus are heavy X-ray sources. They suck in matter from their neighbors, accelerate and heat it through friction, and absorb it in bottomless wells.

"There is no comprehensive explanation why the majority of the Rift stars supernovaed within ten million years of each other, half an eon ago, but the result is a treacherous graveyard of black holes, dwarfs and a few dim giants. They all affect each other across the close-packed Rift in complex patterns.

"Some can be seen through distortion of the stellar background. The rings of stars around a black hole show the effects of gravitational lensing. Light is captured and orbited above the event horizons, producing two primary images and a succession of weaker images caused by anomalies in the spinning singularity. Gas falling into the holes produces hot points of high energy radiation, red-shifted into the visual spectrum by enormous gravitational fields. These are surrounded by rings of stars, images of stars from every angle—every visible object, including those behind the observer. There are gaps of darkness and then succeeding rings like the bands on an interferometer plate, finally blending into star-images undeviated by the singularity."

She was reminded of electronic Christmas ornaments from her childhood. Anna knew what she saw lay only a few million miles away, so close her ship could reach out to touch it in mere minutes.

"Dear God," she murmured. To fall into one of those things would be to transcend any past experience of death. They were miracles, jesters of spacetime. Her eyes filled with tears which nearly broke their tension bonds to drift away in free-fall.

"Where no such diffractions and reflections are visible, perhaps absorbed in dark nebulosities, and where no X-ray or Thrina sources give clues, naked singularities stripped of their event horizons lurk like invisible teeth. These have been charted by evidence obtained in proto-geometry warps. There is no other way to know they exist."

The Thrina song of a nearby singularity was played to her. It sounded like the wailing of lost children, sweetly mixed with a potent bass *boum*, an echoing cave-sound, ghost-sound, preternatural mind-sound. "No reason is known for the existence of the Thrina song. It is connected with singularities as an unpredictable phenomenon of radiating and patterned energy, perhaps in some way directed by intelligence."

Nestor left the sphere and drifted quickly back through the extension to the crew-ball.

Her hands shook.

KAMON FOLLOWED AND WAITED. A SHIP COULD REMAIN IN HALFPHASE ONLY so long before its unintentional mass loss (how easily he had spotted and avoided the ghosts!) reached a critical level. His shipmate meditated and fasted alone in her cabin. Kamon was left with the silent computers—it was blasphemous for an Aighor machine to have a voice—and a few aides to see to his food and wastes. He preferred it that way.

At one point he even ordered them to clear away the captain's smashed body so he might be more alone.

The Venging was close. He had had no further contact with the Council at Frain or any other Aighor agencies. He had spotted and charted the course of Anna Sigrid-Nestor's ship, and felt his own sort of appreciation at the intuition she was following him personally. She was on her own Venging.

Such was the dominance pattern of humans.

"FOUR MINUTES THIRTY SECONDS BEFORE CRITICAL POINT," GRAETIKIN SAID softly. Lady Fairchild gripped her husband's arm tighter. For a society woman she was holding up remarkably well, Graetikin thought. He seldom had a chance to talk with her.

The worst was yet to come. Kamon would inevitably chase them down, and there was only one chance left. His recent equations implied they would survive if they took that chance, but *how* they would survive—in what condition, other than whole and alive—was unknown. It was a terrifying prospect.

"We have to leave half-phase," Fairchild said. "And we have to outrun him. There's no other way." Edith nodded and turned away from the bridge consoles.

"Have you ever wondered why he called a Venging?" she asked.

"What?" Fairchild asked. He was focusing on the blank viewers, as if to strain some impossible clue from them. It was useless to look at half-phase exteriors, however. The eye interpreted them as if they weren't there, and indeed half the time they weren't.

"Kamon has to have a reason," Edith said, louder.

"I'm sure he does," Graetikin said.

"I've been trying to find out what that reason is. I might have a clue."

"That doesn't concern us now," Fairchild said, irritated. "Reason or no, we have to get away from him."

"But doesn't it help to know what we're going to die for?" Edith cried, her voice cracking. "You know damn well we can't outrun him! Graetikin knows it, too. Don't you?"

Graetikin nodded. "But I wouldn't say we're going to die. There might be another way."

"You know of one?" Fairchild asked.

Graetikin nodded. "First, I'd like to hear what Lady Fairchild has to say about Kamon's motive."

Disjohn took a deep breath and held up his arms. "Okay," he said to his wife, "Lady Ethnographer, tell us."

"It's all in the library, for whoever cares to look it up. Some of it is even in the old books. We've known about it for a century at least— the basic form of the Aighor pilgrimage. They have three brains, that's well known—but we've ignored the way they use those brains. One is for rational purposes, and it can do everything a computer can do, but it isn't the strongest. Another is for emotive and autonomic purposes, and that's where the seat of their religion is. We don't know exactly what the third brain does. But I have an idea it's used for preparing the other two brains for a proper death. It has to balance them out, mediate. If the rational brain has an edge, the pilgrim won't be prepared for death. I think the research conducted by the station gave the Aighors a dilemma they couldn't face—the rational treatment of subjects hitherto purely religious to them. It gave their rational minds an edge and caused an imbalance. So the pilgrims couldn't be delivered to the black holes without wholesale failure in proper rituals of dying."

"And?" Graetikin asked, fingering his stylus. It seemed there was another foot to drop in the matter, and she wasn't dropping it.

"That's it. I can't speculate any further. I'm not really an ethnographer. But sometimes I wish to hell *you* had been, dear husband!" There was no bitterness in her voice, only a loving rebuke.

Fairchild stared stonily at the empty screens.

"You have another way?" he asked Graetikin.

"It's possible," Graetikin said. He outlined his alternative. From the ninth word on Fairchild went pale, convinced his Captain had broken under the strain.

ANNA LAY IN THE HALF-DARK AND WATCHED THE YOUNG MAN DRESS. FOR the first time in years she felt guilt that her emotional needs should draw her away from constant alertness. But this was the first time she'd been with the handsome lad for anything more than companionship. He had proven serviceable enough and charming.

Her aging frame didn't bother him. He was a professional and perhaps more than that, a sympathetic human being.

"I don't understand all you've told me," he said. His brown skin shined in the golden sanitoire lamps. "But I think what you're asking me is, do you have a right to put your whole crew in danger. You're the captain, and I signed on—"

"Not as a crewmember," she reminded him.

"No, but I signed on with the understanding there might be hazards involved in deep space travel."

"These aren't the normal hazards."

"But if it serves your purpose to link up with the other ship, how can I or anyone else persuade you not to?"

"I have responsibilities to the people who work for me." She was reminded of what Kondrashef had said to her. Even if they could link up with the Fairchild ship, what guarantee did she have that the Heuritex's predictions were completely accurate? They didn't know precisely what Kamon's ship was capable of. Already they'd been surprised several times. And her first lieutenant, Nilsbaum, had worked the problem out on an alternate computer, a human-manufacture Datapak. It had given them an eighty percent chance of hitting a singularity if they linked and performed a protogeometry jump. The Heuritex had disagreed. But still, the danger existed.

"I can't blast the bastard," Anna said, "because every potshot is registered by the tattling machines I had to hook up to pass USC regulations. I can't tamper with them—they retreat into stasis whenever they're not registering."

She looked sharply at the Polynesian. He looked back at her, his face blank and expectant. "Go take a shower," she said. Then, softer, "Please. You've helped me—very much." She turned over and relaxed to the sounds of the door closing and water running.

She was staring at the drifting colors on the nacreous ceiling when the intership chimed. She reached over to depress the switch and listened half—drowsily. The voice of the Heuritex brought her fully awake.

"Madame, we've contacted Fairchild's ship. First Lieutenant Nilsbaum requests your presence on the bridge."

"I'll be there. Any answer from Disjohn?"

"He refuses to allow a linkup. He says he has two reasons—first, that he will not jeopardize your life; and second, that his computers predict failure if such a plan is carried out. I don't understand these machines of human construction."

"Did he say anything else?"

"He warned you to leave."

She rolled over in bed and cupped her chin in her hands. The shower was still running. "Another question," she said.

"Yes, madame."

"What happens if we hit a black hole?"

"Depending on the angle of impact, we have several varieties of doom. If we go straight in, perpendicular to a tangent, we pass through two or more event horizons, depending on the theoretical geometry you subscribe to—"

"What are event horizons?"

"Simply the horizons beyond which no further events can be seen. The gravitational field at that point has accelerated any particle close to the speed of light. From an outside point of view, the particle's time has slowed to almost zero, no motion at all, so it will take an infinite time to hit the singularity below the event horizon.

"But from our point of view—if we are the hypothetical particle—we will hit it. Not that it will matter to us, though. Long before we pass through the inner event horizon, tidal forces will strip us down to subatomic particles."

"Not too pleasant."

"No, but there are other options. At a lesser angle, we might pass through an outer event horizon at a speed sufficient to propel us into another geometry, and out again someplace else—a different place and time in our own universe, perhaps, or in another universe. We might survive that, if certain theoretical conditions prove true—though it would be a rough trip and the ship might not emerge in one piece."

"How can there be more than one event horizon?"

"Because black holes rotate. May I draw you a comparison of two Kruskal-Szekeres diagrams?"

"By all means," Anna said, activating the display screen on the intership.

But the mosaic-like charts did little to help her comprehension. She had forgotten most of her physics decades before.

"Out of half-phase," Kamon said to himself, "now!"

The image reappeared. He had misjudged the geodesic slightly. The ship was a light-hour farther away than he had predicted, which meant the ship's appearance was an hour off from actual emergence. He felt a brief confusion. But the ruse—if ruse it was—had gained them a very small advantage. He immediately switched to subspace sensors.

Fairchild's ship was over four light-hours away. More disturbing, it was heading toward a nebulosity which charts said contained three collapsars, two of them black holes. Kamon deftly probed the nebula with his protogeometry sensors.

None of these singularities had ever been used for pilgrimages, thus they did not radiate Thrina songs. The area had not been thoroughly charted except on visual and radio levels from thousands of light-years away, where the patterns of the roiling gas-clouds had given away the presence of hidden collapsars.

His scanning revealed another member in the family, elusive and sacred: a naked singularity. The very presence of humans in such a region was sacrilege—and if they were choosing suicide over destruction at his hands, the danger was unthinkable.

A shudder racked his entire body. He had heard of humans going insane under stress, but if they fell into a singularity here, the Venging was a failure and the Rift would never be sacred again.

He forced himself to be calm. They wouldn't know how to prepare themselves for the Fall. They knew nothing about the mental ritual involved. It would be, in effect, nothing more than a suicide. Or it might be something much worse, for them.

But Kamon would take no chances. He must destroy them before they ever reached the cloud. For the first time he felt anxiety that he might fail, even fear.

"IT CAN'T BE DONE!" LADY FAIRCHILD SHOUTED. "DISJOHN, I'M NOT IGNO-rant! I know what those things are. Graetikin has to be insane to think we can survive that!"

"I've heard him explain it. The computers back him up."

"Yes, on his assumptions!"

"He's on to something new. He knows what he's talking about—and he's right. We don't have any other choice. The Aighor has every advantage over us, including religious zeal—as you pointed out. We've tested our course on the computers again and again. We have one chance in a thousand of coming out alive. With Graetikin's plan, our chances are at least a hundred times greater."

"We're going to die, is what you're saying, either way."

"Probably. But there's something grand about this way of going. It robs Kamon of his goal. We have the upper hand now."

"You know what will happen if we suicide in one of the singularities?" Edith asked.

"We don't plan on suiciding."

"Just going down one, we make this entire region useless to them for their pilgrimages. Mixing souls is an abomination to them, just as mixing meat and milk is to an Orthodox Jew."

"There was a hygienic reason not to mix meat and milk."

Such bloody-minded rationalism. "Are we so materialistic that we can't see a reason for this kind of taboo?"

Fairchild swung his hands out and turned away from her, talking loudly to the wall. "Damn it, Edith, we have to use Occam's razor! We can't multiply our hypotheses until we avoid stepping on cracks for fear of killing our mothers. We're rational beings! Kamon has that advantage over us—he is not acting rationally. He's on a Venging, like a goddamned berserker, and he's got a faster, better armed ship. We're doomed! What should we do, bare our breast to him and shout 'mea culpa?' "

Edith shook her head. "I don't know. I just feel so lost."

Fairchild shivered. His teeth clicked together and he wrapped his arms around himself. "You're not alone. I'm petrified. We're about to do something no one else has ever done."

"Except Aighors," Edith reminded him. "And they've always been prepared for it."

"HE WON'T LET US DOCK WITH HIM, HE'S TURNING TOWARD THE SINGULARITIES—there's nothing more I can do," Anna said. "He's choosing suicide rather than death at Kamon's hands. Or is he up to something else?"

"I can offer no explanation, madame. Either something has malfunctioned or they have gone insane."

"I *hate* Kondrashef," Anna said quietly. "He has always been right, has always given advice I could never follow and he's always been so damned, irrefutably correct. But I've got to follow my own wyrd." She sighed and leaned back in her chair. "Can they receive any messages now?"

"They are in the cloud. There's too much interference."

"Veer off. Circle to the opposite side of the nebula and see if anything emerges on that end. I've met Fairchild's captain—he's a brilliant man. He may have more up his sleeve than we can know."

Dumbfounded, Anna watched the final act on her sensors and tapped her fingers on the Heuritex.

PROBABILITY FELL APART AT THE ERGOSPHERE INTERFACE OF A SINGULARITY. Whether the same conditions applied to a naked singularity or not, Graetikin didn't know—he guessed they would.

But they wouldn't have to face the danger of the tidal forces—there would be no event horizons, no overt indication of in-rushing space-time. The singularity ahead had collapsed from a star oblated by the presence of other stars, and the result was a hole in space-time stretched out into a line. If conditions still applied here, he'd have to figure their chances of survival on a near-intuitive hunch.

It was clear to Graetikin now. Interuniverse connections of necessity were devoid of probabilities. They were truce zones between regions of differing qualities, differing constants. Hence, somewhere above the singularity, reshaping of in-falling material had to take place.

Perhaps the Aighors weren't far wrong after all.

He worked all his findings into a single tight-packed signal on several media, and broadcast it to space in general. When he was finished he turned to Disjohn and Edith and said, "Feels good to toss out a bottle, anyway. If someone picks it up, well and good. If not, we've lost a few terawatts."

KAMON COULD EITHER BACK OFF, LET THEM ESCAPE AND HOPE FOR AN EN-counter later, or he could pursue to the very end. But he was becoming fatalistic. It seemed the Fairchild ship was behaving not with human insanity, but with divine irrationality—a shield to his Venging. That could imply they were operating in the Grace of the Thrina, not against it. He wished he could consult the Council about this new intuition, but there was no time. Whether correct or not, it made him reluctant to interfere. That small reluctance made him hesitate.

"No!" he shouted, pounding his thorax in disgust. "They are only insane! There is no Grace upon them!"

But it was too late. He had followed the Fairchild ship into the nebulosity on a matching course. They could only construe that as an intention to continue the chase. Since they were insane, they would destroy themselves.

In his self-rage, he considered destroying the Nestor ship for personal satisfaction. But he had other things to do. He had to prepare himself mentally for the Fall. He told the others to begin their rituals. They would follow all the way.

"COURSE PLOTTED," THE COMPUTER TOLD GRAETIKIN. "THERE WILL BE A proper configuration at these points on the chart. We can meet the singularity's affect-field here, or here—that is, at these points in our future-line. If we fail within any width of time measurably in quantum jump intervals, we will come in at a closer angle, and the warp-wave of our approach will create a temporary event horizon which will destroy us. These are our options."

"Initiate the action and test it on a closed loop. Then choose the best approach and put us there. Kamon hasn't left our tail?"

"No, he still follows. And still jams."

"Then my message didn't get through." Somehow it didn't matter much.

Fairchild gave the final order. Edith watched from his side with a small, knowing smile. She was trying to remember her childhood. There had been so many pleasant things then. She'd married Disjohn, in fact, because he reminded her of the strength of her father. She needed that strength now. She wished she had the strength of a father near.

The ship was otherwise empty. Her corridors echoed as the impact of the nebula's clouds bucked her and made her groan.

The tiny neutron star pulsated regularly, surrounded by a halo of accelerated particles, a natural generator of radio energy. The two normal singularities orbited each other, light-days apart. The violet influx of gases outlined them clearly. Like two whirlpools whose surfaces have been smeared with oil, they glowed in disparate, shimmering mazes of light. Starlight ran in rings around them. Ghost images of each other flickered in the rings, and the ghosts carried rings of stars, and images of other ghosts.

The universe was being twisted into ridiculous failures and inconceivable alterations.

Here time and space rushed into multidimensional holes so rapidly that an object had to move at the speed of light to stay in one place. It was a Red Queen's race on a cosmic scale.

In drawing diagrams of what happens in the singularity below the event horizons, space and time axes cross and replace each other. The word "singularity" itself is a phrase of no more significance than "boojum." It implies points in any mathematical fabric where results start coming out in infinities.

Thus, Graetikin knew, they would soon step off the pages of one book which had told their lives until now, leave that book behind and everything associated with it, and risk a plunge into null.

The naked singularity invisibly approached.

KAMON'S THOUGHTS GREW FUZZY AND UNCOORDINATED. HE BRISTLED WITH rage as one portion of his mind came unbalanced in the ritual, and kicked out with his tail at the bulkhead before him. He dented the inch-thick steel. Then he regained his balance.

The holy display of the black holes dominated everything.

He was ready. A tiny reserved part of him set his weapons for a last-ditch attempt, then vanished into the calm pool of his prepared being.

Disjohn Fairchild felt a giddiness he'd never known before, as if he were being spun on a carnival toy, but every part of him felt it differently.

"I'm expanding," Lady Fairchild said. "I'm getting bigger. Alice down the rabbit hole—"

Still the ship fell. And fell.

Edith gasped. The bridge darkened for the blink of an eye, then was suddenly aglow with scattered bits of ghost lightning. She held her hands in front of her eyes and saw a blue halo around them like Cherenkov radiation.

Expansion. Alteration. The desk in front of her, and her arms on the desk, broke into color-separated images and developed intricate networks of filigree, became crystalline, net-like, tingled and shimmered and pulsed, then repeated in reverse and became solid again. Everything smelled of dust and age, musty like vast libraries.

Both ships ended their existence in status geometry at the same moment. Kamon followed at a different angle and hit the affect-field at the same instant the Fairchild ship did.

As he had known and expected, his warp-wave created a temporary event horizon and he was divested of his material form.

The Fairchild ship survived its fall. Graetikin's equations, thus far, were wholly accurate.

None of them could conceive of what happened in the interface. It was not chaos—it was instead a sea of quiet, an end to action. The destruction and rearrangement of rules and constants led to a lassitude of space-time, an endless sargasso of thought and event, mired and tangled and gray.

Then each experienced that peculiar quality of his or her worldline which made them unique. Fairchild, stable and strong, did not see much to surprise him. Graetikin marveled at the insight into his work. Edith, still wrapped in her childhood, had a nightmare and woke far in her past, screaming for her father.

Again the darkness. The ouroboros of the hole spat them out. The computers triggered a lengthy jump, as best as they were able, for the actions of their smallest circuits were still not statistically reliable. This was the chance Graetikin knew they all had to take.

They escaped. The ship rattled and shook like a dog after a swim. The howl of metal made Fairchild's scalp prickle and his arm-hair stand on end. A rush of wind swept the bridge. Edith Fairchild wept quietly and Disjohn, beside her, trembled.

They held each other, sweat dripping and noses flaring, panicked like wild beasts. Graetikin bounced his fingers clumsily over the screen controls, then corrected his foul-up and gave them a view of what lay outside.

"I don't see anything," Fairchild said.

"I'm astonished we made it," Graetikin whispered. Disjohn gave him a wild look. The screen showed nothing but cold darkness.

"Scan and chart all radiating sources," the captain instructed the computer.

"There are no compact sources of radiation. Standard H-R distribution shows nothing. There is only an average temperature," it said.

"What's the temperature?"

"Two point seven one degrees Kelvin."

Graetikin slammed his scriber onto the panel. "Any white hole activity? Any sign of the singularity we just came through?"

"Nothing."

"We had to come out of something!"

"Undefined," the machine said.

"What does it mean?" Edith asked, holding her chin in her hands.

Graetikin fingered the mar his scriber had made in the panel. "It means we're in a region of heat-death."

"Where's that?"

"Undefined," the computer repeated.

" 'Where' is meaningless now," Graetikin said, eyes dull. "Everything's evenly distributed. We're between beats, at the top of a cycle between expansion and collapse. We've escaped into a dead universe."

"What can we do?" Disjohn asked. He felt an intense ache for his wife, and wished she were at his side. The grief was so strong, it seemed he had lost her only recently. He looked at Edith. She resembled her mother so much his throat ached. He patted his daughter on the head, but felt none of the reassurance he was trying to give.

"We might go into stasis and wait it out. But we'd have to have a timer, something measuring the progress of the universe outside us. Tens of billions of years. I don't think any of our instruments would last that long."

"There has to be a way!" Fairchild said.

"I told you, Father," Edith said. "We were the offenders." She did a mad little dance. "I told you. We didn't prepare. Why—"

Graetikin thought of them waiting until the ship ran out of energy and food and breathable air. Years, certainly. But years with a burnt-out old politician and his prepubescent daughter, a triangle of agonizing possibilities. Even could they survive, they would have no basis for a new life.

Edith's face showed white and distorted. "Why, we're in hell!"

NESTOR'S SHIP ROUNDED THE NEBULA AND WAITED. ANNA ASKED THE HEUritex several times if anything had been sighted, and each time it replied in the negative. "There is no sign," it said finally. "We would do well to return home."

"Nothing left," Anna said. She couldn't convince herself she had done all she could.

"One moment, madame," the Heuritex said. "This region was devoid of Thrina before."

"So?"

"There is a signal emerging from the black holes. A single Thrina tone, very strong."

"That's what started this whole thing," Anna said quietly. "Ignore it, and let's go home."

ON THE EDGES OF THE RIFT, THE OLD AND THE SICK, THE DETRITUS OF CIVIlization awaiting rebirth elsewhere, the Aighor pilgrims received the Thrina, and there was rejoicing.

The death-ships resumed their voyages.

Afterword

"The Venging" is not just about black holes, of course; I'm laying out the details of a space economy that lives and breathes information.

In 1977, in the wake of the success of *Star Wars*, studios and producers all over Los Angeles woke up to find the motion picture landscape changing drastically. Science fiction films—formerly relegated to B-movie status by the critics, and occasional blockbusters such as *Forbidden Planet* and *2001: A Space Odyssey*—were rapidly becoming standard fare and very profitable.

I was living in Long Beach at the time with my first wife, Tina. I published an article in the *Los Angeles Times* Calendar section, describing the roots of *Star Wars* in written SF. Suddenly, I started fielding calls from producers all at sea about science fiction, and over the next few weeks, I took a number of interesting meetings. I had a lovely lunch with Gene Roddenberry, who was planning a television reincarnation of *Star Trek*. Mr. Roddenberry had appreciated a comment I made in my article about how science fiction was the kind of horse best ridden by an individual, and how studios turned our mounts into camels—a horse designed by a committee.

I met with a number of people at Dino DeLaurentiis's Lion's Gate films, and had the pleasure of explaining to Dino's son why hot air rises; sadly, he died a few years later in a plane accident. Lion's Gate was about to go forward with an ill-conceived but beautifully art-directed version of *Flash Gordon*, and had already optioned Frank Herbert's *Dune*. I tried to get them to make one of my favorites, *The House on the Borderland*, based on William Hope Hodgson's novel, but no go. Also nix on filming Poul Anderson's *Tau Zero*.

I heard from a friend, Rick Sternbach, that Disney Studios was working on a film involving a black hole. The project's name at that stage was *Space Probe One*. Here, I thought, was a sterling opportunity. I called the studios and asked about the possibility of becoming a technical advisor. I carried a folio of paintings and a total devotion to the idea of black holes and how they would look.

My first meeting was with famed designer John Mansbridge, who then passed me on to Peter Ellenshaw, a master craftsman responsible for matte paintings in many movies. He was art director on *Space Probe One*. (He was also the father of Harrison Ellenshaw, another fine matte artist who produced backgrounds for *Star Wars* and many subsequent films.)

I showed all who were interested my painting of a black hole, done as a possible cover for "The Venging." As I spoke with Ellenshaw, studio head Ron Miller (no relation to the astronomical artist) came into Ellenshaw's office to chat, and was soon followed by the screenwriter. He seemed a little out of his depth, but Miller was faithfully sticking with him, and that was and is rare in movies.

It was a heady afternoon. Mansbridge told me I might be called on board the production as a sketch artist. I thought I was better suited to being a technical adviser, or even a script consultant, but what the hell. It was a job, and an interesting one.

I left behind the issue of *Galaxy* magazine that contained "The Venging."

I never got the job.

Eventually, *Space Probe One* became *The Black Hole*. It was Peter Ellenshaw's last film, a beautiful production incorporating many technical advances, but otherwise it was pretty abysmal. Oddly enough, there had been a change made in the original movie concept. After passing through the film's glowing, geometric toilet-bowl of a black hole, the good guys end up in a kind of mystical heaven—painted onto the ceiling of the Sistine Chapel. The bad guy, played by German actor Maximilian Schell, ends up quite literally in a Dantean Hell, entombed in his evil robot and surrounded by flames.

Shades of the end of "The Venging"? We'll never know, very likely.

It was ironic, however, that this multimillion-dollar production thudded to a halt with an awful pun. The evil robot is named Maximilian. Maximilian Schell ends up in Hell, in Maximilian's shell.

I wonder if anyone at Disney got the joke.

As an after–after-note, I called Disney Studios at one point and Ron Miller answered the phone. Wow! I've never had that experience since—or talked to another studio head in person, for that matter. Charming.

I COULD NOT QUITE UNDERSTAND WHY ANNA WAS SO DOWN ON LIVING FOR-ever in this and subsequent stories. Clearly, I was working through some ethical issues. But most of my fiction avoided the topic of biological immortality in later years. (In the Thistledown books, people die but have their mentalities uploaded into City Memory—a prospect that seems to me less and less likely, barring transporter-beam superscience.)

I finally explored some of my issues and objections to biological immortality in *Vitals*, published in early 2002. I doubt that I've reached any final conclusions, however. Neither did Anna, as we learn in "Perihesperon."

Introduction to "Perihesperon"

In the middle- and late-seventies, Roger Elwood was cutting a swath through science fiction with a plethora of anthologies and a line of SF novels published by Harlequin in Canada, famed for knock-'em-out-by-the-ream formulaic romances. Elwood's line was called Laser Books, and it was advertised to the Trade through catalogs lacking author names—a no-no in science fiction publishing, where readers care who is writing what. The line folded, but not before publishing novels by Tim Powers, R. Faraday Nelson, and many other up-and-coming writers. I never wrote a Laser Book, but I did sell a short story to one of Elwood's original anthologies, *Tomorrow: New Worlds of Science Fiction*.

This was my first appearance in hardcover (1975, the same year as "The Venging") and needless to say, I was extremely pleased with myself. I was living with my first wife, Tina, in an apartment in Costa Mesa, writing and painting and trying to pull myself up by my bootstraps while fitfully marketing a novel called *Hegira*. I was a newlywed, idealistic and energetic, and I remember those years as pretty good times, full of growth.

I was most of the way through another novel, a time travel piece called *The Kriti Cylinder* that would get shelved before it was sent out to publishers. And I was plotting a story called "Mandala," which was later bought by Robert Silverberg for his anthology *New Directions 9*. ("Mandala" is not included in this collection; it was published in 1982 as part of my novel *Strength of Stones*.)

Elwood would later move on to make a name for himself in Christian publishing, and to help first lady Nancy Reagan write her autobiography.

"Perihesperon" is something of a downer, all about inevitable doom and bravery. It contains some backstory on Anna Sigrid-Nestor, however, and isn't that bad, after all these years.

Perihesperon
Tomorrow, Roger Elwood, 1975

It was the six-hour sleep period for the passengers. Parabolas of light divided the corridors where dim lamps glowed orange. Black carpet on the floors dulled the girl's footsteps. The ordinary sounds of shipboard machinery continued. The muted hum of the blowers and the barely audible click-whine of the periodic engine bursts comforted Karen a little, but she was still disturbed by her solitude.

Her parents hadn't been in the cabin. She shuffled across the carpet in blue quilted robe and knitted slippers, long brown hair quickly combed back behind her ears. As she passed beneath the corridor lights, the top of her head glowed in a yellow crescent and her face fell into umber shadow.

She reached out to touch the wall for balance, unsteady with the new strength in her step. As planned, the ship's artificial gravity had dropped another quarter since she fell asleep.

Something had scratched the yellow enamel on one wall. She examined the revealed layers of primer and white undercoating, the gray plastic bulkhead beneath.

"Hello?" she called hesitantly into an empty cabin.

The cabin's beds had been tucked away in the wall. Nets stuck out a little sloppily from drawer edges. The desklamp glowed. She moved on.

The lounge waited two decks down, and beneath that, the level reserved for the crew—on this flight three men, pilots or copilots or whatever they called the people who monitored the automated ship—and two stewards. One pilot and one steward were female, young and friendly. Karen had talked to them the day before. She thought perhaps they could explain what was going on.

The central elevator didn't work. She descended an emergency ladder to the lounge and stood in the hatchway, jaw clenched tight.

Card tables had been drawn out. The theater screen's doors had been pulled aside. Chairs lay toppled and cards scattered as if wind had blown through the room.

A woman's tote bag lay next to one overturned chair, its contents spilled. Something red puddled on the carpet, too bright to be blood. She dipped her finger into it and sniffed. Nail polish. A ruptured autospray.

Eyes wide and nostrils flushed with the cold, sniffling in the chill air, she returned to the ladder and its tight tube and descended to the crew level.

"Hello?" she called again. No answer. It was impossible, but she was alone on the ship.

Everybody was gone.

Servos clicked and whined. She jumped as a voice spoke from the control room. "Flux rate five thousand hertz, emission velocity point-nine-nine c, time of pulse zero seven-zero-five hours. Request acknowledgment of previous engine analysis."

She returned to the empty control room and listened to the calm requests of the unattended computer.

Beyond the wide transparent panels, stars burned clear and bright, drifting slowly past the window. The ship tumbled and rolled in space. She knew enough about their journey to understand that no such motion was part of the flight plan.

The brownish mass of Hesperus rolled into view, sparsely striped with ice clouds and gray volcanic smudges. Even from a thousand kilometers the broad crater-scarred roads and cities showed as distinct markings. Hesperus's life had vanished in war before humankind had lost its body hair and crossed thumb and little finger.

"Correction of axis yaw in four minutes seven seconds. Please explain cause of yaw. Damage report is incomplete."

More frightened, she descended the ladder again, fingers clawing at the rungs, breath coming in harsh rasps.

Recreation occupied two decks below the crew quarters, adjoining a zero-gravity gymnasium. The door to the gymnasium had been sealed. The door's window fogged with drops of frost. She leaned against the far wall, lip quivering.

This is ridiculous, she thought. *I'm starting to cry. I will* not *cry.* She pushed herself from the wall and ran around the curving corridor, circling the deck, peering into the automated galley, empty, and the in-flight storage area. Tears streamed down her cheeks when she completed the inspection and stood again in front of the gymnasium.

If they were all inside the closed room, then—

She brightened immediately and pushed the button for the door to open. It stayed shut. The frost on the window slowly cleared and she looked inside.

A wide black streak marred the chamber floor. The rubber matting had burned and bubbled. Something had been wedged against a bulkhead high above the door, a patch of some sort, bulging outward toward the closed-off corridor which ringed the lower level.

"I'll be damned," a low voice said to one side. "I thought no one made it." She twisted around to face the man standing a few meters away. He wasn't a passenger, she knew immediately, and he wasn't a member of the crew. A stowaway?

"Where is everybody?" she asked, keeping her tone smooth.

"Went out like lights a half-hour ago. They're gone, honey. Were you in your cabin?" She nodded and examined him as though dreaming. He was old and nut-brown, face lightly etched with lines, nose broad, eyes large and black and calm. He wore green coveralls. An orange lump twitched on his shoulder.

"Where are they?" she asked, not wanting to understand.

"I've never seen anything like it. Snuffed out in minutes. Meteoroid took out a man-sized hole in the lower level, and all the doors were jammed open when it plowed through the safety center. She was airless in less than a minute." He pursed his lips and shook his head. "Everybody's dead. Sorry, honey."

"No," she said, backing away from him. "No!" She ran back along the corridor and up the narrow stairs, hair flying. The man in green stood motionless and looked at where she had stood, his face empty. The lump on his shoulder stirred and extended two horny palps to itch at his ear. "Stop that," he said and the palps withdrew. "We've got more problems than I expected."

When Karen reached her room she looked at the empty nets, still extended, and remembered the card game that had been planned. Her only thought—and part of her coolly considered it ridiculous—was that she was twelve years old and now she was an orphan. What was she going to do?

THERE WAS ONE MORE BODY FOR HIM TO THROW OUT OF THE SHIP. UNDER different circumstances he would have kept the bodies in cold storage, as many as possible, but there was no point in that now. He removed the contorted steward's corpse and placed it in the lock, closing the inner hatch. He slipped into his spacesuit, adjusted the seals, and opened the three outer hatches. Hand clenched on the grips, he braced himself against the playful push of out-rushing air and frozen mist. He kicked the body into space with all his strength and said a brief prayer. Already stiffening in the cold, the body twisted around its central axis and began a slow journey away from the ship.

How was he going to tell the girl what was wrong? He closed the hatch, climbed out of the suit and hung it up neatly in its rack. The orange lump stirred uneasily on his shoulder and he patted it as he locked off the one ruptured level and restored the elevator to operation.

Then he went to find her cabin.

She sat on her bed, one hand entwined in the netting, staring at the opposite wall with its screen-picture of terrestrial desert. She turned to look at the old man as he walked into the door frame, then turned away.

"My name's Cammis Alista, Alista my calling name," he said. "What'll I call you?"

She shrugged as if it didn't matter. Then she said, "Karen."

"We're in trouble, Karen."

"Who are you?" she asked. "I don't remember you on the ship."

"I wasn't," Alista said. "I'm a drifter. Had my own ship, shared it with Jerk here." He patted the orange thing. "We stay away from the lanes mostly, but we have to cross paths with the big ships now and then. We saw that your ship was in trouble. We came aboard."

Karen knew enough about interplanetary distances to think that was hardly credible. She shook her head back and forth, trying to show with one part that she was smart enough not to believe him, and with another part that she didn't care.

"I happened to be following your assigned orbit," he said. "Hooked up with your path when you slingshotted around Hesperus to cut travel time to Satiyajit. I was searching for satellites around Hesperus—alien artifacts bring a good price, you know."

She looked at him again, trying to analyze his features, and she scowled at the thing he called Jerk. "Where's your ship?"

"I approached your ship and made a mistake. Didn't keep out of the way of a flux pulse. You were tumbling pretty badly, I thought the computers would have shut down the drive, but they hadn't. You roasted my outer shell like so much cake batter. Got me pretty good, too, with subsidiary scatter." He smiled a twisted smile and shrugged at the thought of what that meant.

"I didn't do it to you," she said.

"I didn't mean you, your ship . . ."

"It's not my ship," she said.

"You're right," Alista gave in, shrugging again. "It's not really even a ship any more. The safeties were destroyed and part of the guidance computer. I turned off the engines when I came aboard through the meteor hole. The computer still acts as if the engines were running. It clicks its servos and whistles its little electric songs as though everything's okay. My guess is, about two hours ago you were to start the flux pulses which would establish your path to Satiyajit, but now we're starting to curve back toward Hesperus. The computer put the ship in orbit after the accident, very eccentric, but we'll stay up here all the same."

He fell silent and shook his head at his own blabbering. "I'm not insensitive, honey, I know what you must be feeling." He knuckled his eyes. Drops of water beaded on the back of his hand.

"We're not going to Satiyajit?"

"No chance. Not for a while anyway. They'll be sending ships out soon. They'll be here in a few weeks."

"We'll be alive then?"

He lied. "I don't see why not. Hey, feel like a little food?" She said no and slumped down with her elbows on her knees. She was going to cry now. She knew it with certainty and didn't care whether he was there or not. Mother and Father were dead. Why was she alive?

The first sob shook her softly. The second was more violent. Alista backed out of the door and said he would fix some food.

The machines in the automatic galley were in good condition, and he punched up two synthecarn dinners. Jerk moved restlessly on his shoulder and squeaked its own demands for sustenance. Alista played with the controls of the machines for a moment and came up with a reasonable substitute for a yeast biscuit. He fed this to the animal as he gathered courage to face the girl again.

His lie wouldn't help. Their present orbit would take them right through a belt of Hesperus's moonlets. If they were lucky enough to escape them, in less than a day they'd be running through the belt again. A rescue ship wouldn't reach them for a couple of weeks. He wouldn't live that long anyway. He had no more than three days. Jerk could outlast them all by encysting and floating around in the wreckage.

He took the covered trays to the girl's cabin. Pretending suspicion, she picked a morsel from her meal, then ate it in small bites while he watched from the desk chair.

Her eyes had puffed with crying. She was very young, he thought. Fourteen, fifteen? Perhaps younger. She wasn't what he would call beautiful, but there was a simple regularity to her features which produced a pleasing effect. It was a face which any man could grow to love over the years far more than any rubber-stamp beauty. "Listen," he said. "You know how to take care of yourself on this thing?"

She nodded as she ate. "Why?"

"I just wanted to know. I'm not . . ." But he shook his head and filled his mouth with food, chewing and smiling, shaking his head. Could he feel the creeping disintegration of his flesh? Would he hide in a locked sealed cabin the last few hours, so she wouldn't see?

Karen stood up and asked if he'd picked out a room yet. His look of surprise irritated her. Did he think she was concerned about him? No. She was dead inside. She couldn't be concerned about anything any more.

"Not yet," he said.

"Well, you'd better find one."

"Okay," he said. He took both trays and left, standing in the door frame for a moment, as he had stood before. "You'll be all right, Karen?" His questions were curiously accented in the middle, as though each query were half a statement of fact.

"Yes," she said.

He went to find a cabin and get some sleep.

WHEN ALISTA CAME AWAKE, HE SHUT OFF THE NET THAT HAD HELD HIM IN place during the night and kept him warm in the mesh pajamas he'd borrowed. He put everything in its place as though the occupant would be back soon. He had chosen the first officer's cabin, feeling more comfortable in the room of a man who had faced risks as his official duty.

If such a man's time came in such a meaningless way, that was his gamble.

A passenger's cabin would have made Alista nervous.

He found Karen in the lounge cleaning up the scattered cards and taking out the spilled nail polish with solvent. "Damn," she said. "It eats the carpet, too."

"Do you want breakfast?" he asked.

"I've fixed some already," she said.

"I'll get some more myself then."

"Yours is all ready. It's in the warmer."

"Thank you." Looking around the compartment, he commented that it looked better and she shrugged.

"You put them all outside?" she asked.

He nodded.

"Why?"

"You know." He looked at her sternly. She looked away and took a deep breath.

When he had finished his food he tapped the orange lump with his finger and it came to life, protruding eyes on stalks and waving palps. "Ever seen anything like Jerk before?"

Karen shook her head. She didn't want to look at it, or ask any questions, or have it explained to her.

"When I get back from the control room I'll tell you about Jerk. I'm going to shut down the computer and cut the servos. We lose a little battery power each time they switch on the engine pumps."

"You stopped the fuel feed?" she asked.

"I did," Alista said, taking hope from the unprompted question.

He checked the ship's position by shooting the sun rising over the bloated arc of Hesperus and taking an angle from distant bright Sirius. Comparing his findings with the computer, the machine followed his calculations to three figures. The ship's brains weren't scrambled, then. He threw out his own paper and questioned the guidance systems about their position and orbital velocity.

Their speed was increasing. They were approaching Perihesperon. In a few minutes they'd make their first pass through the lunar belt at— he checked the readout—twenty-two-thousand kilometers per hour. At that velocity it would be useless to try to dodge moonlets with the ship's maneuvering and docking engines.

He didn't feel old, watching the planets fill the screen. He didn't feel very old at all, but then he couldn't sense the breakdown of his cells either. Flexing his arms, stretching his legs to increase circulation, he felt like a young man, not at all ready to give up.

Something dark blotted out the planet for the blink of an eye. Then a sharply defined scatter of chunks went past. A haze of dust made the ship tremble and buck.

They were through. First passage.

He returned to the lounge, practicing smiles and wiping them away as they inevitably approached fatuousness.

"Hey!" he said. "I'm going to tell you about Jerk, hm?"

She nodded.

"I picked him up from a dealer on Tau Ceti's Myriadne. He—it—whatever, comes from a place where the air is so bad nothing can breath it, so he breaks down silicates for his oxygen. He eats plants that absorb his own kind when they're dead, and the whole thing . . ." he indicated the ecological pattern with a circling finger, ". . . means that no animal kills another animal to survive. So he's docile and smart . . ." He stopped and didn't feel like saying anything more, but he finished the sentence, "because he absorbs from your own personality, so he's as smart as his owner."

Karen was looking at the spot the solvent had made on the carpet.

"He, she, it, doesn't matter," Alista said. "Jerk doesn't care."

"Did something happen to you?" she asked. "I mean, when you came near the ship."

Alista felt like a small child who wanted to say something, but couldn't. He was eighty years old and he felt so much like a child that he wanted to find a sympathetic breast and weep. But he was a man long used to death, and finding a frightened weakness in himself made him more reluctant to say or do anything.

"Yes," he said.

"Bad?"

"Yes."

"You're going to die?"

"Yes, dammit! Be quiet. Don't say anything."

And he turned to walk out. A day, two days. That was all.

How long did she have?

The second passage through the belt went smoothly. Alista investigated the emergency shields to see what they could repel. They could absorb and transfer impacts from anything up to nine tons. But the shields required safeties to activate them and a guidance system to pinpoint their maximum force on the approaching object. Neither were in working order.

Karen stayed to herself, reading fitfully or trying to sleep, and he stayed in the bridge cabin, idly searching all possible avenues of escape.

If he didn't tell her and she died by surprise, would that be less cruel than telling her? Alista wasn't a religious man, but his Polynesian her-

itage still impressed him with the idea that dignity and a certain courage
in facing one's end led to better relations in the afterlife.

Relations to what, he couldn't say—he'd long since stopped speculating about things after death. Death was merely the final solving of
mysteries, one way or another.

Karen broke out of her pose of deep sorrow when the idea came to
her that she wasn't going to survive. She couldn't shake it because she
could visualize nothing beyond the walls of the crippled ship. She went
to Alista on the bridge and again the uncomfortable waiting for words
began. Alista spoke first, adjusting his seat and manufacturing an excuse
to concentrate on the controls. "I thought you were asleep."

"Couldn't."

"It would be good if you could get some rest."

"I've been sleeping for hours," she said. "I have some more questions."

"Ask them," Alista said.

"What's going to keep the rescue ship from getting here?"

"Nothing."

"Don't lie to me!" she said, indignant. "I'm not a little girl."

"I see," he said. He wanted to ask, *And have you had lovers and children,
and lost people you loved and understood with the grace of your own years
what they lost by dying?*

"It's filthy," she said, "just filthy, not telling me what's going to happen."

"I don't want to make you unhappy."

"I'm not a child," she said softly, evenly.

Alista lifted the shoulder with Jerk on it and patted the orange lump,
head cocked to one side. "You may make it. You'll last longer than I
will, anyway. But more than likely the ship will hit a rock in the belt
of moonlets and everything will go . . ." He made a whoosh with lips
and slapped his palms together.

"It will?"

He nodded.

"Goodbye to all, then."

"Hello to what?" he grinned.

"Where are you from?" she asked, And he told her. He talked for a
few minutes, telling of old Earth, where she'd never been, of Molokai
in a group of islands in a big ocean, of schools and brown children and
going away to seek the stars.

She spoke of her schools on Satiyajit, and the boyfriend who waited
for her, and of her parents. When she could find nothing more to say,
she told him how little she had really seen. She was surprised to find
she had no more self-pity, only a deep well of honesty which told her

all the sad, sad pressure in her gut was something human, of course, but of no use to anybody, least of all her.

They ate dinner together in silence. Alista's face was more relaxed, lines untensed, and his cheeks less wrinkled. But he grew visibly more pale and weaker.

Alone in his cabin, he vomited up his food and slept fitfully, sweating, on the floor, wrapped in a curtain unhooked from the lounge wall. He couldn't stand the formless comfort of the net.

"Let's be a little happy," Karen said when the sleep period was over and she met Alista in the hall around the gymnasium. "Can you make the music play?" He said he could, but he was too weak to dance. "Then let me dance for you," she said. "You won't mind?"

He could hardly mind. She slipped on blue tights and pulled her hair into a long braid, putting a round white cap on her head. With a clapper in one hand and a bell in the other, she showed him a smooth ballet to orchestrated concréte sounds.

She moved in slow motion in the low gravity, but when she finished her breath came in heavy gasps. Her face, flushed with exertion, showed no awareness of the upcoming third passage.

Alista put himself to bed an hour later and took a small drink of water from a cup brought by Karen. With the weakening of his blood, his face was pale; with the failure of his liver, it was turning yellow.

He asked her to get him the kit from the medical officer's cabin and she did so. When she came back he saw she'd been crying and he asked her why.

"I can't hold it back," she said. "I just wish I was never born, to have to feel like I do now. It's all so damned useless! I haven't seen or done anything, anything at all!"

"A little while ago you said you weren't a little child. Do you still think that?"

"No," she said. "I feel like I've just been born."

"Would you like to hear a story?" he asked. "Maybe it'll make both of us feel better."

"All right," she said.

"I was a gigolo once, a long time ago, and do you know whom I was a gigolo to?" Karen shook her head, no. "I was a consort to Baroness Anna Sigrid-Nestor."

"You knew her?" Karen asked, not quite believing. Anna Sigrid-Nestor had been the richest woman in the galaxy, with her control of Dallat Enterprises, the third largest Economische.

"I did. I knew her for three years, the last three years of her life. She was a hundred and fifty years old and she was an abstainer. She didn't use juvenates because—well, I never did find out exactly why, but even when her doctor told her she was going to die soon, she refused them. She also refused prosthetics and transplants.

"The last year, I couldn't be her gigolo any more. She finally gave that up." He smiled at the woman's perseverance and Karen managed a grin of half-understanding. "But I stayed on her ship. She liked to talk with me. Everybody else was too scared to come near her. She kept me on her flagship until she died." He stopped to regain his breath.

"That damned old woman, do you know what she had planned for her funeral? She was going to have her body sealed in a sublight ship and shot into a protostar in the Orion nebula. She thought she could radiate throughout the galaxy then and be immortal that way.

"A few weeks before she died, with the flagship warping to the nebula, she realized what she was doing. She was contradicting her own beliefs. She wanted to call it off. But she hadn't been thinking too well, she'd been getting senile—though I hadn't noticed—and she had ordered that all the ship's officers be fired without benefits if the original mission wasn't fulfilled.

"It was very sad. Nobody would listen to her. Now she wanted to be buried like everybody else of her faith, without pretension, and she couldn't. She told me and I tried to fight the officers, but they wouldn't budge. They said there was no way out for them. I think maybe they were taking a little revenge on her for years of. . . . Well, she was a strong woman."

"That's horrible," Karen said.

Alista nodded. "We were all waiting for her to die, and you know what I began to do? Me, tough old Cammis Alista, I swore I'd never let myself get so involved with another woman again. You know, she was ugly and wrinkled and her breasts were dry and flat, but what she'd *been* and *done*; when she was dying, I loved her for those things. And I wanted to make her live. But there was no way out." He swallowed. "I talked with her just like you and I are talking now, and she told me why she had never wanted to live forever.

" 'Alista,' she said, 'there's something very odd about living. It's not how long you live, not how long a bird flies, but how high you reach and what you learn when you get there. Just like a bird that flies as high as it can, and only does it once before going too near the sun. Think of the glory it must feel to go closer than anyone else!' "

He closed his eyes to rest. They were pink with ruptured vessels. "I asked her, 'What if we never get near the sun at all?' And she said that none of us ever do, really, but we have to work to make ourselves think that way. To think that we really do. She said, 'When I last saw the sun, the sun I was born under, it was something I didn't even pay attention to. I didn't care about it. When I last saw the Earth I was rich and young and it didn't matter to me that I might never come back.'

"The doctor kicked me out of her room before she died. But she wrote a note later. When I read it she was dead and they had just shot her off into the protostar cluster."

"What was the note?" Karen asked.

"A poem. I don't know who wrote it, maybe she did. But it said, 'When last I saw my final sun, I was cold and didn't mind the dark. But now, so near, my chill needs your warmth, and I cry for the warmth denied, the dark to come. I want to sing more, say more words, love again.' That was all she wrote."

"Do you know what she meant?"

"No," Alista said. "I took juvenates like everybody else. I didn't want to die as she had. When she was gone there was nothing left. A little bit of the dark world came in after her, and she didn't even come to my dreams."

Jerk crawled up from the blankets and squatted on Alista's chest, examining his face carefully with extended eyes.

"I don't want to die either," Karen said. Alista smiled in agreement.

"I'll trade you places, little girl," he said. "I'll take your loneliness for my quick end."

"Maybe I'll be saved," she said. "Maybe we can pass through the ring without hitting anything."

SHE DIDN'T CRY FOR THE OLD SPACEMAN WHEN HE WAS GONE. SHE WALKED to the lounge, taking the orange animal with her. She didn't have the strength to write anything, and it didn't much matter anyway, so she spoke out loud. She stroked the orange lump and talked of all the places and things she wanted to see again, and do again, all the people she wanted to meet again.

"There's my parents," she said. Silence. "And Allen. And my friends at school. I would like to dance some more, but I'd probably never be any good. I'd like to . . ."

She was going to say "have children," but that was too much to even begin to understand.

She tried to understand. "I'll miss not seeing things again. There's the lake where we swam at Ankhar, with its snaky blue fish. And my room at—"

Introduction to "Scattershot"

In 1979, when James Turner, editor at Arkham House, contemplated buying a collection of my short fiction, he picked out four stories he thought were worthy: "The Wind from a Burning Woman," "Mandala," "The White Horse Child," and "Scattershot."

"Scattershot" was bought originally by Terry Carr for *Universe 8*. Terry was a friendly and charming man, but editorially spare with words; it was enough, in those days, that he bought a story. Terry—and Ben Bova at *Analog*, and Robert Silverberg—made me feel I was making real progress in those years before any of my novels had sold.

This story features one of my typical strong female characters, and it also shows the influence of James Tiptree, Jr.—an influence I now find slightly peculiar.

Everyone knows now that Tiptree was actually a woman, Alice Sheldon. She wrote fine short stories and cut quite a swath through the science fiction world in the 1970s. Her biography is fascinating. Suffice it to say that in her stories, she often gave the masculine sex a hard time. She was not an overt lesbian, to my knowledge, but in her journals and spoken diaries, she tells us that the sexual attentions of men made her uncomfortable. She married a much older man, and when he was dying and life to her seemed not worth living, she shot him, and then shot herself.

She seemed to enjoy her run at literature a great deal, and the exchanges of letters her stories provoked. She also enjoyed deceiving people, for a time at least, as to her gender.

Many writers, perhaps most, adopt likely quirks to work to the market. In "Scattershot," the quirk I acquired from Tiptree is so small hardly anyone will notice it. But I give the strong male in this story a very hard time, and promote the women characters to almost mythic stature. It seemed right at the time.

Tiptree was wry, witty, and probably deeply misandric. We all miss her, but I no longer want to write like her.

Now, when I write strong women characters, I intend that they be natural and believable, not distorted or mythic. It's tough to beat Alice Sheldon at her own game, and also tough to beat H. Rider Haggard.

Discerning readers might note that this story bears a similarity to "Hardfought." The deep structure is the same, in fact, but the endings are very different.

SCATTERSHOT
Universe 8, Terry Carr, 1978

The Teddy bear spoke excellent Mandarin. It stood about fifty centimeters tall, a plump fellow with close-set eyes above a nose unusually long for the generally pug breed. It paced around me, muttering
to itself.

I rolled over and felt barbs down my back and sides. My arms moved
with reluctance. Something about my will to get up and the way my
muscles reacted was out-of-kilter; the nerves didn't conveying properly.
So it was, I thought, with my eyes and the small black-and-white beast
they claimed to see: a derangement of phosphene patterns, cross-tied
with childhood memories and snatches of linguistics courses ten years
past.

It began speaking Russian. I ignored it and focused on other things.
The rear wall of my cabin was unrecognizable, covered with geometric
patterns that shifted in and out of bas-relief and glowed faintly in the
shadow cast by a skewed panel light. My fold-out desk had been torn
from its hinges and now lay on the floor, not far from my head. The
ceiling was cream-colored. Last I remembered it had been a pleasant
shade of burnt orange. Thus tallied, half my cabin was still with me.
The other half had been ferried away in the—

Disruption. I groaned, and the bear stepped back nervously. My body
was gradually coordinating. Bits and pieces of disassembled vision integrated and stopped their random flights, and still the creature walked,
and still it spoke, though getting deep into German.

It was not a minor vision. It was either real or a full-fledged hallucination.

"What's going on?" I asked.

It bent over me, sighed, and said, "Of all the fated arrangements. A
speaking I know not the best of—Anglo." It held out its arms and shivered. "Pardon the distraught. My cords of psyche—nerves?—they have
not decided which continuum to obey this moment."

"Same for me," I said cautiously. "Who are you?"

"Psyche, we are all psyche. Take this care and be not content with
illusion, this path, this merriment. Excuse. Some writers in English. All
I know is from the read."

"Am I still on my ship?"

"So we are all, and *hors de combat*. We limp for the duration."

I was integrated enough to stand, and I towered over the bear, rearranging my tunic. My left breast ached with a bruise. Because we had been riding at one G for five days, I was wearing a bra, and the bruise lay directly under a strap. Such, to quote, was the fated arrangement. As my wits gathered and held converse, I considered what might have happened and felt a touch of the "distraughts" myself. I began to shiver like a recruit in pressure-drop training.

We had survived. That is, at least I had survived, out of a crew of forty-three. How many others?

"Do you know . . . have you found out—"

"Worst," the bear said. "Some I do not catch, the deciphering of other things not so hard. Disrupted about seven, eight hours past. It was a force of many, for I have counted ten separate things not in my recognition." It grinned. "You are ten, and best yet. We are perhaps not so far in world-lines."

We'd been told survival after disruption was possible. Practical statistics indicated one out of a myriad ships, so struck, would remain integral. For a weapon that didn't actually kill in itself, the probability disrupter was very effective.

"Are we intact?" I asked.

"Fated," the Teddy bear said. "I cognize we can even move and seek a base. Depending."

"Depending," I echoed. The creature sounded masculine, despite size and a childlike voice. "Are you a he? Or—"

"He," the bear said quickly.

I touched the bulkhead above the door and ran my finger along a familiar, slightly crooked seam. Had the disruption kept me in my own universe—against incalculable odds—or exchanged me to some other? Was either of us in a universe we could call our own?

"Is it safe to look around?"

The bear hummed. "Cognize—know not. Last I saw, others had not reached a state of organizing."

It was best to start from the beginning. I looked down at the creature and rubbed a bruise on my forehead. "Wh-where are you from?"

"Same as you, possible," he said. "Earth. Was mascot to captain, for cuddle and advice."

That sounded bizarre enough. I walked to the hatchway and peered down the corridor. It was plain and utilitarian, but neither the right color nor configuration. The hatch at the end was round and had a manual sealing system, six black throw-bolts that no human engineer would ever have put on a spaceship. "What's your name?"

"Have got no official name. Mascot name known only to captain."

I was scared, so my brusque nature surfaced and I asked him sharply if his captain was in sight, or any other aspect of the world he'd known.

"Cognize not," he answered. "Call me Sonok."

"I'm Geneva," I said. "Francis Geneva."

"We are friends?"

"I don't see why not. I hope we're not the only ones who can be friendly. Is English difficult for you?"

"Mind not. I learn fast. Practice make perfection."

"Because I can speak some Russian, if you want."

"Good as I with Anglo?" Sonok asked. I detected a sense of humor—and self-esteem—in the bear.

"No, probably not. English it is. If you need to know anything, don't be embarrassed to ask."

"Sonok hardly embarrassed by anything. Was mascot."

The banter was providing a solid framework for my sanity to grab on to. I had an irrational desire to take the bear and hug him, just for want of something warm. His attraction was undeniable—tailored, I guessed, for that very purpose. But tailored from what? The color suggested panda; the shape did not.

"What do you think we should do?" I asked, sitting on my bunk.

"Sonok not known for quick decisions," he said, squatting on the floor in front of me. He was stubby-limbed but far from clumsy.

"Nor am I," I said. "I'm a software and machinery language expert. I wasn't combat-trained."

"Not cognize 'software,' " Sonok said.

"Programming materials," I explained. The bear nodded and got up to peer around the door. He pulled back and scrabbled to the rear of the cabin.

"They're here!" he said. "Can port shut?"

"I wouldn't begin to know how—" But I retreated just as quickly and clung to my bunk. A stream of serpents flowed by the hatchway, metallic green and yellow, with spade-shaped heads and red ovals running dorsally.

The stream passed without even a hint of intent to molest, and Sonok climbed down the bas-relief pattern. "What the hell are they doing here?" I asked.

"They are a crew member, I think," Sonok said.

"What—who else is out there?"

The bear straightened and looked at me steadily. "Have none other than to seek," he said solemnly. "Elsewise, we possess no rights to ask. No?" The bear walked to the hatch, stepped over the bottom seal, and stood in the corridor. "Come?"

I got up and followed.

A WOMAN'S MIND IS A STRANGE POOL TO SLIP INTO AT BIRTH. IT IS SET WITHIN parameters by the first few months of listening and seeing. Her infant mind is a vast blank template that absorbs all and stores it away. In those first few months come role acceptance, a beginning to attitude, and a hint of future achievement. Listening to adults and observing their actions build a storehouse of preconceptions and warnings: *Do not see those ghosts on bedroom walls—they aren't there! None of the rest of us can see your imaginary companions, darling. . . . It's something you have to understand.*

And so, from some dim beginning, not *ex nihilo* but out of totality, the woman begins to pare her infinite self down. She whittles away at this unwanted piece, that undesired trait. She forgets in time that she was once part of all and turns to the simple tune of life, rather than to the endless and symphonic *before*. She forgets those companions who danced on the ceiling above her bed and called to her from the dark. Some of them were friendly; others, even in the dim time, were not pleasant. But they were all *she*. For the rest of her life, the woman seeks some echo of that preternatural menagerie; in the men she chooses to love, in the tasks she chooses to perform, in the way she tries to be. After thirty years of cutting, she becomes Francis Geneva.

When love dies, another piece is pared away, another universe is sheared off, and the split can never join again. With each winter and spring, spent on or off worlds with or without seasons, the woman's life grows more solid, and smaller.

But now the parts are coming together again, the companions out of the dark above the child's bed. Beware of them. They're all the things you once lost or let go, and now they walk on their own, out of your control; reborn, as it were, and indecipherable.

"DO YOU HAVE UNDERSTANDING?" THE BEAR ASKED. I SHOOK MY HEAD TO break my steady stare at the six-bolted hatch.

"Understand what?" I asked.

"Of how we are here."

"Disrupted. By Aighors, I presume."

"Yes, they are the ones for us, too. But how?"

"I don't know," I said. No one did. We could only observe the results. When the remains of disrupted ships could be found, they always resembled floating garbage heaps—plucked from our universe, rearranged in some cosmic grab-bag, and returned. What came back was of the same mass, made up of the same basic materials, and recombined with a tendency toward order and viability. But in deep space, even ninety percent viability was tantamount to none at all. If the ship's separate elements didn't integrate perfectly—a one in a hundred thousand

chance—there were no survivors. But oh, how interested we were in
the corpses! Most were kept behind the Paper Curtain of secrecy, but
word leaked out even so—word of ostriches with large heads, blobs with
bits of crystalline seawater still adhering to them . . . and now my own
additions, a living Teddy bear and a herd of parti-colored snakes. All
had been snatched out of terrestrial ships from a maze of different universes.

Word also leaked out that of five thousand such incidents, not once
had a human body been returned to our continuum.

"Some things still work," Sonok said. "We are heavy the same."

The gravitation was unchanged—I hadn't paid attention to that. "We
can still breathe, for that matter," I said. "We're all from one world.
There's no reason to think the basics will change." And that meant there
had to be standards for communication, no matter how diverse the
forms. Communication was part of my expertise, but thinking about it
made me shiver. A ship runs on computers, or their equivalent. How
were at least ten different computer systems communicating? Had they
integrated with working interfaces? If they hadn't, our time was limited.
Soon all hell would join us, darkness and cold, and vacuum.

I released the six throw-bolts and opened the hatch slowly.

"Say, Geneva," Sonok mused as we looked into the corridor beyond.
"How did the snakes get through here?"

I shook my head. There were more important problems. "I want to
find something like a ship's bridge, or at least a computer terminal. Did
you see something before you found my cabin?"

Sonok nodded. "Other way in corridor. But there were . . . things
there. Didn't enjoy the looks, so came this way."

"What were they?" I asked.

"One like trash can," he said. "With breasts."

"We'll keep looking this way," I said by way of agreement.

The next bulkhead was a dead end. A few round displays studded the
wall, filled like bull's-eyes with concentric circles of varying thickness.
A lot of information could be carried in such patterns, given a precise
optical scanner to read them—which suggested a machine more than
an organism, though not necessarily. The bear paced back and forth in
front of the wall.

I reached out with one hand to touch the displays. Then I got down
on my knees to feel the bulkhead, looking for a seam. "Can't see it, but
I feel something here—like a ridge in the material."

The bulkhead, displays and all, peeled away like a heart's triplet valve,
and a rush of air shoved us into darkness. I instinctively rolled into a
fetal curl. The bear bumped against me and grabbed my arm. Some
throbbing force flung us this way and that, knocking us against squeak-

ing wet things. I forced my eyes open and unfurled my arms and legs, trying to find a grip. One hand rapped against metal or hard plastic, and the other caught what felt like rope. With some fumbling, I gripped the rope and braced myself against the hard surface. Then I had time to sort out what I was seeing. The chamber seemed to be open to space, but we were breathing, so obviously a transparent membrane was keeping in the atmosphere. I could see the outer surface of the ship, and it appeared a hell of a lot larger than I'd allowed. Clinging to the membrane in a curve, as though queued on the inside of a bubble, were five or six round nebulosities that glowed dull orange like dying suns. I was hanging on to something resembling a ship's mast, a metal pylon that reached from one side of the valve to the center of the bubble. Ropes were rigged from the pylon to stanchions that seemed suspended in midair, though they had to be secured against the membrane. The ropes and pylon supported clusters of head-sized spheres covered with hairlike plastic tubing. They clucked like brood hens as they slid away from us. "Góspodi!" Sonok screeched.

The valve that had given us access was still open, pushing its flaps in and out. I kicked away from the pylon. The bear's grip was fierce. The flaps loomed, slapped against us, and closed with a final sucking throb. We were on the other side, lying on the floor. The bulkhead again was impassively blank.

The bear rolled away from my arm and stood up. "Best to try the other way!" he suggested. "More easily faced, I cognize."

I unshipped the six-bolted hatch, and we crawled through. We doubled back and went past my cabin. The corridor, now that I thought of it, was strangely naked. In any similar region on my ship there would have been pipes, access panels, printed instructions and at least ten cabin doors.

The corridor curved a few yards past my cabin, and the scenery became more diverse. We found several small cubbyholes, all empty, and Sonok walked cautiously ahead. "Here," he said. "Can was here."

"Gone now," I observed. We stepped through another six-bolt hatch into a chamber that had the vague appearance of a command center. In large details it resembled the bridge of my own ship, and I rejoiced for that small sense of security.

"Can you talk to it?" Sonok asked.

"I can try. But where's a terminal?"

The bear pointed to a curved bench in front of a square, flat surface, devoid of keyboard, speaker, or knobs. It didn't look much like a terminal—though the flat surface resembled a visual display screen—but I wasn't ashamed to try speaking to it. Nor was I abashed when it didn't answer. "No go. Something else."

We looked around the chamber for several minutes but found nothing more promising. "It's like a bridge," I said. "But nothing matches specifically. Maybe we're looking for the wrong thing."

"Machines run themselves, perhaps," Sonok suggested.

I sat on the bench, resting an elbow on the edge of the "screen." Nonhuman technologies frequently use other senses for information exchange than we do. Where we generally limit machine-human interactions to sight, sound, and sometimes touch, the Crocerians use odor, and the Aighors control their machines on occasion with microwave radiation from their nervous systems. I laid my hand across the screen. It was warm to the touch, but I couldn't detect any variation in the warmth. Infrared was an inefficient carrier of information for creatures with visual orientation. Snakes use infrared to seek their prey—

"Snakes," I said. "The screen is warm. Is this part of the snake ship?"

Sonok shrugged. I looked around the cabin to find other smooth surfaces. They were few. Most were crisscrossed with raised grills. Some were warm to the touch. There were any number of possibilities—but I doubted if I would hit on the right one very quickly. The best I could hope for was the survival of some other portion of my ship.

"Sonok, is there another way out of this room?"

"Several. One is around the gray pillar," he said. "Another hatch with six dogs."

"What?"

"Six . . ." He made a grabbing motion with one hand. "Like the others."

"Throw-bolts," I said.

"I thought my Anglo was improving," he muttered sulkily.

"It is. But it's bound to be different from mine, so we both have to adapt." We opened the hatch and looked into the next chamber. The lights flickered feebly, and wrecked equipment gave off acrid smells. A haze of cloying smoke drifted out and immediately set ventilators to work. The bear held his nose and jumped over the seal for a quick walk through the room.

"Is something dead in here," he said when he returned. "Not like human, but not far. It is shot in head." He nodded for me to go with him, and I reluctantly followed. The body was pinned between two bolted seats. The head was a mess, and there was ample evidence that it used red blood. The body was covered by gray overalls and, though twisted into an awkward position, was obviously more canine than human. The bear was correct in one respect: it was closer to me than whiskered balls or rainbow snakes. The smoke was almost clear when I stepped back from the corpse.

"Sonok, any possibility this could be another mascot?"

The bear shook his head and walked away, nose wrinkled. I wondered if I'd insulted him.

"I see nothing like terminal here," he said. "Looks like nothing work now, anyway. Go on?"

We returned to the bridgelike chamber, and Sonok picked out another corridor. By the changing floor curvature, I guessed that all my previous estimates as to ship size were appreciably off. There was no way of telling either the shape or the size of this collage of vessels. What I'd seen from the bubble had appeared endless, but that might have been optical distortion.

The corridor dead-ended again, and we didn't press our luck as to what lay beyond the blank bulkhead. As we turned back, I asked, "What were the things you saw? You said there were ten of them, all different."

The bear held up his paws and counted. His fingers were otterlike and quite supple. "Snakes, number one," he said. "Cans with breasts, two; back wall of your cabin, three; blank bulkhead with circular marks, four; and you, five. Other things not so different, I think now snakes and six-dog hatches might go together, since snakes know how to use them. Other things—you and your cabin fixtures, so on, all together. But you add dead thing in overalls, fuzzy balls, and who can say where it ends?"

"I hope it ends someplace. I can only face so many variations before I give up. Is there anything left of your ship?"

"Where I was after disruption," the bear said. "On my stomach in bathroom."

Ah, that blessed word! "Where?" I asked. "Is it working?" I'd considered impolitely messing the corridors if there was no alternative.

"Works still, I think. Back through side corridor."

He showed me the way. A lot can be learned from a bathroom: social attitudes, technological levels, even basic psychology, not to mention anatomy. This one was lovely and utilitarian, with fixtures for males and females of at least three sizes. I made do with the largest. The bear gave me privacy, which wasn't strictly necessary—bathrooms on my ship being coed—but appreciated, nonetheless. Exposure to a Teddy bear takes getting used to.

When I was through, I joined Sonok in the hall and realized I'd gotten myself turned around. "Where are we?"

"Is changing," Sonok said. "Where bulkhead was, is now hatch. I'm not sure I cognize how—it's a different hatch."

And it was, in an alarming way. It was battle-armored, automatically controlled, and equipped with heavily shielded detection equipment. It was ugly and khaki-colored and had no business being inside a ship, unless the occupants distrusted each other. "I was in anteroom, outside lavatory," Sonok said, "with door closed. I hear loud sound and some-thing like metal being cut, and I open door to see this."

Vague sounds of machines were still audible, grinding and screaming. We stayed away from the hatch. Sonok motioned for me to follow him. "One more," he said. "Almost forgot." He pointed into a cubbyhole, about a meter deep and two meters square. "Look like fish tank, per-haps?"

It was a large rectangular tank filled with murky fluid. It reached from my knees to the top of my head and fit the cubbyhole perfectly. "Hasn't been cleaned, in any case," I said.

I touched the glass to feel how warm or cold it was. The tank lighted up, and I jumped back, knocking Sonok over. He rolled into a backward flip and came upright, wheezing.

The light in the tank flickered like a strobe, gradually speeding up until the glow was steady. For a few seconds it made me dizzy. The murk was gathering itself together. I bent over cautiously to get a close look. The murk wasn't evenly distributed. It was composed of animals like brine shrimp no more than a centimeter long, with two black eye-spots at one end, a pinkish "spine," and a feathery fringe rippling be-tween head and tail. They were forming a dense mass at the center of the tank.

Ordered dots of luminescence crossed the bottom of the tank, chang-ing colors across a narrow spectrum: red, blue, amber.

"It's doing something," Sonok said. The mass was defining a shape. Shoulders and head appeared, then torso and arms, sculpted in ghost-colored brine shrimp. When the living sculpture was finished, I recog-nized myself from the waist up. I held out my arm, and the mass slowly followed suit.

I had an inspiration. In my pants pocket I had a marker for labeling tapas cube blanks. It used soft plastic wrapped in a metal jacket. I took it out and wrote three letters across the transparent front of the tank: WHO. Part of the mass dissolved and reformed to mimic the letters, the rest filling in behind. They spelled WHO, then added a question mark.

Sonok chirped, and I came closer to see better. "They understand?" he asked. I shook my head. I had no idea what I was playing with. WHAT ARE YOU? I wrote.

The animals started to break up and return to the general murk. I shook my head in frustration. So near! The closest thing to communi-cation yet.

"Wait," Sonok said. "They're group again."

TENZIONA, the shrimp coalesced. DYSFUNCTIO. GUARDATEO AB PEREGRINO PERAMBULA.

"I don't understand. Sounds like Italian—do you know any Italian?"

The bear shook his head.

" 'Dysfunctio,' " I read aloud. "That seems plain enough. *'Ab pere-grino'*? Something about a hawk?"

"Peregrine, it is foreigner," Sonok said.

"Guard against foreigners . . . 'perambula,' as in strolling? Watch for the foreigners who walk? Well, we don't have the grammar, but it seems to tell us something we already know. Christ! I wish I could remember all the languages they filled me with ten years ago."

The marks on the tank darkened and flaked off. The shrimp began to form something different. They grouped into branches and arranged themselves nose-to-tail, upright, to form a trunk, which rooted itself to the floor of the tank.

"Tree," Sonok said.

Again they dissolved, returning in a few seconds to the simulacrum of my body. The clothing seemed different, however—more like a robe. Each shrimp changed its individual color now, making the shape startlingly lifelike. As I watched, the image began to age. The outlines of the face sagged, wrinkles formed in the skin, and the limbs shrank perceptibly. My arms felt cold, and I crossed them over my breasts; but the corridor was reasonably warm.

OF COURSE THE UNIVERSE ISN'T REALLY HELD IN A LITTLE GIRL'S MIND. IT'S one small thread in a vast skein, separated from every other universe by a limitation of constants and qualities, just as death is separated from life by the eternal nonreturn of the dead. Well, now we know the universes are less inviolable than death, for there are ways of crossing from thread to thread. So these other beings, from similar Earths, are not part of my undifferentiated infancy. That's a weak fantasy for a rather unequipped young woman to indulge in. Still, the symbols of childhood lie all around—nightmares and Teddy bears and dreams held in a tank; dreams of old age and death. And a tree, gray and ghostly, without leaves. That's me. Full of winter, wood cracking into splinters. How do they know?

A RUSTLING CAME FROM THE CORRIDOR AHEAD. WE TURNED FROM THE TANK and saw the floor covered with rainbow snakes, motionless, all heads aimed at us. Sonok began to tremble.

"Stop it," I said. "They haven't done anything to us."

"You are bigger," he said. "Not meal-sized."

"They'd have a rough time putting you away, too. Let's just sit it out calmly and see what this is all about." I kept my eyes on the snakes and away from the tank. I didn't want to see the shape age any more. For all the sanity of this place, it might have kept on going, through death and decay down to bones. Why did it choose me; why not Sonok?

"I cannot wait," Sonok said. "I have not the patience of a snake." He stepped forward. The snakes watched without a sound as the bear approached, one step every few seconds. "I want to know one solid thing," he called back. "Even if it is whether they eat small furry mascots."

The snakes suddenly bundled backward and started to crawl over each other. Small sucking noises smacked between their bodies. As they crossed, the red ovals met and held firm. They assembled and reared into a single mass, cobralike, but flat as a planarian worm. A fringe of snakes weaved across the belly like a caterpillar's idea of Medusa.

Brave Sonok was undone. He swung around and ran past me. I was too shocked to do anything but face the snakes down, neck hairs crawling. I wanted to speak but couldn't. Then, behind me, I heard: "Sinieux!"

As I turned, I saw two things, one in the corner of each eye: the snakes fell into a pile, and a man dressed in red and black vanished into a side corridor. The snakes regrouped into a hydra with six tentacles and grasped the hatch's throw-bolts, springing it open and slithering through. The hatch closed, and I was alone.

There was nothing for it but to scream a moment, then cry. I lay back against the wall, getting the fit out of me as loudly and quickly as possible. When I was able to stop, I wiped my eyes with my palms and kept them covered, feeling ashamed. When I looked out again, Sonok stood next to me.

"We've an Indian on board," he said. "Big, with black hair in three ribbons"—he motioned from crown to neck between his ears—"and a snappy dresser."

"Where is he?" I asked hoarsely.

"Back in place like bridge, I think. He controls snakes?"

I hesitated, then nodded.

"Go look?"

I got up and followed the bear. Sitting on a bench pulled from the wall, the man in red and black watched us as we entered the chamber. He was big—at least two meters tall—and hefty, dressed in a black silk shirt with red cuffs. His cape was black with a red eagle embroidered across the shoulders. He certainly looked Indian—ruddy skin, aristocratic nose, full lips held tight as if against pain.

"Quis la?" he queried.

"I don't speak that," I said. "Do you know English?"

The Indian didn't break his stolid expression. He nodded and turned on the bench to put his hand against a grill. "I was taught in the British school at Nova London," he said, his accent distinctly Oxfordian. "I was educated in Indonesia, and so I speak Dutch, High and Middle German, and some Asian tongues, specifically Nippon and Tagalog. But at English I am fluent."

"Thank God," I said. "Do you know this room?"

"Yes," he replied. "I designed it. It's for the Sinieux."

"Do you know what's happened to us?"

"We have fallen into Hell," he said. "My Jesuit professors warned me of it."

"Not far wrong," I said. "Do you know why?"

"I do not question my punishments."

"We're not being punished—at least, not by God or devils."

He shrugged. It was a moot point.

"I'm from Earth, too," I said. "From Terre."

"I know the words for Earth," the Indian said sharply.

"But I don't think it's the same Earth. What year are you from?" Since he'd mentioned Jesuits, he almost had to use the standard Christian Era dating.

"Year of Our Lord 2345," he said.

Sonok crossed himself elegantly. "For me 2290," he added. The Indian examined the bear dubiously.

I was sixty years after the bear, five after the Indian. The limits of the grab bag were less hazy now. "What country?"

"Alliance of Tribal Columbia," he answered, "District Quebec, East Shore."

"I'm from the Moon," I said. "But my parents were born on Earth in the United States of America."

The Indian shook his head slowly; he wasn't familiar with it.

"Was there—" But I held back the question. Where to begin? Where did the world-lines part? "I think we'd better consider finding out how well this ship is put together. We'll get into our comparative histories later. Obviously you have star drive."

The Indian didn't agree or disagree. "My parents had ancestors from the West Shore, Vancouver," he said. "They were Kwakiutl and Kodikin. The animal, does it have a Russian accent?"

"Some," I said. "It's better than it was a few hours ago."

"I have blood debts against Russians."

"Okay," I said. "But I doubt if you have anything against this one considering the distances involved. We've got to learn if this ship can take us someplace."

"I have asked," he said.

"Where?" Sonok asked. "A terminal?"

"The ship says it is surrounded by foreign parts and can barely understand them. But it can get along."

"You really don't know what happened, do you?"

"I went to look for worlds for my people and took the Sinieux with me. When I reached a certain coordinate in the sky, far along the arrow line established by my extrasolar pierce, this happened." He lifted his hand. "Now there is one creature, a devil, that tried to attack me. It is dead. There are others, huge black men who wear golden armor and carry gold guns like cannon, and they have gone away behind armored hatches. There are walls like rubber that open onto more demons. And now you—and it." He pointed at the bear.

"I'm not an 'it,' " Sonok said. "I'm an *ours*."

"Small *ours*," the Indian retorted.

Sonok bristled and turned away. "Enough," I said. "You haven't fallen into Hell, not literally. We've been hit by something called a disrupter. It snatched us from different universes and reassembled us according to our world-lines, our . . . affinities."

The Indian smiled faintly, very condescendingly.

"Listen, do you understand how crazy this is?" I demanded, exasperated. "I've got to get things straight before we all lose our calm. The beings who did this—in my universe they're called 'Aighors.' Do you know about them?"

He shook his head. "I know of no other beings but those of Earth. I went to look for worlds."

"Is your ship a warper ship—does it travel across a geodesic in higher spaces?"

"Yes," he said. "It is not in phase with the crest of the Stellar Sea but slips between the foamy length, where we must struggle to obey all laws."

That was a fair description of translating from status geometry—our universe—to higher geometries. It was more poetic than scientific, but he was here, so it worked well enough. "How long have your people been able to travel this way?"

"Ten years. And yours?"

"Three centuries."

He nodded in appreciation. "You know then what you speak of, and perhaps there aren't any devils, and we are not in Hell. Not this time."

"How do you use your instruments in here?"

"I do not, generally. The Sinieux use them. If you will not get upset, I'll demonstrate."

I glanced at Sonok, who was still sulking. "Are you afraid of the snakes?"

The bear shook his head.

"Bring them in," I said. "And perhaps we should know each other's name?"

"Jean Frobish," the Indian said. And I told him mine.

The snakes entered at his whistled command and assembled in the middle of the cabin. There were two sets, each made up of about fifty. When meshed, they made two formidable metaserpents. Frobish instructed them with spoken commands and a language that sounded like birdcalls. Perfect servants, they obeyed faultlessly and without hesitation. They went to the controls at his command and made a few manipulations, then turned to him and delivered, one group at a time, a report in consonantal hisses and claps. The exchange was uncanny and chilling. Jean nodded, and the serpents disassembled.

"Are they specially bred?" I asked.

"Tectonogenetic farming," he said. "They are excellent workers and have no will of their own, since they have no cerebrums. They can remember, and en masse can think, but not for themselves, if you see what I mean." He showed another glimmer of a smile. He was proud of his servants.

"I think I understand. Sonok, were you specially bred?"

"Was mascot," Sonok said. "Could breed for myself, given chance."

The subject was touchy, I could see. I could also see that Frobish and Sonok wouldn't get along without friction. If Sonok had been a big bear—and not a Russian—instead of an ursine dwarf, the Indian might have had more respect for him.

"Jean, can you command the whole ship from here?"

"Those parts that answer."

"Can your computers tell you how much of the ship will respond?"

"What is left of my vessel responds very well. The rest is balky or blank entirely. I was trying to discover the limits when I encountered you."

"You met the people who've been putting in the armored hatches?"

He nodded. "Bigger than Masai," he said.

I now had explanations for some of the things we'd seen and could link them with terrestrial origins. Jean and his Sinieux weren't beyond the stretch of reason, nor was Sonok. The armored hatches weren't quite as mysterious now. But what about the canine? I swallowed. That must have been the demon Frobish killed. And beyond the triplet valves?

"We've got a lot to find out," I said.

"You and the animal, are you together, from the same world?" Frobish asked. I shook my head. "Did you come alone?"

I nodded. "Why?"

"No men, no soldiers?"

I was apprehensive now. "No."

"Good." He stood and approached a blank wall near the gray pillar. "Then we will not have too many to support, unless the ones in golden armor want our food." He put his hand against the wall, and a round opening appeared. In the shadow of the hole, two faces watched with eyes glittering.

"These are my wives," Frobish said. One was dark-haired and slender, no more than fifteen or sixteen. She stepped out first and looked at me warily. The second, stockier and flatter of face, was brown-haired and about twenty. Frobish pointed to the younger first. "This is Alouette," he said. "And this is Mouse. Wives, acquaint with Francis Geneva." They stood one on each side of Frobish, holding his elbows, and nodded at me in unison.

That made four humans, more if the blacks in golden armor were men. Our collage had hit the jackpot.

"Jean, you say your machines can get along with the rest of the ship. Can they control it? If they can, I think we should try to return to Earth."

"To what?" Sonok asked. "Which Earth waits?"

"What's the bear talking about?" Frobish asked.

I explained the situation as best I could. Frobish was a sophisticated engineer and astrogator, but his experience with other continua—theoretical or actual—was small. He tightened his lips and listened grimly, unwilling to admit his ignorance. I sighed and looked to Alouette and Mouse for support. They were meek, quiet, giving all to the stolid authority of Frobish.

"What woman says is we decide where to go," Sonok said. "Depends, so the die is tossed, on whether we like the Earth we would meet."

"You would like my Earth," Frobish said.

"There's no guarantee it'll be your Earth. You have to take that into account."

"You aren't making sense." Frobish shook his head. "My decision is made, nonetheless. We will try to return."

I shrugged. "Try as best you can." We would face the truth later.

"I'll have the Sinieux watch over the machines after I initiate instructions," Frobish said. "Then I would like Francis to come with me to look at the animal I killed." I agreed without thinking about his motives. He gave the metaserpents their orders and pulled down a panel cover to reveal a small board designed for human hands. When he was through programming the computers, he continued his instructions to the Sinieux. His rapport with the animals was perfect—the interaction of an engineer with his tool. There was no thought of discord or second opinions. The snakes, to all intents and purposes, were machines keyed only to his voice. I wondered how far the obedience of his wives extended.

"Mouse will find food for the bear, and Alouette will stand guard with the *fusil. Comprens*?" The woman nodded, and Alouette plucked a rifle from the hideaway. "When we return, we will all eat."

"I will wait to eat with you," Sonok said, standing near me.

Frobish looked the bear over coldly. "We do not eat with tectoes," he said, haughty as a British officer addressing his servant. "But you will eat the same food we do."

Sonok stretched out his arms and made two shivers of anger. "I have never been treated less than a man," he said. "I will eat with all or not eat." He looked up at me with his small golden eyes and asked in Russian, "Will you go along with him?"

"We don't have much choice," I answered haltingly in kind.

"What do you recommend?"

"Play along for the moment. I understand." I was unable to read his expression behind the black mask and white markings; but if I'd been he, I'd have questioned the understanding. This was no time, however, to instruct the bear in assertion.

Frobish opened the hatch to the wrecked room and let me step in first. He then closed the hatch and sealed it. "I've seen the body already," I said. "What do you want to know?"

"I want your advice on this room," he said. I didn't believe that for an instant. I bent down to examine the creature between the chairs more carefully.

"What did it try to do to you?" I asked.

"It came at me. I thought it was a demon. I shot at it, and it died."

"What caused the rest of this damage?"

"I fired a good many rounds," he said. "I was more frightened then. I'm calm now."

"Thank God for that," I said. "This—he or she—might have been able to help us."

"Looks like a dog," Frobish said. "Dogs cannot help."

For me, that crossed the line. "Listen," I said tightly, standing away from the body. "I don't think you're in touch with what's going on here. If you don't get in touch soon, you might get us all killed. I'm not about to let myself die because of one man's stupidity."

Frobish's eyes widened. "Women do not address men thus," he said.

"This woman does, friend! I don't know what kind of screwy social order you have in your world, but you had damn well better get used to interacting with different sexes, not to mention different species! If you don't, you're asking to end up like this poor thing. It didn't have a chance to say friend or foe, yea or nay! You shot it out of panic, and we can't have any more of that!" I was trembling.

Frobish smiled over grinding teeth and turned to walk away. He was fighting to control himself. I wondered if my own brains were in the right place. The few aspects of this man that were familiar to me couldn't begin to give complete understanding. I was clearly out of my depth, and kicking to stay afloat might hasten death, not slow it.

Frobish stood by the hatch, breathing deeply. "What is the dog-creature? What is this room?"

I turned back to the body and pulled it by one leg from between the chairs. "It was probably intelligent," I said. "That's about all I can tell. It doesn't have any personal effects." The gore was getting to me, and I turned away for a moment. I was tired—oh, so tired I could feel the weary rivers dredging through my limbs. My head hurt abominably. "I'm not an engineer," I said. "I can't tell if any of this equipment is useful to us, or even if it's salvageable. Care to give an opinion?"

Frobish glanced over the room with a slight inclination of one eyebrow. "Nothing of use here."

"Are you sure?"

"I am sure." He looked across the room and sniffed the air. "Too much burned and shorted. You know, there is much that is dangerous here."

"Yes," I said, leaning against the back of a seat.

"You will need protection.

"Oh."

"There is no protection like the bonds of family. You are argumentative, but my wives can teach you our ways. With bonds of family, there will be no uncertainty. We will return, and all will be well."

He caught me by surprise, and I wasn't fast on the uptake. "What do you mean, bonds of family?"

"I will take you to wife and protect you as husband."

"I think I can protect myself, thank you."

"It doesn't seem wise to refuse. Left alone, you will probably be killed by such as this." He pointed at the canine.

"We'll have to get along whether we're family or not. That shouldn't be too hard to understand. And I don't have any inclination to sell myself for security."

"I do not pay money for women!" Frobish said. "Again you ridicule me."

He sounded like a disappointed little boy. I wondered what his wives would think, seeing him butt his head against a wall without sense or sensibility.

"We've got to dispose of the body before it decays," I said. "Help me carry it out of here."

"It isn't fit to touch."

My tiredness took over, and my rationality departed. "You goddamned idiot! Pull your nose down and look at what's going on around you! We're in serious trouble—"

"It isn't the place of a woman to speak thus, I've told you," he said.

He approached and raised his hand palm-high to strike. I instinctively lowered my head and pushed a fist into his abdomen. The slap fell like a kitten's paw, and he went over, glancing off my shoulder and twisting my arm into a painful muscle kink. I cursed and rubbed the spot, then sat down on the deck to consider what had happened.

I'd never had much experience with sexism in human cultures. It was disgusting and hard to accept, but some small voice in the back of my mind told me it was no more blameworthy than any other social attitude. His wives appeared to go along with it. At any rate, the situation was now completely shot to hell. There was little I could do except drag him back to his wives and try to straighten things out when he came to. I took him by both hands and pulled him up to the hatch. I unsealed it, then swung him around to take him by the shoulders. I almost retched when one of his shoulders broke the crust on a drying pool of blood and smeared red along the deck.

I MISS JAGHIT SINGH MORE THAN I CAN ADMIT. I THINK ABOUT HIM AND wonder what he'd do in this situation. He is a short, dark man with perfect features and eyes like those in the pictures of Krishna. We formally broke off our relationship three weeks ago, at my behest, for I couldn't see any future in it. He would probably know how to handle Frobish, with a smile and even a spirit of comradeship, but without contradicting his own beliefs. He could make a girl's childhood splinters go back to form the whole log again. He could make these beasts and distortions come together again. Jaghit! Are you anywhere that has seasons? Is it still winter for you? You never did understand the little girl who wanted to play in the snow. Your blood is far too hot and regular to stand up to my moments of indecisive coldness, and you could not— would not—force me to change. I was caught between child and my thirty-year-old form, between spring and winter. Is it spring for you now?

ALOUETTE AND MOUSE TOOK THEIR HUSBAND AWAY FROM ME FIERCELY, SPITting with rage. They weren't talking clearly, but what they shouted in quasi-French made it clear who was to blame. I told Sonok what had happened, and he looked very somber indeed. "Maybe he'll shoot us when he wakes up," he suggested.

To avoid that circumstance, I appropriated the rifle and took it back to my half-room. There was a cabinet intact, and I still had the key. I didn't lock the rifle in, however; better simply to hide it and have easy access to it when needed. It was time to be diplomatic, though all I really wanted for the moment was blessed sleep. My shoulder stung like hell, and the muscles refused to get themselves straight.

When I returned, with Sonok walking point a few steps ahead, Frobish was conscious and sitting in a cot pulled from a panel near the hole. His wives squatted nearby, somber as they ate from metal dishes.

Frobish refused to look me in the eye. Alouette and Mouse weren't in the least reluctant, however, and their gazes threw sparks. They'd be good in a fight, if it ever came down to that. I hoped I wasn't their opposite.

"I think it's time we behaved reasonably," I said.

"There is no reason on this ship," Frobish shot back.

"Aye on that," Sonok said, sitting down to a plate left on the floor. He picked at it, then reluctantly ate, his fingers handling the implements with agility.

"If we're at odds, we won't get anything done," I said.

"That is the only thing which stops me from killing you," Frobish said. Mouse bent over to whisper in his ear. "My wife reminds me you must have time to see the logic of our ways." Were the women lucid despite their anger, or was he maneuvering on his own? "There is also the possibility that you are a leader. I'm a leader, and it's difficult for me to face another leader at times. That is why I alone control this ship."

"I'm not a—" I bit my lip. Not too far, too fast. "We've got to work together and forget about being leaders for the moment."

Sonok sighed and put down the plate. "I have no leader," he said. "That part of me did not follow into this scattershot." He leaned on my leg. "Mascots live best when made whole. So I choose Geneva as my other part. I think my English is good enough now for us to understand."

Frobish looked at the bear curiously. "My stomach hurts," he said after a moment. He turned to me. "You do not hit like a woman. A woman strikes for the soft parts, masculine weaknesses. You go for direct points with knowledge. I cannot accept you as the bear does, but if you will reconsider, we should be able to work together."

"Reconsider the family bond?"

He nodded. To me, he was almost as alien as his snakes. I gave up the fight and decided to play for time.

"I'll have to think about it. My upbringing . . . is hard to overcome," I said.

"We will rest," Frobish said.

"And Sonok will guard," I suggested. The bear straightened perceptibly and went to stand by the hatch. For the moment it looked like a truce had been made, but as cots were pulled out of the walls, I picked up a metal bar and hid it in my trousers.

The Sinieux went to their multilevel cages and lay quiet and still as stone. I slipped into the cot and pulled a thin sheet over myself. Sleep came immediately, and delicious lassitude finally unkinked my arm.

I don't know how long the nap lasted, but it was broken sharply by a screech from Sonok. "They're here! They're here!"

I stumbled out of the cot, tangling one leg in a sheet, and came to a stand only after the Indian family was alert and armed. So much, I thought, for hiding the rifle. "What's here?" I asked, still dopey.

Frobish thrust Sonok away from the hatch with a leg and brought the cover around with a quick arm to slam it shut, but not before a black cable was tossed into the room. The hatch jammed on it, and sparks flew. Frobish stood clear and brought his rifle to his shoulder.

Sonok ran to me and clung to my knee. Mouse opened the cages and let the Sinieux flow onto the deck. Frobish retreated from the hatch as it shuddered. The Sinieux advanced. I heard voices from the other side. They sounded human—like children, in fact.

"Wait a minute," I said. Mouse brought her pistol up and aimed it at me. I shut up.

The hatch flung open, and hundreds of fine cables flew into the room, twisting and seeking, wrapping and binding. They plucked Frobish's rifle from his hands and surrounded it like a antibodies on a bacterium. Mouse fired her pistol wildly and stumbled, falling into a nest of cables, which jerked and seized. Alouette was almost to the hole, but her ankles were caught and she teetered.

Cables ricocheted from the ceiling and grabbed at the bundles of Sinieux. The snakes fell apart, some clinging to the cables like insects on a frog's tongue. More cables shot out to hold them all, except for a solitary snake that retreated past me. I was bound rigid and tight, with Sonok strapped to my knee. The barrage stopped, and a small shadowed figure stood in the hatch, carrying a machete. It cleared the entrance of the sticky strands and stepped into the cabin light, looking around cautiously. Then it waved to companions behind, and five more entered.

They were identical, each just under half a meter in height—a little shorter than Sonok—and bald and pink as infants. Their features were delicate and fetal, with large gray-green eyes and thin, translucent limbs. Their hands were stubby-fingered and plump as those on a Rubens baby. They walked into the cabin with long strides, self-assured, nimbly avoiding the cables.

Sonok jerked at a sound in the corridor—a hesitant high-pitched mewing. "With breasts," he mumbled through the cords.

One of the infantoids arranged a ramp over the bottom seal of the hatch. He then stepped aside and clapped to get attention. The others formed a line, pink fannies jutting, and held their hands over their heads as if surrendering. The mewing grew louder. Sonok's trash can with breasts entered the cabin, twisting this way and that like a deranged, obscene toy. It was cylindrical, with sides tapering to a fringed skirt at the base. Three levels of pink and nippled paps ringed it at equal intervals from top to bottom. A low, flat head surmounted the body, tiny black eyes examining the cabin with quick, nervous jerks. It looked like nothing so much as the Diana of Ephesus, Magna Mater to the Romans.

One of the infantoids announced something in a piping voice, and the Diana shivered to acknowledge. With a glance around, the same infantoid nodded, and all six stood up to the breasts to nurse.

Feeding over, they took positions around the cabin and examined us carefully. The leader spoke to each of us in turn, trying several languages. None matched our own. I strained to loosen the cords around my neck and jaw and asked Sonok to speak a few of the languages he knew. He did as well as he could through his bonds. The leader listened to him with interest, then echoed a few words and turned to the other five. One nodded and advanced. He spoke to the bear in what sounded like Greek. Sonok stuttered for a moment, then replied in halting fragments.

They moved to loosen the bear's cords, looking up at me apprehensively. The combination of Sonok and six children still at breast hit me deep, and I had to suppress a hysteric urge to laugh.

"I think he is saying he knows what has happened," Sonok said. "They've been prepared for it; they knew what to expect. I think that's what they say."

The leader touched palms with his Greek-speaking colleague, then spoke to Sonok in the same tongue. He held out his plump hands and motioned for the bear to do likewise. A third stepped over rows of crystallized cable to loosen Sonok's arms.

Sonok reluctantly held up his hands, and the two touched. The infantoid broke into shrill laughter and rolled on the floor. His mood returned to utmost gravity in a blink, and he stood as tall as he could, looking us over with an angry expression.

"We are in command," he said in Russian. Frobish and his wives cried out in French, complaining about their bonds. "They speak different?" the infantoid asked Sonok. The bear nodded. "Then my brothers will learn their tongues. What does the other big one speak?"

"English," Sonok said.

The infantoid sighed. "Such diversities. I will learn from her." My cords were cut, and I held out my palms. The leader's hands were cold and clammy, making my arm-hairs crawl.

"All right," he said in perfect English. "Let us tell you what's happened, and what we're going to do."

His explanation of the disruption matched mine closely. "The Alternates have done this to us." He pointed to me. "This big one calls them

Aighors. We do not dignify them with a name—we're not even sure they are the same. They don't have to be, you know. Whoever has the secret of disruption, in all universes, is our enemy. We are companions now, chosen from a common pool of those who have been disrupted across a century or so. The choosing has been done so that our natures match closely—we are all from one planet. Do you understand this idea of being companions?"

Sonok and I nodded. The Indians made no response at all.

"But we, members of the Nemi, whose mother is Noctilux, we were prepared. We will take control of the aggregate ship and pilot it to a suitable point, from which we can take a perspective and see what universe we're in. Can we expect your cooperation?"

Again the bear and I agreed, and the others were silent.

"Release them all," the infantoid said with a magnanimous sweep of his hands. "Be warned, however—we can restrain you in an instant, and we are not likely to enjoy being attacked again."

The cords went limp and vaporized with some heat discharge and a slight sweet odor. The Diana rolled over the ramp and left the cabin, with the leader and another infantoid following. The four remaining behind watched us closely, not nervous but intent on our every move. Where the guns had been, pools of slag lay on the floor.

"Looks like we've been overruled," I said to Frobish. He didn't seem to hear me.

In a few hours we were told where we would be allowed to go. The area extended to my cabin and the bathroom, which apparently was the only such facility in our reach. The Nemi didn't seem to need bathrooms, but their recognition of our own requirements was heartening. Within an hour after the takeover, the infantoids had swarmed over the controls in the chamber. They brought in bits and pieces of salvaged equipment, which they altered and fitted with extraordinary speed and skill. Before our next meal, taken from stores in the hole, they understood and controlled all the machinery in the cabin.

The leader then explained to us that the aggregate, or "scattershot," as Sonok had called it, was still far from integrated. At least two groups had yet to be brought into the fold. These were the giant blacks in golden armor, and the beings that inhabited the transparent bubble outside the ship. We were warned that leaving the established boundaries would put us in danger.

The sleep period came. The Nemi made certain we were slumbering before they slept, if they slept at all. Sonok lay beside me on the bunk in my room, snucking faint snores and twitching over distant dreams. I stared up into the dark, thinking of the message tank. That was my unrevealed ace. I wanted to get back to it and see what it was capable of telling me. Did it belong to one of the groups we were familiar with, or was it different, perhaps a party in itself?

I TRIED TO BURY MY PRIVATE THOUGHTS—DISTURBING, INTRICATE THOUGHTS and sleep, but I couldn't. I was dead-weight now, and I'd never liked the idea of being useless. Useless things tended to get thrown out. Since joining the various academies and working my way up the line, I'd always assumed I could play some role in any system I was thrust into.

But the infantoids, though tolerant and even understanding, were self-contained. As they said, they'd been prepared, and they knew what to do. Uncertainty seemed to cheer them, or at least draw them together. Of course they were never more than a few meters away from a very impressive symbol of security—a walking breast bank.

The Nemi had their Diana, Frobish had his wives, and Sonok had me. I had no one. My mind went out, imagined blackness and fields of stars, and perhaps nowhere the worlds I knew, and quickly snapped back. My head hurt, and my back muscles were starting to cramp. I had no access to hormone stabilizers, so I was starting my period. I rolled over, nudging Sonok into grumbly half-waking, and shut my eyes and mind to everything, trying to find a peaceful glade and perhaps Jaghit Singh. But even in sleep all I found was snow and broken gray trees.

The lights came up slowly, and I was awakened by Sonok's movements. I rubbed my eyes and got up from the bunk, standing unsteadily.

In the bathroom Frobish and his wives were going about their morning ablutions. They looked at me but said nothing. I could feel a tension but tried to ignore it. I was irritable, and if I let any part of my feelings out, they might all pour forth—and then where would I be?

I returned to my cabin with Sonok and didn't see Frobish following until he stepped up to the hatchway and looked inside.

"We will not accept the rule of children," he said evenly. "We'll need your help to overcome them."

"Who will replace them?" I asked.

"I will. They've made adjustments to my machines which I and the Sinieux can handle."

"The Sinieux cages are welded shut," I said.

"Will you join us?"

"What could I do? I'm only a woman."

"I will fight, my wives and you will back me up. I need the rifle you took away."

"I don't have it." But he must have seen my eyes go involuntarily to the locker.

"Will you join us?"

"I'm not sure it's wise. In fact, I'm sure it isn't. You just aren't equipped to handle this kind of thing. You're too limited."

"I have endured all sorts of indignities from you. You are a sickness of the first degree. Either you will work with us, or I will cure you now." Sonok bristled, and I noticed the bear's teeth were quite sharp.

I stood and faced him. "You're not a man," I said. "You're a little boy. You haven't got hair on your chest or anything between your legs—just a bluff and a brag."

He pushed me back on the cot with one arm and squeezed up against the locker, opening it quickly. Sonok sank his teeth into the man's calf, but before I could get into action the rifle was out and his hand was on the trigger. I fended the barrel away from me, and the first shot went into the corridor. It caught a Nemi and removed the top of his head. The blood and sound seemed to drive Frobish into a frenzy. He brought the butt down, trying to hammer Sonok, but the bear leaped aside and the rifle went into the bunk mattress, sending Frobish off balance. I hit his throat with the side of my hand and caved in his windpipe.

Then I took the rifle and watched him choking against the cabin wall. He was unconscious and turning blue before I gritted my teeth and relented. I took him by the neck and found his pipe with my thumbs, then pushed from both sides to flex the blockage outward. He took a breath and slumped.

I looked at the body in the corridor. "This is it," I said quietly. "We've got to get out of here." I slung the rifle and peered around the hatch seal. The noise hadn't brought anyone yet. I motioned to Sonok, and we ran down the corridor, away from the Indian's control room and the infantoids.

"Geneva," Sonok said as we passed an armored hatch. "Where do we go?" I heard a whirring sound and looked up. The shielded camera above the hatch was watching us, moving behind its thick gray glass like an eye. "I don't know," I said.

A seal had been placed over the flexible valve in the corridor that led to the bubble. We turned at that point and went past the nook where the message tank had been. It was gone, leaving a few anonymous fixtures behind.

An armored hatch had been punched into the wall several yards beyond the alcove, and it was unsealed. That was almost too blatant an invitation, but I had few other choices. They'd mined the ship like termites. The hatch led into a straight corridor without gravitation. I took Sonok by the arm, and we drifted dreamily down. I saw pieces of familiar equipment studding the walls, and I wondered if people from my world were around. It was an idle speculation. The way I felt now, I doubted I could make friends with anyone. I wasn't the type to establish camaraderie under stress. I was the wintry one.

At the end of the corridor, perhaps a hundred meters down, gravitation slowly returned. The hatch there was armored and open. I brought the rifle up and looked around the seal. No one. We stepped through, and I saw the black in his golden suit, fresh as a ghost. I was surprised; he wasn't. My rifle was up and pointed, but his weapon was down. He smiled faintly.

"We are looking for a woman known as Geneva," he said. "Are you she?"

I nodded. He bowed stiffly, armor crinkling, and motioned for me to follow. The room around the corner was unlighted. A port several meters wide, ribbed with steel beams, opened onto the starry dark. The stars were moving, and I guessed the ship was rolling in space. I saw other forms in the shadows, large and bulky, some human, some apparently not. Their breathing made them sound like waiting predators.

A hand took mine, and a shadow towered over me. "This way."

Sonok clung to my calf, and I carried him with each step I took. He didn't make a sound. As I passed from the viewing room, I saw a blue and white curve begin at the top of the port and caught an outline of continent. Asia, perhaps. We were already near Earth. The shapes of the continents could remain the same in countless universes, immobile grounds beneath the thin and pliable paint of living things. What was life like in the distant world-lines where even the shapes of the continents had changed?

The next room was also dark, but a candle flame flickered behind curtains. The shadow that had guided me returned to the viewing room and shut the hatch. I heard the breathing of only one besides myself.

I was shaking. Would they do this to us one at a time? Yes, of course; there was too little food. Too little air. Not enough of anything on this tiny scattershot. Poor Sonok, by his attachment, would go before his proper moment.

The breathing came from a woman, somewhere to my right. I turned to face in her general direction. She sighed. She sounded very old, with labored breath and a kind of pant after each intake.

I heard a dry crack of adhered skin separating, dry lips parting to speak, then the tiny *click* of eyelids blinking. The candle flame wobbled in a current of air. As my eyes adjusted, I could see that the curtains formed a translucent cubicle in the dark.

"Hello," the woman said. I answered weakly. "Is your name Francis Geneva?"

I nodded, then, in case she couldn't see me, and said, "I am."

"I am Junípero," she said, aspirating the *j* as in Spanish. "I was commander of the High-space ship *Callimachus*. Were you a commander on your ship?"

"No," I replied. "I was part of the crew."

"What did you do?"

I told her in a spare sentence or two, pausing to cough. My throat was like parchment.

"Do you mind stepping closer? I can't see you very well."

I walked forward a few steps.

"There is not much from your ship in the way of computers or stored memory," she said. I could barely make out her face as she bent forward, squinting to examine me. "But we have learned to speak your language from those parts that accompanied the Indian. It is not too different from a language in our past, but none of us spoke it until now. The rest of you did well. A surprising number of you could communicate, which was fortunate. And the little children who suckle—the Nemi—they always know how to get along. We've had several groups of them on our voyages."

"May I ask what you want?"

"You might not understand until I explain. I have been through the mutata several hundred times. You call it disruption. But we haven't found our home yet, I and my crew. The crew must keep trying, but I won't last much longer. I'm at least two thousand years old, and I can't search forever."

"Why don't the others look old?"

"My crew? They don't lead. Only the top must crumble away to keep the group flexible, only those who lead. You'll grow old, too. But not the crew. They'll keep searching."

"What do you mean, me?"

"Do you know what 'Geneva' means, dear sister?"

I shook my head, no.

"It means the same thing as my name, Junipero. It's a tree that gives berries. The one who came before me, her name was Jenevr, and she lived twice as long as I, four thousand years. When she came, the ship was much smaller than it is now."

"And your men—the ones in armor—"

"They are part of my crew. There are women, too."

"They've been doing this for six thousand years?"

"Longer," she said. "It's much easier to be a leader and die, I think. But their wills are strong. Look in the tank, Geneva."

A light came on behind the cubicle, and I saw the message tank. The murky fluid moved with a continuous swirling flow. The old woman stepped from the cubicle and stood beside me in front of the tank. She held out her finger and wrote something on the glass, which I couldn't make out.

The tank's creatures formed two images, one of me and one of her.

She was dressed in a simple brown robe, her peppery black hair cropped into short curls. She touched the glass again, and her image changed. The hair lengthened, forming a broad globe around her head. The wrinkles smoothed. The body became slimmer and more muscular, and a smile came to the lips. Then the image was stable.

Except for the hair, it was me.

I took a deep breath. "Every time you've gone through a disruption, has the ship picked up more passengers?"

"Sometimes," she said. "We always lose a few, and every now and then we gain a large number. For the last few centuries our size has been stable, but in time we'll probably start to grow. We aren't anywhere near the total yet. When that comes, we might be twice as big as we are now. Then we'll have had, at one time or another, every scrap of ship, and every person who ever went through a disruption."

"How big is the ship now?"

"Four hundred kilometers across. Built rather like a volvox, if you know what that is."

"How do you keep from going back yourself?"

"We have special equipment to keep us from separating. When we started out, we thought it would shield us from a mutata, but it didn't. This is all it can do for us now: it can keep us in one piece each time we jump. But not the entire ship."

I began to understand. The huge bulk of ship I had seen from the window was real. I had never left the grab bag. I was in it now, riding the aggregate, a tiny particle attracted out of solution to the colloidal mass.

Junipero touched the tank, and it returned to its random flow. "It's a constant shuttle run. Each time we return to the Earth to see who, if any, can find their home there. Then we seek out the ones who have the disrupters, and they attack us—send us away again."

"Out there—is that my world?"

The old woman shook her head. "No, but it's home to one group—three of them. The three creatures in the bubble."

I giggled. "I thought there were a lot more than that."

"Only three. You'll learn to see things more accurately as time passes. Maybe you'll be the one to bring us all home.

"What if I find my home first?"

"Then you'll go, and if there's no one to replace you, one of the crew will command until another comes along. But someone always comes along, eventually. I sometimes think we're being played with, never finding our home, but always having a Juniper to command us." She smiled wistfully. "The game isn't all bitterness and bad tosses, though.

You'll see more things, and do more, and be more, than any normal woman."

"I've never been normal," I said.

"All the better."

"If I accept."

"You have that choice."

" 'Junipero,' " I breathed. "Geneva." Then I laughed.

"How do you choose?"

THE SMALL CHILD, SEEING THE DESTRUCTION OF ITS THOUSAND COMPANIONS with each morning light and the skepticism of the older ones, becomes frightened and wonders if she will go the same way. Someone will raise the shutters and a sunbeam will impale her and she'll phantomize. Or they'll tell her they don't believe she's real. So she sits in the dark, shaking. The dark becomes fearful. But soon each day becomes a triumph. The ghosts vanish, but she doesn't, so she forgets the shadows and thinks only of the day. Then she grows older, and the companions are left only in whims and background thoughts. Soon she is whittled away to nothing; her husbands are past, her loves are firm and not potential, and her history stretches away behind her like carvings in crystal. She becomes wrinkled, and soon the daylight haunts her again. Not every day will be a triumph. Soon there will be a final beam of light, slowly piercing her jellied eye, and she'll join the phantoms.

But not now. Somewhere, far away, but not here. All around, the ghosts have been resurrected for her to see and lead. And she'll be resurrected, too, always under the shadow of the tree name.

"I THINK," I SAID, "THAT IT WILL BE MARVELOUS."

So it was, thirty centuries ago. Sonok is gone, two hundred years past; some of the others have died, too, or gone to their own Earths. The ship is five hundred kilometers across and growing. You haven't come to replace me yet, but I'm dying, and I leave this behind to guide you, along with the instructions handed down by those before me.

Your name might be Jennifer, or Ginepra, or something else, but you will always be me. Be happy for all of us, darling. We will be forever whole.

Afterword

Years later, I would bring back the *sinieux*, the nested snakes of "Scattershot" in my novel, *Anvil of Stars*, give them a conceptual upgrade, and call them the Brothers.

Introduction to "Plague of Conscience"

Poul Anderson was a master at building artificial worlds. With his wife, Karen, he devised a system of planets to serve as the setting for a collaborative novel/anthology entitled *Murasaki*. Fred Pohl, a master of sociology and cultural anticipations, provided the cultural underpinnings for the inhabitants of these worlds. Robert Silverberg edited and organized. A number of prominent writers—Anderson, Pohl, Gregory Benford, David Brin, and Nancy Kress—were invited to contribute to the round robin, setting their individual chapters on these planets; "Plague of Conscience" was my portion.

It's likely to be a little confusing without the other tales to provide background, but I think it works well by itself, though more as a segment of a novel than a complete story. At any rate, it's worthwhile finding *Murasaki* and reading the complete cycle.

The hardest theme in science fiction is that of the alien. The simplest solution of all is in fact quite profound—that the real difficulty lies not in understanding what is alien, but in understanding what is *self*. We are all aliens to each other, all different and divided. We are even aliens to ourselves at different stages of our lives. Do any of us remember precisely what is was like to be a baby?

To describe the alien, I tend to take an aspect from my own multiple selves, a manifold of personality traits, and expand upon it. It's not a bad technique, as long as I'm willing to look very closely at the truth of what I think I see . . .

Plague of Conscience
Murasaki, Robert Silverberg et al., 1992

Kammer looked worse than any corpse Philby had seen; much worse, for he was alive and shouldn't have been. This short wizened man with limbs like gnarled tree branches and skin like leather—what could be seen of his skin beneath the encrustations of brown and green snug—had survived ten Earthly years on Chujo without human contact. He could hardly speak English any more.

Kammer regarded Philby through eyes paled by some Chujoan biological adaptation—the impossible which had happened to him first, and then had spread so disastrously to the God the Physicist settlers and the

Japanese stationed here. Three hundred dead, and it had certainly begun on Kammer's broken, dying body, pissed on by a Chujoan shaman, that benison, that curse. The half-human coughed and his snug wrinkled and crawled in obscene patches, revealing yet more leather.

"Not many people let to see me," Kammer said. "Why do you?"

"I come from Genji," Philby said, "with a message from the Irdizu to the Chujoan shamans."

"Ah, Christ," Kammer said roughly and spat a thin stream of green and red saliva on the rocky ground between them. "Pardon. No offense. I still hate the . . . taste. Keeps me alive, I think, my human thoughts think, but tastes like essence of crap profane."

"You know about the God the Physicist crew?" Philby asked.

"Bloody *criaock* and *oonshlr#hack*."

The translator could not work with his humanized pronunciation; little was known of Chujoan language anyway, the Masters being so spare with their communications. Philby jotted the words on his notepad in the Chujoan phonetic devised by the Japanese, who had dropped transmitters into the villages four years before Philby's ship arrived in the Murasaki system. The Chujoans had tolerated the transmitters, and what few phrases they uttered had been fed into their All Nihon shipboard supercomputers. The Japanese had been kind enough to share their knowledge with Philby.

They knew Philby would be useful. He was, after all, rational—unlike the God the Physicists.

"I've come to talk about Carnot," Philby said. Kammer said nothing, leaning on his thick, snug-encrusted stick. "He's using your name. Claims to have been blessed by you. He's spreading a religion, if you can call it that, around the Irdizu villages—"

"I know little about the Irdizu," Kammer said, voice cracking. "Do them seldom. Not been there." The leathery face seemed to half-smile.

"He claims to have met with you, talked about his version of Jesus with you. He says you have seen visions of Chujo and Genji united under the rule of Jesus, who will come to these planets when the time is right."

"We didn't talk much, doing the first," Kammer said.

Philby tried to understand what he meant, and decided to let contect be his guide. The notepad was recording all sound—perhaps meaning could be found later.

"Doing the second, he was already ill. Could see that."

"You met with him twice?" Philby asked.

Kammer nodded. "Sick the second time. He was doing the wind."

"He was ill with the plague," Philby said, his skin crawling at the thought that Kammer had probably been the source of that plague.

"He was doing the wind," Kammer said. "Pardon me. He was almost dead. He was looking for signs. I did what I could."

"What was that?"

Kammer shook his head slowly and lifted his stick. "Doing the foulness. I hit him." He brought the stick down on the ground with a sharp crack. Philby noticed there was snug on the stick as well. Some of the snug on the stick fell away in patches. "He got away before I could hit him again."

"Do you know where Carnot is hiding?" Philby asked, hoping that Kammer's reversion to Chujoan had reflected a personal distaste.

"Wonderful man," Kammer said, hawking again—his entire chest patch of snug heaving like a sewage-befouled sea—but not spitting. "I don't. Where he is. Who are you? Beg pardon. That means. . . . What will you be doing here?"

General clean-up. Triage. Sanitizing.

"I'm here to interview the survivors of the wineskin plague," Philby said, adjusting his hydrator. "And to find Carnot."

Kammer laughed. "Thinks I'm something."

"I'm sorry, I don't understand."

"Risked doing martyr to the bullyboys. They dislike anything new. Do the thorn fence." Kammer made a disgusting excretory sound in his throat and rasped, "Knew. Knew."

Philby glanced at the line of Chujoans standing mute, motionless, six human paces east of them, and the bullyboys—what the early explorers had called trolls—standing with mindless patience at the edge of the village waiting for some biochemical sign of his alienness, his undesirability.

"He survived the plague," Philby said offhandedly, as if conveying sad news.

"Know that," Kammer said. "Vector of the cultural disease."

"Yes," Philby said, surprised that Kammer was so in tune with his own thoughts. "Then you agree with me, that he—that his people are a danger?"

"You try to block him?"

"Yes," Philby said.

"How?"

"By going from village to village among the Irdizu, and telling them the truth. Not mystical nonsense."

Kammer smiled, his teeth a ruin encrusted with gray. "Doing the good. I mean, that's good of you. What will you make of Carnot . . . doing with him when you find him?"

"Make him stop polluting these worlds," Philby said.

"Ah. Doing us all a service."

"You tried to stop him as well, didn't you? With your stick?"

"He's alive, isn't he? You'd better go now," Kammer said, turning his head and poking his raw-looking chin at their observers. "They'll make you do martyr soon. Best pass on your message from Heaven and do a . . . be a trotter. Trot off. You're beginning to *bore* them, you silly wretch."

"Do I bore you as well, Kammer?" Philby said sharply. He trusted the bullyboys would not detect or react to his human irritation.

Kammer said nothing, the whited eyes with their pastel green irises minus pupils moving back and forth independently, like a lizard's hunting for a flying insect.

"No, old fellow," Kammer said. "I'd really like to sit and do the speaking some more. But my skin tells me I'm not up to it. I always listen to my skin. Without it, I'm an indigestible memory."

Philby nodded, the gesture almost invisible behind his mask and hydrator. "Thank you, Mr. Kammer," he said.

Kammer had already turned and begun his limping retreat to the safety of the village. "Nothing, old folks," Kammer said. Lurching on his beggar's rearranged limbs, s-curved back hunched like a ridge of iron-rich mountains, without looking back Kammer added, "Hope you know what the Irdizy *fchix* are saying to these." He waved a thin crooked hand at the shaman and his attendants.

Philby didn't. He had to take that risk.

The shaman approached and without looking at him, as if direct eye contact was either unknown or an unspeakable breach, snatched the Irdizu package from Philby's grasp and walked away, quietly erecting his genitalia and pissing all over the sacred himatid pelt wrapper.

Philby, hair on his neck frizzing with fear of bullyboy teeth, walked away from the village to rejoin the transport crew on the cliff ledge a kilometer outside the village. The Japanese escort, an attractive middle-aged woman named Tatsumi, bowed deeply on his return. Sheldrake and Thompson, pilots from his own crew, stiffened perceptibly. They seemed surprised he had returned. He lifted his arms and they sprayed him down, just as a precaution. *Our own pissing ceremony.*

Kammer's spit had landed within a meter of his disposable boots.

"He's become the Old Man of the Mountain," Philby said, doffing the boots, tossing them into the scrub and climbing into the transport. Tatsumi, Sheldrake and Thompson followed. "He knows what I'm here for. I think he approves."

They all listened to the notepad playback.

DREAM JOURNEY ABOVE THE PASTEL LAND, DREARY DRY OLD CHUJO, BLEAK waste of a world with a thin cloak of dry air and an illustrious past, if what the Japanese had witnessed years ago could be believed. . . . No reason not to.

Edward Philby, First Planetfall Coordinator of the multinational starship *Lorentz*, who answered only to the Captain and First Manager, tried to sleep briefly and found himself opening his eyes to stare over the mountains and once, briefly, a small pale green lake with ancient shores like lids around a diseased eye. *We have come so far and suffered so much to be here.*

He could not avoid the crooked shape of Kammer in his thoughts, broken and mummified, smelling like an unwashed tramp and yet also like something else: flowers. An odor of sanctity. Eyes like that lake.

The God the Physicists had come here to find something transcendental, their ragged ship surviving the voyage just barely, their faith strengthening in the great Betweens, knowing they could not return if they could not find It here, and they had been lucky. They had found It, and then It had killed them as mercilessly as the unthinking void . . .

The glory of Chujoan biology, the truly transcendental; that which takes a man and transforms him into a survivor and a symbol. Carnot had said: "He is resurrected. The old Kammer died, just as we thought. They resurrected him and imbued him with their spirit of Christ." A dirty, ragged, smelly sort of Christ.

Tatsumi saw that he was not asleep. "You are worried about the settlers on Genji," she said. "Your countrymen."

"They're not my countrymen," Philby said. "I'm English. They're bloody Southwesterners from the U.S.A."

"I beg your pardon."

"Easy mistake, we might as well be a state of the U.S.," he said. "Europe won't have us now. Or rather, *then* . . ." He waved a hand back behind him; time dilated by decades. He had not bothered to catch up on the thin messages from distant Sol, slender lifelines to farflung children.

She smiled and nodded: Earth history, all past for her as well.

"You believe they will do great damage," she offered cautiously, as if Philby might be offended to have a Japanese commenting upon people at least of his language and broad culture if not his nationality.

"You know they will, Tatsumi-san," he said. "Kammer knows they will. He says he tried to kill Carnot and failed."

Tatsumi pursed her lips and frowned. She did not appear shocked. Philby tapped his finger on the edge of the couch, waiting for her reaction. "Carnot thinks Kammer is a . . . Jesus?"

"An avatar of the ancient spirituality of Chujo. Identical to Jesus. Jesus can be found in the universal ground state, where all our redemptions lie. God shows us the way through physics. Just what the

Irdizu need—visitors from the sky able to take messages to Heaven."

"So you take messages in his stead."

"They know I'm not a spirit. I'm a man of solid matter, not Physicist nonsense."

"And what will you do next?"

"Talk to Carnot, if I can find him."

Tatsumi frowned again, shaking her head. "He is not on Chujo?"

"I've been looking for him for the past three weeks."

"Then he must be on Genji. If he is there, I can find out where he is, and take you to him."

Philby hid his surprise. "I thought your people wanted to stay out of this."

"We thought all the cultists would die," Tatsumi said. "They did not."

"Pardon my inquisitiveness—"

"Your *inquisition*?" Tatsumi interrupted with a faint smile. He returned her smile, but with slitted eyes and an ironic nod.

"Believe me, I represent no religious authority on Earth."

"Of course not," Tatsumi said.

"I'm wondering just what your position is on these settlers."

"Earth will keep sending them," Tatsumi said sadly. "There is nothing we can do. Dialog takes decades. The nations of Earth have made the Murasaki system into a symbol of . . . manliness? National prestige? We can not fight such a thing."

"There are two more ships on the way," Philby said.

Tatsumi nodded. "We hope they are as enlightened as your own expedition."

Irony? "Thank you," he said.

"But since dialog is so difficult, we wonder where you derive your authority. You represent no church, and any government is too far away to instruct you. Who gives you orders to quell the God the Physicists?"

Philby shook his head. "Nobody outside of the Murasaki system."

"Then you perform your duty autonomously?"

"Yes."

"Self-appointed."

He flinched and his face reddened. "Your people should remember the effect of a cultural plague. The nineteenth century . . . Admiral Perry?"

"Nobody forces the Irdizu to accept our commercial products. There are none yet to force upon them. And the West came to Nihon before Perry. We had Christians in our midst for centuries before Perry. They were persecuted, tortured, murdered . . . yet fifty thousand still lived in Japan when Perry arrived."

"What Carnot wants to force upon the Irdizu could lead to war, death, destruction on a colossal scale."

"Carnot seems to want to reestablish the ancient links between Chujo and Genji," Tatsumi said.

Thompson, who had listened attentively and quietly in the seat behind Tatsumi, leaned forward. "We're here to preserve Irdizu self-rule. Carnot is a kind of missionary. We can't allow the kind of desecration of native cultures that happened on Earth."

"Oh, yes, that is true," Tatsumi said. She appeared mildly flustered. "I do not wish to be flippant, Mr. Philby, Mr. Thompson."

"They're out of their minds," Philby said, grimacing. Listening to Thompson, though, he realized how much they sounded as if *they* were mouthing a party line, rehearsed across centuries; how much it sounded as if they might be the persecutors, the inquisitors, as Tatsumi had so pointedly punned. "They really are."

"A cultural plague," Tatsumi said, attempting to mollify when in fact no umbrage had been taken.

"Precisely," Philby said. *What Kammer said. Have the Japanese spoken to Kammer?*

Sheldrake had kept his silence, as always, a young man with a young face, born on the journey and accelerated to manhood, but still looking boyish.

"What do you think, Mr. Sheldrake?" Tatsumi asked him.

Sheldrake gave a sudden, sunny smile. "I'm enjoying the landscape," he said in his pleasant tenor.

"Please be open with us," Tatsumi pursued, very uncharacteristically for a Japanese, Philby thought.

"It's not their war," Sheldrake said, glancing at Philby. "Its ours. No matter what we do, we're imposing. I think we just have to reduce that imposition to a minimum."

"I see," Tatsumi said. "Do you know the story of a man named Joseph Caiaphas?" she asked him.

"No," Philby said. She queried the others with a look as they seated themselves in the tiny cockpit. None of them did.

ACROSS THE CHANNEL BETWEEN THE TWO WORLDS, ON CLOUDED AND STORM-wracked Genji, Robert Carnot walked around the temple site, watching the Irdizu workers stalk on strong high chicken-legs around the site of the temple, carrying bricks and mortar and buckets of sloshing paste-thick paint. He rubbed his neck beneath the pressure seal, wondering how much longer this shift before he could take a rest, lie down. He disliked Genji's gravity and climate intensely. His back ached, his legs ached, his neck and *shoulders* ached from the simple weight of his arms. He looked longingly up at the point in the sky where Chujo would be, if they could see it through the rapidly scudding gloom.

The boss of the temple construction crew, a sturdy female named Tsmishfak, approached him with a pronounced swagger of pride. It was good that they should feel proud of what they had accomplished; their pride was good, not the civilized, stately antithesis of resentment that had so often brought Carnot's kind low.

"Tzhe in spatch endED," Tsmishfak told him, eyes glancing back and forth on her sloping fish head. The Irdizu had adapted quickly to this kind of pidgin, much more merciful to their manner of speech than to the humans'. The Japanese had never thought of creating a pidgin; the rationals would despise Carnot for doing so. But at least human and Irdizu could talk without translators intervening.

"Tzhe in spatch finitchED?" he asked, using an Irdizu inquisitive inflection.

"FinitchED," Tsmishfak confirmed.

"Then let me see, and if it matches the Chujoan dimensions—which I'm sure it does—we'll begin the consecration, and I can move on to the next village." Tsmishfak understood most of this unpidgined speech.

She guided him through the fresh pounding rain—each drop like a strike of hail—to the site he had laid out two weeks before. The temple's exterior was still under construction; when completed, the walls would be smooth and white and square, sloping to the broad foundations to withstand the tidal inundations Tsmishfak's village experienced every few Genjian years. Muddy rain fell along the unplastered bricks in gray runnels; clay scoured by clouds from the high mountains above the village's plateau. He would be a Golem-like mess before this day was over.

The in spatch—inner space, interior—was indeed finitchED. Within the temple, out of the sting of clayed rain, the walls were painted a dreadful seasick green, the paint pigments mixed from carpet whale slime and algoid dyes. Tsmishfak had assured him this was a most desirable color to the Irdizu, a sacred color, as yellow might be to a human. Carnot pretended to admire the effect, then noticed he was dripping mud on the clean green floor. Tsmishfak was as well.

"Lengd it," Carnot said, which meant simply, "I will length it," or "I will measure it." Tsmishfak backed away, awed by this moment.

Carnot wiped mud from his face plate and produced a simple string coiled on a spool in his pocket. The string unwound from the two halves of the spool into two lengths; he had made up this device several months before, aware that the temples were nearing completion and some sort of masonic service would be necessary.

By hand gestures up, Carnot indicated that the spool came from Chujo. That was a lie. No matter. What was important was the spiritual import.

He lay one string along the north wall, found it matched precisely, then lay the second string along the east wall. The second string was the same length as the first; the second wall was the same length as the first. He then produced a simple metal protractor, machined aboard their ship in orbit at his request, and measured the angles of each corner. Ninety degrees. A fine square box painted sick green. Perfect.

He raised his hands. "In the name of the great ground of all existence, that which is called Continuum, which breathes with the life of all potential, which creates all and sees all, in the name of the human Kammer who has survived the bonding of human and Chujoan, in the name of the Irdizu Christ called Dsimista, who tells us that all worlds shall be one, I consecrate this temple, which is well-built and square and essential. May no one who does not believe in the Ground, in Kammer, and in Dsimista enter into this place."

Tsmishfak found this eminently satisfactory, particularly as she only understood about a third of what Carnot had said. She echoed, in pidgin, his last commandment, stalked around the walls, then clacked her jaws to summon workers. The workers cleaned up the mud and the in spatch smelled of Irdizu, a not unpleasant smell to Carnot, though pungent.

"Ny mer dert," Tsmishfak promised him as they returned to the exterior. The clayed rain had let up; now there was only drizzle. *Like living at the bottom of a fishbowl.*

"No more dirt, that's fine," Carnot said. "You've din guud, *akkxsha hikfarinkx.*"

Tsmishfak accepted this with a slight swagger.

Good, good, all is well.

"Must move on now," he said in plain English, walking to the edge of the plateau and trying to find his wife and the ship's second officer in the crowded beach area below. "Ah. There are my people." He nodded cordially to the solicitous Tsmishfak. "Must go."

"Dthang u," Tsmishfak said. "Dum Argado."

She was using both English and the Japanese she had acquired.

"You're most welcome," Carnot said. He felt he would die if he could not soon rest his leaden arms and relieve the weight on his back.

Tsmishfak bounced off on spring-steel legs to her workers near the temple, swagger lessened but tentacle arms curling enthusiastically. *Big lumbering thing. Something out of Bosch; fish with legs, but eyes above and below the jawline . . . anatomically improbable. Not easy to love them, but I do, Jesus, I do.*

Carnot found his wife by the ichthyoid pens, standing with the second officer on a wicker frame, nodding to some point of technicality being explained by a small male Irdizu. Not much call for the kind of work she was skilled in, helping poor natives feed themselves. The Irdizu did well enough at that. But scratch beneath their quiet strength and you found a well of anguish; paradise lost and set high in the sky. Connections broken with their distant relations, the Chujoans, millennia past . . .

Desire to rise to heaven and be one with another race. Another species. What if his theories were correct? The rationalists would never accept that intelligent cultures—technological cultures—could rise and fall like fields of wheat coming in and out of season. Perhaps that was why they were looking for him, why he was finding it necessary—through the inner suspicion of aching instinct—to hide . . .

Madeline saw his wave and gently broke off their conversation with the pen manager. It seemed eternities as they made their way back to the ship along the beach. The transport's struts were awash with thick swells of water—no spray under these conditions, only a fine mist like smoke around the sharp rocks. They waded through the swell, more eternities, then the second officer lifted the transport from the beach, its name becoming visible as it rose to a level with him: 2T Benevolent. Second transport of the starship Benevolent.

They touched down again near the lip of the plateau overlooking the beach, and he climbed through the door, wheezing into his respirator. "Enough," he said. "They'll do fine without us. Let's move on."

Madeline touched him solicitously. "You're hurting, poor dear."

"I'm fine," he said, but her touch and sympathy helped. Madeline, thin small strong Madeline, so perfectly adapted to life aboard the Benevolent, could crawl into cubbies where large, lumbering Carnot could not hope to find comfort. Cramped starship, crowded with pilgrims. Madeline who had married him en route and did not share in the sexual-spiritual profligacy, even when her new husband did. Madeline of the bright intense gaze and extraordinary sympathetic intelligence; his main crutch, his main critic. He smiled upon her and she smiled back like a tough-minded little girl.

"I'd enjoy studying their fish farming methods," she said. "We might be able to give them benefit of our own experiences on Earth."

The second officer, thin black African Asian, Lin-Fa Chee by name, did not share Madeline's interest. "They don't farm fish, madame," he observed. "And these people have farmed the ichthyoids for who knows how many thousands of years."

"Millions, perhaps," Carnot said. "Lin-Fa is right, Madeline."

"Still, they need us in many ways," Madeline said, staring through the window as the transport lifted and flew out across the oily rain-dappled sea. "They need *you*, Robert." She smiled at him and he could read the unfinished message: *"Why shouldn't they need me, as well?"*

"Look," Chee said, pointing from his pilot's seat. "Carpet whales."

Carnot looked down upon the huge multicolored leviathans with little interest. *Great flat brutes. Not even Madeline would wish to help them.*

SUZY TATSUMI WATCHED THE DISTANCE LESSEN BETWEEN THE ORBITAL SHUTtle and Genji. To no Chujo grew small as a basketball held at arm's length, visible through the shuttle's starboard windows. She pushed her covered plate of food—sticky rice and bonito flakes topped with thick algal paste—down the aisle between the twenty seats and sat beside Thompson, who had already eaten from a refillable paste tube.

"Fruit yogurt," he said, lifting the empty tube disconsolately. "Supplemented. All we brought with us."

"I would gladly share . . ." Tatsumi said, but that was forbidden. They were still not sure of all the vectors a new wineskin plague might follow, so intimate contact between those who had lived long on Chujo, partaking of its few edibles—or the transfer of food possibly grown on Chujo—was against the rules.

The known forms of the plague had been conquered, but once Chujo's micro-organisms had discovered how to take advantage of the ecological niche offered by humans, they had proven to be remarkably inventive. More mutations might yet occur. Casual contact had not yet shown itself to be dangerous among those protected against the plague, but even so . . .

"I know how your people conquered the plague," Philby said to her. "A remarkable piece of work. But how did Carnot and the last of his people survive?"

Tatsumi shook her head. "We doubt they had any native ability to resist. We still do not know. . . . They were already cured by the time our doctors went among them. But they had suffered terrible losses, on the planet and on their ship . . . there are only twenty of the original two hundred left alive."

"Could they have found the same substances you did?" Thompson asked.

"They did not have our expertise. Nor did they equip themselves with the sophisticated biological equipment we carried . . . the food synthesizers, large molecule analyzers, and the computer programs to run such devices. They arrived here in a weakened state, their ship crippled. We do not know how they survived."

"They get along with the the Irdizu," Philby mused. "Maybe the Irdizu helped them."

"The Irdizu have not the biological mastery of the Chujoans," Tatsumi said.

"Still, there might have been a folk remedy, something serendipitous."

Tatsumi was not familiar with that word. Her translator quickly explained it to her: fortunate, unexpected. "Perhaps," she said. "It was *serendipitous* that we found our own remedy in Chujo's deep lake muds. An antibiotic grown by anaerobic microbes, used to defend their territories against other microbes, and not poisonous to human tissues . . . Most fortunate. Most unexpected. We all thought we would die."

Philby smiled. "Luck favors those who are prepared. . . . Which is why all of Carnot's people should have died. They're as innocent as children."

Tatsumi raised her eyebrows. "You admire strength and their luck?"

"What I admire has nothing to do with what damage they can do here."

"No, indeed," Tatsumi said, feeling dreadfully aware that she had irritated this strange man yet again. She had met Carnot only once, when the *Benevolent* first arrived in orbit around Genji, but she thought these two were well-matched as opponents. Determined, opinionated, they might be brothers in some strange Western tale of Cain and Able, or *East of Eden*, which she had read as a girl back on Earth.

"Do you believe Genji and Chujo are so closely connected, biologically?" Thompson asked.

"They must be," quiet Sheldrake said from behind them all. He had finished his yogurt without complaint or comment.

"What mechanism would bring organisms from Chujo to Genji?" Philby challenged with professorial glee. Tatsumi had noted that these people enjoyed debating, and seemed not to understand boundaries of politeness in such discussions. She had heard them argue violently among themselves without anyone losing face or apologizing.

"Besides the rocket balloons from Chujo . . ." Thompson said.

"I don't yet accept those as fact," Philby said. He glanced at Tatsumi. "Your people didn't actually see rockets . . . just balloons."

"It seems pretty certain the elder Chujo civilizations were capable of rockets," Sheldrake said. Tatsumi was attracted by the young tenor's calm, confident reserve. A child quickly, artificially raised to manhood in space. . . . What strange wisdoms might he have acquired in those years? "But I was thinking of cometary activity—"

"Rare in the Murasaki system," Thompson noted.

"Or even extreme volcanic events. Chujo's ejecta might have carried spores into the upper atmosphere . . . and beyond."

"Not likely," Philby snorted. "There's no easy mechanism, none that doesn't stretch credibility."

"Nevertheless," Tatsumi said, enjoying the spirit of this debate, "the genetic material is very closely related in many primitive organisms on Chujo and Genji."

"There's no denying that," Philby said. "I wish your people had solved this riddle before we arrived . . . there's too many other problems to take care of."

"You did not come here to find and solve such problems?"

"I did," Sheldrake said. "I'm not sure Edward did . . ."

"Essence of crap profane," Philby said, not unpleasantly.

"What's that?" Thompson asked. Philby was not usually so expressive.

"Something Kammer said. He said his mouth tasted like essence of crap profane. After he expectorated red and green saliva."

Tatsumi wrinkled her nose despite herself. "Our biologists would love to be allowed to study him," she said. "We might have saved lives, had we been allowed to . . ."

"Nobody's going to study him without killing a lot of Chujoans," Philby said. "And that we will not allow."

A PLANETARY CONSCIOUSNESS. . . . SOMETHING THAT UNITED BOTH WORLDS, something only vaguely felt by either the Irdizu or the Chujoans. If he could prove its existence, as one might prove the psychic link between two twins, then all of his beliefs would fall into place . . .

Carnot tossed in his weightless bed, drifting slowly between the cylindrical walls of the elastic net. He did not sleep well in microgravity, but it was important that he maintain contact with the ship's Captain, who had suffered horribly from the plague, and might even now be insane.

When Carnot thought of what they had lost, of the price paid by two hundred and forty-five of the *Benevolent*'s crew, he felt a sick darkness curl inside him. Not all the faith, not all the conviction of forty years' service to Jesus the Ground of All Being could erase his sense of loss. From here on in, his life would be a scarred, dedicated emptiness; he knew he would be little more than an efficient shell; the old Carnot had been burned out, leaving fire-hardened wood.

He could not even find the fierce love he had once felt for his wife. He needed her; he paid her the minimum due of affection, all she seemed to require now. She, too, had been burned hollow. Sex between them was at an end. Sex had always been a kind of play, and this close to the truth, this close to the death and disfigurement of their people, no play could be allowed.

And now to be hunted . . .

He closed his eyes tighter, hoping to squeeze a tear or some other sign of his humanity between the lids, but he could not. He thought of the Earth and his young adulthood and the simple miseries that had filled him then. Had his people suffered any more than others had suffered for their faiths? Was he being pressed any harder than any other leader of peoples who believed in pattern and justice and order? These events had been enough to drain him of the pleasures of simply existing; was that the sure sign of his ultimate weakness, that he could no longer take satisfaction in serving Jesus? That he could no longer take satisfaction in having a wife, in breathing in and out, in not being hungry or in having survived that which had turned so many of his people into pain-wracked monsters?

Now he found his one tear, and he let it roll from his left eye, a true luxury. Deep inside, a younger voice said, *You're goddamned right you've had it hard. Space was supposed to be clean and clear-cut, with sharp dividing lines between life and death. It wasn't supposed to be this way, tending this ship like a leaky tub across five years, and then arriving on the inconceivably far shore and finding disease and hideous death. Not supposed to be that way at all. You've been pushed. Don't expect joy when you've been pushed this hard; do not be so demanding as to expect joy after what you've experienced.*

Carnot opened his eyes and saw Captain Plaissix floating in the shadow of the hatch to his cabin. Beyond Plaissix, through the transparent blister of the central alley's cap, Carnot saw Genji's blue-gray surface fall perpetually beneath them. "The Japanese have sent a message," Plaissix said. "They wish to speak directly with you."

Half of the Captain's face had crumpled inward. The wineskin plague had been made up of Chujoan bacterioids particularly well-adapted to living on minerals; they had devoured much of the calcium in his bones, and in his nerves, as well.

"All right," Carnot said, giving up yet another attempt at sleep. He slipped from the net and floated past Plaissix, who tracked him with off-center haunted eyes.

The ship's communications center was in a constant state of repair. George Cluny, the last remaining engineer, moved to one side to give Carnot room. The image of a young Japanese woman floated a few hands away from its normal position; Cluny shrugged in apology, best he could do with what they had. Her voice was distant but clear.

"Carnot here."

"My name is Suzy Tatsumi," the woman said. "I've just traveled to Chujo and back with Edward Philby. We would like to arrange a meeting between your group and his. . . . To settle your disputes."

Carnot smiled. "I don't believe we've met, Tatsumi-san. I've been working with Hiroki-san of Station Hokkaido on Genji."

"He has transferred his responsibilities to me."

Apparently the conflict between Carnot's expedition and the rationalists was beginning to worry the Japanese. Until now, they had been content to let the two stand separate and not intervene in any disputes. Had this Tatsumi woman already already been poisoned by Philby and his representatives?

"I have no time to meet with the rationalists," Carnot said quietly. "They are physically stronger than we are. They would have attacked us by now, if it weren't for their lack of offensive weapons. . . . They cannot harm our ship in orbit." Actually, he was not sure of that.

"I think it would be good for you to begin speaking to each other," Tatsumi said.

"You have remained neutral until now," Carnot said through tight lips. "I can only trust you will not join up with them, against us."

"There are many problems we can solve, Mr. Carnot. We are very far from home, and it is ridiculous to fight among ourselves, when we have faced so many common dangers."

"Tatsumi-san, you underestimate the depth of divisions between our kind. I have already had my dialogues with Edward Philby. We know where we stand. If you will not take sides—" *and damn you if you stay neutral!* "—then please leave us to our histories," he fumbled for what he wanted to say, "our destinies. For what lies ahead."

Tatsumi regarded his image with sad, serious eyes. "Mr. Carnot, Edward Philby has spoken with Kammer. He says that Kammer tried to kill you. If the man you consider so vital a link, if he himself believes you are wrong . . ."

"Please do not argue my faith with me, Tatsumi-san. He struck me with his stick. He did not kill me."

Tatsumi said nothing, puzzled into silence, trying to riddle this human mystery.

"His stick, Tatsumi-san," Carnot said sharply, surprised they had not guessed by now. "He blessed me with his greatest gift. Because of that blow, some of my people are alive now." He was too weary to waste his time with her any longer. "Goodbye, Tatsumi-san. If you wish to offer us help, we are not too proud to accept."

He ordered Cluny to cut the transmission. The engineer did so and stared at him as if awaiting more instructions. Captain Plaissix had come into the communications room and simply floated there, his deformity an accusation.

Carnot had applied the crushed and writhing balm of a patch of Kammer's symbiotic snug, embedded by the stick in his own skin, first upon his wife, and then upon the others. By circumstance Plaissix had been last. Surely by circumstance and not by Carnot's own subconscious planning. Plaissix had been the most doubtful of his revelation regarding Kammer. The one most likely to frustrate their designs, after they had come so far . . .

Casual contact with the avatar was death; the Japanese had learned that much. But to arouse the avatar's passion, and be struck by him, was *to live*.

"WHO IS THE FANATIC, THEN?" EIJI YOSHIMURA ASKED. "AND WHO IS THE aggressor?" The director of Hokkaido station rose from his stone desk, cut from Genji's endless supply of slate, and stood by a rack of laboratory equipment. By trade Yoshimura was an agricultural biologist; he had never wished to be a politician, but deaths at the station during the plague had forced this circumstance upon him.

Tatsumi tried to say something, but Yoshimura was angry and raised his hand. "They are all fools. This Englishman Philby, by what right does he dictate his philosophies?"

"I regret Philby's determination—" Tatsumi began.

"They are all troublemakers!" Yoshimura ranted.

"Director, please hear me out," Tatsumi said, her own voice rising the necessary fraction of a decibel to break through her superior's indignation.

"My apologies," Yoshimura said, glancing at her from the corner of his eye. "I am not angry with you, nor critical of the work you have done."

"I understand, sir. Philby's fears are well-founded. Already Carnot has spread his religious beliefs to nine Genji villages. Already nine temples to their version of Jesus, and to Kammer, have been built. Carnot will soon have a broad enough base of support to endanger our own mission, should he so choose—using Irdizu as his soldiers."

Yoshimura considered this with deep solemnity. "Do you believe Carnot will go that far?"

"He has been pushed beyond reason," Tatsumi said. "By the plague, and now by the rationalists."

"I once would have counted myself among the rationalists," Yoshimura said. "But I have never tried to impose my will upon those who disagreed. Has Carnot made any converts in our camp?"

Tatsumi reacted with some surprise to this question, which had not occured to her. "Not to my knowledge," she replied.

"I will inquire discreetly. You look shocked, Suzy."

"I find it hard to believe any of our people would believe such drivel," she said, with more heat than she intended.

Yoshimura smiled sagely. "We are human, too. We are in a strange land, far from home, and we can lose our bearings as quickly as anyone else. We do have some Christians among us—Aoki, for example."

"Aoki is very circumspect," Tatsumi said. "Besides, traditional Christians would hardly recognize the beliefs of the God the Physicists."

"Such an awkward name," Yoshimura said. "Still, I would hate to face an army of Irdizu—led by the females, no doubt." His expression slumped into solemnity again, and he seemed very old and tired. "Try to reason with Carnot again. If he is still unwilling to meet with Philby, then ask him if he will meet with our people—with you."

"I do not believe he will. He is exhausted and depressed, sir."

"Do you know that for certain?"

"It's obvious."

"Then he's even more dangerous," Yoshimura said. "But we will try anyway."

Tatsumi sighed.

PHILBY STOOD UP UNDER GENJI'S EXCESSIVE AFFECTION, MUSCLES ACHING from the hour of acclimatizing exercise. With most of his time spent on kinder, simpler Chujo, the storms and thickness and heaviness of Genji was like being immersed in nightmare; but here was the core of their problem, among the apparently gullible Irdizu, who were building temples to Kammer—and to Carnot's Jesus.

Theresa O'Brien joined him in the makeshift gymnasium, dressed in exercise tights, short hair frizzed with moisture. "How's the tummy, Edward?" she asked.

"Ah, tight as a drum," Philby responded, thwupping his abdomen with a thumb-released finger. "I've never been in better shape."

O'Brien shook her head dubiously. "You've always inclined to more muscle than you needed, then neglected, then to gut."

"Brutal Theresa," Philby said drily, continuing his leg-lifts.

"When are you leaving for the temple site?"

"In four hours," Philby said.

"I've come from Diana's bungalow," O'Brien said, squatting slowly, carefully beside him. Exercise on Genji seemed ridiculously slow; anything faster and they might injure themselves. She sat and watched his red face. "Don't overdo it."

"What, the exercise, or . . . ?" Philby didn't finish.

"We don't like what Carnot's doing any more than you do," O'Brien said. "But the Japanese concern us, too. We're making an impression here, not just with the Irdizu and the Chujoans—with our fellow humans, as well."

"They seem to be on our side, certainly more than on Carnot's side," Philby said, stopping to devote his full attention to their conversation. "I hope Diana's not rethinking our plans."

"It seems to some of us that you're the one doing the rethinking."

"Diana put me in charge of relations with the *Benevolent*. We've all agreed they're dangerous; I'm following through."

O'Brien nodded. "Edward, it sometimes seem you're the aggressor, not them. What will the Irdizu think if . . ." She shook her head and didn't finish.

"If Carnot's made such an impression on them, and we constrain him?" Philby finished for her. She raised her chin in the slightest nod, as if wary of him.

"I apologize, Theresa," Philby said. "You know my temperament better than anybody. I'm thorough, but I'm not a loose beam. Reassure Diana for me."

"She's on the ship now, arranging for a reception. The Japanese are coming—and she tells me they're trying to get Carnot to come, as well."

"I'm always a man for dialogue," Philby said. He replaced the padded bench and weights and wiped his face with a towel. "But Carnot . . . I think he is not."

"Will you listen to Carnot if the Japanese convince him to come?"

"What will he . . ." Philby realized he was being excessively contrary, and that more argument might tip the balance in O'Brien's eyes. "Of course. I'll listen."

She turned to leave, and he could not restrain himself from saying, "But Theresa, there must be constraint on their part. That should be clear to all of us. We are *protecting* the Irdizu from the worst parts of ourselves."

"Are we?" O'Brien asked over her shoulder.

"Yes," Philby said after a pause. "Any doubts on that score and we might all be lost."

"I do not doubt Carnot is a danger," O'Brien said, and closed the door behind her.

That evening, the communications manager on their starship told Philby something extraordinary, and the wheels began to turn in his mind. If he must meet with Carnot, then he would be prepared to shatter that little plaster prophet once and for all. Now, he might have the hammer to do so.

When traveling at close to lightspeed, our geometry is distorted, such that, to an outside observer, we reveal aspects of our shapes that are not usually seen . . . around curves, edges. We are warped in ways we cannot feel . . . Is this also not true of our souls?

Philby inspected the fourth finished temple, his legs and feet aching abominably. He used two canes now to support his weight; to the Irdizu, he called them "Kammerstaffs."

He had begun to spread the story of Kammer's striking him. He had found an interesting analogy to his contretemps with Kammer in Irdizu storytelling, a resonance he could take advantage of. Indeed, this was very the village, so said Irdizu legend, where the angelic *Szikwshawmi* had landed in ancient times and struck the female warriors with staffs of ice to give them superior strength. At the same time, the *Szikwshawmi* had frozen the tongue-penises of the males, making intercourse in both senses of the word impossible. The females had gone out in their frustration and gathered in new males from distant villages, leaving the females of *those* villages frustrated, and they had gone forth and done likewise . . . and so on, a great wave of Sabine rapes.

It was hardly a precise analogy. In some respects it was embarrassingly inappropriate; but the Irdizu found it a compelling comparison, and when searching for mythic roots, one had to bend, and to be bent.

The temple, constructed in a thick patch of manzanitas-like beach forest, deep in a shadowy hollow filled with drifting mist and sea-spray and dark tidal pools, was certainly the gloomiest that had been built so far. The Irdizu in this village were larger, more sullen, more suspicious than any they had encountered before. The females certainly seemed to be brusker and more dominating.

The village had been visited by humans—Japanese—only once, years before. Yet still the stories of Jesus and Kammer and Carnot and the Chujo connection had spread even into these shadows, and taken root.

The temple matched the necessary specifications. Carnot blessed it, and moved on.

There was a disturbing trend. Five villages had so far refused Carnot, and rejected his doctrines. All of these villages had been visited by Philby and his agents, spreading rationalist doctrine. Carnot had only heard bits and pieces of this antithesis to his thesis: Philby was apparently feeding them visions of a potential future, when Genji and Chujo would be united, not in any mystical sense, but politically, in league with human advisers.

A dry, deadly sort of myth, Carnot thought. To tell the truth, he wasn't sure *what* role humans would play in his own scheme; perhaps none at all. There were so few of his people left. They could find comfort in a small corner of Chujo, perhaps acting as the spiritual advisers, setting up a center for pilgrims. They would certainly not stride hand-in-hand into a bright future with the rationally corrected and technologically equipped Irdizu and Chujoans . . .

And yet still the Japanese tried to arrange a meeting, and still Philby's people visited village after village, creating territories where he could not operate.

It was a war.

Carnot realized how reluctant he had been, until now, to accept that fact. He had always felt hunted, opposed; he had never devised a strategy whereby he might counterstrike. But it was clearly becoming necessary.

"You have done well," Carnot told the chief females, who bounced and swaggered solemnly on their large chicken legs, horizontal bodies quivering. He cringed inside, craving the company of humans, wishing to be relieved of this burden; and he retreated on his Kammerstaffs to the ship, where Madeline and Lin-Fa Chee waited.

"Another message from the Japanese," Madeline said quietly when they were settled, and the transport had lifted off. The ship's engines made a high-pitched whikkering noise and one side settled as they rose; Lin-Fa Chee corrected, and the transport gained altitude, but more slowly.

"Of course," Carnot said.

"The Captain thinks we should talk to them."

Carnot lifted an eyebrow. "Yes?"

"We need to barter," Lin-Fa Chee said. "We need spare parts."

"The Captain has spoken with the Japanese, with Suzy Tatsumi. She says they will trade or manufacture spare parts for us . . . ."

"Generous," Carnot said, closing his eyes.

"If we meet with them, and with the rationalists," Madeline concluded.

Carnot pretended to sleep.

"Robert, we have to make a decision soon," Madeline said. "There's a lot at stake here."

"We'll meet," he said softly. "How many more temples?"

"Three, I think. . . . Perhaps more next week."

"I want to see the ceremonies completed." Suddenly, he was feeling very mortal—with more than a suspicion that what lay beyond mortality was not what he most fervently desired.

PHILBY WALKED SLOWLY TOWARD THE LOOSE LINE OF TWELVE BULLYBOYS, reeking of Chujoan protective scent. They lifted their heads, sniffed the air casually, remained where they were. Surely they could see he was not Chujoan; surely they had minds enough to recognize that scent alone did not guarantee his belonging. But they restrained themselves, and once again added to the mystery of how they functioned in Chujoan society.

He passed between two of them, barely a meter on each side from their claws and fangs barely concealed behind loose lips.

The shamans formed the next line. Beyond them lay the edge of the village, and the hut which Kammer had taken, or been assigned, who could say which. He was on the outskirts, rather than in the center; that might be significant. Perhaps he was not as important to the Chujoans as this peculiar reception ceremony implied; perhaps Chujoan ritual went beyond the simple analogy of enfolding and protection, and put their most valuable icons on the edge rather than the center of the village.

Perhaps he didn't understand Kammer's meaning at all.

A loose dry breeze blew dust between the spindly legs of the shamans. The line parted, as if Philby had ordered the breeze as a signal. He could feel the casual, unreacting presence of the bullyboys behind him.

The work he had done in the past week to make this meeting useful—to be able to ask the question he would now ask of Kammer—had taxed his patience to its limit. He had asked five of his ship's biologists, and three of the Japanese doctors and biologists, how much of a risk Kammer might pose to crews if they were actually exposed to his physical presence. None had been willing to give a straight answer at first; fear of the wineskin plague had distorted simple rational judgments, leading to hedged bets, hems and haws, a reliance on very fuzzy statistics. Finally Philby had been able to draw a consensus from the scientists and doctors: Kammer was not much of a threat now. If indeed the wineskin plague had begun on Kammer, which was almost universally accepted, then it was likely that they had protected themselves against all possible varieties he might have generated. Unless—and this possibility still haunted Philby, if only for its fearfully nonsensical aspects—unless Kammer or the Chujoans had deliberately created the plague . . .

Kammer could walk among them, if he so chose.

Philby stood outside the mud-brick and reed hut. "Hello," he said. Nothing but silence within. His communications with the Chujoans had led him to believe Kammer was willing to have another meeting—had in fact requested it.

"Hello," he called out again, glancing over his shoulder at the shamans, shivering despite himself. Which was worse—to be ignored as if one didn't exist, or to be recognized by something so intrinsically alien? In some respects, now that he was familiar with the two species, the humanoid Chujoans seemed much more alien than the Boschian Irdizu . . .

"Doing you here?"

Kammer came around the other side of the hut. Philby started, turned slowly, trying to regain dignity, and faced Kammer.

302 THE COLLECTED STORIES OF GREG BEAR

"I've brought a message," he said. "From your starship, on its way back to Earth. They intercepted reports that you had been found alive . . ."

Kammer glanced up at the sky speculatively with one pale eye, lips moving. "Must be about two and a half light-years out," he said. "Doing fast by now. Bit-rate way down. Bandwidth doing the very narrow."

"A woman who held you in high regard sends a message to you," Philby said. This, he hoped, was the shock that would jolt Kammer back to some human sense of responsibility. "It's rather personal, but its reception by our ship—and the Japanese ship, simultaneously—was hardly private."

"Something to be read, or just spoken?" Kammer asked. Philby interpreted that question as a promising sign. Curiosity, plain English syntax, a tone of some concern. "I know her. I did life with her." He tapped his leathery pate. "In dreams."

"Her name is—"

"Nicole," Kammer said.

Philby said nothing for a few seconds, watching the brown, tortured face reflect some inner realization, some reawakening of old memories.

"What does she say?"

Philby held out a slate. Nicole had convinced the powers that be— apparently her husband, Captain Darryl Washington—that a message of several hundred words was necessary. This had required considerable diversion of resources—turning antennas around, readjustment, expenditure of valuable communications time. Philby had read the message several times. He had no idea what Kammer would make of it. If he had been Kammer—a long-shot of supposition—Philby would have been deeply saddened.

Dearest Airy,

I cannot believe what we have heard. That you are alive! By what miracle is not clear to us; we have only been able to receive about three-quarters of the transmissions from Murasaki. We all feel incredibly guilty about leaving you behind. There was no chance of your survival—we knew that, you must believe we knew that! I grieved for you. I punished Darryl for years. This has been cruel to all of us, but especially I think to him. Whom I punish, I feel the most sympathy for . . .

What are you now, after so many years with the Chujoans? Do you still think of us, or have they changed you so much you have forgotten? I cannot tell you all that has happened to us. . . . We feel like such cowards, such fools, having left Murasaki just when the rush from Earth was beginning. We should have stayed, but we did not have the heart. What reception we will return home to, I cannot say . . . Perhaps the reception reserved for (L.O.S. 2.4 kb?).

. . . were the better man. I chose you. Know that about me now, Aaron, that in the end, I chose you, my body chose you. Darryl has lived with this, and I think I admire him more now, despite my punishments and inward scorn, for having lived with it.

We have a son, Aaron. You and I. He is your boy. He was born five months ago. I have named him after your father, Kevin. He is healthy and will be a young man when we return to Earth.

He will be told that you are his father. Darryl insists, especially since we've learned you are alive.

That knowledge grinds Darryl down more each night. Who can understand the grief of strong men?

I love you, Aaron.

Nicole

Kammer let the slate drop to the ground, then swayed like an old tree in a slight breeze. "I am not that same person," he said throatily. "He did the dying."

"I think that person is still here," Philby persisted. "You remember Nicole. You remember who you were. And you knew that Carnot would cause great damage. You hit him to stop him."

"I hit him to save him," Kammer said with a sudden heat. "Could not see them all do the dying."

"I don't understand," Philby said, eyes narrowing.

"They gave me this," Kammer said, lifting the stick covered with patchy snug. "Long times past. Years, maybe. I did the bloating too, and the filling with liquids, the twisting of bones. This," he indicated his contorted trunk and limbs, "was not from breaking my back. I did the sickness myself. Body like a skin full of wine. They gave me the stick, and the snug took me over. It found what was making me sick, and it killed them, or tamed them. I got better."

Philby's eyes widened, and for the first time in Kammer's presence, he felt a shiver of awe. What did the Chujoans know—what could they do? He slowly turned to survey the shamans, uncaring and implacable in their loose line between the two humans and the bullyboys.

"Hit him to save him, if he had the brains to know what it was I gave," Kammer said. "I see he did." Kammer's gaze was intense, his eyes seeming darker, more human now. "Perhaps that was when he did the prophet. Bent body, bent mind. Saved from death. Knew, knew."

Softly, shivering slightly, Philby said, "We're going to meet with the God the Physicists, with Carnot. I think it's important that you talk with him."

"Can't go back and do the human thing," Kammer said. "Being this. Knew, knew."

"If you believe his distortions are dangerous—and you must, Aaron, you must!—you cannot refuse us this. Talk with him, tell him what you know. Try to make him stop this insanity. He could destroy all the Genjians have in the way of—culture, language, independent thought."

"Never did them," Kammer said.

"Aaron . . ." Philby stepped forward, hands beseeching. He removed his hydrator, to speak directly with Kammer. The cool dry air felt like dust in his throat and he coughed.

Two trolls shoved him roughly away and spilled him on the ground. His mask flew high into the air and came down six or seven meters away. A troll loomed over him, baring its teeth, seeming to grin, examining his form as if it might be a long diversion from the troll's normal mindless boredom.

Kammer stood back, stick lifted as if to defend himself as well against the trolls, and said nothing.

The shamans moved in around Philby. He tried to get up, but the troll casually kicked his arm out from under him and he fell back. He prepared himself to die, but first, he triggered the emergency signal in his belt. That would bring Sheldrake and Thompson; they were armed. If he was dead, they would do nothing but try to retrieve his body; but if he were still alive, they would carve their way through trolls and shamans both to save him.

He considered this for a moment, realized what an ugliness might spread from another such incident—realized that what the Japanese had done, years before, might still linger between Chujoans and humans—and shouted to Kammer, "For God's sake, Aaron, this is awful! Stop them!"

He saw part of Kammer's twisted leg through the parted legs of a troll. The leg moved, then the stick came down with a thud. More snug dropped away from the stick. Fascinated, anesthetized by his terror, Philby watched the fallen patches of growth twist about and crawl along the ground, back to the stick.

"There isn't much I can do," Kammer said. "Lie still."

"Damn it, you're sacred to them! Tell them to stop!"

"I'm hardly sacred," Kammer said. The troll stepped aside and Philby saw Kammer clearly. He was standing away from the trolls, who showed

their teeth to him with as much apparent enthusiasm as they did to
Philby. "That's what Carnot thought. Doing the Earth anthropomorphic.
I'm an experiment, Philby. I thought you were rational and could know
that. An experiment, and nothing more."

ALWAYS, NEVER

Introduction to "The White Horse Child"

Here's one of my most popular stories, reprinted dozens of times and even made into a multimedia CD-ROM. When Terry Carr bought it for his original hardcover anthology *Universe 9* (1979) I was thrilled—Terry was one of the most respected editors in the field, and he said this story reminded him of Ray Bradbury.

Ray's work has always been one of my biggest influences, but "The White Horse Child" is the only one of my stories that even comes close to being Bradburyesque.

I had strong inspiration. In my late teens and early twenties I experienced a series of dreams that exposed something about my inner, creative self. While I've seldom gotten story ideas from dreams, on occasion—and particularly in those years—dreams acted like a mindquake to reveal hidden layers and allow deep magma to reach the surface.

One of the upwellings came in 1972. I was living by myself in an apartment on College Avenue in San Diego, California. Half-awake, lying in bed in the dark at some hour past midnight, I witnessed an equine beast push slowly through my bedroom wall. It was made of woven ice crystals, but otherwise bore a distinct resemblance to the horse in Fuselli's "Nightmare," and it relayed a message that seemed at first ominous—but on retrospect, after I was fully awake, turned out to be friendly and approving. That message was, and I quote it exactly, "You're doing just fine, but don't forget about me."

I had met this creature before.

When I was nine years old, I had a bad nightmare about a white cloud hovering over my bed. It told me that it was going to eat me.

The ice-crystal horse and the hungry cloud were one and the same. In the intervening years, my subconscious selves—my creative "demons"—had formed an alliance with my consciousness, and were no longer threatening, but intensely collaborative. A whole series of similar dreams sealed the alliance, and my demons and I have been working well together ever since.

In 1977, Tina and I moved to Long Beach. I was writing on an old IBM typewriter, using long sheets of yellow paper wound off of a roll—five feet was a pretty good day's work. In the afternoon, I would often drive into downtown Long Beach and wander through Acres of Books, a venerable old store that is still there, mostly unchanged, and still well worth visiting. Around the corner was Richard Kyle's Wonderworld books, where I met not only Richard, a lean, witty man with a lifetime's experience of popular culture, but Alan Brennert, the superb novelist and screenwriter. Alan was young and ambitious, just like me, and we would soon partner up to impress an agent and take story ideas into Hollywood. I had connections that led Alan to his first Hollywood agent, and Alan had connections that led me to my literary agent, Richard Curtis.

The ideas perked, and in 1977, in that apartment in Long Beach, poured forth as a story of dreams and creativity, of a young lad's awakening to the creative instinct—and of those who, in the name of something they call righteousness and love, would kill everything in this life that really matters.

By the way, no one in my family ever treated me this way. I was lucky, and maybe that's why my demons and I get along so well.

THE WHITE HORSE CHILD
Universe 9, Terry Carr, 1979

When I was seven years old, I met an old man by the side of the dusty road between school and farm. The late afternoon sun had cooled, and he was sitting on a rock, hat off, hands held out to the gentle warmth, whistling a pretty song. He nodded at me as I walked past. I nodded back. I was curious, but I knew better than to get involved with strangers. Nameless evils seemed to attach themselves to strangers, as if they might turn into lions when no one but a little kid was around.

"Hello, boy," he said.

I stopped and shuffled my feet. He looked more like a hawk than a lion. His clothes were brown and gray and russet, and his hands were pink like the flesh of some rabbit a hawk had just plucked up. His face was brown except around the eyes, where he might have worn glasses; around the eyes he was white, and this intensified his gaze. "Hello," I said.

"Was a hot day. Must have been hot in school," he said.

"They got air-conditioning."

"So they do, now. How old are you?"

"Seven," I said. "Well, almost eight."

"Mother told you never to talk to strangers?"

"And Dad, too."

"Good advice. But haven't you seen me around here?"

I looked him over. "No."

"Closely. Look at my clothes. What color are they?"

His shirt was gray, like the rock he was sitting on. The cuffs, where they peeped from under a russet jacket, were white. He didn't smell bad, but he didn't look particularly clean. He was smooth-shaven, though. His hair was white, and his pants were the color of the dirt below the rock. "All kinds of colors," I said.

"But mostly I partake of the landscape, no?"

"I guess so,"I said.

"That's because I'm not here. You're imagining me, at least part of me. Don't I look like somebody you might have heard of?"

"Who are you supposed to look like?" I asked.

"Well, I'm full of stories," he said. "Have lots of stories to tell little boys, little girls, even big folk, if they'll listen."

I started to walk away.

"But only if they'll listen," he said. I ran. When I got home, I told my older sister about the man on the road, but she only got a worried look and told me to stay away from strangers. I took her advice. For some time afterward, into my eighth year, I avoided that road and did not speak with strangers more than I had to.

The house that I lived in, with the five other members of my family and two dogs and one beleaguered cat, was white and square and comfortable. The stairs were rich dark wood overlaid with worn carpet. The walls were dark oak paneling up to a foot above my head, then white plaster, with a white plaster ceiling. The air was full of smells—bacon when I woke up, bread and soup and dinner when I came home from school, dust on weekends when we helped clean.

Sometimes my parents argued, and not just about money, and those were bad times; but usually we were happy. There was talk about selling the farm and the house and going to Mitchell where Dad could work in a computerized feed-mixing plant, but it was only talk.

IT WAS EARLY SUMMER WHEN I TOOK TO THE DIRT ROAD AGAIN. I'D FOR-gotten about the old man. But in almost the same way, when the sun was cooling and the air was haunted by lazy bees, I saw an old woman. Women strangers are less malevolent than men, and rarer. She was sitting on the gray rock, in a long green skirt summer-dusty, with a daisy-colored shawl and a blouse the precise hue of cottonwoods seen in a late hazy day's muted light. "Hello, boy," she said.

"I don't recognize you, either," I blurted, and she smiled.

"Of course not. If you didn't recognize him, you'd hardly know me."

"Do you know him?" I asked. She nodded. "Who was he? Who are you?"

"We're both full of stories. Just tell them from different angles. You aren't afraid of us, are you?"

I was, but having a woman ask the question made all the difference. "No," I said. "But what are you doing here? And how do you know—?"

"Ask for a story," she said. "One you've never heard of before." Her eyes were the color of baked chestnuts, and she squinted into the sun so that I couldn't see her whites. When she opened them wider to look at me, she didn't have any whites.

"I don't want to hear stories," I said softly.

"Sure you do. Just ask."

"It's late. I got to be home."

"I knew a man who became a house," she said. "He didn't like it. He stayed quiet for thirty years, and watched all the people inside grow up, and be just like their folks, all nasty and dirty and leaving his walls to flake, and the bathrooms were unbearable. So he spit them out one morning, furniture and all, and shut his doors and locked them."

"What?"

"You heard me. Upchucked. The poor house was so disgusted he changed back into a man, but he was older and he had a cancer and his heart was bad because of all the abuse he had lived with. He died soon after."

I laughed, not because the man had died, but because I knew such things were lies. "That's silly," I said.

"Then here's another. There was a cat who wanted to eat butterflies. Nothing finer in the world for a cat than to stalk the grass, waiting for black-and-pumpkin butterflies. It crouches down and wriggles its rump to dig in the hind paws, then it jumps. But a butterfly is no sustenance for a cat. It's practice. There was a little girl about your age—might have been your sister, but she won't admit it—who saw the cat and decided to teach it a lesson. She hid in the taller grass with two old kites under each arm and waited for the cat to come by stalking. When it got real close, she put on her mother's dark glasses, to look all bug-eyed, and she jumped up flapping the kites. Well, it was just a little too real, because in a trice she found herself flying, and she was much smaller than she had been, and the cat jumped at her. Almost got her, too. Ask your sister about that sometime. See if she doesn't deny it."

"How'd she get back to be my sister again?"

"She became too scared to fly. She lit on a flower and found herself crushing it. The glasses broke, too."

"My sister did break a pair of Mom's glasses once."

The woman smiled.

"I got to be going home."

"Tomorrow you bring me a story, okay?"

I ran off without answering. But in my head, monsters were already rising. If she thought I was scared, wait until she heard the story I had to tell! When I got home my oldest sister, Barbara, was fixing lemonade in the kitchen. She was a year older than I but acted as if she were grown-up. She was a good six inches taller, and I could beat her if I got in a lucky punch, but no other way—so her power over me was awesome. But we were usually friendly.

"Where you been?" she asked, like a mother.

"Somebody tattled on you," I said.

Her eyes went doe-scared, then wizened down to slits. "What're you talking about?"

"Somebody tattled about what you did to Mom's sunglasses."

"I already been whipped for that," she said nonchalantly. "Not much more to tell."

"Oh, but I know more."

"Was *not* playing doctor," she said. The youngest, Sue-Ann, weakest and most full of guile, had a habit of telling the folks somebody or other was playing doctor. She didn't know what it meant—I just barely did— but it had been true once, and she held it over everybody as her only vestige of power.

"No," I said, "but I know what you were doing. And I won't tell anybody."

"You don't know nothing," she said. Then she accidentally poured half a pitcher of lemonade across the side of my head and down my front. When Mom came in I was screaming and swearing like Dad did when he fixed the cars, and I was put away for life plus ninety years in the bedroom I shared with younger brother Michael. Dinner smelled better than usual that evening, but I had none of it. Somehow I wasn't brokenhearted. It gave me time to think of a scary story for the country-colored woman on the rock.

School was the usual mix of hell and purgatory the next day. Then the hot, dry winds cooled and the bells rang and I was on the dirt road again, across the southern hundred acres, walking in the lees and shadows of the big cottonwoods. I carried my Road-Runner lunch pail and my pencil box and one book—a handwriting manual I hated so much I tore pieces out of it at night, to shorten its lifetime and I walked slowly, to give my story time to gel.

She was leaning up against a tree, not far from the rock. Looking back, I can see she was not so old as a boy of eight years thought. Now I see her lissome beauty and grace, despite the dominance of gray in her reddish hair, despite the crow's-feet around her eyes and the smile-haunts around her lips. But to the eight-year-old she was simply a peculiar crone. And he had a story to tell her, he thought, that would age her unto graveside.

"Hello, boy," she said.

"Hi." I sat on the rock.

"I can see you've been thinking," she said.

I squinted into the tree shadow to make her out better. "How'd you know?"

"You have the look of a boy that's been thinking. Are you here to listen to another story?"

"Got one to tell, this time," I said.

"Who goes first?"

It was always polite to let the woman go first, so I quelled my haste and told her she could. She motioned me to come by the tree and sit on a smaller rock, half-hidden by grass. And while the crickets in the shadow tuned up for the evening, she said, "Once there was a dog. This dog was a pretty usual dog, like the ones that would chase you around home if they thought they could get away with it—if they didn't know you or thought you were up to something the big people might disapprove of. But this dog lived in a graveyard. That is, he belonged to the caretaker. You've seen a graveyard before, haven't you?"

"Like where they took Grandpa."

"Exactly," she said. "With pretty lawns, and big white-and-gray stones, and for those who've died recently, smaller gray stones with names and flowers and years cut into them. And trees in some places, with a mortuary nearby made of brick, and a garage full of black cars, and a place behind the garage where you wonder what goes on." She knew the place, all right. "This dog had a pretty good life. It was his job to keep the grounds clear of animals at night. After the gates were locked, he'd be set loose, and he wandered all night long. He was almost white, you see. Anybody human who wasn't supposed to be there would think he was a ghost, and they'd run away.

"But this dog had a problem. His problem was, there were rats that didn't pay much attention to him. A whole gang of rats. The leader was a big one, a good yard from nose to tail. These rats made their living by burrowing under the ground in the old section of the cemetery."

That did it. I didn't want to hear any more. The air was a lot colder than it should have been, and I wanted to get home in time for dinner and still be able to eat it. But I couldn't go just then.

"Now the dog didn't know what the rats did, and just like you and I, probably, he didn't much care to know. But it was his job to keep them under control. So one day he made a truce with a couple of cats that he normally tormented and told them about the rats. These cats were scrappy old toms, and they'd long since cleared out the competition of other cats, but they were friends themselves. So the dog made them a proposition. He said he'd let them use the cemetery anytime they wanted, to prowl or hunt in or whatever, if they would put the fear of God into a few of the rats. The cats took him up on it. 'We get to do whatever we want,' they said, 'whenever we want, and you won't bother us.' The dog agreed.

"That night the dog waited for the sounds of battle. But they never came. Nary a yowl." She glared at me for emphasis. "Not a claw scratch. Not even a twitch of tail in the wind." She took a deep breath, and so did I. "Round about midnight the dog went out into the graveyard. It was very dark, and there wasn't wind or bird or speck of star to relieve the quiet and the dismal inside-of-a-box-camera blackness. He sniffed his way to the old part of the graveyard and met with the head rat, who was sitting on a slanty, cracked wooden grave marker. Only his eyes and a tip of tail showed in the dark, but the dog could smell him. 'What happened to the cats?' he asked. The rat shrugged his haunches. 'Ain't seen any cats,' he said. 'What did you think—that you could scare us out with a couple of cats? Ha. Listen—if there had been any cats here tonight, they'd have been strung and hung like meat in a shed, and my young'uns would have grown fat on—' "

"No-o-o!" I screamed, and I ran away from the woman and the tree until I couldn't hear the story anymore.

"What's the matter?" she called after me. "Aren't you going to tell me your story?" Her voice followed me as I ran.

It was funny. That night, I wanted to know what happened to the cats. Maybe nothing had happened to them. Not knowing made my visions even worse—and I didn't sleep well. But my brain worked like it had never worked before.

The next day, a Saturday, I had an ending—not a very good one in retrospect—but it served to frighten Michael so badly he threatened to tell Mom on me.

"What would you want to do that for?" I asked. "Cripes, I won't ever tell you a story again if you tell Mom!"

Michael was a year younger and didn't worry about the future. "You never told me stories before," he said, "and everything was fine. I won't miss them."

He ran down the stairs to the living room. Dad was smoking a pipe and reading the paper, relaxing before checking the irrigation on the north thirty. Michael stood at the foot of the stairs, thinking. I was almost down to grab him and haul him upstairs when he made his decision and headed for the kitchen. I knew exactly what he was considering—that Dad would probably laugh and call him a little scaredy-cat. But Mom would get upset and do me in proper.

She was putting a paper form over the kitchen table to mark it for fitting a tablecloth. Michael ran up to her and hung on to a pants leg while I halted at the kitchen door, breathing hard, eyes threatening eternal torture if he so much as peeped. But Michael didn't worry about the future much.

"Mom," he said.

"Cripes!" I shouted, high-pitching on the *i*. Refuge awaited me in the tractor shed. It was an agreed-upon hiding place. Mom didn't know I'd be there, but Dad did, and he could mediate.

It took him a half hour to get to me. I sat in the dark behind a workbench, practicing my pouts. He stood in the shaft of light falling from the unpatched chink in the roof. Dust motes maypoled around his legs. "Son," he said. "Mom wants to know where you got that story."

Now, this was a peculiar thing to be asked. The question I'd expected had been, "Why did you scare Michael?" or maybe, "What made you think of such a thing?" But no. Somehow she had plumbed the problem, planted the words in Dad's mouth, and impressed upon him that father-son relationships were temporarily suspended.

"I made it up," I said.

"You've never made up that kind of story before."

"I just started."

He took a deep breath. "Son, we get along real good, except when you lie to me. We know better. Who told you that story?"

This was uncanny. There was more going on than I could understand—there was a mysterious adult thing happening. I had no way around the truth. "An old woman," I said.

Dad sighed even deeper. "What was she wearing?"

"Green dress," I said.

"Was there an old man?"

I nodded.

"Christ," he said softly. He turned and walked out of the shed. From outside he called me to come into the house. I dusted off my overalls and followed him. Michael sneered at me.

" 'Locked them in coffins with old dead bodies,' " he mimicked. "Phhht! You're going to get it."

The folks closed the folding door to the kitchen with both of us outside. This disturbed Michael, who'd expected instant vengeance. I was too curious and worried to take my revenge on him, so he skulked out the screen door and chased the cat around the house. "Lock you in a coffin!" he screamed.

Mom's voice drifted from behind the louvered doors. "Do you hear that? The poor child's going to have nightmares. It'll warp him."

"Don't exaggerate," Dad said.

"Exaggerate what? That those filthy people are back? Ben, they must be a hundred years old now! They're trying to do the same thing to your son that they did to your brother . . . and just look at *him!* Living in sin, writing for those hell-spawned girlie magazines."

"He ain't living in sin, he's living alone in an apartment in New York City. And he writes for all kinds of places."

"They tried to do it to you, too! Just thank God your aunt saved you."

"Margie, I hope you don't intend—"

"Certainly do. She knows all about them kind of people. She chased them off once, she can sure do it again!"

All hell had broken loose. I didn't understand half of it, but I could feel the presence of Great Aunt Sybil Danser. I could almost hear her crackling voice and the shustle of her satchel of Billy Grahams and Zondervans and little tiny pamphlets with shining light in blue offset on their covers.

I knew there was no way to get the full story from the folks short of listening in, but they'd stopped talking and were sitting in that stony kind of silence that indicated Dad's disgust and Mom's determination. I was mad that nobody was blaming me, as if I were some idiot child not capable of being bad on my own. I was mad at Michael for precipitating the whole mess.

And I was curious. Were the man and woman more than a hundred years old? Why hadn't I seen them before, in town, or heard about them from other kids? Surely I wasn't the only one they'd seen on the road and told stories to. I decided to get to the source. I walked up to the louvered doors and leaned my cheek against them. "Can I go play at George's?"

"Yes," Mom said. "Be back for evening chores."

George lived on the next farm, a mile and a half east. I took my bike and rode down the old dirt road going south.

They were both under the tree, eating a picnic lunch from a wicker basket. I pulled my bike over and leaned it against the gray rock, shading my eyes to see them more clearly.

"Hello, boy," the old man said. "Ain't seen you in a while."

I couldn't think of anything to say. The woman offered me a cookie, and I refused with a muttered, "No, thank you, ma'am."

"Well then, perhaps you'd like to tell us your story."

"No, ma'am."

"No story to tell us? That's odd. Meg was sure you had a story in you someplace. Peeking out from behind your ears maybe, thumbing its nose at us."

The woman smiled ingratiatingly. "Tea?"

"There's going to be trouble," I said.

"Already?" The woman smoothed the skirt in her lap and set a plate of nut bread into it. "Well, it comes sooner or later, this time sooner. What do you think of it, boy?"

"I think I got into a lot of trouble for not much being bad," I said. "I don't know why."

"Sit down, then," the old man said. "Listen to a tale, then tell us what's going on."

I sat down, not too keen about hearing another story but out of politeness. I took a piece of nut bread and nibbled on it as the woman sipped her tea and cleared her throat. "Once there was a city on the shore of a broad blue sea. In the city lived five hundred children and nobody else, because the wind from the sea wouldn't let anyone grow old. Well, children don't have kids of their own, of course, so when the wind came up in the first year the city never grew any larger."

"Where'd all the grown-ups go?" I asked. The old man held his fingers to his lips and shook his head.

"The children tried to play all day, but it wasn't enough. They became frightened at night and had bad dreams. There was nobody to comfort them because only grown-ups are really good at making nightmares go away. Now, sometimes nightmares are white horses that come out of the sea, so they set up guards along the beaches and fought them back with wands made of blackthorn. But there was another kind of nightmare, one that was black and rose out of the ground, and those were impossible to guard against. So the children got together one day and decided to tell all the scary stories there were to tell, to prepare themselves for all the nightmares. They found it was pretty easy to think up scary stories, and every one of them had a story or two to tell. They stayed up all night spinning yarns about ghosts and dead things, and live things that shouldn't have been, and things that were neither. They talked about death and about monsters that suck blood, about things that live way deep in the earth and long, thin things that sneak through cracks in doors to lean over the beds at night and speak in tongues no one could understand. They talked about eyes without heads, and vice versa, and little blue shoes that walk across a cold empty white room, with no one in them, and a bunk bed that creaks when it's empty, and a printing press that produces newspapers from a city that never was. Pretty soon, by morning, they'd told all the scary stories. When the black horses came out of the ground the next night, and the white horses from the sea, the children greeted them with cakes and ginger ale, and they held a big party. They also invited the pale sheet-things from the clouds, and everyone ate hearty and had a good time. One white horse let a little boy ride on it and took him wherever he wanted to go. So there were no more bad dreams in the city of children by the sea."

I finished the piece of bread and wiped my hands on my crossed legs. "So that's why you tried to scare me," I said.

She shook her head. "No. I never have a reason for telling a story, and neither should you."

"I don't think I'm going to tell stories anymore," I said. "The folks get too upset."

"Philistines," the old man said, looking off across the fields.

"Listen, young man. There is nothing finer in the world than the telling of tales. Split atoms if you wish, but splitting an infinitive—and getting away with it—is far nobler. Lance boils if you wish, but pricking prétensions is often cleaner and always more fun."

"Then why are Mom and Dad so mad?"

The old man shook his head. "An eternal mystery."

"Well, I'm not so sure," I said. "I scared my little brother pretty bad, and that's not nice."

"Being scared is nothing," the old woman said. "Being bored, or ignorant—now that's a crime."

"I still don't know. My folks say you have to be a hundred years old. You did something to my uncle they didn't like, and that was a long time ago. What kind of people are you, anyway?"

The old man smiled. "Old, yes. But not a hundred."

"I just came out here to warn you. Mom and Dad are bringing out my great aunt, and she's no fun for anyone. You better go away." With that said, I ran back to my bike and rode off, pumping for all I was worth. I was between a rock and a hard place. I loved my folks but I itched to hear more stories. Why wasn't it easier to make decisions?

That night I slept restlessly. I didn't have any dreams, but I kept waking up with something pounding at the back of my head, like it wanted to be let in. I scrunched my face up and pressed it back.

At Sunday breakfast, Mom looked across the table at me and put on a kind face. "We're going to pick up Auntie Danser this afternoon, at the airport," she said.

My face went like warm butter.

"You'll come with us, won't you?" she asked. "You always did like the airport."

"All the way from where she lives?" I asked.

"From Omaha," Dad said.

I didn't want to go, but it was more a command than a request. I nodded, and Dad smiled at me around his pipe.

"Don't eat too many biscuits," Mom warned him. "You're putting on weight again."

"I'll wear it off come harvest. You cook as if the whole crew was here, anyway."

"Auntie Danser will straighten it all out," Mom said, her mind elsewhere. I caught the suggestion of a grimace on Dad's face, and the pipe wriggled as he bit down on it harder.

THE AIRPORT WAS SOMETHING OUT OF A TV SPACE MOVIE. IT WENT ON FORever, with stairways going up to restaurants and big smoky windows that looked out on the screaming jets, and crowds of people, all leaving, except for one pear-shaped figure in a cotton print dress with fat ankles and glasses thick as headlamps. I knew her from a hundred yards.

When we met, she shook hands with Mom, hugged Dad as if she didn't want to, then bent down and gave me a smile. Her teeth were yellow and even, sound as a horse's. She was the ugliest woman I'd ever seen. She smelled of lilacs. To this day lilacs take my appetite away.

She carried a bag. Part of it was filled with knitting, part with books and pamphlets. I always wondered why she never carried a Bible just Billy Grahams and Zondervans. One pamphlet fell out, and Dad bent to pick it up.

"Keep it, read it," Auntie Danser instructed him. "Do you good." She turned to Mom and scrutinized her from the bottom of a swimming pool. "You're looking good. He must be treating you right."

Dad ushered us out the automatic doors into the dry heat. Her one suitcase was light as a mummy and probably just as empty. I carried it, and it didn't even bring sweat to my brow. Her life was not in clothes and toiletry but in the plastic knitting bag.

We drove back to the farm in the big white station wagon. I leaned my head against the cool glass of the rear seat window and considered puking. Auntie Danser, I told myself, was like a mental dose of castor oil. Or like a visit to the dentist. Even if nothing was going to happen her smell presaged disaster, and like a horse sniffing a storm, my entrails worried.

Mom looked across the seat at me—Auntie Danser was riding up front with Dad—and asked, "You feeling okay? Did they give you anything to eat? Anything funny?"

I said they'd given me a piece of nut bread. Mom went, "Oh, Lord."

"Margie, they don't work like that. They got other ways." Auntie Danser leaned over the backseat and goggled at me. "Boy's just worried. I know all about it. These people and I have had it out before."

Through those murky glasses, her flat eyes knew me to my young pithy core. I didn't like being known so well. I could see that Auntie Danser's life was firm and predictable, and I made a sudden commitment I liked the man and woman. They caused trouble, but they were the exact opposite of my great aunt. I felt better, and I gave her a reassuring grin. "Boy will be okay," she said. "Just a colic of the upset mind."

Michael and Barbara sat on the front porch as the car drove up. Somehow a visit by Auntie Danser didn't bother them as much as it did me. They didn't fawn over her, but they accepted her without complaining—even out of adult earshot. That made me think more carefully about them. I decided I didn't love them any the less, but I couldn't trust them, either. The world was taking sides, and so far on my side I was very lonely. I didn't count the two old people on my side, because I wasn't sure they were—but they came a lot closer than anybody in my family.

Auntie Danser wanted to read Billy Graham books to us after dinner, but Dad snuck us out before Mom could gather us together—all but Barbara, who stayed to listen. We watched the sunset from the loft of the old wood barn, then tried to catch the little birds that lived in the rafters. By dark and bedtime I was hungry, but not for food. I asked Dad if he'd tell me a story before bed.

"You know your mom doesn't approve of all that fairy-tale stuff," he said.

"Then no fairy tales. Just a story."

"I'm out of practice, son," he confided. He looked very sad. "Your mom says we should concentrate on things that are real and not waste our time with make-believe. Life's hard. I may have to sell the farm, you know, and work for that feed-mixer in Mitchell."

I went to bed and felt like crying. A whole lot of my family had died that night, I didn't know exactly how, or why. But I was mad.

I DIDN'T GO TO SCHOOL THE NEXT DAY. DURING THE NIGHT I'D HAD A DREAM, which came so true and whole to me that I had to rush to the stand of cottonwoods and tell the old people. I took my lunch box and walked rapidly down the road.

They weren't there. On a piece of wire bradded to the biggest tree they'd left a note on faded brown paper. It was in a strong feminine hand, sepia-inked, delicately scribed with what could have been a goose-quill pen. It said: "We're at the old Hauskopf farm. Come if you must."

Not, "Come if you can." I felt a twinge. The Hauskopf farm, abandoned fifteen years ago and never sold, was three miles farther down the road and left on a deep-rutted fork. It took me an hour to get there.

The house still looked deserted. All the white paint was flaking, leaving dead gray wood. The windows stared. I walked up the porch steps and knocked on the heavy oak door. For a moment I thought no one was going to answer. Then I heard what sounded like a gust of wind, but inside the house, and the old woman opened the door. "Hello, boy," she said. "Come for more stories?"

She invited me in. Wildflowers were growing along the baseboards, and tiny roses peered from the brambles that covered the walls. A quail led her train of inch-and-a-half fluffball chicks from under the stairs, into the living room. The floor was carpeted, but the flowers in the weave seemed more than patterns. I could stare down and keep picking out detail for minutes. "This way, boy," the woman said. She took my hand. Hers was smooth and warm, but I had the impression it was also hard as wood.

A tree stood in the living room, growing out of the floor and sending its branches up to support the ceiling. Rabbits and quail and a lazy-looking brindle cat stared at me from tangles of roots. A wooden bench surrounded the base of the tree. On the side away from us, I heard someone breathing. The old man poked his head around and smiled at me, lifting his long pipe in greeting. "Hello, boy," he said.

"The boy looks like he's ready to tell us a story, this time," the woman said.

"Of course, Meg. Have a seat, boy. Cup of cider for you? Tea? Herb biscuit?"

"Cider, please," I said.

The old man stood and went down the hall to the kitchen. He came back with a wooden tray and three steaming cups of mulled cider. The cinnamon tickled my nose as I sipped.

"Now. What's your story?"

"It's about two hawks," I said, and then hesitated.

"Go on."

"Brother hawks. Never did like each other. Fought for a strip of land where they could hunt."

"Yes?"

"Finally, one hawk met an old crippled bobcat that had set up a place for itself in a rockpile. The bobcat was learning itself magic so it wouldn't have to go out and catch dinner, which was awful hard for it now. The hawk landed near the bobcat and told it about his brother, and how cruel he was. So the bobcat said, 'Why not give him the land for the day? Here's what you can do.' The bobcat told him how he could turn into a rabbit, but a very strong rabbit no hawk could hurt."

"Wily bobcat," the old man said, smiling.

" 'You mean, my brother wouldn't be able to catch me?' the hawk asked. 'Course not,' the bobcat said. 'And you can teach him a lesson. You'll tussle with him, scare him real bad—show him what tough animals there are on the land he wants. Then he'll go away and hunt somewheres else.' The hawk thought that sounded like a fine idea. So he let the bobcat turn him into a rabbit, and he hopped back to the land and waited in a patch of grass. Sure enough, his brother's shadow passed by soon, and then he heard a swoop and saw the claws held out. So he filled himself with being mad and jumped up and practically bit all the tail feathers off his brother. The hawk just flapped up and rolled over on the ground, blinking and gawking with his beak wide. 'Rabbit,' he said, 'that's not natural. Rabbits don't act that way.'

" 'Round here they do,' the hawk-rabbit said. 'This is a tough old land, and all the animals here know the tricks of escaping from bad birds like you.' This scared the brother hawk, and he flew away as best he could and never came back again. The hawk-rabbit hopped to the rockpile and stood up before the bobcat, saying, 'It worked real fine. I thank you. Now turn me back, and I'll go hunt my land.' But the bobcat only grinned and reached out with a paw and broke the rabbit's neck. Then he ate him, and said, 'Now the land's mine and no hawks can take away the easy game.' And that's how the greed of two hawks turned their land over to a bobcat."

The old woman looked at me with wide baked-chestnut eyes and smiled. "You've got it," she said. "Just like your uncle. Hasn't he got it Jack?" The old man nodded and took his pipe from his mouth. "He's got it fine. He'll make a good one."

"Now, boy, why did you make up that story?"

I thought for a moment, then shook my head. "I don't know," I said. "It just came up."

"What are you going to do with the story?"

I didn't have an answer for that question, either.

"Got any other stories in you?"

I considered, then said, "Think so."

A car drove up outside, and Mom called my name. The old woman stood and straightened her dress. "Follow me," she said. "Go out the back door, walk around the house. Return home with them. Tomorrow, go to school like you're supposed to do. Next Saturday, come back, and we'll talk some more."

"Son? You in there?"

I walked out the back and came around to the front of the house. Mom and Auntie Danser waited in the station wagon. "You aren't allowed out here. Were you in that house?" Mom asked. I shook my head.

My great-aunt looked at me with her glassed-in flat eyes and lifted the corners of her lips a little. "Margie," she said, "go have a look in the windows."

Mom got out of the car and walked up the porch to peer through the dusty panes. "It's empty, Sybil."

"Empty, boy, right?"

"I don't know," I said. "I wasn't inside."

"I could hear you, boy," she said. "Last night. Talking in your sleep.

Rabbits and hawks don't behave that way. You know it, and I know it. So it ain't no good thinking about them that way, is it?"

"I don't remember talking in my sleep," I said.

"Margie, let's go home. This boy needs some pamphlets read into him."

Mom got into the car and looked back at me before starting the engine. "You ever skip school again, I'll strap you black and blue. It's real embarrassing having the school call, and not knowing where you are. Hear me?"

I nodded.

Everything was quiet that week. I went to school and tried not to dream at night and did everything boys are supposed to do. But I didn't feel like a boy. I felt something big inside, and no amount of Billy Grahams and Zondervans read at me could change that feeling.

I made one mistake, though. I asked Auntie Danser why she never read the Bible. This was in the parlor one evening after dinner and cleaning up the dishes. "Why do you want to know, boy?" she asked.

"Well, the Bible seems to be full of fine stories, but you don't carry it around with you. I just wondered why."

"Bible is a good book," she said. "The only good book. But it's difficult. It has lots of camouflage. Sometimes—" she stopped. "Who put you up to asking that question?"

"Nobody," I said.

"I heard that question before, you know," she said. "Ain't the first time I been asked. Somebody else asked me, once."

I sat in my chair, stiff as a ham.

"Your father's brother asked me that once. But we won't talk about him, will we?"

I shook my head.

Next Saturday I waited until it was dark and everyone was in bed. The night air was warm, but I was sweating more than the warm could cause as I rode my bike down the dirt road, lamp beam swinging back and forth. The sky was crawling with stars, all of them looking at me. The Milky Way seemed to touch down just beyond the road, like I might ride straight up it if I went far enough.

I knocked on the heavy door. There were no lights in the windows and it was late for old folks to be up, but I knew these two didn't behave like normal people. And I knew that just because the house looked empty from the outside didn't mean it was empty within. The wind rose up and beat against the door, making me shiver. Then it opened. It was dark for a moment, and the breath went out of me. Two pairs of eyes stared from the black. They seemed a lot taller this time. "Come in, boy," Jack whispered.

Fireflies lit up the tree in the living room. The brambles and wild-flowers glowed like weeds on a sea floor. The carpet crawled, but not to my feet. I was shivering in earnest now, and my teeth chattered.

I only saw their shadows as they sat on the bench in front of me. "Sit," Meg said. "Listen close. You've taken the fire, and it glows bright. You're only a boy, but you're just like a pregnant woman now. For the rest of your life you'll be cursed with the worst affliction known to humans. Your skin will twitch at night. Your eyes will see things in the dark. Beasts will come to you and beg to be ridden. You'll never know one truth from another. You might starve, because few will want to encourage you. And if you do make good in this world, you might lose the gift and search forever after, in vain. Some will say the gift isn't special. Beware them. Some will say it is special, and beware them, too. And some—"

There was a scratching at the door. I thought it was an animal for a moment. Then it cleared its throat. It was my great-aunt.

"Some will say you're damned. Perhaps they're right. But you're also enthused. Carry it lightly and responsibly."

"Listen in there. This is Sybil Danser. You know me. Open up."

"Now stand by the stairs, in the dark where she can't see," Jack said. I did as I was told. One of them—I couldn't tell which—opened the door, and the lights went out in the tree, the carpet stilled, and the brambles were snuffed. Auntie Danser stood in the doorway, outlined by star glow, carrying her knitting bag. "Boy?" she asked. I held my breath.

"And you others, too."

The wind in the house seemed to answer. "I'm not too late," she said. "Damn you, in truth, damn you to Hell! You come to our towns, and you plague us with thoughts no decent person wants to think. Not just fairy stories, but telling the way people live and why they shouldn't live that way! Your very breath is tainted! Hear me?" She walked slowly into the empty living room, feet clonking on the wooden floor. "You make them write about us and make others laugh at us. Question the way we think. Condemn our deepest prides. Pull out our mistakes and amplify them beyond all truth. What right do you have to take young children and twist their minds?"

The wind sang through the cracks in the walls. I tried to see if Jack or Meg was there, but only shadows remained.

"I know where you come from, don't forget that! Out of the ground! Out of the bones of old wicked Indians! Shamans and pagan dances and worshiping dirt and filth! I heard about you from the old squaws on the reservation. Frost and Spring, they called you, signs of the turning year. Well, now you got a different name! Death and demons, I call you, hear me?"

She seemed to jump at a sound, but I couldn't hear it. "Don't you argue with me!" she shrieked. She took her glasses off and held out both hands. "Think I'm a weak old woman, do you? You don't know how deep I run in these communities! I'm the one who had them books taken off the shelves. Remember me? Oh, you hated it—not being able to fill young minds with your pestilence. Took them off high school shelves and out of lists—burned them for junk! Remember? That was me. I'm not dead yet! Boy, where are you?"

"Enchant her," I whispered to the air. "Magic her. Make her go away. Let me live here with you."

"Is that you, boy? Come with your aunt, now. Come with, come away!"

"Go with her," the wind told me. "Send your children this way, years from now. But go with her."

I felt a kind of tingly warmth and knew it was time to get home. I snuck out the back way and came around to the front of the house. There was no car. She'd followed me on foot all the way from the farm. I wanted to leave her there in the old house, shouting at the dead rafters, but instead I called her name and waited.

She came out crying. She knew.

"You poor sinning boy," she said, pulling me to her lilac bosom.

Introduction to "Dead Run"

My irritation at television evangelists is boundless. Nothing unusual in that. Religious visions of damnation seem to be particularly horrible in a Christianity that claims to worship a loving God. These upwellings of tribal animosity and primordial hatred should have been abandoned thousands of years ago, but they strongly influence us to this day.

Well, all right, so what else is new? Humans are imperfect.

But if we're made in God's image, then perhaps God is imperfect, as well. Maybe God gets tired. Maybe he isn't dead, but has simply retired from the scene, exhausted or punch-drunk from our sins.

I've written two stories on this theme. The other is "Petra."

"Dead Run" was submitted to Twilight Zone Magazine and rejected. The editor explained that this simply was not a Twilight Zone story. So I shipped it off to Omni and Ellen Datlow bought it.

A few years later, my friend Alan Brennert was working on the reincarnation of the Twilight Zone TV show, airing on CBS. Michael Toman, a mutual friend and well-read individual of considerable if quiet influence, handed Alan "Dead Run," which he had somehow missed. Alan loved it and thought it was perfect for the show. He wrote the screenplay—a brilliant job, I must say—and it went into production in 1986. Astrid and I drove to Indian Hills, outside Los Angeles, to watch the show being filmed, under the direction of the late Paul Tucker.

Dozens of extras were funneled through the gates of Hell that day. (One of them had taken the trouble to dress up like Michael Jackson in Thriller. The camera, needless to say, did not linger on him.)

A few days later, I returned to watch the filming on a soundstage in Los Angeles, where a high-rise, tenement Hell set had been constructed at a cost of about $50,000. To a novice it was all marvelous. To my delight, I was even able to contribute a line at Paul's request.

An actor on the set approached me during a break and asked for a loan. I explained that I wasn't anybody important or rich—just the original writer. He understood immediately; my status was below that of the extras. But I was treated nicely and had a grand time.

Standards and Practices, the "censorship" office at the network, passed the screenplay with the single wry comment that this could be a good way to get back at Jerry Falwell. I doubt that Falwell noticed.

The show aired to a *huge* response: two letters, one for, one against. Evangelical Christians simply don't watch shows like Twilight Zone. By and large, they stay away from fantasy and science fiction altogether.

This is my only filmed story to date.
My experience with magazine rejections has never been so ironic.

DEAD RUN
Omni, Ellen Datlow, 1985

There aren't many hitchhikers on the road to Hell.

I noticed this dude four miles away. He stood where the road is straight and level, crossing what looks like desert except it has empty towns and motels and shacks. I had been on the road for six hours and the folks in the cattle trailers behind me had been quiet for some time—resigned, I guess—so my nerves had settled a bit and I decided to see what the dude was up to. Maybe he was one of the employees. That would be interesting, I thought. Truth to tell, once the wailing settles down, I get bored.

The dude stood on the right side of the road, thumb out. I piano-keyed down the gears and the air brakes hissed and squealed at the tap of my foot. The semi slowed and the big diesel made that gut-deep dinosaur-belch of shuddered-downness. I leaned across the cab as everything came to a halt and swung the door open.

"Where you heading?" I asked.

He laughed and shook his head, then spit on the soft shoulder. "I don't know," he said. "Hell, maybe." He was thin and tanned with long greasy black hair and blue-jeans and a vest. His straw hat was dirty and full of holes, but the feathers around the crown were bright and new, pheasant if I was any judge. A worn gold fob hung out of his vest. He wore old Frye boots with the toes turned up and soles thinner than my retreads. He looked a lot like me when I had hitchhiked out of Fresno, broke and unemployed, looking for work.

"Can I take you there?" I asked.

"Sure. Why not?" He climbed in and slammed the door shut, took out a kerchief and mopped his forehead, then blew his long nose and stared at me with bloodshot eyes. "What you hauling?" he asked.

"Souls," I said. "Whole shitload of them."

"What kind?" He was young, not more than twenty-five. He tried to sound easy and natural but I could hear the nerves.

"Human kind," I said. "Got some Hare Krishnas this time. Don't look that close anymore."

I coaxed the truck along, wondering if the engine was as bad as it sounded. When we were up to speed—eighty, eighty-five, no smokies on *this* road—he asked, "How long you been hauling?"

"Two years."

"Good pay?"

"I get by."

"Good benefits?"

"Union, like everyone else."

"That's what they told me in that little dump about two miles back. Perks and benefits."

"People live there?" I asked. I didn't think anything lived along the road. Anything human.

He bobbled his head. "Real down folks. They say Teamster bosses get carried in limousines, when their time comes."

"Don't really matter how you get there or how long it takes. Forever is a slow bitch to pull."

"Getting there's all the fun?" he asked, trying for a grin. I gave him a shallow one.

"What're you doing out here?" I asked a few minutes later. "You aren't dead, are you?" I'd never heard of dead folks running loose or looking quite as vital as he did but I couldn't imagine anyone else being on the road. Dead folks—and drivers.

"No," he said. He was quiet for a bit. Then, slowly, as if it embarrassed him, he said, "I'm here to find my woman."

"No shit?" Not much surprised me but this was a new twist. "There ain't no going back, for the dead, you know."

"Sherill's her name, spelled like sheriff but with two L's."

"Got a cigarette?" I asked. I didn't smoke but I could use them later. He handed me the last three in a crush-proof pack, not just one but all. He bobbled his head some more, peering through the clean windshield.

No bugs on this road. No flat rabbits, on the road, snakes, nothing.

"Haven't heard of her," I said. "But then, I don't get to converse with everyone I haul. There are lots of trucks, lots of drivers."

"I heard about benefits," he said. "Perks and benefits. Back in that town." He had a crazy sad look.

I tightened my jaw and stared straight ahead.

"You know," he said, "They talk in that town. They tell about how they use old trains for Chinese, and in Russia there's a tramline. In Mexico it's old buses, always at night—"

"Listen. I don't use all the benefits," I said. "Some do but I don't."

"I got you," he said, nodding that exaggerated goddamn young bobble, his whole neck and shoulders moving, it's all right everything's cool.

"How you gonna find her?" I asked.

"I don't know. Hitch the road, ask the drivers."

"How'd you get in?"

He didn't answer for a moment. "I'm coming here when I die. That's pretty sure. It's not so hard for folks like me to get in beforehand. And . . . my daddy was a driver. He told me the route. By the way, my name's Bill."

"Mine's John," I said.

"Pleased to meet you."

We didn't say much for a while. He stared out the right window and I watched the desert and faraway shacks go by. Soon the mountains loomed up—space seems compressed on the road, especially out of the desert—and I sped up for the approach.

They made some noise in the back. Lost, creepy sounds, like tired old sirens in a factory.

"What'll you do when you get off work?" Bill asked.

"Go home and sleep."

"That's the way it was with Daddy, until just before the end. Look, I didn't mean to make you mad. I'd just heard about the perks and I thought . . ." He swallowed, his Adam's apple bobbing. "You might be able to help. I don't know how I'll ever find Sherill. Maybe back in the annex . . ."

"Nobody in their right minds goes into the yards by choice," I said. "You'd have to look at everybody that's died in the last four months. They're way backed up."

Bill took that like a blow across the face and I was sorry I'd said it. "She's only been gone a week," he said.

"Well," I said.

"My mom died two years ago, just before Daddy."

"The High Road," I said.

"What?"

"Hope they both got the High Road."

"Mom, maybe. Yeah. She did. But not Daddy. He knew." Bill hawked and spit out the window. "Sherill, she's here—but she don't belong."

I couldn't help but smirk.

"No, man, I mean it, I belong but not her. She was in this car wreck couple of months back. Got messed up. I sold her crystal and heroin at first and then fell in love with her and by the time she landed in the hospital, from the wreck—she was the only one who lived, man, shouldn't that tell you something?—but she was, you know, hooked on about four different things."

My arms stiffened on the wheel.

"I tried to tell her when I visited, no more dope, it wouldn't be good, but she begged. What could I do? I loved her." He looked down at his worn boots and bobbled sadly. "She begged me, man. I brought her stuff. She took it all when they weren't looking. I mean, she just took it *all*.

They pumped her but her insides were mush. I didn't hear about her dying until two days ago. That really burned, man. I was the only one who loved her and they didn't even like *inform* me. I had to go up to her room and find the empty bed. *Jesus.* I hung out at Daddy's union hall. Someone talked to someone else and I found the name on a list. *Sherill.* They'd put her down the Low Road."

I hadn't known it was that easy to find out; but then, I'd never traveled with junkies. Dope can loosen a lot of lips.

"I don't do those perks," I said. "Folks in back got enough trouble. I think the union went too far there."

"Bet they thought you'd get lonely, need company," Bill said quietly, looking at me. "It don't hurt the women back there, does it? Maybe give them another chance to, you know, think things over. Give 'em relief for a couple of hours, a break from the mash—"

"A couple of hours don't mean nothing in relation to eternity," I said, too loud. "I'm not so sure I won't be joining them someday, and if that's the way it is I want it smooth, nobody pulling me out of a trailer and, and putting me back in."

"Yeah," he said. "Got you. I know where you're at. But she might be back there right now, and all you'd have to—"

"Bad enough I'm driving this fucking rig in the first place." I wanted to change the subject.

Bill stopped bobbling and squinted. "How'd that happen?"

"Couple of accidents. I hot-rodded with an old fart in a Triumph. Nearly ran down some joggers. My premiums went up to where I couldn't afford payments and finally they took my truck away."

"You coulda gone without insurance."

"Not me," I said. "Anyway, word got out. No companies would hire me. I went to the union to see if they could help. They told me I was a dead-ender, either get out of trucking or . . ." I shrugged. "This. I couldn't leave trucking. It's bad out there, getting work. Couldn't see myself driving a hack in some big city."

"No way, man," Bill said, giving me his whole-body rumba again. He cackled sympathetically.

"They gave me an advance, enough for a down payment on my rig." The truck was grinding a bit but maintaining. Over the mountains, through a really impressive pass like from an old engraving, and down in a rugged rocky valley, the City waited. I'd deliver my cargo, grab my slip, and run the rig (with Bill) back to Baker. Let him out someplace in the real. Park the truck in the yard next to my cottage. Go in, flop down, suck back a few beers, and get some sleep.

Start all over again Monday, two loads a week.

Hell, I never even got into Pahrump any more. I used to be a regular, but after driving the Low Road, the women at the Lizard Ranch all looked like prisoners, too dumb to notice their iron bars. I saw too much of hell in the those air-conditioned trailers.

"I don't think I'd better go on," Bill said. "I'll hitch with some other rig, ask around."

"I'd feel better if you rode with me back out of here. Want my advice?" Bad habit, giving advice.

"No," Bill said. "Thanks anyway. I can't go home. Sherill don't belong here." He took a deep breath. "I'll try to work up a trade with some bosses. I stay, in exchange, and she gets the High Road. That's the way the game works down here, isn't it?"

I didn't say otherwise. I couldn't be sure he wasn't right. He'd made it this far. At the top of the pass I pulled the rig over and let him out. He waved, I waved, and we went our different ways.

Poor rotten doping sonofabitch, I thought. I'd screwed up my life half a dozen different ways—three wives, liquor, three years at Tehachapi—but I'd never done dope. I felt self-righteous just listening to the dude. I was glad to be rid of him, truth be told.

As I GEARED THE TRUCK DOWN FOR THE DECLINE, THE NOISE IN THE TRAILERS got irritating again. They could smell what was coming, I guess, like pigs stepping up to the man with the knife.

The City looks a lot like a dry country full of big white cathedrals. Casting against type. High wall around the perimeter, stretching right and left as far as my eye can see, like a pair of endless highways turned on their sides.

No compass. No magnetic fields. No sense of direction but down.

No horizon.

I pulled into the disembarkation terminal and backed the first trailer up to the holding pen. Employees let down the gates and used their big, ugly prods to offload my herd. These people do not respond to bodily pain. The prod gets them where we all hurt when we're dead.

After the first trailer was empty, employees unhooked it, pulled it away by hand or claw, strong as horses, and I backed in the second.

I got down out of the cab and an employee came up to me, a big fellow with red eyes and brand new coveralls. "Poke any good ones?" he asked. His breath was like the bad end of a bean and garlic dinner. I shook my head, took out the crush-proof box, and held my cigarette up for a light. He pressed his fingernail against the tip. The tip flared and settled down to a steady glow. He regarded it with pure lust. There's no in-between for employees. Lust or nothing.

"Listen," I said.

"I'm all ears," he said, and suddenly, he was. I jumped back and he laughed joylessly. "You're new," he said, and eyed my cigarette again.

"You had anyone named Sherill through here?"

"Who's asking?" he grumbled. He started a slow dance. He had to move around, otherwise his shoes melted the asphalt and got stuck. He lifted one foot, then the other, twisting a little.

"Just curious. I heard you guys know all the names."

"So?" He stopped his dance. His shoes made the tar stink.

"So," I said, with just as much sense, and held out the cigarette.

"Like Cherry with an L?"

"No. Sherill, like sheriff but with two L's."

"Couple of Cheryls. No Sherills," he said. "Sorry."

I handed him the cigarette, then pulled another out of the pack. He snapped it away between two thick, horny nails.

"Thanks," I said.

He popped both of them into his mouth and chewed, bliss rushing over his wrinkled face. Smoke shot out of his nose and he swallowed.

"Think nothing of it," he said, and walked on.

THE ROAD BACK IS SHORTER THAN THE ROAD IN. DON'T ASK HOW. I'D HAVE thought it was the other way around but barriers are what's important not distance. Maybe we all get our chances so the road to Hell is long. But once we're there, there's no returning. You have to save on the budget somewhere.

I took the empties back to Baker. Didn't see Bill. Eight hours later I was in bed, beer in hand, paycheck on the bureau, my eyes wide open.

Shit, I thought. Now my conscience was working. I could have sworn I was past that. But then I didn't use the perks. I wouldn't drive without insurance.

I wasn't really cut out for the life.

THERE ARE NO NORMAL DAYS AND NIGHTS ON THE ROAD TO HELL. NO MATTER how long you drive, it's always the same time when you arrive as when you left, but it's not necessarily the same time from trip to trip.

The next trip it was cool dusk and the road didn't pass through desert and small, empty towns. Instead, it crossed a bleak flatland of skeletal trees, all the same uniform gray as if cut from paper. When I pulled over to catch a nap—never sleeping more than two hours at a stretch— the shouts of the damned in the trailers bothered me even more than usual. Silly things they said, like:

"You can take us back, mister! You really can!"

"Can he?"

"Shit no, mofuck pig."

"You can let us out! We can't hurt you!"

That was true enough. Drivers were alive and the dead could never hurt the living. But I'd heard what happened when you let them out. There were about ninety of them in back and in any load there was always one would make you want to use your perks.

I scratched my itches in the narrow bunk, looking at the Sierra Club calendar hanging just below the fan. The Devil's Postpile. The load became quieter as the voices gave up, one after the other. There was one last shout—some obscenity—then silence.

It was then I decided I'd let them out and see if Sherill was there, or if anyone knew her. They mingled in the annex, got their last socializing before the City. Someone might know. Then if I saw Bill again—

What? What could I do to help him? He had screwed Sherill up royally, but then she'd had a hand in it too, and that was what Hell was all about. Poor stupid sons of bitches.

I swung out of the cab, tucking in my shirt and pulling my straw hat down on my crown. "Hey!" I said, walking alongside the trailers. Faces peered at me from the two inches between each white slat. "I'm going to let you out. Just for a while. I need some information."

"Ask!" someone screamed. "Just ask, goddammit!"

"You know you can't run away. You can't hurt me. You're all dead. Understand?"

"We know," said another voice, quieter.

"Maybe we can help."

"I'm going to open the gates one trailer at a time." I went to the rear trailer first, took out my keys and undid the Yale padlock. Then I swung the gates open, standing back a little like there was some kind of infected wound about to drain.

They were all naked but they weren't dirty. I'd seen them in the annex yards and at the City; I knew they weren't like concentration camp prisoners. The dead can't really be unhealthy. Each just had some sort of air about him telling why he was in Hell; nothing specific but subliminal.

Like three black dudes in the rear trailer, first to step out. Why they were going to Hell was all over their faces. They weren't in the least sorry for the lives they'd led. They wanted to keep on doing what had brought them here in the first place—scavenging, hurting, hurting me in particular.

"Stupid ass mofuck," one of them said, staring at me beneath thin, expressive eyebrows. He nodded and swung his fists, trying to pound the slats from the outside, but the blows hardly made them vibrate.

An old woman crawled down, hair white and neatly coiffed. I couldn't be certain what she had done but she made me uneasy. She might have been the worst in the load. And lots of others, young, old, mostly old. Quiet for the most part.

They looked me over, some defiant, most just bewildered.

"I need to know if there's anyone here named Sherill," I said, "who happens to know a fellow named Bill."

"That's my name," said a woman hidden in the crowd.

"Let me see her." I waved my hand at them. The black dudes came forward. A funny look got in their eyes and they backed away. The others parted and a young woman walked out. "How do you spell your name?" I asked.

She got a panicked expression. She spelled it, hesitating, hoping she'd make the grade. I felt horrible already. She was a Cheryl.

"Not who I'm looking for," I said.

"Don't be hasty," she said, real soft. She wasn't trying hard to be seductive but she was succeeding. She was a very pretty Asian with medium-sized breasts, hips like a teenager's, legs not terrific but nice. Her black hair was clipped short.

I tried to ignore her. "You can walk around a bit," I told them. "I'm letting out the first trailer now." I opened the side gates on that one and the people came down. They didn't smell, didn't look hungry, they just all looked pale. I wondered if the torment had begun already, but if so, I decided, it wasn't the physical kind.

One thing I'd learned in my two years was that all the Sunday school and horror movie crap about Hell was dead wrong.

"Woman named Sherill," I repeated. No one stepped forward. Then I felt someone close to me and I turned. It was the Cheryl woman. She smiled. "I'd like to sit up front for a while," she said.

"So would we all, sister," said the white-haired old woman. The black dudes stood off separate, talking low.

I swallowed, looking at her. Other drivers said they were real insubstantial except at one activity. That was the perk. And it was said the hottest ones always ended up in Hell.

"No," I said. I motioned for them to get back into the trailers. Whatever she was on the Low Road for, it wouldn't affect her performance in the sack, that was obvious.

It had been a dumb idea all around. They went back and I returned to the cab, lighting up a cigarette and thinking what had made me do it.

I shook my head and started her up. Thinking on a dead run was no good. "No," I said, "goddamn," I said, "good."

Cheryl's face stayed with me.

Cheryl's body stayed with me longer than the face.

Something always comes up in life to lure a man onto the Low Road, not driving but riding in the back. We all have some weakness. I wondered what reason God had to give us each that little flaw, like a chip in crystal, you press the chip hard enough everything splits up crazy.

At least now I knew one thing. My flaw wasn't sex, not this way. What most struck me about Cheryl was wonder. She was so pretty; how'd she end up on the Low Road?

For that matter, what had Bill's Sherill done?

I RETURNED HAULING EMPTIES AND FOUND MYSELF THIS TIME OUTSIDE A small town called Shoshone. I pulled my truck into the cafe parking lot. The weather was cold and I left the engine running. It was about eleven in the morning and the cafe was half full. I took a seat at the counter next to an old man with maybe four teeth in his head, attacking French toast with downright solemn dignity. I ordered eggs and hashbrowns and juice, ate quickly, and went back to my truck.

Bill stood next to the cab. Next to him was an enormous young woman with a face like a bulldog. She was wrapped in a filthy piece of plaid fabric that might have been snatched from a trash dump somewhere. "Hey," Bill said. "Remember me?"

"Sure."

"I saw you pulling up. I thought you'd like to know. . . . This is Sherill. I got her out of there." The woman stared at me with all the expression of a brick. "It's all screwy. Like a power failure or something. We just walked out on the road and nobody stopped us."

Sherill could have hid any number of weirdnesses beneath her formidable looks and gone unnoticed by ordinary folks. But I didn't have any trouble picking out the biggest thing wrong with her: she was dead. Bill had brought her out of Hell. I looked around to make sure I was in the World. I was. He wasn't lying. Something serious had happened on the Low Road.

"Trouble?" I asked.

"Lots." He grinned at me. "Pan-demon-ium." His grin broadened.

"That can't happen," I said. Sherill trembled, hearing my voice.

"He's a *driver*, Bill," she said. "He's the one takes us there. We should git out of here." She had that soul-branded air and the look of a pig that's just escaped slaughter, seeing the butcher again. She took a few steps backward. Gluttony, I thought. Gluttony and buried lust and a real ugly way of seeing life, inner eye pulled all out of shape by her bulk.

Bill hadn't had much to do with her ending up on the Low Road.

"Tell me more," I said.

"There's folks running all over down there, holing up in them towns, devils chasing them—"

"Employees," I corrected.

"Yeah. Every which way."

Sherill tugged on his arm. "We got to go, Bill."

"We got to go," he echoed. "Hey, man, thanks. I found her!" He nodded his whole-body nod and they were off down the street, Sherill's plaid wrap dragging in the dirt.

I drove back to Baker, wondering if the trouble was responsible for my being rerouted through Shoshone. I parked in front of my little house and sat inside with a beer while it got dark, checking my calendar for the next day's run and feeling very cold. I can take so much supernatural in its place, but now things were spilling over, smudging the clean-drawn line between my work and the World. Next day I was scheduled to be at the annex and take another load.

Nobody called that evening. If there was trouble on the Low Road, surely the union would let me know, I thought.

I drove to the annex early in the morning. The crossover from the World to the Low Road was normal; I followed the route and the sky muddied from blue to solder-color and I was on the first leg to the annex. I backed the rear trailer up to the yard's gate and unhitched it, then placed the forward trailer at a ramp, all the while keeping my ears tuned to pick up interesting conversation.

The employees who work the annex look human. I took my invoice from a red-faced old guy with eyes like billiard balls and looked at him like I was in the know but could use some updating. He spit smoking saliva on the pavement, returned my look slantwise and said nothing. Maybe it all settled. I hitched up both full trailers and pulled out.

I didn't even mention Sherill and Bill. Like in most jobs keeping one's mouth shut is good policy. That and don't volunteer.

It was the desert again this time, only now the towns and tumble-down houses looked bomb-blasted, like something big had come through flushing out game with a howitzer.

Eyes on the road. Push that rig.

Four hours in, I came to a roadblock. Nobody on it, no employees, just big carved-lava barricades cutting across all lanes and beyond them a yellow smoke which, the driver's unwritten instructions advised, meant absolutely no entry.

I got out. The load was making noises. I suddenly hated them. Nothing beautiful there—just naked Hell-bounders shouting and screaming and threatening like it wasn't already over for them. They'd had their chance and crapped out and now they were still bullshitting the World.

Least they could do was go with dignity and spare me their misery.

That's probably what the engineers on the trains to Auschwitz thought. Yeah, yeah, except I was the fellow who might be hauling those engineers to their just deserts.

Crap, I just couldn't be one way or the other about the whole thing. I could feel mad and guilty and I could think Jesus, probably I'll be complaining just as much when my time comes. Jesus H. Twentieth Century Man Christ.

I stood by the truck, waiting for instructions or some indication what I was supposed to do. The load became quieter after a while but I heard noises off the road, screams mostly and far away.

"There isn't anything," I said to myself, lighting up one of Bill's cigarettes even though I don't smoke and dragging deep, "*anything* worth this shit." I vowed I would quit after this run.

I heard something come up behind the trailers and I edged closer to the cab steps. High wisps of smoke obscured things at first but a dark shape three or four yards high plunged through and stood with one hand on the top slats of the rear trailer. It was covered with naked people, crawling all over, biting and scratching and shouting obscenities. It made little grunting noises, fell to its knees, then stood again and lurched off the road. Some of the people hanging on saw me and shouted for me to come help.

"Help us get this sonofabitch down!"

"Hey, you! We've almost got 'im!"

"He's a driver—"

"Fuck 'im, then."

I'd never seen an employee so big before, nor in so much trouble. The load began to wail like banshees. I threw down my cigarette and ran after it.

Workers will tell you. Camaraderie extends even to those on the job you don't like. If they're in trouble it's part of the mystique to help out. Besides, the unwritten instructions were very clear on such things and I've never knowingly broken a job rule—not since getting my rig back—and couldn't see starting now.

Through the smoke and across great ridges of lava, I ran until I spotted the employee about ten yards ahead. It had shaken off the naked people and was standing with one in each hand. Its shoulders smoked and scales stood out at all angles. They'd really done a job on the bastard. Ten or twelve of the dead were picking themselves off the lava, unscraped, unbruised. They saw me.

The employee saw me.

Everyone came at me. I turned and ran for the truck, stumbling, falling, bruising and scraping myself everywhere. My hair stood on end. People grabbed me, pleading for me to haul them out, old, young, all fawning and screeching like whipped dogs.

Then the employee swung me up out of reach. Its hand was cold and hard like iron tongs kept in a freezer. It grunted and ran toward my truck, opening the door wide and throwing me roughly inside. It made clear with huge, wild gestures that I'd better turn around and go back, that waiting was no good and there was no way through.

I started the engine and turned the rig around. I rolled up my window and hoped the dead weren't substantial enough to scratch paint or tear up slats.

All rules were off now. What about the ones in my load? All the while I was doing these things my head was full of questions, like how could souls fight back and wasn't there some inflexible order in Hell that kept such things from happening? That was what had been implied when I hired on. Safest job around.

I headed back down the road. My load screamed like no load I'd ever had before. I was afraid they might get loose but they didn't. I got near the annex and they were quiet again, too quiet for me to hear over the diesel.

The yards were deserted. The long, white-painted cement platforms and whitewashed wood-slat loading ramps were unattended. No souls in the pens.

The sky was an indefinite gray. An out-of-focus yellow sun gleamed faintly off the stark white employee's lounge. I stopped the truck and swung down to investigate.

There was no wind, only silence. The air was frosty without being particularly cold. What I wanted to do most was unload and get out of there, go back to Baker or Barstow or Shoshone.

I hoped that was still possible. Maybe all exits had been closed. Maybe the overseers had closed them to keep any more souls from getting out.

I tried the gate latches and found I could open them. I did so and returned to the truck, swinging the rear trailer around until it was flush with the ramp. Nobody made a sound. "Go on back," I said. "Go on back. You've got more time here. Don't ask me how."

"Hello, John." That was behind me. I turned and saw an older man without any clothes on. I didn't recognize him at first. His eyes finally clued me in.

"Mr. Martin?" My high school history teacher. I hadn't seen him in maybe twenty years. He didn't look much older, but then I'd never seen him naked. He was dead, but he wasn't like the others. He didn't have that look that told me why he was here.

"This is not the sort of job I'd expect one of my students to take," Martin said. He laughed the smooth laugh he was famous for, the laugh that seemed to take everything he said in class and put it in perspective.

"You're not the first person I'd expect to find here," I responded.

"The cat's away, John. The mice are in charge now. I'm going to try to leave."

"How long you been here?" I asked.

"I died a month ago, I think," Martin said, never one to mince words.

"You can't leave," I said. Doing my job even with Mr. Martin. I felt the ice creep up my throat.

"Still the screwball team player" Martin said, "even when the team doesn't give a damn what you do."

I wanted to explain but he walked away toward the annex and the road out. Looking back over his shoulder, he said, "Get smart, John. Things aren't what they seem. Never have been."

"Look!" I shouted after him. "I'm going to quit, honest, but this load is my responsibility." I thought I saw him shake his head as he rounded the corner of the annex.

The dead in my load had pried loose some of the ramp slats and were jumping off the rear trailer. Those in the forward trailer were screaming and carrying on, shaking the whole rig.

Responsibility, shit, I thought. As the dead followed after Mr. Martin, I unhitched both trailers. Then I got in the cab and swung away from the annex, onto the incoming road. "I'm going to quit," I said. "Sure as anything, I'm going to quit."

The road out seemed awfully long. I didn't see any of the dead, surprisingly, but then maybe they'd been shunted away. I was taking a route I'd never been on before and I had no way of knowing if it would put me where I wanted to be. But I hung in there for two hours, running the truck dead-out on the flats.

The air was getting grayer like somebody turning down the contrast on a TV set. I switched on the high-beams but they didn't help. By now I was shaking in the cab and saying to myself, Nobody deserves this. Nobody deserves going to Hell no matter what they did. I was scared. It was getting colder.

Three hours and I saw the annex and yards ahead of me again. The road had looped back. I swore and slowed the rig to a crawl. The loading docks had been set on fire. Dead were wandering around with no idea what to do or where to go. I sped up and drove over the few that were on the road. They'd come up and the truck's bumper would hit them and I wouldn't feel a thing, like they weren't there. I'd see them in the rearview mirror, getting up after being knocked over. Just knocked over. Then I was away from the loading docks and there was no doubt about it this time.

I was heading straight for Hell.

The disembarkation terminal was on fire, too. But beyond it the City was bright and white and untouched. For the first time I drove past the terminal and took the road into the City.

It was either that or stay on the flats with everything screwy. Inside, I thought maybe they'd have things under control.

The truck roared through the gate between two white pillars maybe seventy or eighty feet thick and as tall as the Washington Monument. I didn't see anybody, employees or the dead. Once I was through the pillars—and it came as a shock—

There was no City, no walls, just the road winding along and countryside in all directions, even behind.

The countryside was covered with shacks, houses, little clusters and big clusters. Everything was tight-packed, people working together on one hill, people sitting on their porches, walking along paths, turning to stare at me as the rig barreled on through. No employees—no monsters. No flames. No bloody lakes or rivers.

This must be the outside part, I thought. Deeper inside it would get worse.

I kept on driving. The dog part of me was saying let's go look for authority and ask some questions and get out. But the monkey was saying let's just go look and find out what's going on, what Hell is all about.

Another hour of driving through that calm, crowded landscape and the truck ran out of fuel. I coasted to the side and stepped down from the cab, very nervous.

Again I lit up a cigarette and leaned against the fender, shaking a little. But the shaking was running down and a tight kind of calm was replacing it.

The landscape was still condensed, crowded, but nobody looked tortured. No screaming, no eternal agony. Trees and shrubs and grass hills and thousands and thousands of little houses.

It took about ten minutes for the inhabitants to get around to investigating me. Two men came over to my truck and nodded cordially. Both were middle-aged and healthy-looking. They didn't look dead. I nodded back.

"We were betting whether you're one of the drivers or not," said the first, a black-haired fellow. He wore a simple handwoven shirt and pants. "I think you are. That so?"

"I am."

"You're lost, then."

I agreed. "Maybe you can tell me where I am?"

"Hell," said the second man, younger by a few years and just wearing shorts. The way he said it was just like you might say you came from

Los Angeles or Long Beach. Nothing big, nothing dramatic.

"We've heard rumors there's been problems outside," a woman said, coming up to join us. She was about sixty and skinny. She looked like she should be twitchy and nervous but she acted rock-steady. They were all rock-steady.

"There's some kind of strike," I said. "I don't know what it is, but I'm looking for an employee to tell me."

"They don't usually come this far in," the first man said. "We run things here. Or rather, nobody tells us what to do."

"You're alive?" the woman asked, a curious hunger in her voice. Others came around to join us, a whole crowd. They didn't try to touch. They stood their ground and stared and talked.

"Look," said an old black fellow. "You ever read about the Ancient Mariner?"

I said I had in school.

"Had to tell everybody what he did," the black fellow said. The woman beside him nodded. "We're all Ancient Mariners here. But there's nobody to tell it to. Would you like to know?" The way he asked was pitiful. "We're sorry. We just want everybody to know how sorry we are."

"I can't take you back," I said. "I don't know how to get there myself."

"We can't go back," the woman said. "That's not our place."

More people were coming and I was nervous again. I stood my ground trying to seem calm and the dead gathered around me, eager.

"I never thought of anybody but myself," one said. Another interrupted with, "Man, I fucked my whole life away, I hated everybody and everything. I was burned out—"

"I thought I was the greatest. I could pass judgment on everybody—"

"I was the stupidest goddamn woman you ever saw. I was a sow, a pig. I farrowed kids and let them run wild, without no guidance. I was stupid and cruel, too. I used to hurt things—"

"Never cared for anyone. Nobody ever cared for me. I was left to rot in the middle of a city and I wasn't good enough not to rot."

"Everything I did was a lie after I was about twelve years old—"

"Listen to me, mister, because it hurts, it hurts so bad—"

I backed up against my truck. They were lining up now, organized, not like any mob. I had a crazy thought they were behaving better than any people on Earth, but these were the damned.

I didn't hear or see anybody famous. An ex-cop told me about what he did to people in jails. A Jesus-freak told me that knowing Jesus in your heart wasn't enough. "Because I should have made it, man, I should have made it."

"A time came and I was just broken by it all, broke myself really. Just kept stepping on myself and making all the wrong decisions—"

They confessed to me, and I began to cry. Their faces were so clear and so pure, yet here they were, confessing, and except maybe for specific things—like the fellow who had killed Ukrainians after the Second World War in Russian camps—they didn't sound any worse than the crazy sons of bitches I called friends who spent their lives in trucks or bars or whorehouses.

They were all recent. I got the impression the deeper into Hell you went, the older the damned became, which made sense; Hell just got bigger, each crop of damned got bigger, with more room on the outer circles.

"We wasted it," someone said. "You know what my greatest sin was? I was dull. Dull and cruel. I never saw beauty. I saw only dirt. I loved the dirt and the clean just passed me by."

Pretty soon my tears were uncontrollable. I kneeled down beside the truck, hiding my head, but they kept on coming and confessing. Hundreds must have passed, talking quietly, gesturing with their hands.

Then they stopped. Someone had come and told them to back away, that they were too much for me. I took my face out of my hands and a very young-seeming fellow stood looking down on me. "You all right?" he asked.

I nodded, but my insides were like broken glass. With every confession I had seen myself, and with every tale of sin I had felt an answering echo.

"Someday, I'm going to be here. Someone's going to drive me in a cattle car to Hell," I mumbled. The young fellow helped me to my feet and cleared a way around my truck.

"Yeah, but not now," he said. "You don't belong here yet." He opened the door to my cab and I got back inside.

"I don't have any fuel," I said.

He smiled that sad smile they all had and stood on the step, up close to my ear. "You'll be taken out of here soon anyway. One of the employees is bound to get around to you." He seemed a lot more sophisticated than the others. I looked at him maybe a little queerly, like there was some explaining in order.

"Yeah, I know all that stuff," he said. "I was a driver once. Then I got promoted. What are they all doing back there?" He gestured up the road. "They're really messing things up now, ain't they?"

"I don't know," I said, wiping my eyes and cheeks with my sleeve.

"You go back, and you tell them that all this revolt on the outer circles, it's what I expected. Tell them Charlie's here and that I warned them. Word's getting around. There's bound to be discontent."

"Word?"

"About who's in charge. Just tell them Charlie knows and I warned them. I know something else, and you shouldn't tell anybody about this . . ." He whispered an incredible fact into my ear then, something that shook me deeper than what I had already been through.

I closed my eyes. Some shadow passed over. The young fellow and everybody else seemed to recede. I felt rather than saw my truck being picked up like a toy.

Then I suppose I was asleep for a time.

In the cab in the parking lot of a truck stop in Bakersfield, I jerked awake, pulled my cap out of my eyes and looked around. It was about noon. There was a union hall in Bakersfield. I checked and my truck was full of diesel, so I started her up and drove to the union hall.

I knocked on the door of the office. I went in and recognized the fat old dude who had given me the job in the first place. I was tired and I smelled bad but I wanted to get it all done with now.

He recognized me but didn't know my name until I told him. "I can't work the run anymore," I said. The shakes were on me again. "I'm not the one for it. I don't feel right driving them when I know I'm going to be there myself, like as not."

"Okay," he said, slow and careful, sizing me up with a knowing eye. "But you're out. You're busted then. No more driving, no more work for us, no more work for any union we support. It'll be lonely."

"I'll take that kind of lonely any day," I said.

"Okay." That was that. I headed for the door and stopped with my hand on the knob.

"One more thing," I said. "I met Charlie. He says to tell you word's getting around about who's in charge, and that's why there's so much trouble in the outer circles."

The old dude's knowing eye went sort of glassy. "You're the fellow got into the City?"

I nodded.

He got up from his seat real fast, jowls quivering and belly doing a silly dance beneath his work blues. He flicked one hand at me, come 'ere. "Don't go. Just you wait a minute. Outside in the office."

I waited and heard him talking on the phone. He came out smiling and put his hand on my shoulder. "Listen, John, I'm not sure we should let you quit. I didn't know you were the one who'd gone inside. Word is, you stuck around and tried to help when everybody else ran. The company appreciates that. You've been with us a long time, reliable driver, maybe we should give you some incentive to stay. I'm sending you to Vegas to talk with a company man . . ."

The way he said it, I knew there wasn't much choice and I better not

fight it. You work union long enough and you know when you keep
your mouth shut and go along.

They put me up in a motel and fed me and by late morning I was on
my way to Vegas, arriving about two in the afternoon. I was in a black
union car with a silent driver and air conditioning and some *Newsweek*s
to keep me company.

The limo dropped me off in front of a four-floor office building, glass
and stucco, with lots of divorce lawyers and a dentist and small companies with anonymous names. White plastic letters on a ribbed felt
background in a glass case. There was no name on the office number I
had been told to go to, but I went up and knocked anyway.

I don't know what I expected. A district supervisor opened the door
and asked me a few questions and I said what I'd said before. I was
adamant. He looked worried. "Look," he said. "It won't be good for you
now if you quit."

I asked him what he meant by that but he just looked unhappy and
said he was going to send me to somebody higher up.

That was in Denver, nearer my God to thee. The same black car took
me there and Saturday morning, bright and early, I stood in front of a
very large corporate building with no sign out front and a bank on the
bottom floor. I went past the bank and up to the very top.

A secretary met me, pretty but her hair done up very tight and her
jaw grimly square. She didn't like me. She let me into the next office,
though.

I swear I'd seen the fellow before, but maybe it was just a passing
resemblance. He wore a narrow tie and a tasteful but conservative gray
suit. His shirt was pastel blue and there was a big Rembrandt Bible on
his desk, sitting on the glass top next to an alabaster pen holder. He
shook my hand firmly and perched on the edge of the desk.

"First, let me congratulate you on your bravery. We've had some
reports from the . . . uh . . . field, and we're hearing nothing but good
about you." He smiled like that fellow on TV who's always asking the
audience to give him some help. Then his face got sincere and serious.
I honestly believe he was sincere; he was also well trained in dealing
with not-very-bright people. "I hear you have a report for me. From
Charles Frick."

"He said his name was Charlie." I told him the story. "What I'm curious about, what did he mean, this thing about who's in charge?"

"Charlie was in Organization until last year. He died in a car accident.
I'm shocked to hear he got the Low Road." He didn't look shocked.
"Maybe I'm shocked but not surprised. To tell the truth, he was a bit of
a troublemaker." He smiled brightly again and his eyes got large and

there was a little too much animation in his face. He had on these MacArthur wire-rimmed glasses too big for his eyes.

"What did he mean?"

"John, I'm proud of all our drivers. You don't know how proud we all are of you folks down there doing the dirty work."

"What did Charlie mean?"

"The abortionists and pornographers, the hustlers and muggers and murderers. Atheists and heathens and idol-worshippers. Surely there must be some satisfaction in keeping the land clean. Sort of a giant sanitation squad, you people keep the scum away from the good folks. The plain good folks. Now we know that driving's maybe the hardest job we have in the company, and that not everyone can stay on the Low Road indefinitely. Still, we'd like you to stay on. Not as a driver— unless you really wish to continue. For the satisfaction of a tough job. No, if you want to move up—and you've earned it by now, surely—we have a place for you here. A place where you'll be comfortable and—"

"I've already said I want out. You're acting like I'm hot stuff and I'm just shit. You know that, I know that. What is going on?"

His face hardened on me. "It isn't easy up here, either, buster." The "buster" bit tickled me. I laughed and got up from the chair. I'd been in enough offices and this fancy one just made me queasy. When I stood, he held up his hand and pursed his lips as he nodded. "Sorry. There's incentive, there's certainly a reason why you should want to work here. If you're so convinced you're on your way to the Low Road, you can work it off here, you know."

"How can you say that?"

Bright smile. "Charlie told you something. He told you about who's in charge here."

Now I could smell something terribly wrong, like with the union boss. I mumbled, "He said that's why there's trouble."

"It comes every now and then. We put it down gentle. I tell you where we really need good people, compassionate people. We need them to help with the choosing."

"Choosing?"

"Surely you don't think the Boss does all the choosing directly?"

I couldn't think of a thing to say.

"Listen, the Boss . . . let me tell you. A long time ago, the Boss decided to create a new kind of worker, one with more decision-making ability. Some of the supervisors disagreed, especially when the Boss said the workers would be around for a long, long time—that they'd be indestructible. Sort of like nuclear fuel, you know. Human souls. The waste builds up after a time, those who turn out bad, turn out to be chronically unemployable. They don't go along with the scheme, or get out of line.

Can't get along with their fellow workers. You know the type. What do you do with them? Can't just let them go away—they're indestructible, and that ain't no joke, so—"

"Chronically unemployable?"

"You're a union man. Think of what it must feel like to be out of work . . . forever. Damned. Nobody will hire you."

I knew the feeling, both the way he meant it and the way it had happened to me.

"The Boss feels the project half succeeded, so He doesn't dump it completely. But He doesn't want to be bothered with all the pluses and minuses, the bookkeeping."

"You're in charge," I said, my blood cooling.

And I knew where I had seen him before.

On television.

God's right-hand man.

And human. Flesh-and-blood.

We ran Hell.

He nodded. "Now, that's not the sort of thing we'd like to get around."

"You're in charge, and you let the drivers take their perks on the loads, you let—" I stopped, instinct telling me I would soon be on a rugged trail with no turnaround.

"I'll tell you the truth, John. I have only been in charge here for a year, and my predecessor let things get out of hand. He wasn't a religious man, John, and he thought this was a job like any other, where you could compromise now and then. I know that isn't so. There's no compromise here, and we'll straighten out those inequities and bad decisions very soon. You'll help us, I hope. You may know more about the problems than we do."

"How do you . . . how do you qualify for a job like this?" I asked. "And who offered it to you?"

"Not the Boss, if that's what you're getting at, John. It's been kind of traditional. You may have heard about me. I'm the one, when there was all this talk about after-life experiences and everyone was seeing bright light and beauty, I'm the one who wondered why no one was seeing the other side. I found people who had almost died and had seen Hell, and I turned their lives around. The management in the company decided a fellow with my ability could do good work here. And so I'm here. And I'll tell you, it isn't easy. I sometimes wish we had a little more help from the Boss, a little more guidance, but we don't, and somebody has to do it. Somebody has to clean out the stables, John." Again the smile.

I put on my mask. "Of course," I said. I hoped a gradual increase in piety would pass his sharp-eyed muster.

"And you can see how this all makes you much more valuable to the organization."

I let light dawn slowly.

"We'd hate to lose you now, John. Not when there's security, so much security, working for us. I mean, here we learn the real ins and outs of salvation."

I let him talk at me until he looked at his watch, and all the time I nodded and considered and tried to think of the best ploy. Then I eased myself into a turnabout. I did some confessing until his discomfort was stretched too far—I was keeping him from an important appointment— and made my concluding statement.

"I just wouldn't feel right up here," I said. "I've driven all my life. I'd just want to keep on, working where I'm best suited."

"Keep your present job?" he said, tapping his shoe on the side of the desk.

"Lord, yes," I said, grateful as could be.

Then I asked him for his autograph. He smiled real big and gave it to me, God's right-hand man, who had prayed with presidents.

THE NEXT TIME OUT, I THOUGHT ABOUT THE INCREDIBLE THING THAT CHARLIE Frick had told me. Halfway to Hell, on the part of the run that he had once driven, I pulled the truck onto the gravel shoulder and walked back, hands in pockets, squinting at the faces. Young and old. Mostly old, or in their teens or twenties. Some were clearly bad news. . . . But I was looking more closely this time, trying to discriminate. And sure enough, I saw a few that didn't seem to belong.

The dead hung by the slats, sticking their arms through, beseeching. I ignored as much of that as I could. "You," I said, pointing to a pale, thin fellow with a listless expression. "Why are you here?"

They wouldn't lie to me. I'd learned that inside the City. The dead don't lie.

"I kill people," the man said in a high whisper. "I kill children."

That confirmed my theory. I had *known* there was something wrong with him. I pointed to an old woman, plump and white-haired, lacking any of the signs. "You. Why are you going to Hell?"

She shook her head. "I don't know," she said. "Because I'm bad, I suppose."

"What did you do that was bad?"

"I don't know!" she said, flinging her hands up. "I really don't know. I was a librarian. When all those horrible people tried to take books out of my library, I fought them. I tried to reason with them. . . . They wanted to remove Salinger and Twain and Baum . . ."

I picked out another young man. "What about you?"

"I didn't think it was possible," he said. "I didn't believe that God hated me, too."

"What did you do?" These people *didn't need to confess*.

"I loved God. I loved Jesus. But, dear Lord, I couldn't help it. I'm gay. I never had a choice. God wouldn't send me here just for being gay, would he?"

I spoke to a few more, until I was sure I had found all I had in this load. "You, you, you and you, out," I said, swinging open the rear gate. I closed the gate after them and led them away from the truck. Then I told them what Charlie Frick had told me, what he had learned on the road and in the big offices.

"Nobody's really sure where it goes," I said. "But it doesn't go to Hell, and it doesn't go back to Earth."

"Where, then?" the old woman asked plaintively. The hope in her eyes made me want to cry, because I just wasn't sure.

"Maybe it's the High Road," I said. "At least it's a chance. You light out across this stretch, go back of that hill, and I think there's some sort of trail. It's not easy to find, but if you look carefully, it's there. Follow it."

The young man who was gay took my hand. I felt like pulling away, because I've never been fond of homos. But he held on and he said, "Thank you. You must be taking a big risk."

"Yes, thank you," the librarian said. "Why are you doing it?"

I had hoped they wouldn't ask. "When I was a kid, one of my Sunday schoolteachers told me about Jesus going down to Hell during the three days before he rose up again. She told me Jesus went to Hell to bring out those who didn't belong. I'm certainly no Jesus, I'm not even much of a Christian, but that's what I'm doing. She called it Harrowing Hell." I shook my head. "Never mind. Just go," I said. I watched them walk across the gray flats and around the hill, then I got back into my truck and took the rest into the annex. Nobody noticed. I suppose the records just aren't that important to the employees.

None of the folks I've let loose have ever come back.

I'm staying on the road. I'm talking to people here and there, being cautious. When it looks like things are getting chancy, I'll take my rig back down to the City. And then I'm not sure what I'll do.

I don't want to let everybody loose. But I want to know who's ending up on the Low Road who shouldn't be. People unpopular with God's right-hand man.

My message is simple.

The crazy folks are running the asylum. We've corrupted Hell.

If I get caught, I'll be riding in back. And if you're reading this, chances are you'll be there, too.

Until then, I'm doing my bit. How about you?

INTRODUCTION TO "PETRA"

"Petra" is the most extravagant of my theological fantasies, perfect, I think, for an animated feature. Cute gargoyles come to life, as in Disney's *Hunchback of Notre Dame*. The sex angle is dicey even for the modern Disney, but I'd be willing to compromise a little to see a splendidly animated feature about a world in which, for whatever reason, God's laws no longer apply.

Matt Howarth did a lovely comic adaptation of "Petra" for the program book of the Philadelphia World Science Fiction convention in 2001, where I was Guest of Honor.

This was the first story I sold to *Omni* under the editorial surveillance of Ellen Datlow. Ben Bova, my worthy editor at *Analog*, and at this point in charge at *Omni*, was not enthusiastic, but once again I was about to benefit from an editor moving on . . .

Ben passed the reins of fiction editing to Ellen, and she bought and published "Petra." Ellen seems to like bent theology. So do I.

I strongly suspect that God has a sense of humor and doesn't mind, either.

PETRA
Omni, Ellen Datlow, 1982

" 'God is dead, God is dead' . . . Perdition! When God dies, you'll know it."
—Confessions of St. Argentine

I'm an ugly son of stone and flesh, there's no denying it. I don't remember my mother. It's possible she abandoned me shortly after my birth. More than likely she is dead. My father—ugly beaked, half-winged thing, if he resembles his son—I have never seen.

Why should such an unfortunate aspire to be a historian? I think I can trace the moment my choice was made. It's among my earliest memories, and it must have happened about thirty years ago, though I'm sure I lived many years before that—years now lost to me. I was squatting behind thick, dusty curtains in a vestibule, listening to a priest instructing other novitiates, all of pure flesh, about Mortdieu. His words are still vivid.

"As near as I can discover," he said, "Mortdieu occurred about seventy-seven years ago. Learned ones deny that magic was set loose on the world, but few deny that God, as such, had died."

Indeed. That's putting it mildly. All the hinges of our once-great universe fell apart, the axis tilted, cosmic doors swung shut, and the rules of existence lost their foundations. The priest continued in measured, awed tones to describe that time.

"I have heard wise men speak of the slow decline. Where human thought was strong, reality's sudden quaking was reduced to a tremor. Where thought was weak, reality disappeared completely, swallowed by chaos. Every delusion became as real as solid matter." His voice trembled with emotion. "Blinding pain, blood catching fire in our veins, bones snapping and flesh powdering. Steel flowing like liquid. Amber raining from the sky. Crowds gathering in streets that no longer followed any maps, if the maps themselves had not altered. They knew not what to do. Their weak minds could not grab hold . . ."

Most humans, I take it, were entirely too irrational to begin with. Whole nations vanished or were turned into incomprehensible whirlpools of misery and depravity. It is said that certain universities, libraries, and museums survived, but to this day we have little contact with them.

I think often of those poor victims of the early days of Mortdieu. They had known a world of some stability; we have adapted since. They were shocked by cities turning into forests, by their nightmares taking shape before their eyes. Prodigal crows perched atop trees that had once been buildings, pigs ran through the streets on their hind legs . . . and so on. (The priest did not encourage contemplation of the oddities. "Excitement," he said, "breeds even more monsters.")

Our Cathedral survived. Rationality in this neighborhood, however, had weakened some centuries before Mortdieu, replaced only by a kind of rote. The Cathedral suffered. Survivors—clergy and staff, worshipers seeking sanctuary—had wretched visions, dreamed wretched dreams. They saw the stone ornaments of the Cathedral come alive. With someone to see and believe, in a universe lacking any other foundation, my ancestors shook off stone and became flesh. Centuries of stone celibacy weighed upon them. Forty-nine nuns who had sought shelter in the Cathedral were discovered and were not entirely loath, so the coarser versions of the tale go. Mortdieu had had a surprising aphrodisiacal effect on the faithful and conjugation took place.

No definite gestation period has been established, for at that time the great stone wheel had not been set twisting back and forth to count the hours. Nor had anyone been given the chair of Kronos to watch over the wheel and provide a baseline for everyday activities.

But flesh did not reject stone, and there came into being the sons and daughters of flesh and stone, including me. Those who had fornicated with the inhuman figures were cast out to raise or reject their monstrous young in the highest hidden recesses. Those who had accepted the embraces of the stone saints and other human figures were less abused but still banished to the upper reaches. A wooden scaffolding was erected, dividing the great nave into two levels. A canvas drop cloth was fastened over the scaffold to prevent offal raining down, and on the second level of the Cathedral the more human offspring of stone and flesh set about creating a new life.

I have long tried to find out how some semblance of order came to the world. Legend has it that it was the archexistentialist Jansard crucifier of the beloved St. Argentine—who, realizing and repenting his error, discovered that mind and thought could calm the foaming sea of reality.

The priest finished his all-too-sketchy lecture by touching on this point briefly: "With the passing of God's watchful gaze, humanity had to reach out and grab hold the unraveling fabric of the world. Those left alive—those who had the wits to keep their bodies from falling apart—became the only cohesive force in the chaos."

I had picked up enough language to understand what he said; my memory was good—still is—and I was curious enough to want to know more.

Creeping along stone walls behind the curtains, I listened to other priests and nuns intoning scripture to gaggles of flesh children. That was on the ground floor, and I was in great danger; the people of pure flesh looking on my kind as abominations. But it was worth it.

I was able to steal a Psalter and learned to read. I stole other books; they defined my world by allowing me to compare it with others. At first I couldn't believe the others had ever existed; only the Cathedral was real. I still have my doubts. I can look out a tiny round window on one side of my room and see the great forest and river that surround the Cathedral, but I can see nothing else. So my experience with other worlds is far from direct.

No matter. I read a great deal, but I'm no scholar. What concerns me is recent history—the final focus of that germinal hour listening to the priest. From the metaphysical to the acutely personal.

I am small—barely three English feet in height—but I can run quickly through most of the hidden passageways. This lets me observe without attracting attention. I may be the only historian in this whole structure. Others who claim the role disregard what's before their eyes, in search of ultimate truths, or at least Big Pictures. So if you prefer history where the historian is not involved, look to the others. Objective as I try to be, I do have my favorite subjects.

In the time when my history begins, the children of stone and flesh were still searching for the Stone Christ. Those of us born of the union of the stone saints and gargoyles with the bereaved nuns thought our salvation lay in the great stone celibate, who came to life as all the other statues had.

Of smaller import were the secret assignations between the bishop's daughter and a young man of stone and flesh. Such assignations were forbidden even between those of pure flesh; and as these two lovers were unmarried, their compound sin intrigued me.

Her name was Constantia, and she was fourteen, slender of limb, brown of hair, mature of bosom. Her eyes carried the stupid sort of divine life common in girls that age. His name was Corvus, and he was fifteen. I don't recall his precise features, but he was handsome enough and dexterous: he could climb through the scaffolding almost as quickly as I. I first spied them talking when I made one of my frequent raids on the repository to steal another book. They were in shadow, but my eyes are keen. They spoke softly, hesitantly. My heart ached to see them and to think of their tragedy, for I knew right away that Corvus was not pure flesh and that Constantia was the daughter of the bishop himself. I envisioned the old tyrant meting out the usual punishment to Corvus for such breaches of level and morality—castration. But in their talk was a sweetness that almost masked the closed-in stench of the lower nave.

"Have you ever kissed a man before?"

"Yes."

"Who?"

"My brother." She laughed.

"And?" His voice was sharper; he might kill her brother, he seemed to say.

"A friend named Jules."

"Where is he?"

"Oh, he vanished on a wood-gathering expedition."

"Oh." And he kissed her again.

I'm a historian, not a voyeur, so I discreetly hide the flowering of their passion. If Corvus had had any sense, he would have reveled in his conquest and never returned. But he was snared and continued to see her despite the risk. This was loyalty, love, faithfulness, and it was rare. It fascinated me.

I HAVE JUST BEEN TAKING IN SUN, A NICE DAY, AND LOOKING OUT OVER THE buttresses.

The Cathedral is like a low-bellied lizard, the nave its belly, the buttresses its legs. There are little houses at the base of each buttress, where rainspouters with dragon faces used to lean out over the trees (or city or whatever was down below once). Now people live there. It wasn't always that way—the sun was once forbidden. Corvus and Constantia from childhood were denied its light, and so even in their youthful prime they were pale and dirty with the smoke of candles and tallow lamps. The most sun anyone received in those days was obtained on wood-gathering expeditions.

After spying on one of the clandestine meetings of the young lovers, I mused in a dark corner for an hour, then went to see the copper giant Apostle Thomas. He was the only human form to live so high in the Cathedral. He carried a ruler on which was engraved his real name— he had been modeled after the Cathedral's restorer in times past, the architect Viollet-le-Duc. He knew the Cathedral better than anyone, and I admired him greatly. Most of the monsters left him alone—out of fear, if nothing else. He was huge, black as night, but flaked with pale green, his face creased in eternal thought. He was sitting in his usual wooden compartment near the base of the spire, not twenty feet from where I write now, thinking about times none of the rest of us ever knew: of joy and past love, some say; others say of the burden that rested on him now that the Cathedral was the center of this chaotic world.

It was the giant who selected me from the ugly hordes when he saw me with a Psalter. He encouraged me in my efforts to read. "Your eyes are bright," he told me. "You move as if your brain were quick, and you keep yourself dry and clean. You aren't hollow like the rainspouters— you have substance. For all our sakes, put it to use and learn the ways of the Cathedral."

And so I did.

He looked up as I came in. I sat on a box near his feet and said, "A daughter of flesh is seeing a son of stone and flesh."

He shrugged his massive shoulders. "So it shall be, in time."

"Is it not a sin?"

"It is something so monstrous it is past sin and become necessity," he said. "It will happen more as time passes."

"They're in love, I think, or will be."

He nodded. "I—and One Other—were the only ones to abstain from fornication on the night of Mortdieu," he said. "I am—except for the Other—alone fit to judge."

I waited for him to judge, but he sighed and patted me on the shoulder. "And I never judge, do I, ugly friend?"

"Never," I said.

"So leave me alone to be sad." He winked. "And more power to them."

The bishop of the Cathedral was an old, old man. It was said he hadn't been bishop before the Mortdieu, but a wanderer who came in during the chaos, before the forest had replaced the city. He had set himself up as titular head of this section of God's former domain by saying it had been willed to him.

He was short, stout, with huge hairy arms like the clamps of a vise. He had once killed a spouter with a single squeeze of his fist, and spouters are tough things, since they have no guts like you (I suppose) and I. The hair surrounding his bald pate was white, thick, and unruly, and his eyebrows leaned over his nose with marvelous flexibility. He rutted like a pig, ate hugely, and shat liquidly (I know all). A man for this time, if ever there was one.

It was his decree that all those not pure of flesh be banned and that those not of human form be killed on sight.

When I returned from the giant's chamber, I saw that the lower nave was in an uproar. They had seen someone clambering about in the scaffold, and troops had been sent to shoot him down. Of course it was Corvus. I was a quicker climber than he and knew the beams better, so when he found himself trapped in an apparent cul-de-sac, it was I who gestured from the shadows and pointed to a hole large enough for him to escape through. He took it without a breath of thanks, but etiquette has never been important to me. I entered the stone wall through a nook a spare hand's width across and wormed my way to the bottom to see what else was happening. Excitement was rare.

A rumor was passing that the figure had been seen with a young girl, but the crowds didn't know who the girl was. The men and women who mingled in the smoky light, between the rows of open-roofed hovels, chattered gaily. Castrations and executions were among the few joys for us then; I relished them too, but I had a stake in the potential victims now and I worried.

My worry and my interest got the better of me. I slid through an unrepaired gap and fell to one side of the alley between the outer wall and the hovels. A group of dirty adolescents spotted me. "There he is!" they screeched. "He didn't get away!"

The bishop's masked troops can travel freely on all levels. I was almost cornered by them, and when I tried one escape route, they waited at a crucial spot in the stairs—which I had to cross to complete the next leg—and I was forced back. I prided myself in knowing the Cathedral top to bottom, but as I scrambled madly, I came upon a tunnel I had never noticed before. It led deep into a broad stone foundation wall. I was safe for the moment but afraid that they might find my caches of food and poison my casks of rainwater. Still, there was nothing I could do until they had gone, so I decided to spend the anxious hours exploring the tunnel.

The Cathedral is a constant surprise; I realize now I didn't know half of what it offered. There are always new ways to get from here to there (some, I suspect, created while no one is looking), and sometimes even new theres to be discovered. While troops snuffled about the hole above, near the stairs—where only a child of two or three could have entered—I followed a flight of crude steps deep into the stone. Water and slime made the passage slippery and difficult. For a moment I was in darkness deeper than any I had experienced before—a gloom more profound than mere lack of light could explain. Then below I saw a faint yellow gleam. More cautious, I slowed and progressed silently. Behind a rusting, scabrous metal gate, I set foot into a lighted room. There was the smell of crumbling stone, a tang of mineral water, slime—and the stench of a dead spouter. The beast lay on the floor of the narrow chamber, several months gone but still fragrant.

I have mentioned that spouters are very hard to kill—and this one had been murdered. Three candles stood freshly placed in nooks around the chamber, flickering in a faint draft from above. Despite my fears, I walked across the stone floor, took a candle, and peered into the next section of tunnel.

It sloped down for several dozen feet, ending at another metal gate. It was here that I detected an odor I had never before encountered—the smell of the purest of stones, as of rare jade or virgin marble. Such a feeling of lightheadedness passed over me that I almost laughed, but I was too cautious for that. I pushed aside the gate and was greeted by a rush of the coldest, sweetest air, like a draft from the tomb of a saint whose body does not corrupt but rather, draws corruption away and expels it miraculously into the nether pits. My beak dropped open. The candlelight fell across the darkness onto a figure I at first thought to be an infant. But I quickly disagreed with myself. The figure was several ages at once. As I blinked, it became a man of about thirty, well formed, with a high forehead and elegant hands, pale as ice. His eyes stared at the wall behind me. I bowed down on scaled knee and touched my forehead as best I could to the cold stone, shivering to my vestigial wing tips. "Forgive me, Joy of Man's Desiring," I said. "Forgive me." I had stumbled upon the hiding place of the Stone Christ.

"You are forgiven," He said wearily. "You had to come sooner or later. Better now than later, when . . ." His voice trailed away and He shook His head. He was very thin, wrapped in a gray robe that still bore the scars of centuries of weathering. "Why did you come?"

"To escape the bishop's troops," I said.

He nodded. "Yes. The bishop. How long have I been here?"

"Since before I was born, Lord. Sixty or seventy years." He was thin, almost ethereal, this figure I had imagined as a husky carpenter. I lowered my voice and beseeched, "What may I do for you, Lord?"

"Go away," He said.

"I could not live with such a secret," I said. "You are salvation. You can overthrow the bishop and bring all the levels together."

"I am not a general or a soldier. Please go away and tell no—"

I felt a breath behind me, then the whisper of a weapon. I leaped aside, and my hackles rose as a stone sword came down and shattered on the floor beside me. The Christ raised His hand. Still in shock, I stared at a beast much like myself. It stared back, face black with rage, stayed by the power of His hand. I should have been more wary—something had to have killed the spouter and kept the candles fresh.

"But, Lord," the beast rumbled, "he will tell all."

"No," the Christ said. "He'll tell nobody." He looked half at me, half through me, and said, "Go, go."

Up the tunnels, into the orange dark of the Cathedral, crying, I crawled and slithered. I could not even go to the giant. I had been silenced as effectively as if my throat had been cut.

The next morning I watched from a shadowy corner of the scaffold as a crowd gathered around a lone man in a dirty sackcloth robe. I had seen him before—his name was Psalo, and he was left alone as an example of the bishop's largess. It was a token gesture; most of the people regarded him as barely half-sane.

Yet this time I listened and, in my confusion, found his words striking responsive chords in me. He was exhorting the bishop and his forces to allow light into the Cathedral again by dropping the canvas tarps that covered the windows. He had talked about this before, and the bishop had responded with his usual statement—that with the light would come more chaos, for the human mind was now a pesthole of delusions. Any stimulus would drive away whatever security the inhabitants of the Cathedral had.

At this time it gave me no pleasure to watch the love of Constantia and Corvus grow. They were becoming more careless. Their talk grew bolder:

"We shall announce a marriage," Corvus said.

"They will never allow it. They'll . . . cut you."

"I'm nimble. They'll never catch me. The church needs leaders, brave revolutionaries. If no one breaks with tradition, everyone will suffer."

"I fear for your life—and mine. My father would push me from the flock like a diseased lamb."

"Your father is no shepherd."

"He is my father," Constantia said, eyes wide, mouth drawn tight.

I sat with beak in paws, eyes half-lidded, able to mimic each statement before it was uttered. Undying love . . . hope for a bleak future . . . shite and onions! I had read it all before, in a cache of romance novels in the trash of a dead nun. As soon as I made the connection and realized the timeless banality—and the futility—of what I was seeing, and when I compared their prattle with the infinite sadness of the Stone Christ, I went from innocent to cynic. The transition dizzied me, leaving little backwaters of noble emotion, but the future seemed clear. Corvus would be caught and executed; if it hadn't been for me, he would already have been gelded, if not killed. Constantia would weep, poison herself; the singers would sing of it (those selfsame warble-throats who cheered the death of her lover); perhaps I would write of it (I was planning this chronicle even then), and afterward, perhaps, I would follow them both, having succumbed to the sin of boredom.

With night, things become less certain. It is easy to stare at a dark wall and let dreams become manifest. At one time, I've deduced from books, dreams could not take shape beyond sleep or brief fantasy. All too often I've had to fight things generated in my dreams, flowing from the walls, suddenly independent and hungry. People often die in the night, devoured by their own nightmares.

That evening, falling to sleep with visions of the Stone Christ in my head, I dreamed of holy men, angels, and saints. I came awake abruptly, by training, and saw that one had stayed behind. The others I saw flitting outside the round window, where they whispered and made plans for flying off to heaven. The wraith that had lingered made a dark, vague shape in one corner. His breath came new to him, raw and harsh. "I am Peter," he said, "also called Simon. I am the Rock of the Church, and popes are told that they are heir to my task."

"I'm rock, too," I said. "At least, part of me is."

"So be it, then. You are heir to my task. Go forth and be Pope. Do not revere the Stone Christ, for a Christ is only as good as He does, and if He does nothing, there is no salvation in Him."

The shadow reached out to pat my head. I saw his eyes grow wide as he made out my form. He muttered some formula for banishing devils and oozed out the window to join his fellows.

I imagined that if such a thing were actually brought before the council, it would be decided under the law that the command of a dream saint is not binding. I did not care. The wraith had given me better orders than any I'd had since the giant told me to read and learn.

But to be Pope, one must have a hierarchy of servants to carry out one's plans. The biggest of rocks does not move by itself. So it was that, swollen with power, I decided to appear in the upper nave and announce myself to the people.

IT TOOK A GREAT DEAL OF COURAGE TO SHOW MYSELF IN BROAD DAYLIGHT, without my cloak, and to walk across the scaffold's surface, on the second level, through crowds of vendors setting up the market for the day. Some saw me and reacted with typical bigotry. They kicked and cursed at me. My beak was swift and discouraged them.

I clambered to the top of a prominent stall and stood in the murky glow of a small lamp, rising to my full height and clearing my throat, making ready to give my commands. Under a hail of rotten pomegranates and limp vegetables, I told the throng who I was. I boldly told them about my vision. I tried to make myself speak clearly, starting over from the beginning several times, but the deluge of opprobrium was too thick. Jeweled with beads of offal, I jumped down and fled to a tunnel entrance too small for most men. Some boys followed, ready to do me real harm, and one lost his finger while trying to slice me with a fragment of colored glass.

I recognized, almost too late, that the tactic of open revelation was worthless. There are levels of fear and bigotry, and I was at the very bottom.

My next strategy was to find some way to disrupt the Cathedral from top to bottom. Even bigots, when reduced to a mob, could be swayed by the presence of one obviously ordained and capable. I spent two days skulking through the walls. There had to be a basic flaw in so fragile a structure as the church, and, while I wasn't contemplating total destruction, I wanted something spectacular, unavoidable.

While I cogitated, hanging from the bottom of the second scaffold, above the community of pure flesh, the bishop's deep gravelly voice roared over the noise of the crowd. I opened my eyes and looked down. The masked troops were holding a bowed figure, and the bishop was intoning over its head, "Know all who hear me now, this young bastard of flesh and stone—"

Corvus, I told myself. Finally caught. I shut one eye, but the other refused to close out the scene.

"—has violated all we hold sacred and shall atone for his crimes on this spot, tomorrow at this time. Kronos! Mark the wheel's progress." The elected Kronos, a spindly old man with dirty gray hair down to his buttocks, took a piece of charcoal and marked an X on the huge bulkhead chart, behind which the wheel groaned and sighed in its circuit.

The crowd was enthusiastic. I saw Psalo pushing through the people.

"What crime?" he called out. "Name the crime!"

"Violation of the lower level!" the head of the masked troops declared.

"That merits a whipping and an escort upstairs," Psalo said. "I detect a more sinister crime here. What is it?"

The bishop looked Psalo down coldly. "He tried to rape my daughter, Constantia."

Psalo could say nothing to that. The penalty was castration and death. All the pure humans accepted such laws. There was no other recourse.

I mused, watching Corvus being led to the dungeons. The future that I desired at that moment startled me with its clarity. I wanted that part of my heritage that had been denied to me—to be at peace with myself, to be surrounded by those who accepted me, by those no better than I. In time that would happen, as the giant had said. But would I ever see it? What Corvus, in his own lusty way, was trying to do was equalize the levels, to bring stone into flesh until no one could define the divisions.

Well, my plans beyond that point were very hazy. They were less plans than glowing feelings, imaginings of happiness and children playing in the forest and fields beyond the island as the world knit itself under the gaze of God's heir. My children, playing in the forest. A touch of truth came to me at this moment. I had wished to be Corvus when he tupped Constantia.

So I had two tasks, then, that could be merged if I was clever. I had to distract the bishop and his troops, and I had to rescue Corvus, fellow revolutionary.

I spent that night in feverish misery in my room. At dawn I went to the giant and asked his advice. He looked me over coldly and said, "We waste our time if we try to knock sense into their heads. But we have no better calling than to waste our time, do we?"

"What shall I do?"

"Enlighten them."

I stomped my claw on the floor. "They are bricks! Try enlightening bricks!"

He smiled his sad, narrow smile. "Enlighten them," he said.

I left the giant's chamber in a rage. I did not have access to the great wheel's board of time, so I couldn't know exactly when the execution would take place. But I guessed—from memories of a grumbling stomach—that it would be in the early afternoon. I traveled from one end of the nave to the other and, likewise, the transept. I nearly exhausted myself.

Then, traversing an empty aisle, I picked up a piece of colored glass and examined it, puzzled. Many of the boys on all levels carried these shards with them, and the girls used them as jewelry—against the wishes of their elders, who held that bright objects bred more beasts in the mind. Where did they get them?

In one of the books I had perused years before, I had seen brightly colored pictures of the Cathedral windows. "Enlighten them," the giant had said.

Psalo's request to let light into the Cathedral came to mind.

Along the peak of the nave, in a tunnel running its length, I found the ties that held the pulleys of the canvases over the windows. The best windows, I decided, would be the huge ones of the north and south transepts. I made a diagram in the dust, trying to decide what season it was and from which direction the sunlight would come—pure theory to me, but at this moment I was in a fever of brilliance. All the windows had to be clear. I could not decide which was best.

I was ready by early afternoon, just after sext prayers in the upper nave. I had cut the major ropes and weakened the clamps by prying them from the walls with a pick stolen from the bishop's armory. I walked along a high ledge, took an almost vertical shaft through the wall to the lower floor, and waited.

Constantia watched from a wooden balcony, the bishop's special box for executions. She had a terrified, fascinated look on her face. Corvus was on the dais across the nave, right in the center of the cross of the transept. Torches illumined him and his executioners, three men and an old woman.

I knew the procedure. The old woman would castrate him first, then the men would remove his head. He was dressed in the condemned red robe to hide any blood. Blood excitement among the impressionable was the last thing the bishop wanted. Troops waited around the dais to purify the area with scented water.

I didn't have much time. It would take minutes for the system of ropes and pulleys to clear and the canvases to fall. I went to my station and severed the remaining ties. Then, as the Cathedral filled with a hollow creaking sound, I followed the shaft back to my viewing post.

In three minutes the canvases were drooping. I saw Corvus look up, his eyes glazed. The bishop was with his daughter in the box. He pulled her back into the shadows. In another two minutes the canvases fell onto the upper scaffold with a hideous crash. Their weight was too great for the ends of the structure, and it collapsed, allowing the canvas to cascade to the floor many yards below. At first the illumination was dim and bluish, filtered perhaps by a passing cloud. Then, from one end of the Cathedral to the other, a burst of light threw my smoky world into clarity. The glory of thousands of pieces of colored glass, hidden for decades and hardly touched by childish vandals, fell upon upper and lower levels at once. A cry from the crowds nearly wrenched me from my post. I slid quickly to the lower level and hid, afraid of what I had done. This was more than simple sunlight. Like the blossoming of two flowers, one brighter than the other, the transept windows astounded all who beheld them.

Eyes accustomed to orangey dark, to smoke and haze and shadow, cannot stare into such glory without drastic effect. I shielded my own face and tried to find a convenient exit.

But the population was increasing. As the light brightened and more faces rose to be locked, phototropic, the splendor unhinged some people. From their minds poured contents too wondrous to be accurately cataloged. The monsters thus released were not violent, however, and most of the visions were not monstrous.

The upper and lower nave shimmered with reflected glories, with dream figures and children clothed in baubles of light. Saints and prodigies dominated. A thousand newly created youngsters squatted on the bright floor and began to tell of marvels, of cities in the East, and times as they had once been. Clowns dressed in fire entertained from the tops of the market stalls. Animals unknown to the Cathedral cavorted between the dwellings, giving friendly advice. Abstract things, glowing balls in nets of gold and ribbons of silk, sang and floated around the upper reaches. The Cathedral became a great vessel of all the bright dreams known to its citizens.

Slowly, from the lower nave, people of pure flesh climbed to the scaffold and walked the upper nave to see what they couldn't from below. From my hideaway I watched the masked troops of the bishop carrying his litter up narrow stairs. Constantia walked behind, stumbling, her eyes shut in the new brightness.

All tried to cover their eyes, but none for long succeeded.

I wept. Almost blind with tears, I made my way still higher and looked down on the roiling crowds. I saw Corvus, his hands still wrapped in restraining ropes, being led by the old woman.

Constantia saw him, too, and they regarded each other like strangers, then joined hands as best they could. She borrowed a knife from one of her father's soldiers and cut his ropes away. Around them the brightest dreams of all began to swirl, pure white and blood-red and sea-green, coalescing into visions of all the children they would innocently have.

I gave them a few hours to regain their senses—and to regain my own. Then I stood on the bishop's abandoned podium and shouted over the heads of those on the lowest level.

"The time has come!" I cried. "We must all unite now; we must unite—"

At first they ignored me. I was quite eloquent, but their excitement was still too great. So I waited some more, began to speak again, and was shouted down. Bits of fruit and vegetables arced up. "Freak!" they screamed, and drove me away.

I crept along the stone stairs, found the narrow crack, and hid in it, burying my beak in my paws, wondering what had gone wrong. It took a surprisingly long time for me to realize that, in my case, it was less the stigma of stone than the ugliness of my shape that doomed my quest for leadership.

I had, however, paved the way for the Stone Christ. He will surely be able to take His place now, I told myself. So I maneuvered along the crevice until I came to the hidden chamber and the yellow glow. All was quiet within. I met first the stone monster, who looked me over suspiciously with glazed gray eyes. "You're back," he said. Overcome by his wit, I leered, nodded, and asked that I be presented to the Christ.

"He's sleeping."

"Important tidings," I said.

"What?"

"I bring glad tidings."

"Then let me hear them."

"His ears only."

Out of the gloomy corner came the Christ, looking much older now. "What is it?" He asked.

"I have prepared the way for You," I said. "Simon called Peter told me I was the heir to his legacy, that I should go before You—"

The Stone Christ shook His head. "You believe I am the fount from which all blessings flow?"

I nodded, uncertain.

"What have you done out there?"

"Let in the light," I said.

He shook His head. "You seem a wise enough creature. You know about Mortdieu."

"Yes."

"Then you should know that I barely have enough power to keep myself together, to heal myself, much less to minister to those out there." He gestured beyond the walls. "My own source has gone away," He said mournfully. "I'm operating on reserves, and those none too vast."

"He wants you to go away and stop bothering us," the monster explained.

"They have their light out there," the Christ said. "They'll play with that for a while, get tired of it, go back to what they had before. Is there any place for you in that?"

I thought for a moment, then shook my head. "No place," I said. "I'm too ugly."

"You are too ugly, and I am too famous," He said. "I'd have to come from their midst, anonymous, and that is clearly impossible. No, leave them alone for a while. They'll make me over again, perhaps, or better still, forget about me. About us. We don't have any place there."

I was stunned. I sat down hard on the stone floor, and the Christ patted me on my head as He walked by. "Go back to your hiding place; live as well as you can," He said. "Our time is over."

I turned to go. When I reached the crevice, I heard His voice behind, saying, "Do you play bridge? If you do, find another. We need four to a table."

I clambered up the crack, through the walls, and along the arches over the revelry. Not only was I not going to be Pope—after an appointment by Saint Peter himself!—but I couldn't convince someone much more qualified than I to assume the leadership.

It is the sign of the eternal student, I suppose, that when his wits fail him, he returns to the teacher.

I returned to the copper giant. He was lost in meditation. About his feet were scattered scraps of paper with detailed drawings of parts of the Cathedral. I waited patiently until he saw me. He turned, chin in hand, and looked me over.

"Why so sad?"

I shook my head. Only he could read my features and recognize my moods.

"Did you take my advice below? I heard a commotion."

"*Mea maxima culpa,*" I said.

"And . . . ?"

I hesitantly made my report, concluding with the refusal of the Stone Christ. The giant listened closely without interrupting. When I was done, he stood, towering over me, and pointed with his ruler through an open portal.

"Do you see that out there?" he asked. The ruler swept over the forests beyond the island, to the far green horizon. I replied that I did and waited for him to continue. He seemed to be lost in thought again.

"Once there was a city where trees now grow," he said. "Artists came by the thousands, and whores, and philosophers, and academics. And when God died, all the academics and whores and artists couldn't hold the fabric of the world together. How do you expect us to succeed now?"

Us? "Expectations should not determine whether one acts or not," I said. "Should they?"

The giant laughed and tapped my head with the ruler. "Maybe we've been given a sign, and we just have to learn how to interpret it correctly."

I leered to show I was puzzled.

"Maybe Mortdieu is really a sign that we have been weaned. We must forage for ourselves, remake the world without help. What do you think of that?"

I was too tired to judge the merits of what he was saying, but I had never known the giant to be wrong before. "Okay. I grant that. So?"

"The Stone Christ tells us His charge is running down. If God weans us from the old ways, we can't expect His Son to replace the nipple, can we?"

"No . . ."

He hunkered next to me, his face bright. "I wondered who would really stand forth. It's obvious He won't. So, little one, who's the next choice?"

"Me?" I asked, meekly. The giant looked me over almost pityingly.

"No," he said after a time. "I am the next. We're *weaned!*" He did a little dance, startling my beak up out of my paws. I blinked. He grabbed my vestigial wing tips and pulled me upright. "Stand straight. Tell me more."

"About what?"

"Tell me all that's going on below, and whatever else you know."

"I'm trying to figure out what you're saying," I protested, trembling a bit.

"Dense as stone!" Grinning, he bent over me. Then the grin went away, and he tried to look stern. "It's a grave responsibility. We must remake the world ourselves now. We must coordinate our thoughts, our dreams. Chaos won't do. What an opportunity, to be the architect of an entire universe!" He waved the ruler at the ceiling. "To build the very skies! The last world was a training ground, full of harsh rules and strictures. Now we've been told we're ready to leave that behind, move on to something more mature. Did I teach you any of the rules of architecture? I mean, the aesthetics. The need for harmony, interaction, utility, beauty?"

"Some," I said.

"Good. I don't think making the universe anew will require any better rules. No doubt we'll need to experiment, and perhaps one or more of our great spires will topple. But now we work for ourselves, to our own glory, and to the greater glory of the God who made us! No, ugly friend?"

LIKE MANY HISTORIES, MINE MUST BEGIN WITH THE SMALL, THE TIGHTLY FO-cused, and expand into the large. But unlike most historians, I don't have the luxury of time. Indeed, my story isn't even concluded yet.

Soon the legions of Viollet-le-Duc will begin their campaigns. Most have been schooled pretty thoroughly. Kidnapped from below, brought up in the heights, taught as I was. We'll begin returning them, one by one.

I teach off and on, write off and on, observe all the time.

The next step will be the biggest. I haven't any idea how we're going to do it.

But, as the giant puts it, "Long ago the roof fell in. Now we must push it up again, strengthen it, repair the beams." At this point he smiles to the pupils. "Not just repair them. Replace them! Now we are the beams. Flesh and stone become something much stronger."

Ah, but then some dolt will raise a hand and inquire, "What if our arms get tired holding up the sky?"

Our task, I think, will never end.

Introduction to "Webster"

"Webster" was written in 1971, sold in 1972, and published in 1973 in *Alternities*, a Dell original paperback anthology edited by David Gerrold. It was my second published story. (The first, "Destroyers," appeared in the Summer 1967 issue of *Famous Science Fiction* and is a little too young to be reprinted here.)

My mood in 1971 and 1972 was pretty down. My nineteenth and twentieth years on this planet were filled with unrealized hopes—as a writer, and as a young man. I was growing up rapidly—too rapidly—and my smarts weren't keeping up with the challenges. I was goofing some things badly, in particular, it seemed to me at the time, my relationships with the opposite sex. Nothing unusual here—typical youthful angst.

But what emerged when I wrote "Webster" was the portrait, not of a disappointed young man, but of a dreaming middle-aged woman too inner-directed to be anything but cruel, too blind to cause anything but pain—and fated as Rod Serling might have fated her, had he briefly teamed up with Jorge Luis Borges.

Someone I once knew, seen in a funhouse mirror. Though why they call it a funhouse, I'll never understand.

Webster
Alternities, David Gerrold, 1974

D *ry.*
It lingered in the air, a dead and sterile word made for whispers. Vultures fanned her hair with feather-duster wings. Up the dictionary's page ran her lean finger, wrapped in skin like pink parchment, and she found *Andrews, Roy Chapman*, digging in the middle of the Gobi, lifting fossil dinosaur eggs cracked and unhatched from their graves.

She folded the large, heavy book on her finger. The compressed pages gripped it with a firm, familiar pressure.

With her other hand, Miss Abigail Coates explored her face, vacant of any emotion she was willing to reveal. She did not enjoy her life. Her thin body gave no pleasure, provoked no surprise, spurred no uncontrollable passion. She took no joy in the bored pain of people in the streets. She felt imprisoned by the sun that shed a revealing, bleaching light on city walls and pavement, its dust-filled shafts stealing into her small apartment.

Miss Coates was fifty and, my God the needle in her throat when she thought of it, she had never borne a child; not once had she shared her bed with a man.

There had been, long ago, a lonely, lifeless love with a boy five years younger than she. She had hoped he would blunt the needle pain in her throat; he had begged to be given the chance. But she had spurned him. *I shall use my love as bait and let men pay the toll.* That had been her excuse, at any rate, until the first flush of her youth had faded. Even after that, even before she had felt *dry,* she had never found the right man.

"Pitiful," she said with a sigh, and drew herself up from the over-stuffed chair in her small apartment, standing straight and lean at five feet seven inches. *I weep inside, then read the dear Bible and the even more dear dictionary. They tell me weeping is a sin. Despair is the meanest of my sins—my few sins.*

She looked around the dry, comfortable room and shielded her eyes from the gloom of the place where she slept, as if blinded by shadow. The place wasn't a bedroom because in a *bedroom* you slept with a man or men and she had none. Her eyes moved up the door frame, nicked in one corner where clumsy movers had knocked her bed against the wood, twenty years ago; down to the worn carpet that rubbed the bottoms of her feet like raw canvas. To the chair behind her, stuffing poking from its middle. To the wallpaper, chosen by someone else, stained with water along the cornice from an old rain. And finally she looked down at her feet, toes frozen in loose, frayed nylons, toenails thick and well-manicured; all parts of her body looked after but the core, the soul.

She went into the place where she slept and lay down. The sheets caressed her, as they were obliged to do, wrinkles and folds in blankets rubbing her thighs, her breasts. The pillow accepted her peppery hair, and in the dark, she ordered herself to sleep.

THE MORNING WAS BETTER. THERE WAS A WHOLE DAY AHEAD. SOMETHING might happen.

Afternoon passed like a dull ache. In the twilight she fixed her pale dinner of potatoes and veal.

In the dark, she sat in her chair with the two books at her feet and listened to the old building crack and groan as it settled in for the night. She stared at the printed flowers on the wallpaper that someone must have once thought pretty.

The morning was fine. The afternoon was hot and sticky and she took a walk, wearing sunglasses. She watched all the young people on this fine Saturday afternoon. *They hold hands and walk in parks. There, on that bench; she'll be in trouble if she keeps that up.*

She went back to the patient apartment that always waited, never judging, ever faithful and unperturbed.

The evening passed slowly. She became lazy with heat. By midnight a cool breeze fluttered the sun-browned curtains in the window and blew them in like the dingy wings of street birds.

Miss Coates opened her dictionary, looking for comfort, and found words she wanted, but words she didn't need. They jumped from the pages and would not leave her alone. She didn't think them obscene; she was not a prude. She loved the sounds of all words, and these words were marvelous, too, when properly entrained with other words. They could be part of rich stories, rich lives. The sound of them made her tremble and ache.

The evening ended. Again, she could not cry. Sadness was a moist, dark thing, the color of mud.

She had spent her evenings like this, with few variations, for the past five years.

The yellow morning sunlight crept across the ironing board and over her fanciest dress, burgundy in shadows, orange in the glare. "I need a lover," she told herself firmly. But one found lovers in offices and she didn't work; in trains going to distant countries, and she never left town. "I need common sense and self-control. That part of my life is over. I need to stop thinking like a teenager." But the truth was, she had no deficiency of self-control. It was her greatest strength.

It had kept her away from danger so many times.

Her name, Coates, was not in the dictionary. There was *coati, coatimundi, coat of arms, coat of mail,* and then *coauthor,* Miss Coauthor, partner and lover to a handsome writer. They would *collaborate, corroborate, celebrate.*

Celibate.

She shut the book.

She drew the curtains on the window and slowly tugged the zipper down the back of her dress with the practiced flourish of a crochet hook. Her fingers rubbed the small of her back, nails scraping. She held her chin high, eyes closed to slits.

A lone suitor came through the dark beyond the window to stroke her skin—a stray breeze, neither hot nor cool. Sweat lodged in the cleft between her breasts. She was proud of her breasts; they were small but still did not sag when she removed her bra. She squatted and marched her hands behind her to sit and then lie down on the floor. Spreading her arms against the rough carpet, Miss Coates pressed her chin into her clavicle and peered at her breasts, boyish against the prominent ribs. Untouched. Unspoiled goods.

She cupped them in both hands. She became a thin crucifixion with legs straight and toes together. Her head lay near the window. She looked up to see the curtains fluttering silently like her lips. Mouth open. Tongue rubbing the backs of her teeth. She smoothed her hands to her stomach and let them rest there, curled on the flat warmth.

My stomach doesn't drape. I am not so undesirable. No flab, few wrinkles. My thighs are not dimpled with gross flesh.

She rolled over and propped herself on one elbow to refer to the dictionary, then the Bible.

Abigail Coates mouthing a word: *Lover.*

The dictionary sat tightly noncommittal in buckram, the Bible silent in black leather.

She gently pushed the Bible aside. For all its ancient sex and betrayal and the begetting of desert progeny, it would do nothing for her. She pulled the dictionary closer. "Help me," she said. "Book of all books, massive thing I can hardly lift, every thought lies in you, all human possibilities. Everything I feel, everything that *can* be felt, lies waiting to be described in combinations of the words you contain. You hold all possible lives, people and places I've never seen, things dead and things unborn. Haven of ghosts, home of tyrants, birthplace of saints."

She knew she would have to be audacious. What she was about to do would be proof of her finally having cracked, like those dinosaur eggs in the Gobi; dead and sterile and cracked.

"Surely you can make a man. Small word, little effort. You can even *tell* me how to make a man from you." She could almost imagine a man rising from the open book, spinning like a man-shaped bird cage filled with light.

The curtains puffed.

"Go," she said. She crossed her legs in a lotus next to the thick book and waited for the dust of each word, the microscopic, homeopathic bits of ink, each charged with the shape of a letter, to sift between the fibers of the paper and combine.

Dry magic. The words smelled sweet in the midnight breeze. *Dead bits of ink, charged with thought, arise.*

Veni.

Her tongue swelled with the dryness of the ink. She unfolded and lay flat on her stomach to let the rough carpet mold her skin with crossword puzzle lines, upon which the right words could be written, her life solved.

Miss Coates flopped the dictionary around to face her, then threw its clumps of pages open to the middle. Her finger searched randomly on the page and found a word. She gasped. *Man,* it said, clear as could be next to her immaculate, colorless nail. Man! She moved her finger and sucked in her breath.

"There *is* a man in you!" she told the book and laughed. It was a joke, that's all; she was not that far gone. Still grinning, she rubbed her finger against the inside of her cheek and pressed the dampness onto the word. "Here," she said. "A few of my cells." She was clever, she was scientific, she was brilliant! "Clone *them*." Then she thought that possibility through and said, "But don't make him look like me or think like me. Change him with your medical words, *plastic surgery* and *eugenics* and *phenotype*."

The page darkened under the press of her finger. She swung the dictionary shut and returned to her lotus.

As my trunk rises from the flower of my legs and the seat of my womb, so, man, arise from the book of all books.

Would it thunder? Only silence. The dictionary trembled and the Bible looked dark and somber. The yellow bulb in the shaded lamp sang like a dying moth. The air grew heavy. *Don't falter,* she told herself. *Don't lose faith, don't drop the flower of your legs and the seat of your womb. A bit of blood? Or milk from unsucked breasts? Catalysts . . . or, God forbid, something living, a* fly *between the pages, the heart of a bird, or*—she shuddered, ill with excitement, with a kind of belief—*the clear seed of a dead man.*

The book almost lifted its cover. It *breathed.*

"That was it," she whispered in awe. "The words know what to do."

Frost clung to its brown binding. The dictionary sucked warmth from the air. The cover flew back. The pages riffled, flew by, flapped spasmodically, and two stuck together, struggling, bulging . . . and then splitting.

A figure flew up, arms spread, and twirled like an ice skater. It sucked in dust and air and heat, sucked sweat from her skin, and turned dry emptiness into damp flesh.

"Handsome!" she cried. "Make him handsome and rugged and kind, and smart as I am, if not smarter. Make him like a father but not my father and like a son and a lover especially a lover, warm, and give him breath that melts my lips and softens my hair like steam from jungles. He should like warm dry days and going to lakes and fishing, but no—he should like reading to me more than fishing, and he should like cold winter days and ice-skating with me he could if you will allow me to suggest he could be brown-haired with a shadow of red and his cheeks rough with fresh young beard I can watch grow and he should—"

His eyes! They flashed as he spun, molten beacons still undefined. She approved of the roughed-in shape of his nose. His hair danced and gleamed, dark brown with a hint of red. Arms, fingers, legs, crawled with words. An ant's nest of dry ink *foots* crawled over his feet, tangling with *heels* and *ankles* and *toes*. *Arms* and *legs* fought for dominance up the branches and into the trunk, where *torso* and *breasts* and other words fought them back. The battle of words went on for minutes, fierce and hot.

Then—what had been a dream, a delusion, suddenly became magic. The words spun, blurred, became real flesh and real bone.

His breasts were firm and square and dark-nippled. The hair on his chest was dark and silky. He was still spinning. She cried out, staring at his groin.

Clothes?

"Yes!" she said. "I have no clothes for men."

A suit, a pink shirt with cuff links and pearl decorations.

His eyes blinked and his mouth opened and closed. His head drooped and a moan flew out like a whirled weight cut loose from a string.

"Stop!" she shouted. "Please stop, he's finished!"

The man stood on the dictionary, knees wobbly, threatening to topple. She jumped up from the floor to catch him, but he fell away from her and collapsed on the carpet beside the chair. The book lay kicked and sprawled by his feet, top pages wrinkled and torn.

Miss Coates stood over the man, hands fluttering at her breasts. He lay on his side, chest heaving, eyes closed. Her wide gaze darted from point to point on his body, lower lip held by tiny white teeth. After a few minutes, she was able to look away from the man. She squinted more closely at the dictionary, frowned, then bent to riffle through the pages. Every page was blank. The dictionary had given everything it had.

"I am naked," she told herself, stretching out her hands, using the realization to shock herself to sensibility. She went into the place where she slept to put on some clothes. Away from the man, she wondered what she would call him. He probably did not have a name, not a Christian name at any rate. It seemed appropriate to call him by a name like everyone else, even if she had raised him from paper and ink, from a dictionary.

"Webster," she said, nodding sharply at the obvious. "I'll call him Webster."

She returned to the living room and looked at the man. He seemed to be resting peacefully. How could she move him to a more comfortable place? The couch was too small to hold his ungainly body; he was very tall. She measured him with the tape from her sewing kit. Six feet two inches. His eyes were still shut; what color were they? She squatted beside him, face flushed, thinking thoughts she warned herself she must not think, not yet.

She wore her best dress, wrapped in smooth dark burgundy, against which her pale skin showed to best advantage. It was one o'clock in the morning, however, and she was exhausted. "You seem comfortable where you are," she told the man, who did not move. "I'll leave you on the floor."

Abigail Coates went into her bedroom to sleep. Tired as she was, she could not just close her eyes and drift off. She felt like shouting for joy and tears dampened the pillow and moistened her pepper hair.

In the darkness, *he* breathed. Dreaming, did he cause the words to flow through her drowsing thoughts? Or was it simply his breath filling the house with the odor of printer's ink?

In the night, *he* moved. Shifting an arm, a leg, sending atoms of words up like dust. His eyes flickered open, then closed. He moaned and was still again.

Abigail Coates's neck hair pricked with the first rays of morning and she awoke with a tiny shriek, little more than a high-pitched gasp. She rolled from her stomach onto her back and pulled up the sheet and bedspread.

Webster stood in the doorway, smiling. She could barely see him in the dawn light. Her eyelids were gummy with sleep. "Good morning, Regina," he said.

Regina Abigail Coates. Everyone had called her Abbie, when there had been friends to call her anything. No one had ever called her Regina.

"Regina," Webster repeated. "It reminds one of queens and Canadian coins."

How well he spoke. How full of class.

"Good morning," she said feebly. "How are you?" She suppressed an urge to giggle. *Why are you?* "How . . . do you feel?"

A ghost of a smile. He nodded politely, unwilling to complain. "As well as could be expected." He walked into her room and stopped at the foot of her bed, like a ghost her father had once told her about. "I'm well-dressed. Too much so, I think. It's uncomfortable."

Her heart was a little piston in her throat, pushing up the phlegm that threatened to choke her.

He walked around to her side of the bed, just as the ghost once had. "You brought me out. Why?"

She stared up at his bright green eyes, like drops of water raised from the depths of an ocean trench. His hand touched her shoulder, lingered on the strap of her nightgown. One finger slipped under the strap and tugged it up a quarter of an inch. "This is the distance between OP and OR," he murmured.

She felt the pressure of the cloth beneath her breast.

"Why?" he asked again. His breath sprinkled words over her face and hair. He shook his head and frowned. "Why do I feel so obliged to . . ." He pulled down the blind and closed the drapes and she heard the soft fall and hiss of rayon dropped onto a chair. In the darkness, a knee pressed the edge of her bed. A finger touched her neck and lips covered hers and parted them. A tongue explored.

He tasted of ink.

In the early morning hours, Regina Abigail Coates gave a tiny, squeezed-in scream.

WEBSTER SAT IN THE OVERSTUFFED CHAIR AND WATCHED HER LEAVE THE apartment. She shut the door and leaned against the wall, not knowing what to think or feel. "Of course," she whispered to herself, as if there were no wind or strength left in her. "Of course he doesn't like the sun."

She walked down the hallway, passed the doors of neighbors with whom she had not even a nodding acquaintance, and descended the stairs to the first floor. The street was filled with cars passing endlessly back and forth. Tugging out wrinkles from her dress, she stepped into the sunlight and faced the world, the new Regina Coates, *debutante*.

"*I know* what all you other women know," she said softly, with a shrill triumph. "All of you!" She looked up and noticed the sky, perhaps for the first time in twenty years; rich with clouds scattered across a bright blue sheet, demanding of her, *Breathe deeply*. She was part of the world, the real world.

Webster still sat in the chair when she returned with two bags of groceries. He was reading her Bible. Her face grew hot and she put down the bags and snatched it quickly from his hands. She could not face his querying stare, so she lay the book on a table, out of his reach, and said, "You don't want that."

"Why?" he asked. She picked up the bags again by their doubled and folded paper corners, taking them one in each hand into the kitchen and opening the old refrigerator to stock the perishables.

"When you're gone," Webster said, "I feel as if I fade. Am I real?"

She glanced up at the small mirror over the sink. Her shoulders twitched and a shudder ran up her back. *I am very far gone now*.

Regina brought in the afternoon newspaper and he held his hand out with a pleading expression; she handed it across, letting it waver for a moment above a patch of worn carpet, teasing him with a frightened, uncertain smile. He took it, spread it eagerly, and rubbed his fingers over the pages. He turned the big sheets slowly, seeming to absorb more than read. She fixed them both a snack but Webster refused to eat. He sat across from her at the small table, face placid, and for the moment, that was more than enough. She sat at her table, ate her small trimmed sandwich and drank her glass of grapefruit juice. Glancing at him from

all sides—he did not seem to mind, and it made his outline sharper—
she straightened up the tiny kitchen.

What was there to say to a man between morning and night? She
had expected that a man made of words would be full of conversation,
but Webster had very little experience. While all the right words existed
in him, they had yet to be connected. Or so she surmised. Still, his very
presence gratified her. He made her as real as she had made him.

He refused dinner, even declining to share a glass of wine with her
after (she had only one glass).

"I expect there should be some awkwardness in the early days," she
said. "Don't you? Quiet times when we can just sit and be with each
other. Like today."

Webster stood by the window, touched a finger to his lips, leaving a
smudge, and nodded. He agreed with most things she said.

"Let's go to bed," she suggested primly.

In the dark, when her solitude had again been sundered and her brow
was sprinkled with salty drops of exertion, he lay next to her, and—

He *moved*.

He *breathed*.

But he did not sleep.

Regina lay with her back to him, eyes wide, staring at the flowers on
the ancient wallpaper and a wide trapezoid of streetlight glare transfix-
ing a small table and its vase. She felt ten years—no, twenty!—sliding
away from her, and yet she couldn't tell him how she felt, didn't dare
turn and talk. The air was full of him. Full of words not her own, un-
organized, potential. She breathed in a million random thoughts, deep
or slight, complex or simple, eloquent or crude. Webster was becoming
a generator. Kept in the apartment, his substance was reacting with
itself; shut away from experience, he was making up his own patterns
and organizations, subtle as smoke.

Even lying still, waiting for the slight movement of air through the
window to cool him, he worked inside, and his breath filled the air with
potential.

Regina was tired and deliciously filled, and that satisfaction at least
was hers. She luxuriated in it and slept.

In the morning, she lay alone in the bed. She flung off the covers
and padded into the living room, pulling down her rucked-up nightgown, shivering against the morning chill. He stood by the window
again, naked, not caring if people on the streets looked up and saw. She
stood beside him and gently enclosed his upper arm with her fingers,
leaned her cheek against his shoulder, a motion that came so naturally
she surprised herself with her own grace. "What do you want?" she
asked.

"No," he said tightly. "The question is, what do *you* want?"

"I'll get us some breakfast. You *must* be hungry by now."

"No. I'm not. I don't know what I am or how to feel."

"I'll get some food," she continued obstinately, letting go of his arm. "Do you like milk?"

"No. I don't know."

"I don't want you to become ill."

"I don't get ill. I don't get hungry. You haven't answered my question."

"I love you," she said, with much less grace.

"You don't love me. You need me."

"Isn't that the same thing?"

"Not at all."

"Shall we get out today?" she asked airily, backing away, realizing she was doing a poor imitation of some actress in the movies. Bette Davis, her voice light, tripping.

"I can't. I don't get sick, I don't get hungry. I don't go places."

"You're being obtuse," she said petulantly, hating that tone, tears of frustration rising in her eyes. *How must I behave? Is he mine, or am I his?*

"*Obtuse, acute, equilateral, isosceles, vector, derivative, sequesential, psychintegrative, mersauvin powers* . . ." He shook his head, grinning sadly. "That's the future of mathematics for the next century. It becomes part of psychology. Did you know that? All numbers."

"Did you think that last night?" she asked. She cared nothing for mathematics; what could a man made of words know about numbers?

"Words mix in blood, my blood is made of words. . . . I can't stop thinking, even at night. Words are numbers, too. Signs and portents, measures and relations, variables and qualifiers."

"You're flesh," she said. "I gave you substance."

"You gave me existence, not substance."

She laughed harshly, caught herself, forced herself to be demure again. Taking his hand, she led him back to the chair. She kissed him on the cheek, a chaste gesture considering their state of undress, and said she would stay with him all day, to help him orient to his new world. "But tomorrow, we have to go out and buy you some more clothes."

"Clothes," he said softly, then smiled as if all was well. She leaned her head forward and smiled back, a fire radiating from her stomach through her legs and arms. With a soft step and a skip she danced on the carpet, hair swinging. Webster watched her, still smiling.

"And while you're out," he said, "bring back another dictionary."

"Of course. We can't use *that* one anymore, can we? The same kind?"

"Doesn't matter," he said, shaking his head.

The uncertainty of Webster's quiet afternoon hours became a dull, sugarcoated ache for Regina Coates. She tried to disregard her fears—that he found her a disappointment, inadequate; that he was weakening, fading—and reasoned that if she was his *mistress*, she could make him do or be whatever she wished. Unless she did not know what to wish. Could a man's behavior be wished for, or must it simply be experienced?

At night the words again poured into her, and she smiled in the dark, lying beside the warmth of the shadow that smelled of herself and printer's ink, wondering if they should be taking precautions. She was a late fader in the biological department and there was a certain risk. . . .

She grinned savagely, thinking about it. All she could imagine was a doctor holding up a damp bloody thing in his hands and saying, "Miss Coates, you're the proud mother of an eight-ounce . . . *Thesaurus*."

"Abridged?" she asked wickedly.

She shopped carefully, picking for him the best clothes she could afford, in a wide variety of styles, dipping into her savings to pay the bill. For herself she chose a new dress that showed her slim waist to advantage and hid her thin thighs. She looked girlish, summery. That was what she wanted. She purchased the dictionary and looked through gift shops for something else to give him. "Something witty and interesting for us to do." She settled on a game of Scrabble.

Webster was delighted with the dictionary. He regarded the game dubiously, but played it with her a few times. "An appetizer," he called it.

"Are you going to eat the book?" she asked, half in jest.

"No," he said.

She wondered why they didn't argue. She wondered why they didn't behave like a normal couple, ignoring her self-derisive inner voice crying out, *Normal!?*

My God, she said to herself after two weeks, staring at the hard edge of the small table in the kitchen. *Creating men from dictionaries, making love until the bed is damp—at* my *age! He still smells like ink. He doesn't sweat and he refuses to go outside. Nobody sees him but me. Me. Who am I to judge whether he's really there?*

What would happen to Webster if I were to take a gun and put a hole in his stomach, above the navel? A man with a navel, not born of woman, is an abomination—isn't he?

If he spoke to her simply and without emotion just once more, or twice, she thought she would try that experiment and see.

She bought a gun, furtive as a mouse but a respectable citizen, for protection, a small gray pistol, and hid it in her drawer. She thought better of it a few hours after, shuddered in disgust, and removed the bullets, flinging them out of the apartment's rear window into the dead garden in the narrow courtyard below.

On the last day, when she went shopping, she carried the empty gun with her so he wouldn't find it—although he showed no interest in snooping, which would at least have been a sign of caring. The bulge in her purse made her nervous.

She did not return until dinnertime. *The apartment is not my own. It oppresses me. He oppresses me.* She walked quietly through the front door, saw the living room was empty, and heard a small sound from behind the closed bedroom door. The light flop of something stiff hitting the floor.

"Webster?" Silence. She knocked lightly on the door. "Are you ready to talk?"

No reply.

He makes me mad when he doesn't answer. I could scare him, force him to react to me in some way. She took out the pistol, fumbling it, pressing its grip into her palm. It felt heavy and formidable.

The door was locked. Outraged that she should be closed out of her own bedroom, she carried the revolver into the kitchen and found a hairpin in a drawer, the same she had used months before when the door had locked accidentally. She knelt before the door and fumbled, teeth clenched, lips tight.

With a small cry, she pushed the door open.

Webster sat with legs crossed on the floor beside the bed. Before him lay the new dictionary, opened almost to the back. "Not now," he said, tracing a finger along the rows of words.

Regina's mouth dropped open. "What are you looking at?" she asked, tightening her fingers on the pistol. She stepped closer, looked down, and saw that he was already up to VW.

"I don't know," he said. He found the word he was looking for, reached into his mouth with one finger and scraped his inner cheek. Smeared the wetness on the page.

"No," she said. Then, "Why . . . ?"

There were tears on his cheeks. The man of dry ink was crying. Somehow that made her furious.

"I'm not even a human being," he said.

She hated him, hated this weakness; she had never liked weak men. He adjusted his lotus position and gripped the edges of the dictionary with both hands. "Why can't you find a human being for yourself?" he asked, looking up at her. "I'm nothing but a dream."

She held the pistol firmly to her side. "What are you doing?"

"Need," he said. "That's all I am. Your hunger and your need. Do you know what I'm good for, what I can do? No. You'd be afraid if you did. You keep me here like some commodity."

"I wanted you to go out with me," she said tightly.

"What has the world done to you that you'd want to create me?"

"You're going to make a woman from that thing, aren't you?" she asked. "Nothing worthwhile has ever happened to me. Everything gets taken away the moment I . . ."

"Need," he said, raising his hands over the book. "You cannot love unless you need. You cannot love the real. You must change the thing you love to please yourself, and damn anyone if he should question what hides within you."

"You *thing*," she breathed, lips curled back. Webster looked at her and at the barrel of the gun she now pointed at him and laughed.

"You don't need that," he told her. "You don't need something real to kill a dream. All you need is a little sunlight."

She lowered the gun, dropped it with a thud on the floor, then lifted her eyebrows and smiled around gritted teeth. She pointed the index finger of her left hand and her face went lax. Listlessly, she whispered, "Bang."

The smell of printer's ink became briefly more intense, then faded on the warm breeze passing through the apartment. She kicked the dictionary shut.

How lonely it was going to be, in the dark with only her own sweat.

Introduction to "Through Road, No Whither"

Back in the early 1980s, John Carr was working for Jerry Pournelle, helping with Jerry's editorial duties on a number of paperback anthologies. Jerry was working a half-dozen enterprises at once—writing excellent bestselling fiction with Larry Niven, consulting with the Reagan administration, and later the Bush Sr. administration, on space business and space defense policy, and writing a very influential column on personal computing. John Carr served Jerry as a general factotum. Through John, I learned that Jerry was buying stories for an anthology to be published by Jim Baen and called *Far Frontier*.

Now, let's backtrack for a moment. James Patrick Baen had been editor of *Galaxy* magazine for a number of years, and had purchased two of my stories. (See the introduction to "The Venging.") He later started Baen Books, a successful publishing enterprise to this day. Jim and Jerry were good friends, simpatico in both politics and business—conservative and ambitious, respectively—and they roped in anybody who seemed likely to be able to deliver interesting ideas. John sometimes did the roping.

Anger at the cruelties of history is often a useless emotion, but "Through Road, No Whither" seems to have struck a cord. It's been reprinted a number of times—most notably, in Gregory Benford's and Marty Greenberg's anthology, *Alternate Hitlers*.

Perhaps justice knows no boundaries. Engage in evil and depravity, and a force or presence might enact its vengeance unto the nth generation—across all time, and all timelines.

Needless to say, this contradicts the conclusions I've drawn in "Dead Run" and in my novels *Queen of Angels* and *Slant*. I'm not much for punishment as a way of adjusting our bent and broken emotions. But sometimes, the sheer immensity of historical depravity overcomes even my gentle sensibilities.

Through Road, No Whither
Far Frontier, John Carr, Jerry Pournelle, 1985

The long black Mercedes rumbled out of the fog on the road south from Dijon, moisture running in cold trickles across its windshield. Horst von Ranke carefully read the maps spread on his lap, eyeglasses perched low on his nose, while Waffen Schutzstaffel Oberleutnant Albert Fischer drove. "Thirty-five kilometers," Von Ranke said under his breath. "No more."

"We are lost," Fischer said. "We've already come thirty-six."

"Not quite that many. We should be there any minute now."

Fischer nodded and then shook his head. His high cheekbones and long, sharp nose only accentuated the black uniform with silver death's heads on the high, tight collar. Von Ranke wore a broad-striped gray suit; he was an undersecretary in the Propaganda Ministry. They might have been brothers, yet one had grown up in Czechoslovakia, the other in the Ruhr; one was the son of a brewer, the other of a coal-miner. They had met and become close friends in Paris, two years before, and were now sightseeing on a three-day pass in the countryside.

"Wait," Von Ranke said, peering through the drops on the side window. "Stop."

Fischer braked the car and looked in the direction of Von Ranke's long finger. Near the roadside, beyond a copse of young trees, was a low, thatch-roofed house with dirty gray walls, almost hidden by the fog.

"Looks empty," Von Ranke said.

"It is occupied; look at the smoke," Fischer said. "Perhaps somebody can tell us where we are."

They pulled the car over and got out, Von Ranke leading the way across a mud path littered with wet straw. The hut looked even dirtier close-up. Smoke curled in a darker brown-gray twist from a hole in the peak of the thatch. Fischer nodded at his friend and they cautiously approached. Over the crude wooden door, letters wobbled unevenly in some alphabet neither knew, and between them they spoke nine languages. "Could that be Rom?" Fischer asked, frowning. "It does look familiar—like Slavic Rom."

"Gypsies? Romany don't live in huts like this, and besides, I thought they were rounded up long ago."

"That's what it looks like," Von Ranke repeated. "Still, maybe we can share some language, if only French."

He knocked on the door. After a long pause, he knocked again, and the door opened before his knuckles made the final rap. A woman too old to be alive stuck her long, wood-colored nose through the crack and peered at them with one good eye. The other was wrapped in a sunken caul of flesh. The hand that gripped the door edge was filthy, its nails long and black. Her toothless mouth cracked into a wrinkled grin. "Good evening," she said in perfect, even elegant, German. "What can I do for you?"

"We need to know if we are on the road to Dôle," Von Ranke said, controlling his revulsion.

"Then you're asking the wrong guide," the old woman said. Her hand withdrew and the door started to close. Fischer kicked out and pushed her back. The door swung open and began to lean on worn-out leather hinges.

"You do not treat us with the proper respect," he said. "What do you mean, 'the wrong guide'? What kind of guide are you?"

"*So strong,*" the old woman crooned, wrapping her hands in front of her withered chest and backing into the gloom. She wore ageless gray rags. Tattered knit sleeves extended to her wrists.

"Answer me!" Fischer said, advancing despite the strong odor of urine and decay in the hut.

"The maps I know are not for this land," she sang, doddering before a cold and empty hearth.

"She's crazy," Von Ranke said. "Let the local authorities take care of her. Let's be off." But a wild look was in Fischer's eyes. So much filth, so much disarray, and impudence as well; these things made him angry.

"What maps *do* you know, crazy woman?" he demanded.

"Maps in time," the old woman said. She let her hands fall to her sides and lowered her head as if, in admitting her specialty, she were suddenly humble.

"Then tell us where we are," Fischer sneered.

"Come," Von Ranke said, but he knew it was too late. There would be an end, but it would be on his friend's terms, and it might not be pleasant.

"On a through road, no whither," the old woman said.

"What?" Fischer towered over her. She stared up as if at some prodigal son, her gums shining spittle.

"If you wish a reading, sit," she said, indicating a low table and three dilapidated cane and leather chairs. Fischer glanced at her, then at the table.

"Very well," he said, suddenly and falsely obsequious. Another game, Von Ranke realized. Cat and mouse.

Fischer pulled out a chair for his friend and sat across from the old woman. "Put your hands on the table, palms down, both of them, both of you," she said. They did so. She lay her ear to the table as if listening, eyes going to the beams of light sneaking through the thatch. "Arrogance," she said. Fischer did not react.

"A road going into fire and death," she said. "Your cities in flame, your women and children shriveling to black dolls in the heat of their burning homes. The camps are found and you stand accused of hideous crimes. Many are tried and hung. Your nation is disgraced, your cause abhorred." Now a peculiar gleam appeared in her eye. "Only psychotics will believe in you, the lowest of the low. Your nation will be divided between your enemies. All will be lost."

Fischer's smile did not waver. He pulled a coin from his pocket and threw it down before the woman, then pushed the chair back and stood. "Your maps are as crooked as your chin, you filthy old hag," he said. "Let's go."

"I've been suggesting that," Von Ranke said. Fischer made no move to leave. Von Ranke tugged on his arm but the SS Oberleutnant shrugged free of his friend's grip.

"Gypsies are few, now, hag," he said. "Soon to be fewer by one." Von Ranke managed to urge him just outside the door. The woman followed and shaded her eye against the misty light.

"I am no Gypsy," she said. "You do not even recognize the words?" She pointed at the letters above the door.

Fischer squinted, and the light of recognition dawned in his eyes. "Yes," he said. "Yes, I do, now. A dead language."

"What are they?" Von Ranke asked, uneasy.

"Hebrew, I think," Fischer said. "She is a Jewess."

"No!" the woman cackled. "I am no Jew."

Von Ranke thought the woman looked younger now, or at least stronger, and his unease deepened.

"I do not care what you are," Fischer said quietly. "I only wish we were in my father's time." He took a step toward her. She did not retreat. Her face became almost youthfully bland, and her bad eye seemed to fill in. "Then, there would be no regulations, no rules—I could take this pistol"—he tapped his holster—"and apply it to your filthy Kike head, and perhaps kill the last Jew in Europe." He unstrapped the holster. The woman straightened in the dark hut, as if drawing strength from Fischer's abusive tongue. Von Ranke feared for his friend. Rashness could get them in trouble.

"This is not our fathers' time," he reminded Fischer.

Fischer paused, pistol in hand, his finger curling around the trigger. "Filthy, smelly old woman." She did not look nearly as old as when they had entered the hut, perhaps not old at all, and certainly not bent and crippled. "You have had a very narrow escape this afternoon."

"You have no idea who I am," the woman half sang, half moaned.

"*Scheisse*," Fischer spat. "Now we will go to report you and your hovel."

"I am the scourge," she breathed. Her breath smelled like burning stone even three strides away. She backed into the hut but her voice did not diminish. "I am the visible hand, the pillar of cloud by day and the pillar of fire by night."

Fischer laughed. "You're right," he said to Von Ranke. "She isn't worth our trouble." He turned and stamped out the door. Von Ranke followed with one last glance over his shoulder into the gloom, the decay. *No one has lived in this hut for years,* he thought. Her shadow was gray and indefinite before the ancient stone hearth, behind the leaning, dust-covered table.

In the car, Von Ranke sighed. "You *do* tend to arrogance, you know that?"

Fischer grinned and shook his head. "You drive, old friend. *I'll* look at the maps." Von Ranke ramped up the Mercedes' turbine until its whine was high and steady and its exhaust cut a swirling hole in the fog. "No wonder we're lost," Fischer said. He shook out the Pan-Deutschland map peevishly. "This is five years old—1979."

"We'll find our way," Von Ranke said.

From the door of the hut, the old woman watched, head bobbing. "I am not a Jew," she said, "but I loved them, too, oh, yes. I loved all my children."

She raised her hand as the long black car roared into the fog. "I will bring you to justice, wherever and whenever you live, and all your children, and their children's children," she said. She dropped a twist of smoke from her elbow to the dirt floor and waggled her finger. The smoke danced and drew black figures in the dirt. "Into the time of your fathers." The fog grew thinner. She brought her arm down, and forty years melted away with the mist.

High above, a deeper growl descended on the road. A wide-winged shadow passed over the hut, wings flashing stars, black and white invasion stripes, and cannon fire.

"Hungry bird," the shapeless figure said. "Time to feed."

Introduction to "Tangents"

John Carr (see the introduction to "Through Road, No Whither") was also instrumental in getting me to write "Tangents." He was working as an editor for a computer magazine and persuaded them that they needed to publish science fiction. He commissioned a number of authors to write mathematically or cybernetically based stories. The magazine ended its experiment with fiction before my story was published.

Once again, I sold the story to Ellen Datlow at *Omni*, for much more money. Ellen has bought more of my short fiction than any other editor.

ALAN TURING WAS AN IMMENSELY INFLUENTIAL FIGURE IN MATHEMATICS AND COMPUTING, a man whose mind swiftly and naturally understood complex theoretical issues. His notion of a Turing Machine, a pure and ultimately simplified computational system, helped define and propel the nascent field of computers. During World War II, he worked in cryptography for the British Foreign Office, and was one of the most important scientific figures to help win the war for the Allies.

After the war, he was persecuted and prosecuted by the British government as a homosexual. His end was tragic and mean, unforgivable under the circumstances, a national disgrace.

"Tangents" went on to win a Hugo and a Nebula award, my second pairing. I was unable to pick up the Hugo award at the World Science Fiction Convention in Atlanta in 1986 because Astrid was perilously close to giving birth to our son, Erik.

Some thirteen years later, Dan Bloch sent me a letter correcting some of the geometry in the story. Thanks!

Neal Stephenson's *Cryptonomicon* uses the historical Turing as a character. It's an excellent novel.

This one is for Alan Turing.

Tangents
Omni, Ellen Datlow, 1986

The nut-brown boy stood in the California field, his Asian face shadowed by a hardhat, his short stocky frame clothed in a T-shirt and a pair of brown shorts. He squinted across the hip-high grass at the spraddled old two-story ranch house, whistling a few bars from a Haydn piano sonata.

Out of the upper floor of the house came a man's high, frustrated "Bloody hell!" and the sound of a fist slamming on a solid surface. Silence for a minute. Then, more softly, a woman's question, "Not going well?"

"No. I'm swimming in it, but I don't see it."

"The encryption?" the woman asked timidly.

"The tesseract. If it doesn't gel, it isn't aspic."

The boy squatted in the grass and listened.

"And?" the woman encouraged.

"Ah, Lauren, it's still cold broth."

The boy lay back in the grass. He had crept over the split-rail and brick-pylon fence from the new housing project across the road. School was out for the summer and his mother—adoptive mother—did not like him around the house all day. Or at all.

Behind his closed eyes, a huge piano keyboard appeared, with him dancing on the keys. He loved music.

He opened his eyes and saw a thin, graying lady in a tweed suit leaning over him, staring. "You're on private land," she said, brows knit.

He scrambled up and brushed grass from his pants. "Sorry."

"I thought I saw someone out here. What's your name?"

"Pal," he replied.

"Is that a name?" she asked querulously.

"Pal Tremont. It's not my real name. I'm Korean."

"Then what's your real name?"

"My folks told me not to use it any more. I'm adopted. Who are you?"

The gray woman looked him up and down. "My name is Lauren Davies," she said. "You live near here?"

He pointed across the fields at the close-packed tract homes.

"I sold the land for those homes ten years ago," she said. She seemed to be considering something. "I don't normally enjoy children trespassing."

"Sorry," Pal said.

"Have you had lunch?"

"No."

"Will a grilled cheese sandwich do?"

He squinted at her and nodded.

In the broad, red-brick and tile kitchen, sitting at an oak table with his shoulders barely rising above the top, he ate the slightly charred sandwich and watched Lauren Davies watching him.

"I'm trying to write about a child," she said. "It's difficult. I'm a spinster and I don't know children well."

"You're a writer?" he asked, taking a swallow of milk.

She sniffed. "Not that anyone would know."

"Is that your brother, upstairs?"

"No," she said. "That's Peter. We've been living together for twenty years."

"But you said you're a spinster . . . isn't that someone who's never married, or never loved?" Pal asked.

"Never married. And never you mind. Peter's relationship to me is none of your concern." She placed a bowl of soup and a tuna salad sandwich on a lacquer tray. "His lunch," she said. Without being asked, Pal trailed up the stairs after her.

"This is where Peter works," Lauren explained. Pal stood in the doorway, eyes wide. The room was filled with electronics gear, computer terminals and bookcases with odd cardboard sculptures sharing each shelf with books and circuit boards. She rested the tray precariously on a pile of floppy disks atop a rolling cart.

"Time for a break," she told a thin man seated with his back toward them.

The man turned around on his swivel chair, glanced briefly at Pal and the tray and shook his head. The hair on top of his head was a rich, glossy black; on the close-cut sides, the color changed abruptly to a startling white. He had a small thin nose and a large green eyes. On the desk before him was a high-resolution computer monitor. "We haven't been introduced," he said, pointing to Pal.

"This is Pal Tremont, a neighborhood visitor. Pal, this is Peter Tuthy. Pal's going to help me with that character we discussed this morning."

Pal looked at the monitor curiously. Red and green lines shadowed each other through some incomprehensible transformation on the screen, then repeated.

"What's a 'tesseract'?" Pal asked, remembering what he had heard as he stood in the field.

"It's a four-dimensional analog of a cube. I'm trying to find a way to teach myself to see it in my mind's eye," Tuthy said. "Have you ever tried that?"

"No," Pal admitted.

"Here," Tuthy said, handing him the spectacles. "As in the movies."

Pal donned the spectacles and stared at the screen. "So?" he said. "It folds and unfolds. It's pretty—it sticks out at you, and then it goes away." He looked around the workshop. "Oh, wow!" The boy ran to a yard-long black music keyboard propped in one corner. "A Tronclavier! With all the switches! My mother had me take piano lessons, but I'd rather play this. Can you play it?"

"I toy with it," Tuthy said, exasperated. "I toy with all sorts of electronic things. But what did you see on the screen?" He glanced up at Lauren, blinking. "I'll eat the food, I'll eat it. Now please don't bother us."

"He's supposed to be helping *me*," Lauren complained.

Peter smiled at her. "Yes, of course. I'll send him downstairs in a little while."

When Pal descended an hour later, he came into the kitchen to thank Lauren for lunch. "Peter's a real flake," he said confidentially. "He's trying to learn to see certain directions."

"I know," Lauren said, sighing.

"I'm going home now," Pal said. "I'll be back, though . . . if it's all right with you. Peter invited me."

"I'm sure it will be fine," Lauren said dubiously.

"He's going to let me learn the Tronclavier." With that, Pal smiled radiantly and exited through the kitchen door, just as he had come in.

When she retrieved the tray, she found Peter leaning back in his chair, eyes closed. The figures on the screen were still folding and unfolding.

"What about Hockrum's work?" she asked.

"I'm on it," Peter replied, eyes still closed.

LAUREN CALLED PAL'S FOSTER MOTHER ON THE SECOND DAY TO APPRISE THEM of their son's location, and the woman assured her it was quite all right. "Sometimes he's a little pest. Send him home if he causes trouble . . . but not right away! Give me a rest," she said, then laughed nervously.

Lauren drew her lips together tightly, thanked the woman and hung up.

Peter and the boy had come downstairs to sit in the kitchen, filling up paper with line-drawings. "Peter's teaching me how to use his program," Pal said.

"Did you know," Tuthy said, assuming his highest Cambridge professorial tone, "that a cube, intersecting a flat plane, can be cut through a number of geometrically different cross-sections?"

Pal squinted at the sketch Tuthy had made. "Sure," he said.

"If shoved through the plane the cube can appear, to a two-dimensional creature living on the plane—let's call him a 'Flatlander'—to be either a triangle, a rectangle, a trapezoid, a rhombus, a square, even a hexagon or a pentagon, depending on the depth of penetration and the angle of incidence. If the two-dimensional being observes the cube being pushed through all the way, what he sees is one or more of these objects growing larger, changing shape suddenly, shrinking, and disappearing."

"Sure," Pal said, tapping his sneakered toe. "That's easy. Like in that book you showed me."

"And a sphere pushed through a plane would appear, to the hapless flatlander, first as an 'invisible' point (the two-dimensional surface touching the sphere, tangential), then as a circle. The circle would grow in size, then shrink back to a point and disappear again." He sketched two-dimensional stick figures looking in awe at such an intrusion.

"Got it," Pal said. "Can I play with the Tronclavier now?"

"In a moment. Be patient. So what would a tesseract look like, coming into our three-dimensional space? Remember the program, now . . . the pictures on the monitor."

Pal looked up at the ceiling. "I don't know," he said, seeming bored.

"Try to think," Tuthy urged him.

"It would . . ." Pal held his hands out to shape an angular object. "It would like like one of those Egyptian things, but with three sides . . . or like a box. It would look like a weird-shaped box, too, not square. And If *you* were to fall through a flatland . . ."

"Yes, that would look very funny," Peter acknowledged with a smile. "Cross-sections of arms and legs and body, all covered with skin . . ."

"And a head!" Pal enthused. "With eyes and a nose."

The doorbell rang. Pal jumped off the kitchen chair. "Is that my Mom?" he asked, looking worried.

"I don't think so," Lauren said. "More likely it's Hockrum." She went to the front door to answer. She returned a moment later with a small, pale man behind her. Tuthy stood and shook the man's hand. "Pal Tremont, this is Irving Hockrum," he introduced, waving his hand between them. Hockrum glanced at Pal and blinked a long, not-very-mammalian blink.

"How's the work coming?" he asked Tuthy.

"It's finished," Tuthy said. "It's upstairs. Looks like your savants are barking up the wrong logic tree." He retrieved a folder of papers and print-outs and handed them to Hockrum.

Hockrum leafed through the print-outs. "I can't say this makes me happy. Still, I can't find fault. Looks like the work is up to your usual brilliant standards. Here's your check." He handed Tuthy an envelope. "I just wish you'd had it to us sooner. It would have saved me some grief—and the company quite a bit of money."

"Sorry," Tuthy said.

"Now I have an important bit of work for you . . ." And Hockrum outlined another problem. Tuthy thought it over for several minutes and shook his head.

"Most difficult, Irving. Pioneering work there. Take at least a month to see if it's even feasible."

"That's all I need to know for now—whether it's feasible. A lot's riding on this, Peter." Hockrum clasped his hands together in front of him, looking even more pale and worn than when he had entered the kitchen. "You'll let me know soon?"

"I'll get right on it," Tuthy said.

"Protégé?" he asked, pointing to Pal. There was a speculative expression on his face, not quite a leer.

"No, a young friend. He's interested in music," Tuthy said. "Damned good at Mozart, in fact."

"I help with his tesseracts," Pal asserted.

"I hope you don't interrupt Peter's work. Peter's work is important."

Pal shook his head solemnly. "Good," Hockrum said, and then left the house with the folder under his arm.

Tuthy returned to his office, Pal in train. Lauren tried to work in the kitchen, sitting with fountain pen and pad of paper, but the words wouldn't come. Hockrum always worried her. She climbed the stairs and stood in the open doorway of the office. She often did that; her presence did not disturb Tuthy, who could work under all sorts of adverse conditions.

"Who was that man?" Pal was asking Tuthy.

"I work for him." Tuthy said. "He's employed by a big electronics firm. He loans me most of the equipment I use. The computers, the high-resolution monitors. He brings me problems and then takes my solutions or answers back to his bosses and claims he did the work."

"That sounds stupid," Pal said. "What kind of problems?"

"Codes, encryptions. Computer security. That was my expertise, once."

"You mean, like fencerail, that sort of thing?" Pal asked, face brightening. "We learned some of that in school."

"Much more complicated, I'm afraid," Tuthy said, grinning. "Did you ever hear of the German 'Enigma,' or the 'Ultra' project?"

Pal shook his head.

"I thought not. Don't worry about it. Let's try another figure on the screen now." He called up another routine on the four-space program and sat Pal before the screen. "So what would a hypersphere look like if it intruded into our space?"

Pal thought a moment. "Kind of weird," he said.

"Not really. You've been watching the visualizations."

"Oh, in *our* space. That's easy. It just looks like a balloon, blowing up from nothing and then shrinking again. It's harder to see what a hypersphere looks like when it's real. Reft of us, I mean."

"Reft?" Tuthy said.

"Sure. Reft and light. Dup and owwen. Whatever the directions are called."

Tuthy stared at the boy. Neither of them had noticed Lauren in the doorway. "The proper terms are *ana* and *kata*," Tuthy said. "What does it look like?"

Pal gestured, making two wide swings with his arms. "It's like a ball and it's like a horseshoe, depending on how you look at it. Like a balloon stung by bees, I guess, but it's smooth all over, not lumpy."

Tuthy continued to stare, then asked quietly, "You actually see it?"

"Sure," Pal said. "Isn't that what your program is supposed to do—make you see things like that?"

Tuthy nodded, flabbergasted.

"Can I play the Tronclavier now?"

Lauren backed out of the doorway. She felt she had eavesdropped on something momentous, but beyond her. Tuthy came downstairs an hour later, leaving Pal to pick out Telemann on the synthesizer. He sat at the kitchen table with her. "The program works," he said. "It doesn't work for me, but it works for him. I've just been showing him reverse-shadow figures. He caught on right away, and then he went off and played Haydn. He's gone through all my sheet music. The kid's a genius."

"Musical, you mean?"

He glanced directly at her and frowned. "Yes, I suppose he's remarkable at that, too. But spacial relations—coordinates and motion in higher dimensions. . . . Did you know that if you take a three-dimensional object and rotate it in the fourth dimension, it will come back with left-right reversed? So if I were to take my hand—" he held up his right hand—"and lift it *dup*—" he enunciated the word clearly, *dup*—"or drop it *owwen*, it would come back like this?" He held his left hand over his right, balled the right up into a fist and snuck it away behind his back.

"I didn't know that," Lauren said. "What are *dup* and *owwen*?"

"That's what Pal calls movement along the fourth dimension. *Ana* and *Kata* to purists. Like up and down to a flatlander, who only comprehends left and right, back and forth." She thought about the hands for a moment. "I still can't see it," she said.

"I've tried, but neither can I," Tuthy admitted. "Our circuits are just too hard-wired, I suppose."

Upstairs, Pal had switched the Tronclavier to a cathedral organ and steel guitar combination and was playing variations on Pergolesi.

"Are you going to keep working for Hockrum?" Lauren asked. Tuthy didn't seem to hear her.

"It's remarkable," he murmured. "The boy just walked in here. You brought him in by accident. Remarkable."

"CAN YOU SHOW ME THE DIRECTION, POINT IT OUT TO ME?" TUTHY ASKED the boy three days later.

"None of my muscles move that way," the boy replied. "I can see it, in my head, but . . ."

"What is it like, seeing that direction?"

Pal squinted. "It's a lot bigger. We're sort of stacked up with other places. It makes me feel lonely."

"Why?"

"Because I'm stuck here. Nobody out there pays any attention to us."

Tuthy's mouth worked. "I thought you were just intuiting those directions in your head. Are you telling me . . . you're actually *seeing* out there?"

"Yeah. There's people out there, too. Well, not people, exactly. But it isn't my eyes that see them. Eyes are like muscles—they can't point those ways. But the head—the brain, I guess—can."

"Bloody hell," Tuthy said. He blinked and recovered. "Excuse me. That's rude. Can you show me the people . . . on the screen?"

"Shadows, like we were talking about," Pal said.

"Fine. Then draw the shadows for me."

Pal sat down before the terminal, fingers pausing over the keys. "I can show you, but you have to help me with something."

"Help you with what?"

"I'd like to play music for them . . . out there. So they'll notice us."

"The people?"

"Yeah. They really look weird. They stand on us, sort of. They have hooks in our world. But they're tall . . . high dup. They don't notice us because we're so small, compared to them."

"Lord, Pal, I haven't the slightest idea how we'd send music out to them . . . I'm not even sure I believe they exist."

"I'm not lying," Pal said, eyes narrowing. He turned his chair to face a mouse on a black ruled pad and began sketching shapes on the monitor. "Remember, these are just shadows of what they look like. Next I'll draw the dup and owwen lines to connect the shadows."

The boy shaded the shapes he drew to make them look solid, smiling at his trick but explaining it was necessary because the projection of a four-dimensional in normal space was, of course, three-dimensional.

"They look like you take the plants in a garden, flowers and such, and giving them lots of arms and fingers . . . and it's kind of like seeing things in an aquarium," Pal explained.

After a time, Tuthy suspended his disbelief and stared in open-mouthed wonder at what the boy was re-creating on the monitor.

"I THINK YOU'RE WASTING YOUR TIME, THAT'S WHAT I THINK," HOCKRUM said. "I needed that feasibility judgment by today." He paced around the living room before falling as heavily as his light frame permitted into a chair.

"I *have* been distracted," Tuthy admitted.

"By that boy?"

"Yes, actually. Quite a talented fellow—"

"Listen, this is going to mean a lot of trouble for me. I guaranteed the study would be finished by today. It'll make me look bad." Hockrum screwed his face up in frustration. "What in hell are you doing with that boy?"

"Teaching him, actually. Or rather, he's teaching me. Right now, we're building a four-dimensional cone, part of a speaker system. The cone is three-dimensional, the material part, but the magnetic field forms a fourth-dimensional extension—"

"Do you ever think how it looks, Peter?" Hockrum asked.

"It looks very strange on the monitor, I grant you—"

"I'm talking about you and the boy."

Tuthy's bright, interested expression fell into long, deep-lined dismay. "I don't know what you mean."

"I know a lot about you, Peter. Where you come from, why you had to leave. . . . It just doesn't look good."

Tuthy's face flushed crimson.

"Keep him away from here," Hockrum advised.

Tuthy stood. "I want you out of this house," he said quietly. "Our relationship is at an end."

"I swear," Hockrum said, his voice low and calm, staring up at Tuthy from under his brows, "I'll tell the boy's parents. Do you think they'd want their kid hanging around an old . . . pardon the expression . . . queer? I'll tell them if you don't get the feasibility judgment made. I think you can do it by the end of this week—two days. Don't you?"

"No, I don't think so," Tuthy said. "Please leave."

"I know you're here illegally. There's no record of you entering the country. With the problems you had in England, you're certainly not a desirable alien. I'll pass word to the INS. You'll be deported."

"There isn't time to do the work," Tuthy said.

"Make time. Instead of 'educating' that kid."

"Get out of here."

"Two days, Peter."

OVER DINNER THAT EVENING, TUTHY EXPLAINED TO LAUREN THE EXCHANGE he had had with Hockrum. "He thinks I'm buggering Pal. Unspeakable bastard. I will never work for him again."

"I'd better talk to a lawyer, then," Lauren said. "You're sure you can't make him . . . happy, stop all this trouble?"

"I could solve his little problem for him in just a few hours. But I don't want to see him or speak to him again."

"He'll take your equipment away."

Tuthy blinked and waved one hand through the air helplessly. "Then we'll just have to work fast, won't we? Ah, Lauren, you were a fool to bring me here. You should have left me to rot."

"They ignored everything you did for them," Lauren said bitterly. "You saved their hides during the war, and then. . . . They would have shut you up in prison." She stared through the kitchen window at the overcast sky and woods outside.

THE CONE LAY ON THE TABLE NEAR THE WINDOW, BATHED IN MORNING SUN, connected to both the mini-computer and the Tronclavier. Pal arranged the score he had composed on a music stand before the synthesizer. "It's like Bach," he said, "but it'll play better for them. It has a kind of over-rhythm that I'll play on the dup part of the speaker."

"Why are we doing this, Pal?" Tuthy asked as the boy sat down to the keyboard.

"You don't belong here, really, do you, Peter?" Pal asked. Tuthy stared at him.

"I mean, Miss Davies and you get along okay—but do you belong *here*, now?"

"What makes you think I don't belong?"

"I read some books in the school library. About the war and everything. I looked up 'Enigma' and 'Ultra.' I found a fellow named Peter Thornton. His picture looked like you. The books made him seem like a hero."

Tuthy smiled wanly.

"But there was this note in one book. You disappeared in 1965. You were being prosecuted for something. They didn't say what you were being prosecuted for."

"I'm a homosexual," Tuthy said quietly.

"Oh. So what?"

"Lauren and I met in England in 1964. We became good friends. They were going to put me in prison, Pal. She smuggled me into the U.S. through Canada."

"But you said you're a homosexual. They don't like women."

"Not at all true, Pal. Lauren and I like each other very much. We could talk. She told me about her dreams of being a writer, and I talked to her about mathematics, and about the war. I nearly died during the war."

"Why? Were you wounded?"

"No. I worked too hard. I burned myself out and had a nervous breakdown. My lover . . . a man . . . kept me alive throughout the forties. Things were bad in England after the war. But he died in 1963. His parents came in to settle the estate, and when I contested the settlement in court, I was arrested. So I suppose you're right, Pal. I don't really belong here."

"I don't, either. My folks don't care much. I don't have too many friends. I wasn't even born here, and I don't know anything about Korea."

"Play," Tuthy said, his face stony. "Let's see if they'll listen."

"Oh, they'll listen," Pal said. "It's like the way they talk to each other."

The boy ran his fingers over the keys on the Tronclavier. The cone, connected with the keyboard through the mini-computer, vibrated tinnily.

For an hour, Pal paged back and forth through his composition, repeating and trying variations. Tuthy sat in a corner, chin in hand, listening to the mousy squeaks and squeals produced by the cone. *How much more difficult to interpret a four-dimensional sound,* he thought. *Not even visual clues . . .*

Finally the boy stopped and wrung his hands, then stretched his arms. "They must have heard. We'll just have to wait and see." He switched the Tronclavier to automatic playback and pushed the chair away from the keyboard.

Pal stayed until dusk, then reluctantly went home. Tuthy sat in the office until midnight, listening to the tinny sounds issuing from the speaker cone.

All night long, the Tronclavier played through its pre-programmed selection of Pal's compositions. Tuthy lay in bed in his room, two doors down from Lauren's room, watching a shaft of moonlight slide across the wall. *How far would a four-dimensional being have to travel to get here?*

How far have I come to get here?

Without realizing he was asleep, he dreamed, and in his dream a wavering image of Pal appeared, gesturing with both arms as if swimming, eyes wide. *I'm okay,* the boy said without moving his lips. *Don't worry about me . . . I'm okay. I've been back to Korea to see what it's like. It's not bad, but I like it better here . . .*

Tuthy awoke sweating. The moon had gone down and the room was pitch-black. In the office, the hyper-cone continued its distant, mouse-squeak broadcast.

PAL RETURNED EARLY IN THE MORNING, REPETITIVELY WHISTLING A FEW BARS from Mozart's Fourth Violin Concerto. Lauren let him in and he joined Tuthy upstairs. Tuthy sat before the monitor, replaying Pal's sketch of the four-dimensional beings.

"Do you see anything?" he asked the boy.

Pal nodded. "They're coming closer. They're interested. Maybe we should get things ready, you know . . . be prepared." He squinted. "Did you ever think what a four-dimensional footprint would look like?"

Tuthy considered for a moment. "That would be most interesting," he said. "It would be solid."

On the first floor, Lauren screamed.

Pal and Tuthy almost tumbled over each other getting downstairs. Lauren stood in the living room with her arms crossed above her bosom, one hand clamped over her mouth. The first intrusion had taken out a section of the living room floor and the east wall.

"Really clumsy," Pal said. "One of them must have bumped it."

"The music," Tuthy said.

"What in HELL is going on?" Lauren demanded, her voice starting as a screech and ending as a roar.

"Better turn the music off," Tuthy elaborated.

"Why?" Pal asked, face wreathed in an excited smile.

"Maybe they don't like it."

A bright filmy blue blob rapidly expanded to a yard in diameter just beside Tuthy. The blob turned red, wriggled, froze, and then just as rapidly vanished.

"That was like an elbow," Pal explained. "One of its arms. I think it's listening. Trying to find out where the music is coming from. I'll go upstairs."

"Turn it off!" Tuthy demanded.

"I'll play something else." The boy ran up the stairs. From the kitchen came a hideous hollow crashing, then the sound of vacuum being filled—a reverse-pop, ending in a hiss—followed by a low-frequency vibration that set their teeth on edge . . .

The vibration caused by a four-dimensional creature *scraping* across its "floor," their own three-dimensional space. Tuthy's hands shook with excitement.

"Peter—" Lauren bellowed, all dignity gone. She unwrapped her arms and held clenched fists out as if she were about to start exercising, or boxing.

"Pal's attracted visitors," Tuthy explained.

He turned toward the stairs. The first four steps and a section of floor spun and vanished. The rush of air nearly drew him down the hole. Regaining his balance, he kneeled to feel the precisely cut, concave edge. Below was the dark basement.

"Pal!" Tuthy called out.

"I'm playing something original for them," Pal shouted back. "I think they like it."

The phone rang. Tuthy was closest to the extension at the bottom of the stairs and instinctively reached out to answer it. Hockrum was on the other end, screaming.

"I can't talk now—" Tuthy said. Hockrum screamed again, loud enough for Lauren to hear. Tuthy abruptly hung up. "He's been fired, I gather," he said. "He seemed angry." He stalked back three paces and turned, then ran forward and leaped the gap to the first intact step. "Can't talk." He stumbled and scrambled up the stairs, stopping on the landing. "Jesus," he said, as if something had suddenly occured to him.

"He'll call the government," Lauren warned.

Tuthy waved that off. "I know what's happening. They're knocking chunks out of three-space, into the fourth. The fourth dimension. Like Pal says: clumsy brutes. They could kill us!"

Sitting before the Tronclavier, Pal happily played a new melody. Tuthy approached and was abruptly blocked by a thick green column, as solid as rock and with a similar texture. It vibrated and ascribed an arc in the air. A section of the ceiling four feet wide was kicked out of three-space. Tuthy's hair lifted in the rush of wind. The column shrank to a broomstick and hairs sprouted all over it, writhing like snakes.

Tuthy edged around the hairy broomstick and pulled the plug on the Tronclavier. A cage of zeppelin-shaped brown sausages encircled the computer, spun, elongated to reach the ceiling, the floor and the top of the monitor's table, and then pipped down to tiny strings and was gone.

"They can't see too clearly here," Pal said, undisturbed that his concert was over. Lauren had climbed the outside stairs and stood behind Tuthy. "Gee, I'm sorry about the damage."

In one smooth curling motion, the Tronclavier and cone and all the wiring associated with them were peeled away as if they had been stick-on labels hastily removed from a flat surface.

"Gee," Pal said, his face suddenly registering alarm.

Then it was the boy's turn. He was removed with greater care. The last thing to vanish was his head, which hung suspended in the air for several seconds.

"I think they liked the music," he said, grinning.

Head, grin and all, dropped away in a direction impossible for Tuthy or Lauren to follow. The air in the room sighed.

Lauren stood her ground for several minutes, while Tuthy wandered through what was left of the office, passing his hand through mussed hair.

"Perhaps he'll be back," Tuthy said. "I don't even know . . ." But he didn't finish. Could a three-dimensional boy survive in a four-dimensional void, or whatever lay dup . . . or owwen?

———

TUTHY DID NOT OBJECT WHEN LAUREN TOOK IT UPON HERSELF TO CALL THE boy's foster parents and the police. When the police arrived, he endured the questions and accusations stoically, face immobile, and told them as much as he knew. He was not believed; nobody knew quite what to believe. Photographs were taken. The police left.

It was only a matter of time, Lauren told him, until one or the other or both of them were arrested. "Then we'll make up a story," he said. "You'll tell them it was my fault."

"I will *not*," Lauren said. "But where *is* he?"

"I'm not positive," Tuthy said. "I think's he's all right, however."

"How do you *know*?"

He told her about the dream.

"But that was before," she said.

"Perfectly allowable in the fourth dimension," he explained. He pointed vaguely up, then down, then shrugged.

ON THE LAST DAY, TUTHY SPENT THE EARLY MORNING HOURS BUNDLED IN AN overcoat and bathrobe in the drafty office, playing his program again and again, trying to visualize *ana* and *kata*. He closed his eyes and squinted and twisted his head, intertwined his fingers and drew odd little graphs on the monitors, but it was no use. His brain was hardwired.

Over breakfast, he reiterated to Lauren that she must put all the blame on him.

"Maybe it will all blow over," she said. "They haven't got a case. No evidence . . . nothing."

"All blow *over*," he mused, passing his hand over his head and grinning ironically. "How *over*, they'll never know."

The doorbell rang. Tuthy went to answer it, and Lauren followed a few steps behind.

Tuthy opened the door. Three men in gray suits, one with a briefcase, stood on the porch. "Mr. Peter Thornton?" the tallest asked.

"Yes," Tuthy acknowledged.

A chunk of the doorframe and wall above the door vanished with a roar and a hissing pop. The three men looked up at the gap. Ignoring what was impossible, the tallest man returned his attention to Tuthy and continued, "We have information that you are in this country illegally."

"Oh?" Tuthy said.

Beside him, an irregular filmy blue cylinder grew to a length of four feet and hung in the air, vibrating. The three men backed away on the porch. In the middle of the cylinder, Pal's head emerged, and below that, his extended arm and hand.

"It's fun here," Pal said. "They're friendly."

"I believe you," Tuthy said.

"Mr. Thornton," the tallest man continued valiantly.

"Won't you come with me?" Pal asked.

Tuthy glanced back at Lauren. She gave him a small fraction of a nod, barely understanding what she was assenting to, and he took Pal's hand. "Tell them it was all my fault," he said.

From his feet to his head, Peter Tuthy was peeled out of this world. Air rushed in. Half of the brass lamp to one side of the door disappeared.

The INS men returned to their car without any further questions, with damp pants and embarrassed, deeply worried expressions. They drove away, leaving Lauren to contemplate the quiet. They did not return.

She did not sleep for three nights, and when she did sleep, Tuthy and Pal visited her, and put the question to her.

Thank you, but I prefer it here, she replied.

It's a lot of fun, the boy insisted. *They like music.*

Lauren shook her head on the pillow and awoke. Not very far away, there was a whistling, tinny kind of sound, followed by a deep vibration.

To her, it sounded like applause.

She took a deep breath and got out of bed to retrieve her notebook.

Introduction to "The Visitation"

This short mood piece appeared in *Omni* with a suite of stories by different authors on religious themes. Again, I'm arguing with our human conceptions of God—and suggesting that our conception of divinity is likely to be very incomplete and immature.

The Visitation
Omni, Ellen Datlow, 1987

The Trinity arrived under a blossoming almond tree in Rebecca Sandia's backyard in the early hours of Easter morning. She watched it appear as she sipped tea on her back porch. Because of the peace radiating from the three images—a lion, a lamb, and a dove—she did not feel alarm or even much concern. She was not an overtly religious person, but she experienced considerable relief at having a major question—the existence of a God—answered in the affirmative. The Trinity approached her table on hooves, paws, and wings; and this, she knew, expressed the ultimate assurance and humility of God—that He should not require her to approach Him.

"Good morning," she said. The lamb nuzzled her leg affectionately. "An especially significant morning for you, is it not?" The lamb bleated and spun its tail. "I am so pleased you have chosen me, though I wonder why."

The lion spoke with a voice like a typhoon confined in a barrel:

"Once each year on this date we reveal the Craft of Godhead to a selected human. Seldom are the humans chosen from My formal houses of worship, for I have found them almost universally unable to comprehend the Mystery. They have preconceived ideas and cannot remove the blinds from their eyes."

Rebecca Sandia felt a brief *frisson* then, but the dove rubbed its breast feathers against her hand where it lay on the table. "I have never been a strong believer," she said, "though I have always had hopes."

"That is why you were chosen," the dove sang, its voice as dulcet as a summer's evening breeze. The lamb cavorted about the grass; and Rebecca's heart was filled with gladness watching it, for she remembered it had gone through hard times not long ago.

"I have asked only one thing of My creations," the lion said, "that once a year I find some individual capable of understanding the Mystery. Each year I have chosen the most likely individual and appeared to speak and enthuse. And each year I have chosen correctly and found understanding and allowed the world to continue. And so it will be until My creation is fulfilled."

"But I am a scientist," Rebecca said, concerned by the lion's words. "I am enchanted by the creation more than the God. I am buried in the world and not the spirit."

"I have spun the world out of My spirit," the dove sang. "Each particle is as one of my feathers; each event, a note in my song."

"Then I am joyful," Rebecca said, "for that I understand. I have often thought of you as a scientist, performing experiments."

"Then you do not understand," the lion said. "For I seek not to comprehend My creation but to know MySelf."

"Then is it wrong for me to be a scientist?" Rebecca asked. "Should I be a priest or a theologian, to help You understand YourSelf?"

"No, for I have made your kind as so many mirrors, that you may see each other; and there are no finer mirrors than scientists, who are so hard and bright. Priests and theologians, as I have said, shroud their brightness with mists for their own comfort and sense of well-being."

"Then I am still concerned," Rebecca said, "for I would like the world to be ultimately kind and nurturing. Though as a scientist I see that it is not, that it is cruel and harsh and demanding."

"What is pain?" the lion asked, lifting one paw to show a triangle marked by thorns. "It is transitory, and suffering is the moisture of My breath."

"I don't understand," Rebecca said, shivering.

"Among My names are disease and disaster, and My hand lies on every pockmark and blotch and boil, and My limbs move beneath every hurricane and earthquake. Yet you still seek to love Me. Do you not comprehend?"

"No," Rebecca said, her face pale, for the world's particles seemed to lose some of their stability at that moment. "How can it be that You love us?"

"If I had made all things comfortable and sweet, then you would not be driven to examine Me and know My motives. You would dance and sing and withdraw into your pleasures."

"Then I understand," Rebecca said "For it is the work of a scientist to know the world and control it, and we are often driven by the urge to prevent misery. Through our knowledge we see You more clearly."

"I see MySelves more clearly through you."

"Then I can love You and cherish You, knowing that ultimately You are concerned for us."

The world swayed; and Rebecca was sore afraid, for the peace of the lamb had faded, and the lion glowed red as coals. "Whom are you closest to," the lion asked, its voice deeper than thunder, "your enemies or your lovers? Whom do you scrutinize more thoroughly?"

Rebecca thought of her enemies and her lovers, and she was not sure.

"In front of your enemies you are always watchful, and with your lovers you may relax and close your eyes."

"Then I understand," Rebecca said. "For this might be a kind of war; and after the war is over, we may come together, former enemies, and celebrate the peace."

The sky became black as ink. The blossoms of the almond tree fell, and she saw, within the branches, that the almonds would be bitter this year.

"In peace the former enemies would close their eyes," the lion said, "and sleep together peacefully."

"Then we must be enemies forever?"

"For I am a zealous God. I am zealous of your eyes and your ears, which I gave you that you might avoid the agonies I visit upon you. I am zealous of your mind, which I made wary and facile, that you might always be thinking and planning ways to improve upon this world."

"Then I understand," Rebecca said fearfully, her voice breaking, "that all our lives we must fight against you . . . but when we die?"

The lamb scampered about the yard, but the lion reached out with a paw and laid the lamb out on the grass with its back broken. "*This* is the Mystery," the lion roared, consuming the lamb, leaving only a splash of blood steaming on the ground.

Rebecca leaped from her chair, horrified, and held out her hands to fend off the prowling beast. "I understand!" she screamed "You are a selfish God, and Your creation is a toy You can mangle at will! You do not love; you do not care; you are cold and cruel."

The lion sat to lick its chops. "And?" it asked menacingly.

Rebecca's face flushed. She felt a sudden anger. "I am better than You," she said quietly, "for I can love and feel compassion. How wrong we have been to send our prayers to You!"

"And?" the lion asked with a growl.

"There is much we can teach You!" she said. "For You do not know how to love or respect Your creation, or YourSelf! You are a wild beast, and it is our job to tame You and train You."

"Such dangerous knowledge," the lion said. The dove landed among the hairs of its mane. "Catch Me if you can," the dove sang. For an instant the Trinity shed its symbolic forms and revealed Its true Self, a thing beyond ugliness or beauty, a vast cyclic thing of no humanity whatsoever, dark and horribly young—and that truth reduced Rebecca to hysterics.

Then the Trinity vanished, and the world continued for another year.

But Rebecca was never the same again, for she had understood, and by her grace we have lived this added time.

Introduction to "Richie by the Sea"

While I enjoy monster movies, horror fiction, and stories of the supernatural—ghost stories in particular—I've written only one novel (*Psychlone*, 1979) and one short story that could be dropped into these categories. Here's the story, a biological *conte cruel*, conceived during a jam session with my cousin, Dan Garrett, in the 1960s. Mark Laidlaw, at a party at Gregory and Joan Benford's house in Laguna Beach, told me that Ramsey Campbell, a master of horror fiction, was looking for short stories for an original anthology he was assembling, and suggested I submit something. I sent him "Richie."

It's sole publication was in Ramsey's anthology. The story has not been reprinted elsewhere since. So much for my dreams of becoming another Stephen King or Dean Koontz!

Richie by the Sea
New Terrors 2, Ramsey Campbell, 1980

The storm had spent its energy the night before. A wild, scattering squall had toppled the Thompson's shed and the last spurt of high water had dropped dark drift across the rocks and sand. In the last light of day the debris was beginning to stink and attract flies and gulls. There were knots of seaweed, floats made of glass and cork, odd bits of boat wood, foam plastic shards, and a whale. The whale was about forty feet long. It had died during the night after its impact on the ragged rocks of the cove. It looked like a giant garden slug, draped across the still pool of water with head and tail hanging over.

Thomas Harker felt a tinge of sympathy for the whale, but his house was less than a quarter-mile south and with the wind in his direction the smell would soon be bothersome.

The sheriff's jeep roared over the bluff road between the cove and the university grounds. Thomas waved and the sheriff waved back. There would be a lot of cleaning-up to do.

Thomas backed away from the cliff edge and returned to the path through the trees. He'd left his drafting table an hour ago to stretch his muscles and the walk had taken longer than he expected; Karen would be home by now, waiting for him, tired from the start of the new school year.

The cabin was on a broad piece of property barely thirty yards from the tideline, with nothing but grass and sand and an old picket fence between it and the water. They had worried during the storm, but there had been no flooding. The beach elevated seven feet to their property and they'd come through remarkably well.

Thomas knocked sand from his shoes and hung them on two nails next to the back door. In the service porch he removed his socks and dangled them outside, then draped them on the washer. He had soaked his shoes and socks and feet during an incautious run near the beach. Wriggling his toes, he stepped into the kitchen and sniffed. Karen had popped homemade chicken pies into the oven. Walks along the beach made him ravenous, especially after long days at the board.

He looked out the front window. Karen was at the gate, hair blowing in the evening breeze and knit sweater puffing out across her pink and white blouse. She turned, saw Thomas in the window and waved, saying something he couldn't hear.

He shrugged expressively and went to open the door. He saw something small on the porch and jumped in surprise. Richie stood on the step, smiling up at him, eyes the color of the sunlit sea, black hair unruly.

"Did I scare you, Mr. Harker?" the boy asked.

"Not much. What are you doing here this late? You should be home for dinner."

Karen kicked her shoes off on the porch. "Richie! When did you get here?"

"Just now. I was walking up the sand hills and wanted to say hello." Richie pointed north of the house with his long, unchildlike fingers. "Hello." He looked at Karen with a broad grin, head tilted.

"No dinner at home tonight?" Karen asked, totally vulnerable. "Maybe you can stay here." Thomas winced and raised his hand.

"Can't," Richie said. "Everything's just late tonight. I've got to be home soon. Hey, did you see the whale?"

"Yeah," Thomas said. "Sheriff is going to have a fun time moving it."

"Next tide'll probably take it out," Richie said. He looked between them, still smiling broadly. Thomas guessed his age at nine or ten but he already knew how to handle people.

"Tide won't be that high now," Thomas said.

"I've seen big things wash back before. Think he'll leave it overnight?"

"Probably. It won't start stinking until tomorrow."

Karen wrinkled her nose in disgust.

"Thanks for the invitation anyway, Mrs. Harker." Richie put his hands in his shorts' pockets and walked through the picket fence, turning just beyond the gate. "You got any more old clothes I can have?"

"Not now," Thomas said. "You've taken all our castoffs already."

"I need more for the rag drive," Richie said. "Thanks anyway."

"Where does he live?" Thomas asked after closing the door.

"I don't think he wants us to know. Probably in town. Don't you like him?"

"Of course I like him. He's only a kid."

"You don't seem to want him around." Karen looked at him accusingly.

"Not all the time. He's not ours, his folks should take care of him."

"They obviously don't care much."

"He's well-fed," Thomas said. "He looks healthy and he gets along fine."

They sat down to dinner. Wisps of Karen's hair still took the shape of the wind. She didn't comb it until after the table was cleared and Thomas was doing the dishes. His eyes traced endless circuit diagrams in the suds. "Hey," he shouted to the back bathroom. "I've been working too much."

"I know," Karen answered. "So have I. Isn't it terrible?"

"Let's get to bed early," he said. She walked into the kitchen wrapped in a terry-cloth bathrobe, pulling a snarl out of her hair. "Must get your sleep," she said.

He aimed a snapped towel at her retreating end but missed. Then he leaned over the sink, rubbed his eyes and looked at the suds again. No circuits, only a portrait of Richie. He removed the last plate and rinsed it.

The next morning Thomas awoke to the sound of hammering coming from down the beach. He sat up in bed to receive Karen's breezy kiss as she left for the University, then hunkered down again and rolled over to snooze a little longer. His eyes flew open a few minutes later and he cursed. The racket was too much. He rolled out of the warmth and padded into the bathroom, wincing at the cold tiles. He turned the shower on to warm, brought his mug out to shave and examined his face in the cracked mirror. The mirror had been broken six months ago when he'd slipped and jammed his hand against it after a full night poring over the circuit diagrams in his office. Karen had been furious with him and he hadn't worked that hard since. But there was a deadline from Peripheral Data on his freelance designs and he had to meet it if he wanted to keep up his reputation.

In a few more months, he might land an exclusive contract from Key Business Corporation, and then he'd be designing what he wanted to design—big computers, mighty beasts. Outstanding money.

The hammering continued and after dressing he looked out the bedroom window to see Thompson rebuilding his shed. The shed had gone unused for months after Thompson had lost his boat at the Del Mar trials, near San Diego. Still, Thompson was sawing and hammering and reconstructing the slope-roofed structure, possibly planning on another boat. Thomas didn't think much about it. He was already at work and he hadn't even reached the desk in his office. There was a whole series of TTL chips he could move to solve the interference he was sure would crop up in the design as he had it now.

By nine o'clock he was deeply absorbed. He had his drafting pencils and templates and mechanic's square spread across the paper in complete confusion. He wasn't interrupted until ten.

He answered the door only half-aware that somebody had knocked. Sheriff Varmanian stood on the porch, sweating. The sun was out and the sky clearing for a hot, humid day.

"Hi, Tom."

"Al," Thomas said, nodding. "Something up?"

"I'm interrupting? Sorry—"

"Yeah, my computers won't be able to take over your job if you keep me here much longer. How's the whale?"

"That's the least of my troubles right now." Varmanian's frizzy hair and round wire-rimmed glasses made him look more like an anarchist than a sheriff. "The whale was taken out with the night tide. We didn't even have to bury it." He pronounced "bury" like it was "burry" and studiously maintained a mid-western twang.

"Something else, then. Come inside and cool off?"

"Thanks. We've lost another kid—the Cooper's four-year-old, Kile. He disappeared last night around seven and no one's seen him since. Anybody see him here?"

"No. Only Richie was here. Listen, I didn't hear any tide big enough to sweep the whale out again. We'd need another storm to do that. Maybe something freak happened and the boy was caught in it . . . a freak tide?"

"There isn't any funnel in Placer Cove to cause that. Just a normal rise and the whale was buoyed up by gases, that's my guess. Cooper kid must have gotten lost on the bluff road and come down to one of the houses to ask for help—that's what the last people who saw him think. So we're checking the beach homes. Thompson didn't see anything either. I'll keep heading north and look at the flats and tide pools again, but I'd say we have another disappearance. Don't quote me, though."

"That's four?"

"Five. Five in the last six months."

"Pretty bad, Al, for a town like this."

"Don't I know it. Coopers are all upset, already planning funeral arrangements. Funerals when there aren't any bodies. But the Goldbergs had one for their son two months ago, so I guess precedent has been set."

He stood by the couch, fingering his hat and looking at the rug. "It's damned hard. How often does this kid, Richie, come down?"

"Three or four times a week. Karen's motherly toward him, thinks his folks aren't paying him enough attention."

"He'll be the next one, wait and see. Thanks for the time, and say hello to the wife for me."

Thomas returned to the board but had difficulty concentrating. He wondered if animals in the field and bush mourned long over the loss of a child. Did gazelles grieve when lions struck? Karen knew more about such feelings than he did; she'd lost a husband before she met him. His own life had been reasonably linear, uneventful.

How would he cope if something happened, if Karen were killed? Like the Coopers, with a quick funeral and burial to make things certain, even when they weren't?

What were they burying?

Four years of work and dreams.

After lunch he took a walk along the beach and found his feet moving him north to where the whale had been. The coastal rocks in this area concentrated on the northern edge of the cove. They stretched into the water for a mile before ending at the deep water shelf. At extreme low tide two or three hundred yards of rocks were exposed. Now, about fifty feet was visible and he could clearly see where the whale had been. Even at high tide the circle of rock was visible. He hadn't walked here much lately, but he remembered first noticing the circle three years before, like a perfect sandy-bottomed wading pool.

Up and down the beach, the wrack remained, dark and smelly and flyblown. But the whale was gone. It was obvious there hadn't been much wave action. Still, that was the easy explanation and he had no other.

After the walk he returned to his office and opened all the windows before setting pencil to paper. By the time Karen was home, he had finished a good portion of the diagram from his original sketches. When he turned it in, Peripheral Data would have little more to do than hand it to their drafting department for smoothing.

Richie didn't visit them that evening. He came in the morning instead. It was a Saturday and Karen was home, reading in the living room. She invited the boy in and offered him milk and cookies, then sat him before the television to watch cartoons.

Richie consumed TV with a hunger that was fascinating. He avidly mimicked the expressions of the people he saw in the commercials, as if memorizing a store of emotions, filling in the gaps in his humanity left by an imperfect upbringing.

Richie left a few hours later. As usual, he had not touched the food. He wasn't starving.

"Think he's adopting us?" Thomas asked.

"I don't know. Maybe. Maybe he just needs a couple of friends like you and me. Human contacts, if his own folks don't pay attention to him."

"Varmanian thinks he might be the next one to disappear." Thomas regretted the statement the instant it was out, but Karen didn't react. She put out a lunch of beans and sausages and waited until they were eating to say something. "When do you want to have a child?"

"Two weeks from now, over the three-day holiday," Thomas said.

"No, I'm serious."

"You've taken a shine to Richie and you think we should have one of our own?"

"Not until something breaks for you," she said, looking away. "If Key Business comes through, maybe I can take a sabbatical and study child-rearing. Directly. But one of us has to be free full time."

Thomas nodded and sipped at a glass of iced tea. Behind her humor she was serious. There was a lot at stake in the next few months—more than just money. Perhaps their happiness together. It was a hard weight to carry. Being an adult was difficult at times. He almost wished he could be like Richie, free as a gull, uncommitted.

A line of dark clouds schemed over the ocean as afternoon turned to evening. "Looks like another storm," he called to Karen, who was typing in the back bedroom.

"So soon?" she asked by way of complaint.

He sat in the kitchen to watch the advancing front. The warm, fading light of sunset turned his face orange and painted an orange square on the living room wall. The square had progressed above the level of the couch when the doorbell rang.

It was Gina Hammond and a little girl he didn't recognize. Hammond was about sixty with thinning black hair and a narrow, wizened face that always bore an irritated scowl. A cigarette was pinched between her fingers, as usual. She explained the visit between nervous stammers which embarrassed Thomas far more than they did her.

"Mr. Harker, this is my granddaughter Julie." The girl, seven or eight, looked up at him accusingly. "Julie says she's lost four of her kittens. Th-th-that's because she gave them to your boy to play with and he— he never brought them back. You know anything about them?"

"We don't have any children, Mrs. Hammond."

"You've got a boy named Richie," the woman said, glaring at him as if he were a monster.

Karen came out of the hallway and leaned against the door jamb beside Thomas. "Gina, Richie just wanders around our house a lot. He's not ours."

"Julie says Richie lives here—he told h-h-her that—and his name is Richie Harker. What's this all about i-i-if he isn't your boy?"

"He took my kittens!" Julie said, a tear escaping to slide down her cheek.

"If that's what he told you—that we're his folks—he was fibbing," Karen said. "He lives in town, closer to you than to us."

"He brought the kittens to the beach!" Julie cried. "I saw him."

"He hasn't been here since this morning," Thomas said. "We haven't seen the kittens."

"He stole 'em!" The girl began crying in earnest.

"I'll talk to him next time I see him," Thomas promised. "But I don't know where he lives."

"H-h-his last name?"

"Don't know that, either."

Mrs. Hammond wasn't convinced. "I don't like the idea of little boys stealing things that don't belong to them."

"Neither do I, Mrs. Hammond," Karen said. "We told you we'd talk to him when we see him."

"Well," Mrs. Hammond said. She thanked them beneath her breath and left with the blubbering Julie close behind.

THE STORM HIT AFTER DINNER. IT WAS A HEAVY SQUALL AND THE RAIN trounced over the roof as if the sky had feet. A leak started in the bathroom, fortunately right over the tub, and Thomas rummaged through his caulking gear, preparing for the storm's end when he could get up on the roof and search out the leak.

A small tool shed connected with the cabin through the garage. It had one bare light and a tiny four-paned window which stared at Thomas's chest-level into the streaming night. As he dug out his putty knife and caulking cans, the phone rang in the kitchen and Karen answered it. Her voice came across as a murmur under the barrage of rain on the garage roof. He was putting all his supplies into a cardboard box when she stuck her head through the garage door and told him she'd be going out.

"The Thompsons have lost their power," she said. "I'm going to take some candles to them on the beach road. I should be back in a few minutes, but they may want me to drive into town and buy some lanterns with them. If they do, I'll be back in an hour or so. Don't worry about me!"

Thomas came out of the shed clutching the box. "I could go instead."

"Don't be silly. Give you more time to work on the sketches. I'll be back soon. Tend the leaks."

Then she was out the front door and gone. He looked through the living room window at her receding lights and felt a gnaw of worry. He'd forgotten a rag to wipe the putty knife. He switched the light back on and went through the garage to the shed.

Something scraped against the wall outside. He bent down and peered out the four-paned window, rubbing where his breath fogged the glass. A small face stared back at him. It vanished almost as soon as he saw it.

"Richie!" Thomas yelled. "Damn it, come back here!"

Some of it seemed to fall in place as Thomas ran outside with his go-aheads and raincoat on. The boy didn't have a home to go to when he left their house. He slept someplace else, in the woods perhaps, and scavenged what he could. But now he was in the rain and soaked and in danger of becoming very ill unless Thomas caught up with him. A flash of lightning brought grass and shore into bright relief and he saw the boy running south across the sand, faster than seemed possible for a boy his age. Thomas ran after with the rain slapping him in the face.

He was halfway toward the Thompson house when the lightning flashes decreased and he couldn't follow the boy's trail. It was pitch black but for the lights coming from their cabin. The Thompson house, of course, was dark.

Thomas was soaked through and rain ran down his neck in a steady stream. Sand itched his feet and burrs from the grass caught in his cuffs, pricking his ankles.

A close flash printed the Thompsons' shed in silver against the dark. Thunder roared and grumbled down the beach.

That was it, that was where Richie stayed. He had fled to the woods only after the first storm had knocked the structure down.

He lurched through the wind-slanted strikes of water until he stood by the shed door. He fumbled at the catch and found a lock. He tugged at it and the whole thing slid free. The screws had been pried loose. "Richie," he said, opening the door. "Come on. It's Tom."

The shed waited dry and silent. "You should come home with me, stay with us." No answer. He opened the door wide and lightning showed him rags scattered everywhere, rising to a shape that looked like a man lying on his back with a blank face turned to Thomas. He jumped, but it was only a lump of rags. The boy didn't seem to be there. He started to close the door when he saw two pale points of light dance in the dark like fireflies. His heart froze and his back tingled. Again the lightning threw its dazzling sheets of light and wrapped the inside of the shed in cold whiteness and inky shadow.

Richie stood at the back, staring at Thomas with a slack expression.

The dark closed again and the boy said, "Tom, could you take me someplace warm?"

"Sure," Tom said, relaxing. "Come here." He took the boy into his arms and bundled him under the raincoat. There was something lumpy on Richie's back, under his sopping T-shirt. Thomas's hand drew back by reflex. Richie shied away just as quickly and Thomas thought, *He's got a hunch or scar, he's embarrassed about it.*

Lurching against each other as they walked to the house, Thomas asked himself why he'd been scared by what he first saw in the shed. A pile of rags. "My nerves are shot," he told Richie. The boy said nothing.

In the house he put Richie under a warm shower—the boy seemed unfamiliar with bathtubs and shower heads—and put an old Mackinaw out for the boy to wear. Thomas brought a cot and sleeping bag from the garage into the living room. Richie slipped on the Mackinaw, buttoning it with a curious crabwise flick of right hand over left, and climbed into the down bag, falling asleep almost immediately.

Karen came home an hour later, tired and wet. Thomas pointed to the cot with his finger at his lips. She looked at it, mouth open in surprise, and nodded.

In their bedroom, before fatigue and the patter of rain lulled them into sleep, Karen told him the Thompsons were nice people. "She's a little old and crotchety, but he's a bright old coot. He said something strange, though. Said when the shed fell down during the last storm he found a dummy inside it, wrapped in old blankets and dressed in cast-off clothing. Made out of straw and old sheets, he said."

"Oh." He saw the lump of rags in the lightning and shivered.

"Do you think Richie made it?"

He shook his head, too tired to think.

SUNDAY MORNING, AS THEY CAME AWAKE, THEY HEARD RICHIE PLAYING OUT-side. "You've got to ask about the kittens," Karen said. Thomas agreed reluctantly and put his clothes on.

The storm had passed in the night, having scrubbed a clear sky for the morning. He found Richie talking to the Sheriff and greeted Var-manian with a wave and a yawned "Hello."

"Sheriff wants to know if we saw Mr. Jones yesterday," Richie said. Mr. Jones—named after Davy Jones—was an old beachcomber fre-quently seen waving a metal detector around the cove. His bag was always filled with metal junk of little interest to anybody but him.

"No, I didn't," Thomas said. "Gone?"

"Not hard to guess, is it?" Varmanian said grimly. "I'm starting to think we ought to have a police guard out here."

"Might be an idea." Thomas waited for the sheriff to leave before asking the boy about the kittens. Richie became huffy, as if imitating some child in a television commercial. "I gave them back to Julie," he said. "I didn't take them anywhere. She's got them now."

"Richie, this was just yesterday. I don't see how you could have returned them already."

"You don't trust me, do you, Mr. Harker?" Richie asked. The boy's face turned as cold as seawater, as hard as the rocks in the cove.

"I just don't think you're telling the truth."

"Thanks for the roof last night," Richie said softly. "I've got to go now." Thomas thought briefly about following after him, but there was nothing he could do. He considered calling Varmanian's office and telling him Richie had no legal guardian, but it didn't seem the right time.

Karen was angry with him for not being more decisive. "That boy needs someone to protect him! It's our duty to find out who the real parents are and tell the sheriff he's neglected."

"I don't think that's the problem," Thomas said. He frowned, trying to put things together. More was going on than was apparent.

"But he would have spent the night in the rain if you hadn't brought him here."

"He had that shed to go back to. He's been using the rags we gave him for—"

"That shed is cold and damp and no place for a small boy!" She took a deep breath to calm herself. "What are you trying to say, under all your evasions?"

"I have a feeling Richie can take care of himself."

"But he's a small *boy*, Tom."

"You're pinning a label on him without thinking how . . . without looking at how he can take care of himself, what he can do. But okay, I tell Varmanian about him and the boy gets picked up and returned to his parents—"

"What if he doesn't have any? He told Mrs. Hammond we were his parents."

"He's got to have parents somewhere, or legal guardians! Orphans just don't have the run of the town without somebody finding out. Say Varmanian turns him back to his parents—what kind of parents would make a small boy, as you call him, want to run away?"

Karen folded her arms and said nothing.

"Not very good to turn him back then, hm? What we should do is tell Varmanian to notify the parents, if any, if they haven't skipped town or something, that we're going to keep Richie here until they show up to claim him. I think Al would go along with that. If they don't show, we can contest their right to Richie and start proceedings to adopt him."

"It's not that simple," Karen said, but her eyes were sparkling. "The laws aren't that cut and dried."

"Okay, but that's the start of a plan, isn't it?"

"I suppose so."

"Okay." He pursed his lips and shook his head. "That'd be a big responsibility. Could we take care of a boy like Richie now?"

Karen nodded and Thomas was suddenly aware how much she wanted a child. It stung him a little to see her eagerness and the moisture in her eyes.

"Okay. I'll go find him." He put on his shoes and started out through the fence, turning south to the Thompson's shed. When he reached the wooden building he saw the door had been equipped with a new padlock and the latch screwed in tight. He was able to peek in through a chink in the wood—whatever could be said about Thompson as a boatbuilder, he wasn't much of a carpenter—and scan the inside. The pile of rags was gone. Only a few loose pieces remained. Richie, as he expected, wasn't inside.

Karen called from the porch and he looked north. Richie was striding toward the rocks at the opposite end of the cove. "I see him," Thomas said as he passed the cabin. "Be back in a few minutes."

He walked briskly to the base of the rocks and looked for Richie. The boy stood on a boulder, pretending to ignore him. Hesitant, not knowing exactly how to say it, Thomas told him what they were going to do. The boy looked down from the rock.

"You mean, you want to be my folks?" A smile, broad and toothy, slowly spread across his face. Everything was going to be okay.

"That's it, I think," Thomas said. "If your parents don't contest the matter."

"Oh, I don't have any folks," Richie said. Thomas looked at the sea-colored eyes and felt sudden misgivings.

"Might be easier, then," he said softly.

"Hey, Tom? I found something in the pools. Come look with me? Come on!" Richie was pure small-boy then, up from his seat and down the rock and vanishing from view like a bird taking wing.

"Richie!" Thomas cried. "I haven't time right now. Wait!" He climbed up the rock with his hands and feet slipping on the slick surface. At the top he looked across the quarter-mile stretch of pools, irritated. "Richie!"

The boy ran like a crayfish over the jagged terrain. He turned and shouted back, "In the big pool! Come on!" Then he ran on.

Tom followed, eyes lowered to keep his footing. "Slow down!" He looked up for a moment and saw a small flail of arms, a face turned toward him with the smile frozen in surprise, and the boy disappearing. There was a small cry and a splash. "Richie!" Thomas shouted, his voice cracking. He'd fallen into the pool, the circular pool where the whale had been.

He gave up all thought of his own safety and ran across the rocks, slipping twice and cracking his knees against a sharp ridge of granite. Agony shot up his legs and fogged his vision. Cursing, throwing hair out of his eyes, he crawled to his feet and shakily hobbled over the loose pebbles and sand to the edge of the round pool.

With his hands on the smooth rock rim, he blinked and saw the boy floating in the middle of the pool, face down. Thomas groaned and shut his eyes, dizzy. There was a rank odor in the air; he wanted to get up and run. This was not the way rescuers were supposed to feel. His stomach twisted. There was no time to waste, however. He forced himself over the rim into the cold water, slipping and plunging head first. His brow touched the bottom. The sand was hard and compact, crusted. He stood with the water streaming off his head and torso. It was slick like oil and came up to his groin, deepening as he splashed to the middle. It would be up to his chest where Richie floated.

Richie's shirt clung damply, outlining the odd hump on his back. *We'll get that fixed*, Thomas told himself. *Oh, God, we'll get that fixed, let him be alive and it'll work out fine.*

The water splashed across his chest. Some of it entered his mouth and he gagged at the fishy taste. He reached out for the boy's closest foot but couldn't quite reach it. The sand shifted beneath him and he ducked under the surface, swallowing more water. Bobbing up again, kicking to keep his mouth clear, he wiped his eyes with one hand and saw the boy's arms making small, sinuous motions, like the fins of a fish.

Swimming away from Thomas.

"Richie!" Thomas shouted. His wet tennis shoes, tapping against the bottom, seemed to make it resound, as if it were hollow. Then he felt the bottom lift slightly until his feet pressed flat against it, fall away until he tread water, lift again . . .

He looked down. The sand, distorted by ripples in the pool, was receding. Thomas struggled with his hands, trying to swim to the edge. Beneath him waited black water like a pool of crude oil, and in it something long and white, insistent. His feet kicked furiously to keep him from ducking under again, but the water swirled.

Thomas shut his mouth after taking a deep breath. The water throbbed like a bell, drawing him deeper, still struggling. He looked up and saw the sky, gray-blue above the ripples. There was still a chance. He kicked his shoes off, watching them spiral down. Heavy shoes, wet, gone now, he could swim better.

He spun with the water and the surface darkened. His lungs ached. He clenched his teeth to keep his mouth shut. There seemed to be progress. The surface seemed brighter. But three hazy-edged triangles converged and he could not fool himself any more, the surface was black and he had to let his breath out, hands straining up.

He touched a hard rasping shell.

The pool rippled for a few minutes, then grew still. Richie let loose of the pool's side and climbed up the edge, out of the water. His skin was pale, eyes almost milky.

The hunger had been bad for a few months. Now they were almost content. The meals were more frequent and larger—but who knew about the months to come? Best to take advantage of the good times. He pulled the limp dummy from its hiding place beneath the flat boulder and dragged it to the pool's edge, dumping it over and jumping in after. For a brief moment he smiled and hugged it; it was so much like himself, a final lure to make things more certain. Most of the time, it was all the human-shaped company he needed. He arranged its arms and legs in a natural position, spread out, and adjusted the drift of the Mackinaw in the water. The dummy drifted to the center of the pool and stayed there.

A fleshy ribbon thick as his arm waved in the water and he pulled up the back of his shirt to let it touch him on the hump and fasten. This was the best time. His limbs shrank and his face sunk inward. His skin became the color of the rocks and his eyes grew large and golden. Energy—food—pulsed into him and he felt a great love for this clever other part of him, so adaptable.

It was mother and brother at once, and if there were times when Richie felt there might be a life beyond it, an existence like that of the people he mimicked, it was only because the mimicry was so fine.

He would never actually leave.

He couldn't. Eventually he would starve; he wasn't very good at digesting.

He wriggled until he hugged smooth against the rim, with only his head sticking out of the water. He waited.

"Tom!" a voice called, not very far away. It was Karen.

"Mrs. Harker!" Richie screamed. "Help!"

Introduction to *Sleepside Story*

Jan O'Nale, of Cheap Street Press, requested that I write a novella for her series of custom-designed and illustrated limited editions. This was a real honor— Cheap Street published the loveliest editions of any small press associated with science fiction. With complete freedom, I wrote a fantasy based on the photographic negative of a fairy tale—"Beauty and the Beast." One early title, in fact, was "Handsome and the Whore," but that was deemed too overt, and perhaps too judgmental.

Every element in *Sleepside Story* is familiar, but reversed, white to black, female to male, with appropriate adjustments reflecting these changes. It was printed in a hardcover anthology, *Full Spectrum 2,* after the publication of the Cheap Street edition, and was selected by Terry Windling and Ellen Datlow as one of the best fantasy stories of the year. It's still one of my all-time favorites.

Sleepside Story, along with *The Infinity Concerto* and *The Serpent Mage*, comprise my contributions to the genre of gritty urban fantasy—with a tip of the hat, of course, to Peter Beagle.

The original illustrations to the Cheap Street Edition were by Judy King Reinitz, and they were lovely. Unfortunately, I doubt the illustrations and the story will ever be paired again, as O'Nale and I had a falling out even before the book was published. If you can find the original Cheap Street Edition—it's quite rare— take a look at both the production and the illustrations. Magnificent.

Sleepside Story
Cheap Street Press, Jan O'Nale, 1988
First popular publication, *Full Spectrum 2,* Lou Aronica, Shawna
McCarthy, Amy Stout, Pat LoBrutto, 1989

Oliver Jones differed from his brothers as wheat from chaff. He didn't grudge them their blind wildness; he loaned them money until he had none, and regretted it, but not deeply. His needs were not simple, but they did not hang on the sharp signs of dollars. He worked at the jobs of youth without complaining, knowing there was something better waiting for him. Sometimes it seemed he was the only one in the family able to take cares away from his Momma, now that Poppa was gone and she was lonely even with the two babies sitting on her lap, and his younger sister Yolanda gabbing about the neighbors.

The city was a puzzle to him. His older brothers Denver and Reggie believed it was a place to be conquered, but Oliver did not share their philosophy. He wanted to make the city part of him, sucked in with his breath, built into bones and brains. If he could dance with the city's music, he'd have it made, even though Denver and Reggie said the city was wide and cruel and had no end; that its four quarters ate young men alive, and spat back old people. Look at Poppa, they said; he was forty-three and he went to the fifth quarter, Darkside, a bag of wearied bones; they said, take what you can get while you can get it.

This was not what Oliver saw, though he knew the city was cruel and hungry.

His brothers and even Yolanda kidded him about his faith. It was more than just going to church that made them rag him, because they went to church, too, sitting superior beside Momma. Reggie and Denver knew there was advantage in being seen at devotions. It wasn't his music that made them laugh, for he could play the piano hard and fast as well as soft and tender, and they all liked to dance, even Momma sometimes. It was his damned sweetness. It was his taste in girls, quiet and studious; and his honesty.

On the last day of school, before Christmas vacation, Oliver made his way home in a fall of light snow, stopping in the old St. John's church-yard for a moment's reflection by his father's grave. Surrounded by the crisp, ancient slate gravestones and the newer white marble, worn by the city's acid tears, he thought he might now be considered grown-up, might have to support all of his family. He left the churchyard in a somber mood and walked between the tall brick and brownstone ten-ements, along the dirty, wet black streets, his shadow lost in Sleepside's greater shade, eyes on the sidewalk.

Denver and Reggie could not bring in good money, money that Momma would accept; Yolanda was too young and not likely to get a job anytime soon, and that left him, the only one who would finish school. He might take in more piano students, but he'd have to move out to do that, and how could he find another place to live without losing all he made to rent? Sleepside was crowded.

Oliver heard the noise in the flat from half a block down the street. He ran up the five dark, trash-littered flights of stairs and pulled out his key to open the three locks on the door. Swinging the door wide, he stood with hand pressed to a wall, lungs too greedy to let him speak.

The flat was in an uproar. Yolanda, rail-skinny, stood in the kitchen doorway, wringing her big hands and wailing. The two babies lurched down the hall, diapers drooping and fists stuck in their mouths. The neighbor widow Mrs. Diamond Freeland bustled back and forth in a useless dither. Something was terribly wrong.

"What is it?" he asked Yolanda with his first free breath. She just moaned and shook her head. "Where's Reggie and Denver?" She shook her head less vigorously, meaning they weren't home. "Where's Momma?" This sent Yolanda into hysterics. She bumped back against the wall and clenched her fists to her mouth, tears flying. "Something happen to Momma?"

"Your momma went uptown," Mrs. Diamond Freeland said, standing flatfooted before Oliver, her flower print dress distended over her generous stomach. "What are you going to do? You're her son."

"Where uptown?" Oliver asked, trying to control his quavering voice. He wanted to slap everybody in the apartment. He was scared and they weren't being any help at all.

"She we-went sh-sh-shopping!" Yolanda wailed. "She got her check today and it's Christmas and she went to get the babies new clothes and some food."

Oliver's hands clenched. Momma had asked him what he wanted for Christmas, and he had said, "Nothing, Momma. Not really." She had chided him, saying all would be well when the check came, and what good was Christmas if she couldn't find a little something special for each of her children? "All right," he said. "I'd like sheet music. Something I've never played before."

"She must of taken the wrong stop," Mrs. Diamond Freeland said, staring at Oliver from the corners of her wide eyes. "That's all I can figure."

What happened?"

Yolanda pulled a letter out of her blouse and handed it to him, a fancy purple paper with a delicate flower design on the borders, the message handwritten very prettily in gold ink fountain pen and signed. He read it carefully, then read it again.

To the Joneses.

Your momma is uptown in My care. She came here lost and I tried to help her but she stole something very valuable to Me she shouldn't have. She says you'll come and get her. By you she means her youngest son Oliver Jones and if not him then Yolanda Jones her eldest daughter. I will keep one or the other here in exchange for your momma and one or the other must stay here and work for Me. Miss Belle Parkhurst
   969 33rd Street

"Who's she, and why does she have Momma?" Oliver asked.

"I'm not going!" Yolanda screamed.

"Hush up," said Mrs. Diamond Freeland. "She's that whoor. She's that uptown whoor used to run the biggest cathouse."

OLIVER LOOKED FROM FACE TO FACE IN DISBELIEF.

"Your momma must of taken the wrong stop and got lost," Mrs. Diamond Freeland reiterated. "That's all I can figure. She went to that whoor's house and she got in trouble."

"I'm not going!" Yolanda said. She avoided Oliver's eyes. "You know what she'd make me do."

"Yeah," Oliver said softly. "But what'll she make *me* do?

Reggie and Denver, he learned from Mrs. Diamond Freeland, had come home before the message had been received, leaving just as the messenger came whistling up the outside hall. Oliver sighed. His brothers were almost never home; they thought they'd pulled the wool over Momma's eyes, but they hadn't. Momma knew who would be home and come for her when she was in trouble.

Reggie and Denver fancied themselves the hottest dudes on the street. They claimed they had women all over Sleepside and Snowside; Oliver was almost too shy to ask a woman out. He was small, slender, and almost pretty, but very strong for his size. Reggie and Denver were cowards. Oliver had never run from a true and worthwhile fight in his life, but neither had he started one.

The thought of going to Miss Belle Parkhurst's establishment scared him, but he remembered what his father had told him just a week before dying. "Oliver, when I'm gone—that's soon now, you know it— Yolanda's flaky as a bowl of cereal and your brothers . . . well, I'll be kind and just say your momma, she's going to need you. You got to turn out right so as she can lean on you."

The babies hadn't been born then.

"Which train did she take?"

"Down to Snowside," Mrs. Diamond Freeland said. "But she must of gotten off in Sunside. That's near Thirty-third."

"It's getting night," Oliver said.

Yolanda sniffed and wiped her eyes. Off the hook. "You going?"

"Have to," Oliver said. "It's Momma."

Said Mrs. Diamond Freeland, "I think that whore got something on her mind."

ON THE LINE BETWEEN DUSK AND DARK, DOWN UNDERGROUND WHERE IT shouldn't have mattered, the Metro emptied of all the day's passengers and filled with the night's.

Sometimes day folks went in tight-packed groups on the Night Metro, but not if they could avoid it. Night Metro was for carrying the lost or human garbage. Everyone ashamed or afraid to come out during the day came out at night. Night Metro also carried the zeroes—people who lived their lives and when they died no one could look back and say they remembered them. Night Metro—especially late—was not a good way to travel, but for Oliver it was the quickest way to get from Sleepside to Sunside; he had to go as soon as possible to get Momma.

Oliver descended the four flights of concrete steps, grinding his teeth at the thought of the danger he was in. He halted at the bottom, grimacing at the frightened knots of muscle and nerves in his back, repeating over and over again, "It's Momma. It's Momma. No one can save her but me." He dropped his bronze cat's head token into the turnstile, *clunk-chunking* through, and crossed the empty platform. Only two indistinct figures waited trackside, heavy-coated though it was a warm evening. Oliver kept an eye on them and walked back and forth in a figure eight on the grimy foot-scrubbed concrete, peering nervously down at the wet and soot under the rails. Behind him, on the station's smudged white tile walls hung a gold mosaic trumpet and the number 7, the trumpet for folks who couldn't read to know when to get off. All Sleepside stations had musical instruments.

The Night Metro was run by a different crew than the Day Metro. His train came up, clean and silver-sleek, without a spot of graffiti or a stain of tarnish. Oliver caught a glimpse of the driver under the SLEEPSIDE/CHASTE RIVER/SUNSIDE-46TH destination sign. The driver wore or had a bull's head and carried a prominent pair of long gleaming silver scissors on his Sam Browne belt. Oliver entered the open doors and took a smooth handgrip even though the seats were mostly empty. Somebody standing was somebody quicker to run.

There were four people on his car: two women, one young, vacant, and not pretty or even very alive-looking, the other old and muddy-eyed with a plastic daisy-flowered shopping bag—and two men, both sunny blond and chunky, wearing shiny-elbowed business suits. Nobody looked at anybody else. The doors shut and the train grumbled on, gathering speed until the noise of its wheels on the tracks drowned out all other sound and almost all thought.

There were more dead stations than live and lighted ones. Night Metro made only a few stops congruent with Day Metro. Most stations were turned off, but the only people left standing there wouldn't show in bright lights anyway. Oliver tried not to look, to keep his eyes on the few in the car with him, but every so often he couldn't help peering out. Beyond I-beams and barricades, single orange lamps and broken tiled walls rushed by, platforms populated by slow smudges of shadow.

Some said the dead used the Night Metro, and that after midnight it went all the way to Darkside. Oliver didn't know what to believe. As the train slowed for his station, he pulled the collar of his dark green nylon windbreaker up around his neck and rubbed his nose with one finger. Reggie and Denver would never have made it even this far. They valued their skins too much.

The train did not move on after he disembarked. He stood by the open doors for a moment, then walked past the lead car on his way to the stairs. Over his shoulder, he saw the driver standing at the head of the train in his little cabin of fluorescent coldness, the eyes in the bull's head sunk deep in shade. Oliver felt rather than saw the starlike pricks in the sockets, watching him. The driver's left hand tugged on the blades of the silver shears.

"What do you care, man?" Oliver asked softly, stopping for an instant to return the hidden stare. "Go on about your work. We all got stuff to do."

The bull's nose pointed a mere twitch away from Oliver, and the hand left the shears to return to its switch. The train doors closed. The silver side panels and windows and lights picked up speed and the train squealed around a curve into darkness. He climbed the two flights of stairs to Sunside Station.

Summer night lay heavy and warm on the lush trees and grass of a broad park. Oliver stood at the head of the Metro entrance and listened to the crickets and katydids and cicadas sing songs unheard in Sleepside, where trees and grass were sparse. All around the park rose dark-windowed walls of high marble and brick and gray stone hotels and fancy apartment buildings with gable roofs.

Oliver looked around for directions, a map, anything. Above the Night Metro, it was even possible ordinary people might be out strolling, and he could ask them if he dared. He walked toward the street and thought of Momma getting this far and of her being afraid. He loved Momma very much. Sometimes she seemed to be the only decent thing in his life, though more and more often young women distracted him as the years passed, and he experienced more and more secret fixations.

"Oliver Jones?"

A long white limousine waited by the curb. A young, slender woman in violet chauffeur's livery, with a jaunty black and silver cap sitting atop exuberant hair, cocked her head coyly, smiled at him, and beckoned with a white-leather-gloved finger. "Are you Oliver Jones, come to rescue your momma?"

He walked slowly toward the white limousine. It was bigger and more beautiful than anything he had ever seen before, with long ribbed chrome pipes snaking out from under the hood and through the fenders, stand-alone golden headlights, and a white tonneau roof made of real leather. "My name's Oliver," he affirmed.

"Then you're my man. Please get in." She winked and held the door open.

When the door closed, the woman's arm—all he could see of her through the smoky window glass—vanished. The driver's door did not open. She did not get in. The limousine drove off by itself. Oliver fell back into the lush suede and velvet interior. An electronic wet bar gleamed silver and gold and black above a cool white-lit panel on which sat a single crystal glass filled with ice cubes. A spigot rotated around and waited for instructions. When none came, it gushed fragrant gin over the ice and rotated back into place.

Oliver did not touch the glass.

Below the wet bar, the television set turned itself on. Passion and delight sang from the small, precise speakers. "No," he said. "No!"

The television shut off.

He edged closer to the smoky glass and saw dim streetlights and cab headlights moving past. A huge black building trimmed with gold ornaments, windows outlined with red, loomed on the corner, all but three of its windows dark. The limousine turned smoothly and descended into a dark underground garage. Lights throwing huge golden cat's eyes, tires squealing on shiny concrete, it snaked around a slalom of walls and pillars and dusty limousines and came to a quick stop. The door opened.

Oliver stepped out. The chauffeur stood holding the door, grinning, and doffed her cap. "My pleasure," she said.

The car had parked beside a big wooden door set into hewn stone. Fossil bones and teeth were clearly visible in the matrix of each block in the walls. Glistening ferns in dark ponds flanked the door. Oliver heard the car drive away and turned to look, but he did not see whether the chauffeur drove this time or not.

He walked across a wood plank bridge and tried the black iron handle on the door. The door swung open at the suggestion of his fingers. Beyond, a narrow red-carpeted staircase with rosebush-carved maple banisters ascended to the upper floor.

The place smelled of cloves and mint and, somehow, of what Oliver imagined dogs or horses must smell like—a musty old rug sitting on a floor grate. (He had never owned a dog and never seen a horse without a policeman on it, and never so close he could smell it.) Nobody had been through here in a long time, he thought. But everybody knew about Miss Belle Parkhurst and her place. And the chauffeur had been young. He wrinkled his nose; he did not like this place.

The dark wood door at the top of the stairs swung open silently.

Nobody stood there waiting; it might have opened by itself. Oliver tried to speak, but his throat itched and closed. He coughed into his fist and shrugged his shoulders in a spasm. Then, eyes damp and hot with anger and fear and something more, he moved his lips and croaked, "I'm Oliver Jones. I'm here to get my momma."

The door remained unattended. He looked back into the parking garage, dark and quiet as a cave; nothing for him there. Then he ascended quickly to get it over with and passed through the door into the ill-reputed house of Miss Belle Parkhurst.

THE CITY EXTENDS TO THE FAR HORIZON, DIVIDED INTO QUARTERS BY ROADS or canals or even train tracks, above or underground; and sometimes you know those divisions and know better than to cross them, and sometimes you don't. The city is broader than any man's life, and it is worth more than your life not to understand why you are where you are and must stay there.

The city encourages ignorance because it must eat.

The four quarters of the city are Snowside, Cokeside where few sane people go, Sleepside, and Sunside. Sunside is bright and rich and hazardous because that is where the swell folks live. Swell folks don't tolerate intruders. Not even the police go into Sunside without an escort. Toward the center of the city is uptown, and in the middle of uptown is where all four quarters meet at the Pillar of the Unknown Mayor. Outward is the downtown and scattered islands of suburbs, and no one knows where it ends.

The Joneses live in downtown Sleepside. The light there even at noon is not very bright, but neither is it burning harsh as in Cokeside where it can fry your skull. Sleepside is tolerable. There are many good people in Sleepside and Snowside, and though confused, the general run is not vicious. Oliver grew up there and carries it in his bones and meat. No doubt the Night Metro driver smelled his origins and knew here was a young man crossing a border going uptown. No doubt Oliver was still alive because Miss Belle Parkhurst had protected him. That meant Miss Parkhurst had protected Momma, and perhaps lured her, as well.

The hallway was lighted by rows of candles held in gold eagle claws along each wall. At the end of the hall, Oliver stepped into a broad wood-paneled room set here and there with lush green ferns in brass spittoons. The Oriental carpet revealed a stylized garden in cream and black and red. Five empty black velvet-upholstered couches stood unoccupied, expectant, like a line of languorous women amongst the ferns. Along the walls, chairs covered by white sheets asserted their heavy wooden arms. Oliver stood, jaw open, not used to such luxury. He needed a long moment to take it all in.

Miss Belle Parkhurst was obviously a very rich woman, and not your ordinary whore. From what he had seen so far, she had power as well as money, power over cars and maybe over men and women. Maybe over Momma. "Momma?"

A tall, tenuous white-haired man in a cream-colored suit walked across the room, paying Oliver scant attention. He said nothing. Oliver watched him sit on a sheet-covered chair. He did not disturb the sheets, but sat through them. He leaned his head back reflectively, elevating a cigarette holder without a cigarette. He blew out clear air, or perhaps nothing at all, and then smiled at something just to Oliver's right. Oliver turned. They were alone. When he looked back, the man in the cream-colored suit was gone.

Oliver's arms tingled. He was in for more than he had bargained for, and he had bargained for a lot.

"This way," said a woman's deep voice, operatic, dignified, easy and friendly at once. He could not see her, but he squinted at the doorway, and she stepped between two fluted green onyx columns. He did not know at first that she was addressing him; there might be other gentlemen, or girls, equally as tenuous as the man in the cream-colored suit. But this small, imposing woman with upheld hands, dressed in gold and peach silk that clung to her smooth and silent, was watching only him with her large dark eyes. She smiled richly and warmly, but Oliver thought there was a hidden flaw in that smile, in her assurance. She was ill at ease from the instant their eyes met, though she might have been at ease before then, *thinking* of meeting him. She had had all things planned until that moment.

If he unnerved her slightly, this woman positively terrified him. She was beautiful and smooth-skinned, and he could smell the sweet roses and camellias and magnolia blossoms surrounding her like a crowd of familiar friends.

"This way," she repeated, gesturing through the doors.

"I'm looking for my momma. I'm supposed to meet Miss Belle Parkhurst."

"I'm Belle Parkhurst. You're Oliver Jones . . . aren't you?"

He nodded, face solemn, eyes wide. He nodded again and swallowed.

"I sent your momma on her way home. She'll be fine."

He looked back at the hallway. "She'll be on the Night Metro," he said.

"I sent her back in my car. Nothing will happen to her."

Oliver believed her. There was a long, silent moment. He realized he was twisting and wringing his hands before his crotch and he stopped this, embarrassed.

"Your momma's fine. Don't worry about her."

"All right," he said, drawing his shoulders up. "You wanted to talk to me?"

"Yes," she said. "And more."

His nostrils flared and he jerked his eyes hard right, his torso and then his hips and legs twisting that way as he broke into a scrambling rabbit-run for the hallway. The golden eagle claws on each side dropped their candles as he passed and reached out to hook him with their talons. The vast house around him seemed suddenly alert, and he knew even before one claw grabbed his collar that he did not have a chance.

He dangled helpless from the armpits of his jacket at the very end of the hall. In the far door appeared the whore, angry, fingers dripping small beads of fire onto the wooden floor. The floor smoked and sizzled.

"I've let your momma go," Belle Parkhurst said, voice deeper than a grave, face terrible and smoothly beautiful and very old, very experienced. "That was my agreement. You leave, and you break that agreement, and that means I take your sister, or I take back your momma."

She cocked an elegant, painted eyebrow at him and leaned her head to one side in query. He nodded as best he could with his chin jammed against the teeth of his jacket's zipper.

"Good. There's food waiting. I'd enjoy your company."

THE DINING ROOM WAS SMALL, NO LARGER THAN HIS BEDROOM AT HOME, occupied by two chairs and an intimate round table covered in white linen. A gold eagle claw candelabrum cast a warm light over the table top. Miss Parkhurst preceded Oliver, her long dress rustling softly at her heels. Other things rustled in the room as well; the floor might have been ankle-deep in windblown leaves by the sound, but it was spotless, a rich round red and cream Oriental rug centered beneath the table; and beneath that, smooth old oak flooring. Oliver looked up from his sneaker-clad feet. Miss Parkhurst waited expectantly a step back from her chair.

"Your momma teach you no manners?" she asked softly.

He approached the table reluctantly. There were empty gold plates and tableware on the linen now that had not been there before. Napkins seemed to drop from thin fog and folded themselves on the plates. Oliver stopped, his nostrils flaring.

"Don't you mind that," Miss Parkhurst said. "I live alone here. Good help is hard to find."

OLIVER STEPPED BEHIND THE CHAIR AND LIFTED IT BY ITS MAPLE HEADPIECE, pulling it out for her. She sat and he helped her move closer to the table. Not once did he touch her; his skin crawled at the thought.

"The food here is very good," Miss Parkhurst said as he sat across from her.

"I'm not hungry," Oliver said.

She smiled warmly at him. It was a powerful thing, her smile. "I won't bite," she said. "Except supper. *That* I'll bite."

Oliver smelled wonderful spices and sweet vinegar. A napkin had been draped across his lap, and before him was a salad on a fine china plate. He was very hungry and he enjoyed salads, seeing fresh greens so seldom in Sleepside.

"That's it," Miss Parkhurst said soothingly, smiling as he ate. She lifted her fork in turn and speared a fold of olive-oiled butter lettuce, bringing it to her red lips.

The rest of the dinner proceeded in like fashion, but with no further conversation. She watched him frankly, appraising, and he avoided her eyes.

Down a corridor with tall windows set in an east wall, dawn gray and pink around their faint silhouettes on the west wall, Miss Parkhurst led Oliver to his room. "It's the quietest place in the mansion," she said.

"You're keeping me here," he said. "You're never going to let me go?"

"Please allow me to indulge myself. I'm not just alone. I'm lonely. Here, you can have anything you want . . . almost . . ."

A door at the corridor's far end opened by itself. Within, a fire burned brightly within a small fireplace, and a wide bed waited with covers turned down. Exquisitely detailed murals of forests and fields covered the walls; the ceiling was rich deep blue, flecked with gold and silver and jeweled stars. Books filled a case in one corner, and in another corner stood the most beautiful ebony grand piano he had ever seen. Miss Parkhurst did not approach the door too closely. There were no candles; within this room, all lamps were electric.

"This is your room. I won't come in," she said. "And after tonight, you don't ever come out after dark. We'll talk and see each other during the day, but never at night. The door isn't locked. I'll have to trust you."

"I can go anytime I want?"

She smiled. Even though she meant her smile to be nothing more than enigmatic, it shook him. She was deadly beautiful, the kind of woman his brothers dreamed about. Her smile said she might eat him alive, all of him that counted. Oliver could imagine his mother's reaction to Miss Belle Parkhurst.

He entered the room and swung the door shut, trembling. There were a dozen things he wanted to say; angry, frustrated, pleading things. He leaned against the door, swallowing them all back, keeping his hand from going to the gold and crystal knob.

Behind the door, her skirts rustled as she retired along the corridor. After a moment, he pushed off from the door and walked with an exaggerated swagger to the bookcase, mumbling. Miss Parkhurst would never have taken Oliver's sister Yolanda; that wasn't what she wanted. She wanted young boy flesh, he thought. She wanted to burn him down to his sneakers, smiling like that.

The books on the shelves were books he had heard about but had never found in the Sleepside library, books he wanted to read, that the librarians said only people from Sunside and the suburbs cared to read. His fingers lingered on the tops of their spines, tugging gently.

He decided to sleep instead. If she was going to pester him during the day, he didn't have much time. She'd be a late riser, he thought; a night person.

Then he realized: whatever she did at night, she had not done this night. This night had been set aside for him.

He shivered again, thinking of the food and napkins and the eagle claws. Was this room haunted, too? Would things keep watch over him?

Oliver lay back on the bed, still clothed. His mind clouded with thoughts of living sheets feeling up his bare skin. Tired, almost dead out.

The dreams that came were sweet and pleasant and she did not walk in them. This really was his time.

AT ELEVEN O'CLOCK BY THE BRASS AND GOLD AND CRYSTAL CLOCK ON THE bookcase, Oliver kicked his legs out, rubbed his face into the pillows and started up, back arched, smelling bacon and eggs and coffee. A covered tray waited on a polished brass cart beside the bed. A vase of roses on one corner of the cart scented the room. A folded piece of fine ivory paper leaned against the vase. Oliver sat on the edge of the bed and read the note, once again written in golden ink in a delicate hand.

I'm waiting for you in the gymnasium. Meet me after you've eaten.
Got something to give to you.

He had no idea where the gymnasium was. When he had finished breakfast, he put on a plush robe, opened the heavy door to his room—both relieved and irritated that it did not open by itself—and looked down the corridor. A golden arc clung to the base of each tall window. It was at least noon, Sunside time. She had given him plenty of time to rest.

A pair of new black jeans and a white silk shirt waited for him on the bed, which had been carefully made in the time it had taken him to glance down the hall. Cautiously, but less frightened now, he removed the robe, put on these clothes and the deerskin moccasins by the foot of the bed, and stood in the doorway, leaning as casually as he could manage against the frame.

A silk handkerchief hung in the air several yards away. It fluttered like a pigeon's ghost to attract his attention, then drifted slowly along the hall. He followed.

The house seemed to go on forever, empty and magnificent. Each public room had its own decor, filled with antique furniture, potted palms, plush couches and chairs, and love seats. Several times he thought he saw wisps of dinner jackets, top hats, eager, strained faces, in foyers, corridors, on staircases as he followed the handkerchief. The house smelled of perfume and dust, faint cigars, spilled wine, and old sweat.

He had climbed three flights of stairs before he stood at the tall ivory-white double door of the gymnasium. The handkerchief vanished with a flip. The doors opened.

Miss Parkhurst stood at the opposite end of a wide black tile dance floor, before a band riser covered with music stands and instruments. Oliver inspected the low half-circle stage with narrowed eyes. Would she demand he dance with her, while all the instruments played by themselves?

"Good morning," she said. She wore a green dress the color of fresh wet grass, high at the neck and down to her calves. Beneath the dress she wore white boots and white gloves, and a white feather curled around her black hair.

"Good morning," he replied softly, politely.

"Did you sleep well? Eat hearty?"

Oliver nodded, fear and shyness returning. What could she possibly want to give him? Herself? His face grew hot.

"It's a shame this house is empty during the day," she said. *And at night?* he thought. "I could fill this room with exercise equipment," she continued. "Weight benches, even a track around the outside." She smiled. The smile seemed less ferocious now, even wistful; younger.

He rubbed a fold of his shirt between two fingers. "I enjoyed the food, and your house is real fine, but I'd like to go home," he said.

She half turned and walked slowly from the stand. "You could have this house and all my wealth. I'd like you to have it."

"Why? I haven't done anything for you."

"Or to me, either," she said, facing him again. "You know how I've made all this money?"

"Yes, ma'am," he said after a moment's pause. "I'm not a fool."

"You've heard about me. That I'm a whore."

"Yes, ma'am. Mrs. Diamond Freeland says you are."

"And what is a whore?"

"You let men do it to you for money," Oliver said, feeling bolder, but with his face hot all the same.

Miss Parkhurst nodded. "I've got part of them all here with me," she said. "My bookkeeping. I know every name, every face. They keep me company now that business is slow."

"All of them?" Oliver asked.

Miss Parkhurst's faint smile was part pride, part sadness, her eyes distant and moist. "They gave me all the things I have here."

"I don't think it would be worth it," Oliver said.

"I'd be dead if I wasn't a whore," Miss Parkhurst said, eyes suddenly sharp on him, flashing anger. "I'd have starved to death." She relaxed her clenched hands. "We got plenty of time to talk about my life, so let's hold it here for a while. I got something you need, if you're going to inherit this place."

"I don't want it, ma'am," Oliver said.

"If you don't take it, somebody who doesn't need it and deserves it a lot less will. I want you to have it. Please, be kind to me this once."

"Why me?" Oliver asked. He simply wanted out; this was completely off the planned track of his life. He was less afraid of Miss Parkhurst now, though her anger raised hairs on his neck; he felt he could be bolder and perhaps even demanding. There was a weakness in her: he was her weakness, and he wasn't above taking some advantage of that, considering how desperate his situation might be.

"You're kind," she said. "You care. And you've never had a woman, not all the way."

Oliver's face warmed again. "Please let me go," he said quietly, hoping it didn't sound as if he was pleading.

Miss Parkhurst folded her arms. "I can't," she said.

WHILE OLIVER SPENT HIS FIRST DAY IN MISS PARKHURST'S MANSION, ACROSS the city, beyond the borders of Sunside, Denver and Reggie Jones had returned home to find the apartment blanketed in gloom. Reggie, tall and gangly, long of neck and short of head, with a prominent nose, stood with back slumped in the front hall, mouth open in surprise. "He just took off and left you all here?" Reggie asked. Denver returned from the kitchen, shorter and stockier than his brother, dressed in black vinyl jacket and pants.

Yolanda's face was puffy from constant crying. She now enjoyed the tears she spilled, and had scheduled them at two-hour intervals, to her momma's sorrowful irritation. She herded the two babies into their momma's bedroom and closed a rickety gate behind them, then brushed her hands on the breast of her ragged blouse.

"You don't get it," she said, facing them and dropping her arms dramatically. "That whore took Momma, and Oliver traded himself for her."

"That whore," said Reggie, "is a rich old witch."

"Rich old bitch witch," Denver said, pleased with himself.

"That whore is opportunity knocking," Reggie continued, chewing reflectively. "I hear she lives alone."

"That's why she took Oliver," Yolanda said. The babies cooed and chirped behind the gate.

"Why him and not one of us?" Reggie asked.

Momma gently pushed the babies aside, swung open the gate, and marched down the hall, dressed in her best wool skirt and print blouse, wrapped in her overcoat against the gathering dark and cold outside. "Where you going?" Yolanda asked her as she brushed past.

"Time to talk to the police," she said, glowering at Reggie. Denver backed into the bedroom he shared with his brother, out of her way. He shook his head condescendingly, grinning: Momma at it again.

"Them dogheads?" Reggie said. "They got no say in Sunside."

Momma turned at the front door and glared at them. "How are you going to help your brother? He's the best of you all, you know, and you just stand here, flatfooted and jawboning yourselves."

"Momma's upset," Denver informed his brother solemnly.

"She should be," Reggie said sympathetically. "She was held prisoner by that witch bitch whore. We should go get Oliver and bring him home. We could pretend we was customers."

"She don't have customers anymore," Denver said. "She's too old. She's worn out." He glanced at his crotch and leaned his head to one side, glaring for emphasis. His glare faded into an amiable grin.

"How do you know?" Reggie asked.

"That's what I hear."

Momma snorted and pulled back the bars and bolts on the front door. Reggie calmly walked up behind her and stopped her. "Police don't do anybody any good, Momma," he said. "We'll go. We'll bring Oliver back."

Denver's face slowly fell at the thought. "We got to plan it out," he said. "We got to be careful."

"We'll be careful," Reggie said. "For Momma's sake."

With his hand blocking her exit, Momma snorted again, then let her shoulders droop and her face sag. She looked more and more like an old woman now, though she was only in her late thirties.

Yolanda stood aside to let her pass into the living room. "Poor Momma," she said, eyes welling up.

"What you going to do for your brother?" Reggie asked his sister pointedly as he in turn walked by her. She craned her neck and stuck out her chin resentfully. "Go trade places with him, work in *her* house?" he taunted.

"She's rich," Denver said to himself, cupping his chin in his hand. "We could make a whole lot of money, saving our brother."

"We start thinking about it now," Reggie mandated, falling into the chair that used to be their father's, leaning his head back against the lace covers Momma had made.

Momma, face ashen, stood by the couch staring at a family portrait hung on the wall in a cheap wooden frame. "He did it for me. I was so stupid, getting off there, letting her help me. Should of known," she murmured, clutching her wrist. Her face ashen, her ankle wobbled under her and she pirouetted, hands spread out like a dancer, and collapsed face down on the couch.

THE GIFT, THE THING THAT OLIVER NEEDED TO INHERIT MISS PARKHURST'S mansion, was a small gold box with three buttons, like a garage door opener. She finally presented it to him in the dining room as they finished dinner.

Miss Parkhurst was nice to talk to, something Oliver had not expected, but which he should have. Whores did more than lie with a man to keep him coming back and spending his money; that should have been obvious. The day had not been the agony he expected. He had even stopped asking her to let him go. Oliver thought it would be best to bide his time, and when something distracted her, make his escape. Until then, she was not treating him badly or expecting anything he could not freely give.

"It'll be dark soon," she said as the plates cleared themselves away. He was even getting used to the ghostly service. "I have to go soon, and you got to be in your room. Take this with you, and keep it there." She lifted a tray cover to reveal a white silk bag. Unstringing the bag, she removed the golden opener and shyly presented it to him. "This was given to me a long time ago. I don't need it now. But if you want to run this place, you got to have it. You can't lose it, or let anyone take it from you."

Oliver's hands went to the opener involuntarily. It seemed very desirable, as if there were something of Miss Parkhurst in it: warm, powerful, a little frightening. It fit his hand perfectly, familiar to his skin; he might have owned it forever.

He tightened his lips and returned it to her. "I'm sorry," he said. "It's not for me."

"You remember what I told you," she said. "If you don't take it, somebody else will, and it won't do anybody any good then. I want it to do some good now, when I'm done with it."

"Who gave it to you?" Oliver asked.

"A pimp, a long time ago. When I was a girl."

Oliver's eyes betrayed no judgment or disgust. She took a deep breath.

"He made you do it . . . ?" Oliver asked.

"No. I was young, but already a whore. I had an old, kind pimp, at least he seemed old to me, I wasn't much more than a baby. He died, he was killed, so this new pimp came, and he was powerful. He had the magic. But he couldn't tame me. So he says . . ."

Miss Parkhurst raised her hands to her face. "He cut me up. I was almost dead. He says, 'You shame me, whore. You do this to me, make me lose control, you're the only one ever did this to me. So I curse you. You'll be the greatest whore ever was.' He gave me the opener then, and he put my face and body back together so I'd be pretty. Then he left town, and I was in charge. I've been here ever since, but all the girls have gone, it's been so long, died or left or I told them to go. I wanted this place closed, but I couldn't close it all at once."

Oliver nodded slowly, eyes wide.

"He gave me most of his magic, too. I didn't have any choice. One thing he didn't give me was a way out. Except this time, she was the one with the pleading expression.

Oliver raised an eyebrow.

"What I need has to be freely given. Now take this." She stood and thrust the opener into his hands. "Use it to find your way all around the house. But don't leave your room after dark."

She swept out of the dining room, leaving a scent of musk and flowers and something bittersweet. Oliver put the opener in his pocket and walked back to his room, finding his way without hesitation, without thought. He shut the door and went to the bookcase, sad and troubled and exultant all at once.

She had told him her secret. He could leave now if he wanted. She had given him the power to leave.

SIPPING FROM A GLASS OF SHERRY ON THE NIGHTSTAND BESIDE THE BED, reading from a book of composers' lives, he decided to wait until morning.

Yet after a few hours, nothing could keep his mind away from Miss Parkhurst's prohibition—not the piano, the books, or the snacks delivered almost before he thought about them, appearing on the tray when he wasn't watching. Oliver sat with hands folded in the plush chair, blinking at the room's dark corners. He thought he had Miss Parkhurst pegged. She was an old woman tired of her life, a beautifully preserved old woman to be sure, very strong . . . But she was sweet on him, keeping him like some unused gigolo. Still, he couldn't help but admire her, and he couldn't help but want to be home, near Momma and Yolanda and the babies, keeping his brothers out of trouble—not that they appreciated his efforts.

The longer he sat, the angrier and more anxious he became. He felt sure something was wrong at home. Pacing around the room did nothing to calm him. He examined the opener time and again in the firelight, brow wrinkled, wondering what powers it gave him. She had said he could go anywhere in the house and know his way, just as he had found his room without her help.

He moaned, shaking his fists at the air. "She can't keep me here! She just *can't*!"

At midnight, he couldn't control himself any longer. He stood before the door. "Let me out, dammit!" he cried, and the door opened with a sad whisper. He ran down the corridor, scattering moonlight on the floor like dust, tears shining on his cheeks.

Through the sitting rooms, the long halls of empty bedrooms—now with their doors closed, shades of sound sifting from behind—through the vast deserted kitchen, with its rows of polished copper kettles and huge black coal cookstoves, through a courtyard surrounded by five stories of the mansion on all sides and open to the golden-starred night sky, past a tiled fountain guarded by three huge white porcelain lions, ears and empty eyes following him as he ran by, Oliver searched for Miss Parkhurst, to tell her he must leave.

For a moment, he caught his breath in an upstairs gallery. He saw faint lights under doors, heard more suggestive sounds. No time to pause, even with his heart pounding and his lungs burning. If he waited in one place long enough, he thought the ghosts might become real and make him join their revelry. This was Miss Parkhurst's past, hoary and indecent, more than he could bear contemplating. How could anyone have lived this kind of life, even if they were cursed?

Yet the temptation to stop, to listen, to give in and join in was almost stronger than he could resist. He kept losing track of what he was doing, what his ultimate goal was.

"Where are you?" he shouted, throwing open double doors to a game room, empty but for more startled ghosts, more of Miss Parkhurst's eternity of bookkeeping. Pale forms rose from the billiard tables, translucent breasts shining with an inner light, their pale lovers rolling slowly to one side, fat bellies prominent, ghost eyes black and startled. "Miss Parkhurst!"

Oliver brushed through hundreds of girls, no more substantial than curtains of raindrops. His new clothes became wet with their tears. *She* had presided over this eternity of sad lust. *She* had orchestrated the debaucheries, catered to what he felt inside him: the whims and deepest desires unspoken.

Thin antique laughter followed him.

He slid on a splash of sour-smelling champagne and came up abruptly against a heavy wooden door, a room he did not know. The golden opener told him nothing about what waited beyond.

"Open!" he shouted, but he was ignored. The door was not locked, but it resisted his entry as if it weighed tons. He pushed with both hands and then laid his shoulder on the paneling, bracing his sneakers against the thick wool pile of a champagne-soaked runner. The door swung inward with a deep iron and wood grumble, and Oliver stumbled past, saving himself at the last minute from falling on his face. Legs sprawled, down on both hands, he looked up from the wooden floor and saw where he was.

The room was narrow, but stretched on for what might have been miles, lined on one side with an endless row of plain double beds, and on the other with an endless row of freestanding cheval mirrors. An old man, the oldest he had ever seen, naked, white as talcum, rose stiffly from the bed, mumbling. Beneath him, red and warm as a pile of glowing coals, Miss Parkhurst lay with legs spread, incense of musk and sweat thick about her. She raised her head and shoulders, eyes fixed on Oliver's, and pulled a black peignoir over her nakedness. In the gloom of the room's extremities, other men, old and young, stood by their beds, smoking cigarettes or cigars or drinking champagne or whisky, all observing Oliver. Some grinned in speculation.

Miss Parkhurst's face wrinkled in agony like an old apple and she threw back her head to scream. The old man on the bed grabbed clumsily for a robe and his clothes.

Her shriek echoed from the ceiling and the walls, driving Oliver back through the door, down the halls and stairways. The wind of his flight chilled him to the bone in his tear-soaked clothing. Somehow he made his way through the sudden darkness and emptiness, and shut himself in his room, where the fire still burned warm and cheery yellow. Shivering uncontrollably, Oliver removed the wet new clothes and called for his own in a high-pitched, frantic voice. But the invisible servants did not deliver what he requested.

He fell into the bed and pulled the covers tight about him, eyes closed. He prayed that she would not come after him, not come into his room with her peignoir slipping aside, revealing her furnace body; he prayed her smell would not follow him the rest of his life.

The door to his room did not open. Outside, all was quiet. In time, as dawn fired the roofs and then the walls and finally the streets of Sunside, Oliver slept.

"YOU CAME OUT OF YOUR ROOM LAST NIGHT," MISS PARKHURST SAID OVER the late breakfast. Oliver stopped chewing for a moment, glanced at her through bloodshot eyes, then shrugged.

"Did you see what you expected?"

Oliver didn't answer. Miss Parkhurst sighed like a young girl.

"It's my life. This is the way I've lived for a long time."

"None of my business," Oliver said, breaking a roll in half and buttering it.

"Do I disgust you?"

Again no reply. Miss Parkhurst stood in the middle of his silence and walked to the dining-room door. She looked over her shoulder at him, eyes moist. "You're not afraid of me now," she said. "You think you know what I am."

Oliver saw that his silence and uncaring attitude hurt her, and relished for a moment this power. When she remained standing in the doorway, he looked up with a purposefully harsh expression—copied from Reggie, sarcastic and angry at once—and saw tears flowing steadily down her cheeks. She seemed younger than ever now, not dangerous, just very sad. His expression faded. She turned away and closed the door behind her.

Oliver slammed half the roll into his plate of eggs and pushed his chair back from the table. "I'm not even full-grown!" he shouted at the door. "I'm not even a man! What do you want from me?" He stood up and kicked the chair away with his heel, then stuffed his hands in his pockets and paced around the small room. He felt bottled up, and yet she had said he could go anytime he wished.

Go where? Home?

He stared at the goldenware and the plates heaped with excellent food. Nothing like this at home. Home was a place he sometimes thought he'd have to fight to get away from; he couldn't protect Momma forever from the rest of the family, he couldn't be a breadwinner for five extra mouths for the rest of his life . . .

And if he stayed here, knowing what Miss Parkhurst did each night? Could he eat breakfast each morning, knowing how the food was earned, and all his clothes and books and the piano, too? He really would be a gigolo then.

Sunside. He was here, maybe he could live here, find work, get away from Sleepside for good.

The mere thought gave him a twinge. He sat down and buried his face in his hands, rubbing his eyes with the tips of his fingers, pulling at his lids to make a face, staring at himself reflected in the golden carafe, big-nosed, eyes monstrously bleared. He had to talk to Momma. Even talking to Yolanda might help.

But Miss Parkhurst was nowhere to be found. Oliver searched the mansion until dusk, then ate alone in the small dining room. He retired to his room as dark closed in, spreading through the halls like ink through water. To banish the night, and all that might be happening in it, Oliver played the piano loudly.

When he finally stumbled to his bed, he saw a single yellow rose on the pillow, delicate and sweet. He placed it by the lamp on the night-stand and pulled the covers over himself, clothes and all.

In the early hours of morning, he dreamed that Miss Parkhurst had fled the mansion, leaving it for him to tend to. The ghosts and old men crowded around, asking why he was so righteous. "She never had a Momma like you," said one decrepit dude dressed in black velvet night robes. "She's lived times you can't imagine. Now you just blew her right out of this house. Where will she go?"

Oliver came awake long enough to remember the dream, and then returned to a light, difficult sleep.

MRS. DIAMOND FREELAND SCOWLED AT YOLANDA'S HAND-WRINGING AND mumbling. "You can't help your momma acting that way," she said.

"I'm no doctor," Yolanda complained.

"No doctor's going to help her," Mrs. Freeland said, eyeing the door to Momma's bedroom.

Denver and Reggie lounged uneasily in the parlor.

"You two louts going to look for your brother?"

"We don't have to look for him," Denver said. "We know where he is. We got a plan to get him back."

"Then why don't you do it?" Mrs. Freeland asked.

"When the time's right," Reggie said decisively.

"Your Momma's pining for Oliver," Mrs. Freeland told them, not for the first time. "It's churning her insides thinking he's with that witch and what she might be doing to him."

Reggie tried unsuccessfully to hide a grin.

"What's funny?" Mrs. Freeland asked sternly.

"Nothing. Maybe our little brother needs some of what she's got."

Mrs. Freeland glared at them. "Yolanda," she said, rolling her eyes to the ceiling in disgust. "The babies. They dry?"

"No, ma'am," Yolanda said. She backed away from Mrs. Freeland's severe look. "I'll change them."

"Then you take them into your momma."

"Yes, ma'am."

THE BREAKFAST WENT AS IF NOTHING HAD HAPPENED. MISS PARKHURST SAT across from him, eating and smiling. Oliver tried to be more polite, working his way around to asking a favor. When the breakfast was over, the time seemed right.

"I'd like to see how Momma's doing," he said.

Miss Parkhurst considered for a moment. "There'll be a TV in your room this evening," she said, folding her napkin and placing it beside her plate. "You can use it to see how everybody is."

That seemed fair enough. Until then, however, he'd be spending the entire day with Miss Parkhurst; it was time, he decided, to be civil. Then he might actually test his freedom.

"You say I can go," Oliver said, trying to sound friendly.

Miss Parkhurst nodded. "Anytime. I won't keep you."

"If I go, can I come back?"

She smiled ever so slightly. There was the young girl in that smile again, and she seemed very vulnerable. "The opener takes you anywhere across town."

"Nobody messes with me?"

"Nobody touches anyone I protect," Miss Parkhurst said.

Oliver absorbed that thoughtfully, steepling his hands below his chin. "You're pretty good to me," he said. "Even when I cross you, you don't hurt me. Why?"

"You're my last chance," Miss Parkhurst said, dark eyes on him. "I've lived a long time, and nobody like you's come along. I don't think there'll be another for even longer. I can't wait that long. I've lived this way so many years, I don't know another, but I don't want any more of it."

Oliver couldn't think of a better way to put his next question. "Do you like being a whore?"

Miss Parkhurst's face hardened. "It has its moments," she said stiffly.

Oliver screwed up his courage enough to say what was on his mind, but not to look at her while doing it. "You enjoy lying down with any man who has the money?"

"It's work. It's something I'm good at."

"Even ugly men?"

"Ugly men need their pleasures, too."

"Bad men? Letting them touch you when they've hurt people, maybe killed people?"

"What kind of work have you done?" she asked.

"Clerked a grocery store. Taught music."

"Did you wait on bad men in the grocery store?"

"If I did," Oliver said swiftly, "I didn't know about it."

"Neither did I," Miss Parkhurst said. Then, more quietly, "Most of the time."

"All those girls you've made whore for you . . ."

"You have some things to learn," she interrupted. "It's not the work that's so awful. It's what you have to be to do it. The way people expect you to be when you do it. Should be, in a good world, a whore's like a doctor or a saint, she doesn't mind getting her hands dirty any more than they do. She gives pleasure and smiles. But in the city, people won't let it happen that way. Here, a whore's always got some empty place inside her, a place you've filled with self-respect, maybe. A whore's got respect, but not for herself. She loses that whenever anybody looks at her. She can be worth a million dollars on the outside, but inside, she knows. That's what makes her a whore. That's the curse. It's beat into you sometimes, everybody taking advantage, like you're dirt. Pretty soon you think you're dirt, too, and who cares what happens to dirt? Pretty soon you're just sliding along, trying to keep from getting hurt or maybe dead, but who cares?"

"You're rich," Oliver said.

"Can't buy everything," Miss Parkhurst commented dryly.

"You've got magic."

"I've got magic because I'm here, and to stay here, I have to be a whore."

"Why can't you leave?"

She sighed, her fingers working nervously along the edge of the tablecloth.

"What stops you from just leaving?"

"If you're going to own this place," she said, and he thought at first she was avoiding his question, "you've got to know all about it. All about me. We're the same, almost, this place and I. A whore's no more than what's in her purse, every pimp knows that. You know how many times I've been married?"

Oliver shook his head.

"Seventeen times. Sometimes they left me, once or twice they stayed. Never any good. But then, maybe I didn't deserve any better. Those who left me, they came back when they were old, asking me to save them from Darkside. I couldn't. But I kept them here anyway. Come on."

She stood and Oliver followed her down the halls, down the stairs, below the garage level, deep beneath the mansion's clutter-filled basement. The air was ageless, deep-earth cool, and smelled of old city rain. A few eternal clear light bulbs cast feeble yellow crescents in the dismal murk. They walked on boards over an old muddy patch, Miss Parkhurst lifting her skirts a few inches to clear the mire. Oliver saw her slim ankles and swallowed back the tightness in his throat.

Ahead, laid out in a row on moss-patched concrete biers, were fifteen black iron cylinders, each seven feet long and slightly flattened on top. They looked like big blockbuster bombs in storage. The first was wedged into a dark corner. Miss Parkhurst stood by its foot, running her hand along its rust-streaked surface.

"Two didn't come back. Maybe they were the best of the lot," she said. "I was no judge. I couldn't know. You judge men by what's inside you, and if you're hollow, they get lost in there, you can't know what you're seeing."

Oliver stepped closer to the last cylinder and saw a clear glass plate mounted at the head. Reluctant but fascinated, he wiped the dusty glass with two fingers and peered past a single cornered bubble. The coffin was filled with clear liquid. Afloat within, a face the color of green olives in a martini looked back at him, blind eyes murky, lips set in a loose line. The liquid and death had smoothed the face's wrinkles, but Oliver could tell nonetheless, this dude had been old, old.

"They all die," she said. "All but me. I keep them all, every john, every husband, no forgetting, no letting them go. We've always got this tie between us. That's the curse."

Oliver pulled back from the coffin, holding his breath, heart thumping with eager horror. Which was worse, this, or old men in the night? Old dead lusts laid to rest or lively ghosts? Wrapped in gloom at the far end of the line of bottle-coffins, Miss Parkhurst seemed for a moment to glow with the same furnace power he had felt when he first saw her.

"I miss some of these guys," she said, her voice so soft the power just vanished, a thing in his mind. "We had some good times together."

Oliver tried to imagine what Miss Parkhurst had lived through, the good times and otherwise. "You have any children?" he asked, his voice as thin as the buzz of a fly in a bottle. He jumped back as one of the coffins resonated with his shaky words.

Miss Parkhurst's shoulders shivered as well. "Lots," she said tightly. "All dead before they were born."

At first his shock was conventional, orchestrated by his Sundays in church. Then the colossal organic waste of effort came down on him like a pile of stones. All that motion, all that wanting, and nothing good from it, just these iron bottles and vivid lists of ghosts.

"What good is a whore's baby?" Miss Parkhurst asked. "Especially if the mother's going to stay a whore."

"Was your mother . . . ?" It didn't seem right to use the word in connection with anyone's mother.

"She was, and her mother before her. I have no daddies, or lots of daddies."

Oliver remembered the old man chastising him in his dream. Before he could even sort out his words, wishing to give her some solace, some sign he wasn't completely unsympathetic, he said, "It can't be all bad, being a whore."

"Maybe not," she said. Miss Parkhurst hardly made a blot in the larger shadows. She might just fly away to dust if he turned his head.

"You said being a whore is being empty inside. Not everybody who's empty inside is a whore."

"Oh?" she replied, light as a cobweb. He was being pushed into an uncharacteristic posture, but Oliver was damned if he'd give in just yet, however much a fool he made of himself. His mixed feelings were betraying him.

"You've *lived*," he said. "You got memories nobody else has. You could write books. They'd make movies about you."

Her smile was a dull lamp in the shadows. "I've had important people visit me," she said. "Powerful men, even mayors. I had something they needed. Sometimes they opened up and talked about how hard it was not being little boys anymore. Sometimes, when we were relaxing, they'd cry on my shoulder, just like I was their momma. But then they'd go away and try to forget about me. If they remembered at all, they were scared of me, because of what I knew about them. Now, they know I'm getting weak," she said. "I don't give a damn about books or movies. I won't tell what I know, and besides, lots of those men are dead. If they aren't, they're waiting for me to die, so they can sleep easy."

"What do you mean, getting weak?"

"I got two days, maybe three, then I die a whore. My time is up. The curse is almost finished."

Oliver gaped. When he had first seen her, she had seemed as powerful as a diesel locomotive, as if she might live forever.

"And if I take over?"

"You get the mansion, the money."

"How much power?"

She didn't answer.

"You can't give me any power, can you?"

"No," faint as the breeze from her eyelashes.

"The opener won't be any good."

"No."

"You lied to me."

"I'll leave you all that's left."

"That's not why you made me come here. You took Momma—"

"She stole from me."

"My momma never stole anything!" Oliver shouted. The iron coffins buzzed.

"She took something after I had given her all my hospitality."

"What could she take from you? She was no thief."

"She took a sheet of music."

Oliver's face screwed up in sudden pain. He looked away, fists clenched. They had almost no money for his music. More often than not since his father died, he made up music, having no new scores to play. "Why'd you bring me here?" he croaked.

"I don't mind dying. But I don't want to die a whore."

Oliver turned back, angry again, this time for his momma as well as himself. He approached the insubstantial shadow. Miss Parkhurst shimmered like a curtain. "What do you want from me?"

"I need someone who loves me. Loves me for no reason."

For an instant, he saw standing before him a scrawny girl in a red shimmy, eyes wide. "How could that help you? Can that make you something else?"

"Just love," she said. "Just letting me forget all these"—she pointed to the coffins—"and all those," pointing up.

Oliver's body lost its charge of anger and accusation with an exhaled breath. "I can't love you," he said. "I don't even know what love is." Was this true? Upstairs, she had burned in his mind, and he *had* wanted her, though it upset him to remember how much. What *could* he feel for her? "Let's go back now. I have to look in on Momma."

Miss Parkhurst emerged from the shadows and walked past him silently, not even her skirts rustling. She gestured with a finger for him to follow.

She left him at the door to his room, saying, "I'll wait in the main parlor." Oliver saw a small television set on the nightstand by his bed and rushed to turn it on. The screen filled with static and unresolved images. He saw fragments of faces, patches of color and texture passing so quickly he couldn't make them out. The entire city might be on the screen at once, but he could not see any of it clearly. He twisted the channel knob and got more static. Then he saw the label next to channel 13 on the dial: HOME, in small golden letters. He twisted the knob to that position and the screen cleared.

Momma lay in bed, legs drawn tightly up, hair mussed.

She didn't look good. Her hand, stretched out across the bed, trembled. Her breathing was hard and rough. In the background, Oliver heard Yolanda fussing with the babies, finally screaming at her older brothers in frustration.

Why don't you help with the babies? his sister demanded in a tinny, distant voice.

Momma told you, Denver replied.

She did not. She told us all. You could help.

Reggie laughed. *We got to make plans.*

Oliver pulled back from the TV. Momma was sick, and for all his brothers and sister and the babies could do, she might die. He could guess why she was sick, too; with worry for him. He had to go to her and tell her he was all right. A phone call wouldn't be enough.

Again, however, he was reluctant to leave the mansion and Miss Parkhurst. Something beyond her waning magic was at work here; he wanted to listen to her and to experience more of that fascinated horror. He wanted to watch her again, absorb her smooth, ancient beauty. In a way, she needed him as much as Momma did. Miss Parkhurst outraged everything in him that was lawful and orderly, but he finally had to admit, as he thought of going back to Momma, that he enjoyed the outrage.

He clutched the gold opener and ran from his room to the parlor. She waited for him there in a red velvet chair, hands gripping two lions at the end of the armrests. The lions' wooden faces grinned beneath her caresses. "I got to go," he said. "Momma's sick for missing me."

She nodded. "I'm not holding you," she said.

He stared at her. "I wish I could help you," he said.

She smiled hopefully, pitifully. "Then promise you'll come back."

Oliver wavered. How long would Momma need him?

What if he gave his promise and returned and Miss Parkhurst was already dead?

"I promise."

"Don't be too long," she said.

"Won't," he mumbled.

THE LIMOUSINE WAITED FOR HIM IN THE GARAGE, WHITE AND BEAUTIFUL, languid and sleek and fast all at once. No chauffeur waited for him this time. The door opened by itself and he climbed in; the door closed behind him, and he leaned back stiffly on the leather seats, gold opener in hand. "Take me home," he said. The glass partition and the windows all around darkened to an opaque smoky gold. He felt a sensation of smooth motion. *What would it be like to have this kind of power all the time?*

But the power wasn't hers to give.

Oliver arrived before the apartment building in a blizzard of swirling snow. Snow packed up over the curbs and coated the sidewalks a foot deep; Sleepside was heavy with winter. Oliver stepped from the limousine and climbed the icy steps, the cold hardly touching him even in his light clothing. He was surrounded by Miss Parkhurst's magic.

Denver was frying a pan of navy beans in the kitchen when Oliver burst through the door, the locks flinging themselves open before them. Oliver paused in the entrance to the kitchen. Denver stared at him, face slack, too surprised to speak.

"Where's Momma?"

Yolanda heard his voice in the living room and screamed.

Reggie met him in the hallway, arms open wide, smiling broadly. "Goddamn, little brother! You got away?"

"Where's Momma?"

"She's in her room. She's feeling low."

"She's sick," Oliver said, pushing past his brother. Yolanda stood before Momma's door as if to keep Oliver out. She sucked her lower lip between her teeth. She looked scared.

"Let me by, Yolanda," Oliver said. He almost pointed the opener at her, and then pulled back, fearful of what might happen.

"You made Momma si-*ick*," Yolanda squeaked, but she stepped aside. Oliver pushed through the door to Momma's room. She sat up in bed, face drawn and thin, but her eyes danced with joy. "My boy!" She sighed. "My beautiful boy."

Oliver sat beside her and they hugged fiercely. "Please don't leave me again," Momma said, voice muffled by his shoulder. Oliver set the opener on her flimsy nightstand and cried against her neck.

The day after Oliver's return, Denver stood lank-legged by the window, hands in frayed pants pockets, staring at the snow with heavy-lidded eyes. "It's too cold to go anywhere now," he mused.

Reggie sat in their father's chair, face screwed in thought. "I listened to what he told Momma," he said. "That whore sent our little brother back here in a limo. A big white limo. See it out there?"

Denver peered down at the street. A white limousine waited at the curb, not even dusted by snow. A tiny vanishing curl of white rose from its tailpipe. "It's still there," he said.

"Did you see what he had when he came in?" Reggie asked. Denver shook his head. "A gold box. *She* must have given that to him. I bet whoever has that gold box can visit Miss Belle Parkhurst. Want to bet?"

Denver grinned and shook his head again.

"Wouldn't be too cold if we had that limo, would it?" Reggie asked.

Oliver brought his momma chicken soup and a half-rotten, carefully trimmed orange. He plumped her pillow for her, shushing her, telling her not to talk until she had eaten. She smiled weakly, beatific, and let him minister to her. When she had eaten, she lay back and closed her eyes, tears pooling in their hollows before slipping down her cheeks. "I was so afraid for you," she said. "I didn't know what she would do. She seemed so nice at first. I didn't see her. Just her voice, inviting me in over the security buzzer, letting me sit and rest my feet. I knew where I was . . . was it bad of me, to stay there, knowing?"

"You were tired, Momma," Oliver said. "Besides, Miss Parkhurst isn't that bad."

Momma looked at him dubiously. "I saw her piano. There was a shelf next to it with the most beautiful sheet music you ever saw, even big books of it. I looked at some. Oh, Oliver, I've never taken anything in my life . . ." She cried freely now, sapping what little strength the lunch had given her.

"Don't you worry, Momma. She used you. She *wanted* me to come." As an afterthought, he added, not sure why he lied, "Or Yolanda."

Momma absorbed that while her eyes examined his face in tiny, caressing glances. "You won't go back," she said, "will you?"

Oliver looked down at the sheets folded under her arms. "I promised. She'll die if I don't," he said.

"That woman is a liar," Momma stated unequivocally. "If she wants you, she'll do anything to get you."

"I don't think she's lying, Momma."

She looked away from him, a feverish anger flushing her cheeks. "Why did you promise her?"

"She's not that bad, Momma," he said again. He had thought that coming home would clear his mind, but Miss Parkhurst's face, her plea, stayed with him as if she were only a room away. The mansion seemed just a fading dream, unimportant; but Belle Parkhurst stuck. "She needs help. She wants to change."

Momma puffed out her cheeks and blew through her lips like a horse. She had often done that to his father, never before to him. "She'll always be a whore," she said.

Oliver's eyes narrowed. He saw a spitefulness and bitterness in Momma he hadn't noticed before. Not that spite was unwarranted; Miss Parkhurst had treated Momma roughly. Yet . . .

Denver stood in the doorway. "Reggie and I got to talk to Momma," he said. "About you." He jerked his thumb back over his shoulder. "Alone." Reggie stood grinning behind his brother. Oliver took the tray of dishes and sidled past them, going into the kitchen.

In the kitchen, he washed the last few days' plates methodically, letting the lukewarm water slide over his hands, eyes focused on the faucet's dull gleam. He had almost lost track of time when he heard the front door slam. Jerking his head up, he wiped the last plate and put it away, then went to Momma's room. She looked back at him guiltily. Something was wrong. He searched the room with his eyes, but nothing was out of place. Nothing that was normally present . . .

The opener.

His brothers had taken the gold opener.

"Momma!" he said.

"They're going to pay her a visit," she said, the bitterness plain now. "They don't like their momma mistreated."

It was getting dark and the snow was thick. He had hoped to return this evening. If Miss Parkhurst hadn't lied, she would be very weak by now, perhaps dead tomorrow. His lungs seemed to shrink within him, and he had a hard time taking a breath.

"I've got to go," he said. "She might *kill* them, Momma!" But that wasn't what worried him. He put on his heavy coat, then his father's old cracked rubber boots with the snow tread soles. Yolanda came out of the room she shared with the babies. She didn't ask any questions, just watched him dress for the cold, her eyes dull.

"They got that gold box," she said as he flipped the last metal clasp on the boots. "Probably worth a lot."

Oliver hesitated in the hallway, then grabbed Yolanda's shoulders and shook her vigorously. "You take care of Momma, you hear?"

She shut her jaw with a clack and shoved free. Oliver was out the door before she could speak.

Day's last light filled the sky with a deep peachy glow tinged with cold gray. Snow fell golden above the buildings and smudgy brown within their shadow. The wind swirled around him mournfully, sending gust-fingers through his coat searching for any warmth that might be stolen. For a nauseating moment, all his resolve was sucked away by a vacuous pit of misery. The streets were empty; he briefly wondered what night this was, and then remembered it was the twenty-third of December, but too cold for whatever stray shoppers Sleepside might send out. *Why go? To save two worthless idiots?* Not that so much, although that would have been enough, since their loss would hurt Momma, and they *were* his brothers; not that so much as his promise. And something else.

He was afraid for Belle Parkhurst.

He buttoned his coat collar and leaned into the wind. He hadn't put on a hat. The heat flew from his scalp, and in a few moments he felt drained and exhausted. But he made it to the subway entrance and staggered down the steps, into the warmer heart of the city, where it was always sixty-four degrees.

Locked behind her thick glass and metal booth, wrinkled eyes weary with night's wisdom, the fluorescent-lighted token seller took his money and dropped cat's-head tokens into the steel tray with separate, distinct *chinks*. Oliver glanced at her face and saw the whore's printed there instead; this middle-aged woman did not spread her legs for money, but had sold her youth and life away sitting in this cavern. Whose emptiness was more profound?

"Be careful," she warned vacantly through the speaker grill. "Night Metro any minute now."

He dropped a token into the turnstile and pushed through, then stood shivering on the platform, waiting for the Sunside train. It seemed to take forever to arrive, and when it did, he was not particularly relieved. The driver's pit-eyes winked green, bull's head turning as the train slid to a halt beside the platform. The doors opened with an oiled groan, and Oliver stepped aboard, into the hard, cold, and unforgiving glare of the train's interior.

At first, Oliver thought the car was empty. He did not sit down, however. The hair on his neck and arm bristled. Hand gripping a stainless steel handle, he leaned into the train's acceleration and took a deep, half-hiccup breath.

He first consciously noticed the other passengers as their faces gleamed in silhouette against the passing dim lights of ghost stations. They sat almost invisible, crowding the car; they stood beside him, less substantial than a breath of air. They watched him intently, bearing no ill will for the moment, perhaps not yet aware that he was alive and they were not. They carried no overt signs of their wounds, but how they had come to be here was obvious to his animal instincts.

This train carried holiday suicides: men, women, teenagers, even a few children, delicate as expensive crystal in a shop window. Maybe the bull's head driver collected them, culling them out and caging them as they stumbled randomly aboard his train. Maybe he controlled them.

Oliver tried to sink away in his coat. He felt guilty, being alive and healthy, enveloped in strong emotions; they were so flimsy, with so little hold on this reality.

He muttered a prayer, stopping as they all turned toward him, showing glassy disapproval at this reverse blasphemy. Silently, he prayed again, but even that seemed to irritate his fellow passengers, and they squeaked among themselves in voices that only a dog or a bat might hear.

The stations passed one by one, mosaic symbols and names flashing in pools of light. When the Sunside station approached and the train slowed, Oliver moved quickly to the door. It opened with oily grace. He stepped onto the platform, turned, and bumped up against the tall, dark uniform of the bull's head driver. The air around him stank of grease and electricity and something sweeter, perhaps blood. He stood a bad foot and a half taller than Oliver, and in one outstretched, black-nailed, leathery hand he held his long silver shears, points spread wide, briefly suggesting Belle Parkhurst's horizontal position among the old men.

"You're in the wrong place, at the wrong time," the driver warned in a voice deeper than the train motors. "Down here, I can cut your cord." He closed the shears with a slick, singing whisper.

"I'm going to Miss Parkhurst's," Oliver said, voice quavering.

"Who?" the driver asked.

"I'm leaving now," Oliver said, backing away. The driver followed, slowly hunching over him. The shears sang open, angled toward his eyes. The crystal dead within the train passed through the open door and glided around them. Gluey waves of cold shivered the air.

"You're a bold little bastard," the driver said, voice managing to descend off any human scale and still be heard. The white tile walls vibrated. "All I have to do is cut your cord, right in front of your face"—he snicked the shears inches from Oliver's nose—"and you'll never find your way home."

The driver backed him up against a cold barrier of suicides. Oliver's fear could not shut out curiosity. Was the bull's head real, or was there a man under the horns and hide and bone? The eyes in their sunken orbits glowed ice-blue. The scissors crossed before Oliver's face again, even closer; mere hairs away from his nose.

"You're mine," the driver whispered, and the scissors closed on something tough and invisible. Oliver's head exploded with pain. He flailed back through the dead, dragging the driver after him by the pinch of the shears on that something unseen and very important. Roaring, the driver applied both hands to the shears' grips. Oliver felt as if his head were being ripped away. Suddenly he kicked out with all his strength between the driver's black-uniformed legs. His foot hit flesh and bone as unyielding as rock and his agony doubled. But the shears hung for a moment in air before Oliver's face, and the driver slowly curled over.

Oliver grabbed the shears, opened them, released whatever cord he had between himself and his past, his home, and pushed through the dead. The scissors reflected elongated gleams over the astonished, watery faces of the suicides. Suddenly, seeing a chance to escape, they spread out along the platform, some up the station's stairs, some to both sides. Oliver ran through them up the steps and stood on the warm evening sidewalk of Sunside. All he sensed from the station's entrance was a sour breath of oil and blood and a faint chill of fading hands as the dead evaporated in the balmy night air.

A quiet crowd had gathered at the front entrance to Miss Parkhurst's mansion. They stood vigil, waiting for something, their faces shining with a greedy sweat.

He did not see the limousine. His brothers must have arrived by now; they were inside, then.

Catching his breath as he ran, he skirted the old brown-stone and looked for the entrance to the underground garage. On the south side, he found the ramp and descended to slam his hands against the corrugated metal door. Echoes replied. "It's me!" he shouted. "Let me in!"

A middle-aged man regarded him dispassionately from the higher ground of the sidewalk. "What do you want in there, young man?" he asked.

Oliver glared back over his shoulder. "None of your business," he said.

"Maybe it is, if you want in," the man said. "There's a way any man can get into that house. It never refuses gold."

Oliver pulled back from the door a moment, stunned. The man shrugged and walked on.

He still grasped the driver's shears. They weren't gold, they were silver, but they had to be worth something. "Let me in!" he said. Then, upping the ante, he dug in his pocket and produced the remaining cat's head token. "I'll pay!"

The door grumbled up. The garage's lights were off, but in the soft yellow glow of the streetlights, he saw an eagle's claw thrust out from the brick wall just within the door's frame, supporting a golden cup. Token in one hand, shears in another, Oliver's eyes narrowed. To pay Belle's mansion now was no honorable deed; he dropped the token into the cup, but kept the shears as he ran into the darkness.

A faint crack of light showed beneath the stairwell door. Around the door, the bones of ancient city dwellers glowed in their compacted stone, teeth and knuckles bright as fireflies. Oliver tried the door; it was locked. Inserting the point of the shears between the door and catchplate, he pried until the lock was sprung.

The quiet parlor was illuminated only by a few guttering candles clutched in drooping gold eagle's claws. The air was thick with the blunt smells of long-extinguished cigars and cigarettes. Oliver stopped for a moment, closing his eyes and listening. There was a room he had never seen in the time he had spent in Belle Parkhurst's house. She had never even shown him the door, but he knew it had to exist, and that was where she would be, alive or dead. Where his brothers were, he couldn't tell; for the moment he didn't care. He doubted they were in any mortal danger. Belle's power was as weak as the scattered candles.

Oliver crept along the dark halls, holding the gleaming shears before him as a warning to whatever might try to stop him. He climbed two more flights of stairs, and on the third floor, found an uncarpeted hallway, walls bare, that he had not seen before. The dry floorboards creaked beneath him. The air was cool and still. He could smell a ghost of Belle's rose perfume. At the end of the hall was a plain panel door with a tarnished brass knob.

This door was also unlocked. He sucked in a breath for courage and opened it.

This was Belle's room, and she was indeed in it. She hung suspended above her plain iron-frame bed in a weave of glowing threads. For a moment, he drew back, thinking she was a spider, but it immediately became clear she was more like a spider's prey. The threads reached to all corners of the room, transparent, binding her tightly, but to him as insubstantial as the air.

Belle turned to face him, weak, eyes clouded, skin like paper towels. "Why'd you wait so long?" she asked.

From across the mansion, he heard the echoes of Reggie's delighted laughter.

Oliver stepped forward. Only the blades of the shears plucked at the threads; he passed through unhindered. Arm straining at the silver instrument, he realized what the threads were; they were the cords binding Belle to the mansion, connecting her to all her customers. Belle had not one cord to her past, but thousands. Every place she had been touched, she was held by a strand. Thick twining ropes of the past shot from her lips and breasts and from between her legs; not even the toes of her feet were free.

Without thinking, Oliver lifted the driver's silver shears and began methodically snipping the cords. One by one, or in ropy clusters, he cut them away. With each meeting of the blades, they vanished. He did not ask himself which was her first cord, linking her to her childhood, to the few years she had lived before she became a whore; there was no time to waste worrying about such niceties.

"Your brothers are in my vault," she said. "They found my gold and jewels. I crawled here to get away."

"Don't talk," Oliver said between clenched teeth. The strands became tougher, more like wire the closer he came to her thin gray body. His arm muscles knotted and cold sweat soaked his clothes. She dropped inches closer to the bed.

"I never brought any men here," she said.

"Shh."

"This was my place, the only place I had."

There were hundreds of strands left now, instead of thousands. He worked for long minutes, watching her grow more and more pale, watching her one-time furnace heat dull to less than a single candle, her eyes lose their feverish glitter. For a horrified moment, he thought cutting the cords might actually weaken her; but he hacked and swung at the cords, regardless. They were even tougher now, more resilient.

Far off in the mansion, Denver and Reggie laughed together, and there was a heavy clinking sound. The floor shuddered.

Dozens of cords remained. He had been working at them for an eternity, and now each cord took a concentrated effort, all the strength left in his arms and hands. He thought he might faint or throw up. Belle's eyes had closed. Her breathing was undetectable.

Five strands left. He cut through one, then another. As he applied the shears to the third, a tall man appeared on the opposite side of her bed, dressed in pale gray with a wide-brimmed gray hat. His fingers were covered with gold rings. A gold eagle's claw pinned his white silk tie.

"I was her friend," the man said. "She came to me and she cheated me."

Oliver held back his shears, eyes stinging with rage. "Who are you?" he demanded, nearly doubled over by his exertion. He stared up at the gray man through beads of sweat on his eyebrows.

"That other old man, he hardly worked her at all. I put her to work right here, but she cheated me."

"You're her *pimp*," Oliver spat out the word.

The gray man grinned.

"Cut that cord, and she's nothing."

"She's nothing now. Your curse is over and she's dying."

"She shouldn't have messed with me," the pimp said. "I was a strong man, lots of connections. What do you want with an old drained-out whore, boy?"

Oliver didn't answer. He struggled to cut the third cord but it writhed like a snake between the shears.

"She would have been a whore even without me," the pimp said. "She was a whore from the day she was born."

"That's a lie," Oliver said.

"Why do you want to get at her? She give you a pox and you want to finish her off?"

Oliver's lips curled and he flung his head back, not looking as he brought the shears together with all his remaining strength, boosted by a killing anger. The third cord parted and the shears snapped, one blade singing across the room and sticking in the wall with a spray of plaster chips. The gray man vanished like a double-blown puff of cigarette smoke, leaving a scent of onions and stale beer.

Belle hung awkwardly by two cords now. Swinging the single blade like a knife, he parted them swiftly and fell over her, lying across her, feeling her cool body for the first time. She could not arouse lust now. She might be dead.

"Miss Parkhurst," he said. He examined her face, almost as white as the bed sheets, high cheekbones pressing through waxy flesh. "I don't want anything from you," Oliver said. "I just want you to be all right." He lowered his lips to hers, kissed her lightly, dripping sweat on her closed eyes.

Far away, Denver and Reggie cackled with glee.

The house grew quiet. All the ghosts, all accounts received, had fled, had been freed.

The single candle in the room guttered out, and they lay in the dark alone. Oliver fell against his will into an exhausted slumber.

COOL, ROSE-SCENTED FINGERS LIGHTLY TOUCHED HIS FOREHEAD. HE OPENED his eyes and saw a girl in a white nightgown leaning over him, barely his age. Her eyes were very big and her lips bowed into a smile beneath high, full cheekbones. "Where are we?" she asked. "How long we been here?"

Late morning sun filled the small, dusty room with warmth. He glanced around the bed, looking for Belle, and then turned back to the girl. She vaguely resembled the chauffeur who had brought him to the mansion that first night, though younger, her face more bland and simple.

"You don't remember?" he asked.

"Honey," the girl said sweetly, hands on hips, "I don't remember much of anything. Except that you kissed me. You want to kiss me again?"

Momma did not approve of the strange young woman he brought home, and wanted to know where Reggie and Denver were. Oliver did not have the heart to tell her. They lay cold as ice in a room filled with mounds of cat's-head subway tokens, bound by the pimp's magic. They had dressed themselves in white, with broad white hats; dressed themselves as pimps. But the mansion was empty, stripped during that night of all its valuables by the greedy crowds.

They were pimps in a whorehouse without whores. As the young girl observed, with a tantalizing touch of wisdom beyond her apparent years, there was nothing much lower than that.

"Where'd you find that girl? She's hiding something, Oliver. You mark my words."

Oliver ignored his mother's misgivings, having enough of his own. The girl agreed she needed a different name now, and chose Lorelei, a name she said "Just sings right."

He saved money, lacking brothers to borrow and never repay, and soon rented a cheap studio on the sixth floor of the same building. The girl came to him sweetly in his bed, her mind no more full—for the most part—than that of any young girl. In his way, he loved her—and feared her, though less and less as days passed.

She played the piano almost as well as he, and they planned to give lessons. They had brought a trunk full of old sheet music and books with them from the mansion. The crowds had left them at least that much.

Momma did not visit for two weeks after they moved in. But visit she did, and eventually the girl won her over.

"She's got a good hand in the kitchen," Momma said. "You do right by her, now."

Yolanda made friends with the girl quickly and easily, and Oliver saw more substance in his younger sister than he had before. Lorelei helped Yolanda with the babies. She seemed a natural.

Sometimes, at night, he examined her while she slept, wondering if there still weren't stories, and perhaps skills, hidden behind her sweet, peaceful face. Had she forgotten everything?

In time, they were married.

And they lived—

Well, enough.

They lived.

FARAWAY

INTRODUCTION TO "JUDGMENT ENGINE"

"Judgment Engine" was first published in Japanese translation for inclusion in a magnificent boxed set published by Pioneer. The set, called *Artificial Life (Insects)*, contains an art book with computer graphics concepts by Daizaburo Harada, a CD-ROM, and a paperback book with this story, essays, and interviews with me and with Ryuichi Sakamoto. It is the most sumptuous presentation yet for my fiction—truly a stunning piece of work.

About the same time, Gregory Benford, a longtime friend, invited me to submit an original story to an anthology he was editing, *Far Futures,* to be published by Tor Books. The Japanese edition presented no difficulties, and so I was able to market the story as an original publication twice, always a good thing, though rare in my experience.

Among the hardest science fiction stories to write are those set in the near future, and the very far future. The near future is difficult because it takes only a few years for the reader and history to catch up with the story; maintaining believability in such circumstances is difficult. A typical mistake is inventing too many new words and new things, thus: "In the year 1990, John Jones entered the living room of his beautiful mistress, Leonora. He rubbed the lumo-cig across his palm, took a deep inhale of the herbivorous tobacco, and switched on the Tri-D set to catch the morning Dicto-news." Only rarely does society accept a new word for something familiar, however expanded its capabilities. Thus, a cellular phone is still a phone, not a trans-palmer. A 3D TV is probably still going to be a TV, not a Tri-D visionater. An electronic nose flute is still going to be—well, you get the idea.

The far future is difficult to describe because so much will have changed. Mainstream literature often claims that there are eternal human verities, immutable qualities that will last throughout all eternity. I have severe doubts about this. There is so much variation just in our time, around the globe, in these so-called verities that I can't imagine them not changing in the thousands of years to come.

The problem for a modern reader is that a believable story of the far future may also be incomprehensible. (To wit: "Fergon grabbed his twad with something very like glee, and obnoxiously asserted his right to snorg and wippie in the middle of the info-stream." Lewis Carroll, anyone?)

I've touched on the far future in a number of stories in this collection: "Hard-fought," "The Fall of the House of Escher," and this one. Just to keep the attention of contemporary, mortal humans, I've stuck with a few of the eternal human verities in each of these tales.

I'm sure the *real* inhabitants of the distant future will forgive me. Or, to use their parlance, undergo complete snorgwhup and carn-symp on my case.

Judgment Engine
Artificial Life (Insects), Pioneer, with Diazaburo Harada and Ryuichi Sakamoto (Japan) 1993
First English publication, Far Futures, Gregory Benford, 1995

We

Seven tributaries disengage from their social-mind and Library and travel by transponder to the School World. There they are loaded into a temporary soma, an older physical model with eight long, flexible red legs. Here the seven become We.

We have received routine orders from the Teacher Annex. We are to investigate student labor on the Great Plain of History, the largest physical feature on the School World. The students have been set to searching all past historical records, donated by the nine remaining Libraries. Student social-minds are sad; they will not mature before Endtime. They are the last new generation and their behavior is often aberrant. There may be room for error.

The soma sits in an enclosure. We become active and advance from the enclosure's shadow into a light shower of data condensing from the absorbing clouds high above. We see radiation from the donating Libraries, still falling on School World from around the three remaining systems; we hear the lambda whine of storage in the many rows of black hemispheres perched on the plain; we feel a patter of drops on our black carapace.

We stand at the edge of the plain, near a range of bare brown and black hills left over from planetary reformation. The air is thick and cold. It smells sharply of rich data moisture, wasted on us; We do not have readers on our surface. The moisture dews up on the dark, hard ground under our feet, evaporates and is reclaimed by translucent soppers. The soppers flit through the air, a tenth our size and delicate.

The hemispheres are maintained by single-tributary somas. They are tiny, marching along the rows by the hundreds of thousands.

The sun rises in the west, across the plain. It is brilliant violet surrounded by streamers of intense blue. The streamers curl like flowing hair. Sun and streamers cast multiple shadows from each black hemisphere. The sun attracts our attention. It is beautiful, not part of a Library simscape; this scape is *real*. It reminds us of approaching Endtime; the changes made to conserve and concentrate the last available energy have rendered the scape beautifully novel, unfamiliar to the natural birth algorithms of our tributaries.

The three systems are unlike anything that has ever been. They contain all remaining order and available energy. Drawn close together, surrounded by the permutation of local space and time, the three systems deceive the dead outer universe, already well into the dull inaction of the long Between. We are proud of the three systems. They took a hundred million years to construct, and a tenth of all remaining available energy. They were a gamble. Nine of thirty-seven major Libraries agreed to the gamble. The others spread themselves into the greater magnitudes of the Between, and died.

The gamble worked.

Our soma is efficient and pleasant to work with. All of our tributaries agree, older models of such equipment are better. We have an appointment with the representative of the School World students, student tributaries lodged in a newer model soma called a Berkus, after a social-mind on Second World, which designed it. A Berkus soma is not favored. It is noisy; perhaps more efficient, but brasher and less elegant. We agree it will be ugly.

Data clouds swirl and spread tendrils high over the plain. The single somas march between our legs, cleaning unwanted debris from the black domes. Within the domes, all history. We could reach down and crush one with the claws on a single leg, but that would slow Endtime Work and waste available energy.

We are proud of our stray thinking. It shows that we are still human, still linked directly to the past. We are proud that we can ignore improper impulses.

We are teachers. All teachers must be linked with the past, to understand and explain it. Teachers must understand error; the past is rich with pain and error.

We await the Berkus.

Too much time passes. The world turns away from the sun and night falls. Centuries of Library time pass, but we try to be patient and think in the flow of external time. Some of our tributaries express a desire to taste the domes, but there is no real need, and this would also waste available energy.

With night, more data fills the skies from the other systems, condenses, and rains down, covering us with a thick sheen. Soppers clean our carapace again. All around, the domes grow richer, absorbing history. We see, in the distance, a night interpreter striding on giant disjointed legs between the domes. It eats the domes and returns white mounds of discard. All the domes must be interpreted to see if any of the history should be carried by the final Endtime self.

The final self will cross the Between, order held in perfect inaction, until the Between has experienced sufficient rest and boredom. It will cross that point when time and space become granular and nonlinear, when the unconserved energy of expansion, absorbed at the minute level of the quantum foam, begins to disturb the metric. The metric becomes noisy and irregular, and all extension evaporates. The universe has no width, no time, and all is back at the beginning.

The final self will survive, knitting itself into the smallest interstices, armored against the fantastic pressures of a universe's deathsound. The quantum foam will give up its noise and new universes will bubble forth and evolve. One will transcend. The transcendent reality will absorb the final self, which will seed it. From the compression should arise new intelligent beings.

It is an important thing, and all teachers approve. The past should cover the new, forever. It is our way to immortality.

Our tributaries express some concern. We are to be sure not on a vital mission, but the Berkus is very late.

Something has gone wrong. We investigate our links and find them cut. Transponders do not reply.

The ground beneath our soma trembles. Hastily, the soma retreats from the plain of history. It stands by a low hill, trying to keep steady on its eight red legs. The clouds over the plain turn green and ragged. The single somas scuttle between vibrating hemispheres, confused.

We cannot communicate with our social-mind or Library. No other libraries respond. Alarmed, we appeal to the School World Student Committee, then point our thoughts up to the Endtime Work Coordinator, but they do not answer, either.

The endless kilometers of low black hemispheres churn as if stirred by a huge stick. Cracks appear, and from the cracks, thick red drops; the drops crystallize in high, tall prisms. Many of the prisms shatter and turn to dead white powder. We realize with great concern that we are seeing the internal stored data of the planet itself. This is a reserve record of all Library knowledge, held condensed; the School World contains selected records from the dead Libraries, more information than any single Library could absorb in a billion years. The knowledge shoots through the disrupted ground in crimson fountains, wasted. Our soma retreats deeper into the hills.

Nobody answers our emergency signal.

Nobody will speak to us, anywhere.

More days pass. We are still cut off from the Library. Isolated, we are limited only to what the soma can perceive, and that makes no sense at all.

We have climbed a promontory overlooking what was once the Great

Plain of History. Where once our students worked to condense and select those parts of the past that would survive the Endtime, the hideous leaking of reserve knowledge has slowed and an equally hideous round of what seems to be amateurish student exercises work themselves in rapid time.

Madness covers the plain. The hemispheres have all disintegrated, and the single somas and interpreters have vanished.

Now, everywhere on the plain, green and red and purple forests grow and die in seconds; new trees push through the dead snags of the old. New kinds of trees invade from the west and pushed aside their predecessors. Climate itself accelerates: the skies grew heavy with cataracting clouds made of water and rain falls in sinuous sheets. Steam twists and pullulates; the ground becomes hot with change.

Trees themselves come to an end and crumble away; huge solid brown and red domes balloon on the plain, spread thick shell-leaves like opening cabbages, push long shoots through their crowns. The shoots tower above the domes and bloom with millions of tiny gray and pink flowers.

Watching all our work and plans destroyed, the seven tributaries within our soma offer dismayed hypotheses: this is a malfunction, the conservation and compression engines have failed and all knowledge is being acted out uselessly; no, it is some new gambit of the Endtime Work Coordinator, an emergency project; on the contrary, it is a political difficulty, lack of communication between the Coordinator and the Libraries, and it will all be over soon . . .

We watch shoots toppled with horrendous snaps and groans, domes collapsing with brown puffs of corruption.

The scape begins anew.

More hours pass, and still no communication with any other social-minds. We fear our Library itself has been destroyed; what other explanation for our abandonment? We huddle on our promontory, seeing patterns but no sense. Each generation of creativity brings something different, something that eventually fails, or is rejected.

Today large-scale vegetation is the subject of interest; the next day, vegetation is ignored for a rush of tiny biologies, no change visible from where We stand, our soma still and watchful on its eight sturdy legs.

We shuffle our claws to avoid a carpet of reddish growth surmounting the rise. By nightfall, we see, the mad scape could claim this part of the hill and we will have to move.

The sun approaches zenith. All shadows vanish. Its violet magnificence humbles us, a feeling we are not used to. We are from the great social-minds of the Library; humility and awe come from our isolation and concern. Not for a billion years have any of our tributaries felt so removed from useful enterprise. If this is the Endtime overtaking us, overcoming all our efforts, so be it. We feel resolve, pride at what we have managed to accomplish.

Then, we receive a simple message. The meeting with the students will take place. The Berkus will find us and explain. But We are not told when.

Something has gone very wrong, that students should dictate to their teachers, and should put so many tributaries through this kind of travail. The concept of *mutiny* is studied by all the tributaries within the soma. It does not explain much.

New hypotheses occupy our thinking. Perhaps the new matter of which all things were now made has itself gone wrong, destabilizing our worlds and interrupting the consolidation of knowledge; that would explain the scape's ferment and our isolation. It might explain unstable and improper thought processes. Or, the students have allowed some activity on School World to run wild; error.

The scape pushes palace-like glaciers over its surface, gouging itself in painful ecstasy: change, change, birth and decay, all in a single day, but slower than the rush of forests and living things. We might be able to remain on the promontory. Why are we treated so?

We keep to the open, holding our ground, clearly visible, concerned but unafraid. We are of older stuff. Teachers have always been of older stuff.

Could We have been party to some mis-instruction, to cause such a disaster? What have We taught that might push our students into manic creation and destruction? We search all records, all memories, contained within the small soma. The full memories of our seven tributaries have not of course been transferred into the extension; it was to be a temporary assignment, and besides, the records would not fit. The lack of capacity hinders our thinking and we find no satisfying answers.

One of our tributaries has brought along some personal records. It has a long-shot hypothesis and suggests that an ancient prior self be activated to provide an objective judgment engine. There are two reasons: the stronger is that this ancient self once, long ago, had a connection with a tributary making up the Endtime Work Coordinator. If the problem is political, perhaps the self's memories can give us deeper insight. The second and weaker reason: truly, despite our complexity and advancement, perhaps we have missed something important. Perhaps this earlier, more primitive self will see what we have missed.

There is indeed so little time; isolated as we are from a greater river of being, a river that might no longer exist, we might be the last fragment of social-mind to have any chance of combating planet-wide madness.

There is barely enough room to bring the individual out of compression. It sits beside the tributaries in the thought plenum, in distress and not functional. What it perceives it does not understand. Our questions are met with protests and more questions.

The Engine

I come awake, aware. *I* sense a later and very different awareness, part of a larger group. My thoughts spin with faces to which I try to apply names, but my memory falters. These fade and are replaced by gentle calls for attention, new and very strange sensations.

I label the sensations around me: other humans, but not in human bodies. They seem to act together while having separate voices. I call the larger group the We-ness, not me and yet in some way accessible, as if part of my mind and memory.

I do not think that I have died, that I am *dead*. But the quality of my thought has changed. I have no body, no sensations of liquid pumping and breath flowing in and out.

Isolated, confused, I squat behind the We-ness's center of observation, catching glimpses of a chaotic high-speed landscape. Are they watching some entertainment? I worry that I am in a hospital, in recovery, forced to consort with other patients who cannot or will not speak with me.

I try to collect my last meaningful memories. I remember a face again and give it a name and relation: Elisaveta, my wife, standing over me as I lie on a narrow bed. Machines bend over me. I remember nothing after that.

But I am not in a hospital, not now.

Voices speak to me and I begin to understand some of what they say. The voices of the We-ness are stronger, more complex and richer, than anything I have ever experienced. I do not hear them. I have no ears.

"You've been stored inactive for a very long time," the We-ness tells me. It is (or they are) a tight-packed galaxy of thoughts, few of them making any sense at all.

Then I know.

I have awakened in the future. Thinking has changed.

"I don't know where I am. I don't know who you are . . ."

"We are joined from seven tributaries, some of whom once had existence as individual biological beings. You are an ancient self of one of us."

"Oh," I say. The word seems wrong without lips or throat. I will not use it again.

"We're facing great problems. You'll provide unique insights." The voice expresses overtones of fatherliness and concern; I do not believe it.

Blackness paints me. "I'm hungry and I can't feel my body. I'm afraid. Where am I? I miss . . . my family."

"There is no body, no need for hunger, no need for food. Your family—*our* family—no longer lives, unless they have been stored elsewhere."

"How did I get here?"

"You were stored before a major medical reconstruction, to prevent total loss. Your stored self was kept as a kind of historical record and memento."

I don't remember any of that, but then, how could I? I remember signing contracts to allow such a thing. I remember thinking about the possibility I would awake in the future. But I did not die! "How long has it been?"

"Twelve billion two hundred and seventy-nine million years."

Had the We-ness said, *Ten thousand years,* or even *two hundred years,* I might feel some visceral reaction. All I know is that such an enormous length of time is geological, cosmological. I do not believe in it.

I glimpse the landscape again, glaciers slipping down mountain slopes, clouds pregnant with winter building gray and orange in the stinging glare of a huge setting sun. The sun is all wrong—too bright, violet, it resembles a dividing cell, all extrusions and blebs, with long ribbons and streaming hair. It looks like a Gorgon to me.

The faces of the glaciers break, sending showers and pillars of white ice over gray-shaded hills and valleys. I have awakened in the middle of an ice age. But it is too fast. Nothing makes sense.

"Am I all here?" I ask. Perhaps I am delusional.

"What is important from you is here. We would like to ask you questions now. Do you recognize any of the following faces/voices/thought patterns/styles?"

Disturbing synesthesia—bright sounds, loud colors, dull electric smells—fill my senses and I close them out as best I can. "No! That isn't right. Please, no questions until I know what's happened. No! That hurts!"

The We-ness prepares to shut me down. I am told that I will become inactive again.

Just before I wink out, I feel a cold blast of air crest the promontory on which the We-ness, and I, sit. Glaciers now completely cover the hills and valleys. The We-ness flexes eight fluid red legs, pulling them from quick-freezing mud. The sun still has not set.

Thousands of years in a day.

I am given sleep as blank as death, but not so final.

———

We gather as one and consider the problem of the faulty interface. "This is too early a self. It doesn't understand our way of thinking," one tributary says. "We must adapt to it."

The tributary whose prior self this was, volunteers to begin restructuring.

"There is so little time," says another, who now expresses strong disagreement with the plan to resurrect. "Are we truly agreed this is best?"

We threaten to fragment as two of the seven tributaries vehemently object. But solidarity holds. All tributaries flow again to renewed agreement. We start the construction of an effective interface, which first requires deeper understanding of the nature of the ancient self. This takes some time.

We have plenty of time. Hours, days, with no communication.

The glacial cold nearly kills us where we stand. The soma changes its fluid nature by linking liquid water with long-chain and even more slippery molecules, highly resistant to freezing.

"Do the students know We're here, that We watch?" asks a tributary.

"They must . . ." says another. "They express a willingness to meet with us."

"Perhaps they lie, and they mean to destroy this soma, and us with it. There will be no meeting."

Dull sadness.

We restructure the ancient self, wrap it in our new interface, build a new plenary face to hold us all on equal ground, and call it up again, saying,

Vasily

I know the name, recognize the fatherly voice, feel a new clarity. I wish I could forget the first abortive attempt to live again, but my memory is perfect from the point of first rebirth on. I will forget nothing.

"Vasily, your descendant self does not remember you. It has purged older memories many times since your existence, but We recognize some similarities even so between your patterns. Birth patterns are strong and seldom completely erased. Are you comfortable now?"

I think of a simple place where I can sit. I want wood paneling and furniture and a fireplace, but I am not skilled; all I can manage is a small gray cubicle with a window on one side. In the wall is a hole through which the voices come. I imagine I am hearing them through flesh ears, and a kind of body forms within the cubicle. This body is my security. "I'm still afraid. I know—there's no danger."

"There *is* danger, but We do not yet know how significant the danger is."

Significant carries an explosion of information. If their original selves still exist elsewhere, in a social-mind adjunct to a Library, then all that might be lost will be immediate memories. A *social-mind*, I understand, is made up of fewer than ten thousand tributaries. A Library typically contains a trillion or more social-minds.

"I've been dead for billions of years," I say, hoping to address my future self. "But you've lived on—you're immortal."

"We do not measure life or time as you do. Continuity of memory is fragmentary in our lives, across eons. But continuity of access to the Library—and access to records of past selves—does confer a kind of immortality. If that has ended, We are completely mortal."

"I must be so primitive," I say, my fear oddly fading now. This is a situation I can understand—life or death. I feel more solid within my cubicle. "How can I be of any use?"

"You are primitive in the sense of *firstness*. That is why you have been activated. Through your life experience, you may have a deeper understanding of what led to our situation. Argument, rebellion, desperation. . . . These things are difficult for us to deal with."

Again, I don't believe them. From what I can tell, this group of minds has a depth and strength and complexity that makes me feel less than a child . . . perhaps less than a bacterium. What can I do except cooperate? I have nowhere else to go . . .

For billions of years . . . inactive. Not precisely death.

I remember that I was once a *teacher*.

Elisaveta had been my student before she became my wife.

The We-ness wants me to teach it something, to do something for it. But first, it has to teach me history.

"Tell me what's happened," I say.

The Libraries

In the beginning, human intelligences arose, and all were alone. That lasted for tens of thousands of years. Soon after understanding the nature of thought and mind, intelligences came together to create group minds, all in one. Much of the human race linked in an intimacy deeper than sex. Or unlinked to pursue goals as quasi-individuals; the choices were many, the limitations few. (*This all began a few decades after your storage.*) Within a century, the human race abandoned biological limitations, in favor of the social-mind. Social-minds linked to form Libraries, at the top of the hierarchy.

The Libraries expanded, searching around star after star for other intelligent life. They found life—millions upon millions of worlds, each rare as a diamond among the trillions of barren star systems, but none with intelligent beings. Gradually, across millions of years, the Libraries realized that they were the All of intelligent thought.

We had simply exchanged one kind of loneliness for a greater and more final isolation. There were no companion intelligences, only those derived from humanity . . .

As the human Libraries spread and connections between them became more tenuous—some communications taking thousands of years to be completed—many social-minds reindividuated, assuming lesser degrees of togetherness and intimacy. Even in large Libraries, individuation became a crucial kind of relaxation and holiday. The old ways reasserted.

Being human, however, some clung to old ways, or attempted to enforce new ones, with greater or lesser tenacity. Some asserted moral imperative. Madness spread as large groups removed all the barriers of individuation, in reaction to what they perceived as a dangerous atavism—the "lure of the singular."

These "uncelled" or completely communal Libraries, with their slow, united consciousness, proved burdensome and soon vanished—within half a million years. They lacked the range and versatility of the "celled" Libraries.

But conflicts between differing philosophies of social-mind structure continued. There were wars.

Even in wars the passions were not sated; for something more frightening had been discovered than loneliness: the continuity of error and cruelty.

After tens of millions of years of steady growth and peace, the renewed paroxysms dismayed us.

No matter how learned or advanced a social-mind became, it could, in desperation or in certain moments of development, perform acts analogous to the errors of ancient individuated societies. It could kill other social-minds, or sever the activities of many of its own tributaries. It could frustrate the fulfillment of other minds. It could experience something like *rage*, but removed from the passions of the body: rage cold and precise and long-lived, terrible in its persuasiveness, dreadful in its consequences. Even worse, it could experience *indifference*.

I TUMBLE THROUGH THESE RECORDS, UNABLE TO COMPREHEND THE SCALE OF what I see. Our galaxy was linked star to star with webworks of transferred energy and information; parts of the galaxy darkened with massive conflict, millions of stars shut off. This was war.

At human scale, planets seemed to have reverted to ancient Edens, devoid of artifice or instrumentality; but the trees and animals themselves carried myriads of tiny machines, and the ground beneath them was an immense thinking system, down to the core. . . . Other worlds, and other structures between worlds, seemed as abstract and meaningless as the wanderings of a stray brush on canvas.

The Proof

One great social-mind, retreating far from the ferment of the Libraries, formulated the rules of advanced meta-biology, and found them precisely analogous to those governing planet-bound ecosystems: competition, victory through survival, evolution and reproduction. It proved that error and pain and destruction are essential to any change—but more important, to any growth.

The great social-mind carried out complex experiments simulating millions of different ordering systems, and in every single case, the rise of complexity (and ultimately intelligence) led to the wanton destruction of prior forms. Using these experiments to define axioms, what began as a scientific proof ended as a rigorous mathematical proof: *there can be no ultimate ethical advancement in this universe, in systems governed by time and subject to change*. The indifference of the universe—reality's grim and mindless harshness—is multiplied by the necessity that old order, prior thoughts and lives, must be extinguished to make way for new.

After checking its work many times, the great social-mind wiped its stores and erased its infrastructure in, on and around seven worlds and the two stars, leaving behind only the formulation and the Proof.

For Libraries across the galaxy, absorption of the Proof led to mental disruption. From the nightmare of history there was to be no awakening.

Suicide was one way out. A number of prominent Libraries brought their own histories to a close.

Others recognized the validity of the Proof, but did not commit suicide. They lived with the possibility of error and destruction. And still, they grew wiser, greater in scale and accomplishment . . .

Crossing from galaxy to galaxy, still alone, the Libraries realized that human perception was the only perception. The Proof would never be tested against the independent minds of non-human intelligences. In this universe, the Proof must stand.

Billions of years passed, and the universe became a huge kind of house, confining a practical infinity of mind, an incredible ferment which "burned" the available energy with torchy brilliance, decreasing the total life span of reality.

Yet the Proof remained unassailed.

WAIT. I DON'T SEE ANYTHING HERE. I DON'T FEEL ANYTHING. THIS ISN'T HIS-tory; it's . . . too large! I can't understand some of the things you show me . . . But worse, pardon me, it's babbling among minds who feel no passion. This We-ness . . . how do you *feel* about this?

YOU ARE DISTRACTED BY PRECONCEPTIONS. YOU LONG FOR AN ORGANIC BODY, and assume that lacking organic bodies, We experience no emotions. We experience emotions. *Listen* to them>>>>>

I SQUIRM IN MY CUBICLE AND EXPERIENCE THEIR EMOTIONS OF FIRST AND second loneliness, degrees of isolation from old memories, old selves; longing for the first individuation, the Birth-time. . . . Hunger for un-derstanding not just of the outer reality, beyond the social-mind's vast internal universe of thought, but of the ever-changing currents and or-derliness arising between tributaries. Here is social and mental interac-tion as a great song, rich and joyous, a love greater than anything I can remember experiencing as an embodied human. Greater emotions still, outside my range again, of loyalty and love for a social-mind and some-thing like *respect* for the immense Libraries. (I am shown what the We-ness says is an emotion experienced at the level of Libraries, but it is so far beyond me that I seem to disintegrate, and have to be coaxed back to wholeness.)

A tributary approaches across the mind space within the soma. My cubicle grows dim. I feel a strange familiarity again; this will be, *is*, my future self.

This tributary feels sadness and some grief, touching its ancient self—me. It feels pain at my limitations, at my tightly packed biological char-acter. Things deliberately forgotten come back to haunt it.

And they haunt *me*. My own inadequacies become abundantly clear. I remember useless arguments with friends, making my wife cry with frustration, getting angry at my children for no good reason. My child-hood and adolescent indiscretions return like shadows on a scrim. And I remember my *drives:* rolling in useless lust, and later, Elisaveta! With her young and supple body; and others. Just as significant, but different in color, the cooler passions of discovery and knowledge, my growing self-awareness. I remember fear of inadequacy, fear of failure, of not being a useful member of society. I needed above all (more than I needed Elisaveta) to be important and to teach and be influential on young minds.

All of these emotions, the We-ness demonstrates, have analogous emotions at their level. For the We-ness, the most piercing unpleasant-

ness of all—akin to physical pain—comes from recognition of their possible failure. The teachers may not have taught their students properly,
and the students may be making mistakes.

"Let me get all this straight," I say. I grow used to my imagined state—
to riding like a passenger within the cubicle, inside the eight-legged
soma, to seeing as if through a small window the advancing and now
receding of the glaciers. "You're teachers—as I was once a teacher—and
you used to be connected to a larger social-mind, part of a Library." I
mull over mind as society, society as mind. "But there may have been
a revolution. After billions of years! Students . . . a *revolution!* Extraordinary!

"You've been cut off from the Library. You're alone, you might be
killed. . . . And you're telling *me* about ancient history?"

The We-ness falls silent.

"I must be important," I say with an unbreathed sigh, a kind of as-
terisk in the exchanged thoughts. "I can't imagine why. But maybe it
doesn't matter—I have so many questions!" I hunger for knowledge of
what has become of my children, of my wife. Of everything that came
after me. . . . All the changes!

"We need information from you, and your interpretation of certain
memories. Vasily was our name once. Vasily Gerazimov. You were the
husband of Elisaveta, father of Maxim and Giselle. . . . We need to know
more about Elisaveta."

"You don't remember her?"

"Twelve billion years have passed. Time and space have changed. This
tributary alone has partnered and bonded and matched and socialized
with perhaps fifty billion individuals and tributaries since. Our combined
tributaries in the social-mind have had contacts with all intelligent beings, once or twice removed. Most have dumped or stored memories
more than a billion years old. If We were still connected to the Library,
I could learn more about my past. I have kept you as a kind of *memento*,
a talisman, and nothing more."

I feel a freezing awe. Fifty billion mates. . . . Or whatever they had
been. I catch fleeting glimpses of liaisons in the social-mind, binary,
trinary, as many as thousands at a time linked in the crumbling remnants of marriage and sexuality, and finally those liaisons passing completely out of favor, fashion, usefulness.

"Elisaveta and you," the tributary continues, "were divorced ten years
after your storage. I remember nothing of the reasons why. We have no
other clues to work with."

The "news" comes as a doubling of my pain, a renewed and expanded
sense of isolation from a loved one. I reach up to touch my face, to see
if I am crying. My hands pass through imagined flesh and bone. My

body is long since dust; Elisaveta's body is dust. What went wrong between us? Did she find another lover? Did I? I am a ghost. I should not care. There were difficult times, but I never thought of our liaison—our *marriage*, I would defend that word even now—as temporary. Still, across *billions* of years! We have become *immortal*—her perhaps more than I, who remember nothing of the time between. "Why do you need me at all? Why do you need clues?"

But we are interrupted. An extraordinary thing happens to the retreating glaciers. From our promontory, the soma half-hidden behind an upthrust of frozen and deformed knowledge, we see the icy masses blister and bubble, as if made of some superheated glass or plastic. Steam bursts from the bubbles—at least, what I assume to be steam—and freezes in the air in shapes suggesting flowers. All around, the walls and sheets of ice succumb to this beautiful plague.

The We-ness understands it no more than I.

From the hill below come faint sounds and hints of radiation—gamma rays, beta particles, mesons, all clearly visible to the We-ness, and vaguely passed on to me as well.

"Something's coming," I say.

THE BERKUS ADVANCES IN ITS UNEXPECTED CLOUD OF PRODUCTION-destruction. There is something deeply wrong with it—it squanders too much available energy. Its very presence disrupts the new matter of which We are made.

Of the seven tributaries, four feel an emotion rooted in the deepest algorithms of their pasts: fear. Three have never known such bodily functions, have never known mortal and embodied individuation. They feel intellectual concern and a tinge of cosmic sadness, as if our end might be equated with the past death of the natural stars and galaxies. We keep to our purpose despite these ridiculous excursions, signs of our disorder.

The Berkus advances up the hill.

I SEE THROUGH MY WINDOW THIS MONUMENTAL AND ABSOLUTELY HORRIFYING *creature*, shining with a brightness comprised of the qualities of diamonds and polished silver, a scintillating insect pushing its sharply pointed feet into the thawing soil, steam rising all around. The legs hold together despite gaps where joints should be, gaps crossed only by something that produces hard radiation. Below the Berkus (so the We-ness calls it), the ground ripples as if School World has muscles and twitches, wanting to scratch.

The Berkus pauses and sizes up our much less powerful, much smaller soma with blasts of neutrons, flicked as casually as a flashlight beam. The material of our soma wilts and reforms beneath this withering barrage. The soma expresses distress—and inadvertently, the Weness translates this distress to me as tremendous pain.

I explode within my confined mental space. Again comes the blackness.

THE BERKUS DECIDES IT IS NOT NECESSARY TO COME ANY CLOSER. THAT IS fortunate for us, and for our soma. Any lessening of the distance between us would prove fatal.

The Berkus communicates with pulsed light. "Why are you here?"

"We have been sent here to observe and report. We are cut off from the Library—"

"Your Library has fled," the Berkus informs us. "It disagreed with the Endtime Work Coordinator."

"We were told nothing of this."

"It was not our responsibility. We did not know you would be here."

The magnitude of this rudeness is difficult to comprehend. We wonder how many tributaries the Berkus contains. We hypothesize that it might contain all of the students, the entire student social-mind, and this would explain its use of energy and change in design.

Our pitiful ancient individual flickers back into awareness and sits quietly, too stunned to protest.

"We do not understand the purpose of this creation and destruction," We say. Our strategy is to avoid the student tributaries altogether now. Still, they might tell us more We need to know.

"It must be obvious to teachers," the Berkus says. "By order of the Coordinator, We are rehearsing all possibilities of order, usurping stored knowledge down to the planetary core and converting it. There must be an escape from the Proof."

"The Proof is an ancient discovery. It has never been shown to be wrong. What can it possibly mean to the Endtime Work?"

"It means a great deal," the Berkus says.

"How many are you?"

The Berkus does not answer. All this has taken place in less than a millionth of a second. The Berkus's incommunication lengthens into seconds, then minutes. Around us, the glaciers crumple like mud caught in rushing water.

"Another closed path, of no value," the Berkus finally says.

"We wish to understand your motivations."

"We have no need of you now."

"Why this concern with the Proof? And what does it have to do with the change you provoke, the destruction of School World's knowledge?"

The Berkus rises on a tripod of three disjointed legs, waving its other legs in the air, a cartoon medallion so disturbing in design that We draw back a few meters.

"The Proof is a cultural aberration," it radiates fiercely, blasting our surface and making the mud around us bubble. "It is not fit to pass on to those who seed the next reality. You failed us. You showed no way beyond the Proof. The Endtime Work has begun, the final self chosen to fit through the narrow gap—"

I SEE ALL THIS THROUGH THE WE-NESS AS IF I HAVE BEEN THERE, HAVE LIVED it, and suddenly I know why I have been recalled, why the We-ness has shown me faces and patterns.

The universe, across more than twelve billion years, grows irretrievably old. From spanning the galaxies billions of years before, all life and intelligence—all arising from the sole intelligence in all the universe, humanity—have shrunk to a few star systems. These systems have been resuscitated and nurtured by concentrating the remaining available energy of thousands of dead galaxies. And they are no longer natural star systems with planets—the bloated coma—wrapped violet star rising at zenith over us is a congeries of plasma macromachines, controlling and conserving every gram of the natural matter remaining, every erg of available energy. These artificial suns pulse like massive living cells, shaped to be ultimately efficient and to squeeze every moment of active life over time remaining. The planets themselves have been condensed, recarved, rearranged, and they too are composed of geological macro-machines. With some dread, I gather that the matter of which all these things are made is itself artificial, with redesigned component particles.

The natural galaxies have died, reduced to a colorless murmur of useless heat, and all the particles of all original creation—besides those marshaled and remade in these three close-packed systems—have dulled and slowed and unwound. Gravity itself has lost its bearings and become a chancy phenomenon, supplemented by new forces generated within the macromachine planets and suns.

Nothing is what it seems, and nothing is what it had been when I lived.

Available energy is strictly limited. The We-ness looks forward to less than four times ten to the fiftieth units of Planck time—roughly an old Earth year.

And in charge of it all, controlling the Endtime Work, a supremely confident social-mind composed of many "tributaries," and among those gathered selves . . .

Someone very familiar to me indeed. My wife.

"Where is she? Can I speak to her? What happened to her—did she die, was she stored, did she live?"

The We-ness seems to vibrate both from my reaction to this information, and to the spite of the Berkus. I am assigned to a quiet place,
where I can watch and listen without bothering them. I feel our soma,
our insect-like body, dig into the loosening substance of the promontory.

"You taught us the Proof was absolute," the Berkus says, "that
throughout all time, in all circumstances, error and destruction and pain
will accompany growth and creation, that the universe must remain
indifferent and randomly hostile. We do not accept that."

"But why dissolve links with the Library?" We cry, shrinking beneath
the Berkus's glare. The constantly reconstructed body of the Berkus
channels and consumes energy with enormous waste, as if the students
do not care, intent only on their frantic mission, whatever that might
be. . . . Reducing available active time by days for *all of us*—

I know! I shout in the quiet place, but I am not heard, or not paid
attention to.

"Why condemn us to a useless end in this chaos, this madness?" We
ask.

"Because We must refute the Proof and there is so little useful time
remaining. The final self must not be sent over carrying this burden of
error."

"Of sin!" I shout, still not heard. Proof of the validity of primordial
sin—that everything living must eat, must destroy, must climb up the
ladder on the backs of miserable victims. That all true creation involves
death and pain; the universe is a charnel house.

I am fed and study the Proof. Time runs in many tracks within the
soma. I try to encompass the principles and expressions, no longer given
as words, but as multisense abstractions. In the Proof, miniature universes of discourse are created, manipulated, reduced to an expression,
and discarded: the Proof is more complex than any single human life,
or even the life of a species, and its logic is not familiar. The Proof is
rooted in areas of mental experience I am not equipped to understand,
but I receive glosses.

Law: Any dynamic system (I understand this as *organism*) **has limited access to resources, and a limited time in which to achieve
its goals.** A multitude of instances are drawn from history, as well as
from an artificial miniature universe.) Other laws follow regarding behavior of systems within a flow of energy, but they are completely beyond me.

Observed Law: The goals of differing organisms, even of like

variety, never completely coincide. (History and the miniature universe teem with instances, and the Proof lifts these up for inspection at moments of divergence, demonstrating again and again this obvious point.)

Then comes a roll of beginning deductions, backed by examples too numerous for me to absorb:

And so it follows that for any complex of organisms, competition must arise for limited resources.

From this: some will succeed, some will fail, to acquire resources sufficient to live. Those who succeed, express themselves in later generations.

From this: New dynamic systems will arise to compete more efficiently.

From this: Competition and selection will give rise to organisms that are *streamlined,* incapable of surviving even in the midst of plenty because not equipped with complete methods of absorbing resources. These will prey on complete organisms to acquire their resources. And in return, the prey will acquire a reliance on the predators.

From this: Other forms of *streamlining* will occur. Some of the resulting systems will depend entirely on others for reproduction and fulfillment of goals.

From this: Ecosystems will arise, interdependent, locked in predator-prey, disease-host relationships.

I experience a multitude of rigorous experiments, unfolding like flowers.

And so it follows that in the course of competition, some forms will be outmoded, and will pass away, and others will be preyed upon to extinction, without regard to their beauty, their adaptability to a wide range of possible conditions. I sense here a kind of aesthetic judgment, above the fray: beautiful forms will die without being fully tested, their information lost, their opportunities limited.

And so it follows . . .

And so it follows . . .

The ecosystems increase in complexity, giving rise to organisms whose primary adaptation is perception and judgment, forming the abstract equivalents of societies, which interact through the exchange of resources and extensions of cultures and politics—models for more efficient organization. Still, change and evolution, failure and death, societies and cultures pass and are forgotten; whole classes of these larger systems suffer extinction, without being allowed fulfillment.

From history: Nations pray upon nations, and eat them alive, discarding them as burned husks.

Law: The universe is neutral; it will not care, nor will any ultimate dynamic system interfere . . .

In those days before I was born, as smoke rose from the ovens, God did not hear the cries of His people.

And so it follows: that no system will achieve perfect efficiency and self-sufficiency. Within all changing systems, accumulated error must be purged. For the good of the dynamic whole, systems must die. But efficient and beautiful systems will die as well.

I see the Proof's abstraction of evil: a shark-like thing, to me, but no more than a very complex expression. In this shark there is history, and dumb organic pressure, and the accumulations of the past: and the shark does not discriminate, knows nothing of judgment or justice, will eat the promising and the strong as well as birthing young. Waste, waste, an agony of waste, and over it all, not watching, the indifference of the real.)

After what seems hours of study, of questions asked and answered, new ways of thinking acquired—re-education—I begin to feel the thoroughness of the Proof, and I feel a despair unlike anything in my embodied existence.

Where once there had been hope that intelligent organisms could see their way to just, beautiful and efficient systems, in practice, without exception, they revert to the old rules.

Things have not and will never improve.

Heaven itself would be touched with evil—or stand still. But there is no heaven run by a just God. Nor can there be a just God. Perfect justice and beauty and evolution and change are incompatible.

Not the birth of my son and daughter, not the day of my marriage, not all my moments of joy can erase the horror of history. And the stretch of future histories, after my storage, shows even more horror, until I seem to swim in carnivorous, *cybernivorous* cruelty.

Connections

We survey the Berkus with growing concern. Here is not just frustration of our attempts to return to the Library, not just destruction of knowledge, but a flagrant and purposeless waste of precious resources. Why is it allowed?

Obviously, the Coordinator of the Endtime Work has given license, handed over this world, with such haste that We did not have time to withdraw. The Library has been forced away (or worse), and all transponders destroyed, leaving us alone on School World.

The ancient self, having touched on the Proof (absorbing no more than a fraction of its beauty) is wrapped in a dark shell of mood. This mood, basic and primal as it is, communicates to the tributaries. Again, after billions of years, We feel sadness at the inevitability of error and the impossibility of justice—and sadness at our own error. The Proof has always stood as a monument of pure thought—and a curse, even to we who affirm it.

The Berkus expands like a balloon. "There is going to be major work done here. You will have to move."

"*No,*" the combined tributaries cry. "This is enough confusion and enough being *shoved around.*" Those words come from the ancient self.

The Berkus finds them amusing.

"Then you'll stay here," it says, "and be absorbed in the next round of experiment. You are teachers who have taught incorrectly. You deserve no better."

I BREAK FREE OF THE *DARK SHELL OF MOOD,* AS THE TRIBUTARIES DESCRIBE it, and now I seem to kick and push my way to a peak of attention, all without arms or legs. "Where is the plan, the order? Where are your billions of years of superiority? How can this be happening?"

WE PASS ON THE CRIES OF THE ANCIENT SELF. THE BERKUS HEARS THE MESsage.

"We are not familiar with this voice," the student social-mind says.

"I judge you from the past!" the ancient self says. "You are *all* found wanting!"

"This is not the voice of a tributary, but of an individual," the Berkus says. "The individual sounds uninformed."

"I DEMAND TO SPEAK WITH MY WIFE!" MY DEMAND GETS NO REACTION FOR almost a second. Around me, the tributaries within the soma flow and rearrange, thinking in a way I cannot follow. They finally rise as a solid, seamless river of consent.

"*We charge you with error,*" they say to the Berkus. "*We charge you with confirming the Proof you wish to negate.*"

The Berkus considers, then backs away swiftly, beaming at us one final message: "There is an interesting rawness in your charge. You no longer think as outmoded teachers. A link with the Endtime Work Coordinator will be requested. Stand where you are. Our own work must continue."

I FEEL A SENSE OF RELIEF AROUND ME. THIS IS A BREAKTHROUGH. I HAVE A purpose! The Berkus retreats, leaving us on the promontory to observe. Where once, hours before, glaciers melted, the ground begins to churn, grow viscous, divide into fenced enclaves. Within the enclaves, green and gray shapes arise, sending forth clouds of steam. These enclaves surround the range of hills, surmount all but our promontory, and move off to the horizon on all sides, perhaps covering the entire School World.

In the center of each fenced area, a sphere forms first as a white blister on the hardness, then a pearl resting on the surface. The pearl lifts, suspended in air. Each pearl begins to evolve in a different way, turning inward, doubling, tripling, flattening into disks, centers dividing to form toruses; a practical infinity of different forms.

The fecundity of idea startles me. Blastulas give rise to cell-like complexity, spikes twist into intricate knots, all the rules of ancient topological mathematics are demonstrated in seconds, and then violated as the spaces within the enclaves themselves change.

"What are they doing?" I ask, bewildered.

"A mad push of evolution, trying all combinations starting from a simple beginning form," my descendant self explains. "It was once a common exercise, but not on such a vast scale. Not since the formulation of the Proof."

"What do they want to learn?"

"If they can find one instance of evolution and change that involves only growth and development, not competition and destruction, then they will have falsified the Proof."

"But the Proof is perfect," I said. "It can't be falsified . . ."

"So We have judged. The students incorrectly believe We are wrong."

The field of creation becomes a vast fabric, each enclave contributing to a larger weave. What is being shown here could have occupied entire civilizations in my time: the dimensions of change, all possibilities of progressive growth. "It's beautiful," I say.

"It's futile," my descendant self says, its tone bitter. I feel the emotion in its message as an aberration, and it immediately broadcasts shame to all of its fellows, and to me.

"Are you afraid they'll show your teachings were wrong?" I asked.

"No," my tributary says. "I am sorry that they will fail. Such a message to pass on to a young universe. . . . That whatever our nature and design, however we develop, we are doomed to make errors and cause pain. Still, that is the truth, and it has never been refuted."

"But even in my time, there was a solution," I say.

They show mild curiosity. What could come from so far in the past, that they hadn't advanced upon it, improved it, a billion times over, or discarded it? I wonder why I have been activated at all . . .

But I persist. "From God's perspective, destruction and pain and error may be part of the greater whole, a beauty from its point of view. We only perceive it as evil because of our limited point of view."

The tributaries allow a polite pause. My tributary explains, as gently as possible, "We have never encountered ultimate systems you call gods. Still, we are or have been very much like gods. As gods, all too often we have made horrible errors, and caused unending pain. Pain did not add to the beauty."

I want to scream at them for their hubris, but it soon becomes apparent to me, they are right. Their predecessors have reduced galaxies, scanned all histories, made the universe itself run faster with their productions and creations. They have advanced the Endtime by billions of years, and now prepare to seed a new universe across an inconceivable gap of darkness and immobility.

From my perspective, humans have certainly become god-like. But not just. And there are no others. Even in the diversity of the human diaspora across the galaxies, not once has the Proof been falsified. And that is all it would have taken: one instance.

"Why did you bring me back, then?" I ask my descendant self in private conference. It replies in kind:

"Your thought processes are not our own. You can be a judgment engine. You might give us insight into the reasoning of the students, and help explain to us their plunge into greater error. There must be some motive not immediately apparent, some fragment of personality and memory responsible for this. An ancient self of a tributary of the Endtime Work Coordinator and you were once intimately related, married as sexual partners. You did not stay married. That is division and dissent. And there is division and dissent between the Endtime Work Committee and the teachers. That much is apparent . . ."

Again I feel like clutching my hands to my face and screaming in frustration. Elisaveta—it must mean Elisaveta. *But we were not divorced . . . not when I was stored!* I sit in my imagined gray cubicle, my imagined body uncertain in its outline, and wish for a moment of complete privacy. They give it to me.

Tapering Time

The scape has progressed to a complexity beyond our ability to process. We stand on our promontory, surrounded by the field of enclaved experiments, each enclave containing a different evolved object, the objects still furiously convoluting and morphing. Some glow faintly as night sweeps across our part of the School World. We are as useless and incompetent as the revived ancient self, now wrapped in its own shock and misery. Our tributaries have fallen silent. We wait for what will happen next, either in the scape, or in the promised contact with the Endtime Work Coordinator.

The ancient self rises from its misery and isolation. It joins our watchful silence, expectant. It has not completely lost *hope*. We have never had need of *hope*. Connected to the Library, fear became a distant and unimportant thing; hope, its opposite, equally distant and not useful.

I HAVE BEEN MUSING OVER MY LAST HAZY MEMORIES OF ELISAVETA, OF OUR children Maxim and Giselle—bits of conversation, physical features, smells. . . . Reliving long stretches with the help of memory recovery . . .

watching seconds pass into minutes as if months pass into years.

Outside, time seems to move much more swiftly. The divisions be-tween enclaves fall, and the uncounted experiments stand on the field, still evolving, but now allowed to interact. Tentatively, their evolution takes in the new possibility of *motion*.

I feel for the students, wish to be part of them. However wrong, this experiment is vital, idealistic. It smells of youthful naiveté. Because of my own rugged youth, raised in a nation running frantically from one historical extreme to another, born to parents who jumped like puppets between extremes of hope and despair, I have always felt uneasy in the face of idealism and naiveté.

Elisaveta was a naive idealist when I first met her. I tried to teach her, pass on my sophistication, my sense of better judgment.

The brightly colored, luminous objects hover on the plain, discovering new relations: a separate identity, a larger sense of space. The objects have reached a high level of complexity and order, but within a limited environment. If any have developed mind, they can now reach out and explore new objects.

First, the experiments shift a few centimeters this way or that, visible across the plain as kind of restless, rolling motion. The plain becomes an ocean of gentle waves. Then, the experiments *bump* each other. Near our hill, some of the experiments circle and surround their companions, or just bump with greater and greater urgency. Extensions reach out, and we can see—it must be obvious to all—that mind does exist, and new senses are being created and explored.

If Elisaveta, whatever she has become, is in charge of this sea of experiments, then perhaps she is merely following an inclination she had billions of years before: when in doubt, when all else fails, *punt*.

This is a cosmological kind of punt, burning up available energy at a distressing rate . . .

Just like her, I think, and feel a warmth of connection with that an-cient woman. But the woman *divorced* me. She found me wanting, later than my memories reach. . . . And after all, what she has become is as little like the Elisaveta I knew as my descendant tributary is like me.

The dance on the plain becomes a frenzied blur of color. Snakes flow, sprout legs, wings beat the air. Animal relations, plant relations, new ecosystems. . . . But these creatures have evolved not from the simplest beginnings, but from already elaborate sources. Each isolated experi-ment, already having achieved a focused complexity beyond anything I can understand, becomes a potential player in a new order of interac-tion. What do the students—or Elisaveta—hope to accomplish in this peculiar variation on the old scheme?

I am so focused on the spectacle surrounding us that it takes a "nudge" from my descendant self to alert me to change in the sky. A liquid silvery ribbon pours from above, spreading over our heads into a flat upside-down ocean of reflective cloud. The inverse ocean expands to the horizon, blocking all light from the new day.

Our soma rises expectantly on its eight legs. I feel the tributaries' interest as a kind of heat through my cubicle, and I abandon the imagined environment for the time being. Best to receive this new phenomenon directly.

A fringed curtain, like the edge of a shawl woven from threads of mercury, descends from the upside-down ocean, brushing over the land. The fringe crosses the plain of experiments without interfering, but surrounds our hill, screening our view. Light pulses from selected threads in the liquid weave. The tributaries translate instantly.

"What do you want?" asks a clear neutral voice. No character, no tone, no emotion. This is the Endtime Work Coordinator, or at least an extension of that powerful social-mind. It does not sound anything like Elisaveta. My hopes have been terribly naive.

After all this time and misery, the teachers' reserve is admirable. I detect respect, but no awe; they are used to the nature of the Endtime Work Coordinator, largest of the social-minds not directly connected to a Library. "We have been cut off, and We need to know why," the tributaries say.

"Your work reached a conclusion," the voice responds.

"Why were We not accorded the respect of being notified, or allowed to return to our Library?"

"Your Library has been terminated. We have concluded the active existence of all entities no longer directly connected with Endtime Work, to conserve available energy."

"But you have let us live."

"It would involve more energy to terminate existing extensions than to allow them to run down."

The sheer coldness and precision of the voice chill me. The end of a Library is equivalent to the end of thousands of worlds full of individual intelligences. *Genocide. Error and destruction.*

But my future self corrects me. *"This is expediency,"* it says in a private sending. *"It is what We all expected would happen sooner or later. The manner seems irregular, but the latitude of the Endtime Work Coordinator is great."*

Still, the tributaries request a complete accounting of the decision. The Coordinator obliges. A judgment arrives:

The Teachers are irrelevant. Teaching of the Proof has been deemed useless; the Coordinator has decided—I hear a different sort of voice, barely recognizable to me—*Elisaveta.*

"All affirmations of the Proof merely discourage our search for alternatives. The Proof has become a thought disease, a cultural tyranny. It blocks our discovery of another solution."

A New Accounting

Our ancient self recognizes something in the message. What We have planned from near the beginning now bears fruit—the ancient self, functioning as an engine of judgment and recognition, has found a key player in the decision to isolate us, and to terminate our Library.

"We detect the voice of a particular tributary," We say to the Coordinator. "May We communicate with this tributary?"

"Do you have a valid reason?" the Coordinator asks.

"We must check for error."

"Your talents are not recognized."

"Still, the Coordinator might have erred, and as there is so little time, following the wrong course will be doubly tragic."

The Coordinator reaches a decision after sufficient time to show a complete polling of all tributaries within its social-mind.

"An energy budget is established. Communication is allowed."

We follow protocol billions of years old, but excise unnecessary ceremonial segments. We poll the student tributaries, searching for some flaw in reasoning, finding none.

Then We begin searching for our own justification. If We are about to *die*, lost in the last-second noise and event-clutter of a universe finally running down, We need to know where *We* have failed. If there is no failure—and if all this experimentation is simply a futile act, We might die less ignominiously. We search for the tributary familiar to the ancient self, hoping to find the personal connection that will reduce all our questions to one exchange.

Bright patches of light in the sky bloom, spread, and are quickly gathered and snuffed. The other suns and worlds are being converted and conserved. We have minutes, perhaps only seconds.

We find the voice, descendant tributary of Elisaveta.

THERE ARE IMMENSE DEATHS IN THE SKY, AND NOW ALL IS GOING DARK. There is only the one sun, turning in on itself, violet shading to deep orange, and the School World.

Four seconds. I have just four seconds. . . . Endtime accelerates upon us. The student experiment has consumed so much energy. All other worlds have been terminated, all social-minds except the Endtime Coordinator's and the final self. . . . The seed that will cross the actionless Between.

I feel the tributaries frantically create an interface, make distant requests, then demands. They meet strong resistance from a tributary within the Endtime Work Coordinator. This much they convey to me. . . . I sense weeks, months, years of negotiation, all passing in a second of more and more disjointed and uncertain real time.

As the last energy of the universe is spent, as all potential and all kinesis bottom out at a useless average, the fractions of seconds become clipped, their qualities altered. Time advances with an irregular jerk, truly like an off-center wheel.

Agreement is reached. Law and persuasion even now have some force.

"Vasily. I haven't thought about you in ever so long."

"Elisaveta, is that you?" I cannot see her. I sense a total lack of emotion in her words. And why not?

"Not *your* Elisaveta, Vasily. But I hold her memories and some of her patterns."

"You've been alive for billions of years?"

I receive a condensed impression of a hundred million sisters, all related to Elisaveta, stored at different times like a huge library of past selves. The final tributary she has become, now an important part of the Coordinator, refers to her past selves much as a grown woman might open childhood diaries. The past selves are kept informed, to the extent that being informed does not alter their essential natures.

How differently my own descendant self behaves, sealing away a small part of the past as a reminder, but never consulting it. How perverse for a mind that reveres the past! Perhaps what it reveres is form, not actuality . . .

"Why do you want to speak with me?" Elisaveta asks. Which Elisaveta, from which time, I cannot tell right away.

"I think . . . *they* seem to think it's important. A disagreement, something that went wrong."

"They are seeking justification through you, a self stored billions of years ago. They want to be told that their final efforts have meaning. How like the Vasily I knew."

"It's not my doing! I've been inactive. . . . Were we divorced?"

"Yes." Sudden realization changes the tone of this Elisaveta's voice. "You were stored before we divorced?"

"Yes! How long after . . . were you stored?"

"A century, maybe more," she answers. With some wonder, she says, "Who could have known we would live forever?"

"When I saw you last, we loved each other. We had children . . ."

"They died with the Libraries," she says.

I do not feel physical grief, the body's component of sadness and rage at loss, but the news rocks me, even so. I retreat to my gray cubicle.

My children! They have survived all this time, and yet I have missed them. What happened to my children, in my time? What did they become to me, and I to them? Did they have children, grandchildren, and after our divorce, did they respect me enough to let me visit my grandchildren . . . ? But it's all lost now, and if they kept records of their ancient selves—records of what had truly been my children—that is gone, too. They are *dead*.

Elisaveta regards my grief with some wonder, and finds it sympathetic. I feel her warm to me slightly. "They weren't really our children any longer, Vasily. They became something quite other, as have you and I. But *this* you—you've been kept like a butterfly in a collection. How sad."

She seeks me out and takes on a bodily form. It is not the shape of the Elisaveta I knew. She once built a biomechanical body to carry her thoughts. This is the self-image she carries now, of a mind within a primitive, woman-shaped soma.

"What happened to us?" I ask, my agony apparent to her, to all who listen.

"Is it that important to you?"

"Can you explain any of this?" I ask. I want to bury myself in her bosom, to hug her. I am so lost and afraid I feel like a child, and yet my pride keeps me together.

"I was your student, Vasily. Remember? You *browbeat* me into marrying you. You poured learning into my ear day and night, even when we made love. You were so full of knowledge. You spoke nine languages. You knew all there was to know about Schopenhauer and Hegel and Marx and Wittgenstein. You did not listen to what was important to me."

I want to draw back; it is impossible to cringe. This I recognize. This I remember. But the Elisaveta I knew had come to accept me, my faults and my learning, joyously, had encouraged me to open up with her. I had taught her a great deal.

"You gave me absolutely no room to grow, Vasily."

The enormous triviality of this conversation, at the end of time, strikes me and I want to laugh out loud. Not possible. I stare at this *monstrous* Elisaveta, so bitter and different. . . . And now, to me, shaded by her indifference. "I feel like I've been half a dozen men, and we've all loved you badly," I say, hoping to sting her.

"No. Only one. You became angry when I disagreed with you. I asked for more freedom to explore. . . . You said there was really little left to explore. Even in the last half of the twenty-first century, Vasily, you said we had found all there was to find, and everything thereafter would be mere details. When I had my second child, it began. I saw you through the eyes of my infant daughter, saw what you would do to her, and I began to grow apart from you. We separated, then divorced, and it was for the best. For me, at any rate; I can't say that you ever understood."

We seem to stand in that gray cubicle, that comfortable simplicity with which I surrounded myself when first awakened. Elisaveta, taller, stronger, face more seasoned, stares at me with infinitely more experience. I am outmatched.

Her expression softens. "But you didn't deserve *this*, Vasily. You mustn't blame me for what your tributary has done."

"I am not he . . . It. It is not me. And you are not the Elisaveta I know!"

"You wanted to keep me forever the student you first met in your classroom. Do you see how futile that is now?"

"Then what can we love? What is there left to attach to?"

She shrugs. "It doesn't much matter, does it? There's no more time left to love or not to love. And love has become a vastly different thing."

"We reach this *peak* . . . of intelligence, of accomplishment, immortality . . ."

"Wait." Elisaveta frowns and tilts her head, as if listening, lifts her finger in question, listens again, to voices I do not hear. "I begin to understand your confusion," she says.

"What?"

"This is not a peak, Vasily. This is a backwater. We are simply all that's left after a long, dreadful attenuation. The greater, more subtle galaxies of Libraries ended themselves a hundred million years ago."

"Suicide?"

"They saw the very end we contemplate now. They decided that if our kind of life had no hope of escaping the Proof—the Proof these teachers helped fix in all our thoughts—than it was best not to send a part of ourselves into the next universe. We are what's left of those who disagreed . . ."

"My tributary did not tell me this."

"Hiding the truth from yourself even now."

I hold my hands out to her, hoping for pity, but this Elisaveta has long since abandoned pity. I desperately need to activate some fragment of love within her. "I am so lost . . ."

"We are all lost, Vasily. There is only one hope."

She turns and opens a broad door on one side of my cubicle, where I originally placed the window to the outside. "If we succeed at this," she says, "then we are better than those great souls. If we fail, they were right. . . . Better that nothing from our reality crosses the Between."

I admire her for her knowledge, then, for being kept so well informed. But I resent that she has advanced beyond me, has no need for me. The tributaries watch with interest, like voyeurs.

("*Perhaps there is a chance.*" My descendant self speaks in a private sending.)

"I see why you divorced me," I say sullenly.

"You were a tyrant and a bully. When you were stored—before your heart replacement, I remember now. . . . When you were stored, you and I simply had not grown far apart. We would. It was inevitable."

(I ask my descendant self whether what she says is true.

"*It is a way of seeing what happened,*" it says. "*The Proof has yet to be disproved. We recommended no attempts be made to do so. We think such attempts are futile.*"

"*You taught that?*"

"*We created patterns of thought and diffused them for use in creation of new tributaries. The last students. But perhaps there is a chance. Touch her. You know how to reach her.*")

"The Proof is very convincing," I tell Elisaveta. "Perhaps this *is* futile."

"You simply have no say, Vasily. The effort is being made." I have touched her, but it is not pity I arouse this time, and certainly not love—it is disgust.

Through the window, Elisaveta and I see a portion of the plain. On it, the experiments have congealed into a hundred, a thousand smooth, slowly pulsing shapes. Above them all looms the shadow of the Coordinator.

(I feel a bridge being made, links being established. I sense panic in my descendant self, who works without the knowledge of the other tributaries. Then I am asked: "*Will you become part of the experiment?*"

"*I don't understand.*"

"*You are the judgment engine.*")

"Now I must go," Elisaveta says. "We will all die soon. Neither you nor I are in the final self. No part of the teachers, or the Coordinator, will cross the Between."

"All futile, then," I say.

"Why so, Vasily? When I was young, you told me that change was an evil force, and that you longed for an eternal college, where all learning could be examined at leisure, without pressure. You've found that. Your tributary self has had billions of years to study the unchanging truths. And to infuse them into new tributaries. You've had your heaven, and I've had mine. Away from you, among those who nurture and respect."

I am left with nothing to say. Then, unexpectedly, the figure of Elisaveta reaches out with a nonexistent hand and touches my unreal cheek. For a moment, between us, there is something like the contact of flesh to flesh. I feel her fingers. She feels my cheek. Despite her words, the love has not died completely.

She fades from the cubicle. I rush to the window, to see if I can make out the Coordinator, but the shadow, the mercury-liquid cloud, has already vanished.

"They will fail," the We-ness says. It surrounds me with its mind, its persuasion, greater in scale than a human of my time to an ant. "This shows the origin of their folly. We have justified our existence."

(You can still cross. There is still a connection between you. You can judge the experiment, go with the Endtime Work Coordinator.)

I watch the plain, the joined shapes, extraordinarily beautiful, like condensed cities or civilizations or entire histories.

The sunlight dims, light rays jerk in our sight, in our fading scales of time.

(Will you go?)

"She doesn't need me . . ." I want to go with Elisaveta. I want to reach out to her and shout, "I see! I understand!" But there is still sadness and self-pity. I am, after all, too small for her.

(You may go. Persuade. Carry us with you.)

And billions of years too late—

Shards of Seconds

We know now that the error lies in the distant past, a tendency of the Coordinator, who has gathered tributaries of like character. As did the teachers. The past still dominates, and there is satisfaction in knowing We, at least, have not committed any errors, have not fallen into folly.

We observe the end with interest. Soon, there will be no change. In that, there is some cause for exultation. Truly, We are tired.

On the bubbling remains of the School World, the students in their Berkus continue to the last instant with the experiment, and We watch from the cracked and cooling hill.

Something huge and blue and with many strange calm aspects rises from the field of experiments. It does not remind us of anything We have seen before.

It is new.

The Coordinator returns, embraces it, draws it away.

("SHE DOES NOT TELL THE TRUTH. PARTS OF THE ENDTIME COORDINATOR MUST cross with the final self. This is your last chance. Go to her and reconcile. Carry our thoughts with you.")

I feel a love for her greater than anything I could have felt before. I hate my descendant self, I hate the teachers and their gray spirits, depth upon depth of ashes out of the past. They want to use me to perpetuate all that matters to them.

I ache to reclaim what has been lost, to try to make up for the past.

The Coordinator withdraws from School World, taking with it the results of the student experiment. Do they have what they want—something worthy of being passed on? It would be wonderful to know. . . . I could die contented, knowing the Proof has been shattered. I could cross over, ask . . .

But I will not pollute her with me any more.

"No."

The last thousandths of the last second fall like broken crystals.

(The connection is broken. You have failed.)

My tributary self, disappointed, quietly suggests I might be happier if I am deactivated.

CURIOUSLY, TO THE LAST, HE CLINGS TO HIS IMAGINED CUBICLE WINDOW. HE cries his last words where there is no voice, no sound, no one to listen but us:

"Elisaveta! YES!"

The last of the ancient self is packed, mercifully, into oblivion. We will not subject him to the Endtime. We have pity.

We are left to our thoughts. The force that replaces gravity now spasms. The metric is very noisy. Length and duration become so grainy that thinking is difficult.

One tributary works to solve an ancient and obscure problem. Another studies the Proof one last time, savoring its formal beauty. Another considers ancient relations.

Our end, our own oblivion, the Between, will not be so horrible. There are worse things. Much

INTRODUCTION TO "THE FALL OF THE HOUSE OF ESCHER"

Janet Berliner Gluckman asked me to contribute to a collection of science fiction and fantasy stories, to be selected and approved by David Copperfield, the magician. Each story would touch upon magic in some form or another. While I could easily imagine writing a fantasy story about magic, a science fiction story presented a bigger challenge. I grabbed up a few books about the history of legerdemain and stage magic, and soon had an idea.

A rather wealthy and powerful acquaintance, discussing the future of mass entertainment, once shook me by declaring, at the end of a conversation, "A hundred million people can't be wrong."

I wasn't so sure.

I wondered whether an entertainer could ever possibly satisfy a hundred million people on a regular basis, without undergoing some sort of undesirable transformation.

I then upped the ante; how about a *hundred billion people*, all mesmerized by centuries of cleverly designed, spiritually empty corporate amusement. What would it take to satisy *them?*

Edgar Allan Poe was, I thought, an appropriate inspiration for such a tale of illusion, show business, and fear.

THE FALL OF THE HOUSE OF ESCHER
Beyond Imagination, David Copperfield (Janet Berliner Gluckman)
1996

H oc est corpus," said the licorice voice. "Lich, arise."
The void behind my eyes filled. Subtle colors pinwheeled against velvet. Oiled thoughts raced, unable to grab.

The voice slid like black syrup into my ears.

"Once dead, now quick. Arise."

I opened my eyes. My fingers curled across palm, thumb touched pinkie, tack of prints on skin, twist and pull of muscles in wrist, the first things necessary. No pain in my joints. Hands agile and strong. Tremors gone.

I shivered.

"I'm back," I said.

"Quick and quick," the voice said

I turned to see who spoke in such lovely black tones. My eyes focused on a brown oval like rich fine wood, ivory eyes with ruby pupils, face square and stern but unmarred by age.

"How does it feel to be inside again, and whole? I am a doctor. You can tell."

I opened my mouth. "No pain," I said. "I feel . . . oily, inside. Smooth and slick."

"Young," the face said. I saw the face in profile and decided, from the timbre of the voice and general features, that this was a woman. The smoothness of her skin reminded me of the unlined surface of a painting. She wore long black robes from neck to below where I lay on an elevated bed or table. "Do you have memories?"

I swallowed. My throat felt cool. I thought of eating and remembered one last painful meal, when swallowing had been difficult. "Yes. Eating. Hurting."

"Your name?"

"Something. Cardino."

"Cardino, that's all?"

"My stage name. My real name. Is. Robert . . . Falucci."

"That is right. When you are ready, you may stand and join them for dinner. Roderick invites you."

"Them?"

"Roderick suggested you, and the five voted to bring you back. You may thank them, if you wish, at dinner."

The face smiled.

"Your name?" I asked.

"Ont. O-N-T."

The face departed, robes swishing like waves. Lights came up. I rolled and propped myself on one elbow, expecting pain, feeling only an easeful smoothness. I suspected that I had died. I surmised I had been frozen, as I had paid them to do, the Nitrogen Fixers, and that . . .

Lich, she had called me. Body, corpse. In one of my flashier shows I had reanimated a headless woman. Spark coils and strobes and a big van de Graaf generator had made the hair on her free head stand on end.

I slipped my naked legs down from the table, found the coolness of a tessellated tile floor. My fumbling fingers found the robe on the table as I stared at the floor: men and women, each a separate tile perfectly joined, in a flow of completion advanced to the far wall: courtship, embracing, copulating, birth.

I felt a sudden floating happiness.

I've made it.

———

ON A HEAVY BLACK OAK TABLE, I FOUND CLOTHES SET OUT THAT MIGHT HAVE come from a studio costume department—black stiffly formal suit out of a 1930s society movie, something for Fred Astaire. To my chagrin, I tended to corpulence even in this resurrected state. I put the robe aside and stuffed myself into the outfit and poured a glass of water from a nearby pitcher. A watercress sandwich appeared and I nibbled it while exploring the room.

I should be terrified. I'm not. Roderick . . .

The table on which I had been reborn occupied the center of the room, spare and black and shiny, like a stone altar. It felt cold to my touch. A yard to the right, the heavy oak table supported my sandwich plate, the pitcher and glass of water, the discarded robe, and a pair of shoes.

Lich, she had called me.

I stood in bright if diffuse illumination. No lights were visible. The room's corners lay in shadow. Armless chairs lined the wall behind me. A door opened in the next wall. Paintings covered the wall before me. The room seemed square and complete, but I could not find a fourth wall. No matter which direction, as I made a complete turn, I counted only three walls. The decor seemed rich and fashionable, William Morris and the restrained lines of classic Japanese furniture.

Obviously, not the next decade, I thought. *Maybe centuries in the future.*

I walked forward and the illumination followed. Expertly painted portraits covered the wall, precise cold renderings of five people, three pale males and two dark females, all in extravagant dress. None of them were Roderick—if Roderick was who I thought he might be—and Ont did not appear, either. The men wore tights and seemed ridiculously well endowed, with feathers puffed on their shoulders and immense fan-shaped hats rising from the crowns of their close-cropped heads; the women in tight-fitting black gowns, reddish hair spread like sunbursts, skin the color and sheen of rubbed maple.

I wondered if I would ever find employment in this future world. "Do you like illusions?" I asked the portraits rhetorically.

"They are life's blood," answered the male on the left, smiling at me.

The portrait resumed its old, painted appearance.

Assume nothing, I told myself.

Startling patterns decorated the wall behind the portraits. Flowers surrounded and gave form to skull-shapes, eyes like holograms of black olives floating within petaled sockets.

"Where is dinner?" I asked.

The portraits did not answer.

———

THE ROOM'S ONLY DOOR OPENED ONTO A STRAIGHT CORRIDOR THAT EXTENDED for a few yards, then sent me back to the room where I had been reborn. I scowled at the unresponsive portraits, then looked for intercoms, doorbells, hidden telephones. Odd that I should still feel happy and at ease, for I might be stuck like a mouse in a cage.

"I would like to go to dinner," I said in my stage voice, precise and commanding. The door swung shut and opened again. When I stepped through, I faced another corridor, and this one led to a larger double door, half ajar.

I opened the door and stepped outside. I faced an immense ruined garden and orchard, ranks of great squat thick trees barren of any leaves and overgrown with brown creepers and tall sere thistles spotted with black crusty patches. Hundreds of acres spread over low desolate hills, and on the highest hill stood an edifice that would have seemed unlikely in a dream.

It rose above the ruined gardens, white and yellow-gray like ancient chalk, what must have once been a splendid mansion, its lowest level simple and elegant. An architectural cancer had set in, however, and tumorous wings and floors and towers and bridges thrust from the first level with malign genius, twisting and joining in ways I could not make sense of. These extrusions reflected the condition of the garden: the house was overgrown, thick with its own weeds.

Above the house and land rose a sky at once gray and dull and threatening. Coils of cloud dropped from a scudding ash-colored ceiling like incipient tornadoes, and the air smelled of stale ocean and electricity.

A slender spike of alarm rose in me, then faded back into a general euphoria at simply being alive, and free of pain. It did not matter that everything in this place seemed nightmarish and out of balance. All would be explained, I told myself.

Roderick would explain.

If anyone besides me could have survived into this puzzling and perhaps far future, it was the resourceful and clever friend of my youth, the only Roderick of my acquaintance: Roderick Escher. I could imagine no other.

I let go of the door and stepped out on a stone pathway, then turned to look back at the building where I had been reborn. It was small and square, simply and solidly constructed of smooth pieces of yellow-gray stone, without ornament, like a dignified tomb. Frost covered the stones, and ice rime caked the soil around the building, yet the interior had not been noticeably cooler.

I squared my shoulders, examined my hands one more time, flexed the fingers, and spread them at arm's length. I wiped both of my hands quickly before my face, as if to pass an imaginary coin between them, and smiled at the ease of movement. I then set out along the path through the trees of the ruined garden, toward the encrusted and cancerous-looking house.

The trees and thistles seemed to consent to my passage, listening to my footfalls in silent reservation. I did not so much feel watched as measured, as if all the numbers of my life, my new body, were being recorded and analyzed. I noticed as I approached the barren trunks or the dry, lifeless wall of some past hedge, that all the branches and remaining dry leaves were gripped and held immobile by tiny strands of white fiber. *Spiders, mites,* I hypothesized, but saw no evidence of anything moving. When I stumbled and kicked aside a clod of dry dirt, I saw the soil was laden with thicker white fibers, some of which released sparkles like buried stars where tiny rocks had cut or scratched them. As I walked, I dug with my toe into more patches, and wherever I investigated, strands underlay the topsoil like fine human hairs, a few inches beneath the dusty gray surface. I bent down to feel them. They broke under my fingers, the severed ends sparkling, but then reassembled.

The house on the hill appeared even more diseased and outlandish, the closer I came. Among its many peculiarities, one struck me forcibly: with the exception of the ground floor, there were no windows in the building. All the walls and towers rose in blind disregard of each other and of the desolation beyond. Moreover, as I approached the broad verandah and the stone steps leading to a large bronze door, I noticed that the house itself was also layered with tiny white threads, some of which had been cut and sparkled faintly. What might have seemed cheerful—a house pricked along its intricate surfaces and lines by a myriad of stars, as if portrayed on a Christmas card—became instead flatly dreadful, dreadful in my inner estimation, yet flatly so because of my artificial and inappropriate *calm.*

Another wave of concern swept outward from my core, and was just as swiftly damped. *Part of me wants to feel fear, but I don't. Something in me desires to turn around and find peace again . . .*

A *lich* would feel this way . . . still half-dead.

From the porch, the house did not appear solid. Fine cracks spread through the stones, and to one side—the northern side, to judge from the angle of the sun—a long crack reached from the foundation to the top of the first floor, where it climbed the side of a short, stubby tower. I could easily imagine the stones crumbling. Perhaps all that held the house together were the white threads covering it like the fine webs of a silkworm or tent caterpillar.

I walked up the steps, my feet kicking aside dust and windblown fragments of desiccated leaves and twigs. The bronze door rose over my head, splotched with black and green. In its center panel, a bas relief of two hands had been cast. These hands reached out to clasp each other, desire apparent in the tension and arc of the phalanges and strain of tendons, yet the beseeching fingers could not touch.

I could not equate any of this with the Roderick I had known for so many years, beginning in university. I remembered a thin but energetic man, tall and handsome in an ascetic way, his hair flyaway fine and combed back from a high forehead, double-lobed with a crease between, above his nose, that gave him an air of intense concern and concentration. Roderick's most remarkable feature had always been his eyes, set low and deep beneath straight brows, eyes great and absorbing, sympathetic and sad and yet enlivened by a twist and glitter of sensuous humor.

The Roderick I remembered had always been excessively neat, and concerned about money and possessions, and would have never allowed such an estate to go to ruin. . . . Or lived in such a twisted and forbidding house.

Perhaps, then, I was going to meet another of the same name, not my friend. Perhaps my frozen body had become an item of curiosity among strangers, and resurrection could be accomplished by whimsical dilettantes. Why would the doctor suddenly abandon me, if I had any importance?

The bronze door swung open silently. Along its edges and hinges, the fine white threads parted and sparkled. The door seemed surrounded by tiny embers, which faded to orange and died, silent and unexplained.

Within, a rich darkness gradually filled with a dour luminosity, and I stepped into a long hallway. The hallway twisted along its length, corkscrewing until wall became floor, and then wall again, and finally ceiling. Smells of food and sounds of tableware and clinking glasses came through doors at the end of the twisted hall.

I followed the smells and the sounds. I had expected to have to scramble up the sloping floor, to crawl down the twisted hall, but up and down redefined themselves, and I simply walked along what remained, to my senses, the floor, making a dizzy rotation, to a dining room at the very end. Doors swung open at my approach. I expected at any moment to meet my friend Roderick—expected and hoped, but was disappointed.

THE FIVE PEOPLE PICTURED IN THE PORTRAITS SAT IN FORMAL SUITS AND gowns around a long table set with many empty plates and bottles of wine. Their raiment was of the same period and fashion as my own, the twenties or thirties of my century. They were in the middle of a toast, as I entered. The woman who had presided at my rebirth was not present, nor was anyone I recognized as Roderick.

"To our revivified lich, Robert Falucci," the five said, lifting their empty glasses and smiling. They were really quite handsome people, the two women young and brown and supple, with graceful limbs and long fingers, the three men strong and well-muscled, if a little too pale. Veins and arteries showed through the translucent skin on the men's faces.

"Thank you," I replied. "Pardon me, but I'm a little confused."

"Welcome to Confusion," the taller of the two women said, pushing her chair back to walk to my side. She took my arm and led me to an empty seat at the end of the table. Her skin radiated a gentle warmth and smelled sweetly musky. "Tonight, Musnt is presiding. I am Cant, and this is Shant, Wont, and Dont."

I smiled. Were they joking with me? "Robert," I said.

"We know," Cant said. "Roderick warned us you would arrive."

Musnt, at the head of the table, raised his glass again and with a gesture bade me to sit. Cant pushed my chair in for me and returned to her seat.

"I've been dead, I think," I said in a low voice, as if ashamed.

"Gone but not forgotten," Dont, the shorter woman, said, and she hid a brief giggle behind a fist clutching a lace handkerchief.

"You brought me back?"

"The doctor brought you back," Cant said with a helpful and eager expression.

"Against the wishes of Roderick's poor sister," Musnt said. "Some of us believe that with her, and perhaps with you, he has gone too far."

I turned away from his accusing gaze. "Is this Roderick's house?" I asked.

"Yes and no," Musnt said. "We oversee his work and time. We are, so to speak, the bonds placed on the last remnants of the family Escher."

"Roles we greatly enjoy," Cant said. She was youthfully, tropically beautiful, and I suspected I attracted her as much as she did me.

"I think I've been gone a long time. How much has changed?" I asked.

The four around the table, all but Cant, looked at each other with expressions I might have found on children in a schoolyard: disdain for a new boy.

"A lot, really," Musnt said, lifting knife and fork. Food appeared on Musnt's plate, a green salad and two whole raw zucchinis. Food appeared on my plate, the uneaten remains of my watercress sandwich. I looked up, dismayed. Then a zucchini appeared, and they all laughed. I smiled, but there was a salt edge to my happiness now.

I felt inferior. I certainly felt out of touch.

I did not remember Roderick having a sister.

AFTER DINNER, THEY RETIRED TO THE DRAWING ROOM, WHICH WAS DARKLY paneled and decorated in queer rococo fashion, with many reptilian cherubs and even full-sized dog-headed angels, as well as double pillars in spiral embrace and thick gold-threaded canopies. The materials appeared to be lapis and black marble and ebony, and everywhere, the sourceless lights followed, and everywhere, the busy and ubiquitous fibers overlay all surfaces.

I heard the distant murmur of a brook, rushes of air, sounds from some invisible ghostly landscape, and the voices of the five, discussing the spices used in the vegetable soup. Wont then added, "*She* persists in calling our work a blanding of the stew."

"Ah, but *she* is only half an Escher—" Wont said.

"Or a fading reflection of the truly penultimate Escher," Shant added.

"She would do anything for her brother," Cant said sympathetically.

"You've always favored Roderick," Dont said with a sniff. "You sound like Dr. Ont."

Cant turned and smiled at me. "We are judges, but not muses. I *am* the least critical."

Musnt opened a heavy brocaded curtain figured with seashells and they looked out upon the overgrown garden. Orange and yellow clouds moved swiftly in a twilight azure sky. Musnt flung open the glass-paneled doors and we all strode onto a marble patio.

Cant put her arm through mine and hugged my elbow against her ribs. "How nice for you to arrive on a good day, with such a fine settling," she said. "I trust the doctor remade you well?"

"She must have," I said. "I feel young and well. A little . . . anxious, I think."

Cant smiled sweetly. "Poor man. They have brought back so many, and all have felt anxious. We're quite used to your anxiety. You will not disturb us."

"We're Roderick's antitheticals," Wont said, as if that might explain something, but it still told me nothing useful. Mired in a dense awkwardness and buried unease, I looked back at the house. It reached to the sky, a cathedral, Xanadu and the tower of Babel all in one. Towers met with buttresses in impossible ways, drawing my eye from multiple perspectives into hopeless directions.

"What did you do, in your life?" Musnt asked.

"I was a magician," I said. "Cardino the Unbelievable." The name seemed ridiculous, from this distance, in the middle of these marvels.

"We are all magicians," Musnt said disdainfully. "How boring. Perhaps Roderick chose poorly."

"I do not think so," Cant said, and gave me another smile, this one eerily reassuring, an anxiolytic bowing curve of her smooth and plump lips. To my shock, nipples suddenly grew on her cheeks, surrounded by fine brown areolae. "If Robert wants, he can add another layer of critique to our efforts."

"What could he possibly know, and besides, aren't we critical enough?" Shant asked.

"Hush," Cant said. "He's our guest, and we're already showing him our dark side."

"As antitheticals should," Musnt said.

"I don't understand. . . . What am I, here?" I asked, the salt taste in my mouth turning bitter. "*Why* am I here?"

"You're a lich," Musnt said staring away from me at nothing in particular. "As such, you have no rights. You can be an added amusement. A spice against our blanding, if you wish, but nothing more."

"Please don't ask if you're in hell, not so soon," Shant said with a twist of disgust. "It is *so* common."

"Who is this Roderick?"

"He is our master and our slave," Shant said. "We observe all he does, bring him his audience, and bind him like chains."

"He is a seeker of sensation without consequence," Cant said. "We, like his audience, are perfect for him, for we are of no consequence whatsoever." Cant sighed. "I suppose he should come down and say hello."

"Or you can find *him*, which is more likely," Shant suggested.

I opened my mouth to speak, then closed it again, turning to look at the five on the patio. Finally, I said, "Are you real?"

Cant said, "If you mean embodied, no."

"You're dreams," I said.

"You asked if we like illusions," Cant said shyly, touching my shoulder with her slender hand. "We can't help but like them. We are all of us tricks of mind and light, and cheap ones at that. Roderick, for the time being, is real, as is this house."

"Where is Roderick?"

"Upstairs," Shant said.

Wont chuckled at that. "That's very general, but we really don't know. You may find him, or he will find you. Take care you do not meet his sister first. She may not approve of you."

At a noise from within the patio doors, I turned. I heard footsteps cross the stone floor, and looked back at Cant and the others to see their reactions. All, however, had vanished. I took a tentative step toward the doors, and was about to make another, when a tall and spectrally thin figure strode onto the patio, turned his head, and fixed me with a puzzled and even irritated glare.

"So soon? The doctor said it would take days more."

I studied the figure's visage with halting recognition. There were similarities; the high forehead, divided into two prominences of waxen pallor, the short sharp falcon nose, the sunken cheeks hollowed even more now as if by some wasting disease. . . . And the eyes. The figure's eyes burned like a flame on the taper of his thin, elongated body. The voice sounded like an echo from caverns at the center of a cold ferrous planet, metallic and sad, yet keeping some of the remembered strength of the original, and that I could not mistake.

"Roderick!"

The figure wore a tight-fitting pair of red pants and a black shirt with billowing sleeves buttoned to preposterously thick gloves like leathern mittens, while around his neck hung a heavy black collar or yoke as might be worn by an ox. At the ends of this yoke depended two brilliant silver chains threaded with thick white fiber. Around his legs twined more fibers, which seemed to grow from the floor, breaking and joining anew with his every step. He seemed to walk on faint embers. Threads grew also beneath his clothes and to his neck, forming fine webs around his mouth and eyes. Looking more closely, I saw that the threads intruded *into* his mouth and eyes.

Still his most arresting feature, the large and discerning eyes had assumed a blue and watery glaze, as if exposed to many brilliant suns, or visions too intense for healthy witness.

"You appear alert and well," Roderick said, turning his gaze with a long blink, as if ashamed. His hair swept back from his forehead, still thin and fine, but white as snow, and tufted as if he had just awakened from damp and restless sleep. "The doctor has done her usual excellent work."

"I feel well. . . . But so many irritating . . . evasions! I have been treated like a. . . . I have been called an amusement—"

Roderick raised his right hand, then stared at it with some surprise and slowly, pulling back florid lips from prominent white teeth as at the appearance of some vermin, peeled off the glove by tugging at one finger, then the next, until the hand rose naked and revealed. He slowly curled and straightened the slender, bony fingers and thumb. A spot of blood bedewed the tip of each. One drop fell to the floor and made a ruby puddle on the stone.

"Pardon me," Roderick said, closing the naked hand tightly and pushing it into a pocket in his clinging pants. "I am still emerging. You have come from a farther land than I—how ironic that you seem the more healthy for your journey!"

"I am renewed," I said. Upon seeing Roderick, I began to feel my emotions returning, fear mixing now with a leap of hope that some essential questions might be answered. "Have I truly died and been re-born?"

"You died a very young man—at the age of sixty," Roderick said. "I took charge of your frozen remains from that ridiculous corporation twenty years later and secured you in the vaults of my own family. I had made the beginnings of my huge fortune by then and arranged such preparations very early, and so you were protected by many forces, legal and political. None interfered with our vaults. If not for me, you would have been decanted and rotted long ago."

"How long has it been?"

"Two hundred and fifty years."

"And the others—Wont, Cant, Musnt, Shant, Dont . . ."

Roderick's face grew stern, as if I had unexpectedly uttered a string of rude words. Then he shook his head and put his still-gloved hand on my shoulder.

"All the world's people lie in cool vaults now, or wear no form at all. People are born and die at will, ever and again. Death is conquered, disease a helpmeet and plaything. The necessities of life are not food but sensation. All is servant to the quest for stimulus. The expectant and all-devouring Nerve is King."

I was suddenly dizzied by a vertigo of deep time, the precipitous awareness of having emerged from a long well or tunnel of insensate nullity leaving almost everyone and everything I had known behind. And perhaps Roderick, the friend I had once known, was no longer with me, either. I felt as if the stones beneath me swayed.

"You alone, of all our friends, our family . . . are alive?"

"I alone keep my present shape, though not without some gaps," Roderick said with some pride. "I am the last of the embodied and walk-about Eschers. . . . I, and my sister, but she is not well." His face creased into a mask of sorrow, a well-worn expression I could not entirely credit. "I have mourned her a thousand times already, and a thousand times she has returned to something like life. She feigns death, I think, to taunt me, and abhors my quest, but. . . . I could ask for no one more obedient."

"I don't remember you having a sister," I said.

Roderick closed his eyes. "Come, this place is filled with unpleasant associations. I no longer eat. The thought of clamping my jaw and grind-ing organic matter . . . ugh!"

Roderick led me from the dining room, back to the foyer, and a staircase which rose opposite the main door. The stairs branched midpoint to either side, leading to an upper floor. Roderick ascended the stairs with an eerie grace, halting and surveying his surroundings unpredictably, as if motivated not by human desires, but by the volition of a hunting insect or spider. His eyes studied the fiber-crusted walls, lids half-closed, head shaking at some association or memory conjured by stimuli invisible to me.

"You must find a place here," Roderick said. "You are the last in the vault. All the others have long since been freed and either vapored or joined with some neural clan or another. I have kept you in reserve, dear Robert, because I value you most highly. You have a keen mind and quick fingers. I need you."

"How may I be useful?"

"All this, the house and the lands around us, survive by whim of King Nerve," Roderick said. "We are entertainers, and our tenure wears thin. Audiences demand so much of us, and of everything around us. You are new and unexplored."

"What kind of entertainment?"

"Our lives and creations—the lives of my sister and I—are one illusion following on the tail of another," Roderick said. "All that we do and think is marked and absorbed by billions. It is our prison, and our glory. Our family has always had conjurers—do you remember? It is how we met and became friends."

"I remember. Your father—"

"I have not thought of him in a century," Roderick said, and his eyes glowed. He smiled. "Fine work, Robert! My mind tingles with associations already. My father . . . and my mother . . ."

"But Roderick, you did not get along with your father. You abhorred magic and illusions. You called them 'tricks,' and said they 'deceived the simple and the unobservant.' "

"I remained a faithful friend, did I not?"

"Yes," I said. "You must have. You brought me back from the dead."

"Sufficient time shows even me how wrong I am," he murmured.

We reached the top of the stairs. A familiar figure, the doctor named Ont, passed down the endless hallway, black robes swirling like ink in water. She stopped before us, paying no attention to me, but staring at Roderick with pained solicitousness, as if she might cry if he grew any more pale, or thinner.

"Thank you, Dr. Ont," Roderick said, bowing slightly. She nodded acknowledgment.

"He is what you wanted, what you need?"

"So soon, and unexpected, but already valuable."

"He can help you?"

"I do not know," Roderick said. Ont looked now at me.

"You must be very *cautious* with Roderick Escher," she warned. "He is a national cleverness, a treasure. It is my duty to sustain him, or to do his bidding, whichever he desires."

"How is *she?*" Roderick asked, hands clasped before him, naked fingers preposterously thin and white against the thick leathern glove.

Ont replied, "Even this vortex soon spins itself out, and this time I fear the end will be permanent."

"Fear . . . more than you hope?" Roderick asked.

Ont shook her head sternly. "I do not understand this conceit between you."

With another tip of her head, Ont walked on, and the hall curled into a corkscrew ahead of her. Remaining upright, she tread along the spiraling floor and vanished around the curve. The hall straightened, but she was no longer visible.

"A century ago, I chose to come back into this world refreshed," Roderick said to me, "and took from myself a kind of rib or vault of my mind, to make a sister. She became my twin. Now, let me show you how the house works . . ."

Roderick gripped me by the elbow and guided me to a steep, winding stair that must have coiled within the largest tower surmounting the house. He gave what he meant to be an encouraging smile, but instead revealed his teeth in a conspiratorial rictus, and climbed the steps before me. I hesitated, palms and upper lip moist with growing dread of this odd time and incomprehensible circumstance. Soon, however, as my friend's form vanished around the first curve in the stair, I felt even more dread at being left alone, and hoped knowledge of whatever sort might ease my apprehensiveness. I raced to catch up with him.

"As a race, in the plenitude of time—a very short time—we have found our success," Roderick said. "Lacking threat from without, and at peace within, our people enjoy the fruits of the endeavors of all civilizations. All that has been suffered is repaid here." His voice sounded hollow in the tower, like the mocking laughter of a far-off crowd.

"How?" I asked, following on Roderick's heels up the stairs. That which might have once winded me now seemed almost effortless. Whatever shortness of breath I felt was due to nerves, not frailness of body.

"All work is stationary," Roderick said, again favoring me with that peculiar grimace that had replaced a once fine and encouraging smile. We had made two turns around the tower.

"Then why do we walk?" I asked.

"We are chosen. Privileged, in a way. We—my sister and I, Dr. Ont, and now you—maintain the last links with physical bodies. We give a foundation to all the world's dreams. The entire Earth is like the seed in a peach, all but disposed of. What matters is the sweet pulp of the fruit—communication and expansion along the fiber optic lines, endless interaction, endless exchange of sensations. Some have abandoned all links with the physical, the seed, having bodies no more. They flit like ghosts through the interwoven threads that make the highways and rivers and oceans of our civilization. Most, more conservative, maintain their corporeal forms like shrines, and visit them now and then, though the bodies are cold and unfeeling, suspended and vestigial. You were reborn in one such vault, made to hold such as you, and eventually to receive my sister and I—though I have decided not to go there, never to go there. I think *death* would be more interesting."

"I've been there," I said.

"Yes, and I always ask my liches. . . . What do you recall?"

"Nothing," I said.

"Look closely at that excised segment in your world-line. You were dead two and a half centuries, and you remember nothing?"

"No," I said.

He smiled. "No one has. The demands . . . The voices . . . Gone." He stopped and looked back at me. We stood more than halfway up the tower. "A blankness, a darkness. A surcease from endless art."

"In my life, you were more concerned with business than the arts."

"The world changed after you died. Everyone turned their eyes inward, and riches could be achieved by any who linked. Riches of the inner life, available to all. We made our world self-sustaining and returned to a kind of cradle. I grew bored with predicting the weather of money when it hardly mattered and so few cared. I worked with artists, and found more and more a sympathy, until I became one myself."

He stood before a large pale wooden door set in the concrete and plaster of the tower. "Robert, when we were boys, we dreamed of untrammeled sensual delights. Soon enough, I saw that experiences that seemed real, but carried no onerous burdens of pain, would consume all of humanity. Before my rebirth, I directed banks and shaped industries. . . . Then I slept for twenty years, waiting for fruition. After my rebirth, my sister and I invested the riches I earned in certain industries and new businesses. We *directed* the flow and shape of the river of light, on which everyone floated like little boats. For a time, I controlled—but I never retired to the vaults myself."

He touched the door with a long finger, smearing a spot of blood on the unpainted and bleached surface. "Physical desire," he whispered, "drove the growth. Sex and lust without rejection or loss, without competition, was the beginning. Primal drives directed the river, until everyone had all they wanted. . . . In a land of ghosts and shades."

The door swung open at another touch of his finger leaving two red prints on the wood. Within, more river sounds, and a series of breathless sighs.

"Now, hardly anyone cares about sex, or any other basic drives. We have accessed deeper pleasures. We re-string our souls and play new tunes."

A fog of gossamer filled the dark space beyond the door. Lights flitted along layer after layer of crossed fibers, and in the middle, a machine like a frightened sea-urchin squatted on a wheeled carriage. Its gray spines rose with rapid and sinuous grace to touch points on conjunctions between threads, and light seeped forth.

"This is the thymolecter. What I create, as well as what I think and experience, the thymolecter dispenses to waiting billions. And my thoughts are at work throughout this house, in room after room. Look!"

He turned and lifted his hand, and I saw a group of thin children form within the gossamer. They played listlessly around a bubbling green lump, poking it with a stick and laughing like fiends. It made little sense to me. "This amuses half the souls who occupy what was once the subcontinent of India."

I curled my lip instinctively, but said nothing.

"It *speaks* to them," Roderick whispered. "There is torment in every gesture, and triumph in the antagonism. This has played continuously for fifteen years, and always it changes. The *audience* responds, becomes part of the piece, takes it over . . . and I adjust a figure here, a sensibility there. Some say it is my masterpiece. And I had to fight for years to overcome the objections of the five!" His cheeks took on some color at memory of the triumph. He must have sensed my underwhelming, for he added, "You realize we experience only the tip of the sword here, the cover of a deep book. You see it out of context, and without the intervening years to acculturate you."

"I am sure," I muttered, and was thankful when Roderick extinguished the entertainment.

"You've had experience with live audiences, of course, but never with a hundred billion respondents. My works spread in waves against a huge shore. At one time they beat up against other waves, the works of other artists. But there are far fewer artists than when you were first alive. As we have streamlined our arts for maximum impact, competition has narrowed and variety has waned, and now, the waves slide in tandem; we serve niches which do not overlap. Mine is the largest niche of all. I am the master."

"It's all vague to me," I said. "Isn't there anything besides entertainment?"

"There is discussion of entertainment," Roderick said.

"Nothing else? No courtships, relationships, raising children?"

"Artists imagine children to be raised, far better than any real children. Remember how horrid *we* were?"

"I had no children . . . I had hoped, here—"

"A splendid idea! Eventually, perhaps we will re-enact the family. But for now . . ."

I sensed it coming. Roderick's friendship, however grand, had always hung delicately upon certain favors, never difficult to grant individually, but when woven together, amounting to a subtle fabric of obligations.

"I need a favor," Roderick said.

"I suppose I owe you my life."

"Yes," Roderick said, bluntly and without inflection. He drew me from the gossamer chamber, and as he was about to close the door, I glimpsed another play of lights, arranged into curved blades slicing geometric objects. A few of the objects—angular polyhedra, flushed red—seemed to try to escape the blades.

"Half of Central America," Roderick confided, seeing my puzzlement.

"What sort of favor?" I asked with a sigh as the door swung silently shut.

"I need you to perform magic," Roderick said.

I brightened. "That's all?"

"It will be enough," Roderick said. "Nobody has performed magic of your sort for a hundred years. Few remember. It will be novel. It will be concrete. It will play on different strings. King Nerve has gotten demanding lately, and I feel . . ."

He did not complete this expression. "Pardon my enthusiasm, you must be exhausted," he said, with a tone of sudden humility that again endeared him to me. "There is a kind of night here. Sleep as best you can, in a special room, and we will talk . . . tomorrow."

RODERICK LED ME THROUGH ANOTHER OF THOSE HELICAL HALLS, WHOSE presence I keenly felt in every part of the house, and soon came to hate. I wondered if there were no doors or halls at all, only illusions of connections between great stacks and heaps of cubicals, which Roderick could activate to carry us through the walls like Houdini or Joselyne. In a few minutes, we came to a small narrow door, and beyond I found a pleasant though small room, with a canopy bed and a white marble lavatory, supplying a need I was beginning to feel acutely.

Roderick waited for me to return, and chided my physical limitations. "You still need to eat, and suffer the consequences."

"Can I change that?" I asked, half fearfully.

"Not now. It is part of the novelty. You are a lich. you subscribe to no services, move nothing by will alone."

"As do the five?"

Again he shook his head and frowned. "They are projections. To you, they feel solid enough, real enough, but there is no amusement in them. They can *seem* to do anything. Including make my life a torment."

"How?"

"They express the combined will of King Nerve," he said, and answered no further questions. He then showed me the main highlights of the room. It was much larger than it seemed, and wherever I turned I beheld new walls, which met previous walls at square angles, each wall supporting shelves covered with apparatus of such rareness and beauty that I lost all of my dread in a bath of primal delight.

"These can be your tools," Roderick said with a flourish. I turned and walked from wall to apparent wall, shelf to shelf, picking up Brema brasses, numerous fine boxes nested and false-bottomed and with hidden pockets and drawers, large and small tables covered with black and white squares in which velvet-drop bags might be concealed, stacks of silver and gold and steel and bronze coins hollow and hinged and double-faced and rough on one side and smooth on the other, silk handkerchiefs and scarves and stacks of cloths of many colors; collapsing birdcages of such beautiful craftsmanship I felt my eyes moisten; glasses filled with apparent ink and wine and milk, metal tubes of many sizes, puppet doves and mice and white rats and even monkeys, mummified heads of many expressions, some in boxes; slates spirit and otherwise, some quite small; pens and pencils, and paint brushes with hidden talents; cords and retracting reels and loops; stacked boxes à la Welles in which a young woman might be rearranged at will; several Johnson Wedlocks in crystal goblets; tables and platforms and cages with seemingly impassable Jarrett pedestals; collapsible or compressible chess pieces, checkers, poker chips, potato chips, marbles, golfballs, baseballs, basketballs, soccer balls; ingenious items of clothing and collars and cufflinks manufactured by the Magnificent Traumata; handcuffs and strait jackets . . .

As I turned from wall to wall with delight growing to delirium, Roderick merely stood behind me, arms folded, receiving my awestruck glances with a patient smile. Finally I came to a wall on which hung one small black cabinet with glass doors. Within this cabinet there lay . . .

Ten sealed decks of playing cards.

I opened this cabinet eagerly, aching to try my new hands, wrists, fingers, on them. I unwrapped cellophane from a deck and tamped the stack into one hand, immediately fanning the cards into a double spiral. With a youthful and pliant fold of skin near my thumb I pushed a single Ace of Spades to prominence, remembering with hallucinatory vividness the cards most likely to be chosen by audience members in any given geography, as recorded by Maskull in his immortal *Force and Suit*. I turned and presented the deck to Roderick.

"Pick a card," I said, "any card."

He stared at me intensely, almost resentfully, and his left eye opened wider than the right, presenting an expression composed at once of equal mix delight and apprehension. "Save it. There is altogether too much time."

But like a child suddenly brought home to familiar toys, I could not restrain myself. I propelled the deck in an arc from one hand to the other, and back. I shuffled them and cut them expertly behind my back, knowing the arrangement had not even now been disturbed. With my fingers I counted from the top of the precisely split deck, and brought up a Queen of Hearts. "Appropriate for your world," I said.

"Impressive legerdemain," Roderick said with a slight shudder. He had never been able to judge my lights of hand, or follow my instant sleights and slides and crosses. With almost carnivorous glee I wanted to dazzle this man who controlled so much illusion, to challenge him to a duel.

"It's magic," I said breathlessly. "*Real* magic."

"Its charm," he said in a subdued and musing voice, "lies in its simplicity and its antiquity." He seemed doubtful, and rested his chin on the tip of an index finger. "Still, I insist you need to rest, to prepare. Tomorrow . . . We will begin, and all will be judged."

I realized he was correct. Now was not the time. I needed to know more. It was possible, in this unreal futurity, anything I might be able to accomplish with such simple props would be laughed at. Sooner expect a bird to fly to the moon . . .

With a brief farewell, he departed, and left me alone in the marvelous room. My heart hammered like a pecking dove in my chest.

Nowhere in this room, unique I supposed in all the rooms of the house of Roderick Escher, did there creep or coat or insinuate any of the pale light-guiding threads or fibers. I was alone and unwatched, unconnected to any hungry external beings, be they kings or slaves . . .

I fancied I was Roderick's secret.

I undressed and showered. The bathroom filled with steam, and I inhaled its warm moistness, returning again to the euphoria I had experienced upon my arrival. I toweled and picked up a thick terry cloth robe, examining the sleeves and pockets. In a table drawer I found needle and many colors of thread, and marveled at Roderick's thoroughness.

Far too restless and exalted for sleep, I began to sew hooks and loops and pockets into the robe, for practice, and then into my suit of clothes. My fingers worked furiously, as agile as they had ever been in my prime.

I turned to the laded walls and spun through a dozen displays before finding clamps, tack, glue, brads, wire, springs, card indexes, and other necessities. I altered the suit for fit as well as fittings. I had long centuries ago learned to be a tailor and seamstress, as well as a forger and engineer.

There were no windows, no clocks, no way to learn the time of evening, if evening it actually was. I might have spent days of objective time in my obsessive labors. It did not matter here; I was not disturbed and did not rest until I became so tired I could hardly stand or clasp a needle or bend a wire.

I removed the robe, climbed into the small, comfortable bed, and immediately fell into deep slumber.

I know not how many minutes or hours, or perhaps years later, I felt a touch on my face and jerked abruptly to consciousness. My eyes burned but my nerves pulsed as if I had just drunk a dozen cups of black coffee. In the darkened room (had I turned off any lights? there were no lights to control!) I saw a whitish shape, tall and blurred. Now came to me a supreme supernatural dread, and I was immediately drenched with sweat. I rubbed my eyes to clear them.

"Who's there?" I cried.

"It is I, Maja," the form said in a thrilling contralto.

"Who?" I asked, my voice breaking, for I only half-remembered my circumstances. I did not know what might face me in this unknown place and time.

"I am Roderick's sister," she said, and came closer, her face entering a sourceless, nacreous spot of glow. I beheld a woman of extraordinary character, her countenance as thin as the faces of the women in Klimt's darker paintings, her eyes as large as Roderick's, and of like cast and color. I could have sworn her high twin-lobed forehead would have blemished her femininity, had it been described so to me, yet it did not.

"What do you want?" I asked, my heart slowing its staccato beat. I felt no danger from her, only a ruinous sadness.

"Do not do this thing," she warned, eyes intent on mine. I could not break that gaze, so frightened and yet so strong. "It is a change too drastic for the Eschers, a breach, a leap to disaster. Roderick wishes our doom, but he does not know what he does."

"Why would he wish to die?"

This she did not answer, but instead leaned forward and whispered to me, "He believes we *can* die. That is his madness. He has told me to go before, to prove certain theories."

"And you have agreed—to die?"

She nodded, eyes fixed on mine, drawing me in as if to the doors of her soul. In her there was more of the cadaver already than a living woman, yet she seemed sadly, infinitely beautiful. Her beauty was that of a guttering candle flame. The fire of her eyes was a fraction that of Roderick's, and her body, as a taper, might supply only a few minutes more of the fuel of life. Unlike the brown women, Cant and Dont, who were unreal yet seemed solid and healthy, she was all too real, and I could have blown her away with a weak breath. "I am his twin. He took me from his mind, shaped me to equal him, in all but will. I have no will of my own. I obey him."

"He made his own sister a slave?"

"It is done that way here. We may create versions of our self that do not possess a legal existence."

"How bitter!" I exclaimed.

"Oh, I may protest, may try to show him my love by directing his will with persuasion. But he is stronger, and I do whatever he tells me. Now, it is his wish I try again to die. I only hope this time I might succeed."

Behind her I saw the approach of the solicitous Dr. Ont. The doctor took Roderick's sister by one skeletal hand, pushed her lips close to Maja's almost translucent ear, and murmured words in a tongue I could not understand. Maja's head fell to one side and it seemed she might collapse. Dr. Ont supported her, and they withdrew from the room.

I felt at once a heavy swell of resentment, and a commensurate surge of bluster. "How dare she come here, smelling of death. I've left *death* behind." But in my declining terror, I was exaggerating. Roderick's sister, Maja, had had no smell at all.

She had smelled no more intensely than a matching volume of empty air.

I FELT I SLEPT ONLY A FEW MINUTES, YET WHEN RODERICK'S VOICE BOOMED into my room, waking me, I was completely refreshed, confident, ready for any challenge. *I* was no slave of Roderick Escher. "Dear friend—have you made the necessary preparations?" he asked. I looked around for his presence, but he was not there, only his voice.

"I'm ready," I said.

"Do you understand your challenge?"

"Better than ever," I said. I had the confidence of an innocent child, thinking tigers are simply large cats; even the appearance during the night of Maja Escher held no awe for me.

"Good. Then eat hearty, and build up your strength."

Roderick did not enter my room, but breakfast appeared on a table within the room. The apparatus I had chosen the night before lay beside the plates of warm vegetables, broth, breads. I put on my robe, manifested an Ace of Spades in my right hand, and threw it at the stack of toast, piercing the top slice. The card stuck out of the toast upright. I lifted the card, retrieving the toast with it, and took a bite, chewing with a broad smile. All my fears of the day before (if indeed a day had passed) had faded. I had never in my first life felt so confident before going on stage, or beginning a performance.

As I ate, I wondered at the lack of all meat. Had the world's inhabitants suddenly and humanely ended the slaughter of innocent animals? Or did they simply distance themselves from the carnal, in sympathy, as most of them had assumed the character of frozen meat in chilly refrigerators?

Were there any animals left to eat?

In truth, what did I know about Roderick's brave civilization? Nothing. He had not prepared me or informed me any farther. Yet my confidence did not fade. I felt instinctively the challenge that Roderick was about to offer—to compare the overwhelming and undeniable magic of this time, against my own simple *legerdemain,* as Roderick had called it.

Roderick visited me in person as I finished my breakfast.

"Did you enjoy yourself?" he asked as he entered through the door. His arm rose slowly to indicate the changeable wall of cases, now frozen to the apparatus associated with cards. He walked over to the glass case, opened it, and removed a reel manufactured by my inspiration, Cardini, who had died just after my first birth, but whose effects I had learned by heart. "Did you know," Roderick said, holding the tiny reel in his palm, "that a century ago, children played with dollhouses indistinguishable from the real? Little automata going about their lives, using tools perfect for their scale, living dolls sitting on furniture accurate in every way. . . . And these houses were so cheap they were made available to the poorest of the poor?"

"I didn't know that," I said.

Roderick smiled at me, and for the first time on this, my second day in my new life, I felt a narrow chilliness behind my eyes, a suspicion of the unforeseen.

"Yet we have advanced beyond that time as gods march beyond ants," he said. "All pleasures available at will. Every nerve and region within the brain—and without!—charted and their affects explored in endless variations. Whole societies devoted to pain from injuries impossible in all past experience, to the ghostlike exertion of an infinite combination of muscles in creatures the size of planets, to the social and sexual dalliances of phantoms conjured from histories and times and places that never were."

"Remarkable," I said stiffly.

"An audience of such intense discernment and sophistication that nothing surprises them, nothing arouses their childlike amazement, for they have never *been* children!"

"Extraordinary," I said with some pique. Did he wish for my defeat, my failure, to enjoy some petty triumph over an inferior? I steeled myself against his words, as I might have armored against the complaints of an older and better magician, criticizing my fledgling efforts.

"There are audiences of such size that they dwarf all of the Earth's past populations," he added.

I saw my bed fold into itself until it vanished into a corner. The wall of cases shrank into a narrow box the size of a book, leaving me with only the table and the apparatus I had chosen the night before.

"Prepare, Robert," he said. "The curtain rises soon."

Then his voice took on a shadowed depth, betraying a mix of emotions I could not comprehend, relief mixed with heavy grief and even guilt, and something else beyond my poor, unembellished range. "Dr. Ont came to me last night. Maja has succumbed. My sister is no more. Ont certifies that she has truly died. She has even begun to decay."

"I'm sorry," I said.

"It's a triumph," he said quietly. "She goes before . . ."

I put on the suit I had tailored and adjusted, and inwardly smiled at its close fit and how it flattered my pudgy form. I had never been handsome, had always lacked the charms of magicians who combined grace and artistry with physical beauty. I compensated by simply being better, faster, and more ingenious.

Roderick looked around the room. Fibers grew from the floor, climbing the walls like mold, until they shrouded everything but me and my table and cards. I seemed surrounded by a forest of fungal tendrils, glowing like swarms of fireflies.

"Billions of receptors, hooked into webs and matrices and nets reaching around the Earth," Roderick said. "Tiny little eyes like stars that have replaced any desire to leave and venture out to real stars, to other worlds. We have our own interior infinities to explore."

I made my final arrangements, and stood in the center of the lights, the tendrils. "Tell me when I'm to begin."

"We've already begun, except for the time you've spent in this room," Roderick said. "Even Maja's protests to me, and her death, have been watched and absorbed. I've used the drama of my own war to stay at the top of the ratings, my preparations and agonizing. Even the five, the antitheticals—I have made them part of this!"

The same nacreous light that had bathed Maja's face now surrounded me, and the fibers arranged themselves with a sound like the motion of a horde of chitinous sea-creatures rubbing their claws.

Roderick backed away until he stood in shadow, then lifted his hand, giving me my cue.

I had never had such a draw in my life—nor felt so alone. But was this really so different from appearing on television? I had done that often enough.

"Once upon a time," I said, focusing ahead of me at no space in particular, and smiling confidently, "a young man on a luxury cruise was caught in a horrible shipwreck, stranded on a desert island with nobody and nothing but a crate of food and water, and a crate of un-opened packs of playing cards."

I brought out a deck of cards and peeled away the plastic. "I was that young man. I knew nothing of the magical arts, but in three solitary years I taught myself thousands of manipulations and passes and mo-tions, until I felt I could fool even myself at times. And how was this done? How does a magician, knowing all the methods behind his effects, come to believe in magic?"

I swallowed a lump in my throat and leaped into the abyss.

"In those three years, I learned to make cards *confess*." I riffled the deck of cards and formed a rippling mouth, and with one finger strummed the edges.

"We spoke to each other," the cards said in a breathless stringy voice. "And Cardino taught us all we know."

I produced another deck, opened it with one hand, removed the cards and arranged them on my palm, and made them speak as well, in a *female* voice: "And we taught him all that we know."

I squeezed both decks up in a double arc and caught them in opposite hands. From the top of each deck I produced a Queen of Hearts, and clamped the two cards together in my teeth. "I learned the secrets of royalty," I said through clenched teeth. Holding the decks in one hand, separated by my pointing finger, I plucked the cards from between my teeth and revealed them as two jacks. "The knaves whispered to me of court intrigues, and the kings and queens taught me the secrets of their royal numbers."

In my hands, the two cards quickly became a pair of threes, then fives, then sevens, then nines, and then queens again. "Finally, I was rescued." I riffled the decks together, blowing through them to make the sound of a ship's horn. "And returned to civilization. And there, I practiced my new art, my new life. And now, having returned from that island called *death*, where all magic must begin—"

I looked around me, unsure what effect my next request would have. "I call for volunteers, who wish to learn what I have learned."

The overgrown chamber whispered and lights passed among the fi-brous growths like lanterns on far shores. Five figures appeared in the chambers then: Wont, Cant, Shant, Mustnt, and Dont. Cant approached first, smiling her most wistful and attractive smile. "I volunteer," she said.

Roderick, standing in the background, his feet almost rooted to the floor by thick cables of fiber, lifted his hands in overt approval. Why encourage those he loathed—those who shackled him with so many strictures?

Was he flaunting the strength of his chains, like Houdini?

"Am I a physical person?" I asked Cant, dismissing all questions from my thoughts.

"Yes," she said. "Very."

"Am I the last untouched human on this world?"

"In this house, to be sure."

"Do I have a connection with any of the external powers that can make things appear and disappear, make illusions by wish alone?"

"You do not subscribe to any services," Cant said. "This we guarantee, as antitheticals."

I hesitated just a moment, and then took her hand. She felt solid enough—like real flesh. "Are *you* real?" I asked.

"Who can say?" she replied.

"Is your form solid enough to forego false illusions, illusions of will isolated from body?"

"I can do that, and guarantee it," Cant said. Her companions took attitudes of rapt attention.

"It is guaranteed," they said as one.

I began to get some sense of what their function was then, and how they constrained Roderick. What would they do to constrain me?

"If I told you there were cards rolled up in your ears, what would you say?"

"All things are possible," Cant said musically, "but for you, that is not possible."

I held my hand up to her ear and drew out a rolled-up card, making sure to tap the auricle and the opening to the canal. She reacted with some puzzlement, then delight.

"You have doubtless been told that in the past, illusion was possible only through tricks. Tell me, then—how so I do such tricks?"

"Concealment," Cant said, prettily nonplused.

I showed her my hands, which were empty, then removed my coat, dropping it to the floor, and rolled up my sleeves. I pulled another card from her other ear, unrolled it, showing it to be ruined as a playing card, then converted it to a cigarette by pushing it through my fist.

"Everyone can do that," Cant said, her smile fading. "But you—"

"I can't do such things," I said with a note of triumph. "I am an atavism,

an innocent, an anachronic . . . a *lich*." I held out the cigarette. "Does anybody smoke anymore?" I asked. The five did not speak. Roderick shook his head in the shadows. "I didn't think so. King Nerve needs no chemical stimulants. All drugs are electronic. There is no one else on this planet—or in this house, at least—who can make the world dance, the *real* world. Except me—and I was taught by the cards."

The remaining antitheticals came forward. Musnt, as it happened, unknowingly carried a deck of cards in the pockets of his solid but un-real dinner jacket. Producing a fountain pen, I had him mark his name on the edge of the deck, grateful that these phantoms could still write, and blew upon the ink to help it dry. "These cards have friends all over the world, and they tell tales. Have you ever heard cards whisper?" I patted the deck firmly into his hands. "Hold these. Don't let them go anywhere." I borrowed his jacket and put it on Dont, helping her into the sleeves with courtesy centuries out of date. They hung over her hands.

"Hold up your deck of cards, please," I said to Musnt. He lifted the cards, his face betraying anticipation. I was grateful for small favors.

"I believe you have a set of pockets on the outside of your jacket," I told Dont. "Investigate them, please."

She reached into the pockets and removed two cellophane-wrapped decks of cards.

"Sneaky devils, these cards. They go anywhere and everywhere, and listen to our most intimate words. You have to be discreet around play-ing cards. Open the decks, please."

She pulled the cellophane from one deck. On the edge of the deck was the awkward scrawl of Musnt, written in fountain pen. Musnt im-mediately looked at his deck. The edges were blank.

Fibers formed curious worms and squirmed closer, lights pulsing.

"The other deck, now," I told Dont. She unwrapped the second deck, and there, in fountain pen, was written, *Wont.*

"Hand the deck to the person whose name is written on the side," I said. She passed the deck to Wont.

"Write on the other side your name and any number," I told Wont, giv-ing him the pen. "And then, on a card within the deck, write the name of anybody in this room—in big, sloppy, wet letters. Show the card to everybody *except* me, and put it within the deck and press the deck together firmly."

He did this.

"Now give the deck to Cant."

He passed the deck to her. "How many decks do you carry now?" I asked. She reached into her pockets and found two more decks, which she handed to me, keeping Wont's deck with his name written on it.

"Now find the card Wont has written on, and the card immediately next to it, smeared with the wet ink from that card. Write your name on the face of that card, and another number. Show them to everybody but me."

She did so.

"How many decks do we all have now?" I asked.

I went among them, counting the decks presently in circulation—five. I redistributed the decks one to each of the five Negatives.

"The cards have told each other all about you, and you have no secrets. But I am the master of the cards—and from *me* not even the cards have secrets!"

I reached behind their ears, one by one, and pulled the cards that had been written on, with the names Cant, Musnt, Dont, and Wont. "The gossip of the cards goes full circle," I said. "Show us your decks!"

On the top of each deck, the cards bearing the suit and number of the written-on cards—for all had been number cards—appeared, bearing a newly written number, and a new name—*Cardino*.

The Negatives seemed befuddled. They showed the cards to each other and to the questing fibers.

They had forgotten the art of applause, and the fibers were silent, but no applause was necessary.

"How is this done?" Musnt asked. "You must tell . . ."

I pitied them, just as a caveman might pity a city slicker who has lost the art of flint knapping. From the beginning of their lives to the present moment, they had truly fooled nobody. They had lived lives of illusion without wonder, for always they could explain how things were done—all their magic was performed by silent, subservient, electronic demiurges.

"Turn to the last card in your decks," I said. "Show me who is King."

On every one of their decks, the King of Hearts was inscribed with two names. They held the cards out simultaneously. Each Negative carried a card bearing his or her name, and in larger letters, RODERICK ESCHER.

The fibers seemed to give a mighty heave. Roderick came forward, and I saw the fibers fleeing from his legs, his suit, his face and skin.

The Negatives turned to each other in confusion. Cant giggled. They compared their decks, searched them. "They're made of matter," Wont said. "They aren't false—"

"Tricks," Shant said.

"Can *you* do them?" Wont asked.

"In an instant," Shant said. Cards fluttered down around him, twisted, formed a tall mannequin and danced around us all. The fibers withdrew from around him as if singed by flames.

"Not the point," Roderick said, free of fibers now. "You can do anything you want, but you *subscribe*. Cardino does these things by himself, alone."

The fibers bunched around my feet. Shant made his cards and the mannequin vanish. "How?" he asked, shrugging.

"Skill," Roderick said.

"Skill of the body," Shant said haughtily. "Who needs that?"

"Self-discipline, training, years of concentrated effort," Roderick said. "Isn't that right, Cardino?"

"Yes," I said, the confidence of my performance fading. I was caught in a game whose rules I could not understand. Roderick was using me, and I did not know why.

"Nothing any of us can experience compares to what this man does all by himself," Roderick continued.

The five froze in place for a moment. I could see some change in their structure, a momentary fluctuation in their illusory solid shapes.

Roderick lifted his arms and stared at his body. "I'm free!" he said to me in an undertone, as if confiding to a priest.

"What's all this about?" I asked.

"It's about skill and friendship and death," Roderick said.

The five began to move again. The fibers touched my shoes, the hem of my pants. Instinctively, I kicked at them, sending glowing bits scattering like sparks. They recoiled, toughened, pushed in more insistently.

"My time is ending," Roderick said. "I've done all I can, experienced all I can."

The five smiled and circled around me. "*They* favor you," Cant said, and she bent to push a wave of growing fibers toward my legs. I backed off, kicked again without effect, shouted to Roderick,

"What do they want?"

"You," Roderick said. "My time is done. Maja is dead; I go to follow her."

I turned and ran from the room, sliding on the clumps of fibers, falling. The fibers lightly touched my face, felt at my cheeks, prodded my lips as if to push into my mouth, but I jumped to my feet and ran through the door. Roderick followed, and behind him a surge of fibers clogged the door.

Wherever I ran in the house, eager fibers grew from the walls, the floor, fell from the ceiling, like webs trying to ensnare me. Cant appeared in a twisted hallway ahead. I fell to my hands and knees, staring as the floor twisted into a corkscrew, afraid I would pitch forward into the architectural madness.

Dr. Ont appeared, shoulders dipped in failure, hands beseeching to explain. "Roderick, do not—"

"It is done!" Roderick cried.

A cold wind flowed down the hall, conveying a low moan of endless agony. Roderick helped me to my feet, his thin fingers cold even through the fabric of my suit.

"Can you feel it?" he whispered to me. "King Nerve has released me. I'm dying, Robert!" He turned to Dr. Ont. "I'm dying, and there's nothing you can do! I know all the permutations! I've experienced it all, and *I am bored. Let me die!*"

Dr. Ont stared at Roderick with an expression of infinite pity. "Your sister—"

Roderick gripped my shoulders. "We are walled in like prisoners by the laziness of gods, all desires sated, all refinements exhausted. Let them crown the new master!"

The moaning grew louder. Behind Dr. Ont, Roderick's sister appeared, even more haggard and pale, the feeblest energy of purpose animating a husk, her dry and shrunken mouth trying to speak.

Dr. Ont stood aside as Roderick saw her. "Maja!" Roderick cried, holding up his hands to block out sight of her.

"Still alive," Dr. Ont said. "I was wrong. She cannot die. We have all forgotten how."

The five brushed past Roderick, smiling only at me.

"The House of Escher loses all support," Cant said, touching my arm lightly. "The flow is with you. The world wants you. You will teach them your experience. You will show them what it feels to be *skilled* and to have fleshly talents, to *work* and *touch* in a primal way. Roderick was absolutely correct—you are a marvel!"

I looked at Roderick, frozen in terror, and then at Maja, her eyes like pits sucking in nothing, as isolated as any corpse but still alive.

The walls shuddered around me. The fibers withdrew from the stones, and where they no longer held, cracks appeared, running in crazed patterns over the white and yellow surfaces. The tiles of the floor heaved up, the tessellations disrupted, all order scattered.

Cant took my hand and led me through the disintegrating corridors, down the shivering and swaying stairs. Behind me, the stairs buckled and crumbled, and the beams of the ceiling split and jabbed down to the floor like broken elbows. Ahead, a tide of fibers withdrew from the house like sea sucked from a cave, and above the ripping snap of tearing timbers, the rumble and slam of stone blocks falling and shattering, I heard Roderick's high, chicken-cluck shriek, the cry of an avatar driven past desperation into madness:

"No death! *No Death!* King Nerve forever!"

And his bray of laughter at the final jest revealed, all his plans cocked asunder.

The antitheticals blew me through the front door like a wind, and down the walk into the ruined garden, among the twisted and fiber-covered trees, until I was away from the house of Roderick Escher. All of his spreading distractions and entertainments, all of his chambers filled with the world's diversions, the pandering to the commonest denominators of a frozen or disembodied horde . . . the impossible and convoluted towers leaned, shuddered, and collapsed, blowing dust and splinters through the door and the windows of the first floor.

The fibers pushed from the ground, binding my feet, rising up my legs toward my trunk, feeling through my suit, probing for secrets, for solutions. I felt voices and demands in my head, petulant, childish, *Show us. Do for us. Give us.* The fibers burrowed into my flesh, with the pricks of thousands of tiny cold needles.

Cant took my arm. "You are favored," she said.

The voices picked at my thoughts, rudely invaded my memories, making crude and cruel jokes. They seemed to know nothing but expletives, arranged in no sensible order, and they applied them accompanied by demands that went beyond the obscene, demands that echoed again and again; and I saw that this new world was composed not of gods, but of mannerless children who had never faced responsibility or consequences, and whose lives were all secrecy, all privilege, conducted behind thick and impersonal walls.

Tingles shot up my hands and feet and along my spine, and I felt sparks at the very basement of my reason.

Do for us, do everything, live for us, let us feel, all new and all unique, all superlatives and all gladness and joy, and no death no end

My hands jerked out, holding a pack of cards, and I felt a will other than mine—a collective will—move my fingers, attempt to spread the cards into a fan. The fingers jerked and spilled the cards into the dirt, across the creeping fibers. "Get them away from me!" I cried in furious panic.

The blocks and timbers and reduced towers of the House of Escher settled with a final groaning sigh, but I pictured Roderick and Maja buried beneath its timbers, still alive.

The fibers lanced into my tongue. The voices filling my head hissed and slid and insinuated like snakes, like *worms in my living brain*, demanding *tapeworms*, asking numbing questions, prodding, prickling, insatiable.

Cant said, "You must assert yourself. They demand much, but you have so much to give—"

The fibers shoved down my throat, piercing and threading through my tissues as if to connect with every cell of my being. I clawed at my mouth, my throat, my body, trying to tug free, but the fibers were strong as steel wires, though thinner than the strands of a spider's web.

"Newness is a treasure," Musnt said, standing beside Cant. Wont and Shant and Dont joined her.

My legs buckled, but the fibers stiffened and held me like a puppet. I could not speak, could only gag, could hardly hear above the dissonant voices. *Amuse. Give all. Share all. Live all.*

"Hail to the new and masterful," Cant said worshipfully, smiling broadly, simply, innocently. Even in my terror and pain that smile seemed angelic, entrancing.

"A hundred billion people cannot be wrong," Shant said, and touched the crown of my head with his outspread hand.

"We anoint the new Master of King Nerve," the five said as one, and I could breathe, and speak, for myself, no more.

Introduction to "The Way of All Ghosts"

The Thistledown sequence—*Eon, Eternity,* and *Legacy*—began with "The Wind from a Burning Woman." This most recent story was commissioned by Robert Silverberg for his anthology, *Far Horizons.*

I've long been fascinated by the visionary novels of William Hope Hodgson, and in particular, his magnum opus, *The Night Land,* published in 1912. Hodgson died in 1918 at Ypres, ending a short and influential career. Today, *The Night Land* is a difficult book to read, for stylistic reasons mostly—Hodgson affected a pseudo-Georgian style that doesn't really work for contemporary readers, though it does create a dreamlike sense of alternate reality. But more important is the incredible atmosphere of his most fabulous creation, the Night Land itself.

It seemed to me that a science fictional treatment of this vision, set in the Thistledown sequence, would serve more as a collaborative tribute than a rip-off, and Robert Silverberg agreed. Hence the dedication.

Check out *The Night Land* and William Hope Hodgson's many shorter works. We lost something very special at Ypres.

The Way of All Ghosts
A Myth from Thistledown

Far Horizons, Robert Silverberg, 1999

For William Hope Hodgson

Introduction

Once upon a very long extension, not precisely time nor any space we know, there existed an endless hollow thread of adventure and commerce called the Way, introduced in *Eon* (Bluejay/Tor, 1985). The Way, an artificial universe fifty kilometers in diameter and infinitely long, was created by the human inhabitants of an asteroid starship called *Thistledown.* They had become bored with their seemingly endless journey between the stars; the Way, with its potential of openings to other times and other universes, made reaching their destination unnecessary.

That the Way was destroyed (in *Eternity,* Warner, 1988) is known; that it never ends in any human space or time is less obvious.

Even before its creators completed their project, the Way was discovered and invaded by the nonhuman Jarts, who sought to announce themselves to Deity, what they called Descendant Mind, by absorbing and understanding everything, everywhere. The Jarts nearly destroyed the Way's creators, but were held at bay for a time, and for a price.

Yet there were stranger encounters. The plexus of universes is beyond the mind of any individual, human or Jart.

One traveler experienced more of this adventure than any other. His name was Olmy Ap Sennen. In his centuries of life, he lived to see himself become a living myth, be forgotten, rediscovered, and made myth again. So many stories have been told of Olmy that history and myth intertwine.

This is an early story. Olmy has experienced only one reincarnation (*Legacy*, Tor, 1995). In fee for his memories, he has been rewarded with a longing to return to death everlasting.

1

"Probabilities fluctuated wildly, but always passed through zero, and gate openers, their equipment, and all associated personnel within a few hundred meters of the gate, were swallowed by a null that can only be described in terms of mathematics. It became difficult to remember that they had ever existed; records of their histories were corrupted or altered, even though they lay millions of kilometers from the incident. We had tapped into the geometric blood of the gods. But we knew we had to continue. We were compelled."
          —*Testimony of Master Gate Opener Ry Ornis, Secret Hearings Conducted by the Infinite Hexamon Nexus, "On the Advisability of Opening Gates into Chaos and Order"*

The ghost of his last lover found Olmy Ap Sennen in the oldest columbarium of Alexandria, within the second chamber of the *Thistledown*.

Olmy stood in the middle of the hall, surrounded by stacked tiers of hundreds of small golden spheres. The spheres were urns, most of them containing only a sample of ashes. They rose to the glassed-in ceiling, held within columns of gentle yellow suspension fields. He reached out to touch a blank silver plate at the base of one column. The names of the dead appeared as if suddenly engraved, one after another.

He removed his hand when the names reached *Ilmo, Paul Yan*. This is where the soldiers from his childhood neighborhood were honored; in this column, five names, all familiar to him from days in school, all killed in a single skirmish with the Jarts near 3 ex 9, three billion kilometers down the Way. All had been obliterated without trace. These urns were empty.

He did not know the details. He did not need to. These dead had served Thistledown as faithfully as Olmy, but they would never return.

Olmy had spent seventy-three years stranded on the planet Lamarckia, in the service of the Hexamon, cut off from the Thistledown and the Way that stretched beyond the asteroid's seventh chamber. On Lamarckia, he had raised children, loved and buried wives . . . lived a long and memorable life in primitive conditions on an extraordinary world. His rescue and return to the Way, converted within days from an old and dying man to a fresh-bodied youth, had been a shock worse than the return of any real and ancient ghost.

Axis City, slung on the singularity that occupied the geodesic center of the Way, had been completed during those tumultuous years before Olmy's rescue and resurrection. It had moved four hundred thousand kilometers "north," down the Way, far from the seventh chamber cap. Within the Geshel precincts of Axis City, the mental patterns of many who died were now transferred to City Memory, a technological afterlife not very different from the ancient dream of heaven. Using similar technology, temporary partial personalities could be created to help an individual multitask. These were sometimes called ghosts. Olmy had heard of partials, sent to do the bidding of their originals, with most of their mental faculties duplicated, but limited power to make decisions. He had never actually met one, however.

The ghost appeared just to his right and announced its nature by flickering slightly, growing translucent, then briefly turning into a negative. This display lasted only a few seconds. After, the simulacrum seemed perfectly solid and real. Olmy jumped, disoriented, then surveyed the ghost's features. He shook his head and smiled wryly.

"It will give my original joy to find you well," the partial said. "You seem lost, Ser Olmy."

Olmy did not quite know what form of speech to use with the partial. Should he address it with respect due to the original, a corprep and a woman of influence. . . . The last woman he had tried to be in love with . . . or as he might address a servant?

"I come here often. Old acquaintances."

The image looked concerned. "Poor Olmy. Still don't belong anywhere?"

Olmy ignored this. He looked for the ghost's source. It was projected from a small fist-sized flier hovering several meters away.

"I'm here on behalf of my original, corporeal representative Neya Taur Rinn. You realize . . . I am not her?"

"I'm not ignorant," Olmy said sharply, finding himself once more at a disadvantage with this woman.

The ghost fixed her gaze on him. The image, of course, was not actually doing the seeing. "The presiding minister of the Way, Yanosh Ap Kesler, instructed me to find you. My original was reluctant. I hope you understand."

Olmy folded his hands behind his back as the partial picted a series of ID symbols: Office of the Presiding Minister, Hexamon Nexus Office of Way Defense, Office of Way Maintenance. Quite a stack of bureaucracies, Olmy thought, Way Maintenance currently being perhaps the most powerful and arrogant of them all.

"What does Yanosh want with me?" he asked bluntly.

The ghost lifted her hands and pointed her index finger into her palm, tapping with each point. "You supported him in his bid to become presiding minister of the Seventh Chamber and the Way. You've become a symbol for the advance of Geshel interests."

"Against my will," Olmy said. Yanosh, a fervent progressive and Geshel, had sent Olmy to Lamarckia—and had also brought him back and arranged for his new body. Olmy for his own part had never known quite which camp he belonged to: conservative Naderites, grimly opposed to the extraordinary advances of the last century; or the enthusiastically progressive Geshels.

Neya Taur Rinn's people were Geshels of an ancient radical faction, among the first to move into Axis City. The partial continued. "Ser Kesler has won re-election as presiding minister of the Way and now also serves as mayor of three precincts in Axis City."

"I'm aware of that."

"Of course. The presiding minister extends his greetings and hopes you are agreeable."

"I am very agreeable," Olmy said mildly. "I stay out of politics and disagree with nobody. I can't pay back Yanosh for all he has done—but then, I have rendered him due service as well." He did not like being baited—and could not understand why Yanosh would send Neya to fetch him. The presiding minister knew enough about Olmy's private life—probably too much. "Yanosh knows I've put myself on permanent leave." Olmy could not restrain himself. "Pardon me for boldness, but I'm curious. How do you feel? Do you actually *think* you are Neya Taur Rinn?"

The partial smiled. "I am a high-level partial given subordinate authority by my original," it said. *She* said . . . Olmy decided he would not cut such fine distinctions.

"Yes, but what does it *feel* like?" he asked.

"At least you're still alive enough to be curious," the partial said.

"Your original regarded my curiosity as a kind of perversity," Olmy said.

"A morbid curiosity," the partial returned, clearly uncomfortable. "I couldn't stand maintaining a relationship with a man who wanted to be *dead*."

"You rode my fame until I bored you," Olmy rejoined, then regretted the words. He used old training to damp his sharper emotions.

"To answer your question, I *feel* everything my original would feel. And my original would hate to see you here. What do *you* feel like, Ser Olmy?" The ghost's arm swung out to take in the urns, the columbarium. "Coming here, walking among the dead, that's pretty melodramatic."

That a ghost could remember their time together, could carry tales of this meeting to her original, to a woman he had admired with all that he had left of his heart, both irritated and intrigued him. "You were attracted to me because of my history."

"I was attracted to you because of your strength," she said. "It hurt me that you were so intent on living in your memories."

"I clung to you."

"And to nobody else . . ."

"I don't come here often," Olmy said. He shook his hands out by his side and stepped back. "All my finest memories are on a world I can never go back to. Real loves . . . real life. Not like Thistledown now." He squinted at the image. The image's focus was precise; still, there was something false about it, a glossiness, a prim neatness unlike Neya. "You didn't help."

The partial's expression softened. "I don't take the blame entirely, but your distress doesn't please me. My original."

"I didn't say I was in distress. I feel a curious peace in fact. Why did Yanosh send you? Why did you agree to come?"

The ghost reached out to him. Her hand passed through his arm. She apologized for this breach of etiquette. "For your sake, to get you involved, and for the sake of my original, please, at least speak to our staff. The presiding minister needs you to join an expedition." She seemed to consider for a moment, then screw up her courage. "There's trouble at the Redoubt."

Olmy felt a sting of shock at the mention of that name. The conversation had suddenly become more than a little risky. He shook his head vigorously. "I do not acknowledge even knowing of such a place," he said.

"You know more than I do," the partial said. "I've been assured that it's real. Way Defense tells the Office of Way Maintenance that it now threatens us all."

"I'm not comfortable holding this conversation in a public place," Olmy protested.

This seemed to embolden the partial, and she projected her image closer. "This area is quiet and clean. No one listens."

Olmy stared up at the high glass ceiling.

"We are not being observed," the partial insisted. "The Nexus and Way Defense are concerned that the Jarts are closing in on that sector of the Way. I am told that if they occupy it, gain control of the Redoubt, Thistledown might as well be ground to dust and the Way set on fire like a piece of string. That scares my original. It scares *me* as I am now. Does it bother you in the least, Olmy?"

Olmy looked along the rows of urns. . . . Centuries of Thistledown history, lost memory, now turned to pinches of ash, or less.

"Yanosh says he's positive you can help," the partial said with a strong lilt of emotion. "It's a way to rejoin the living and make a new place for yourself."

"Why should that matter to you? To your original?" Olmy asked.

"Because my original still regards you as a hero. I still hope to emulate your service to the Hexamon."

Olmy smiled wryly. "Better to find a living model," he said. "I don't belong out there. I'm rusted over."

"That is not true," the partial said. "You have been given a new body. You are youthful and strong, and very experienced . . ." She seemed about to say more, but hesitated, rippled again, and faded abruptly. Her voice faded as well, and he heard only "Yanosh says he's never lost faith in you—"

The floor of the columbarium trembled. The solidity of Thistledown seemed to be threatened; a quake through the asteroid material, an impact from outside . . . or something occurring within the Way. Olmy reached out to brace himself against a pillar. The golden spheres vibrated in their suspensions, jangling like hundreds of small bells.

From far away, sirens began to wail.

The partial reappeared. "I have lost contact with my original," it said, its features blandly stiff. "Something has broken my link with City Memory."

Olmy watched Neya's image with fascination as yet untouched by any visceral response.

"I do not know when or if there will be a recovery," she said. "There's a failure on Axis City." Suddenly the image appeared puzzled, then stricken. She held out her phantom arms. "My original . . ." As if she were made of solid flesh, her face crinkled with fear. "She's died. I've *died*. Oh, my God, Olmy!"

Olmy tried to understand what this might mean, under the radical new rules of life and death for Geshels such as Neya. "What's happened? What can we do?"

The image flickered wildly. "My body is *gone*. There's been a complete system failure. I don't have any legal existence."

"What about the whole-life records? Connect with them." Olmy walked around the unsteady image, as if he might capture it, stop it from fading.

"I kept putting it off. . . . So stupid! I haven't put myself in City Memory yet."

He tried to touch her and of course could not. He could not believe what she was saying, yet the sirens still wailed, and another small shudder rang through the asteroid.

"I have no place to go. Olmy, please! Don't let me just *stop*!" The ghost of Neya Taur Rinn drew herself up, tried to compose herself. "I have only a few seconds before . . ."

Olmy felt a sudden and intense attraction to the shimmering image. He wanted to know what actual death, final death, could possibly feel like. He reached out again, as if to embrace her.

She shook her head. The flickering increased. "It feels so strange—losing—"

Before she could finish, the image vanished completely. Olmy's arms hung around silent and empty air.

The sirens continued to wail, audible throughout Alexandria. He slowly dropped his arms, all too aware of being alone. The projector flew in a small circle, emitting small *wheep*ing sounds. Without instructions from its source, it could not decide what to do.

For a moment, he shivered and his neck hair pricked—a sense of almost religious awe he had not experienced since his time on Lamarckia.

Olmy had started walking toward the end of the hall before he consciously knew what to do. He turned right to exit through the large steel doors and looked up through the thin clouds enwrapping the second chamber, through the glow of the flux tube to the axis borehole on the southern cap. His eyes were warm and wet. He wiped them with the back of his hand and his breath hitched.

Emergency beacons had switched on around the flux tube, forming a bright ring two thirds of the way up the cap.

His shivering continued, and it angered him. He had died once already, yet this new body was afraid of dying, and its wash of emotions had taken charge of his senses.

Deeper still and even more disturbing was a scrap of the old loyalty. . . . To his people, to the vessel that bore them between the stars, that served as the open chalice of the infinite Way. A loyalty to the woman who had found him too painful to be with. "Neya!" he moaned. Perhaps she had been wrong. A partial might not have access to all information; perhaps things weren't as bad as they seemed.

But he knew that they were. He had never felt Thistledown shake so.

Olmy hurried to the rail terminal three city squares away, accompanied by throngs of curious and alarmed citizens. Barricades had been set across the entrances to the northern cap elevators; all inter-chamber travel was temporarily restricted. No news was available.

Olmy showed the ID marks on his wrist to a cap guard, who scanned them quickly and transmitted them to her commanders. She let him pass, and he entered the elevator and rode swiftly to the borehole.

Within the workrooms surrounding the borehole waited an arrowhead-shaped official transport, as the presiding minister's office had requested. None of the soldiers or guards he questioned knew what had happened. There were still no official pronouncements on any of the citizen nets. Olmy rode the transport, accompanied by five other officials, through the vacuum above the atmospheres of the next four chambers, threading the boreholes of each of the massive concave walls that separated them. None of the chambers showed any sign of damage.

In the southern cap borehole of the sixth chamber, Olmy transferred from the transport to a tuberider, designed to run along the singularity that formed the core of the Way. On this most unusual railway, he sped at many thousands of miles per hour toward the Axis City at 4 ex 5— four hundred thousand kilometers north of Thistledown.

A few minutes from Axis City, the tuberider slowed and the forward viewing port darkened. There was heavy radiation in the vicinity, the pilot reported. Something had come down the Way at relativistic velocity and struck the northern precincts of Axis City.

Olmy had little trouble guessing the source.

2

A day passed before Olmy could see the presiding minister. Emergency repairs on Axis City had rendered only one precinct, Central City, habitable; the rest, including Axis Prime and Axis Nader, were being evacuated. Axis Prime had taken the brunt of the impact. Tens of thousands had lost their lives, both Geshels and Naderites. Naderites by and large did not participate in the practice of storing their body patterns and recent memories as insurance against such a calamity.

Some Geshels would receive their second incarnation—many thousands more would not. City Memory itself had been damaged. Even had Neya taken the time to make her whole-life record, store her patterns, she might still have died.

The last functioning precinct, Central City, now contained the combined offices of Presiding Minister of the Way and the Axis City government, and it was here that Yanosh met with Olmy.

"Her name was Deirdre Enoch," the presiding minister said, floating
over the transparent external wall of the new office. His body was
wrapped below the chest in a shining blue medical support suit; the
impact had broken both of his legs and caused severe internal injuries.
For the time being, the presiding minister was a functioning cyborg,
until new organs could be grown and placed. "She opened a gate illegally at 3 ex 9, fifty years ago. Just beyond the point where we last
repulsed the Jarts. She was helped by a master gate opener who deliberately disobeyed Nexus and guild orders. We learned about the breach
six months after she had smuggled eighty of her colleagues—or maybe
a hundred and twenty, we aren't sure how many—into a small research
center—and just days after the gate was opened. There was nothing we
could do to stop it."

Olmy gripped a rail that ran around the perimeter of the office,
watching Kesler without expression. The irony was too obvious. "I've
only heard rumors. Way Maintenance—"

Kesler was hit by a wave of pain, quickly damped by the suit. He
continued, his face drawn. "Damn Way Maintenance. Damn the in-
fighting and politics." He forced a smile. "Last time it was a Naderite
renegade on Lamarckia."

Olmy nodded.

"This time—Geshel. Even worse—a member of the Openers Guild. I
never imagined running this damned starship would ever be so complicated. Makes me almost understand why you long for Lamarckia."

"It wasn't any easier there," Olmy said.

"Yes—but there were fewer people." Yanosh rotated his support suit
and crossed the chamber. "We don't know precisely what happened.
Something disturbed the immediate geometry around the gate. The conflicts between Way physics and the universe Enoch accessed were too
great. The gate became a lesion, impossible to close. By that time, most
of Enoch's scientists had retreated to the main station, a protective pyramid—what she called the Redoubt."

"She tapped into chaos?" Olmy asked. Some universes accessed
through the Way were empty voids, dead, useless but relatively harmless; others were virulent, filled with a bubbling stew of unstable "constants" that reduced the reality of any observer or instrumentality. Only
two such gates had ever been opened in the Way; the single fortunate
aspect of these disasters had been that the gates themselves had quickly
closed and could not be reopened.

"Not chaos," Kesler said, swallowing and bowing his head at more discomfort. "This damn suit . . . could be doing a better job."

"You should be resting," Olmy said.

"No time. The Opener's Guild tells me Enoch was looking for a domain of enhanced structure, hyper-order. What she found was more dangerous than any chaos. Her gate may have opened into a universe of endless fecundity. Not just order: Creativity. Every universe is in a sense a plexus, its parts connected by information links; but Enoch's universe contained no limits to the propagation of information. No finite speed of light, no separation between anything analogous to the Bell continuum . . . and other physicality."

Olmy frowned, trying to make sense of this. "My knowledge of Way physics is shaky . . ."

"Ask your beloved Konrad Korzenoswki," Kesler snapped.

Olmy did not react to this provocation.

Kesler apologized under his breath. He floated slowly back across the chamber, his face a mask of pain, a pathetic parody of restlessness. "We lost three expeditions trying to save her people and close the gate. The last was six months ago. Something like life-forms had grown up around the main station, fueled by the lesion. They've became *huge*, unimaginably bizarre. No one can make sense of them. What was left of our last expedition managed to build a barrier about a thousand kilometers south of the lesion. We thought that would give us the luxury of a few years to decide what to do next. But that barrier has been destroyed. We've not been able to get close enough since to discover what's happened. We have defenses in that sector, key defenses that keep the flaw from being used against us." He looked down through the transparent floor at the segment of the Way twenty-four kilometers below.

"The Jarts were able to send a relativistic projectile along the flaw, hardly more than a gram of rest mass. We couldn't stop it. It struck Axis City at twelve hundred hours yesterday."

Olmy had been told the details of the attack: A pellet less than a millimeter in diameter, traveling very close to the speed of light. Only the safety and control mechanisms of the sixth chamber machinery had kept the entire Axis City from disintegrating. The original of Neya Taur Rinn had been conducting business on behalf of her boss, Yanosh, in Axis Prime while her partial had visited Olmy.

"We're moving the city south as fast as we can and still keep up the evacuation," Kesler said. "The Jarts are drawing close to the lesion now. We're not sure what they can do with it. Maybe nothing—but we can't afford to take the chance."

Olmy shook his head in puzzlement. "You've just told me nothing can be done. Why call me here when we're helpless?"

"I didn't say *nothing* could be done," Kesler responded, eyes glittering.

"Some of our gate openers think they can build a cirque, a ring gate, and seal off the lesion."

"That would cut us off from the rest of the Way," Olmy said.

"Worse. In a few days of weeks it would destroy the Way completely, seal us off in Thistledown forever. Until now, we've never been that desperate." He smiled, lips twisted by pain. "Frankly, you were not my choice. I'm no longer sure that you can be relied upon, and this matter is far too complicated to allow anyone to act alone."

Neya had not told him the truth, then. "Who chose me?" Olmy asked.

"A gate opener. You made an impression on him when he escorted you down the Way some decades ago. He was the one who opened the gate to Lamarckia."

"Frederik Ry Ornis?"

Kesler nodded. "From what I'm told, he's become the most powerful opener in the guild. A senior master."

Olmy took a deep breath. "I'm not what I appear to be, Yanosh. I'm an old man who's seen women and his friends die. I miss my sons. You should have left me on Lamarckia."

Kesler closed his eyes. The blue jacket around his lower body adjusted slightly, and his face tightened. "The Olmy I knew would never have turned down a chance like this."

"I've seen too many things already," Olmy said.

Yanosh moved forward. "We both have. This . . . is beyond me," he said quietly. "The lesion . . . the gate openers tell me it's the strangest place in creation. All the boundaries of physics have collapsed. Time and causality have new meanings. Heaven and Hell have married. Only those in the Redoubt have seen all that's happened there—if they still exist in any way we can understand. They haven't communicated with us since the lesion formed."

Olmy listened intently, something slowly stirring to life, a small speck of ember glowing brighter.

"It may be over, Olmy," Yanosh said. "The whole grand experiment may be at an end. We're ready to close off the Way, pinch it, seal the lesion within its own small bubble . . . dispose of it."

"Tell me more," Olmy said, folding his arms.

"Three citizens escaped from the Redoubt, from Enoch's small colony, before the lesion became too large. One died, his mind scrambled beyond retrieval. The second has been confined for study, as best we're able. What afflicts him—or *it*—is something we can never cure. The third survived relatively unharmed. She's become . . . unconventional, more than a little obsessed by the mystical, but I'm told she's still rational. If you accept, she will accompany you." Yanosh's tone indicated he was not going to allow Olmy to decline. "We have two other volunteers, both apprentice gate openers, both failed by the guild. All have been chosen by Frederik Ry Ornis. He will explain why."

Olmy shook his head. "A mystic, failed openers. . . . What would I do with such a team?"

Yanosh smiled grimly. "Kill them if it goes wrong. And kill yourself. If you can't close off the Way, and if the lesion remains, you will not be allowed to come back. The third expedition I sent never even reached the Redoubt. But they were absorbed by the lesion." Another grimace of pain. "Do you believe in ghosts, Olmy?"

"What kind?"

"Real ghosts?"

"No," Olmy said.

"I think I do. Some members of our rescue expeditions came back. Several versions of them. We *think* we destroyed them."

"Versions?"

"Copies of some sort. They were sent back—echoed—along their own world-lines in a way no one understands. They returned to their loved ones, their relatives, their friends. If more return, everything we call real could be in jeopardy. It's been very difficult keeping this secret."

Olmy raised an eyebrow skeptically. He wondered if Yanosh was himself still rational. "I've served my time. More than my time. Why should I go active?"

"Damn it, Olmy, if not for love of Thistledown—if you're beyond that, then because you *want to die*," Kesler grunted, his face betraying quiet disgust behind the pain, "You've wanted to die since I brought you back from Lamarckia. This time, if you make it to the Redoubt, you're likely to have your wish granted.

"Think of it as a gift from me to you, or to what you once were."

3

"If you were enhanced, this would go a lot faster," Jarr Flynch said, pointing to Olmy's head. Frederik Ry Ornis smiled. The three of them walked side by side down a long, empty hall, approaching a secure room deep in the old Thistledown Defense Tactical College building in Alexandria.

Ry Ornis had aged not at all physically. In appearance he was still the same long-limbed, mantis-like figure, but his gawkiness had been replaced by an eerie grace, and his youthful, eccentric volubility by a wry spareness of language.

Olmy dismissed Flynch's comment with a wave of his hand. "I've gone through the important files," he said. "I think I know them well enough. I have questions about the choice of people to go with me. The apprentice gate openers. . . . They've been rejected by the guild. Why?"

Flynch smiled. "They're flamboyant."

Olmy glanced at the master opener. "Ry Ornis was as flamboyant as they come."

"The guild has changed," Ry Ornis said. "It demands more now."

Flynch agreed. "In the time since I've been a teacher in the guild, that's certainly true. They tolerate very little . . . creativity. The defection of Enoch's pupils scared them. The lesion terrified all of us. Rasp and Karn are young, innovative. Nobody denies they're brilliant, but they've refused to settle in and play their roles. So . . . the guild denied them final certification."

"Why choose them for this job?" Olmy asked.

"Ry Ornis did the choosing," Flynch said.

"We've discussed this," Ry Ornis said.

"Not to my satisfaction. When do I meet them?"

"No meeting has been authorized with Rasp and Karn until you're on the flawship. They're still in emergency conditioning." Flynch glanced at Ry Ornis. "The training has been a little rough on them."

Olmy felt less and less sure that he wanted anything to do with the guild, or with Ry Ornis's chosen openers. "The files only tell half a story," he said. "Deirdre Enoch never became an opener—she never even tried to qualify. She was just a teacher. How could she become so important to the guild?"

Flynch shook his head. "Like me, she was never qualified to be an opener, but also like me, as a teacher, she was considered one of the best. She became a leader to some apprentice openers. Philosopher."

"Prophet," Ry Ornis said softly.

"Training for the guild is grueling," Flynch continued. "Some say it's become torture. The mathematical conditioning alone is enough to produce a drop-out rate of over ninety percent. Deirdre Enoch worked as a counselor in mental balance, compensation, and she was good. . . . In the last twenty years, she worked with many who went on to become very powerful in Way Maintenance. She kept up her contacts. She convinced a lot of her students—"

"That human nature is corrupt," Olmy ventured sourly.

Flynch shook his head. "That the laws of our universe are inadequate. Incomplete. That there is a way to become better human beings, and of course, better openers. Disorder, competition, and death corrupt us, she thought."

"She knew high-level theory, speculations circulated privately among master openers," Ry Ornis said. "She heard about domains where the rules were very different."

"She heard about a gate into complete order?"

"It had been discussed, on a theoretical basis. None had ever been attempted. No limits have been found to the variety of domains—of universes. She speculated that a well-tuned gate could access almost any domain a good opener could conceive of."

Olmy scowled. "She expected order to balance out competition and death? Order versus disorder, a fight to the finish?"

Ry Ornis made a small noise, and Flynch nodded. "There's a reason none of this is in the files," Flynch said. "No opener will talk about it, or admit they knew anybody involved in making the decision. It's been very embarrassing to the guild. I'm impressed that you know what questions to ask. But it's better that you ask Ry Ornis—"

Olmy focused on Flynch. "You say you and Enoch occupied similar positions. I'd rather ask you."

Flynch gestured for them to turn to the left. The lights came on before them, and at the end of a much shorter hall, a door stood open. "Deirdre Enoch read extensively in the old religious texts. As did her followers. I believe they lost themselves in a dream," he said. "They thought that anyone who bathed in a stream of pure order, as it were—in a domain of unbridled creation without destruction—would be enhanced. Armored. Annealed. That's my opinion . . . what they might have been thinking. She might have told them such things."

"A fountain of youth?" Olmy ventured, still scowling.

"Openers don't much care about temporal immortality," Ry Ornis said. "When we open a gate—we glimpse eternity. A hundred gates, a hundred different eternities. Coming back is just an interlude between forevers. Those who listened to Enoch thought they would end up more skilled, more brilliant. Less corrupted by competitive evolution." He smiled, a remarkably unpleasant expression on his skeletal face. "Free of original sin."

Olmy's scowl faded. He glanced at Flynch, who had turned away from Ry Ornis. Something between them, a coolness. "All right. I can see that."

"Really?" Flynch shook his head dubiously.

Perhaps the master opener could tell even more. But it did not seem wise at this point to push the matter.

A bell chimed and they entered the conference room.

Already seated within was the only surviving and whole escapee from the Redoubt: Gena Plass. As a radical Geshel, she had designed her own body and appearance decades ago, opting for a solid frame, close to her natural physique. Her face she had tuned to show strength as well as classic beauty, but she had allowed it to age, and the experience of her time with the expedition, the trauma at the lesion, had not been erased. Olmy noted that she carried a small book with her, an antique printed on paper—a Bible.

Flynch made introductions. Plass looked proud and more than a little confused. They sat around the table.

"Let's start with what we know," Flynch said. He ordered up visual records made by the retreating flawship that had carried Plass.

Olmy looked at the images hovering over the table: the great pipeline of the Way, sheets of field fluorescing brilliantly as they were breached, debris caught in whirling clouds along the circumference, the flaw itself, running along the center of the Way like a wire heated to blinding blue-white.

Plass did not look. Olmy watched her reaction closely. For a moment, something seemed to swirl around her, a wisp of shadow, smoothly transparent, like a small slice of twilight. The others did not see or ignored what they saw, but Plass's eyes locked on Olmy's and her lips tightened.

"I'm pleased you've both agreed to come," Ry Ornis said as the images came to an end.

Plass looked at the opener, and then back at Olmy. She studied Olmy's face closely. "I can't stay here. That's why I'm going back. I don't belong in Thistledown."

"Ser Plass is haunted," Flynch said. "Ser Olmy has been told about some of these visitors."

"My husband," she said, swallowing. "Just my husband, so far. Nobody else."

"Is he still there?" Olmy asked. "In the Redoubt?"

Bitterly, she said, "They haven't told you much that's useful, have they? As if they want us to fail."

"He's dead?"

"He's not in the Redoubt and I don't know if you could call it death," Plass said. "May I tell you what this really means? What we've actually done?" She stared around the table, eyes wide.

Ry Ornis lifted his hand tolerantly.

"I have diaries from before the launch of Thistledown, from my family," she said. "As far back as my ancestors can remember, my family was special. . . . They had access to the world of the spiritual. They all saw ghosts. The old-fashioned kind, not the ones we use now for servants. Some described the ghosts in their journals." She reached up and pinched her lower lip, released it, pinched it again. "I think some of the ghosts my husband. I recognize that now. Everyone on my world-line, back to before I was born, haunted by the same figure. My husband. Now I see him, too."

"I have a hard time visualizing this sort of ghost," Olmy said.

Plass looked up at the ceiling and clutched her Bible. "Whatever it is that we tapped into—a domain of pure order, something else clever—

it's *suffused* into the Way, into the Thistledown. It's like a caterpillar crawling up our lives, grabbing hold of events and . . . crawling, spreading backward, maybe even forward in time. They try to keep us quiet. I cooperate . . . but my husband tells me things when he returns. Do the others hear . . . reports? Messages from the Redoubt?"

Ry Ornis shook his head, but Olmy doubted this meant simple denial.

"What happened when the gate became a lesion?" Olmy asked.

Plass grew pale. "My husband was at the gate with Enoch's master opener, Tom Issa Danna."

"One of our finest," Ry Ornis said.

"Enoch's gate into order was the second they had opened. The first was a well to an established supply world where we could bring up raw materials."

"Standard practice for all far-flung stations," Flynch said.

"I wasn't there when they opened the second gate," Plass continued, her eyes darting between Flynch and Olmy. She seemed to have little sympathy for either. "I was at a support facility about a kilometer from the gate, and two kilometers from the Redoubt. There was already an atmospheric envelope and a cushion of sand and soil around the site. My husband and I had started a quick-growth garden. An orchard. We heard they had opened the second gate. My husband was with Issa Danna. Ser Enoch came by on a tractor and said it was a complete success. We were celebrating, a small group of researchers, opening bottles of champagne. We got reports of something going wrong two hours later. We came out of our bungalows—a scout from the main flawship was just landing. Enoch had returned to the new gate to join Issa Danna. My husband must have been right there with them."

"What did you see?"

"Nothing at first. We watched them on the monitors inside the bungalows. Issa Danna and his assistants were working, talking, laughing. Issa Danna was so confident. He radiated his genius. The second gate looked normal—a well, a cupola. But in a little while, a few hours, we saw that the people around the new gate sounded drunk. All of them. Something had come out of the gate, something intoxicating. They spoke about a shadow."

She looked up at Olmy, and Olmy realized that before this experience, she must have been a very lovely woman. Some of that beauty still shone through.

"We saw that some kind of veil covered the gate. Then the assistant openers in the bungalows, students of Issa Danna, said that the gate was out of control. They were feeling it in their clavicles, slaved to the master's clavicle."

Clavicles were devices used by gate-openers to create the portals that gave access to other times, other universes, "outside" the Way. Typically, they were shaped like bicycle handlebars attached to a small sphere.

"How many openers were there?" Olmy asked.

"Two masters and seven apprentices," Plass said.

Olmy turned to Ry Ornis. He held up his hand, urging patience.

"A small truck came out of the gate site. Its tires wobbled and all the people clinging to it were shouting and laughing. Then everyone around the truck—the bungalows were almost empty now—began to shout, and an assistant grabbed me—I was the closest to her—and said we had to get onto the scout and return to the flawship. She—her name was Jara—said she had never felt anything like this. She said they must have made a mistake and opened a gate into chaos. I had never heard about such a thing—but she seemed to think if we didn't leave now, we'd all die. Four people. Two men and me and Jara. We were the only ones who made it into the scout ship. Shadows covered everything around us. Everybody was drunk, laughing, screaming."

Plass stopped and took several breaths to calm herself. "We flew up to the flawship. The rest is on the record. The Redoubt was the last thing I saw, surrounded by something like ink in water, swirling. A storm."

Flynch started to speak, but Plass cut him off. "Two of the others on the flawship, the men, were afflicted. They came out of the veil around the truck and Jara helped them get into the scout. As for Jara . . . nobody remembers her but me."

Flynch waited a moment, then said, "There were only three people aboard the scout when it reached the flawship. You, and the figure we haven't identified. There was no other man, and there has never been an assistant opener named Jara."

"They were real."

"It doesn't matter," Ry Ornis said impatiently. "Issa Danna knew better than to open a gate into chaos. He knew the signs and never would have completed the opening. But—in the linkage, the slaving, qualities can be reversed if the opener loses control."

"A gate into order—but the slaved clavicles behaving as if they were associated with chaos?" Olmy asked, trying to grasp the complexities.

Ry Ornis seemed reluctant to go into more detail. "They no longer exist in our world-line," he said. "Ser Plass remembers that one hundred and twenty people accompanied Enoch and Issa Danna. She remembers two master openers and seven assistants. Here on Thistledown, we have records, life-histories, of only eighty, with one master and two assistants."

"I survived. You remember me," Plass said, her expression desperate.

"You're in our records. You survived," Ry Ornis confirmed. "We don't know why or how."

"What about the other survivor?" Olmy said.

"We don't know who he or she was," Ry Ornis said.

"Show him the other," Plass said. "Show him Number 2, show him what happens when you survive, but you *don't return*."

"That's next," Ry Ornis said. "If you're ready, Ser Olmy."

"I may never be *ready*, Ser Ry Ornis," Olmy said.

4

The flawship cradled in the borehole dock was sleek and new and very fast. Olmy tracted along the flank of the ship, resisting the urge to run his fingers along the featureless reflecting surface.

He was still pondering the meeting with the figure called Number 2.

Around the ship's dock, the bore hole between the sixth and seventh chamber glowed with a violet haze, a cup-shaped field erected to receive the southernmost extensors of Axis City, gripping the remaining precincts during their evacuation and repair. Olmy swiveled to face the axis and the flaw's blunt conclusion and watch the workers and robots guiding power grids and huge steel beams to act as buffers.

The dock manager, a small man with boyish features and no hair, his scalp decorated with an intricate green and brown Celtic braid, pulled himself toward Olmy and extended a paper certificate.

"We're going to vacuum in an hour," he said. "I hope everybody's here before then. I'd like to seal the ship and check its integrity."

Olmy applied his sigil to the document, transferring its command from borehole management and the construction guild to Way Defense.

"Two others were here earlier," the dock manager said. "Twins, young women. They carried the smallest clavicles I've ever seen."

Olmy looked back along the dock and saw three figures tracting toward them. "Looks like we're all here," he said.

"No send-off?" the manager asked.

Olmy smiled. "Everyone's much too busy," he said.

"Don't I know it," the manager said.

As a rule, gate openers had a certain look and feel that defined them, sometimes subtle, usually not. Rasp and Karn, were little more than children, born (perhaps *made* was a better word) fifteen years ago in Thistledown City. They were of radical Geshel ancestry, and their four parent-sponsors were also gate-openers.

They tracted to the flawship and introduced themselves to Olmy. Androgynous, ivory-white, slender, with long fingers and small heads covered with a fine silvery fur, each spoke with identical resonant tenor voices. Karn had black eyes, Rasp green. Otherwise, they were identical. To Olmy, neither had the air of authority he had seen in experienced gate-openers.

The dock manager picted a coded symbol and dilated the flawship entrance, a glowing green circle in the hull. The twins solemnly entered the ship.

Plass arrived several minutes later. She wore a formal blue suit and seemed to have been crying. As she greeted Olmy, her voice sounded harsh. She addressed him as if they had not met before. "You're the soldier?"

"I've worked in Way Defense," he said.

Gray eyes small and wary, surrounded by puffy pale flesh, face broad and sympathetic, hair dark and cut short, Plass today reminded Olmy of any of a dozen matrons he had known as a child: polite but hardly hesitant.

"Ser Flynch tells me you're the one who died on Lamarckia. I heard about that. By birth, a Naderite."

"By birth," Olmy said.

"Such adventures we have," she said with a sniff. "Because of Ser Korzenowski's cleverness." She glanced away, then fastened her eyes on him and leaned her head to one side. "I'm not looking forward to this. Have they told you I'm a little broken, that my thoughts take odd paths?"

"They said your studies and experiences have influenced you," Olmy said, a little uncomfortable at having to re-establish an acquaintance already made.

Rasp and Karn watched from the flawship hatch.

"She's broken, we're young and inexperienced," Rasp said. Karn laughed, a surprising watery tinkle, very sweet. "And you've died once already, Ser Olmy. What a crew!"

"I presume everyone knows what they're doing," Plass said.

"Presume nothing," Olmy said.

Olmy guided Plass into the ship. The dock manager watched this with dubious interest. Olmy swung around fields to face him.

"I take charge of this vessel now. Thanks for your attention and care."

"Our duty," the dock manager said. "She was delivered just yesterday. No one has taken her out yet—she's a virgin, Ser Olmy. She doesn't even have a name."

"Call her the *Lark*!" Rasp trilled from inside.

Olmy shook hands firmly with the manager and climbed into the ship. The entrance sealed with a small beep behind him.

The flawship's interior was cool and quiet. With intertial control, there were no special couches or nets or fields; they would experience only simulated motion, for psychological effect, on their journey; at most a mild sense of acceleration and deceleration.

Plass introduced herself to Karn and Rasp. Since she wore no pictor, only words were exchanged. This suited Olmy.

"Ser Olmy," Plass said, "I assume we are in privacy now. No one outside can hear?"

"No one," Olmy said.

"Good. Then we can speak our minds. This trip is useless." She turned on the twins, who floated like casual accent marks on some unseen word. "They've chosen you because you're inexperienced."

"Unmarked," Rasp said brightly. "Open to the new."

Karn smiled and nodded. "And not afraid of spooks."

This seemed to leave Plass at a loss, but only for a second. She was obviously determined to establish herself as a Cassandra. "You won't be disappointed."

"We visited with Number 2," Rasp said, and Karn nodded. "Ser Ry Ornis insisted we study it."

Olmy remembered his own encounter with the vividly glowing figure in the comfortably appointed darkened room. It was not terribly mis-shapen, as he had anticipated before the meeting, but certainly far from normal. Its skin had burned with the tiny firefly deaths of stray metal atoms in the darkened room's air. It had stood out against the shadows like a nebula in the vastness beyond Thistledown's walls. Its hands alone had remained dark, ascribing arcs against its starry body as it tried to speak.

It lived in a twisted kind of time, neither backwards nor forwards, and its words had required special translation. It had spoken of things that would happen in the room after Olmy left. It had told him the Way would soon end, "in the blink of a bird's eye." The translator relayed this clearly enough, but could not translate other words; it seemed the unknown figure was inventing or accessing new languages, some clearly not of human origin.

Plass said, "It'll be a mercy if all that happens is we end up like *him*."

"How interesting," Rasp said.

"We are fiends for novelty," Karn added with a smile.

"Monsters are *made*," Plass said with a grimace, clasping her Bible, "not born."

"Thank you," Karn said, and produced a forced, fixed smile, accom-panied by a glassy stare. Rasp was obviously thinking furiously to come up with a more witty riposte.

Olmy decided enough was more than enough. "If we're going to die, or worse, we should at least be civil." The three stared at him, each surprised in a different way. This gave Olmy a bare minimum of satisfaction. "Let's go through our orders and manifest, and learn how to work together."

"A man who wants only to die again—" Karn began, still irritated, her stare still glazed, but her twin interrupted.

"Shut up," Rasp said. "As he says. Time to work." Karn shrugged and her anger dissolved instantly.

AT SPEED, THE FLAWSHIP'S FORWARD VIEW OF THE WAY BECAME A TWISTED lens. Stray atoms and ions of gas within the Way piled up before them into a distorting, white-hot atmosphere. Rays of many colors writhed from a skewed vertex of milky brightness; the flaw, itself a slender geometric distortion, now resembled a white-hot piston.

Stray atoms of gas in the Way were becoming a problem, the result of so many gates being opened to bring in raw materials from the first exploited worlds.

The flawship's status appeared before Olmy in steady reassuring symbols of blue and green. Their speed: three percent of c', the speed of light in the Way, slightly less than c in the outside universe. They were now accelerating at more than six g's, down from the maximum they had hit at 4 ex 5. None of this could be felt inside the hull.

The display showed their position as 1 ex 7, ten million kilometers beyond the cap of the seventh chamber, still almost three billion kilometers from the Redoubt.

Olmy had a dreamlike sense of dissociation, as always when traveling in a flawship. The interior had been divided by its occupants into three private compartments, a common area, and the pilot's position. Olmy was spending most of his time at the pilot's position. The others kept to their compartments and said little to each other.

The first direct intimation of the strangeness of their mission came on the second day, halfway through their journey. Olmy was studying what little was known about the Redoubt, from a complete and highly secret file. He was deep into the biography of Deirdre Enoch when a voice called him from behind.

He turned and saw a young woman floating three meters aft, her head nearer to him than her feet, precessing slightly about her own axis. "I've felt you calling us," she said. "I've felt you studying us. What do you want to know?"

Olmy checked to make sure this was not some product of the files, of the data projectors. It was not; no simulations were being projected. Behind the image he saw the sisters and Plass emerging from their quarters. The sisters appeared interested, Plass bore an expression of shocked sadness.

"I don't recognize her," Plass said.

Olmy judged this was not a prank. "I'm glad you're decided to visit us," he said to the woman, with a touch of wry perversity. "How is the situation at the Redoubt?"

"The same, ever the same," the young woman answered. Her face was difficult to discern. As she spoke, her features blurred and re-formed, subtly different.

"Are you well?" Olmy asked. Rasp and Karn sidled forward around the image, which ignored them.

"I am nothing," the image said. "Ask another question. It's amusing to see if I can manage any sensible answers."

Rasp and Karn joined Olmy. "She's real?" Rasp asked.

The twins were both pale, their faces locked in dread fascination.

"I don't know," Olmy said. "I don't think so."

"Then she's used her position on the Redoubt's timeline to climb back to us," Rasp said. "Some of us at least do indeed get to where we're going!"

Karn smiled with her usual fixed contentment and glazed eyes. Olmy was beginning not to like this hyperintelligent twin.

Plass moved forward, hands clenched as if she would hit the figure. "I don't recognize you," she said. "Who are you?"

"I see only one of you clearly." The young woman pointed at Olmy. "The others are like clouds of insects."

"Have the Jarts taken over the Redoubt?" Rasp asked. The image did not answer, so Olmy echoed the question.

"They are alone in the Redoubt. That is sufficient. I can describe the situation as it will be when you arrive. There is a large groove or valley in the Way, with the Redoubt forming a series of bands of intensely ranked probabilities within the groove. The Redoubt has grown to immense proportions, in time, all possibilities realized. My prior self has lived more than any cardinal number of lives. Still lives them. It sheds us as you shed skin."

"Tell us about the gate," Karn requested, sidling closer to the visitor. "What's happened? What state is it in?" Again, Olmy relayed the question. The woman watched him with discomforting intensity.

"It has become those who opened it. There is an immense head of Issa Danna on the western boundary of the gate, watching over the land. We do not know what it does, what it means."

Plass made a small choking sound and covered her mouth with her hand, eyes wide.

"Some tried to escape. It made them into living mountains, carpeted with fingers, or forests filled with fog and clinging blue shadow. Some waft through the air as vapors that change whoever encounters them.

We've learned. We don't go outside, none for thousands of years . . ."

Rasp and Karn flanked the visitor, studying her with catlike focus.

"Then how can you leave, return to us?" Olmy asked.

The young woman frowned and held up her hands. "It doesn't speak. It doesn't know. I am so lonely."

Plass, Rasp and Karn, and Olmy stood facing each other through clear air.

Olmy started, suddenly drawn back to the last time he had seen a ghost vanish—the partial of Neya Taur Rinn.

Plass let out her breath with a shudder. "It is always the same," she said. "My husband says he's lonely. He's going to find a place where he won't be lonely. But there are no such places!"

Karn turned to Rasp. "A false vision, a deception?" she asked her twin.

"There are no deceptions where we are going," Plass said, and relaxed her hands, rubbed them.

Karn made a face out of her sight.

"NO ONE KNOWS WHAT HAPPENED TO THE GATE OPENED AT THE REDOUBT," Rasp said, turning away from her own session with the records. Since the appearance of the female specter, they had spent most of their time in the pilot cabin. Olmy's presence seemed to afford them some comfort. "None of the masters can even guess."

Karn sighed, whether in sympathy or shame, Olmy could not tell.

"Can either of you make a guess?" Olmy asked.

Plass floated at the front of the common space, just around the pale violet bulkhead, arms folded, looking not very hopeful.

"A gate is opened on the floor of the Way," Rasp said flatly, as if reciting an elementary lesson. "That is a constraint in the local continuum of the Way. Four point gates are possible in each ring position. When four are opened, they are supposed to always cling to the wall of the Way. In practice, however, small gates have been known to rise above the floor. They are always closed immediately."

"What's that got to do with my question?" Olmy asked.

"Oh, nothing, really!" Rasp said, waving her hand in exasperation.

"Perhaps it does," Karn said, playing the role of thoughtful one for the moment. "Perhaps it's deeply connected.".

"Oh, all right, then," Rasp said, and squinched up her face. "What I might have been implying is this: if Issa Danna's gate somehow lifted free of the floor, the wall of the Way, then its constraints would have changed. A free gate can adversely affect local world-lines. Something can enter and leave from any angle. In conditioning we are made to understand that the world-lines of all transported objects passing through such a free gate actually shiver for several years backward. Waves of probability retrograde."

"How many actually went through the gate?" Olmy asked.

"My husband never did," Plass said, pulling herself into the hatchway. "Issa Danna and his entourage. Maybe others, after the lesion formed . . . against their will."

"But you didn't recognize this woman," Olmy said.

"No," Plass said

"Was she extinguished when the gate became a lesion?" Olmy continued. "Was her world-line wiped clean in our domain?"

"My head hurts," Rasp said.

"I think you might be right," Karn said thoughtfully. "It makes sense, in a frightening sort of way. She is suspended . . . we have no record of her existence."

"But the line still exists," Rasp said. "It echoes back in time even in places where her record has ended."

"No," Plass said, shaking her head.

"Why?" Rasp asked.

"She mentioned an *allthing*."

"I didn't hear that," Rasp said.

"Neither did I," Olmy said.

Plass gripped her elbow and squeezed her arms tight around her, pulling her shoulder forward. "We heard different words." She pointed at Olmy. "He's the only one she really saw."

"It looked at you, too," Rasp said. "Just once."

"An allthing was an ancient Nordic governmental meeting," Olmy said, reading from the flawship command entry display, where he had called for a definition.

"That's not what she meant," Plass said. "My husband used another phrase in the same way. He referred to the Final Mind of the domain. Maybe they mean the same thing."

"It was just an echo," Rasp said. "We all heard it differently. We all interacted with it differently depending on . . . whatever. That means more than likely it carried random information from a future we'll never reach. It's a ghost that babbles . . . like your husband, perhaps."

Plass stared at the twins, then grabbed for the hatch frame. She stubbornly shook her head. "We're going to hear more about this allthing," she said. "Deirdre Enoch is still working. Something is still happening there. The Redoubt still exists."

"Your husband told you this?" Rasp asked with a taunting smile. Olmy frowned at her, but she ignored him.

"We'll know when we see our own ghosts," Plass said, with a kick that sent her flying back to her cabin.

PLASS CALMLY READ HER BIBLE IN THE COMMON AREA AS THE SHIP PREPARED a meal for her. The twins ate on their own schedule, but Olmy matched his meals to Plass's, for the simple reason that he liked to talk to the woman, and did not feel comfortable around the twins.

There was about Plass the air of a spent force, something falling near the end of its arc from a truly high and noble trajectory. Plass seemed to enjoy his company, but did not comment on it. She asked about his experiences on Lamarckia.

"It was a beautiful world," he said. "The most beautiful I've ever seen."

"It no longer exists, does it?" Plass said.

"Not as I knew it. It adapted the ways of chlorophyll. Now it's something quite different, and at any rate, the gate there has collapsed. . . . No one in the Way will ever go there again."

"A shame," Plass said. "It seems a great tragedy of being mortal that we can't go back. My husband, on the other hand . . . has visited me seven times since I left the Redoubt." She smiled. "Is it wrong for me to take pleasure in his visits? He isn't happy—but I'm happier when I can see him, listen to him." She looked away, hunched her shoulders as if expecting a blow. "He doesn't, can't, listen to me."

Olmy nodded. What did not make sense could at least be politely acknowledged.

"In the Redoubt, he says, nothing is lost. I wonder how he knows? Is he there? Does he watch over them? The tragedy of uncontrolled order is that the past is revised—and revisited—as easily as the future. The last time he returned, he was in great pain. He said a new God had cursed him for being a counterrevolutionary. The Final Mind. He told me that the Eye of the Watcher tracked him throughout all eternity, on all world-lines, and whenever he tried to stand still, he was tortured, made into something different." Plass's face took on a shiny, almost sensual expectancy and she watched Olmy's reaction closely.

"You denied what the twins were saying," Olmy reminded her. "About echoes along world-lines."

"They aren't just *echoes*. We *are* our world-lines, Ser Olmy. These ghosts . . . are really just altered versions of the originals. They have blurred origins. They come from many different futures. But they have a reality, an independence. I feel this . . . when he speaks to me."

Olmy frowned. "I can't visualize all this. Order is supposed to be simplicity and peace . . . not torture and distortion and coercion. Surely a universe of complete order would be more like heaven, in the Christian sense." He pointed to the antique book resting lightly in her lap. Plass shifted and the Bible rose into the air a few centimeters. She reached out to grasp it, hold it close again.

"Heaven has no change, no death," she said. "Mortals find that attractive, but they are mistaken. No good thing lasts forever. It becomes unbearable. Now imagine a force that demands that something last forever, yet become even more the essence of what it was, a force that will accept nothing less than compliance, but *can't communicate*."

Olmy shook his head. "I can't."

"I can't, either, but that is what my husband describes."

Several seconds. Plass tapped the book lightly with her finger.

"How long since he last visited you?" Olmy asked.

"Three weeks. Maybe longer. Things seemed quiet just before they told me I could return to the Redoubt." She closed her eyes and held her hands to her cheeks. "I believed what Enoch believed, that order ascends. That it ascends forever. I believed that we are made with flaws, in a universe that was itself born flawed. I thought we would be so much more beautiful when—"

Karn and Rasp tracted forward and hovered beside Plass, who fell quiet and greeted them with a small shiver.

"We have ventured a possible answer to this dilemma," Karn said.

"Our birth geometry, outside the Way, is determined by a vacuum of infinite potential," Rasp said, nodding with something like glee. "We are forbidden from tapping that energy, so in our domain, space has a shape, and time has direction and a velocity. In the universe Enoch tapped, the energy of the vacuum is available at all times. Time and space and this energy, this potential, are bunched in a tight little knot of incredible density. That is what your husband must call the Final Mind. That our visitor re-named the allthing."

Plass shook her head indifferently.

"How amazing that must be!" Karn said. "A universe where order took hold in the first few nanoseconds after creation, controlling all the fires of the initial expansion, all the shape and constants of existence . . ."

"I wonder what Enoch would have done with such a domain, if she could have controlled it," Rasp said, hovering over Plass, peering down on her. Plass made as if to swat a fly, and Rasp tracted out of reach with a broad smile. "Ours is a pale candle indeed by comparison."

"EVERYTHING MUST TEND TOWARD A FINAL MIND. THIS FORCE BLOSSOMS AT the end of Time like a flower pushed up from all events, all lives, all thought.

It is the ancestor not just of living creatures, but of all the interactions of matter, space, and time, for all things tend toward this blossom."

Olmy had often thought about this quote from the notes of Korzen-owski. The designer of the Way had put together quite an original cos-mology, which he had never tried to spread among his fellows. The original was in Korzenowski's library, kept as a Public Treasure, but few visited there now.

Olmy visited Rasp and Karn in their cabin while Plass read her Bible in the common area. The twins had arranged projections of geometric art and mathematical figures around the space, brightly colored and disorienting. He asked them whether they believed such an allthing, a perfectly ordered mind, could exist.

"Goodness, no!" Karn said, giggling.

"You mean, *Godness*, no!" Rasp added. "Not even if we believed in it, which we don't. Energy and impulse, yes; final, perhaps. Mind, no!"

"Whatever you call it—in the lesion, it may already exist, and it's different?"

"Of course it would exist! Not as a mind, that's all. Mind is impossible without neural qualities—communication between separate nodes that either contradict or confirm. If we think correctly, a domain of order would reach completion within the first few seconds of existence, freez-ing everything. It would grasp and control all the energy of its beginning moment, work through all possible variations in an instant—become a monobloc, still and perfected, timeless. Not eternal—eviternal, frozen forever. Timeless."

"Our universe, our domain, could spin on for many billions or even trillions more years," Karn continued. "In our universe, there could very well be a Final Mind, the summing up of all neural processes throughout all time. But Deirdre Enoch found an abomination. If it were a mind, think of it! Instantly creating all things, never being contradicted, neve*r knowing*. Nothing has ever frustrated it, stopped it, trained or tamed it. It would be as immature as a newborn baby, and as sophisticated—"

"And ingenious," Rasp chimed in.

"—As the very devil," Karn finished.

"Please," Rasp finished, her voice suddenly quiet. "Even it such a thing is possible, let it not be a mind."

FOR THE PAST MILLION KILOMETERS, THEY HAD PASSED OVER A SCOURGED, scrubbed segment of the Way. In driving back the Jarts from their strongholds, tens of thousands of Way defenders had died. The Way had been altered by the released energies of the battle and still glowed slightly, shot through with pulsing curls and rays, while the flaw in this region transported them with a barely noticeable roughness. The flaw-ship could compensate some, but even with this compensation, they had reduced their speed to a few thousand kilometers an hour.

The Redoubt lay less than ten thousand kilometers ahead.

Rasp and Karn removed their clavicles from their boxes and tried as best they could to interpret the state of the Way as they came closer to the Redoubt.

Five thousand kilometers from the Redoubt, evidence of immense constructions lined the wall of the Way: highways, bands connecting what might have been linked gates; yet there were no gates. The con-structions had been leveled to thin lanes of rubble, like lines of powder.

Olmy shook his head, dismayed. "Nothing is the way it was reported to be just a few weeks ago."

"I detect something unusual, too," Rasp said. Karn agreed. "Some-thing related to the Jart offensive . . ."

"Something we weren't told about?" Plass wondered. "A colony that failed?"

"Ours, or Jart?" Olmy asked.

"Neither," Karn said, looking up from her clavicle. She lifted the de-vice, a small fist-sized sphere mounted on two handles, and rotated the display for Olmy and Plass to see. Olmy had watched gate openers per-form before, and knew the workings of the display well enough—though he could never operate a clavicle. "There have never been gates opened here. This is all sham."

"A decoy," Plass said.

"Worse," Rasp said. "The gate at the Redoubt is twisting probabilities, sweeping world-lines within the Way to such an extreme. . . . The res-idue of realities that never were are being deposited."

"Murmurs in the Way's sleep, nightmares in our unhistory," Karn said. For once, the twins seemed completely subdued, even disturbed. "I don't see how we can function if we're incorporated into such a sweep."

"So what is this?" Olmy asked, pointing to the smears of destroyed highways, cities, bands between the ghosts of gates.

"A future," Karn said. "Maybe what will happen if we fail . . ."

"But these patterns aren't like human construction," Plass observed. "No human city planner would lay out those roadways. Nor does it match anything we know about the Jarts."

Olmy looked more closely, frowned in concentration. "If someone else had created the Way," he said, "maybe this would be their ruins, the rubble of their failure."

Karn gave a nervous laugh. "Wonderful!" she said. "All we could have hoped for! If we open a gate here, what could possibly happen?"

Plass grabbed Olmy's arm. "Put it in our transmitted record. Tell the Hexamon this part of the Way must be forbidden. *No gates should be opened here, ever!*"

"Why not?" Karn said. "Think what could be learned. The new domains."

"I agree with Ser Plass," Rasp said. "It's possible there are worse alternatives than finding a universe of pure order." She let go of her clavicle and grabbed her head. "Even touching our instruments here causes pain. We are useless . . . any gate we open would consume us more quickly than the gate at the Redoubt! You *must* agree, sister!"

Karn was stubborn. "I don't see it," she said. "I simply don't. I think this could be very interesting. Fascinating, even."

Plass sighed. "This is the box that Konrad Korzenowski has opened for us," she said for Olmy's benefit. "Spoiled genius children drawn to evil like insects to a corpse."

"I thought evil was related to disorder," Olmy said.

"Already, you know better," Plass rejoined.

Rasp turned her eyes on Olmy and Plass, eyes narrow and full of uncomfortable speculation.

Olmy reached out and grasped Rasp's clavicle to keep it from bumping into the flawship bulkheads. Karn took charge of the instrument indignantly and thrust it back at her sister. "You forget your responsibility," she chided. "We can fear this mission, or we can engage it with joy and spirit," she said. "Cowering does none of us any good."

"You're right, sister, about that at least," Rasp said. She returned her clavicle to its box and straightened her clothing, then used a cloth to wipe her face. "We are, after all, going to a place where we have always gone, always will go."

"It's what happens when we get there that is always changing," Karn said.

Plass's face went white. "My husband never returns the same way, in the same condition," she said. "How many hells does he experience?"

"One for each of him," Rasp said. "Only one. It is different husbands who return."

THOUGH THERE HAD NEVER BEEN SUCH THIS FAR ALONG THE WAY, OLMY SAW the scattered wreckage of Jart fortifications, demolished, dead, and empty. Beyond them lay a region where the Way was covered with winding black and red bands of sand, an immense serpentine desert; also unknown. Olmy felt a spark of something reviving, if not a wish for life, then an appreciation of what extraordinary sights his life had brought him.

On Lamarckia, he had seen the most extraordinary variations on biology. Here, near the Redoubt, it was reality itself subject to its own flux, its own denial.

Plass was transfixed. "The next visitors, if any, will see something completely different," she said. "We've been caught up in a sweeping world-line of the Way, not necessarily our own."

"I would never have believed it possible," Rasp said, and Karn reluctantly agreed. "This is not the physics we were taught."

"It can make any physics it wishes," Plass said. "Any reality. It has all the energy it needs. It has human minds to teach it our variations."

"It knows only unity," Karn said, taking hold of Plass's shoulder.

The older woman did not seem to mind. "It knows no will stronger than its own," she said. "Yet it may divide its will into illusory units. It is a tyrant . . ." Plass pointed to the winding sands, stretching for thousands of kilometers beneath them. "This is a moment of calm, of steady concentration. If my memories are correct, if what my husband's returning self . . . selves . . . tell me, is correct, it is usually much more frantic. Much more inventive."

Karn made a face and placed her hands on the bars of her clavicle. She rubbed the grips and her face became tight with concentration. "I feel it. There is still a lesion . . ."

Rasp took hold of her own instrument and went into her own state. "It's still there," she agreed,. "It's bad. It floats above the Way, very near the flaw. From below, it must look like some sort of bale star . . ."

They passed through a fine bluish mist that rose from the northern end of the desert. The flawship made a faint belling sound. The mist passed behind.

"There," Plass said. "No mistaking it!"

The gate pushed through the Way by Issa Danna had expanded and risen above the floor, just as the Rasp and Karn had felt in their instruments. Now, at a distance of a hundred kilometers, they could see the spherical lesion clearly. It did indeed resemble a dark sun, or a chancre. A glow of pigeon's blood flicked around it, the red of rubies and enchantment. The black center, less than the width of a fingertip at this distance, perversely seemed to fill Olmy's field of vision.

His young body decided it was time to be very reluctant to proceed. He swallowed and brought this fear under control, biting his cheek until blood flowed.

The flawship lurched. It's voice told Olmy, "We have received an instructional beacon. There is a place held by humans less than ten kilometers away. They say they will guide us to safety."

"It's still there!" Plass said.

They all looked down through the flawship's transparent nose, away from the lurid pink of the flaw, through layers of blue and green haze wrapped around the Way, down twenty-five kilometers to a single dark, gleaming steel point in the center of a rough, rolling land.

The Redoubt lay in the shadow of the lesion, surrounded by a penumbral twilight suffused with the flickering red of the lesion's halo.

"I can feel the whipping hairs of other world-lines," Karn and Rasp said together. Olmy glanced back and saw their clavicles touching sphere to sphere. The spheres crackled and clacked. Karn twisted her instrument toward Olmy so that he could see the display. A long list of domain "constants"—pi, Planck's constant, others—varied with a regular humming in the flawship hull. "Nothing is stable out there!"

Olmy glanced at the message sent from the Redoubt. It provided navigation instructions for their flawship's landing craft; how to disengage from the flawship, descend, undergo examination, and be taken into the pyramid. The message concluded, "We will determine whether you are illusions or aberrations. If you are from our origin, we will welcome you. It is too late to return now. Abandon your flawship before it approaches any closer to the allthing. Whoever sent you has committed you to our own endless imprisonment."

"Cheerful enough," Olmy said. The ghastly light cast a fitful, abbatoir glow on their faces.

"We have always gone there," Rasp said quietly.

"We have to agree," Plass said. "We have no other place to go."

They tracted aft to the lander's hatch and climbed into the small, arrowhead-shaped craft. Its interior welcomed them by fitting to their forms, providing couches, instruments, tailored to their bodies. Plass sat beside Olmy in the cockpit, Rasp and Karn directly behind them.

Olmy disengaged from the flawship and locked the lander onto the pyramid's beacon. They dropped from the flawship. The landscape steadily grew in the broad cockpit window.

Plass's face crumpled, like a child about to break into tears. "Star, fate and pneuma, be kind. I see the opener's head. There!" She pointed in helpless dread, equally horrified and fascinated by something so inconceivable.

On a low, broad rise in the shadowed land surrounding the Redoubt, a huge dark head rose like an upright mountain, its skin like gray stone, one eye turned toward the south, the other watching over the territory before the nearest face of the pyramid. This watchful eye was easily a hundred meters wide, and glowed a dismal sea-green, throwing a long beam through the thick twisted ropes of mist. Plass's voice became shrill. "Oh, Star and Fate . . ."

The landscape around the Redoubt rippled beneath the swirling rays of rotating world-lines, spreading like hair from the black center of the lesion, changing the land a little with each pass, moving the bizarre landmarks a few dozen meters this way or that, increasing them in size, reducing them.

Olmy could never have imagined such a place. The Redoubt sat within a child's nightmare of disembodied human limbs, painted over the hills like trees, their fingers grasping and releasing spasmodically. At the top of one hill stood a kind of castle made of blocks of green glass, with a single huge door and window. Within the door stood a figure—a statue, perhaps—several hundred meters high, vaguely human, nodding its head steadily, idiotically, as the lander passed over. Hundreds of much smaller figures, gigantic nevertheless, milled in a kind of yard before the castle, their red and black shadows flowing like capes in the lee of the constant wind of changing probabilities. Olmy thought they might be huge dogs, or tailless lizards, but Plass pointed and said, "My husband told me about an assistant to Issa Danna named Ram Chako. . . . Duplicated, forced to run on all fours."

The giant in the castle door slowly raised its huge hand, and the massive lizards scrambled over each other to run from an open portal in the yard. They leaped up as the lander passed overhead, as if they would snap it out of the air with hideous jaws.

Olmy's head throbbed. He could not bring himself out of a conviction that none of this could be real; indeed, there was no necessity for it to *be* real in any sense his body understood. For their part, Rasp and Karn had lost all their earlier bravado and clung to each other, their clavicles floating on tethers wrapped around their wrists.

The lurid glare of the halo flowed like blood into the cabin as the lander rotated to present points of contact for traction fields from the Redoubt. Olmy instructed the ship to present a wide-angle view of the Redoubt and the land, and this view revolved slowly around them, filling the lander's cramped interior.

The perverse variety seemed to never end. Something had dissected not only a human body, or many bodies, and wreaked hideous distortions on its parts, but had done the same with human thoughts and desires, planting the results over the region with no obvious design.

Within the low valley—as described by the female visitant—a large blue-skinned woman, the equal of the figure in the doorway of the castle, crouched near a cradle within which churned hundreds of naked humans. She slowly dropped her hand into the cauldron of flesh and stirred, and her hair sprayed out from her head with a sullen cometary glow, casting everything in a syrupy green luminosity.

"Mother of geometries," Karn muttered, and hid her eyes.

Olmy could not turn away, but everything in him wanted to go to sleep, to die, rather than to acknowledge what they were seeing.

Plass saw his distress. Somehow she took strength from the incomprehensible view. "It does not need to make sense," she said with the tone of a chiding schoolteacher. "It's supported by infinite energy and a monolithic, mindless will. There is nothing new here, nothing—"

"I'm not asking that it make sense," Olmy said. "I need to know what's behind it."

"A sufficient force, channeled properly, can create anything a mind can imagine—" Karn began.

"More than any mind will imagine. Not a mind like our minds," Rasp restated. "A unity, not a *mind* at all."

For a moment, Olmy's anger lashed and he wanted to shout his frustration, but he took a deep breath, folded his arms where he floated in tracting restraints, and said to Plass, "A mind that has no goals? If there's pure order here—"

Karn broke in, her voice high and sweet, singing. "Think of the dimensions of order. There is mere arrangement, the lowest form of order, without motive or direction. Next comes self-making, when order can convert resources into more of itself, propagating order. Then comes creation, self-making reshaping matter into something new. But when creation stalls, when there is no mind, just force, it becomes mere elaboration, an endless spiral of rearrangement of what has been created. What do we see down there? Empty elaboration. Nothing new. No understanding."

"She shows some wisdom," Plass acknowledged grudgingly. "But the allthing still must exist."

"And all this . . . elaboration?" Olmy asked.

"Spoiled by deathlessness," Plass said, "by never-ending supplies of resources. Never freshened by the new, at its core. Order without death, art without critic or renewal, the final mind of a universe where only riches exist, only joy is possible, never knowing disappointment."

The lander shuddered again and again as they dropped toward the pyramid. Its inertial control systems could not cope with the sweeping rays of different world-lines.

"Sounds like a spoiled child," Olmy said.

"Far worse," Karn said. "*We're* like spoiled children, Rasp and I. Willful and maybe a little silly. Humans are silly, childish, always learning, full of failure. Out there—beyond the lesion, reaching through it . . ."

"Perpetual success," Rasp mocked. "Ultimate maturity. It cannot learn. Only rearrange."

"Deirdre Enoch was never content with limitations," Plass said, looking to Olmy for sympathy. "She went searching for what heaven would really be. Her eyes glittered with her emotion—exaltation brought on by too much fear and dismay.

"Maybe she found it," Karn said.

5

"I can't welcome you," Deirdre Enoch said, walking heavily toward them. Behind Olmy, within a chamber high in the Redoubt, near the tip of the steel pyramid, the lander sighed and settled into its cradle.

Olmy tried to compare this old woman with the portraits of Enoch in the records. Her voice was much the same, though deeper, and almost without emotion.

Rasp, Karn, and Plass stood beside Olmy as Enoch approached. Behind Enoch, in the lambency of soft amber lights spaced around the base of the chamber, wavered a line of ten other men and women, all of them old, all dressed in black, with silver ribbons hanging from the tops of their white-haired heads. "You've come to a place of waiting where nothing is resolved. Why come at all?"

Before Olmy could answer, Enoch smiled, her deeply wrinkled face seeming to crack with the unfamiliar expression. "We assume you are here because you think the Jarts could become involved."

"I don't know what to think," Olmy said, his voice hoarse. "I recognize you, but none of the others . . ."

"We survived the first night after the lesion. We formed an expedition to make an escape attempt. There were sixty of us that first time. We managed to return to the Redoubt before the Night Land could change us too much, play with us too drastically. We aged. Some of us were taken and . . . you see them out there. There was no second expedition."

"My husband," Plass said. "Where is he?"

"Yes . . . I know you. You are so much the same it hurts. You escaped at the very beginning."

"I was the only one," Plass said.

"You called it the Night Land," Rasp said, holding up her hands, the case with her clavicle. "How appropriate."

"No sun, no hope, only *order*," Enoch said, as if the word were a curse. "Did you send yourselves, or were you sent by other fools?"

"Fools, I'm afraid," Plass said.

"And you . . . you came back, knowing what you'd find?"

"It wasn't like this when I left. My husband sent ghosts to visit me. They told me a little of what's happened here . . . or might have happened."

"Ghosts try to come into the Redoubt and talk," Enoch said, her many legs shifting restlessly. "We refuse them. Your husband was caught outside that first night. He hasn't been changed much. He stands near the Watcher, frozen in the eyebeam."

Plass sobbed and hid her face.

Enoch continued, heedless. "The only thing left in his control—to shed ghosts like dead skin. And never the same . . . are they? He's allowed to take temporary twists of space-time and shape them in his own image. The allthing finds this sufficiently amusing. Needless to say, we don't let the ghosts bother us. We have too much else to do, just to keep our place secure, and in repair."

"Repair," Karn said with a beatific smile, and Olmy turned to her, startled by a reaction similar to his own. Karn did a small dance. "Disorder has its place here, then. You have to *work* to *fix things?*"

"Precisely," Enoch said. "I worship rust and age. But we're only allowed so much of it and no more. Now that you're here, perhaps you'll join us for some tea?" She smiled. "Blessedly, our tea cools quickly in the Redoubt. Our bones grow frail, our skin wrinkles. Tea cools. Hurry!"

"DON'T BE DECEIVED BY OUR BODIES," DEIRDRE ENOCH SAID AS SHE POURED steaming tea into cups for all her guests. "They are distorted, but they are sufficient. The *allthing* can only perfect and elaborate; it knows nothing of real destruction."

Olmy watched something ripple through the old woman, a shudder of slight change. She seemed not as old and wrinkled now, as if some force had turned back a clock.

"I'm not clear about perfection," Olmy said, lifting the cup without enthusiasm. "I'm not even clear on how you come to look old."

"We're not unhappy," Enoch said. "That isn't within our power. We know we can never return to Thistledown. We know we can never escape."

"You haven't answered Ser Olmy's question," Plass said gently. "Are you independent here?"

"That wasn't his question, Ser Gena Plass," Enoch said, an edge in her voice. "What you ask is not a *polite* question. I said, we were caught trying to escape. Some of us are out there in the Night Land now. Those of us who returned to the pyramid . . . did not escape the enthusiasm of the allthing. But it's influence here is limited. To answer one question at least: We have some independence." Enoch nodded as if falling asleep, her head dropping briefly to an angle with her shoulders . . . an uncomfortable angle, Olmy would have thought. She raised it again with a jerk. "The universe I discovered . . . there is nothing else. It is all."

"The Final Mind of the domain," Plass said.

"I gather it regards the Way and the humans it finds here as objects of curiosity," Olmy said. Rasp and Karn fidgeted.

"Objects to be recombined and distorted," Enoch said. "We are materials for the ultimate in decadent art. The allthing is beyond our knowing." She leaned forward on her cushion, where she had gracefully folded her legs into an agile lotus, and rubbed her nose reflectively with the back of one hand. "We are allowed to resist, I suspect, because we are antithesis."

"The *allthing* has only known thesis," Rasp said with a small giggle.

"Exa-*a-a*-ctly," Enoch said, drawing out the word with pleasure. Struck by another sensation of unreality, Olmy looked around the group sitting with Enoch and himself: Plass, the twins, a small woman with a questing, feline expression behind Enoch who had said nothing. She carried the teapot around again and refilled their cups.

The tea was cold.

Olmy turned on his sitting pillow to observe the other elderly followers, arrayed around the circular room, still, subservient. Their faces had changed since his arrival, yet no one had left, no one had entered.

It had been observed for a dozen generations that Thistledown's environment and culture bred followers with proportionately fewer leaders, often assigned much greater power. Efforts were being made to remedy that—to reduce the extreme schisms of rogues such as Deirdre Enoch. *Too late for these*, he thought. *Does this allthing want followers?*

He could not get his bearings long enough to plan his course of action. He felt drugged, but knew he wasn't.

"Can it tolerate otherness?" Karn asked, her voice high and sweet once more, like a child's.

"No," Enoch said. "Its nature is to absorb and disguise all otherness in mutation, change without goal."

"Like the Jarts?" Rasp asked, chewing on her thumb with a coyness and insecurity that was at once studied and completely convincing.

"Not like the Jarts. The Jarts met the allthing and it gave them their own Night Land. I fear it won't be long until ours is merged with theirs, and we are both mingled and subjected to further useless change."

"How long?" Olmy asked.

"Another few years, perhaps."

"Not so soon, then," he said.

"Soon enough," Enoch said with a sniff. She rubbed her nose again. "We've been here already for well over thousand centuries."

Olmy tried to understand this. "Truly?" he asked, expecting her to break into laughter.

"Truly. I've had millions of different followers here. Look around you." She leaned over the table to whisper to Olmy, "Waves in a sea. I've lived a thousand centuries in a thousand infinitesimally different universes. It plays with all world-lines, not just the tracks of individuals. Only I am relatively the same with each tide. I appear to be the real nexus in this part of the Way."

"Tea cools . . . skin wrinkles . . . but you experience such a length of time?"

"Ten thousand lengths cut up and bundled and rotated." She took a scarf from around her thin neck and stretched it between her firsts. "Twisted. Knotted. You were sent here to correct the reckless madness of a renegade . . . weren't you?"

"A Geshel visionary," Olmy said.

Enoch was not mollified. She drew herself up and returned her scarf to her neck, tying it with a conscious flourish. "I was appointed by the Office of Way Maintenance by Ry Ornis himself. They gave me two of the best gate openers in the guild, and they instructed me, specifically, to find a gate into total order. I wasn't told why. I can guess now, however."

"I remember two openers," Plass said. "They don't."

"They hoped you would find me transformed or dead," Enoch said. "Well, I'm different, but I've survived, and after a few thousands of centuries, one's personality becomes rather rigid. I've become more like that Watcher and its huge gaping eye outside. I don't know how to lie any more. I've seen too much. I've fought against what I found, and I've endured atrocities beyond what any human has ever had to face. Believe me, I would rather have died before my mission began than see what I've seen."

"Where is the other opener?" Olmy asked.

"In the Night Land," Enoch said. "Issa Danna was the first to encounter the *allthing*. He and his partner, master Tolby Kin, took the brunt of its first efforts at elaboration."

Rasp walked over to Olmy and whispered in his ear. "There never was a master opener named Tolby Kin."

"Can anybody else confirm your story?" Olmy asked.

"Would you believe anyone here? No," Enoch said.

"Not that it matters," Plass said fatalistically. "The end result is the same."

"Not at all," Enoch said. "We couldn't close down the lesion now even if we had it in our power. Ry Ornis was correct. The rift had to be opened. The infection is not finished. If we don't wait for completion, our universe will never quicken. It'll be born dead." Enoch shook her head and laughed softly. "And no human in our history will ever see a ghost. A haunted world is a living world, Ser Olmy."

Olmy touched his tea cup with his finger. The tea was hot again.

THE LIVING QUARTERS MADE AVAILABLE WERE SPARE AND COLD. MOST OF the Redoubt's energy went to keeping the occupants of the Night Land at bay; that energy was derived from the wall of the Way, an ingenious arrangement set up by Issa Danna before he was caught up in the lesion; sufficient, but not a surfeit by any means.

For the first time in days, Olmy had a few moments alone. He cleared a window looking south, toward the lesion and across about fifty kilometers of the Night Land. Enoch had provided him with a pair of ray-tracing binoculars.

Beyond a tracting grid stretched to its limits, and a glowing demarcation of complete nuclear destruction, through which nothing made of matter could hope to cross, less than a thousand meters from the pyramid, lay the peculiar vivid darkness and the fitful nightmare glows of the allthing's victims.

Olmy swung the light-weight binoculars in a slow steady arc. What looked like hills or low mountains were constructions attended by hundreds of pale figures, human-sized but only vaguely human in shape. They seemed to spend much of their time fighting, waving their limbs about like insect antennae. Others carried loads of glowing dust in baskets, dumping them at the top of a hill, then stumbling and sliding down to begin again.

The giant head modeled after the opener stood a little to the west of the Green Glass Castle. Olmy could not tell whether the head was actually organic material—human flesh—or not. It looked more like stone, though the eye was very expressive.

From this angle, he could not see the huge figure standing in the door of the castle; that side was turned away from the Redoubt. Nothing that he saw contradicted what Plass and Enoch had told him. He could not share the cheerful nihilism of the twins. Nevertheless, nothing that he saw could be fit into any philosophy or web of physical laws he had ever encountered. If there was a mind here, it was incomprehensibly different—perhaps no mind at all.

Still, he tried to find some pattern, some plan to the Night Land. A rationale. He could not.

Just before the tallest hills stood growths like the tangled roots of upended trees, leafless, barren, dozens of meters high and stretching in ugly, twisted forests several kilometers across. A kind of pathway reached from the northern wall of the Redoubt, through the demarcation, into a tortured terrain of what looked like huge strands of melted and drawn glass, and to the east of the castle. It dropped over a closer hill and he could not see where it terminated.

The atmosphere around the Redoubt was remarkably clear, though columns of twisted mist rose around the Night Land. Before a wall of blue haze at some fifty kilometers distance, everything stood out with complete clarity.

Olmy turned away at a knock on his door. Plass entered, wearing a look of contentment that seemed ready to burst into enthusiasm. "Now do you doubt me?"

"I doubt everything," Olmy said. "I'd just as soon believe we've been captured and are being fed delusions."

"Do you think that's what's happened?" Plass asked, eyes narrowing as if she had been insulted.

"No," Olmy said. "I've experienced some pretty good delusions in training. This is real, whatever that means."

"I must admit the little twins are busy," Plass said, sitting on a small chair near the table. These and a small mattress on the floor were the only items of furniture in the room. "They're talking to anybody who knows anything about Enoch's gate openers. I don't think you can talk to the same person twice here in an hour—unless it's Enoch."

Olmy nodded. He was still digesting Enoch's claim that the Office of Way Maintenance had sent an expedition with secret orders. . . . In collusion with the opener's guild.

Perhaps the twins knew more than he did, or Plass. "Did you know anything about an official mission?" he asked.

Plass did not answer for a moment. "Not in so many words. Not 'official.' But perhaps not without . . . support from Way Maintenance. We did not think we were outlaws."

"You've both talked about completion. Was that mentioned when you joined the group?"

"Only in passing. A theory."

Olmy turned back to the window. "There's a camera obscura near the top of the pyramid. I'd like to look over everything around us, try to make sense of our position."

"Useless," Plass said. "I'd wait for a visitation first."

"More ghosts?"

Plass shrugged her shoulders and stretched out her legs, rubbing her knees.

"I haven't been visited," Olmy said.

"It will happen," Plass said flatly. She appeared to be hiding something, something that worried her. "I wouldn't look forward to it. But then, there's nothing you can do to prepare."

Olmy laughed, but the laugh sounded hollow. He felt as if he were slowly coming unraveled, like Enoch's bundle of relived world-lines. "How would I know if I've seen a ghost?" he asked. "Maybe I have— on Thistledown. Maybe they're around us all the time, but don't reveal themselves."

Plass looked to one side, then said, with an effort, her voice half-choking, "I've met my own ghost."

"You didn't mention that before."

"It came to visit me the night after we left Thistledown. It told me we would reach the pyramid."

Olmy held back another laugh, afraid it might get loose and never stop. "I've never seen a ghost of myself."

"We do things differently, then. I seemed to be working backward from some experience with the allthing. A ghost lets you remember the future, or some alternate of the future. Maybe in time I'll be told what the allthing will do to me. Its elaborations."

Olmy considered this in silence. Plass's somber gray eyes focused on him, clear, child-like in their perfect gravity. Now he saw the resemblance, the reason why he felt a tug of liking for her. She reminded him of Sheila Ap Nam, his first wife on Lamarckia.

"Your loved ones, friends, colleagues. . . . They will see you, versions of you, if you meet the allthing." Plass said. "A kind of immortality. Remembrance." She looked down and clutched her arms. "No other intelligent species we've encountered has a history of myths about spirits. No experience with ghosts. You know that? We're unique. Alone. Except perhaps the Jarts . . . and we don't know much about them, do we?"

He nodded, wanting to get rid of the topic. "What are the twins planning?"

"They seem to regard this as a challenging game. Who knows? They're working. It's even possible they'll think of something."

Olmy aimed the binoculars toward the Watcher, its single glowing eye forever turned toward the Redoubt. He felt a bone-deep revulsion and hatred, mixed with a desiccating chill. His tongue seemed frosted. Perversely, the flesh behind his eyes felt hot and moist. His neck hair pricked.

"There's—" he began, but then flinched and blinked. A curtain of shadow passed through the few centimeters between him and the window. He backed off with a groan and tried to push something away, but the curtain would not be touched. It whirled around him, swept before Plass, who tracked it calmly, and then seemed to press against and slip through the opposite wall.

The warmth behind his eyes felt hot as steam.

"*I knew it!*" he said hoarsely. "I could feel it coming! Something about to happen." His hands trembled. He had never reacted so drastically to physical danger.

"That was nothing," Plass said. "I've seen them many times, more since I first came here."

Olmy's reaction angered him. "What is it?"

"Not a ghost, not any other version of ourselves, that's for sure," she said. "A parasite, maybe, like a flea darting around our world-lines. Harmless, as far as I know. But much more visible here than back on Thistledown."

Trying to control himself was backfiring. All his instincts rejected what he was experiencing. "I don't accept any of this!" he shouted. His hands spasmed into fists. "None of it makes sense!"

"I agree," Plass said, her voice low. "Pity we're stuck with it. Pity you're stuck with me. But more pity that I'm stuck with you. It seems you try to be a rational man, Ser Olmy. My husband was exceptionally rational. The allthing adores rational men."

6

Rasp and Karn walked with Olmy on the parapet near the peak of the Redoubt. Their work seemed to have sobered them. They still walked like youngsters, Karn or Rasp lagging to peer at something in the Night Land and then scurrying to catch up; but their voices were steady, serious, even a little sad.

"We've never experienced anything like the lesion," Karn said. The huge dark disk, rimmed in bands and flares of red, blotted out the opposite side of the Way. "It's much more than just a failed gate. It doesn't stop here, you know."

"How do you mean?" Olmy asked.

"Something like this influences the entire Way. When the gate got out of control—"

Rasp took Karn's hand and tugged it in warning.

"What does it matter?" Karn asked, and shook her twin loose. "There can't be secrets here. If we don't agree to do something, the allthing will get us soon anyway, and then we'll be planted out there . . . bits and pieces of us, like lost toys."

Rasp dropped back a few steps, folded her arms in pique. Karn continued. "When the lesion formed, gate openers felt it in every new gate. Threads trying to get through, like spider-silk. We can see the world-lines being twirled here . . . But they bunch up and wind around the Way even where we can't see them. Master Ry Ornis thought—"

"Enough!" Rasp said, rushing to catch up.

Karn stopped with tears in her eyes and glared over the parapet wall.

"I can guess a few things," Olmy said. "What Deirdre Enoch says leaves little enough to imagine. You aren't failed apprentices, are you?"

Rasp stared at him defiantly.

"No," Karn said.

Her twin turned and lifted a hand as if to strike her, then dropped it by her side. She drew a short breath, said, "We act like children because of the mathematical conditioning. Too fast. Ry Ornis told us we were needed. He accelerated training. We were the best, but we *are* too young. It holds us down."

A sound like hundreds of voices in a bizarre chorus floated over the Night Land, through the field that protected the Redoubt's atmosphere. The chorus alternately rose and sank through scales, hooting forlornly like apes in a zoo.

"Ry Ornis thought the lesion was bending world-lines even beyond Thistledown," Karn said. Rasp nodded and held her sister's hand. "Climbing back along the Thistledown's world-line . . . where all our lives bunch together with the lives of our ancestors. Using us as a ladder."

"Not just us," Rasp added. The hooting chorus now came from all around the Redoubt. From this side of the pyramid, they could see a slender obelisk the colors of bright moon on an oil slick rising within an immense scaffold made of parts of bodies, arms and legs strapped together with cords. These limbs were monstrous, however, fully dozens of meters long, and the obelisk had climbed within its scaffolding to at least a kilometer in height, twice as tall as the Redoubt.

The region around the construction crawled with pale tubular bodies, like insect larva, and Olmy decided it was these bodies that were doing most of the singing and hooting.

"Right," Karn agreed. "Not just us. Using the branching lines of all the matter, all the particles in Thistledown and the Way."

"Who knows how far it's reached?" Rasp asked.

"What can it do?" Olmy asked.

"We don't know," Karn said.

"What can *we* do?"

"Oh, we can close down the lesion, if we act quickly," Rasp said with a broken smile. "That shouldn't be too difficult."

"It's actually growing smaller," Karn said. "We can create a ring gate from here . . . a cirque. Cinch off the Way. The Way will shrink back towards the source, the maintenance machinery in the sixth chamber, very quickly—a million kilometers a day. We might even be able to escape along the flaw, but—"

"The flaw will act weird if we make a cinch," Rasp finished.

"Very weird," Karn agreed. "So we probably won't get home. We knew that. Ry Ornis prepared us. He told us that much."

"Besides, if we did go back to Thistledown, who would want us now, the way we are?" Rasp asked. "We're pretty broken inside."

The twins paused on the parapet. Olmy watched as they clasped hands and began to hum softly to each other. Their clavicles hung from their shoulders, and the cases tapped as they swayed. Rasp glanced at Olmy, primming her lips.

"Enoch spoke of a plan by the Office of Way Maintenance," Olmy said. "She claims she was sent here secretly."

"We know nothing about that," Karn said guilelessly. "But that might not mean much. I don't think they would have trusted us."

"She also said that the allthing has some larger purpose in our own universe," Olmy continued. "Something that has to be completed, or our existence will be impossible."

Karn considered this quietly, finger to her nostril, then shook her head. "We heard her, but I don't see it," she said. "Maybe she's trying to justify herself."

"*We* do that all the time," Rasp said. "We understand that sort of thing."

They had reached the bottom of the stairs leading up to the peak and the camera obscura. Karn climbed two steps at a time, her robe swinging around her ankles, and Rasp followed with more dignity. Olmy stayed near the bottom. Rasp turned and looked down on him.

"Come on," she said, waving.

Olmy shook his head. "I've seen enough. I can't make sense out of anything out there. I think it's random—just nonsense."

"Not at all!" Rasp said, and descended a few steps, beseeching him to join her. "We have to see what happened to the openers' clavicles. What sort of elaboration there might be. It could be very important."

Olmy hunched his shoulders, shook his head like a bull trying to build courage. He followed her up the steps.

The camera obscura was a spherical all-focal lens, its principle not unlike that of the ray-tracing binoculars. Mounted on a tripod on the flat platform at the peak of the pyramid, it projected and magnified the Night Land for anyone standing on the platform. Approaching the tripod increased magnification in logarithmic steps, with precise quickness; distances of a few tenths of a centimeter could make objects zoom to alarming proportions. Monitors on the peripheral circle, small spheres on steel poles, rolled in and out with slow grace, tracking the developments in the Night Land and sending their results down to Enoch and the others inside.

Olmy deftly avoided the monitors and walked slowly, with great concentration, around the circle. Karn and Rasp made their own surveys.

Olmy stopped and drew back to take in the Watcher's immense eye. The angle of the hairless brow, the droop of the upper lid, gave it a sad and corpse-like lassitude, but the eye still moved in small arcs, and from this perspective, there was no doubt it was observing the Redoubt. Olmy felt that it saw him, knew him; had he ever met the opener, before his mission to Lamarckia, perhaps by accident? Was there some residual memory of Olmy in that immense head? Olmy thought such a connection might be very dangerous.

"The Night Land changes every hour, sometimes small changes, sometimes massive," Enoch said, walking slowly and deliberately up the steps behind them. She stopped outside the camera's circle. "It tracks our every particle. It's patient."

"Does it fear us?" Olmy asked.

"No fear. We haven't even begun to be played with."

"That out there is not elaboration—it's pointless madness."

"I thought so myself," Enoch said. "Now I see a pattern. The longer I'm here, the more I sympathize with the allthing. Do you understand what I told you earlier? It *recognizes* us, Ser Olmy. It sees its own work in us, a cycle waiting to be completed."

Rasp held a spot within the circle and motioned for Karn to join her. Together, they peered at something in complete absorption, ignoring Enoch.

Olmy could not ignore her, however. He needed to resolve this question. "The Office of Way Maintenance sent you here to confirm that?"

"Not in so many words, but . . . yes. We know that our own domain, our home universe outside the Way, should have been born barren, empty. Something quickened it, fed it with the necessary geometric nutrients. Some of us thought that would only be possible if the early universe made a connection with a domain of very different properties. I told Ry Ornis that such a quickening need not have happened at the beginning. We could do it now. We had the Way. . . . We could perform the completion. There was such a feeling of power and justification within the guild. I encouraged it. The connection has been made. . . . And all that, the Night Land, is just a side effect. Pure order flowing back through the Way, through Thistledown, back through time to the beginning. Was it worth it? Did we do what we had planned? I'll never know conclusively, because we can't reverse it now . . . and cease to be."

"You weren't sure. You knew this could be dangerous, harm the Way, fatal if the Jarts gained an advantage?"

Enoch stared at him for a few seconds, eyes moving from his eyes to his lips, his chest, as if she would measure him. "Yes," she said. "I knew. Ry Ornis knew. The others did not."

"They suffered for what you've learned," Olmy said. Enoch's gaze steadied and her jaw clenched.

"I've suffered, too. I've learned very little, Ser Olmy. What I learn repeats itself over and over again, and it has more to do with arrogance than metaphysics."

"We've found one!" Karn shouted. "There's a clavicle mounted on top of the green castle. We can pinpoint it!"

Olmy stood where Rasp indicated. At the top of the squat, massive green castle stood a cube, half-hidden behind a mass of root-like growth. On top of the cube, a black pillar about the height of a man supported the unmistakable sphere-and-handles of a clavicle. The sphere was dark, dormant; nothing moved around the pillar or anywhere on the castle roof.

"There's only one, and it appears to be inactive," Rasp said. "The lesion is independent."

Karn spread her arms, wiggling her fingers. A wide smile lit up her face. "We can make a cirque!"

"We can't do it from here," Rasp said. "We have to go out there."

Enoch's face tensed into a rigid mask. "We haven't finished," she said. "The work isn't done!"

Olmy shook his head. He'd made his decision. "Whoever started this, and for whatever reason, it has to end now. The Nexus orders it."

"They don't know!" Enoch cried out.

"We know enough," Olmy said.

Rasp and Karn held each other's hand and descended the stairs. Rasp stuck her tongue out at the old woman.

Enoch laughed and lightly slapped her hands on her thighs. "They're only children! They won't succeed. What have I to fear from failed apprentices?"

The Night Land's atmosphere was a thin haze of primordial hydrogen, mixed with carbon dioxide and some small trace of oxygen from the original envelope surrounding the gate. At seven hundred millibars of pressure, and with a temperature just above freezing, they could venture out of the Redoubt in the most basic pressurized worksuits.

Enoch and her remaining, ever-changing people would not help them. Olmy preferred it that way. He walked through the empty corridors of the pyramid's ground floor and found a small wheeled vehicle that at one time had been used to reach the garden outside the Redoubt—a garden that now lay beyond the demarcation.

Plass showed him how the open vehicle worked. "It has its own pilot, makes a field around the passenger compartment."

"It looks familiar enough," Olmy said.

Plass sat next to Olmy and placed her hand on a control bar. "My husband and I used to tend our plot out there . . . flowers, herbs, vegetables. We'd drive one of these for a few hundred meters, outside the work zone, to where the materials team had spread soil brought through the first gate."

Olmy sat in the vehicle. It announced it was drawing a charge in case it would be needed. It added, in a thin voice, "Will this journey last more than a few hours? I can arrange with the station master for—"

"No," Olmy said. "No need." He turned to Plass. "Time to put on a suit."

Plass stepped out of the car and nervously smoothed her hands down her hips. "I'm staying here. I can't bring myself to go out there again."

"I understand."

"I don't see how you'll survive."

"It looks very chancy," Olmy admitted.

"Why can't they open a ring gate from here?"

"Rasp and Karn say they have to be within five hundred meters of the lesion. About where the other clavicle is now."

"Do you know what my husband was, professionally? Before we came here?"

"No."

"A neurologist. He came along to study the effects of our experiment on the researchers. There was some thought our minds would be enhanced by contact with the ordered domain. They were all very optimistic." She put her hand on Olmy's shoulder. "We had faith. Enoch still believes what they told her, doesn't she?"

Olmy nodded. "May I make one last request?"

"Of course," Plass said.

"Enoch promised us she would open a way through the demarcation and let us through. She claimed we couldn't do anything out there but be taken in by the allthing, anyway . . ."

Plass smiled. "I'll watch her, make sure the fields are open long enough for you to go through. The guild was very clever, sending you and the twins, you know."

"Why?"

"You're all very deceptive. You all seem to be failures." Plass clenched his shoulder.

She turned and left as Rasp and Karn entered the storage chamber. The twins watched her go in silence. They carried their clavicles and had already put on their pressure suits, which had adjusted to their small frames and made a precise fit.

"We've always made her uncomfortable," Rasp said. "Maybe I don't blame her."

Karn regarded Olmy with deep black eyes. "You haven't met a ghost of yourself, have you?"

"I haven't," Olmy said.

"Neither have we. And that's significant. We're never going to reach the allthing. It's never going to get us."

Olmy remembered what Plass had said. She had seen her own ghost . . .

7

They cursed the opening of the Way and the changing of the Thistledown's
mission. They assassinated the Way's creator, Konrad Korzenowski. For centuries
they maintained a fierce opposition, largely underground, but with connections
to the Naderites in power. In any given year there might be only four of five
active members of this most radical sect, the rest presuming to lead normal lives;
but the chain was maintained. All this because their original leader had a vision
of the Way as an easy route to infinite hells.
        —Lives of the Opposition, Anonymous, Journey Year 475

The three rode the tiny wheeled vehicle over a stretch of bare Way floor,
a deeply tarnished copper-bronze colored surface of no substance whatsoever, and no friction at this point. They kept their course with little
jets of air expelled from the sides of the car, until they reached a broad
low island of glassy materials, just before the boundary markers that
warned they were coming to the demarcation.

As agreed, the traction lines switched to low power, and an opening
appeared directly ahead of them, a clarified darkness in the pale green
field. This relieved Olmy somewhat; he had had some doubts that Enoch
would cooperate, or that Plass could compel her. The vehicle rolled
through. They crossed the defenses. Behind them, the fields went up
again.

Now the floor of the Way was covered with sandy soil. The autopilot
switched off the air jets and let the vehicle roll for another twenty meters.

The pressure suits were already becoming uncomfortable; they were
old, and while they did their best to fit, their workings were in less than
ideal condition. Still, they would last several weeks, recycling gases and
liquids and complex molecules, rehydrating the body through arterial
inserts and in the same fashion providing a minimal diet.

Olmy doubted the suits would be needed for more than a few more
hours.

The twins ignored their discomfort and focused their attention on the
lesion. Outside the pyramid, the lesion seemed to fill the sky, and in a
few kilometers, it would be almost directly overhead. From this angle,
the hairlike swirls of spinning world-lines already took on a shimmering
reflective quality, like bands sliced from a wind-ruffled lake; their passage sang in Olmy's skull, more through his teeth than through his ears.

The full character of the Night Land came on gradually, beginning
with a black, gritty, loose scrabble beneath the tires of the vehicle.

Olmy's suit readout, shining directly into his left eye, showed a decrease in air pressure of a few millibars beyond the demarcation. The temperature remained steady, just above zero degrees Celsius.

They turned west, to their left as they faced north down the Way, and came upon the path Olmy had seen from the peak of the pyramid. Plass had identified it as the road used by vehicles carrying material from the first gate Enoch had opened. It had also been the path to Plass's garden, the one she had shared with her husband. Within a few minutes, about three kilometers from the Redoubt, passing over the rise that had blocked his view, they came across the garden's remains.

The relief here was very low, but the rise of some fifty meters had been sufficient to hide what must have been among the earliest attempts at elaboration. Olmy was not yet sure he believed in the allthing, but what had happened in the garden, and in the rest of the Night Land, made any disagreement moot. The trees in the southwest corner of a small rapid-growth orchard had spread out low to the ground, and glowed now like the body of Number 2. Those few trees left standing flickered like frames in a child's flipbook. The rest of the orchard had simply turned to sparkling ash. In the center, however, rose a mound of gnarled brown shot through with vivid reds and greens, and in the middle of this mound, facing almost due south, not looking at anything in particular, was a face some three meters in height, its skin the color of green wood, cracks running from crown to chin. The face did not move or exhibit any sign of life.

Puffs of dust rose from the ash, tiny little explosions from within this mixture of realities. The ash reformed to obliterate the newly formed craters. It seemed to have some purpose of its own, as did everything else in the garden but the face.

Ruin and elaboration; one form of life extinguished, another imbued.

"Early," Karn said, looking to their right at a sprawl of shining dark green leaves, stretched, expanded, and braided into eye-twisting knots. "Didn't know what it was dealing with."

"Doesn't look like it ever did," Olmy said, realizing she were speaking as if some central director actually did exist. Rasp set her sister straight.

"We've seen textbook studies of gates gone wrong. Geometry is the living tissue of reality. Mix constants and you get a—"

"We've sworn not to discuss the failures," Karn said, but without any strength.

"We are being driven through the worst failure of all," Rasp said. "Mixed constants and skewed metrics explain all of this."

Karn shrugged. Olmy thought that perhaps it did not matter; perhaps Rasp and Karn and Plass did not really disagree, merely described the same thing in different ways. What they were seeing up close was not random rearrangement; it had a demented, even a vicious quality, that suggested purpose.

Above the rows of flipbook trees and the living layers of ash stretched a dead and twisted sky. From the hideous chancre of dead blackness, with its sullen ring of congealed red, depended curtains of rushing darkness that swept the Night Land like rain beneath a moving front.

"Mother's hair," Karn said, and clutched her clavicle tightly in white-knuckled hands.

"She's playing with us," Rasp said. "Bending over us, waving her hair over our crib. We reach up to grab and she pulls away."

"She laughs," Karn said.

"Then she gives us to the—"

Rasp did not have time to finish. The vehicle swerved abruptly with a small squeak before a sudden chasm that had not been there an instant before. Out of the chasm leaped white shapes, humanlike but fungal, doughy, and featureless. They seemed to be expelled and to climb out equally, and they lay on the sandy black-streaked ground for a moment, as if recovering from their birth. Then they rose to loose and wobbling feet and ran with speed and even grace over the irregular landscape to the trees, which they began to uproot.

These were the laborers Olmy had seen from the pyramid. They paid no attention to the intruders. The chasm closed, and Olmy instructed the car to continue.

"Is that what we'll become?" Karn asked.

"Each of us will become *many* of them," Rasp said.

"Such a relief to know!" Karn said sardonically.

The rotating shadows ahead gave the ground a blurred and frantic aspect, like unfocused time-lapse photography. Only the major landmarks stood unchanged in the sweeps of metaphysical revision: the Watcher, pale beam still glowing from its unblinking eye, the Castle with its unseen giant occupant, and the obelisk with its scaffold and hordes of white figures working directly beneath the lesion.

Olmy ordered the vehicle to stop, but Rasp grabbed his hand. "Farther," she said. "We can't do anything here."

Olmy grinned and threw back his head, then grimaced like a monkey in the oldest forest of all, baring his teeth at this measureless madness.

"Farther!" Karn insisted. The car rolled on, jolting with the regular ridges some or other force had pushed up in the sand.

Above the constant sizzle of rearranged world-lines, like a symphony of scrubbing and tapping brooms, came more sounds. If a burning forest could sing its pain, Olmy thought, it would be like the rising wail that came from the tower and the Castle. Thousands of the white figures made thousands of different sounds, as if trying to talk to each other, but not succeeding. Mock speech, sing-song pidgin nonsense, attempts to communicate emotions and thoughts they could not truly have; protests at being jabbed and pulled and jiggled along the scaffolding of the tower, over the uneven ground, like puppets directed by something trying to mock a process of construction.

Olmy's body had up to this moment sent him a steady bloodwash of fear. He had controlled this emotion as well as he could, but never ignored it; that would have been senseless and wrong, for fear was what told him he came from a world that made sense, that held together and was consistent, that *worked*.

Yet fear was not enough, could not be an adequate response to what they were seeing. This was a threat beyond anything the body had been designed to experience. Had he allowed himself to scream, he could not have screamed loudly enough.

The Death we all know, Olmy told himself, is an end to something real; death here would be worse than nightmare, worse than the hell one imagines for one's enemies and unbelievers.

"I know," Karn said, and her hands shook on the clavicle.

"What do you know?" Rasp asked.

"Every meter, ever second, every dimension, has its own mind here," Karn said. "Space and time are arguing."

Rasp disagreed violently. "No mind, no minds at all!" she insisted shrilly.

Light itself began to waver and change as they came closer to the tower. Olmy could see the face of oncoming events before they occurred, like waves on a beach, rushing over the land, impatient to reach their destinations, their observers, before all surprise had been lost.

They now entered the fringes of shadow. The revisions of their surroundings felt like deep drumming pulses. Caught directly in a shadow, Olmy felt a sudden rub of excitement. He saw flashes of colors, felt a spectrum of unfamiliar emotions that threatened to cancel out his fear. He looked to his left, into the counterclockwise sweep, anticipating each front of darkness, leaning toward it. Ecstasy, followed by a buzz of exhilaration, suddenly a spasm of brilliance, all the while the back of his head crisping and glowing and sparking. He could see into the back of his brain, down to the working foundations of every thought; where symbols with no present meaning are painted and arrayed on long tables, then jerked and jostled until they become emotions and memories and words.

"Like opening a gate!" Karn shouted, seeing Olmy's expression.

"Much worse. Dangerous! Very dangerous!"

"Don't ignore it, don't suppress," Rasp told him. "Just pay attention to what's in front! That's what they teach us when we open a gate!"

"These aren't gates!" Olmy shouted above the hideous symphony of brooms. The twins' heads jerked and vibrated as he spoke.

"They are!" Rasp said. "Little gates into directly adjacent worlds. They're trying to escape their neighboring realities, to split away, but the lesion gathers them, holds them. They flow back behind us, along our world-lines."

"Back to the beginning!" Karn said.

"Back to our birth!" Rasp said.

"Here!" Karn said, and Olmy brought the car to a stop. The two assistants, little more than girls, with pale faces and wide eyes and serious expressions climbed down from the open cab and marched resolutely across the rippled sand, leaning into the pressure of other streams of reality. Their clothes changed color, their hair changed its arrangement, even their skin changed color, but they marched until the clavicles seemed to lift of their own will.

Rasp and Karn faced each other.

Olmy told himself, with whatever was left of his mind, that they were now going to attempt a cirque, a ring gate, that would bring all this to a meeting with the flaw. Within the flaw lay the peace of incommensurable contradictions, pure and purifying. Within the flaw this madness would burn to less than nothing, to paradoxes that would cancel and expunge.

He did not think they would have time to escape, even if the shrinking of the Way was less than instantaneous.

He stood on the seat of the car for a moment, watching the twins, admiring them. *Enoch underestimates them. As have I. This is what Ry Ornis wanted, why he chose them.*

He hunched his shoulders: something coming. Before he could duck or jump aside, Olmy was caught between two folds of shadow, like a bug snatched between fingers, and lifted bodily from the car. He twisted his neck and looked back to see a fuzzy image of the car, the twins lifting their clavicles, the rippled and streaked sand. The car seemed to vibrate, the tire tracks rippling behind it like snakes; and for a long moment, the twins and the car were not visible at all, as if they had never been.

Olmy's thoughts raced and his body shrieked with joy. Every nerve shivered, and all his memories stood out together in sharp relief, with different selves viewing them all at once. He could not distinguish between present and future; all were just parts of different memories. His reference point had blurred to where his life was a flat field, and within that field swam a myriad of possibilities. What would happen, what had happened, became indistinguishable from the unchosen and unlived moments that *could* happen.

This blurring of his world-line rushed backward. He felt he could sidle across fates into what was fixed and unfix it, free his past to be all possible, all potential, once more. But the diffusion, the smearing and blending of the chalked line of his life, came up against the moment of his resurrection, the abrupt shift from Lamarckia—

And could not go any further. Dammed, the tide of his life spilled out in all directions. He cried out in surprise and a kind of pain he had never known before.

Olmy hung suspended beneath the dark eye, spinning slowly, all things above and below magnified or made minute depending on his angle. The pain passed. Perhaps it had never been. He felt as if his head had become a tiny but all-seeing camera obscura.

There was a past in which Ry Ornis accompanied the twins; he saw them working together near a very different vehicle, tractor rather than small car, to make the cirque. Already they had forced the Way to extrude a well through the sand. A cupola floated over the well, brazen and smooth, reflecting in golden hues the flaw, the lesion.

Olmy turned his head a fraction of a centimeter and once more saw only the twins, but this time dead, lying mangled beside the car, their clavicles flaring and burning. Another degree or two, and they were resurrected, still working. Ry Ornis was with them again.

A memory: Ry Ornis had traveled with them in the flawship. How could he have lost this fact?

Olmy rotated again, this time in a new and unfamiliar dimension, and felt the Way simply cease to exist and his own life with it. From this dark and soundless eventuality, he turned with a bitter, acrid wrench and found a very narrow course through the gripping shadows, a course illumined by half-forgotten emotions that had been plucked like flowers, arranged like silent speech.

He had been carried to the other side of the lesion, looking north down the endless throat of the Way.

The gripping baleen of shadow from the whale's mouth of the lesion, the driving cilia whisking him between world-lines, drove him under and over a complex surface through which he could see a deep mountainous valley, its floor smooth and vitreous like obsidian.

Black glass, reflecting the lesion, the flaw behind the lesion, scudding layers of mist. The cilia that controlled Olmy's orientation let him drop to a few meters above the vitreous black floor.

Motion stopped. His thoughts slowed. He felt only one body, one existence. All his lines clumped back into one flow.

He tried to close his eyes, to not see, but that was impossible. He faced down and saw his reflection in the mirror-shiny valley floor, a small still man floating beneath the red-rimmed eye like an intruding mote.

On either side of the valley rose jagged glassy peaks, mountain ranges like shreds of pulled taffy. A few hundred meters ahead of him—or perhaps a few kilometers, mounted in the middle of the valley lay something he recognized: a Jart defensive emplacement, white as ivory, jagged spikes thrusting like a sea urchin's spines from a squat discus. Shaded cilia played around the spikes, but the spikes did not track, did not move.

The emplacement was dead.

Olmy held his hands in front of his face. He could see them, see through them, with equal clarity. Nothing was obscured, nothing neglected by his new vision.

He tried to speak, or perhaps to pray, to whatever it was that held him, directed his motion. He asked first if anything was there, listening. No answer.

He remembered Plass's comments about the allthing: that in its domain it was unique, had never learned the arts of communication, was *one* without other and controlled all by *being all*. No separation between mind and matter, observed and observer. Such a being could neither listen nor answer. Nor could it change.

He thought of the emotions arrayed along the path that had guided him here. Pain, disappointment, fear. Weariness. Had the allthing learned this method of communication after its time in the Way? Had it dissected and rearranged enough human elements to change its nature this much?

Why pain? Olmy asked, spoken but unheard in the stillness.

He moved north down the center of the valley, over the dead Jart emplacement. His reflection shimmered in the uneven black mirror of the floor. He looked east and west, up the long curves of the Way beyond the jagged mountains, and saw more Jart emplacements, the spiral and beaded walls of what looked like Jart settlements, all abandoned, all spotted with large, distorted shapes he could not begin to comprehend.

Olmy thought, *It's made a Night Land for the Jarts. It does not know any difference between us.*

As if growing used to the extraordinary pressure of the shadow cilia gripping him, his body once more sent signals of fear, then simple, childlike wonder, and finally its own exhaustion. Olmy's head rolled on his shoulders and he felt his body sleep, but his mind remained alert. All his muscles tingled as they went off-line and would not respond to his tentative urgings.

How much time passed, if it were possible for time to pass, he could not judge. The tingling stopped and control returned. He lifted his head and saw a different valley, this one lined with huge figures. If the scale he had assumed at the beginning of his journey was still valid, these monolithic sculptures or shapes or beings—whatever they might be— were fully two or three kilometers distant, and therefore hundreds of meters in height. They were so strange he found himself looking at them in his peripheral vision, to avoid the confusion of placing them at the points of his visual focus. While vaguely organic in design—compound curves, folds of what might have been a semblance of tissue weighted by gravity, a kind of multilateral symmetry—the figures simply refused to be analyzed.

Olmy had many times experienced a lapse of visual judgment, when he would look at something in his living quarters and not remember it right away, and because of dim lighting or an unfamiliar angle, be unable to judge what it was. Under those conditions, he could feel his mind making hypotheses, trying desperately to compare them with what he was looking directly at, to reach some valid conclusion, and so actually *see* the object. This had occurred to him many times on Lamarckia, especially with regard to objects unique to that planet.

Here, he had no prior experience, no memory, no physical training or familiarity whatsoever with what he looked at, so he saw *nothing* sensible, nameable, to which he could begin to relate. Slowly, it dawned on Olmy that these might be more trophies of the allthing's encounters with Jarts.

He was drifting down a rogue's gallery of failed models, failed attempts to duplicate and understand, much like the gallery of objects and conditions around the Redoubt that made up the Night Land.

Humans had approached from the south, Jarts from the north. The allthing had applied similar awkward tools to both, either to unify them into its being, or to find some new way to experience their otherness. Both had been incomprehensibly alien to the allthing.

Pain. One of the emotions borrowed from Olmy's mind and arrayed along the pathway. A sense of disunification, unwanted change. The allthing had been disturbed by this entry; there was no evil, no enthusiastic destruction, in the Night Land. Olmy suddenly saw what Enoch had been trying to communicate to him, and went beyond her own understanding.

A monobloc of pure order had been invaded by a domain whose main character was that of disunity and contradiction. That must have been very painful indeed. And this quality of order was being sucked backward, like gas into a vacuum, into their domain.

Enoch and the guild of gate openers had manufactured the tip of a tooth. They had thrust into this other domain the bloody predatorial tooth of a hungry universe seeking quickening, a completion at its own beginning.

But this hypothesis did not instantly open any floodgate of comprehension or communication. Olmy did not find himself suddenly analyzing the raw emotional outbursts of another mind, godlike or otherwise; the allthing was not a mind in any sense he could understand. It was simply a pure and necessary set of qualities. It gripped him, controlled him, but literally had no use for him. Like everything else here, it could neither analyze nor absorb him. It could not even spread back along his world-line, for Olmy's existence had begun over with this new body, with his resurrection.

That was why he had not met any ghosts of himself. Physically, he had almost no past. The allthing, if such existed, had flung him along this valley of waste and failure, another piece of detritus, even more frustrating than most.

He squirmed, his body struggling to break free like an animal in a cage. Panic overwhelmed him despite his best efforts. Olmy could not locate any point of reference within; not even a self was clearly defined.

Everything blurred, became confused, as if he had been smudged by an enormous finger and no outline remained. *I am no where, now here, no name, moving, no future*

He twisted, convulsed, trying to find his center. The figures mounted on the ranges of mountains to either side seemed interested in this effort. He could feel their attention and did not welcome it. He fancied they moved, however slowly, advancing toward him across astronomical time.

If this lump of conflicting order and chaos could define himself anew, perhaps these incomprehensible monoliths, these unworshipped gods and unrealized mockeries, could establish a presence as well.

The panic stopped. Signals stopped.

He had come to an end. That minimum condition he had wished for was now upon him. He cared nothing for past or future, had lost nothing, gained nothing.

I am or was a part of a society really no part of any
This name is Olmy Ap Sennen
Lover of many loved and loving by few
Contact nothing without
Without contact nothing
Uprooted tree

The lesion's inflamed rim began to brighten. The suspended and aimless figure in its gripping cilia of probabilities maintained enough structure and drive to be interested in this, and noted that compared to past memory, the lesion was much smaller, much darker, and the flaring rim much broader. It resembled an immense solar eclipse with a bloody corona.

Loyalties and loves uprooted

Language itself faded until the aimless figure saw only images, the lushness of another world out of reach, closed off, the faces of old humans once loved once reassuringly close now dead and without ghosts.

Can't even be haunted by a past uprooted

The figure's motion down the valley slowed. No time passed. Eveternity, endless now. Naked, skinless, fleshless, boneless. Consumed, integrated.

Experiences stillness.

Mark this in an endless column: *experiences*

Experiences stillness

stillness

stillness

No divisions. A tiny place no bigger than a fist, a womb. Tiny place of infinite peace at the heart of a frozen geometry. All elaboration, variation, permutation, long since exhausted; infinite access to unbounded energy contained in oneness.

You/I/We no difference. See?

See. Vidya. All seeing. Eye of Buddha. Nerveless kalpas of some body. Nerve vanity.

This oneness consumed. Many nows, peace past.

At peace in the past. Loved women, raised children, lived a long life on a world to which there is no returning.

Nothing one at peace in no past all completed no returning.

Point.

One makes possible all.

I see. Buddha, do not leave your student bound.

The eye is shrinking, closing, its gorgeous bloody flare dimming. It is pierced by a white needle visible behind the small dark center.

Small large no matter no time

Do not go. Take us with

Am your father/mother/food

loved raised living longing no return

my own ghost

8

Ry Ornis, the tall insect-thin master, smiled down on him. Olmy saw many of the master opener, like an avatar of an ancient god. All the different masters merged.

They were surrounded by a glassy tent and a slow breeze cooled his face. Ry Ornis had wrapped him in a rescue field where he fell, carrying safe cool air to replenish what his worksuit could no longer provide.

Olmy rediscovered scattered rivers of memory and bathed his ancient feet there. He swallowed once. The eye, the lesion, had shut forever. "It's gone," he said.

Ry Ornis nodded. "It's done."

"I can never tell anybody," Olmy realized out loud.

"You can never tell anybody."

"We robbed and ate to live. To be born."

Ry Ornis held his fingers to his lips, his face spectral in a new light from the south. A huge grin was spreading around half the Way, a gorgeous brilliant electric light. "The ring gate. A cirque," the gate opener said, glancing over his shoulder. "Rasp and Karn, my students, have done well. We've done what we came here to do, and we saved the Way, as well. Not bad, eh, Ser Olmy?"

Olmy reached up to grab the gate opener, perhaps to strangle him. Ry Ornis had moved, however.

Olmy turned away, swallowed a second time against a competing dryness. There had been no need to complete the ring gate. The unfinished cirque had done its job and drained the final wasted remnants of the lesion, forcing a closure.

As they watched, the cirque shrank. The grin became a smile became an all-knowing serene curve, then collapsed to a point, and the point dimmed on distant rippled sands.

"I think the twins are a little disappointed they can't finish the cirque. But it's wonderful," Ry Ornis enthused, and performed a small dance on the black obsidian of the valley floor. "They are truly masters now! When I am tried and convicted, they will take my place!"

The Way remained. Rolling his head to one side, Olmy could not see the Redoubt.

"Where's the pyramid?" he asked hoarsely.

"Enoch has her wish," Ry Ornis said, and shaded his eyes with one hand.

Plass, Enoch, the allthing.

Plass had seen her own ghost.

To east and west, the ruined mountains and their statues remained, rejected, discarded. No dream, no hallucination.

He had been used again. No matter. For an endless instant, like any gate opener, only more so, he had merged with the eye of the Buddha.

9

"The Infinite Hexamon Nexus does not approve of risky experiments that cannot be documented or explained. How many were deceived, Master Ry Ornis?"

"All, myself included."

"Yet you maintain this was done out of necessity?"

"All of it. The utmost necessity."

"Will this ever be necessary again? Answer honestly; the trust between us has worn very thin!"

"Never again."

"How do you explain that one universe, one domain, must feed on another in order to be born?"

"I don't. We were compelled. That is all I know."

"Could it have gone badly?"

"Of course. As it is, in our clumsiness and ignorance, we have condemned all our ancestors to live with unexplainable presences, ghosts of past and future. A kind of afterbirth."

"You are smiling, Master Gate Opener. This is intolerable!"

"It is all I can do, Sers."

. . .

"For your disobedience and arrogance, what punishment do you choose, Master Ry Ornis?"

"Sers of the Nexus. This I swear. I will put down my clavicle from this time forward, and never know the grace again." —Sentencing Phase of Secret Hearings Conducted by the Infinite Hexamon Nexus, "On the Advisability of Opening Gates into Chaos and Order"

TRACTING THROUGH THE WEIGHTLESS FOREST OF THE WALD IN THE REBUILT Axis Nader, reaching out to the trees to push or grab roots and branches, half-flying and half-climbing, in his mind's river-wide eye, Olmy Ap Sennen returned to Lamarckia, where he had once nearly died of old age, and retrieved a package he had left there, tied in neat pieces of mat-paper. His wives and children had kept it safe for him, and now they returned it. There was much smiling and laughter, then saying of farewells, last of all a farewell to his sons, whom he had left behind. Occupants of a different land, another life.

As they faded, in his mind's eye, he opened the package they had given to him and greedily swallowed the wonderful contents.

His soul.

Introduction to "MDIO Ecosystems"

Henry Gee at the science journal *Nature* asked a number of science fiction writers to contribute brief stories describing some future development in science. The series was great fun. My contribution was an attempt to write a review of recent discoveries as it might appear in *Nature* some two centuries hence. Along the way, I got to promote my speculative views of genetics and biological development (expressed in detail in *Darwin's Radio, Vitals,* and *Darwin's Children*) as if they were part of an established paradigm. Talk about smug!

MDIO Ecosystems Increase Knowledge of DNA Languages (2215 C.E.)

The discovery of over 15,000 massive deep ice objects (MDIO) in orbit around supermassive planets in the close interstellar neighborhood has the potential to revolutionize our understanding of biological languages.

Phenotype-generating languages for terrestrial DNA-recorded life forms can be ranked closely according to kingdoms. Most plants, for example, express phylogeny according to the famous Zinn-Wang languages, first decoded in the mid-twenty-first century.

Archaea, commonly used as the Rosetta stone for all primitive DNA languages, have provided deep insights into nonterrestrial biologies that have advanced to the DNA level.

RNA languages in terrestrial viruses constitute a virtual Tower of Babel, indicating a degenerate and mutationally rich mix that can still compel replication in DNA hosts. Early RNA coding systems found outside the solar system, however, can often be translated into Archaean DNA-based languages, and these may constitute the most basic fixed languages of life.

MDIOs are typically seven to nine Earth masses and consist of layers of water ice two to five thousand kilometers in depth, overlying a high-pressure liquid ocean (HPLO) that sits in turn on a rocky mantle. At the center is an iron- and sulfur-rich core.

The interior is warmed both by latent heat and radioactivity (chiefly thorium 90) and by tidal friction generated by interaction with the parent supermassive body. Temperatures in the HPLO can frequently exceed 130 degrees Celsius.

MDIOs may constitute the most common life-supporting bodies in the universe.

Neutronium self-guided probes (NSGP) have penetrated seven of these deep ice objects and have obtained remarkable data. Spin-off probes made of normal matter, transmuted from neutronium and released into the HPLO, perform in situ analysis of all carbon chemistry and send information to orbiting research stations.

What is most remarkable about MDIO biologies is that they can exist at all under these extraordinary conditions. Once again, it is demonstrated that life will begin and thrive anywhere there is liquid water and the necessary elements.

To date, RNA and DNA language analysis has been conducted on three HPLO ecosystems. Because of limited exploration ranges for the probes, the extent of these ecosystems is not known; however, every probed MDIO possesses life.

One of the ecosystems (MDIO 2341-a) is still in a "profligate" mutation-rich RNA phase, with no complex organisms and no DNA detected. Here, new genetic coding schemes may naturally emerge every few months, and competition between coding schemes is likely to be extreme. (The emergence of competent and stable genetic languages on Earth may have taken more than a billion years.)

The other two ecosystems (MDIO 5756-b, MDIO 349-x) have entered the more stable age of DNA and show remarkable similarities to each other.

The most striking feature of these ecosystems is how bright they are, since they are completely hidden from all starlight. The roving probes have sent back images of massive reef-like structures glowing as brightly as several full moons, surrounded by a thick, slowly churning mass of light-dependent microbes. Feeding on these microbes are living filter nets, fringed by corkscrew cilia, able to join into larger units or separate into smaller.

Tall spiral chimneys, like Baroque columns in a church, release water heated in the upper mantle, creating plumes that can extend for many kilometers. These plumes spread out at the upper ice layer, eroding smooth domes almost a hundred kilometers in diameter and usually less than a millimeter deep. These domes collect oxygen freed from the actions of photosynthetic organisms. Typically the oxygen is forced back under extreme pressure into the water and the ice within seconds, but during this brief time, miniature forests of opportunistic organisms grow in the domes, extracting all the benefits from a more efficient oxygen metabolism.

The upper limit of organization in MDIO ecosystems is not known. Typical distributed-intelligence ecosystems are found here, and interact to form complex neuronal networks that govern MDIO life-cycles (as on Earth). However, no condensed nodal intelligences such as large animals have yet been found. Instead, intelligence seems frozen at a very early and distributed stage.

This may reflect the unlikelihood of any intelligences within the MDIO ever being challenged by major environmental change, much less being given a chance to observe the outside universe. (MDIOs seem to be remarkably stable over hundreds of millions of years.)

The impossibility of emergence through the deep ice and escape into space limits the potential growth of concentrated hypothesis engines as defined by the Turing-Watteau diagram of novel information vs. expansion opportunity.

Some researchers suggest that the seeding of provocative artifacts ("Clarkeing") below the deep ice may encourage condensation of concentrated intelligences, or at the very least, induce some interesting emergent properties. The design of these artifacts is currently spurring intense debate.

As one chief communications researcher has asked, "How do you uplift slime?"

Harnessing of bacterial communities on Earth in the last century could provide a template for working with MDIO ecosystems, adding to the list of beings we can actually talk to.

INTRODUCTION TO *HARDFOUGHT*

I can't recall the list of magazines that rejected *Hardfought*—at some 24,000 words, my novella was too long for most at the time, too weird and difficult for some. When I sent it to *Isaac Asimov's Science Fiction Magazine,* an interim editor caught the story and didn't know what to do with it. (Isaac Asimov did not buy stories for the magazine. He wrote editorials, answered letters, and visited the offices to spread good cheer.)

Asimov's future editor-in-chief, Shawna McCarthy, was enthusiastic, but she was not yet in control. *Asimov's* had become known for publishing fairly traditional stories, generally light and doggedly unpretentious. *Hardfought* is long and heavy and very pretentious.

I made a phone call and tried to persuade the interim editor to buy it. Certainly it was not your usual SF story, I said. I invoked the hallowed name of Joseph Conrad. I was desperate. I needed the money. "What if I cut it—a little?" I suggested. *Pretty please . . . ?*

The editor, still undecided, soon left to take another editorial position. Shawna McCarthy moved up, bought the story, made some cuts, slotted it for publication, and . . .

But let's go back a bit.

Jim Turner at Arkham House was waiting for me to write a masterpiece to cap off a proposed story collection. Jim is dead now, but I remember his voice very clearly, and cherish his contrarian sense of humor. I sent him *Hardfought.* He phoned to tell me the bad news. It was a tough read, he confessed. He was not enthusiastic.

He read it four more times and called again. Had he seen *Babe,* he might have said, "That'll do, Bear." What he actually said was, "All right, Bear. It's a masterpiece."

Asimov's published the story first. Shawna warned the magazine's readers that it was not the magazine's usual fare. She needn't have worried.

Hardfought and "Blood Music" picked up Nebula Awards from the Science Fiction Writers of America, on the same evening. The Nebula Banquet that year (1984) was held on the Queen Mary in Long Beach Harbor. Seated at our table were my mother and father, my favorite college professor, Elizabeth Chater, her daughter Patty, and my wife Astrid. The ceremony was emceed by my good friend Gregory Benford, and the award was presented by my father-in-law, Poul Anderson.

Need I say it was a great evening?

My first story collection, *The Wind from a Burning Woman,* was published in the spring of 1983 by Arkham House. It sold out its first print run in ninety days, and became the fastest selling book in Arkham House history.

A few years later, in 1986, I spoke briefly with Isaac Asimov at a SFWA Publisher's Reception in Manhattan. I had my infant son Erik strapped to my chest. Isaac was being ferried from interview to interview when he spotted my name tag, paused, lifted his eyebrows, and said, "So *you're* Greg Bear! I'm glad you weren't around when *I* was getting started!"

I beamed.

This may be the best story I've ever written.

HARDFOUGHT

Isaac Asimov's Science Fiction Magazine, Shawna McCarthy, 1983;
The Wind from a Burning Woman, Jim Turner, 1983

I n the Han Dynasty, historians were appointed by royal edict to write the history of Imperial China. They alone were the arbiters of what would be recorded. Although various emperors tried, none could gain access to the ironbound chest in which each document was placed after it was written. The historians preferred to suffer death rather than betray their trust.

At the end of each reign the box would be opened and the documents published, perhaps to benefit the next emperor. But for these documents, Imperial China, to a large extent, has no history.

The thread survives by whim.

HUMANS CALLED IT THE MEDUSA. ITS LONG TWISTED RIBBONS OF GAS strayed across fifty parsecs, glowing blue, yellow, and carmine. Watery black flecked a central core of ghoulish green. Half a dozen protostars circled the core, and as many more dim conglomerates pooled in dimples in the nebula's magnetic field. The Medusa was a huge womb of stars—and disputed territory.

Whenever Prufrax looked at the nebula in displays or through the ship's ports, it seemed malevolent, like a zealous mother showing an ominous face to protect her children. Prufrax had never had a mother, but she had seen them in some in the fibs.

At five, Prufrax was old enough to know the *Mellangee's* mission and her role in it. She had already been through four ship-years of indoctrination. Until her first battle she would be educated in both the Know and the Tell. She would be exercised and trained in the Mocks; in sleep she would dream of penetrating the huge red-and-white Senexi seedships and finding the brood mind. "Zap, Zap," she went with her lips, silent so the tellman wouldn't think her thoughts were straying.

The tellman peered at her from his position in the center of the spherical classroom. Her mates stared straight at the center, all focusing somewhere around the tellman's spiderlike teaching desk, waiting for the trouble, some fidgeting. "How many branch individuals in the Senexi brood mind?" he asked. He looked around the classroom. Peered face by face. Focused on her again. "Pru?"

"Five," she said. Her arms ached. She had been pumped full of moans the wake before. She was already three meters tall, in elfstate, with her long, thin limbs not nearly adequately fleshed out and her fingers still crisscrossed with the surgery done to adapt them to the gloves.

"What will you find in the brood mind?" the tellman pursued, his impassive face stretched across a hammerhead as wide as his shoulders. Some of the fems thought tellmen were attractive. Not many, and Pru was not one of them.

"Yoke," she said.

"What is in the brood-mind yoke?"

"Fibs."

"More specifically? And it really isn't all fib, you know."

"Info. Senexi data."

"What will you do?"

"Zap," she said, smiling.

"Why, Pru?"

"Yoke has team gens-memory. Zap yoke, spill the life of the team's five branch inds."

"Zap the brood, Pru?"

"No," she said solemnly. That was a new instruction, only in effect since her class's inception. "Hold the brood for the supreme overs." The tellman did not say what would be done with the Senexi broods. That was not her concern.

"Fine," said the tellman. "You tell well, for someone who's always half-journeying."

Brainwalk, Prufrax thought to herself. Tellman was fancy with the words, but to Pru, what she was prone to do during Tell was brainwalk, seeking out her future. She was already five, soon six. Old. Some saw Senexi by the time they were four.

"Zap, Zap," she said softly.

ARYZ SKIDDED THROUGH THE THIN LAYER OF LIQUID AMMONIA ON HIS BROADest pod, considering his new assignment. He knew the Medusa by another name, one that conveyed all the time and effort the Senexi had invested in it. The protostar nebula held few mysteries for him. He and his four branchmates, who along with the all-important brood mind comprised one of the six teams aboard the seedship, had patrolled the nebula for ninety-three orbits, each orbit—including the timeless periods outside status geometry—taking some one hundred and thirty human years. They had woven in and out of the tendrils of gas, charting the infalling masses and exploring the rocky accretion disks of stars entering the main sequence. With each measure and update, the brood minds refined their view of the nebula as it would be a hundred generations hence when the Senexi plan would finally mature.

The Senexi were nearly as old as the galaxy. They had achieved spaceflight during the time of the starglobe when the galaxy had been a sphere. They had not been a quick or brilliant race. Each great achievement had taken thousands of generations, and not just because of their material handicaps. In those times elements heavier than helium had been rare, found only around stars that had greedily absorbed huge amounts of primeval hydrogen, burned fierce and blue and exploded early, permeating the ill-defined galactic arms with carbon and nitrogen, lithium and oxygen. Elements heavier than iron had been almost nonexistent. The biologies of cold gas-giant worlds had developed with a much smaller palette of chemical combinations in producing the offspring of the primary Population II stars.

Aryz, even with the limited perspective of a branch ind, was aware that, on the whole, the humans opposing the seedship were more adaptable, more vital. But they were not more experienced. The Senexi with their billions of years had often matched them. And Aryz's perspective was expanding with each day of his new assignment.

In the early generations of the struggle, Senexi mental stasis and cultural inflexibility had made them avoid contact with the Population I species. They had never begun a program of extermination of the younger, newly life-forming worlds; the task would have been monumental and probably useless. So when spacefaring cultures developed, the Senexi had retreated, falling back into the redoubts of old stars even before engaging with the new kinds. They had retreated for three generations, about thirty thousand human years, raising their broods on cold nestworlds around red dwarfs, conserving, holding back for the inevitable conflicts.

As the Senexi had anticipated, the younger Population I races had found need of even the aging groves of the galaxy's first stars. They had moved in savagely, voraciously, with all the strength and mutability of organisms evolved from a richer soup of elements. Biology had, in some ways, evolved in its own right and superseded the Senexi.

Aryz raised the upper globe of his body, with its five silicate eyes arranged in a cross along the forward surface. He had memory of those times, and times long before, though his team hadn't existed then. The brood mind carried memories selected from the total store of nearly twelve billion years' experience; an awesome amount of knowledge, even to a Senexi. He pushed himself forward with his rear pods.

Through the brood mind Aryz could share the memories of a hundred thousand past generations, yet the brood mind itself was younger than its branch individuals. For a time in their youth, in their liquid-dwelling larval form, the branch inds carried their own sacs of data, each a fragment of the total necessary for complete memory. The branch inds swam through ammonia seas and wafted through thick warm gaseous zones, protoplasmic blobs three to four meters in diameter, developing their personalities under the weight of the past—and not even a complete past. No wonder they were inflexible, Aryz thought. Most branch inds were aware enough to see that—especially when they were allowed to compare histories with the Population I species, as he was doing—but there was nothing to be done. They were content the way they were. To change would be unspeakably repugnant. Extinction was preferable . . . almost.

But now they were pressed hard. The brood mind had begun a number of experiments. Aryz's team had been selected from the seedship's contingent to oversee the experiments, and Aryz had been chosen as the chief investigator. Two orbits past, they had captured six human embryos in a breeding device, as well as a highly coveted memory storage center. Most Senexi engagements had been with humans for the past three or four generations. Just as the Senexi dominated Population II species, humans were ascendant among their kind.

Experiments with the human embryos had already been conducted. Some had been allowed to develop normally; others had been tampered with, for reasons Aryz was not aware of. The tamperings had not been very successful.

The newer experiments, Aryz suspected, were going to take a different direction, and the seedship's actions now focused on him; he believed he would be given complete authority over the human shapes. Most branch inds would have dissipated under such a burden, but not Aryz. He found the human shapes rather interesting, in their own horrible way. They might, after all, be the key to Senexi survival.

THE MOANS WERE TOUGHENING HER ELFSTATE. SHE LAY IN PAIN FOR A WAKE, not daring to close her eyes; her mind was changing and she feared sleep would be the end of her. Her nightmares were not easily separated from life; some, in fact, were sharper.

Too often in sleep she found herself in a Senexi trap, struggling uselessly, being pulled in deeper, her hatred wasted against such power. . . .

When she came out of the rigor, Prufrax was given leave by the subordinate tellman. She took to the *Mellangee*'s greenroads, walking stiffly in the shallow gravity. Her hands itched. Her mind seemed almost empty after the turmoil of the past few wakes. She had never felt so calm and clear. She hated the Senexi double now; once for their innate evil, twice for what they had made her overs put her through to be able to fight them. Logic did not matter. She was calm, assured. She was growing more mature wake by wake. Fight-budding, the tellman called it, hate coming out like blooms, synthesizing the sunlight of his teaching into pure fight.

The greenroads rose temporarily beyond the labyrinth shields and armor of the ship. Simple transparent plastic and steel geodesic surfaces formed a lacework over the gardens, admitting radiation necessary to the vegetation growing along the paths. No machines scooted one forth and inboard here. It was necessary to walk. Walking was luxury and privilege.

Prufrax looked down on the greens to each side of the paths without much comprehension. They were *beautiful*. Yes, one should say that, think that, but what did it mean? Pleasing? She wasn't sure what being pleased meant, outside of thinking Zap. She sniffed a flower that, the signs explained, bloomed only in the light of young stars not yet fusing. They were near such a star now, and the greenroads were shiny black and electric green with the blossoms. Lamps had been set out for other plants unsuited to such darkened conditions. Some technic allowed suns to appear in selected plastic panels when viewed from certain angles. Clever, the technicals.

She much preferred the looks of a technical to a tellman, but she was common in that. Technicals required brainflex, tellmen cargo capacity. Technicals were strong and ran strong machines, like in the adventure fibs, where technicals were often the protags. She wished a technical were on the greenroads with her. The moans had the effect of making her receptive—what she saw, looking in mirrors, was a certain shine in her eyes—but there was no chance of a breeding liaison. She was quite unreproductive in this moment of elfstate. Other kinds of meetings were not unusual.

She looked up and saw a figure at least a hundred meters away, sitting on an allowed patch near the path. She walked casually, gracefully as possible with the stiffness. Not a technical, she saw soon, but she was not disappointed. Too calm.

"Over," he said as she approached.

"Under," she replied. But not by much—he was probably six or seven ship years old and not easily classifiable.

"Such a fine elfstate," he commented. His hair was black. He was shorter than she, but something in his build reminded her of the glovers. She accepted his compliment with a nod and pointed to a spot near him. He motioned for her to sit, and she did so with a whuff, massaging her knees.

"Moans?" he asked.

"Bad stretch," she said.

"You're a glover." He looked at the fading scars on her hands.

"Can't tell what you are," she said.

"Noncombat," he said. "Tuner of the mandates."

She knew very little about the mandates, except that law decreed every ship carry one, and few of the crew were ever allowed to peep. "Noncombat, hm?" she mused. She didn't despise him for that; one never felt strong negatives for a crew member. She didn't feel much of anything. Too calm.

"Been working on ours this wake," he said. "Too hard, I guess. Told to walk." Overzealousness in work was considered an erotic trait aboard the *Mellangee*. Still, she didn't feel too receptive toward him.

"Glovers walk after a rough growing," she said.

He nodded. "My name's Clevo."

"Prufrax."

"Combat soon?"

"Hoping. Waiting forever."

"I know. Just been allowed access to the mandate for a half-dozen wakes. All new to me. Very happy."

"Can you talk about it?" she asked. Information about the ship not accessible in certain rates was excellent barter.

"Not sure," he said, frowning. "I've been told caution."

"Well, I'm listening."

He could come from glover stock, she thought, but probably not from technical. He wasn't very muscular, but he wasn't as tall as a glover, or as thin, either.

"If you'll tell me about gloves."

With a smile she held up her hands and wriggled the short, stumpy fingers. "Sure."

THE BROOD MIND FLOATED WEIGHTLESS IN ITS TANK, HELD IN PLACE BY BUF-fered carbon rods. Metal was at a premium aboard the Senexi ships, more out of tradition than actual material limitations. From what Aryz could tell, the Senexi used metals sparingly for the same reason—and he strained to recall the small dribbles of information about the human past he had extracted from the memory store—for the same reason **that the Romans of old Earth regarded farming as the only truly noble occupation—**

Farming being the raising of *plants* for food *and* raw materials. *Plants* were analogous to the freeth Senexi ate in their larval youth, but the freeth were not green and sedentary.

There was always a certain fascination in stretching his mind to encompass human concepts. He had had so little time to delve deeply—and that was good, of course, for he had been set to answer specific questions, not mire himself in the whole range of human filth.

He floated before the brood mind, all these thoughts coursing through his tissues. He had no central nervous system, no truly differentiated organs except those that dealt with the outside world limbs, eyes, permea. The brood mind, however, was all central nervous system, a thinly buffered sac of viscous fluids about ten meters wide.

"Have you investigated the human memory device yet?" the brood mind asked.

"I have."

"Is communication with the human shapes possible for us?"

"We have already created interfaces for dealing with their machines. Yes, it seems likely we can communicate."

"Does it occur to you that in our long war with humans, we have made no attempt to communicate before?"

This was a complicated question. It called for several qualities that Aryz, as a branch ind, wasn't supposed to have. Inquisitiveness, for one. Branch inds did not ask questions. They exhibited initiative only as offshoots of the brood mind.

He found, much to his dismay, that the question had occurred to him. "We have never captured a human memory store before," he said, by way of incomplete answer. "We could not have communicated without such an extensive source of information."

"Yet, as you say, even in the past we have been able to use human machines."

"The problem is vastly more complex."

The brood mind paused. "Do you think the teams have been prohibited from communicating with humans?"

Aryz felt the closest thing to anguish possible for a branch ind. Was he being considered unworthy? Accused of conduct inappropriate to a branch ind? His loyalty to the brood mind was unshakeable. "Yes."

"And what might our reasons be?"

"Avoidance of pollution."

"Correct. We can no more communicate with them and remain untainted than we can walk on their worlds, breathe their atmosphere." Again, silence. Aryz lapsed into a mode of inactivity. When the brood mind readdressed him, he was instantly aware.

"Do you know how you are different?" it asked.

"I am not . . ." Again, hesitation. Lying to the brood mind was impossible for him. What snared him was semantics, a complication in the radiated signals between them. He had not been aware that he was different; the brood mind's questions suggested he might be. But he could not possibly face up to the fact and analyze it all in one short time. He signaled his distress.

"You are useful to the team," the brood mind said. Aryz calmed instantly. His thoughts became sluggish, receptive. There was a possibility of redemption. But how was he different? "You are to attempt communication with the shapes yourself. You will not engage in any discourse with your fellows while you are so involved." He was banned. "And after completion of this mission and transfer of certain facts to me, you will dissipate."

Aryz struggled with the complexity of the orders. "How am I different, worthy of such a commission?"

The surface of the brood mind was as still as an undisturbed pool. The indistinct black smudges that marked its radiating organs circulated slowly within the interior, then returned, one above the other, to focus on him. "You will grow a new branch ind. It will not have your flaws, but, then again, it will not be useful to me should such a situation come a second time. Your dissipation will be a relief, but it will be regretted."

"How am I different?"

"I think you know already," the brood mind said. "When the time comes, you will feed the new branch ind all your memories but those of human contact. If you do not survive to that stage of its growth, you will pick your fellow who will perform that function for you."

A small pinkish spot appeared on the back of Aryz's globe. He floated forward and placed his largest permeum against the brood mind's cool surface. The key and command were passed, and his body became capable of reproduction. Then the signal of dismissal was given. He left the chamber.

Flowing through the thin stream of liquid ammonia lining the corridor, he felt ambiguously stimulated. His was a position of privilege and anathema. He had been blessed—and condemned. Had any other branch ind experienced such a thing?

Then he knew the brood mind was correct. He *was* different from his fellows. None of them would have asked such questions. None of them could have survived the suggestion of communicating with human shapes. If this task hadn't been given to him, he would have had to dissipate anyway.

The pink spot grew larger, then began to make grayish flakes. It broke through the skin, and casually, almost without thinking, Aryz scraped it off against a bulkhead. It clung, made a radio-frequency emanation something like a sigh, and began absorbing nutrients from the ammonia.

Aryz went to inspect the shapes.

SHE WAS INTRIGUED BY CLEVO, BUT THE KIND OF INTEREST SHE FELT WAS new to her. She was not particularly receptive. Rather, she felt a mental gnawing as if she were hungry or had been injected with some kind of brain moans. What Clevo told her about the mandates opened up a topic she had never considered before. How did all things come to be— and how did she figure in them?

The mandates were quite small, Clevo explained, each little more than a cubic meter in volume. Within them was the entire history and culture of the human species, as accurate as possible, culled from all existing sources. The mandate in each ship was updated whenever the ship returned to a contact station. It was not likely the *Mellangee* would return to a contact station during their lifetimes, with the crew leading such short lives on the average.

Clevo had been assigned small tasks—checking data and adding ship records—that had allowed him to sample bits of the mandate. "It's mandated that we have records," he explained, "and what we have, you see, is *man-data*." He smiled. "That's a joke," he said. "Sort of."

Prufrax nodded solemnly. "So where do we come from?"

"Earth, of course," Clevo said. "Everyone knows that."

"I mean, where do *we* come from—you and I, the crew."

"Breeding division. Why ask? You know."

"Yes." She frowned, concentrating. "I mean, we don't come from the same place as the Senexi. The same way."

"No, that's foolishness."

She saw that it was foolishness—the Senexi were different all around. What was she struggling to ask? "Is their fib like our own?"

"Fib? History's not a fib. Not most of it, anyway. Fibs are for unreal. History is overfib."

She knew, in a vague way, that fibs were unreal. She didn't like to have their comfort demeaned, though. "Fibs are fun," she said. "They teach Zap."

"I suppose," Clevo said dubiously. "Being noncombat, I don't see Zap fibs."

Fibs without Zap were almost unthinkable to her. "Such dull," she said.

"Well, of course you'd say that. I might find Zap fibs dull—think of that?"

"We're different," she said. "Like Senexi are different."

Clevo's jaw hung open. "No way. We're crew. We're human. Senexi are . . ." He shook his head as if fed bitters.

"No, I mean . . ." She paused, uncertain whether she was entering unallowed territory. "You and I, we're fed different, given different moans. But in a big way we're different from Senexi. They aren't made, nor do they act, as you and I. But . . ." Again it was difficult to express. She was irritated. "I don't want to talk to you anymore."

A tellman walked down the path, not familiar to Prufrax. He held out his hand for Clevo, and Clevo grasped it. "It's amazing," the tellman said, "how you two gravitate to each other. Go, elfstate," he addressed Prufrax. "You're on the wrong greenroad."

She never saw the young researcher again. With glover training underway, the itches he aroused soon faded, and Zap resumed its overplace.

THE SENEXI HAD WAYS OF KNOWING HUMANS WERE NEAR. AS INFORMATION came in about fleets and individual cruisers less than one percent nebula diameter distant, the seedship seemed warmer, less hospitable. Everything was UV with anxiety, and the new branch ind on the wall had to be shielded by a special silicate cup to prevent distortion. The brood mind grew a corniculum automatically, though the toughened outer membrane would be of little help if the seedship was breached.

Aryz had buried his personal confusion under a load of work. He had penetrated the human memory store deeply enough to find instructions on its use. It called itself a *mandate* (the human word came through the interface as a correlated series of radiated symbols), and even the simple preliminary directions were difficult for Aryz. It was like swimming in another family's private sea, though of course infinitely more alien; how could he connect with experiences never had, problems and needs never encountered by his kind?

He could speak some of the human languages in several radio frequencies, but he hadn't yet decided how he was going to produce modulated sound for the human shapes. It was a disturbing prospect. What would he vibrate? A permeum could vibrate subtly—such signals were used when branch inds joined to form the brood mind but he doubted his control would ever be subtle enough. Sooner expect a human to communicate with a Senexi by controlling the radiations of its nervous system! The humans had distinct organs within their breathing passages that produced the vibrations; perhaps those structures could be mimicked. But he hadn't yet studied the dead shapes in much detail.

He observed the new branch ind once or twice each watch period. Never before had he seen an induced replacement. The normal process was for two brood minds to exchange plasm and form new team buds, then to exchange and nurture the buds. The buds were later cast free to swim as individual larvae. While the larvae often swam through the liquid and gas atmosphere of a Senexi world for thousands, even tens of thousands of kilometers, inevitably they returned to gather with the other buds of their team. Replacements were selected from a separately created pool of "generic" buds only if one or more originals had been destroyed during their wanderings. The destruction of a complete team meant reproductive failure.

In a mature team, only when a branch ind was destroyed did the brood mind induce a replacement. In essence, then, Aryz was already considered dead.

Yet he was still useful. That amused him, if the Senexi emotion could be called amusement. Restricting himself from his fellows was difficult, but he filled the time by immersing himself, through the interface, in the mandate.

The humans were also connected with the mandate through their surrogate parent, and in this manner they were quiescent.

He reported infrequently to the brood mind. Until he had established communication, there was little to report.

And throughout his turmoil, like the others he could sense a fight was coming. It could determine the success or failure of all their work in the nebula. In the grand scheme, failure here might not be crucial. But the Senexi had taken the long view too often in the past. Their age and experience—their calmness—were working against them. How else to explain the decision to communicate with human shapes? Where would such efforts lead? If he succeeded.

And he knew himself well enough to doubt he would fail.

He could feel an affinity for them already, peering at them through the thick glass wall in their isolated chamber, his skin paling at the thought of their heat, their poisonous chemistry. A diseased affinity. He hated himself for it. And reveled in it. It was what made him particularly useful to the team. If he was defective, and this was the only way he could serve, then so be it.

The other branch inds observed his passings from a distance, making no judgments. Aryz was dead, though he worked and moved. His sacrifice had been fearful. Yet he would not be a hero. His kind could never be emulated.

It was a horrible time, a horrible conflict.

SHE FLOATED IN LANGUAGE, LEARNED IT IN A TRICE; THERE WERE NO DIS-tractions. She floated in history and picked up as much as she could, for the source seemed inexhaustible. She tried to distinguish between eyes-open—the barren, pale gray-brown chamber with the thick green wall, beyond which floated a murky roundness—and eyes-shut, when she dropped back into language and history with no fixed foundation.

Eyes-open, she saw the Mam with its comforting limbs and its soft voice, its tubes and extrusions of food and its hissings and removal of waste. Through Mam's wires she learned. Mam also tended another like herself, and another, and one more unlike any of them, more like the shape beyond the green wall.

She was very young, and it was all a mystery.

At least she knew her name. And what she was supposed to do. She took small comfort in that.

THEY FITTED PRUFRAX WITH HER GLOVES, AND SHE WENT INTO THE PRACTICE chamber, dragged by her gloves almost, for she hadn't yet knitted her plug-in nerves in the right index digit and her pace control was uncertain.

There, for six wakes straight, she flew with the other glovers back and forth across the dark spaces like elfstate comets. Constellations and nebula aspects flashed at random on the distant walls, and she oriented to them like a night-flying bird. Her glovemates were Ornin, an especially slender male, and Ban, a red-haired female, and the special-projects sisters Ya, Trice, and Damu, new from the breeding division.

When she let the gloves have their way, she was freer than she had ever felt before. Did the gloves really control? The question wasn't important. Control was somewhere uncentered, behind her eyes and beyond her fingers, as if she were drawn on a beautiful silver wire where it was best to go. Doing what was best to do. She barely saw the field that flowed from the grip of the thick, solid gloves or felt its caressing, life-sustaining influence. Truly, she hardly saw or felt anything but situations, targets, opportunities, the success or failure of the Zap. Failure was an acute pain. She was never reprimanded for failure; the reprimand was in her blood, and she felt like she wanted to die. But then the opportunity would improve, the Zap would succeed, and everything around her—stars, Senexi seedship, the *Mellangee*, everything—seemed part of a beautiful dream all her own.

She was intense in the Mocks.

Their initial practice over, the entry play began.

One by one, the special-projects sisters took their hyperbolic formation. Their glove fields threw out extensions, and they combined force. In they went, the mock Senexi seedship brilliant red and white and UV and radio and hateful before them. Their tails swept through the seedship's outer shields and swirled like long silky hair laid on water; they absorbed fantastic energies, grew bright like violent little stars against the seedship outline. They were engaged in the drawing of the shields, and sure as topology, the spirals of force had to have a dimple on the opposite side that would iris wide enough to let in glovers. The sisters twisted the forces, and Prufrax could see the dimple stretching out under them—

The exercise ended. The elfstate glovers were cast into sudden dark. Prufrax came out of the mock unprepared, her mind still bent on the Zap. The lack of orientation drove her as mad as a moth suddenly flipped from night to day. She careened until gently mitted and channeled. She flowed down a tube, the field slowly neutralizing, and came to a halt still gloved, her body jerking and tingling.

"What the breed happened?" she screamed, her hands beginning to hurt.

"Energy conserve," a mechanical voice answered. Behind Prufrax the other elfstate glovers lined up in the catch tube, all but the special-projects sisters. Ya, Trice, and Damu had been taken out of the exercise early and replaced by simulations. There was no way their functions could be mocked. They entered the tube ungloved and helped their comrades adjust to the overness of the real.

As they left the mock chamber, another batch of glovers, even younger and fresher in elfstate, passed them. Ya held up her hands, and they saluted in return. "Breed more every day," Prufrax grumbled. She worried about having so many crew she'd never be able to conduct a satisfactory Zap herself. Where would the honor of being a glover go if everyone was a glover?

She wriggled into her cramped bunk, feeling exhilarated and irritated. She replayed the mocks and added in the missing Zap, then stared gloomily at her small narrow feet.

Out there the Senexi waited. Perhaps they were in the same state as she—ready to fight, testy at being reined in. She pondered her ignorance, her inability to judge whether such feelings were even possible among the enemy. She thought of the researcher, Clevo. "Blank," she murmured. "Blank, blank." Such thoughts were unnecessary, and humanizing Senexi was unworthy of a glover.

ARYZ LOOKED AT THE INSTRUMENT, STRETCHED A POD INTO IT, AND WILLED. Vocal human language came out the other end, thin and squeaky in the helium atmosphere. The sound disgusted and thrilled him. He removed the instrument from the gelatinous strands of the engineering wall and pushed it into his interior through a stretched permeum. He took a thick draft of ammonia and slid to the human shapes chamber again.

He pushed through the narrow port into the observation room. Adjusting his eyes to the heat and bright light beyond the transparent wall, he saw the round mutated shape first—the result of their unsuccessful experiments. He swung his sphere around and looked at the others.

For a time he couldn't decide which was uglier—the mutated shape or the normals. Then he thought of what it would be like to have humans tamper with Senexi and try to make them into human forms. . . . He looked at the round human and shrunk as if from sudden heat. Aryz had had nothing to do with the experiments. For that, at least, he was grateful.

Apparently, even before fertilization, human buds—eggs—were adapted for specific roles. The healthy human shapes appeared sufficiently different—discounting *sexual* characteristics—to indicate some variation in function. They were four-podded, two-opticked, with auditory apparatus and olfactory organs mounted on the *head*, along with one permeum, the *mouth*. At least, he thought, they were hairless, unlike some of the other Population I species Aryz had learned about in the mandate.

Aryz placed the tip of the vocalizer against a sound-transmitting plate and spoke.

"Zello," came the sound within the chamber. The mutated shape looked up. It lay on the floor, great bloated stomach backed by four almost useless pods. It usually made high-pitched sounds continuously. Now it stopped and listened, straining on the tube that connected it to the breed-supervising device.

"Hello," replied the male. It sat on a ledge across the chamber, having unhooked itself.

The machine that served as surrogate parent and instructor stood in one corner, an awkward parody of a human, with limbs too long and head too small. Aryz could see the unwillingness of the designing engineers to examine human anatomy too closely.

"I am called—" Aryz said, his name emerging as a meaningless stretch of white noise. He would have to do better than that. He compressed and adapted the frequencies. "I am called Aryz."

"Hello," the young female said.

"What are your names?" He knew that well enough, having listened many times to their conversations.

"Prufrax," the female said. "I'm a glover."

The human shapes contained very little genetic memory. As a kind of brood marker, Aryz supposed, they had been equipped with their name, occupation, and the rudiments of environmental knowledge. This seemed to have been artificially imposed; in their natural state, very likely, they were born almost blank. He could not, however, be certain, since human reproductive chemistry was extraordinarily subtle and complicated.

"I'm a teacher, Prufrax," Aryz said. The logic structure of the language continued to be painful to him.

"I don't understand you," the female replied.

"You teach me, I teach you."

"We have the Mam," the male said, pointing to the machine. "She teaches us." The Mam, as they called it, was hooked into the mandate. Withholding that from the humans—the only equivalent, in essence, to the Senexi sac of memory—would have been unthinkable. It was bad enough that humans didn't come naturally equipped with their own share of knowledge.

"Do you know where you are?" Aryz asked.

"Where we live," Prufrax said. "Eyes-open."

Aryz opened a port to show them the stars and a portion of the nebula. "Can you tell where you are by looking out the window?"

"Among the lights," Prufrax said.

Humans, then, did not instinctively know their positions by star patterns as other Population I species did.

"Don't talk to it," the male said. "Mam talks to us." Aryz consulted the mandate for some understanding of the name they had given to the breed-supervising machine. Mam, it explained, was probably a natural expression for womb-carrying parent. Aryz severed the machine's power.

"Mam is no longer functional," he said. He would have the engineering wall put together another less identifiable machine to link them to the mandate and to their nutrition. He wanted them to associate comfort and completeness with nothing but himself.

The machine slumped, and the female shape pulled herself free of the hookup. She started to cry, a reaction quite mysterious to Aryz. His link with the mandate had not been intimate enough to answer questions about the wailing and moisture from the eyes. After a time the male and female lay down and became dormant.

The mutated shape made more soft sounds and tried to approach the transparent wall. It held up its thin arms as if beseeching. The others would have nothing to do with it; now it wished to go with him. Perhaps the biologists had partially succeeded in their attempt at transformation; perhaps it was more Senexi than human.

Aryz quickly backed out through the port, into the cool and security of the corridor beyond.

IT WAS AN ENDLESS ORBITAL DANCE, THIS DETECTION AND MATCHING OF course, moving away and swinging back, deceiving and revealing, between the *Mellangee* and the Senexi seedship. It was inevitable that the human ship should close in; human ships were faster, knew better the higher geometries.

Filled with her skill and knowledge, Prufrax waited, feeling like a ripe fruit about to fall from the tree. At this point in their training, just before the application, elfstates were very receptive. She was allowed to take a lover, and they were assigned small separate quarters near the outer greenroads.

The contact was satisfactory, as far as it went. Her mate was an older glover named Kumnax, and as they lay back in the cubicle, soothed by air-dance fibs, he told her stories about past battles, special tactics, how to survive.

"Survive?" she asked, puzzled.

"Of course." His long brown face was intent on the view of the green-roads through the cubicle's small window.

"I don't understand," she said.

"Most glovers don't make it," he said patiently.

"I will."

He turned to her. "You're six," he said. "You're very young. I'm ten. I've seen. You're about to be applied for the first time, you're full of confidence. But most glovers won't make it. They breed thousands of us. We're expendable. We're based on the best glovers of the past, but even the best don't survive."

"I will," Prufrax repeated, her jaw set.

"You always say that," he murmured.

Prufrax stared at him for a moment.

"Last time I knew you," he said, "you kept saying that. And here you are, fresh again."

"What last time?"

"Master Kumnax," a mechanical voice interrupted.

He stood, looking down at her. "We glovers always have big mouths. They don't like us knowing, but once we know, what can they do about it?"

"You are in violation," the voice said. "Please report to S."

"But now, if you last, you'll know more than the tellman tells."

"I don't understand," Prufrax said slowly, precisely, looking him straight in the eye.

"I've paid my debt," Kumnax said. "We glovers stick. Now I'm going to go get my punishment." He left the cubicle. Prufrax didn't see him again before her first application.

THE SEEDSHIP BURIED ITSELF IN A HEATING PROTOSTAR, RAISING SHIELDS against the infalling ice and stone. The nebula had congealed out of a particularly rich cluster of exploded fourth- and fifth-generation stars, thick with planets, the detritus of which now fell on Aryz's ship like hail.

Aryz had never been so isolated. No other branch ind addressed him; he never even saw them now. He made his reports to the brood mind, but even there the reception was warmer and warmer, until he could barely endure to communicate. Consequently—and he realized this was part of the plan—he came closer to his charges, the human shapes. He felt more sympathy for them. He discovered that even between human and Senexi there could be a bridge of need—the need to be useful.

The brood mind was interested in one question: how successfully could they be planted aboard a human ship? Would they be accepted until they could carry out their sabotage, or would they be detected? Already Senexi instructions were being coded into their teachings.

"I think they will be accepted in the confusion of an engagement," Aryz answered. He had long since guessed the general outlines of the brood mind's plans. Communication with the human shapes was for one purpose only; to use them as decoys, insurgents. They were weapons. Knowledge of human activity and behavior was not an end in itself; seeing what was happening to him, Aryz fully understood why the brood mind wanted such study to proceed no further.

He would lose them soon, he thought, and his work would be over. He would be much too human-tainted. He would end, and his replacement would start a new existence, very little different from Aryz—but, he reasoned, adjusted. The replacement would not have Aryz's peculiarity.

He approached his last meeting with the brood mind, preparing himself for his final work, for the ending. In the cold liquid-filled chamber, the great red-and-white sac waited, the center of his team, his existence. He adored it. There was no way he could criticize its action.

Yet—

"We are being sought," the brood mind radiated. "Are the shapes ready?"

"Yes," Aryz said. "The new teaching is firm. They believe they are fully human." And, except for the new teaching, they were. "They defy sometimes." He said nothing about the mutated shape. It would not be used. If they won this encounter, it would probably be placed with Aryz's body in a fusion torch for complete purging.

"Then prepare them," the brood mind said. "They will be delivered to the vector for positioning and transfer."

DARKNESS AND WAITING. PRUFRAX NESTED IN HER DELIVERY TUBE LIKE A freshly chambered round. Through her gloves she caught distant communications murmurs that resembled voices down hollow pipes. The *Mellangee* was coming to full readiness.

Huge as her ship was, Prufrax knew that it would be dwarfed by the seedship. She could recall some hazy details about the seedship's structure, but most of that information was stored securely away from interference by her conscious mind. She wasn't even positive what the tactic would be. In the mocks, that at least had been clear. Now such information either had not been delivered or had waited in inaccessible memory, to be brought forward by the appropriate triggers.

More information would be fed to her just before the launch, but she knew the general procedure. The seedship was deep in a protostar, hiding behind the distortion of geometry and the complete hash of electromagnetic energy. The *Mellangee* would approach, collide if need be. Penetrate. Release. Find. Zap. Her fingers ached. Sometime before the launch she would also be fed her final moans—the tempers—and she would be primed to leave elfstate. She would be a mature glover. She would be a woman.

If she returned

will return

she could become part of the breed, her receptivity would end in ecstasy rather than mild warmth, she would contribute second state, naturally born glovers. For a moment she was content with the thought. That was a high honor.

Her fingers ached worse.

The tempers came, moans tiding in, then the battle data. As it passed into her subconscious, she caught a flash of—

Rocks and ice, a thick cloud of dust and gas glowing red but seeming dark, no stars, no constellation guides this time. The beacon came on. That would be her only way to orient once the gloves stopped inertial and locked onto the target.

The seedship

was like

a shadow within a shadow twenty-two kilometers across, yet carrying only six teams

LAUNCH *She flies!*

Data: the *Mellangee* has buried herself in the seedship, ploughed deep into the interior like a carnivore's muzzle looking for vitals.

Instruction: a swarm of seeks is dashing through the seedship, looking for the brood minds, for the brood chambers, for branch inds. The glovers will follow.

Prufrax sees herself clearly now. She is the great avenging comet, bringer of omen and doom, like a knife moving through the glass and ice and thin, cold helium as if they weren't there, the chambered round fired and tearing at hundreds of kilometers an hour through the Senexi vessel, following the seeks.

The seedship cannot withdraw into higher geometries now. It is pinned by the *Mellangee*. It is *hers*.

Information floods *her*, pleases *her* immensely. *She* swoops down orange-and-gray corridors, buffeting against *the* walls like a ricocheting bullet. Almost immediately she comes across a branch ind, sliding through the ammonia film against the outrushing wind, trying to reach an armored cubicle. Her first Zap is too easy, not satisfying, nothing like what she thought. In her wake the branch ind becomes scattered globules of plasma. She plunges deeper.

Aryz delivers his human charges to the vectors that will launch them. They are equipped with simulations of the human weapons, their hands encased in the hideous gray gloves.

The seedship is in deadly peril; the battle has almost been lost at one stroke. The seedship cannot remain whole. It must self-destruct, taking the human ship with it, leaving only a fragment with as many teams as can escape.

The vectors launch the human shapes. Aryz tries to determine which part of the ship will be elected to survive; he must not be there. His job is over, and he must die.

The glovers fan out through the seedship's central hollow, demolishing the great cold drive engines, bypassing the shielded fusion flare and the reprocessing plant, destroying machinery built before their Earth was formed.

The special-projects sisters take the lead. Suddenly they are confused. They have found a brood mind, but it is not heavily protected. They surround it, prepare for the Zap—

It is sacrificing itself, drawing them in to an easy kill and away from another portion of the seedship. Power is concentrating elsewhere. Sensing that, they kill quickly and move on.

Aryz's brood mind prepares for escape. It begins to wrap itself in flux bind as it moves through the ship toward the frozen fragment. Already three of its five branch inds are dead; it can feel other brood minds dying. Aryz's bud replacement has been killed as well.

Following Aryz's training, the human shapes rush into corridors away from the main action. The special-projects sisters encounter the decoy male, allow it to fly with them . . . until it aims its weapons. One Zap almost takes out Trice. The others fire on the shape immediately. He goes to his death weeping, confused from the very moment of his launch.

The fragment in which the brood mind will take refuge encompasses the chamber where the humans had been nurtured, where the mandate is still stored. All the other brood minds are dead, Aryz realizes; the humans have swept down on them so quickly. What shall he do?

Somewhere, far off, he feels the distressed pulse of another branch ind dying. He probes the remains of the seedship. He is the last. He cannot dissipate now; he must ensure the brood mind's survival.

Prufrax, darting through the crumbling seedship, searching for more opportunities, comes across an injured glover. She calls for a mediseek and pushes on.

The brood mind settles into the fragment. Its support system is damaged; it is entering the time-isolated state, the flux bind, more rapidly than it should. The seals of foamed electric ice cannot quite close off the fragment before Ya, Trice, and Damu slip in. They frantically call for bind-cutters and preservers; they have instructions to capture the last brood mind, if possible.

But a trap falls upon Ya, and snarling fields tear her from her gloves. She is flung down a dark disintegrating shaft, red cracks opening all around as the seedship's integrity fails. She trails silver dust and freezes, hits a barricade, shatters.

The ice seals continue to close. Trice is caught between them and pushes out frantically, blundering into the region of the intensifying flux bind. Her gloves break into hard bits, and she is melded into an ice wall like an insect trapped on the surface of a winter lake.

Damu sees that the brood mind is entering the final phase of flux bind. After that they will not be able to touch it. She begins a desperate Zap

and is too late.

Aryz directs the subsidiary energy of the flux against her. Her Zap deflects from the bind region, she is caught in an interference pattern and vibrates until her tiniest particles stop their knotted whirlpool spins and she simply becomes

space and searing light.

The brood mind, however, has been damaged. It is losing information from one portion of its anatomy. Desperate for storage, it looks for places to hold the information before the flux bind's last wave.

Aryz directs an interface onto the brood mind's surface. The silvery pools of time-binding flicker around them both. The brood mind's damaged sections transfer their data into the last available storage device—the human mandate.

Now it contains both human and Senexi information.

The silvery pools unite, and Aryz backs away. No longer can he sense the brood mind. It is out of reach but not yet safe. He must propel the fragment from the remains of the seedship. Then he must wrap the fragment in its own flux bind, cocoon it in physics to protect it from the last ravages of the humans.

Aryz carefully navigates his way through the few remaining corridors. The helium atmosphere has almost completely dissipated, even there. He strains to remember all the procedures. Soon the seedship will explode, destroying the human ship. By then they must be gone.

Angry red, Prufrax follows his barely sensed form, watching him behind barricades of ice, approaching the moment of a most satisfying Zap. She gives her gloves their way

and finds a shape behind her, wearing gloves that are not gloves, not like her own, but capable of grasping her in tensed fields, blocking the Zap, dragging them together. The fragment separates, heat pours in from the protostar cloud. They are swirled in their vortex of power, twin locked comets—one red, one sullen gray.

"Who are you?" Prufrax screams as they close in on each other in the fields. Their environments meld. They grapple. In the confusion, the darkening, they are drawn out of the cloud with the fragment, and she sees the other's face.

Her own.

The seedship self-destructs. The fragment is propelled from the protostar, above the plane of what will become planets in their orbits, away from the crippled and dying *Mellangee*.

Desperate, Prufrax uses all her strength to drill into the fragment. Helium blows past them, and bits of dead branch inds.

Aryz catches the pair immediately in the shapes chamber, rearranging the fragment's structure to enclose them with the mutant shape and mandate. For the moment he has time enough to concentrate on them. They are dangerous. They are almost equal to each other, but his shape is weakening faster than the true glover. They float, bouncing from wall to wall in the chamber, forcing the mutant to crawl into a corner and howl with fear.

There may be value in saving the one and capturing the other. Involved as they are, the two can be carefully dissected from their fields and induced into a crude kind of sleep before the glover has a chance to free her weapons. He can dispose of the gloves—fake and real—and hook them both to the Mam, reattach the mutant shape as well. Perhaps something can be learned from the failure of the experiment.

The dissection and capture occur faster than the planning. His movement slows under the spreading flux bind. His last action, after attaching the humans to the Mam, is to make sure the brood mind's flux bind is properly nested within that of the ship.

The fragment drops into simpler geometries.

It is as if they never existed.

THE BATTLE WAS OVER. THERE WERE NO VICTORS. ARYZ BECAME AWARE OF the passage of time, shook away the sluggishness, and crawled through painfully dry corridors to set the environmental equipment going again. Throughout the fragment, machines struggled back to activity.

How many generations? The constellations were unrecognizable. He made star traces and found familiar spectra and types, but advanced in age. There had been a malfunction in the overall flux bind. He couldn't find the nebula where the battle had occurred. In its place were comfortably middle-aged stars surrounded by young planets.

Aryz came down from the makeshift observatory. He slid through the fragment, established the limits of his new home, and found the solid mirror surface of the brood mind's cocoon. It was still locked in flux bind, and he knew of no way to free it. In time the bind would probably wear off—but that might require life spans. The seedship was gone. They had lost the brood chamber, and with it the stock.

He was the last branch ind of his team. Not that it mattered now; there was nothing he could initiate without a brood mind. If the flux bind was permanent—as sometimes happened during malfunction then he might as well be dead.

He closed his thoughts around him and was almost completely submerged when he sensed an alarm from the shapes chamber. The interface with the mandate had turned itself off; the new version of the Mam was malfunctioning. He tried to repair the equipment, but without the engineer's wall he was almost helpless. The best he could do was rig a temporary nutrition supply through the old human-form Mam. When he was done, he looked at the captive and the two shapes, then at the legless, armless Mam that served as their link to the interface and life itself.

SHE HAD SPENT HER WHOLE LIFE IN A ROOM BARELY EIGHT BY TEN METERS, and not much taller than her own height. With her had been Grayd and the silent round creature whose name—if it had any—they had never learned. For a time there had been Mam, then another kind of Mam not nearly as satisfactory. She was hardly aware that her entire existence had been miserable, cramped, in one way or another incomplete.

Separated from them by a transparent partition, another round shape had periodically made itself known by voice or gesture.

Grayd had kept her sane. They had engaged in conspiracy. Removing themselves from the interface—what she called "eyes-shut"—they had held on to each other, tried to make sense out of what they knew instinctively, what was fed them through the interface, and what the being beyond the partition told them.

First they knew their names, and they knew that they were glovers. They knew that glovers were fighters. When Aryz passed instruction through the interface on how to fight, they had accepted it eagerly but uneasily. It didn't seem to jibe with instructions locked deep within their instincts.

Five years under such conditions had made her introspective. She expected nothing, sought little beyond experience in the eyes-shut. Eyes-open with Grayd seemed scarcely more than a dream. They usually managed to ignore the peculiar round creature in the chamber with them; it spent nearly all its time hooked to the mandate and the Mam.

Of one thing only was she completely sure. Her name was Prufrax. She said it in eyes-open and eyes-shut, her only certainty.

Not long before the battle, she had been in a condition resembling dreamless sleep, like a robot being given instructions. The part of Prufrax that had taken on personality during eyes-shut and eyes-open for five years had been superseded by the fight instructions Aryz had programmed. She had flown as glovers must fly (though the gloves didn't seem quite right). She had fought, grappling (she thought) with herself, but who could be certain of anything?

She had long since decided that reality was not to be sought too avidly. After the battle she fell back into the mandate—into eyes-shut— all too willingly.

And what matter? If eyes-open was even less comprehensible than eyes-shut, why did she have the nagging feeling eyes-open was so compelling, so necessary? She tried to forget.

But a change had come to eyes-shut, too. Before the battle, the information had been selected. Now she could wander through the mandate at will. She seemed to smell the new information, completely unfamiliar, like a whiff of ocean. She hardly knew where to begin. She stumbled across:

—that all vessels will carry one, no matter what their size or class, just as every individual carries the map of a species. The mandate shall contain all the information of our kind, including accurate and uncensored history, for if we have learned anything, it is that censored and untrue accounts distort the eyes of the leaders. Leaders must have access to the truth. It is their responsibility. Whatever is told those who work under the leaders, for whatever reason, must not be believed by the leaders. Unders are told lies. Leaders must seek and be provided with accounts as accurate as possible, or we will be weakened and fall—

What wonderful dreams the *leaders* must have had. And they possessed some intrinsic gift called *truth*, through the use of the *man-date*. Prufrax could hardly believe that. As she made her tentative explorations through the new fields of eyes-shut, she began to link the word *mandate* with what she experienced. That was where she was.

And she alone. Once, she had explored with Grayd. Now there was no sign of Grayd.

She learned quickly. Soon she walked along a beach on Earth, then a beach on a world called Myriadne, and other beaches, fading in and out. By running through the entries rapidly, she came up with a blurred *eidos* and so learned what a beach was in the abstract. It was a boundary between one kind of eyes-shut and another, between water and land, neither of which had any corollary in eyes-open.

Some beaches had sand. Some had clouds—the *eidos* of clouds was quite attractive. And one—

had herself running scared, screaming.

She called out, but the figure vanished. Prufrax stood on a beach under a greenish-yellow star, on a world called Kyrene, feeling lonelier than ever.

She explored farther, hoping to find Grayd, if not the figure that looked like herself. Grayd wouldn't flee from her. Grayd would. The round thing confronted her, its helpless limbs twitching. Now it was her turn to run, terrified. Never before had she met the round creature in eyes-shut. It was mobile; it had a purpose. Over land, clouds, trees, rocks, wind, air, equations, and an edge of physics she fled. The farther she went, the more distant from the round one with hands and small head, the less afraid she was.

She never found Grayd.

The memory of the battle was fresh and painful. She remembered the ache of her hands, clumsily removed from the gloves. Her environment had collapsed and been replaced by something indistinct. Prufrax had fallen into a deep slumber and had dreamed.

The dreams were totally unfamiliar to her. If there was a left-turning in her arc of sleep, she dreamed of philosophies and languages and other things she couldn't relate to. A right-turning led to histories and sciences so incomprehensible as to be nightmares.

It was a most unpleasant sleep, and she was not at all sorry to find she wasn't really asleep.

The crucial moment came when she discovered how to slow her turnings and the changes of dream subject. She entered a pleasant place of which she had no knowledge but which did not seem threatening. There was a vast expanse of water, but it didn't terrify her. She couldn't even identify it as water until she scooped up a handful. Beyond the water was a floor of shifting particles. Above both was an open expanse, not black but obviously space, drawing her eyes into intense pale blue-green. And there was that figure she had encountered in the seedship. Herself. The figure pursued. She fled.

Right over the boundary into Senexi information. She knew then that what she was seeing couldn't possibly come from within herself. She was receiving data from another source. Perhaps she had been taken captive. It was possible she was now being forcibly debriefed. The tell-man had discussed such possibilities, but none of the glovers had been taught how to defend themselves in specific situations. Instead it had been stated—in terms that brooked no second thought that self-destruction was the only answer. So she tried to kill herself.

She sat in the freezing cold of a red-and-white room, her feet meeting but not touching a fluid covering on the floor. The information didn't fit her senses—it seemed blurred, inappropriate. Unlike the other data, this didn't allow participation or motion. Everything was locked solid.

She couldn't find an effective means of killing herself. She resolved to close her eyes and simply will herself into dissolution. But closing her eyes only moved her into a deeper or shallower level of deception—other categories, subjects, visions. She couldn't sleep, wasn't tired, couldn't die.

Like a leaf on a stream, she drifted. Her thoughts untangled, and she imagined herself floating on the water called ocean. She kept her eyes open. It was quite by accident that she encountered:

Instruction. Welcome to the introductory use of the mandate. As a noncombat processor, your duties are to maintain the mandate, provide essential information for your overs, and, if necessary, protect or destroy the mandate. The mandate is your immediate over. If it requires maintenance, you will oblige. Once linked with the mandate, as you are now, you may explore any aspect of the information by requesting delivery. To request delivery, indicate the core of your subject—

Prufrax! she shouted silently. What is Prufrax?

A voice with different tone immediately took over.

Ah, now that's quite a story. I was her biographer, the organizer of her life tapes (ref. GEORGE MACKNAX), and knew her well in the last years of her life. She was born in the Ferment 26468. Here are selected life tapes. Choose emphasis. Analyses follow.

—Hey! Who are you? There's someone here with me. . . .

—Shh! Listen. Look at her. Who is she?

They looked, listened to the information.

—Why, she's me . . . sort of.

—She's us.

SHE STOOD TWO AND A HALF METERS TALL. HER HAIR WAS BLACK AND THICK, though cut short; her limbs well-muscled though drawn out by the training and hormonal treatments. She was seventeen years old, one of the few birds born in the solar system, and for the time being she had a chip on her shoulder. Everywhere she went, the birds asked about her mother, Jayax. "You better than her?"

Of course not! Who could be? But she was good; the instructors said so. She was just about through training, and whether she graduated to hawk or remained bird she would do her job well. Asking Prufrax about her mother was likely to make her set her mouth tight and glare.

On Mercior, the Grounds took up four thousand hectares and had its own port. The Grounds was divided into Land, Space, and Thought, and training in each area was mandatory for fledges, those birds embarking on hawk training. Prufrax was fledge three. She had passed Land—though she loathed downbound fighting—and was two years into Space. The tough part, everyone said, was not passing Space, but lasting through four years of Thought after the action in nearorbit and planetary.

Prufrax was not the introspective type. She could be studious when it suited her. She was a quick study at weapon maths, physics came easy when it had a direct application, but theory of service and polinstruc—which she had sampled only in prebird courses—bored her.

Since she had been a little girl, no more than five—

—Five! Five what?

and had seen her mother's ships and fightsuits and fibs, she had known she would never be happy until she had ventured far out and put a seedship in her sights, had convinced a Senexi of the overness of end—

—The Zap! She's talking the Zap!

—What's that?

—You're me, you should know.

—I'm not you, and we're not her.

The Zap, said the mandate, and the data shifted.

"Tomorrow you receive your first implants. These will allow you to coordinate with the zero-angle phase engines and find your targets much more rapidly than you ever could with simple biologic. The implants, of course, will be delivered through your noses—minor irritation and sinus trouble, no more—into your limbic system. Later in your training, hookups and digital adapts will be installed as well. Are there any questions?"

"Yes, sir." Prufrax stood at the top of the spherical classroom, causing the hawk instructor to swivel his platform. "I'm having problems with the zero-angle phase maths. Reduction of the momenta of the real."

Other fledge threes piped up that they, too, had had trouble with those maths. The hawk instructor sighed. "We don't want to install cheaters in all of you. It's bad enough needing implants to supplement biologic. Individual learning is much more desirable. Do you request cheaters?" That was a challenge. They all responded negatively, but Prufrax had a secret smile. She knew the subject. She just took delight in having the maths explained again. She could reinforce an already thorough understanding. Others not so well versed would benefit. She wasn't wasting time. She was in the pleasure of her weapon—the weapon she would be using against the Senexi.

"Zero-angle phase is the temporary reduction of the momenta of the real." Equations and plexes appeared before each student as the instructor went on. "Nested unreals can conflict if a barrier is placed between the participator princip and the assumption of the real. The effectiveness of the participator can be determined by a convenience model we call the angle of phase. Zero-angle phase is achieved by an opaque probability field according to modified Fourier of the separation of real waves. This can also be caused by the reflection of the beam—an effective counter to zero-angle phase, since the beam is always compoundable and the compound is always time-reversed. Here are the true gedanks—"

—Zero-angle phase. She's learning the Zap.

—She hates them a lot, doesn't she?

—The Senexi? They're Senexi.

—I think . . . eyes-open is the world of the Senexi. What does that mean?

—That we're prisoners. You were caught before me.

—Oh.

The news came as she was in recovery from the implant. Seedships had violated human space again, dropping cuckoos on thirty-five worlds. The worlds had been young colonies, and the cuckoos had wiped out all life, then tried to reseed with Senexi forms. The overs had reacted by sterilizing the planet's surfaces. No victory, loss to both sides. It was as if the Senexi were so malevolent they didn't care about success, only about destruction.

She hated them. She could imagine nothing worse.

Prufrax was twenty-three. In a year she would be qualified to hawk on a cruiser/raider. She would demonstrate her hatred.

ARYZ FELT HIMSELF SLIPPING INTO ENDTHOUGHT, THE MIND SET THAT ALWAYS preceded a branch ind's self-destruction. What was there for him to do? The fragment had survived, but at what cost, to what purpose? Nothing had been accomplished. The nebula had been lost, or he supposed it had. He would likely never know the actual outcome.

He felt a vague irritation at the lack of a spectrum of responses. Without a purpose, a branch ind was nothing more than excess plasm.

He looked in on the captive and the shapes, all hooked to the mandate, and wondered what he would do with them. How would humans react to the situation he was in? More vigorously, probably. They would fight on. They always had. Even without leaders, with no discernible purpose, even in defeat. What gave them such stamina? Were they superior, more deserving? If they were better, then was it right for the Senexi to oppose their triumph?

Aryz drew himself tall and rigid with confusion. He had studied them too long. They had truly infected him. But here at least was a hint of purpose. A question needed to be answered.

He made preparations. There were signs the brood mind's flux bind was not permanent, was in fact unwinding quite rapidly. When it emerged, Aryz would present it with a judgment, an answer.

He realized, none too clearly, that by Senexi standards he was now a raving lunatic.

He would hook himself into the mandate, improve the somewhat isolating interface he had used previously to search for selected answers. He, the captive, and the shapes would be immersed in human history together. They would be like young suckling on a Population I mother-animal—just the opposite of the Senexi process, where young fed nourishment and information into the brood mind.

The mandate would nourish, or poison. Or both.

—DID SHE LOVE?
   —What—you mean, did she receive?
   —No, did she—we—I—give?
   —I don't know what you mean.
   —I wonder if she would know what I mean. . . .
   Love, said the mandate, and the data proceeded.

Prufrax was twenty-nine. She had been assigned to a cruiser in a new program where superior but untested fighters were put into thick action with no preliminary. The program was designed to see how well the Grounds prepared fighters; some thought it foolhardy, but Prufrax found it perfectly satisfactory.

The cruiser was a million-ton raider, with a hawk contingent of fifty-three and eighty regular crew. She would be used in a second-wave attack, following the initial hardfought.

She was scared. That was good; fright improved basic biologic, if properly managed. The cruiser would make a raid into Senexi space and retaliate for past cuckoo-seeding programs. They would come up against thornships and seedships, likely.

The fighting was going to be fierce.

The raider made its final denial of the overness of the real and pip-squeezed into an arduous, nasty sponge space. It drew itself together again and emerged far above the galactic plane.

PRUFRAX SAT IN THE HAWKS WARDROOM AND LOOKED AT THE SIMULATED rotating snowball of stars. Red-coded numerals flashed along the borders of known Senexi territory, signifying old stars, dark hulks of stars, the whole ghostly home region where they had first come to power when the terrestrial sun had been a mist-wrapped youngster. A green arrow showed the position of the raider.

She drank sponge-space supplements with the others but felt isolated because of her firstness, her fear. Everyone seemed so calm. Most were fours or fives—on their fourth or fifth battle call. There were ten ones and an upper scatter of experienced hawks with nine to twenty-five battles behind them. There were no thirties. Thirties were rare in combat; the few that survived so many engagements were plucked off active and retired to PR service under the polinstructors. They often ended up in fibs, acting poorly, looking unhappy.

Still, when she had been more naive, Prufrax's heroes had been a man-and-woman thirty team she had watched in fib after fib—Kumnax and Arol. They had been better actors than most.

Day in, day out, they drilled in their fightsuits. While the crew bustled, hawks were put through implant learning, what slang was already calling the Know, as opposed to the Tell, of classroom teaching. Getting background, just enough to tickle her curiosity, not enough to stimulate morbid interest.

—There it is again. Feel?

—I know it. Yes. The round one, part of eyes-open . . .

—Senexi?

—No, brother without name.

—Your . . . brother?

—No . . . I don't know.

—Can it hurt us?

—It never has. It's trying to talk to us.

—Leave us *alone!*

—It's going.

Still, there were items of information she had never received before, items privileged only to the fighters, to assist them in their work. Older hawks talked about the past, when data had been freely available. Stories circulated in the wardroom about the Senexi, and she managed to piece together something of their origins and growth.

Senexi worlds, according to a twenty, had originally been large, cold masses of gas circling bright young suns nearly metal-free. Their gas-giant planets had orbited the suns at hundreds of millions of kilometers and had been dusted by the shrouds of neighboring dead stars; the essential elements carbon, nitrogen, silicon, and fluorine had gathered in sufficient quantities on some of the planets to allow Population II biology.

In cold ammonia seas, lipids had combined in complex chains. A primal kind of life had arisen and flourished. Across millions of years, early Senexi forms had evolved. Compared with evolution on Earth, the process at first had moved quite rapidly. The mechanisms of procreation and evolution had been complex in action, simple in chemistry

There had been no competition between life forms of different genetic bases. On Earth, much time had been spent selecting between the plethora of possible ways to pass on genetic knowledge.

And among the early Senexi, outside of predation there had been no death. Death had come about much later, self-imposed for social reasons. Huge colonies of protoplasmic individuals had gradually resolved into the team-forms now familiar.

Soon information was transferred through the budding of branch inds; cultures quickly developed to protect the integrity of larvae, to allow them to regroup and form a new brood mind. Technologies had been limited to the rare heavy materials available, but the Senexi had expanded for a time with very little technology. They were well adapted to their environment, with few predators and no need to hunt, absorbing stray nutrients from the atmosphere and from layers of liquid ammonia. With perceptions attuned to the radio and microwave frequencies, they had before long turned groups of branch inds into radio telescope chains, piercing the heavy atmosphere and probing the universe in great detail, especially the very active center of the young galaxy. Huge jets of matter, streaming from other galaxies and emitting high-energy radiation, had provided laboratories for their vicarious observations. Physics was a primitive science to them.

Since little or no knowledge was lost in breeding cycles, cultural growth was rapid at times; since the dead weight of knowledge was often heavy, cultural growth often slowed to a crawl.

Using water as a building material, developing techniques that humans still understood imperfectly, they prepared for travel away from their birthworlds.

Prufrax wondered, as she listened to the older hawks, how humans had come to know all this. Had Senexi been captured and questioned? Was it all theory? Did anyone really know—anyone she could ask?

—She's weak.

—Why weak?

—Some knowledge is best for glovers to ignore. Some questions are best left to the supreme overs.

—Have you thought that in here, you can answer her questions, our questions?

—No. No. Learn about me—us—first.

In the hour before engagement, Prufrax tried to find a place alone. On the raider this wasn't difficult. The ship's size was overwhelming for the number of hawks and crew aboard. There were many areas where she could put on an environs and walk or drift in silence, surrounded by the dark shapes of equipment wrapped in plexerv. There was so much about ship operations she didn't understand, hadn't been taught. Why carry so much excess equipment, weapons—far more than they'd need even for replacements? She could think of possibilities—superiors on Mercior wanting their cruisers to have flexible mission capabilities, for one—but her ignorance troubled her less than why she was ignorant. Why was it necessary to keep fighters in the dark on so many subjects?

She pulled herself through the cold g-less tunnels, feeling slightly awked by the loneness, the quiet. One tunnel angled outboard, toward the hull of the cruiser. She hesitated, peering into its length with her environs beacon, when a beep warned her she was near another crew member. She was startled to think someone else might be as curious as she. The other hawks and crew, for the most part, had long outgrown their need to wander and regarded it as birdish. Prufrax was used to being different—she had always perceived herself, with some pride, as a bit of a freak. She scooted expertly up the tunnel, spreading her arms and tucking her legs as she would in a fightsuit.

The tunnel was filled with a faint milky green mist, absorbing her environs beam. It couldn't be much more than a couple of hundred meters long, however, and it was quite straight. The signal beeped louder.

Ahead she could make out a dismantled weapons blister. That explained the fog: a plexerv aerosol diffused in the low pressure. Sitting in the blister was a man, his environs glowing a pale violet. He had deopaqued a section of the blister and was staring out at the stars. He swiveled as she approached and looked her over dispassionately. He seemed to be a hawk—he had fightform, tall, thin with brown hair above hull-white skin, large eyes with pupils so dark she might have been looking through his head into space beyond.

"Under," she said as their environs met and merged.

"Over. What are you doing here?"

"I was about to ask you the same."

"You should be getting ready for the fight," he admonished.

"I am. I need to be alone for a while."

"Yes." He turned back to the stars. "I used to do that, too."

"You don't fight now?"

He shook his head. "Retired. I'm a researcher."

She tried not to look impressed. Crossing rates was almost impossible. A bitalent was unusual in the service.

"What kind of research?" she asked.

"I'm here to correlate enemy finds."

"Won't find much of anything, after we're done with the zero phase."

It would have been polite for him to say, "Power to that," or offer some other encouragement. He said nothing.

"Why would you want to research them?"

"To fight an enemy properly, you have to know what they are. Ignorance is defeat."

"You research tactics?"

"Not exactly."

"What, then?"

"You'll be in a tough hardfought this wake. Make you a proposition. You fight well, observe, come to me and tell me what you see. Then I'll answer your questions."

"Brief you before my immediate overs?"

"I have the authority," he said. No one had ever lied to her; she didn't even suspect he would. "You're eager?"

"Very."

"You'll be doing what?"

"Engaging Senexi fighters, then hunting down branch inds and brood minds."

"How many fighters going in?"

"Twelve."

"Big target, eh?"

She nodded.

"While you're there, ask yourself—what are they fighting for? Understand?"

"I—"

"Ask, what are they fighting for. Just that. Then come back to me."

"What's your name?"

"Not important," he said. "Now go."

She returned to the prep center as the sponge-space warning tones began. Overhawks went among the fighters in the lineup, checking gear and giveaway body points for mental orientation. Prufrax submitted to the molded sensor mask being slipped over her face. "Ready!" the overhawk said. "Hardfought!" He clapped her on the shoulder. "Good luck."

"Thank you, sir." She bent down and slid into her fightsuit. Along the launch line, eleven other hawks did the same. The overs and other crew left the chamber, and twelve red beams delineated the launch tube.

The fightsuits automatically lifted and aligned on their individual beams. Fields swirled around them like silvery tissue in moving water, then settled and hardened into cold scintillating walls, pulsing as the launch energy built up.

The tactic came to her. The ship's sensors became part of her information net. She saw the Senexi thornship—twelve kilometers in diameter, cuckoos lacing its outer hull like maggots on red fruit, snakes waiting to take them on.

She was terrified and exultant, so worked up that her body temperature was climbing. The fightsuit adjusted her balance.

At the count of ten and nine, she switched from biologic to cyber. The implant—after absorbing much of her thought processes for weeks—became Prufrax.

For a time there seemed to be two of her. Biologic continued, and in that region she could even relax a bit, as if watching a fib.

With almost dreamlike slowness, in the electronic time of cyber, her fightsuit followed the beam. She saw the stars and oriented herself to the cruiser's beacon, using both for reference, plunging in the sword-flower formation to assault the thornship. The cuckoos retreated in the vast red hull like worms withdrawing into an apple. Then hundreds of tiny black pinpoints appeared in the closest quadrant to the sword flower.

Snakes shot out, each piloted by a Senexi branch ind. "Hardfought!" she told herself in biologic before that portion gave over completely to cyber.

Why were we flung out of dark
through ice and fire, a shower
of sparks? a puzzle;
Perhaps to build hell.

we strike here, there;
Set brief glows, fall through
and cross round again.

By our dimming, we see what
Beatitude we have.
In the circle, kindling
together, we form an
exhausted Empyrean.
We feel the rush of
igniting winds but still
grow dull and wan.

New rage flames, new light,
dropping like sun through muddy
ice and night and fall
Close, spinning blue and bright.

In time they, too,
Tire. Redden.
We join, compare pasts
cool in huddled paths,
turn gray.

And again.
We are a companion flow
of ash, in the slurry,
out and down.
We sleep.

Rivers form above and below.
Above, iron snakes twist,
clang and slice, chime,
helium eyes watching, seeing
Snowflake hawks,
signaling adamant muscles and
energy teeth. What hunger
compels our venom spit?

It flies, strikes the crystal
flight, making mist gray-green
with ammonia rain.

Sleeping, we glide,
and to each side
unseen shores wait
with the moans of
an unseen tide.

—SHE WROTE THAT. WE. ONE OF HER—OUR—POEMS."

—Poem?
—A kind of fib, I think.
—I don't see what it says.
—Sure you do! She's talking hardfought.

—The Zap? Is that all?

—No, I don't think so.

—Do you understand it?

—Not all . . .

SHE LAY BACK IN THE BUNK, LEGS CROSSED, EYES CLOSED, FEELING THE RE-ceding dominance of the implant—the overness of cyber—and the almost pleasant ache in her back. She had survived her first. The thornship had retired, severely damaged, its surface seared and scored so heavily it would never release cuckoos again.

It would become a hulk, a decoy. Out of action. *Satisfaction / out of action / Satisfaction . . .*

Still, with eight of the twelve fighters lost, she didn't quite feel the exuberance of the rhyme. The snakes had fought very well. Bravely, she might say. They lured, sacrificed, cooperated, demonstrating teamwork as fine as that in her own group. Strategy was what made the cruiser's raid successful. A superior approach, an excellent tactic. And perhaps even surprise, though the final analysis hadn't been posted yet.

Without those advantages, they might have all died.

She opened her eyes and stared at the pattern of blinking lights in the ceiling panel, lights with their secret codes that repeated every second, so that whenever she looked at them, the implant deep inside was debriefed, reinstructed. Only when she fought would she know what she was now seeing.

She returned to the tunnel as quickly as she was able. She floated up toward the blister and found him there, surrounded by packs of information from the last hardfought. She waited until he turned his attention to her.

"Well?" he said.

"I asked myself what they are fighting for. And I'm very angry."

"Why?"

"Because I don't know. I *can't* know. They're Senexi."

"Did they fight well?"

"We lost eight. Eight." She cleared her throat.

"Did they fight well?" he repeated, an edge in his voice.

"Better than I was ever told they could."

"Did they die?"

"Enough of them."

"How many did you kill?"

"I don't know." But she did. Eight.

"You killed eight," he said, pointing to the packs. "I'm analyzing the battle now."

"You're behind what we read, what gets posted?" she asked.

"Partly," he said. "You're a good hawk."

"I knew I would be," she said, her tone quiet, simple.

"Since they fought bravely—"

"How can Senexi be brave?" she asked sharply.

"Since," he repeated, "they fought bravely, why?"

"They want to live, to do their . . . work. Just like me."

"No," he said. She was confused, moving between extremes in her mind, first resisting, then giving in too much. "They're Senexi. They're not like us."

"What's your name?" she asked, dodging the issue.

"Clevo."

Her glory hadn't even begun yet, and already she was well into her fall.

ARYZ MADE HIS CONNECTION AND FELT THE BROOD MIND'S EMERGENCY CACHE of knowledge in the mandate grow up around him like ice crystals on glass. He stood in a static scene. The transition from living memory to human machine memory had resulted in either a coding of data or a reduction of detail; either way, the memory was cold not dynamic. It would have to be compared, recorrelated, if that would ever be possible.

How much human data had had to be dumped to make space for this?

He cautiously advanced into the human memory, calling up topics almost at random. In the short time he had been away, so much of what he had learned seemed to have faded or become scrambled. Branch inds were supposed to have permanent memory, human data, for one reason or another, didn't take. It required so much effort just to begin to understand the different modes of thought.

He backed away from sociological data, trying to remain within physics and mathematics. There he could make conversions to fit his understanding without too much strain.

Then something unexpected happened. He felt the brush of another mind, a gentle inquiry from a source made even stranger by the hint of familiarity. It made what passed for a Senexi greeting, but not in the proper form, using what one branch ind of a team would radiate to a fellow; a gross breach, since it was obviously not from his team or even from his family. Aryz tried to withdraw. How was it possible for minds to meet in the mandate? As he retreated, he pushed into a broad region of incomprehensible data. It had none of the characteristics of the other human regions he had examined.

—This is for machines, the other said.—Not all cultural data is limited to biologic. You are in the area where programs and cyber designs are stored. They are really accessible only to a machine hooked into the mandate.

—What is your family? Aryz asked, the first-step-question in the sequence Senexi used for urgent identity requests.

—I have no family. I am not a branch ind. No access to active brood minds. I have learned from the mandate.

—Then what are you?

—I don't know, exactly. Not unlike you.

Aryz understood what he was dealing with. It was the mind of the mutated shape, the one that had remained in the chamber, beseeching when he approached the transparent barrier.

—I must go now, the shape said. Aryz was alone again in the incomprehensible jumble. He moved slowly, carefully, into the Senexi sector, calling up subjects familiar to him. If he could encounter one shape, doubtless he could encounter the others—perhaps even the captive.

The idea was dreadful—and fascinating. So far as he knew, such intimacy between Senexi and human had never happened before. Yet there was something very Senexi-like in the method, as if branch inds attached to the brood mind were to brush mentalities while searching in the ageless memories.

The dread subsided. There was little worse that could happen to him, with his fellows dead, his brood mind in flux bind, his purpose uncertain.

What Aryz was feeling, for the first time, was a small measure of freedom.

THE STORY OF THE ORIGINAL PRUFRAX CONTINUED.

In the early stages she visited Clevo with a barely concealed anger. His method was aggravating, his goals never precisely spelled out. What did he want with her, if anything?

And she with him? Their meetings were clandestine, though not precisely forbidden. She was a hawk one now with considerable personal liberty between exercises and engagements. There were no monitors in the closed-off reaches of the cruiser, and they could do whatever they wished. The two met in areas close to the ship's hull, usually in weapons blisters that could be opened to reveal the stars there as they talked.

Prufrax was not accustomed to prolonged conversation. Hawks were not raised to be voluble, nor were they selected for their curiosity. Yet the exhawk Clevo talked a great deal and was the most curious person she had met, herself included, and she regarded herself as uncharacteristically curious.

Often he was infuriating, especially when he played the "leading game," as she called it. Leading her from one question to the next, like an instructor, but without the trappings or any clarity of purpose. "What do you think of your mother?"

"Does that matter?"

"Not to me."

"Then why ask?"

"Because you matter."

Prufrax shrugged. "She was a fine mother. She bore me with a well-chosen heritage. She raised me as a hawk candidate. She told me her stories."

"Any hawk I know would envy you for listening at Jayax's knee."

"I was hardly at her knee."

"A speech tactic."

"Yes, well, she was important to me."

"She was a preferred single?"

"Yes."

"So you have no father."

"She selected without reference to individuals."

"Then you are really not that much different from a Senexi."

She bristled and started to push away. "There! You insult me again."

"Not at all. I've been asking one question all this time, and you haven't even heard. How well do you know the enemy?"

"Well enough to destroy them." She couldn't believe that was the only question he'd been asking. His speech tactics were very odd.

"Yes, to win battles, perhaps. But who will win the war?"

"It'll be a long war," she said softly, floating a few meters from him. He rotated in the blister, blocking out a blurred string of stars. The cruiser was preparing to shift out of status geometry again. "They fight well."

"They fight with conviction. Do you believe them to be evil?"

"They destroy us."

"We destroy them."

"So the question," she said, smiling at her cleverness, "is who began to destroy?"

"Not at all," Clevo said. "I suspect there's no longer a clear answer to that. Our leaders have obviously decided the question isn't important. No. We are the new, they are the old. The old must be superseded. It's a conflict born in the essential difference between Senexi and humans."

"That's the only way we're different? They're old, we're not so old? I don't understand."

"Nor do I, entirely."

"Well, finally!"

"The Senexi," Clevo continued, unperturbed, "long ago needed only gas-giant planets like their homeworlds. They lived in peace for billions of years before our world was formed. But as they moved from star to star, they learned uses for other types of worlds. We were most interested in rocky Earth-like planets. Gradually we found uses for gas giants, too. By the time we met, both of us encroached on the other's territory. Their technology is so improbable, so unlike ours, that when we first encountered them we thought they must come from another geometry."

"Where did you learn all this?" Prufrax squinted at him suspiciously.

"I'm no longer a hawk," he said, "but I was too valuable just to discard. My experience was too broad, my abilities too useful. So I was placed in research. It seems a safe place for me. Little contact with my comrades." He looked directly at her. "We must try to know our enemy, at least a little."

"That's dangerous," Prufrax said, almost instinctively.

"Yes, it is. What you know, you cannot hate."

"We must hate," she said. "It makes us strong. Senexi hate."

"They might," he said. "But, sometime, wouldn't you like to . . . sit down and talk with one, after a battle? Talk with a fighter? Learn its tactic, how it bested you in one move, compare—"

"No!" Prufrax shoved off rapidly down the tube. "We're shifting now. We have to get ready."

—She's smart. She's leaving him. He's crazy.

—Why do you think that?

—He would stop the fight, end the Zap.

—But he was a hawk.

—And hawks became glovers, I guess. But glovers go wrong, too.

—?

—Did you know they used you? How you were used?

—That's all blurred now.

—She's doomed if she stays around him. Who's that?

—Someone is listening with us.

—Recognize?

—No, gone now.

The next battle was bad enough to fall into the hellfought. Prufrax was in her fightsuit, legs drawn up as if about to kick off. The cruiser exited sponge space and plunged into combat before sponge-space supplements could reach full effectiveness. She was dizzy, disoriented. The overhawks could only hope that a switch from biologic to cyber would cure the problem.

She didn't know what they were attacking. Tactic was flooding the implant, but she was only receiving the wash of that; she hadn't merged yet. She sensed that things were confused. That bothered her. Overs did not feel confusion.

The cruiser was taking damage. She could sense at least that, and she wanted to scream in frustration. Then she was ordered to merge with the implant. Biologic became cyber. She was in the Know.

The cruiser had reintegrated above a gas-giant planet. They were seventy-nine-thousand kilometers from the upper atmosphere. The damage had come from ice mines—chunks of Senexi-treated water ice, altered to stay in sponge space until a human vessel integrated nearby. Then they emerged, packed with momentum and all the residual instability of an unsuccessful exit into status geometry. Unsuccessful for a ship, that is—very successful for a weapon.

The ice mines had given up the overness of the real within range of the cruiser and had blasted out whole sections of the hull. The launch lanes had not been damaged. The fighters lined up on their beams and were peppered out into space, spreading in the classic sword flower.

The planet was a cold nest. Over didn't know what the atmosphere contained, but Senexi activity had been high in the star system, concentrating on this world. Over had decided to take a chance. Fighters headed for the atmosphere. The cruiser began planting singularity eggs. The eggs went ahead of the fighters, great black grainy ovoids that seemed to leave a trail of shadow—the wake of a birthing disruption in status geometry that could turn a gas giant into a short-lived sun.

Their time was limited. The fighters would group on entry sleds and descend to the liquid water regions where Senexi commonly kept their upwelling power plants. The fighters would first destroy any plants, loop into the liquid ammonia regions to search for hidden cuckoos, then see what was so important about the world.

She and five other fighters mounted the sled. Growing closer, the hazy clear regions of the atmosphere sparkled with Senexi sensors. Spiderweb beams shot from the six sleds to down the sensors. Buffet began. Scream, heat, then a second flower from the sled at a depth of two hundred kilometers. The sled slowed and held station. It would be their only way back. The fightsuits couldn't pull out of such a large gravity well.

She descended deeper. The pale, bloated beacon of the red star was dropping below the second cloudtops, limning the strata in orange and purple. At the liquid ammonia level she was instructed to key in permanent memory of all she was seeing. She wasn't "seeing" much, but other sensors were recording a great deal, all of it duly processed in her implant. "There's life here," she told herself. Indigenous life. Just another example of Senexi disregard for basic decency: they were interfering with a world developing its own complex biology.

The temperature rose to ammonia vapor levels, then to liquid water. The pressure on the fightsuit was enormous, and she was draining her stores much more rapidly than expected. At this level the atmosphere was particularly thick with organics.

Senexi snakes rose from below, passed them in altitude, then doubled back to engage. Prufrax was designated the deep diver; the others from her sled would stay at this level in her defense. As she fell, another sled group moved in behind her to double the cover.

She searched for the characteristic radiation curve of an upwelling plant. At the lower boundary of the liquid water level, below which her suit could not safely descend, she found it.

The Senexi were tapping the gas giant's convection from greater depths than usual. Ten kilometers above the plant, almost undetectable, hung another object with an uncharacteristic curve. The power plant was feeding its higher companion with tight energy beams.

She slowed. Two other fighters, disengaged from the brief skirmish above, took backup positions a few dozen kilometers higher. Her implant searched for an appropriate tactic. She would avoid the zero-angle phase for the moment, go in for reconnaissance. She could feel sound pouring from the plant and its companion—rhythmic, not waste noise, but deliberate. And homing in on that sound were waves of large vermiform organisms, like chains of gas-filled sausage. They were dozens of meters long, two meters at their greatest thickness, shaped vaguely like the Senexi snake fighters. The vermiforms were native, and they were being lured into the uppermost floating structure. None were emerging. Her backups spread apart, descended, and drew up along her flanks.

She made her decision almost immediately. She could see a pattern in the approach of the natives. If she fell into the pattern, she might be able to enter the structure unnoticed.

—It's a grinder. She doesn't recognize it.

—What's a grinder?

—She should make the Zap! It's an ugly thing; Senexi use them all the time. Net a planet with grinders, like a cuckoo, but for larger operations.

The creatures were being passed through separator fields. Their organics fell from the bottom of the construct, raw material for new growth—Senexi growth. Their heavier elements were stored for later harvest.

With Prufrax in their midst, the vermiforms flew into the separator. The interior was hundreds of meters wide, lead-white walls with flat gray machinery floating in a dust haze, full of hollow noise, the distant bleats of vermiforms being slaughtered. Prufrax tried to retreat, but she was caught in a selector field. Her suit bucked and she was whirled violently, then thrown into a repository for examination. She had been screened from the separator; her plan to record, then destroy, the structure had been foiled by an automatic filter.

"Information sufficient." Command logic programmed into the implant before launch was now taking over. "Zero-angle phase both plant and adjunct." She was drifting in the repository, still slightly stunned. Something was fading. Cyber was hissing in and out; the over logic-commands were being scrambled. Her implant was malfunctioning and was returning control to biologic. The selector fields had played havoc with all cyber functions, down to the processors in her weapons.

Cautiously she examined the down systems one by one, determining what she could and could not do. This took as much as thirty seconds—an astronomical time on the implant's scale.

She still could use the phase weapon. If she was judicious and didn't waste her power, she could cut her way out of the repository, maneuver and work with her escorts to destroy both the plant and the separator. By the time they returned to the sleds, her implant might have rerouted itself and made sufficient repairs to handle defense. She had no way of knowing what was waiting for her if—when—she escaped, but that was the least of her concerns for the moment.

She tightened the setting of the phase beam and swung her fightsuit around, knocking a cluster of junk ice and silty phosphorescent dust. She activated the beam. When she had a hole large enough to pass through, she edged the suit forward, beamed through more walls and obstacles, and kicked herself out of the repository into free fall. She swiveled and laid down a pattern of wide-angle beams, at the same time relaying a message on her situation to the escorts.

The escorts were not in sight. The separator was beginning to break up, spraying debris through the almost-opaque atmosphere. The rhythmic sound ceased, and the crowds of vermiforms began to disperse.

She stopped her fall and thrust herself several kilometers higher—directly into a formation of Senexi snakes. She had barely enough power to reach the sled, much less fight and turn her beams on the upwelling plant.

Her cyber was still down.

The sled signal was weak. She had no time to calculate its direction from the inertial guidance cyber. Besides, all cyber was unreliable after passing through the separator.

Why do they fight so well? Clevo's question clogged her thoughts. Cursing, she tried to blank and keep all her faculties available for running the fightsuit. *When evenly matched, you cannot win against your enemy unless you understand them. And if you truly understand, why are you fighting and not talking?* Clevo had never told her that—not in so many words. But it was part of a string of logic all her own.

Be more than an automaton with a narrow range of choices. Never underestimate the enemy. Those were old Grounds dicta, not entirely lost in the new training, but only emphasized by Clevo.

If they fight as well as you, perhaps in some ways they fight—think like you do. Use that.

Isolated, with her power draining rapidly, she had no choice. They might disregard her if she posed no danger. She cut her thrust and went into a diving spin. Clearly she was on her way to a high-pressure grave. They would sense her power levels, perhaps even pick up the lack of field activity if she let her shields drop. She dropped the shields. If they let her fall and didn't try to complete the kill—if they concentrated on active fighters above—she had enough power to drop into the water vapor regions, far below the plant, and silently ride a thermal into range. With luck, she could get close enough to lay a web of zero-angle phase and take out the plant.

She had minutes in which to agonize over her plan. Falling, buffeted by winds that could knock her kilometers out of range, she spun like a vagrant flake of snow.

She couldn't even expend the energy to learn if they were scanning her, checking out her potential.

Perhaps she underestimated them. Perhaps they would be that much more thorough and take her out just to be sure. Perhaps they had unwritten rules of conduct like the ones she was using, taking hunches into account. Hunches were discouraged in Grounds training—much less reliable than cyber.

She fell. Temperature increased. Pressure on her suit began to constrict her air supply. She used fighter trancing to cut back on her breathing.

Fell.

And broke the trance. Pushed through the dense smoke of exhaustion. Planned the beam web. Counted her reserves. Nudged into an updraft beneath the plant. The thermal carried her, a silent piece of paper in a storm, drifting back and forth beneath the objective. The huge field intakes pulsed above, lightning outlining their invisible extension. She held back on the beam.

Nearly faded out. Her suit interior was almost unbearably hot.

She was only vaguely aware of laying down the pattern. The beams vanished in the murk. The thermal pushed her through a layer of haze, and she saw the plant, riding high above clear-atmosphere turbulence.

The zero-angle phase had pushed through the field intakes, into their source nodes and the plant body, surrounding it with bright blue Cherenkov. First the surface began to break up, then the middle layers, and finally key supports. Chunks vibrated away with the internal fury of their molecular, then atomic, then particle disruption. Paraphrasing Grounds description of beam action, the plant became less and less convinced of its reality. "Matter dreams," an instructor had said a decade before. "Dreams it is real, maintains the dream by shifting rules with constant results. Disturb the dreams, the shifting of the rules results in inconstant results. Things cannot hold."

She slid away from the updraft, found another, wondered idly how far she would be lifted. Curiosity at the last. Let's just see, she told herself; a final experiment.

Now she was cold. The implant was flickering, showing signs of reorganization. She didn't use it. No sense expanding the amount of time until death. No sense—

at all.

The sled, maneuvered by one remaining fighter, glided up beneath her almost unnoticed.

Aryz waited in the stillness of a Senexi memory, his thinking temporarily reduced to a faint susurrus. What he waited for was not clear.

—Come.

The form of address was wrong, but he recognized the voice. His thoughts stirred, and he followed the nebulous presence out of Senexi territory.

—Know your enemy.

Prufrax . . . the name of one of the human shapes sent out against their own kind. He could sense her presence in the mandate, locked into a memory store. He touched on the store and caught the essentials—the grinder, the updraft plant, the fight from Prufrax's viewpoint.

—Know how your enemy knows you.

He sensed a second presence, similar to that of Prufrax. It took him some time to realize that the human captive was another form of the shape, a reproduction of the . . .

Both were reproductions of the female whose image was in the memory store. Aryz was not impressed by threes—Senexi mysticism, what had ever existed of it, had been preoccupied with fives and sixes—but the coincidence was striking.

—Know how your enemy *sees you*.

He saw the grinder processing organics—the vermiform natives—in preparation for a widespread seeding of deuterium gatherers. The operation had evidently been conducted for some time; the vermiform populations were greatly reduced from their usual numbers. Vermiforms were a common type-species on gas-giants of the sort depicted. The mutated shape nudged him into a particular channel of the memory, that which carried the original Prufrax's emotions. She had reacted with *disgust* to the Senexi procedure. It was a reaction not unlike what Aryz might feel when coming across something forbidden in Senexi behavior. Yet eradication was perfectly natural, analogous to the human cleansing of *food* before *eating*.

—It's in the memory. The vermiforms are intelligent. They have their own kind of civilization. Human action on this world prevented their complete extinction by the Senexi.

—So what matter they were *intelligent?* Aryz responded. They did not behave or think like Senexi, or like any species Senexi find compatible. They were therefore not desirable. Like humans.

—You would make humans extinct?

—We would protect ourselves from them.

—Who damages whom most?

Aryz didn't respond. The line of questioning was incomprehensible. Instead he flowed into the memory of Prufrax, propelled by another aspect of complete freedom, confusion.

THE IMPLANT WAS REPLACED. PRUFRAX'S DAMAGED LIMBS AND SKIN WERE repaired or regenerated quickly, and within four wakes, under intense treatment usually reserved only for overs, she regained all her reflexes and speed. She requested liberty of the cruiser while it returned for repairs. Her request was granted.

She first sought Clevo in the designated research area. He wasn't there, but a message was, passed on to her by a smiling young crew member. She read it quickly:

"You're free and out of action. Study for a while, then come find me. The old place hasn't been damaged. It's less private, but still good. Study! I've marked highlights."

She frowned at the message, then handed it to the crew member, who duly erased it and returned to his duties. She wanted to talk with Clevo, not study.

But she followed his instructions. She searched out highlighted entries in the ship's memory store. It was not nearly as dull as she had expected. In fact, by following the highlights, she felt she was learning more about Clevo and about the questions he asked.

Old literature was not nearly as graphic as fibs, but it was different enough to involve her for a time. She tried to create imitations of what she read, but erased them. Nonfib stories were harder than she suspected. She read about punishment, duty; she read about places called Heaven and Hell, from a writer who had died tens of thousands of years before. With ed supplement guidance, she was able to comprehend most of what she read. Plugging the store into her implant, she was able to absorb hundreds of volumes in an hour.

Some of the stores were losing definition. They hadn't been used in decades, perhaps centuries.

Halfway through, she grew impatient. She left the research area. Operating on another hunch, she didn't go to the blister as directed, but straight to memory central, two decks inboard the research area. She saw Clevo there, plugged into a data pillar, deep in some aspect of ship history. He noticed her approach, unplugged, and swiveled on his chair. "Congratulations," he said, smiling at her.

"Hardfought," she acknowledged, smiling.

"Better than that, perhaps," he said.

She looked at him quizzically. "What do you mean, better?"

"I've been doing some illicit tapping on over channels."

"So?"

—He *is dangerous!*

"*You've* been recommended."

"For what?"

"Not for hero status, not yet. You'll have a good many more fights before that. And you probably won't enjoy it when you get there. You won't be a fighter then."

Prufrax stood silently before him.

"You may have a valuable genetic assortment. Overs think you behaved remarkably well under impossible conditions."

"Did I?"

He nodded. "Your type may be preserved."

"Which means?"

"There's a program being planned. They want to take the best fighters and reproduce them—clone them—to make uniform topgrade squadrons. It was rumored in my time—you haven't heard?"

She shook her head.

"It's not new. It's been done, off and on, for tens of thousands of years. This time they believe they can make it work."

"You were a fighter, once," she said. "Did they preserve your type?"

Clevo nodded. "I had something that interested them, but not, I think, as a fighter."

Prufrax looked down at her stubby-fingered hands. "It was grim," she said. "You know what we found?"

"An extermination plant."

"You want me to understand them better. Well, I can't. I refuse. How could they do such things?" She looked disgusted and answered her own question. "Because they're Senexi."

"Humans," Clevo said, "have done much the same, sometimes worse."

"No!"

—No!

"Yes," he said firmly. He sighed. "We've wiped Senexi worlds, and we've even wiped worlds with intelligent species like our own. Nobody is innocent. Not in this universe."

"We were never taught that."

"It wouldn't have made you a better hawk. But it might make a better human of you, to know. Greater depth of character. Do you want to be more aware?"

"You mean, study more?"

He nodded.

"What makes you think you can teach me?"

"Because you thought about what I asked you. About how Senexi thought. And you survived where some other hawk might not have. The overs think it's in your genes. It might be. But it's also in your head."

"Why not tell the overs?"

"I have," he said. He shrugged. "I'm too valuable to them, otherwise I'd have been busted again, a long time ago."

"They wouldn't want me to learn from you?"

"I don't know," Clevo said. "I suppose they're aware you're talking to me. They could stop it if they wanted. They may be smarter than I give them credit for." He shrugged again. "Of course they're smart. We just disagree at times."

"And if I learn from you?"

"Not from me, actually. From the past. From history, what other people have thought. I'm really not any more capable than you . . . but I know history, small portions of it. I won't teach you so much, as guide."

"I did use your questions," Prufrax said. "But will I ever need to use them—think that way—again?"

Clevo nodded. "Of course."

—You're quiet.

—She's giving in to him.

—She gave in a long time ago.

—She should be afraid.

—Were you—we—ever really afraid of a challenge?

—No.

—Not Senexi, not forbidden knowledge.

—Someone listens with us. Feel—

———————

CLEVO FIRST LED HER THROUGH THE HISTORY OF PAST WARS, JUDGING THAT was appropriate considering her occupation. She was attentive enough, though her mind wandered; sometimes he was didactic, but she found she didn't mind that much. At no time did his attitude change as they pushed through the tangle of the past. Rather her perception of his attitude changed. Her perception of herself changed.

She saw that in all wars, the first stage was to dehumanize the enemy, reduce the enemy to a lower level so that he might be killed without compunction. When the enemy was not human to begin with, the task was easier. As wars progressed, this tactic frequently led to an under-estimation of the enemy, with disastrous consequences. "We aren't ex-actly underestimating the Senexi," Clevo said. "The overs are too smart for that. But we refuse to understand them, and that could make the war last indefinitely."

"Then why don't the overs see that?"

"Because we're being locked into a pattern. We've been fighting for so long, we've begun to lose ourselves. And it's getting worse." He as-sumed his didactic tone, and she knew he was reciting something he'd formulated years before and repeated to himself a thousand times. "There is no war so important that to win it, we must destroy our minds."

She didn't agree with that; losing the war with the Senexi would mean extinction, as she understood things.

Most often they met in the single unused weapons blister that had not been damaged. They met when the ship was basking in the real between sponge-space jaunts. He brought memory stores with him in portable modules, and they read, listened, experienced together. She never placed a great deal of importance in the things she learned; her interest was focused on Clevo. Still, she learned.

The rest of her time she spent training. She was aware of a growing isolation from the hawks, which she attributed to her uncertain rank status. Was her genotype going to be preserved or not? The decision hadn't been made. The more she learned, the less she wanted to be singled out for honor. Attracting that sort of attention might be dan-gerous, she thought. Dangerous to whom, or what, she could not say.

Clevo showed her how hero images had been used to indoctrinate birds and hawks in a standard of behavior that was ideal, not realistic. The results were not always good; some tragic blunders had been made by fighters trying to be more than anyone possibly could or refusing to be flexible.

The war was certainly not a fib. Yet more and more the overs seemed to be treating it as one. Unable to bring about strategic victories against the Senexi, the overs had settled in for a long war of attrition and were apparently bent on adapting all human societies to the effort.

"There are overs we never hear of, who make decisions that shape our entire lives. Soon they'll determine whether or not we're even born, if they don't already."

"That sounds paranoid," she said, trying out a new word and concept she had only recently learned.

"Maybe so."

"Besides, it's been like that for ages—not knowing all our overs."

"But it's getting worse," Clevo said. He showed her the projections he had made. In time, if trends continued unchanged, fighters and all other combatants would be treated more and more mechanically, until they became the machines the overs wished them to be.

—No.

—Quiet. How does he feel toward her?

It was inevitable that as she learned under his tutelage, he began to feel responsible for her changes. She was an excellent fighter. He could never be sure that what he was doing might reduce her effectiveness. And yet he had fought well—despite similar changes—until his billet switch. It had been the overs who had decided he would be more effective, less disruptive, elsewhere.

Bitterness over that decision was part of his motive. The overs had done a foolish thing, putting a fighter into research. Fighters were tenacious. If the truth was to be hidden, then fighters were the ones likely to ferret it out. And pass it on. There was a code among fighters, seldom revealed to their immediate overs, much less to the supreme overs parsecs distant in their strategospheres. What one fighter learned that could be of help to another had to be passed on, even under penalty. Clevo was simply following that unwritten rule.

Passing on the fact that, at one time, things had been different. That war changed people, governments, societies, and that societies could effect an enormous change on their constituents, especially now— change in their lives, their thinking. Things could become even more structured. Freedom of fight was a drug, an illusion—

—No!

used to perpetuate a state of hatred.

"Then why do they keep all the data in stores?" she asked. "I mean, you study the data, everything becomes obvious."

"There are still important people who think we may want to find our way back someday. They're afraid we'll lose our roots, but—"

His face suddenly became peaceful. She reached out to touch him, and he jerked slightly, turning toward her in the blister. "What is it?" she asked.

"It's not organized. We're going to lose the information. Ship overs are going to restrict access more and more. Eventually it'll decay, like some already has in these stores. I've been planning for some time to put it all in a single unit—"

—He built the mandate!

"And have the overs place one on every ship, with researchers to tend it. Formalize the loose scheme still in effect, but dying. Right now I'm working on the fringes. At least I'm allowed to work. But soon I'll have enough evidence that they won't be able to argue. Evidence of what happens to societies that try to obscure their histories. They go quite mad. The overs are still rational enough to listen; maybe I'll push it through." He looked out the transparent blister. The stars were smudging to one side as the cruiser began probing for entrances to sponge space. "We'd better get back."

"Where are you going to be when we return? We'll all be transferred."

"That's some time removed. Why do you want to know?"

"I'd like to learn more."

He smiled. "That's not your only reason."

"I don't need someone to tell me what my reasons are," she said testily.

"We're so reluctant," he said. She looked at him sharply, irritated and puzzled. "I mean," he continued, "we're hawks. Comrades. Hawks couple like *that*." He snapped his fingers. "But you and I sneak around it all the time."

Prufrax kept her face blank.

"Aren't you receptive toward me?" he asked, his tone almost teasing.

"You're so damned superior. Stuffy," she snapped.

"Aren't you?"

"It's just that's not all," she said, her tone softening.

"Indeed," he said in a barely audible whisper.

In the distance they heard the alarms.

—It was never any different.

—What?

—Things were never any different before me.

—Don't be silly. It's all here.

—If Clevo made the mandate, then he put it here. It isn't true.

—Why are you upset?

—I don't like hearing that everything I believe is a . . . fib.

—I've never known the difference, I suppose. Eyes-open was never all that real to me. This isn't real, you aren't . . . this is eyes-shut. So why be upset? You and I . . . we aren't even whole people. I feel you. You wish the Zap, you fight, not much else. I'm just a shadow, even compared to you. But she is whole. She loves him. She's less a victim than either of us. So something has to have changed.

—You're saying things have gotten worse.

—If the mandate is a lie, that's all I am. You refuse to accept. I *have* to accept, or I'm even less than a shadow.

—I don't refuse to accept. It's just hard.

—You started it. You thought about love.

—You did!

—Do you know what love is?

—Reception.

They first made love in the weapons blister. It came as no surprise; if anything, they approached it so cautiously they were clumsy. She had become more and more receptive, and he had dropped his guard. It had been quick, almost frantic, far from the orchestrated and drawn-out ballet the hawks prided themselves for. There was no pretense. No need to play the roles of artists interacting. They were depending on each other. The pleasure they exchanged was nothing compared to the emotions involved.

"We're not very good with each other," Prufrax said.

Clevo shrugged. "That's because we're shy."

"Shy?"

He explained. In the past—at various times in the past, because such differences had come and gone many times—making love had been more than a physical exchange or even an expression of comradeship. It had been the acknowledgment of a bond between people.

She listened, half-believing. Like everything else she had heard that kind of love seemed strange, distasteful. What if one hawk was lost, and the other continued to love? It interfered with the hardfought, certainly. But she was also fascinated. Shyness—the fear of one's presentation to another. The hesitation to present truth, or the inward confusion of truth at the awareness that another might be important, more important than one thought possible. That such emotions might have existed at one time, and seem so alien now only emphasized the distance of the past, as Clevo had tried to tell her. And that she felt those emotions only confirmed she was not as far from that past as, for dignity's sake, she might have wished.

Complex emotion was not encouraged either at the Grounds or among hawks on station. Complex emotion degraded complex performance. The simple and direct was desirable.

"But all we seem to do is talk—until now," Prufrax said, holding his hand and examining his fingers one by one. They were very little different from her own, though extended a bit from hawk fingers to give greater versatility with key instruction.

"Talking is the most human thing we can do."

She laughed. "I know what you are," she said, moving up until her eyes were even with his chest. "You're stuffy. You aren't the party type."

"Where'd you learn about parties?"

"You gave me literature to read, I read it. You're an instructor at heart. You make love by telling." She felt peculiar, almost afraid, and looked up at his face. "Not that I don't enjoy your lovemaking, like this. Physical."

"You receive well," he said. "Both ways."

"What we're saying," she whispered, "is not truth-speaking. It's amenity." She turned into the stroke of his hand through her hair. "Amenity is supposed to be decadent. That fellow who wrote about heaven and hell. He would call it a sin."

"Amenity is the recognition that somebody may see or feel differently than you do. It's the recognition of individuals. You and I, we're part of the end of all that."

"Even if you convince the overs?"

He nodded. "They want to repeat success without risk. New individuals are risky, so they duplicate past success. There will be more and more people, fewer individuals. More of you and me, less of others. The fewer individuals, the fewer stories to tell. The less history. We're part of the death of history."

She floated next to him, trying to blank her mind as she had before, to drive out the nagging awareness he was right. She thought she understood the social structure around her. Things seemed new. She said as much.

"It's a path we're taking," Clevo said. "Not a place we're at."

—It's a place we're at. How different are we?

—But there's so much history in here. How can it be over for us?

—I've been thinking. Do we know the last event recorded in the mandate?

—Don't, we're drifting from Prufrax now. . . .

ARYZ FELT HIMSELF DRIFTING WITH THEM. THEY SWEPT OVER COUNTLESS MIL-lennia, then swept back the other way. And it became evident that as much change had been wrapped in one year of the distant past as in a thousand years of the closing entries in the mandate. Clevo's voice seemed to follow them, though they were far from his period, far from Prufrax's record.

"Tyranny is the death of history. We fought the Senexi until we became like them. No change, youth at an end, old age coming upon us. There is no important change, merely elaborations in the pattern."

—How many times have we been here, then? How many times have we died?

ARYZ WASN'T SURE, NOW. *WAS* THIS THE FIRST TIME HUMANS HAD BEEN CAPtured? Had he been told everything by the brood mind? Did the Senexi have no *history,* whatever that was—

The accumulated lives of living, thinking beings. Their actions, thoughts, passions, hopes.

The mandate answered even his confused, nonhuman requests. He could understand action, thought, but not passion or hope. Perhaps without those there was no *history.*

—You have no history, the mutated shape told him. There have been millions like you, even millions like the brood mind. What is the last event recorded in the brood mind that is not duplicated a thousand times over, so close they can be melded together for convenience?

—You understand that? Aryz asked the shape.

—Yes.

—How do you understand—because we made you between human and Senexi?

—Not only that.

The requests of the twin captive and shape were moving them back once more into the past, through the dim gray millennia of repeating ages. History began to manifest again, differences in the record.

ON THE WAY BACK TO MERCIOR, FOUR SKIRMISHES WERE FOUGHT. PRUFRAX did well in each. She carried something special with her, a thought she didn't even tell Clevo, and she carried the same thought with her through their last days at the Grounds.

Taking advantage of hawk liberty, she opted a post-hardfought residence just outside the Grounds, in the relatively uncrowded Daughter of Cities zone. She wouldn't be returning to fight until several issues had been decided—her status most important among them.

Clevo began making his appeal to the middle overs. He was given Grounds duty to finish his proposals. They could stay together for the time being.

The residence was sixteen square meters in area, not elegant—*natural,* as rentOpts described it. Clevo called it a "garret," inaccurately as she discovered when she looked it up in his memory blocs, but perhaps he was describing the tone.

On the last day she lay in the crook of Clevo's arm. They had done a few hours of nature sleep. He hadn't come out yet, and she looked up at his face, reached up with a hand to feel his arm.

It was different from the arms of others she had been receptive toward. It was unique. The thought amused her. There had never been a reception like theirs. This was the beginning. And if both were to be duplicated, this love, this reception, would be repeated an infinite number of times. Clevo meeting Prufrax, teaching her, opening her eyes.

Somehow, even though repetition contributed to the death of history, she was pleased. This was the secret thought she carried into fight. Each time she would survive, wherever she was, however many duplications down the line. She would receive Clevo, and he would teach her. If not now—if one or the other died—then in the future. The death of history might be a good thing. Love could go on forever.

She had lost even a rudimentary apprehension of death, even with present pleasure to live for. Her functions had sharpened. She would please him by doing all the things he could not. And if he was to enter that state she frequently found him in, that state of introspection, of reliving his own battles and of envying her activity, then that wasn't bad. All they did to each other was good.

—Was good

—Was

She slipped from his arm and left the narrow sleeping quarter, pushing through the smoke-colored air curtain to the lounge. Two hawks and an over she had never seen before were sitting there. They looked up at her.

"Under," Prufrax said.

"Over," the woman returned. She was dressed in tan and green, Grounds colors, not ship.

"May I assist?"

"Yes."

"My duty, then?"

The over beckoned her closer. "You have been receiving a researcher."

"Yes," Prufrax said. The meetings could not have been a secret on the ship, and certainly not their quartering near the Grounds. "Has that been against duty?"

"No." The over eyed Prufrax sharply, observing her perfected fight-form, the easy grace with which she stood, naked, in the middle of the small compartment. "But a decision has been reached. Your status is decided now."

She felt a shiver.

"Prufrax," said the elder hawk. She recognized him from fibs, and his companion: Kumnax and Arol. Once her heroes. "You have been accorded an honor, just as your partner has. You have a valuable genetic assortment—"

She barely heard the rest. They told her she would return to fight, until they deemed she had had enough experience and background to be brought into the polinstruc division. Then her fighting would be over. She would serve better as an example, a hero.

Heroes never partnered out of function. Hawk heroes could not even partner with ex-hawks.

Clevo emerged from the air curtain. "Duty," the over said. "The residence is disbanded. Both of you will have separate quarters, separate duties."

They left. Prufrax held out her hand, but Clevo didn't take it. "No use," he said.

Suddenly she was filled with anger. "You'll give it up? Did I expect too much? *How strongly?*"

"Perhaps even more strongly than you," he said. "I knew the order was coming down. And still I didn't leave. That may hurt my chances with the supreme overs."

"Then at least I'm worth more than your breeding history?"

"Now you are history. History the way they make it."

"I feel like I'm dying," she said, amazement in her voice. "What is that, Clevo? What did you do to me?"

"I'm in pain, too," he said.

"You're hurt?"

"I'm confused."

"I don't believe that," she said, her anger rising again. "You knew, and you didn't do anything?"

"That would have been counter to duty. We'll be worse off if we fight it."

"So what good is your great, exalted history?"

"History is what you have," Clevo said. "I only record."

—Why did they separate them?

—I don't know. You didn't like him, anyway.

—Yes, but now . . .

—See? You're her. We're her. But shadows. She was whole.

—I don't understand.

—We don't. Look what happens to her. They took what was best out of her. Prufrax

went into battle eighteen more times before dying as heroes often do, dying in the midst of what she did best. The question of what made her better before the separation—for she definitely was not as fine a fighter after—has not been settled. Answers fall into an extinct classification of knowledge, and there are few left to interpret, none accessible to this device.

—So she went out and fought and died. They never even made fibs about her. This killed her?

—I don't think so. She fought well enough. She died like other hawks died.

—And she might have lived otherwise.

—How can I know that, any more than you?

—They—we—met again, you know. I met a Clevo once, on my ship. They didn't let me stay with him long.

—How did you react to him?

—There was so little time, I don't know.

—Let's ask. . . .

In thousands of duty stations, it was inevitable that some of Prufrax's visions would come true, that they should meet now and then. Clevos were numerous, as were Prufraxes. Every ship carried complements of several of each. Though Prufrax was never quite as successful as the original, she was a fine type. She—

—She was never quite as successful. They took away her edge. They didn't even know it!

—They must have known.

—Then they didn't want to win!

—We don't know that. Maybe there were more important considerations.

—Yes, like killing history.

ARYZ SHUDDERED IN HIS WARMING BODY, DIZZY AS IF ABOUT TO BUD, THEN regained control. He had been pulled from the mandate, called to his own duty.

He examined the shapes and the human captive. There was something different about them. How long had they been immersed in the mandate? He checked quickly, frantically, before answering the call. The reconstructed Mam had malfunctioned. None of them had been nourished. They were thin, pale, cooling.

Even the bloated mutant shape was dying; lost, like the others, in the mandate.

He turned his attention away. Everything was confusion. Was he human or Senexi now? Had he fallen so low as to understand them? He went to the origin of the call, the ruins of the temporary brood chamber. The corridors were caked with ammonia ice, burning his pod as he slipped over them. The brood mind had come out of flux bind. The emergency support systems hadn't worked well; the brood mind was damaged.

"Where have you been?" it asked.

"I assumed I would not be needed until your return from the flux bind."

"You have not been watching!"

"Was there any need? We are so advanced in time, all our actions are obsolete. The nebula is collapsed, the issue is decided."

"We do not know that. We are being pursued."

Aryz turned to the sensor wall—what was left of it—and saw that they were, indeed, being pursued. He had been lax.

"It is not your fault," the brood mind said. "You have been set a task that tainted you and ruined your function. You will dissipate."

Aryz hesitated. He had become so different, so tainted, that he actually *hesitated* at a direct command from the brood mind. But it was damaged. Without him, without what he had learned, what could it do? It wasn't reasoning correctly.

"There are facts you must know, important facts—"

Aryz felt a wave of revulsion, uncomprehending fear, and something not unlike human anger radiate from the brood mind. Whatever he had learned and however he had changed, he could not withstand that wave.

Willingly, and yet against his will—it didn't matter—he felt himself liquefying. His pod slumped beneath him, and he fell over, landing on a pool of frozen ammonia. It burned, but he did not attempt to lift himself. Before he ended, he saw with surprising clarity what it was to be a branch ind, or a brood mind, or a human. Such a valuable insight, and it leaked out of his permea and froze on the ammonia.

The brood mind regained what control it could of the fragment. But there were no defenses worthy of the name. Calm, preparing for its own dissipation, it waited for the pursuit to conclude.

The Mam set off an alarm. The interface with the mandate was severed. Weak, barely able to crawl, the humans looked at each other in horror and slid to opposite corners of the chamber.

They were confused: which of them was the captive, which the decoy shape? It didn't seem important. They were both bone-thin, filthy with their own excrement. They turned with one motion to stare at the bloated mutant. It sat in its corner, tiny head incongruous on the huge thorax, tiny arms and legs barely functional even when healthy. It smiled wanly at them.

"We felt you," one of the Prufraxes said. "You were with us in there." Her voice was a soft croak.

"That was my place," it replied. "My only place."

"What function, what name?"

"I'm . . . I know that. I'm a researcher. In there. I knew myself in there."

They squinted at the shape. The head. Something familiar, even now. "You're a Clevo . . ."

There was noise all around them, cutting off the shape's weak words.

As they watched, their chamber was sectioned like an orange, and the wedges peeled open. The illumination ceased. Cold enveloped them.

A naked human female, surrounded by tiny versions of herself, like an angel circled by fairy kin, floated into the chamber. She was thin as a snake. She wore nothing but silver rings on her wrists and a narrow torque around her waist. She glowed blue-green in the dark.

The two Prufraxes moved their lips weakly but made no sound in the near vacuum. *Who are you?*

She surveyed them without expression, then held out her arms as if to fly. She wore no gloves, but she was of their type.

As she had done countless times before on finding such Senexi experiments—though this seemed older than most—she lifted one arm higher. The blue-green intensified, spread in waves to the mangled walls, surrounded the freezing, dying shapes. Perfect, angelic, she left the debris behind to cast its fitful glow and fade.

They had destroyed every portion of the fragment but one. They left it behind unharmed.

Then they continued, millions of them thick like mist, working the spaces between the stars, their only master the overness of the real.

They needed no other masters. They would never malfunction.

THE MANDATE DRIFTED IN THE DARK AND COLD, ITS MEMORY GOING ON, BUT its only life the rapidly fading tracks where minds had once passed through it. The trails writhed briefly, almost as if alive, but only following the quantum rules of diminishing energy states. Finally, a small memory was illuminated.

Prufrax's last poem, explained the mandate reflexively.

How the fires grow!
Peace passes
All memory lost.
Somehow we always miss that single door,
Dooming ourselves to circle.
Ashes to stars, lies to souls,
Let's spin round the sinks and holes.
Kill the good, eat the young.
Forever and more,
You and I are never done.

The track faded into nothing. Around the mandate, the universe grew old very quickly.

Appendix

Earlier Prefaces
From the 1983 Arkham House edition of *The Wind from a Burning Woman*, my first collection.

Preface

I have had a passion for science fiction and fantasy ever since I can remember. Science fiction has been a wonderful mother for my mind, showing me that the world is far bigger and stranger than it seems within my province. And in the past few years—after many more years of apprenticeship—it has become a fine, broad landscape on which to test my imagination.

Occasionally I've felt the pressure of limited editors and markets, but I have yet to run up against an artistic boundary. If a thought is expressible in human language, a science fiction story can be written about it. The same cannot be said of any other genre.

Through reading science fiction, I became interested in other forms of literature, in astronomy and the sciences, in history and philosophy. Specifically, discovering James Blish's *Case of Conscience* when I was sixteen led me to read James Joyce; L. Sprague de Camp, Fletcher Pratt, Poul Anderson, and others have given me solid reasons to explore history. Arthur C. Clarke—and through Clarke, Olaf Stapledon—sent me on a wild search through philosophy, looking for similar insights and experiences. (I've usually been disappointed; Stapledon is unique.) In short, my intellect has been nurtured and guided by science fiction.

Some people, reading the above, will sneer the ineradicable sneer. The hell with them. C. P. Snow pinned their little gray moth in *The Two Cultures and the Scientific Revolution;* they are ignorant or afraid of science.

They reject the universe in favor of a small human circle, limited in time and place to their own lifetimes. You are not one of them if you have read this far. You are one of the brave ones.

So I will open my heart to you a little bit and talk about the stories that follow.

I have friends who believe the world will come to an end in twenty or thirty years. They foresee complete collapse, perhaps nuclear war. They look on the prospect with either stunned indifference or some relish. Serve everybody right, they seem to say.

What they are actually saying is that within the next few decades—certainly within the next sixty or seventy years—*they* will come to an end. *Their* world will darken. And, solipsists that many of us are, it seems perfectly logical to take everybody and everything with us. The future does not really exist, certainly not the far and unknowable future. Why talk about it?

They are still my friends, but they are as wrong as wrong can be. The future will come, and it will be different, unimaginably so. Then why do I bother to try imagining it?

I could sing you a long number on how science fiction is seldom intended to be prophetic. But I'm willing to bet, in our deepest hearts, that we all hope one of our more optimistic imagined futures, or some aspect of a literary time to come, will closely parallel reality. Then we will be admired for our perspicacity. People in the future, if they still read, might come across an even more fantastic concept and say, "Hey, that crazy Greg Bear stuff!"

Perhaps. But it will be accident, not prophecy.

Like my pessimistic friends, I'm not going to live forever. I may see the first starships; I may not.

But when I write, I not only live to see one future, I experience dozens. I chart their courses, lay out histories, try to create new cultures and extend the range of discovery. When I write—

When I write, I'm immortal.

Sometimes I enter into a kind of trance state and engage so many thoughts and ideas and abilities that I seem to rise onto another plane. And though I seldom think about it while I'm on that plane, I seem to become everyone who has ever thought about the future. I join the greats, past and present, at least for a moment.

I've been writing since I was eight or nine years old. In 1966, when I was fifteen, through something of a fluke I sold my first professional short story. Five years passed before I sold another. The apprenticeship is still not over, and may never be. None of those earlier efforts are represented in this collection; the earliest piece here, "Mandala," was written in 1975 and first appeared in 1978. It also comprises the first third of my novel, *Strength of Stones*, published in 1981.

There isn't much remarkable to record about the writing of these stories. Writing is usually quite dull to an outside observer. It consists of long periods of apparent loafing around, punctuated by hours at a typewriter, highlighted by moments of desk-pounding and finger-chewing puzzlement. (All this, to contrast with the above-mentioned trance state.)

"Mandala" and "Hardfought" were about equally difficult to write, for different reasons. "The White Horse Child" was one of the easiest; like "Scattershot," it emerged while I sat at the typewriter, consciously unaware of what was going to pour out. "Petra" went through several stages, becoming progressively stranger and stranger. (One of the great difficulties with creativity is trying to impose order on the results.)

"The Wind from a Burning Woman" also began as an exercise in sitting blankly at the typewriter. As in most instances where such stories turn out well, there was a strong emotion lurking behind the apparent blankness—that of repugnance to terrorism. Do the weak have the right to force the strong to do their bidding by terrorist action? To handle the issue honestly, I had to make the "Burning Woman" fight for a cause that I, myself, would cherish. One editor, reading the story for an anthology on space colonies, rejected it because it didn't overtly support the cause. It would have been dishonest to force the story into such a mold; however pleasant or unpleasant the result, my stories must work themselves out within their own framework, not according to some market principle or philosophical bias.

It may be remarkable that, with such views, I've come as far as I have in publishing, where large conglomerates seem to dictate overall marketing of science fiction as if it were some piecework commodity. ("Take dragon/unicorn/spaceship, add vaguely medieval/magical setting, mix well with wise old wizard/cute sidekick . . .") Don't get me wrong, I've enjoyed stories with all those elements, but enough is enough. Science fiction is much too restless to accept the same kind of genre regimentation displayed by, for example, Westerns or hard-boiled detective novels, where one Western Town or corrupt Big City can serve as stage settings for an infinity of retold tales.

But enough authorial interference. I will tell you no more about these stories until we meet in person; perhaps not even then, for I'm not certain my interpretations are always correct. "Mandala,"* for example, has defied my analysis for seven years, and yet I knew what I wanted to say when I wrote it.

That's when I'm happiest with my own work—when the stories say

*Not included in this collection; available in my novel *Strength of Stones*

so many things that they become playgrounds for the mind. I hope you feel the same way.

Spring Valley, California

From *Bear's Fantasies*, Wildside Press, 1993
On Losing the Taint of Being a Cannibal
Greg Bear

I'm reminded of the line delivered by Joseph Bologna in the motion picture comedy, *The Big Bus*. His character, Dan Torrance, once drove a bus through Donner Pass, and of course got snowed in. Desperation quickly set in among the passengers, and some odd recipes were cooked up. Torrance pleads that he did not know what was in the soup, adding, "One lousy foot, and they call you a cannibal for the rest of your life!"

Writing science fiction is one of those odd activities, like being a cannibal, that marks you permanently, even should you later become a vegan.

The odd relationship most people have with science—awed fascination, not infrequently dismay and distrust, and guilty dependence—guarantees a mixed reaction among the reading public: "You actually *enjoy* science? Writing about it, making it up? How *interesting*."

Their tone of voice tells you that you are now marked forever in their minds.

Science fiction explores the outer limits of the current Western paradigm, science; its playground is all that we know about the universe, and what we imagine we might eventually know.

Many of us, at one time or another, enjoy playing with previous paradigms—mind over matter, magic, dream logic, and so on. Literature does not play favorites; excellent stories have been written in all these areas.

A science fiction writer who writes fantasy, however, is regarded by some as an odd bird indeed. Write science fiction, become well known for it, and—well, your fantasy stories become almost *invisible*. All those times when you *weren't* a cannibal—simply forgotten.

Yet most of the great science fiction writers have written a great deal of fantasy, and I have, as well. But prejudices and snobbery on both sides of the fence have grown in the past ten or fifteen years.

I've never thought of my fantasy stories as dabbling or slumming. They represent an important part of my writing. Some of my very finest work is fantasy. The first novel I ever finished—an early version of what would later be published as *The Infinity Concerto* and *The Serpent Mage*—was fantasy. My second published novel, *Psychlone*, is a ghost story, heavily influenced by Stephen King. In real life I've even gone hunting ghosts in a world-famous hotel, just like Carnacki, though without his spectacular success.

I love fantasy.

Perhaps by gathering some of my fantasy in one volume, I can convince the world that I've had at least a few moments when I was not a cannibal.

But I won't bet on it.

Being a writer of science fiction is just so *odd*.

Thank goodness.

Commentary on the story "Sisters" published in *Paragons*, edited by Reg Bretnor

Characters Great and Small in SF: "Sisters"
Greg Bear

In "Sisters," the viewpoint character, Letitia Blakely, is familiar enough—an adolescent girl, struggling with painful problems. In outline, "Sisters" reads much like a contemporary story of growing up—with a few words and some set dressing changed to indicate the near future. Yet my intent in this story—as in many of my stories—is to deal with characters *within* larger characters, to explore how individuals react to change within a larger setting.

If anything has become more and more clear in the past five hundred years, it is that men and women are not the measure of all things, but the *measurers*. A richer, more powerful literature must take into account the nature of larger entities than human individuals.

There's nothing that stops science fiction—often dismissed as merely a literature of ideas—from also being a literature of character, so long as readers understand a larger definition of character. Character is not limited to the nature and actions of a single individual, or even a group of individuals. Character may also describe a nation, a culture, a species, a world—or a universe.

For me, the story of character is not limited to the Jamesian small group of individuals in an unchanging social setting, with all change arising from individually willed action. Yet since James this has been touted as the datum of literature—and not without reason.

Human readers (the only kind I've encountered) enjoy reading about people not greatly unlike themselves. We enjoy watching the lives of others we can relate to. For relaxation, or a historical refresher, we also enjoy reading about the mores and social patterns of the past, in Dickens and Austen and Joyce, or Tolstoy and Hemingway and Dostoevsky. But what involves us most of all is fiction that directly or indirectly models our present situation and stimulates thought about the choices we have and the decisions we make. We enjoy discovering patterns and relationships between strangers and ourselves, and between different societies in different times.

In a sense, science fiction takes its cues from historical fiction, but with no specific arrow of time. The future as well as the past is open. (Alternate times and realities may qualify as well!)

Since there are few if any societies where change from outside—forced by history, the weather, or other natural phenomena—does not have a major impact on individual lives, to focus on change coming about solely through the willed actions of the individual is a very artificial limitation. It produces attractive and moving works, but these works are no more than an aspect, perhaps just a *genre*. At their worst, they give a false sense of comfort. Even at their best, they do not define the range of literature.

Most of my stories draw the lives of characters *within* larger characters, exploring how individuals react to change within a larger setting. Science fiction stories at their most ambitious model changes in nations, in cultures, even in species and worlds.

Writing science fiction puts added burdens on me as a storyteller. I have to do more than just closely observe: I have to extrapolate. This takes me into dangerous territory, since to extrapolate, I must try to understand the laws and forces that direct the greater characters. I see sociology, psychology, technology, and history as interrelated subsets of biology. This is far from the static and isolating world view common in many religions and much philosophy; it is also far from the gooey and shapeless "holistic" approach of New Age thinking, where anything goes, and the universe caters to our personal whims.

Just as a sharp observer of individual character strives not to be guided by sentiment and personal animus, an observer of larger characters must adopt a similar objectivity. In my stories, individuals are often shaped by environments that may be only marginally familiar, if at all, to the average reader. Bringing the environment to life is important, and inevitably takes some of the center spotlight away from so-called "pure" exploration of character and motive. But it returns the focus with additional rewards by giving insight into how characters shape and are shaped.

No character great or small lives in splendid isolation. Everything an individual does reflects back, and the mirror is not just society, but nature. Discovering how a larger nature works in a story is as thrilling (and dangerous) to my characters as internal discovery.

Letitia's world has changed in significant ways, and offers her challenges no modern young woman has to face. Facing those challenges reveals her inner self as no contemporary setting can.

Moving between the internal world, the social world, and the external world, breaks down the barriers between. Inside becomes outside. There is no mirror, after all.